"Miss Agres."

Selina had turned away from him. Standing before the fire, only her silhouette, outlined in sparks and tongues of curling flame, was visible to Edward's gaze. He could see the tension in her back and knew it was only by sheer willpower she was maintaining her composure.

"Yes."

"I think I may have a solution to your current dilemma, depending on your answers to two questions."

"Have you." Her tone was flat and devoid of curiosity. "And what would those be?"

Edward ignored how dull she sounded, his own hopes beginning to build. "The first—what is your age?"

She didn't turn to look at him, her eyes still fixed on the flames before her. "How is that of any relevance?"

"Please. Humor me."

She sighed as though it was an effort to find the words to reply. "Very well. I am recently turned twenty." The fire crackled, sending sparks swirling into the night sky. "Your second question?"

Edward reached for her. At the first touch of his hand on her shoulder Selina jumped and swung around to face him, a frown of distrust clouding her features. Edward smiled as the expression in her dark eyes, at first ⬚⬚⬚⬚⬚⬚⬚⬚⬚⬚⬚⬚⬚⬚ rozen astonishme⬚⬚⬚⬚⬚⬚⬚⬚⬚⬚⬚⬚⬚⬚ ne knee and take he⬚⬚⬚

"Selina Agr⬚⬚⬚

Author Note

For this, my debut Harlequin Historical novel, I was delighted to have an excuse to do some research into a corner of social history I have always found fascinating: Roma culture, and the differences between the lives of travelers and the gentry across whose land they might have passed. I wanted to look deeper into the way of life of those on the road, their customs and traditions, and contrast them with what might be more familiar.

Life in a horse-drawn caravan is often painted in a rosy light, but the nineteenth-century Romani would not have had an easy existence. Often facing prejudice and abuse, they had more obstacles to overcome than many in search of that happily-ever-after.

In *The Marriage Rescue*'s Romani heroine, Selina, we have a combination of everything I've always loved most in female Romance characters—kindness, determination and enough spirit to keep the hero on his toes! Edward, a newly inherited squire in dire need of a wife, more than meets his match in his independent new bride, although both realize they have a lot to learn about the secret sorrows of the other. I hope you enjoy meeting them.

JOANNA JOHNSON

The Marriage Rescue

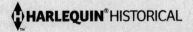

HARLEQUIN® HISTORICAL

Recycling programs
for this product may
not exist in your area.

ISBN-13: 978-1-335-63514-3

The Marriage Rescue

Copyright © 2019 by Joanna Johnson

Printed in U.S.A.

www.Harlequin.com

Joanna Johnson lives in a pretty Wiltshire village with her husband and as many books as she can sneak into the house. Being part of the Harlequin Historical family is a dream come true. She has always loved writing, starting at five years old with a series about a cat imaginatively named Cat, and she keeps a notebook in every handbag—just in case. In her spare time she likes finding new places to have a cream tea, stroking scruffy dogs and trying to remember where she left her glasses.

The Marriage Rescue **is Joanna Johnson's gripping debut for Harlequin Historical!**

Visit the Author Profile page at Harlequin.com.

Chapter One

Selina Agres was going to die, and it was all her own fault. Hadn't she been warned, time and time again, to stay as far away as possible from those upper-class English animals?

Grandmother Zillah's words echoed in her ears as she rode for her life, her horse Djali's hooves pounding over waterlogged ground and leaving deep tracks in their fleeing wake.

Stupid girl.

It wasn't as though she hadn't seen the proof of their wickedness for herself, either.

The last clear memory she had of her mother was the way her eyes had changed at the moment of her death. Many of the other details she could recall were blurred: snatches of lullabies sung on summer nights, when the rhythmic swaying of their creaking caravan had rocked young Selina to sleep; the barest suggestion of a comforting floral scent she could never quite pin down. But the memory of those eyes—so bright and sharp in life, missing nothing, holding a world of wisdom and humour—had clouded to a flat black, staring unseeing at the little girl who had gazed back, who had wondered where the light had gone from Mama's face…

She bent lower over the horse's neck, urging him onwards ever faster. A swift glance behind showed her pursuers losing ground, hindered by their own far clumsier mounts. Selina grasped at a tentative new hope: stubborn and scarred he might be, but nobody was as fast as her Djali over level terrain. He had been her mother's horse before she'd passed, then barely more than a colt, and Selina blessed Mama in that moment for training the bad-tempered creature so well. Perhaps they might survive this after all.

The wind tore at her clothes, an autumn squall that threatened the rapid approach of winter tugging her riot of midnight curls free from their ribbon and tossing the heavy tresses into her face. She flung them aside with desperate haste, her other hand tightening its death grip on the horse's reins.

She couldn't stop now. Just one more fence to jump and then it was all downhill to a thick copse of trees, if her memories of this wretched place were correct, and there she might just be able to hide—if she could only put enough distance between herself and those behind her… Twelve years had passed since she had last set foot on this land, and all she could do was pray her scattered recollections were right.

'Come on, Djali!' Her voice was loud, battling against the roar of the wind, belying the way her heart railed against her ribs like a trapped animal.

The horse plunged onwards, his breath coming short and fast in a pattern that matched Selina's own.

She hadn't even *wanted* to get so close. But what else could she have done? Left the poor girl alone in the forest? Perhaps she should have; look at where taking pity on a landowner's child had got her.

Seeing a Roma woman carrying a sobbing English child through the woods—Squire Ambrose Fulbrooke's own daughter, no less—of *course* his men had jumped to the wrong conclusion. The idea that the little girl had escaped her governess and got herself lost would never have occurred to them, whereas everybody had heard how the Roma were a community of thieves and vagrants. Of course she was stealing the child; what other explanation could there be?

Selina knew from bitter experience the prejudices that existed against her people. Shunned and almost feared, the Roma were well used to living on the fringes, making do in whatever ways they could. But they were strong, and that characteristic spirit was more than evident in Selina.

Almost from her first steps she had worked hard: foraging food for the pot, fetching water, helping Papa break in horses to sell. Her hands had grown calloused and her skin tanned, and with each passing year she had become more and more like the kind, capable mother ripped so cruelly from her.

Even Papa had commented on the resemblance once, years ago, on a camp a hundred miles from this damned estate, as he'd watched her lunge a new pony. The animal had been skittish and afraid, but with gentleness and determination Selina had brought him on well, and her father had nodded at her as he'd sat on the back porch of their wagon, pipe in hand.

'What do you think, Lina? Will you make a mount of him yet?'

'I believe so, Papa.' Selina had smiled across at him

and wiped the sweat from her brow with the back of a hand. 'He's clever, and a good worker.'

'I think you might be right. You've a good eye for horses. You get that from me.'

He'd pulled on his pipe for a moment and Selina had seen the smile fade from his weathered face.

'Everything else comes from your mother. You're looking more and more like her every day.'

'Thank you, Papa.'

Selina's voice had been quiet and she'd turned back to the pony, wishing with all her heart she hadn't noticed her strong, tall Papa quickly pat a tear from his face with his old red neckerchief. The picture had stayed with her ever since, and never failed to bring a lump to her throat.

The fence was looming fast—a straggling construction that leaned back drunkenly at an angle that would make it difficult to jump. Selina cursed beneath her breath and chanced another raking glare backwards. They were still coming, three of them now. Two were dressed in the usual muddy colours of gamekeepers, riding out in front of a third too distant to see in any real detail. She thought she made out a flash of blue, stark against the muted grey of the sullen autumn sky. When had *he* joined the chase?

But it didn't matter how many there were. She would escape them all or die trying.

'Get up, Djali—good boy!' Clicking her teeth in command, Selina touched the horse with her heels. He was galloping flat out, lips pulled back from ivory teeth and mane flying, ready to take the jump.

She felt the rush of air as they left the ground. It hit her squarely in the face—a stinging slap that brought tears to her eyes—but they were sailing over the lolling fence and nobody would catch them now.

And then they went down.

Djali struck the fence with a back hoof and veered to one side, stumbling to right himself. Selina pitched forward, tumbling from the saddle in a tangle of crimson skirts and bright woollen shawls.

She lay gasping, winded and dazed. She'd fallen from horses before, many times, but never from one so tall as Djali—one of the reasons he had been officially given over to her ownership on her eighteenth birthday, aside from sentiment, had been his surefootedness. After the fate that had befallen her mother, Papa hadn't wanted to take any chances with his only child.

What a cruel irony if I were to die here, too.

The thought crossed Selina's racing mind before she could stop it. A fresh bolt of terror tore through her heaving chest and her head swam as she struggled to regain her breath.

We never should have come back here, even if that murdering devil Charles Fulbrooke is on the other side of the ocean.

Her pursuers had seen her fall. She could hear them now, the unmistakable beat of hooves growing closer as she lay prone on the sodden ground, one arm flung out and the other twisted beneath her.

She pushed herself up, wincing as she felt a dart of pain crackle through the wrist that had borne her weight. *Where's Djali?* A wild scan of the grass showed him standing a short distance away, ears back as he eyed the approaching horses.

There was no time to reach him, Selina calculated. By the time she managed to get back into the saddle her hunters would be upon her and she would have nowhere else to turn. There was only one option open to her and she seized the lifeline with both hands.

Selina ran.

The copse lay mere feet away from her now; if she could reach the safety of the trees she would be able to climb high enough to conceal herself among the orange canopy of leaves that swayed in the chill wind. Djali would be fine, she knew. The obstinate creature was well capable of defending himself and would likely trot back to the campsite if she didn't reappear to guide him home herself.

Grandmother Zillah would be beside herself with worry when the horse came back without his rider, but there was nothing Selina could do about that now as she reached the first line of trees and plunged headlong through the rusty carpet of fallen leaves.

'After her!'

'Don't let her get away!'

Selina heard the rough shouts at her back and fought onwards, crashing through the undergrowth. Sharp boughs whipped at her face, drawing blood, but she kept running, searching for a tree whose lower branches would allow her enough purchase to haul herself up.

There! As if by divine providence a huge oak reared up in front of her, its gnarled roots thrust out and wide boughs sweeping down to hold out their arms to her. It was the work of moments to heave herself up, and she lunged upwards, ignoring the scream of her jarred wrist, moving through the leaves just as her pursuers lurched into view, now on foot, with faces flushed red with exertion.

'Which way did she go?'

'I didn't see!'

'You mean you *lost* her?'

Selina peered down through the branches at the two gamekeepers standing just metres from her hiding place. Secreted among the boughs, her crimson skirt blending with the autumnal colours of the leaves, she felt her palms prickle with sweat. If they looked up…

Why hadn't she just pointed the child in the right direction and then left? She hated the landowners for their wealthy arrogance, their hypocrisy, for the way they treated her people and, of course, for their part in Mama's death. It hardly mattered that the Squire himself— owner of this vast estate and the imposing Blackwell Hall that sat within it—had not been directly responsible for the fate of Diamanda Agres; the upper classes were all cut from the same cloth.

For all Selina knew, Squire Ambrose had aided his brother Charles's flight to the Continent after the events of twelve years before that had scarred her young life so violently, allowing him to neatly avoid any unsavoury accusations. If only Selina had treated the girl with the disdain she deserved, coming from such a family, and hadn't tried to return her to the great Hall, less than a mile away…

Damn. Selina sighed to herself. *You always were too soft.*

The sight of the little thing in her muddy gown, clutching a tow-headed doll, had moved Selina in a way she couldn't explain. Perhaps having lost her own mother at just eight years old had made her more sympathetic. The child had sobbed as she'd called for her mama, and Selina had had only a moment of hesitation before bundling the mite up in her own shawl and making for Djali.

It wasn't the child's fault she'd been born to such a man, she'd reasoned. Not that the girl's father could do much harm now, Selina had thought grimly as she settled into the saddle. Squire Ambrose Fulbrooke had been six feet under for the best part of a month—a deadly combination of port and rich food had caused his heart to give out in the middle of a poker game, if the rumours that had reached the Romani were to be believed.

Apparently his son was in line to inherit, but no sign of the man had yet been seen, and in the absence of a master the Romani had judged it safe enough to make camp temporarily on Fulbrooke land—a judgement that, given her current situation, Selina now regretted with every fibre of her being.

The third man was approaching, kicking his way through the fallen leaves. One of the gamekeepers groaned, just loudly enough for Selina to hear. 'I knew he'd follow us. I said so, didn't I? And now he's going to see we let her get away...'

'Harris! Milton! What happened?'

Selina curled her lip instinctively at the sound of the man's voice. Cut-glass vowels and the confidence of a man born into luxury. He was one of *them*—she was sure of it.

A peep down through the branches confirmed her suspicions: the tall man standing with his back to her was the epitome of a well-bred English gentleman, dressed in a well-cut blue coat with breeches tucked into immaculate leather riding boots and with hair of a distinctive dark burnished gold. She frowned as a flicker of something stirred in the back of her mind, like a gentle breeze through long grass. That unique hair colour, so different from the Roma darkness…had she seen it somewhere before?

'Well? Don't keep me in suspense!' The voice was deep and edged with humour. 'I see my sister being carted off in the direction of the house by your wife, Milton, and then you two on horseback in hot pursuit of somebody—I ask again: What happened?'

'Well, sir,' began one of the gamekeepers, sounding nervous, 'we were just doing our rounds when we saw Miss Ophelia being carried off by a gypsy woman— sobbing her heart out, wasn't she, Harris?'

'Fit to burst, sir,' continued the other. 'So we snatched her back. The girl tried to tell us she came upon Miss Ophelia wandering all on her own, but of course we knew that wasn't true. Trying to steal her, she was.'

'So you gave chase, did you? Two of you against one woman and she still gave you the slip?'

The other men shuffled slightly. 'You know what they're like, sir, those gypsies. Eels they are. Too tricky by half.'

'Yes. I can see how she would be difficult quarry.'

Although Selina couldn't see his face, she was sure the man was smiling. 'Never mind. All's well that ends well—my sister is back safely with her governess.'

'Thank you, sir. But you know…' The other man's voice lowered menacingly; the hairs on the back of Selina's neck stirred in response. 'If we ever come across her again, or find where those gypsies' grubby little nest is, well…'

'We wouldn't hesitate to teach them a lesson, sir. Be happy to do it.'

'Yes, Milton. I think I quite catch your drift.' The educated voice was cool—bordering on cold. 'Let's hope for everybody's sake that the woman in question is far away by now.'

'Yes, sir.'

'I think we should all be on our way. Bid you good day, gents.'

'Good day, sir.'

The men moved off. Selina listened to them go: footsteps on damp earth, then the telltale jingle of their horses' tack as they rode away, growing fainter and fainter until only the swaying creak of the forest remained.

She exhaled, long and loud. She was safe. She'd ventured into the lion's den and escaped by the skin of her teeth.

'You can come down now, miss. It's quite safe.'

Selina froze. *There was still someone down there!*

Her heart checked for the briefest of painful moments before slamming back into a pounding rhythm so hard she was sure the man standing below her must be able to hear it.

She drew herself sharply against the oak's knotted trunk, pressing herself closely to the bark. A quick look down through the leaves allowed her nothing more than a view of the back of the uncannily familiar fair-haired head, its owner resolutely positioned at the base of her tree.

'I know you're up there. Don't be afraid. I won't harm you.'

Selina swallowed—a quick convulsion of her dry throat. *Celebrating too soon.* She was trapped. There was only one way down and he was guarding it; there was no way she could pass without being seen.

'Please, miss. You have nothing to fear from me.'

Selina's pulse was racing as she registered his words. What kind of simpleton did he think she was? Surely that was exactly the sort of claim he *would* make.

'Nothing to fear? You just hunted me for three miles like an animal—please excuse me if I don't hop down at the click of your fingers.'

There was a huff of laughter from below. 'I understand why it may have appeared that way. I'd be more than happy to explain if you would just come down.'

'I think not.'

Peering down through the leaves once more, Selina trained her eyes on her captor's blond curls. He hadn't moved so much as an inch, blast him. She herself was beginning to feel the sharp texture of the bark digging into her skin, forcing her to shift her position, and she could have cursed aloud when the movement sent a rotten branch crashing down through the canopy.

Hearing the sudden noise, the man whipped his head round, searching for the direction of the sound, and as his profile turned Selina saw the face of her tormentor clearly for the first time.

It was as though she had been winded all over again.

She *knew* him. Not by name—it hadn't seemed the right time for formal introductions many years ago, when Selina had come across a strange boy in these very woods and held a pad of moss against his cheek to stem the flow of blood that had seeped between his fingers.

How old had he been then? Perhaps twelve to Selina's eight? He had been the first gentry boy she'd ever seen up close, and the rare combination of his hazel eyes and golden hair, so foreign to Selina's childish mind, had burned itself into her memory. There could be no mistaking the fact that this man was the same person, and

Selina felt a thrill of some unknown feeling tingle down the length of her spine as she watched him searching upwards, confusion rushing in to replace where moments previously she had felt only fear.

He's handsome. The thought came out of nowhere, taking her by surprise, and she shook her head slightly as if to clear it. *Don't be absurd*, she admonished herself fiercely, although nothing could stop the slow creep of colour she knew was stealing over her cheeks as she took in his defined jaw, in turn well matched by a straight nose and a mouth just teetering on the brink of a smile, and she felt another dart of the same unexplained feeling lance through her.

It was uncomfortably, unacceptably similar to the admiration she had felt once or twice before when confronted with an attractive man. On those occasions, however, she hadn't felt her heart rate pick up speed, and neither had she felt such a disturbingly instinctive appreciation for the fine colour of his eyes. How this gentleman managed to affect her in such a powerfully unexpected way she had no clue, but she knew she didn't like it.

He was hunting through the branches in earnest now, and Selina forced herself closer against the tree's rough trunk. She screwed her eyes closed, trying to bully her brain into ordering her whirling thoughts while her pulse skipped ever faster.

Who is he? Why is he here?

It was exactly her luck to have such an unlikely encounter, she acknowledged helplessly, even as the strange feeling crackled beneath her skin and she felt the urge to look down pull at her once again. *He* wouldn't remember *her*, that was for certain. She had been a skinny, dirt-streaked child, and he...

He now bore a scar, exactly where she had staunched the bleeding gash on his cheek—a pale crescent that somehow only served to enhance the otherwise unblemished perfection of his features...features that looked as though they had been designed to be traced by female fingertips.

Selina's own face felt uncomfortably warm as she sat motionless, horrified by the spontaneous reaction of her body. Each nerve tingled with the desire to take another peep at the man below, to make doubly sure her disbelieving eyes had been correct and he truly was the same person she had encountered all those years before—as well as to take another glimpse of the face that made her heart beat a frenzied tattoo against her ribs.

If it was him, could there be a slim chance her predicament might not be as dire as she had feared?

As a boy he had accepted her help and seemed grateful for it, she was forced to recall. There had been no sign of any upper-class prejudice then, only two children, both too young to fully grasp the social gulf that would divide them so completely as adults. Perhaps he might be as gracious now he was fully grown, and allow her to leave without too much trouble?

It was the most Selina could hope for, and she clung to that hope as she prayed for his disconcerting effect on her to wane.

Edward Fulbrooke frowned lightly as he craned his neck upwards. Where exactly *was* she? He'd known she was there the whole time. Poor Harris and Milton...it was the most obvious hiding place imaginable.

He'd arrived on the scene just after the two game-keepers had thundered off, his own horse blowing powerfully from their afternoon ride. Milton's wife, Ada, had been attempting to drag a wailing Ophelia towards the Hall, and Edward had dismounted swiftly to aid her.

'Oh, Mr Fulbrooke. I'm that glad you're here!' Ada's voice had been barely audible above Ophelia's sobs, and Edward scooped the child up immediately in one strong arm.

'Ophie. That's enough. What's the matter?'

The little girl quieted at once, though her eyes—the same hazel as Edward's own—had glittered with unshed tears. 'Ned, the lady was only trying to help, and now they're going to *hurt* her!'

Ophelia had told him the full story. She'd been 'exploring' again, having escaped from the watchful gaze of her governess, and had walked so far she'd been unable to find her way back home. She had been about to give up all hope of ever seeing her mama again when a lady had appeared through the trees, dressed in strange clothes and singing a song Ophelia hadn't understood.

When she had seen the child she'd stopped and looked almost frightened, but after Ophelia burst into tears and explained that she was lost and alone the lady had wrapped her up snug in a shawl and taken her towards a waiting horse—a huge grey stallion, with great scars marring his flanks—and said she would take Ophelia safely home.

'But then Harris and Milton came, and they were so *angry*. Harris pulled me away and Milton tried to take hold of the lady. But she ran—and nobody would *listen* to me!'

Edward had set Ophelia back on her feet and leapt

back into the saddle without a word. He hadn't doubted for a moment that the child was telling the truth; there wasn't a moment to lose.

He peered upwards yet again. Was that a scrap of fabric? It was hard to tell against the leafy backdrop.

'What is it that concerns you? Are you afraid I'll come chasing after you again?'

There was only silence from above, and Edward forced back a grin.

The pert creature. Sitting pretty as a picture up her tree, deciding whether the Squire's own son is worth coming down for.

The smile faded and a small crease formed between his eyebrows. The *late* Squire's son, now. He was still getting used to that, having returned from London only two days prior to find the Hall quieter than he had ever known it before.

'I can't deny I have some slight misgivings.'

The smoky voice was edged with an undercurrent of something Edward could not identify, and his frown deepened.

'Well, what if I gave you my word as a gentleman that I won't? Would you allow me the honour of an introduction then?'

Another silence stretched out, this time less amusing, and Edward raised an eyebrow. This was getting a little out of hand. He was well within his rights to *order* her down, trespassing as she was on his own land—or what *would* be his land once he took formal possession of his inheritance.

'Miss, I would have you know my word is my law. I would think myself beyond contempt if, once given, I were to break it.'

There was a moment's quiet. Then, 'I suppose there's no chance you'd leave and let me go about my business without an audience?'

'None whatsoever, I'm afraid.'

'Not very *gentlemanly* of you.'

'Alas, I remain unmoved.'

There was another pause. Edward was certain he could hear the grinding of teeth and allowed himself a small smile at her reluctance. She really was an unusual woman.

The branches above his head swayed suddenly, and then with a shower of falling leaves the woman dropped to the ground in front of him.

Edward felt his eyes widen in surprise. She was younger than he had expected: her tawny face, flecked with mud and with a long scratch across one cheek, belonged to a woman no older than twenty. Perhaps it had been the modest clothing that had confused him—she was certainly dressed like no fashionable young lady *he* had ever met. Her bright skirt was paired with a loose-fitting blouse, half hidden beneath a number of colourful tasselled shawls, and raven hair hung in thick waves about her shoulders.

Her effect on him was both immediate and startling. A distant part of his mind knew it was rude to stare, but for some reason he didn't seem able to tear his gaze away as he took in the vibrancy of the scarlet wool against the deep black of her curls, the delicacy of the bone structure beneath the dirt on her face and even the oddly intriguing lack of a wedding ring on the hand that clutched her shawls to her chest.

There was something about her that seemed to call to him, to make him want to drink her in, and he felt a sharp pang of surprise at the very thought. There she stood, a complete stranger and an intruder on his land. He ought to be unmoved by their chance encounter and yet there *he* stood, a full-grown man, apparently struck dumb by the power of a lovely countenance. For lovely it most certainly was.

Where had he ever seen its equal?

It was the strangest sensation—almost as though he had surrendered control of his senses for the briefest of moments before coming back down to earth with a bump. So she was handsome—what was that to him? He was only human, and now his rational mind must take charge again. Her beauty counted for nothing—just the same as any other woman's. He would not be making that mistake again.

She stood watching him with eyes as mistrustful as a feral cat's. There was a feline grace to her posture, too, in the way she held herself, ready to run at the slightest provocation, and it highlighted the contrast between her lithe elegance and his broad stature. Although he easily topped her by a good head and a half, the tense wariness of her frame radiated an untouchability that would have stopped most men in their tracks.

Thrusting his moment of madness firmly to the back of his mind, Edward offered a short bow. 'Thank you for indulging me.'

The woman inclined her head slightly but said nothing.

This might be a little more difficult than I thought, Edward mused. He wanted to thank her for trying to help Ophelia, but apparently conversing with her was destined to be like drawing blood from a stone.

She couldn't know who he was, he was sure. If she

did she would be far more interested in conversation. The young women of his acquaintance always seemed to open up at the first hint of his name and prospects.

Not that it was necessarily a good thing. Edward had lost count of the number of ladies who had breezed up to him at balls and revels, affecting shyness, confiding that they had a dance reserved for him in the event that he might be 'inclined to take a turn'. Bitter experience had taught him not to be tempted.

'My name is Edward Fulbrooke,' Edward continued. 'I'm the son of the late Squire of Blackwell Hall, and this is my family estate.' He watched as something sparked in the woman's eyes—something akin to fear. 'Might I have the pleasure of knowing your name?'

He saw her throat move as she swallowed, his gaze drawn there by some impulse he couldn't control. The look in her eyes had been fleeting, but there had definitely been a reaction. *Was it something I said?* Far from impressing her, the revelation of his name had seemed to unnerve her even more. Why *was* that?

'Selina. Selina Agres.'

'Delighted to make your acquaintance, Miss Agres.'

The woman nodded again. An odd expression flickered across her face, mingling with the ever-present wariness; it was half watchful, half curious. She seemed on the brink of saying something before evidently thinking better of it, instead folding her full lips into a tight line.

'I'm afraid I might have frightened you earlier.' Edward spoke quietly, his voice uncharacteristically gentle; the last thing he wanted was for her to bolt before he'd had a chance to explain. That was the least he could do, given the circumstances. 'Please allow me to apologise for the misunderstanding.'

'Misunderstanding?' Selina's eyebrows almost disappeared into her hair. 'You and your men wanted nothing more than to hunt me down like a fox running from hounds!'

Edward frowned. 'That's not quite right. Ophelia told me what happened, and what your motives were. I went after Harris and Milton to—' He broke off. *To stop them from lynching you*, he concluded internally. Not a fit topic of conversation for a lady, traditional or not. 'They're very fond of her, and I was uneasy that in their concern for her safety they might get carried away. It was my intention to defend you, if necessary.'

Edward watched a spark of surprise kindle in Selina's eyes and felt another jolt of that unwelcome electricity as he saw how it enhanced their beguiling darkness. Their rich ebony was a colour rarely seen, and so entirely different from the china-blue set he had once thought the finest in the county.

Even if Harris and Milton hadn't told him Edward would have known at once that she was Romani. The realisation was oddly pleasing. Surely her presence indicated an encampment nearby? A fact that flew directly in the face of his late father's orders?

Passing groups of Roma had been a familiar sight to him on this land years ago, and Edward was momentarily lost in fond memories of brightly painted caravans pulled by gleaming horses, and the dark-haired boys his own age who had invited him, a shy, affection-starved child, to join their games. Although each group had rarely stayed for very long before moving on, Edward could still recall the brief happiness he had felt at their acceptance of him, all of them too young to have yet developed the prejudices of their parents.

His own father had disapproved enormously when Edward had told him of his newfound friends—but then, as usual, Ambrose's attention had been caught by something far more interesting than his lonely young son, and it had been an older Roma boy who had taught Edward to fish, and how to play cards, and any number of other things his father should have taken the time to share with his child so desperate for some tenderness.

A vivid pang of nostalgia hit him like a sudden blow as he remembered the friend he had made the last year the Roma had crossed Fulbrooke land—a little girl, younger than himself, who had cared for him after his fight with the neighbouring family's two sons. Edward felt a dull ache spread through his chest as he recalled how the pain of his cheek had been nothing compared to the crushing realisation that the other boys had been right: his mother was *not* going to return, and perhaps the unkind things they had said about her were more accurate than he'd wanted to accept.

Still, he'd given as good as he'd got. One cut cheek had been a fair price to pay for doling out a black eye and a broken tooth, and Edward almost smiled at the memory of his young nurse. She'd shown him more kindness in their short encounter than he had experienced in months, and again shown him the warmth of the Romani, almost unheard of among the upper classes.

There had been some unpleasantness soon after that incident, he recalled—some trouble with Uncle Charles and a Roma woman—and his father's reluctant permission for the travellers to cross his land had been swiftly revoked. If they had returned it meant Ambrose's grip on the estate was loosening, and Edward could truly step into his place.

He realised he was staring again. Selina returned his gaze uncertainly, a trace of a blush crossing her cheeks under his scrutiny, and Edward looked away swiftly, cursing his apparent lack of self-control.

'My sister has a bad habit of escaping. If you hadn't found her who knows what would have happened?'

Ophelia was the precocious daughter of Maria, the Squire's second, much younger wife. Little Ophelia had breathed new life into the ancient house and, at just seven years old to Edward's twenty-four, she held the key to her half-brother's heart in one tiny hand. She'd been quick enough to take advantage of her mother's absence from the Hall, visiting friends in Edinburgh, and go tramping about the estate on one of her 'expeditions'.

'It was never my intention to frighten you. Please forgive me if that was the case and accept my heartfelt thanks for your service to my sister.'

Selina shrugged—a fleeting movement of one slight shoulder. 'It was what anybody would have done under the circumstances.'

Edward nodded as though she had said something more gracious. She really did have the most disarming manner, he thought. Not at all polished, or even very polite, but there was honesty in her words, a lack of affectation that was oddly refreshing.

He shouldn't admire it; indeed, his interest in her was unnerving. *Get a hold of yourself, man*, he chastised himself uncomfortably. *You're not some green lad, swooning over a milkmaid.*

'Well. Thank you all the same.' After a moment's

pause Edward delved into his waistcoat pocket, wrestling with something contained within.

Selina flinched backwards at the movement, glancing this way and that; she seemed on the point of darting away through the trees—

'No! Wait.' Edward held up both hands. Bunched in his right was a snowy handkerchief, which he held out to Selina as gingerly as he might on approaching a wild bird.

'You have some mud on your face, and a scratch—it's been bleeding.' He smiled wryly, one hand moving to the moon-shaped scar below his right eye. 'I know from experience that it's best to treat such a wound as soon as possible.'

Selina stiffened, and Edward saw another complex look dart across her countenance before she regained her composure.

'Oh. Thank you.'

She tentatively took the handkerchief from Edward's outstretched hand, her eyes never leaving his face. He watched as she dabbed at her cheek and cleared the dirt from her skin.

She may well be the most beautiful woman I've ever seen.

For all the scratches that marred her face, she was strikingly lovely in a way totally apart from the celebrated society belles of his circle. The notion was unsettling: hadn't he long thought himself immune to the charms of women? The fact that in that moment, with the trees whispering around him and leaves strewn at his feet, he found himself as vulnerable as any other man was alarming in the extreme.

He would disregard it. She confused him, straying

dangerously close to stirring something deep within him that he wanted left undisturbed, and *that* he couldn't allow.

When she tried to return the handkerchief, he backed away with a shake of his head. 'You keep it. Call it a memento.'

'I'm not sure how much of today I'm like to want to remember.'

Edward bowed. 'I understand. Whatever else you might feel, I hope you won't forget that you have a friend in me. If I'm ever able to repay your kindness I shall endeavour to do so. I pay my debts.'

Selina's answering smile was strange and still mistrustful, as though she knew a secret she didn't intend to share. She was moving away from him, backing out of his reach in the direction of the place where Edward had seen her horse waiting for her. He watched her go, wishing the graceful movement of her stride wasn't so damnably intriguing.

'If that's the case, you owe me twice over.'

'Twice?'

She was almost out of sight. Edward frowned as she turned away from him, confusion clouding into his mind. *Twice? How was that?*

'Once for today. Once for before.'

She threw the words over her shoulder and with a whisk of her crimson skirt disappeared between the trees.

Chapter Two

Selina gazed up at the ceiling of the darkened caravan, arching in a perfect curve above her head. Orange embers glowed in the grate of the compact stove set against one wall, dimly illuminating the gilt-painted woodwork of the shelves and bunks to gleam like real gold. A sliver of moonlight fell from one not quite shuttered window, slicing down to leave a pale splash on the polished floor.

Like all Roma women, Selina kept her *vardo* spotlessly clean, and even Papa, when he came to call for a cup of tea, knew to wipe his boots before he was allowed to cross the threshold.

A sideways glance across the narrow cabin showed her grandmother was asleep, the mound of colourful crochet blankets she slept under rising and falling with each breath. In the eerie stillness of the night even that small movement was a comfort.

Selina sighed. *It's no use.*

Sleep evaded her, just as it had on the previous three nights. Each time she closed her eyes pictures rose up to chase each other through her mind: Edward as a young lad, on the day she had first encountered him all those years ago, attempting to smile through gritted teeth as she cleaned his wounded face, and then his adult counterpart, the blond curls just as vivid but his shoulders so impressively broad beneath his fine coat that Selina felt her heart beat a little faster at the memory.

Would that distinctive hair have been soft beneath her fingertips, she wondered, if she'd leaned down from her tree to touch?

The very notion made her breath hitch in her throat before she slammed the brakes on that train of thought, horrified by its wayward direction.

You can stop that this moment, Selina. What's the matter with you?

At least the mystery of who he was and why she had encountered him there had been solved. *Edward Fulbrooke. Ambrose's son and Charles' nephew.* Perhaps she should have suspected, she mused as the image of his face drifted unstoppably across her mind's eye once again, wearing the same dazzling smile he had flashed her mere days previously. But Edward's father and uncle shared the same chestnut hair and ruddy complexion, quite unlike his cool fairness. There was no physical resemblance. And as for character...

Certainly as a boy he had been agreeable, she recalled as she lay in the darkness. He'd looked surprised to see her there in the woods, hunting for wild mushrooms, and she herself had felt nothing but sympathy for him at the state of his bloodied cheek. In those days she'd had no real reason to fear the gentry; Mama had still been alive, and in her childish innocence it had felt the most natural thing in the world to go to him, to help tend to his wound and to feel a slow creep of pleasure at having made a new friend who delighted her with his strange old-fashioned manners.

But then they had killed Mama. The Roma had left the Fulbrooke estate, never intending to return—and Selina's hatred of the gentry had been burned into her heart like a brand.

It was just as well he didn't remember me. He might have wanted to talk, otherwise, and that would never have done.

Selina shifted beneath her bedclothes, attempting to make her body more comfortable than her mind. The fact Edward had been just as courteous as a grown man as he had been as a lad was as surprising as her apparently instinctive attraction to him—and almost as confusing. The upper classes were renowned among her people for their contempt of the Romani, fostering the animosity that raged on both sides.

Had her care of Edward as a child opened his mind to the possibility the Roma were more civilised than he would otherwise have believed? she wondered. Or perhaps she was giving herself too much credit, Selina thought wryly. Certainly she was giving *him* too much space in her head.

The fact that she had slipped Edward's handkerchief beneath her pillow meant nothing. There just wasn't anywhere else to keep it. Zillah, with her hawk-like eyes, would spy it at once if she left it on her shelf, and carrying it upon her person seemed unduly intimate. Perhaps she should just get rid of it, wad it into the stove, but the thought made her uncomfortable in a way she couldn't quite identify.

Beneath her pillow it would have to stay, incriminating embroidered initials and all, and Selina could only pray nobody would find it.

'You're still awake, child.'

Selina jumped, and sat up so quickly she almost hit her head on the low shelf above her bunk. 'I thought you were sleeping, Grandmother.'

'So I was—until you decided the early hours would be a good time to begin talking to yourself. A sign of madness, as well you know.'

'Sorry. I didn't realise I'd spoken aloud.'

'You didn't.' Zillah rose up in her bunk, arthritic bones creaking. 'You've been tossing and turning all night; any fool could tell you have something on your mind. I'd wager it's the reason why you rode back into camp three days ago as if the devil himself was after you.'

'It's nothing, Grandmother. Go back to sleep.'

'I will not. Make a cup of tea, girl, and tell me what ails you.'

Selina groaned inwardly. There really was no stopping Zillah once she got the bit between her teeth. A lifetime on the road—a hard path for any woman—had instilled in her an almost legendary resolve. There was no room for weakness in a *vardo*. At past eighty years old, with silver hair and a face lined with the countless creases of age, Zillah had a mind that was still sharp as a knife, and she was revered among the Roma for her experience and wisdom.

Of course she'd noticed Selina's absence from camp, and how distracted she had been for the past few days— how could Selina have expected anything less?

She swung her legs down from her bunk and shuffled, still cocooned in blankets, the few steps towards the stove. She could have made a fire in her sleep by now, she was sure, and it wasn't long before their copper kettle was whistling shrilly. Two doses of strong, sweet tea were poured into china cups, and she conveyed them back to where her grandmother sat, swathed in a thick woollen shawl and regarding her expectantly.

'Well?'

'Well, what, Grandmother?' Selina hopped up into her bunk, cup clutched to her chest.

'I would like to know what it is that bothers you. Start from the beginning, and don't leave anything out.'

'I don't know what you want me to say.' Selina glanced at Zillah from beneath her lashes. Even in the darkness she could see her grandmother's eyes were fixed on her, gleaming bright as a pair of new pins. 'There isn't anything I can think of.'

Edward's face rose up before her mind's eye before she could stop it, his hazel gaze locked onto hers, and she frowned down into her teacup. How was it that the only man ever to make her blush was a gentleman, and a Fulbrooke at that? She had every reason to loathe his family, and yet the pull of Edward's powerful appeal was impossible for her to ignore.

No Roma man had ever tempted her so much, that was for sure. Although plenty had vied for the hand of Tomas Agres's pretty daughter, Selina had never felt more than a passing flicker of interest in any of them beyond a stolen kiss or two.

The only one who had ever made her think twice was a handsome youth named Sampson, and even his charms had quickly vanished when she'd overheard him boast of his confidence in winning her without even needing to try. Since her swift and loud rejection of him nobody else had dared approach her, for which Selina felt nothing but relief.

The only man whose good opinion she needed to consider was Papa, and that had suited her just fine—until Edward Fulbrooke had come striding back into her life, his handsome face making her question every rational thought she'd ever had.

'Are you absolutely sure?'

'Yes.'

'You lie,' stated the old woman flatly. 'Do you think I'm blind? That I've finally lost my aged mind after all these years?'

'Of course not!'

'Then don't play games with me, girl. I can read you like a book.'

Selina sighed, shoulders slumping in resignation. *Perhaps it wouldn't be such a terrible idea to talk things over,* she mused. There had never been any secrets between the two of them; living in such close quarters didn't really leave much room for intrigue. Besides, she had too much respect for Zillah to continue with such an unconvincing lie.

Edward's image surfaced once again, all disarming smile and broad shoulders, and she forced it back roughly. It was definitely because she was overtired. She wouldn't waste a single, solitary second thinking about him *or* the musculature hidden beneath his coat under usual circumstances. The distress of that day must have disturbed her more than she'd realised, and now her mind was playing tricks on her. Perhaps the benefit of her grandmother's wisdom would help her regain her mental equilibrium. She just wouldn't tell her every detail.

'Very well.' Selina took a sip of tea and braced herself for the inevitable. She had no doubt it would not be pleasant. 'There was an incident while I was scouting for food.'

'What kind of incident, child?'

'I was set upon by two men. They chased me for a few miles, then I managed to climb a tree and hide until they left.'

'Did they hurt you?' Zillah's voice was soft in the darkness—ominously so.

'No. No doubt they would have done, had they caught me, but another man came and threw them off the scent. I suppose it's to him I owe my escape.' She hadn't thought of it that way before, she had to confess, and, looking at events in such a light, didn't it make her earlier behaviour towards Edward seem a little ungrateful?

Not to mention rude, she chided herself. *You didn't do much to show him Roma aren't really insolent and ill-mannered.*

But, no. One good act could never hope to negate generations of malice. Even if Edward *had* surprised her that day, there was nothing to say he wouldn't revert to his class type on any other. Besides, she thought grimly, if he'd known where they were camping would he have acted entirely less chivalrously?

'I see. And this heroic figure of a man—what of him?'

'What do you mean?'

'I mean what of him, Lina? Why did he intervene? What manner of person was he? Roma?'

'No, Grandmother.' Selina's mouth twitched at the thought as a sudden recollection of Edward's refined features flitted through her mind, his lips curved yet again into a distressingly attractive smile. 'Most definitely not Roma.'

Zillah's eyes narrowed. 'Come along, Selina. At my age I don't have time for guessing games. What is it you think you cannot tell me?'

Selina took a deep breath.

'He was gentry.'

There was silence.

'Grandmother...?'

'Speak on, girl.'

The mound of crochet blankets shifted as Zillah turned to face her directly with a close scrutiny Selina could have done without.

'What strange circumstances led such a high and mighty gentleman to concern himself with the likes of you?'

'I found his sister lost in the woods. I was trying to return her to where she came from and I was seen. The men who saw me assumed I was trying to steal her—and they weren't pleased.' Selina shivered suddenly and drew her blankets round her more tightly. What exactly would they have done if they'd caught her? The endless possibilities made her feel sick. 'The gentleman saw where I was hiding but sent the men away before they realised. He said his sister had told him what happened, and if I ever needed help I was to call on him.'

Zillah gave a short caw of laughter. 'Call on him? What does he think we would ever need *him* for?'

She clucked to herself for a few moments, evidently tickled. Selina tried to smile, but found her face was cold.

'And did he have a name, your new friend?'

'He—yes. Grandmother, he was the late Squire's own son.'

Every trace of mirth died from the old woman's face. 'Selina! Say you didn't tell him we were camped on his land?' Her voice was earnest, and her eyes fixed on Selina's own. 'I had not thought he would come so soon. If he learns we're here we'll have to move. With winter coming, and the babies so ill, we can't—'

'I would never endanger our people,' Selina breathed. 'I gave no clue where I had come from. He has no reason to suspect we're on his land.'

Zillah gazed at her a moment longer, before exhaling slowly. 'Good.'

It would be disastrous to move the camp now, and both women knew it. Winter was approaching fast—the hardest time of year for those living on the road, whose lives were a trial at the best of times.

All their menfolk, with the exception of just two elderly grandfathers, were away working on the Oxford Canal, undertaking the backbreaking labour of widening it. Even their adolescent boys had gone, taking up shovels and picks and toiling alongside the grown men. The work was hard, and the hours long, but they were able to make a few coppers to take back to the waiting women on their short visits home that would allow them to buy provisions for the entire winter— including costly coal to feed the stoves that kept their caravans warm.

Such opportunities didn't arise every day, and Selina's father had jumped at the chance. Even the prospect of returning to the Blackwell estate, with all its nightmarish memories, would be worthwhile if it meant securing the survival of the camp. If the Roma moved on now the men would have to give up this precious source of reliable income.

It isn't just the men's jobs at stake, though, is it?

Selina bit her lip as she thought of the women who'd had the misfortune to bear autumn babies: three of them, all born within a few days of each other, struggling to breathe in the raw mornings and coughing their hearts out at the first suggestion of a frost. They would never survive the jolting journey along pitted roads if the camp had to move. The chill would get into their tiny lungs and one of the women would be sewing a miniature shroud before they knew what had happened.

No. There was no way they could leave now.

'I mean it, Grandmother.'

With a supreme effort Selina once again attempted to banish Edward from her mind. He had no place in her world; their chance encounter could so easily have ended in disaster.

'You know nothing in this world is more important to me than the safety of our people.'

Zillah seemed about to reply when the silent night was shattered by a terrible scream.

Edward couldn't sleep.

That damned letter from Father certainly hadn't helped, he reflected drily. How unfortunate that even now the Squire's missives brought so little happiness to their recipients.

Edward's mouth set in a grim line as he recalled the weight that had settled in his stomach when he'd heard the news of his father's passing. Their relationship had been strained in life. Each had been as stubborn as the other, and Ambrose's unsuccessful attempts to control his son had damaged their already shaky bond.

Edward remembered the many times his father had pushed him to the limits of his patience with his demands. His move to London, ostensibly to take care of their business in the capital, had allowed Edward to put a distance between them, and that was the only reason their relationship had managed to survive at all. They had disagreed on so many things, and their heated arguments had been the cause of more than one servant running for cover.

But Ambrose was the only father Edward would ever have, and in his own way he had begun to mourn the man who had caused him so much frustration; or at least he had, until anger had seeped in to mingle with his complicated grief.

He threw back the red coverlet and left his bed. The cold night air raised goosebumps on his skin and he shrugged his way into his best brocade dressing gown. The fire in the grate had burned down to ash, and he toyed momentarily with the idea of calling for a maid to bring it back to life before dismissing the thought in irritation. When had he become the kind of man to consider dragging a girl from her warm bed in the middle of the freezing night solely to pander to his own needs?

He'd been in London too long; it was as well he'd returned to Warwickshire when he had. The capital, with all its diversions and frivolous pursuits, had threatened to turn him into a 'perfect' gentleman—selfish, hedonistic and mainly decorative. Now he was back where he belonged he could feel the countryside and its ways seeping back into his bones, gently erasing the hardness city living had threatened to instil in him.

Edward struck a match and lit the candle standing on his desk. The light illuminated the Squire's final letter, lying on the green leather top, and Edward picked it up. He'd read it a dozen times already, and it did not improve with further scrutiny.

His father's solicitor had seemed almost apologetic when he'd handed it over, having taken it from his ancient safe at the reading of Ambrose's will. It was written in a bold and flowing hand, and Edward ran his eye over the last communication he would ever receive from the man to whom he had been so deeply vexing.

> *As my only son and heir, you have repeatedly disappointed me in your duty to continue the line of our great and noble family. Nothing in your life could be more important, and your persistent failure to marry has provoked me to act.*
>
> *I have instructed Mr Lucas to amend the terms of my will and add a condition on your inheritance. If you have not taken a wife within two months of my death the entirety of your inheritance will revert to my brother, your Uncle Charles, in his position as next in line.*

He dropped the letter back onto the desk and extinguished the candle. He'd half expected it. His reluctance to marry had been like a red rag to a bull for Ambrose, for whom the continuation of the family name had been almost an obsession. Pretty heiress after pretty heiress had been paraded under Edward's nose, but of course the damage had been done long before then.

His mother had been the first to crush his faith in gentry women, but the Right Honourable Letitia James had driven the lesson home with brutal clarity. With her blonde ringlets and china-blue eyes Letitia had the face of an angel but not the morals to match, and her thoughtless betrayal of Edward with a richer suitor had opened the wounds he had hoped she would help him to heal. She was the only woman he had ever entertained marrying, and her actions had only proved to Edward his reticence had been justified.

Edward felt a hot pulse of anger course through him as he wrenched his mind away from past pains and recalled the full contents of the letter. Unable to dictate terms while alive, Ambrose had in death finally managed to find a way to bend Edward to his will, and recognition of the fact that he had no choice but to obey caused Edward's hands to curl into fists. He wasn't a simpleton; he knew he would have to wed eventually. It was the notion of being ordered, instructed like a child, that turned Edward's blood to fire.

In fairness, I suppose my bride might not be entirely like Mother or Letitia, he mused grimly as he dropped into his favourite armchair by the cold hearth. *You never know. Her pretty ringlets might be dark instead of blonde, for instance.*

The thought of dark hair stirred something in the back of his mind.

The girl from the woods. Selina. Now, that's the sort of woman a man might be persuaded to marry, were such a feat ever to be managed.

What had she meant, he owed her twice? The words had puzzled him ever since their chance meeting. Surely they had never met before. Edward knew he would never have forgotten one such as her. It must have been simple mischief on her part, doubtless for her own amusement, and he had resolved to put her from his mind.

Unfortunately the Romani girl had persisted in working her way into his thoughts with vexing regularity since their encounter three days before. The memory had troubled him to begin with—what was he doing, allowing a woman so much space in his mind?—until he had reassured himself that it meant nothing.

It was simple human nature to admire a pretty face, and that was surely all his idle thoughts amounted to. Couldn't a man enjoy the mental picture of a handsome woman without it meaning anything more? He was in little danger of ever seeing her again—and besides, his disinclination for spending too long in the company of young ladies ran deep.

Thoughts as to her suitability as a wife were as laughable as they were entirely hypothetical. Still... She wouldn't be self-centred and idle like the women of his class, he was sure of it. She certainly wouldn't spend too much money on dresses and amusements—in a stark contrast to the wasteful extravagance of the gentry. Of course it helped that she was beautiful, but a beautiful wife was often more trouble than she was worth—and besides, it wasn't as though he had any intention of *loving* a woman. He doubted he was even capable anymore, his heart having twice been battered by thoughtless rejection.

The only female with any sort of claim to his affections was little Ophelia, and he resolved there and then never to allow her to be moulded into an upperclass Miss. If she were to be subjected to endless lessons in etiquette and how to be a true lady he feared his sister would one day become conditioned to be more concerned with herself than other people. Just like his mother.

Edward grimaced. *Now you're getting maudlin,* he chided himself. Ophelia was nothing like the first mistress of Blackwell Hall and thank goodness for it. His sister would never be so cruel as to abandon her own child and run away with another man, leaving without so much as a goodbye for the boy she'd left behind, who had spent months waiting in vain for her return and defending her reputation with his fists.

At least she'd done him one favour—even if accidentally. From her harsh teaching he had learned a valuable lesson: he knew never to fall in love with a woman lest she leave and shatter his heart all over again. That was his mother's legacy.

Letitia had been the only one to break through, and Edward had dared to believe she might be a better woman than the one who had given him life. But instead she had proved herself almost a copy of his mother, and after her duplicity he had rebuilt his defences with even higher walls.

Edward drummed his fingers on the arm of his chair as thoughts of Letitia flitted through his mind. The notion that he had once thought she could be his bride seemed so ridiculous now he might almost have seen the humour in it if she hadn't ripped open the emotional scars he'd borne since childhood.

She knew how Mother's leaving had affected me, and yet she betrayed me in exactly the same way Mother betrayed Father.

If what he'd felt for Letitia had been love he could do without it. For when the loved one left—as apparently was inevitable—the pain was almost too much to bear.

The gilt clock on the mantelpiece struck two, but Edward was only half listening to the feeble chimes. The idea of another fashionable young lady parading around his countryside sanctuary appalled him. This was where he came to escape the cloying falseness of high society—the notion of inviting it into this last outpost of peace was unthinkable.

He sighed and rubbed his aching forehead with one hand. 'Think, Ned,' he said aloud. 'Put that Cambridge education to use for once in your life.'

Inspiration wouldn't come.

Edward got to his feet and paced the floor, boards creaking as he moved. 'Think! This is your future. Do you really want to be bound to such a creature for the rest of your life?'

Anger at his father's last actions churned within him once again, and he felt his chest tighten with the now familiar mixture of grief and rage. The Squire had been dead almost one month already; only a few weeks remained for Edward to find a suitable match or risk forfeiting his inheritance forever.

He could barely even remember Uncle Charles, the man to whom all his future could be lost. The only communication they had shared in the twelve years since Charles had left for the Continent was the occasional letter, never concerning anything warmer than news of business affairs. The injustice of his situation made Edward curse out loud.

He crossed to the window and drew aside one heavy curtain. There was no sign of dawn. Darkness would cover the estate for hours yet—until the sun sulked into view and its pale autumn rays signalled the start of a new day.

His rooms were at the front of the Hall, positioned to make the most of the natural light, and from the window Edward could just make out the line of manicured trees that stood to attention on either side of the long drive leading up to the Hall's imposing front door. He gazed out at the night, watching the trees stir gently in the moonlight.

A movement further down the drive caught his eye. He frowned. Even from a distance he could tell that whatever was out there was approaching the house at some speed, and getting ever closer. Edward squinted, straining his eyes against the gloom. Was it an animal of some kind?

Yes, he could just see it now: a great horse, bleached bone-white by the moon, galloping towards the Hall as though fleeing the fires of hell. Its rider was swathed in a cloak, with only her hair uncovered, flying out behind her like streamers in a storm—

'*Selina?*'

A thrill of something unknown flared in Edward's chest. It was definitely her—the closer she drew, the more Edward's certainty grew that the figure flying towards him was the girl from the woods. Now she was in range he could even recognise her horse: a huge grey beast, flecked with scars and knotted with hard muscle, speeding down the gravelled drive with a gracefulness that belied its size.

Momentarily frozen in surprise, all Edward could do was watch her approach, his confusion growing with every moment. He hadn't expected to see her again, and yet here she was. A less sensible man might have called it fate, and the unwanted suggestion was enough to galvanise him into action.

His heart pounded in his ears as he wrenched on his

breeches, a rapid succession of thoughts chasing each other through his mind. Why was she here? At this hour? And why had she approached so swiftly? Something must be gravely wrong. She had given the impression that she distrusted his offer of friendship. What events could the intervening few days have wrought to bring about such a change?

A disloyal corner of his consciousness registered the thought that he was, despite his rational mind, *pleased* she had sought him out. Whatever it was she wanted, it was to him that she was turning. He dismissed the thought as soon as it arose—*ridiculous notion!*—but the echo of it stubbornly remained.

A thunderous sound at the front door drove him onwards in even greater haste. *She'll break it in two if she's not careful*, he thought in wry amusement as he thrust his feet into long leather boots.

The creak of an inner door being hurriedly flung open signalled the emergence of Blackwell's aged butler, Evans, and Edward couldn't restrain a grin at the prospect of the faithful retainer confronted with Selina.

Poor Evans. He smiled. *He won't know what's hit him.*

She was trying to pull away from the butler's firm grip when Edward reached the top of the grand sweeping staircase that led down into the entrance hall, all the while waving something in Evans's heated face—something white. Or at least it might have been white originally, but now it was streaked with mud and perhaps...dried blood?

'Mr Fulbrooke!' Selina spotted him and her attempts at escape doubled. Her hair was windswept and tangled from riding and her eyes were wild. 'Mr Fulbrooke! Please, sir, I must speak with you—let me *go!*'

Evans was trying manfully to restrain her, but the woman appeared to be as strong as an ox. The older man's face was puce with effort, and one of his slippers had come clean off in the fracas.

'You can't just push in here, waking the whole house—'

Selina paid him about as much attention as Edward would have paid a gnat. 'I brought this with me. We met in the woods—do you remember? You gave me this— this handkerchief!'

'Of course, Miss Agres.' Edward reached the bottom step and gently laid a hand on the butler's heaving shoulder. 'Thank you, Evans, you've done very well, but Miss Agres is a friend of mine. Please let go of her.'

The other man's face was a picture of surprise, and he opened his mouth as if to argue. Edward watched as the butler took a good look at Selina, taking in her disordered hair and unusual dress, but years of unfailing service prevailed and he hesitated for only a moment before sweeping into a low bow and stepping away.

'Please forgive me, miss. I should never have laid hands on you had I realised you were known to the master.'

Edward turned back to her, a smile forming on his lips. But it flickered and died when he saw the expression on her face, and he registered for the first time how her entire body trembled as though she suffered from an ague. Her slim form, so perturbingly attractive to him upon his first sight of her, now seemed to radiate a vulnerability unlike the defiance of their previous meeting. Was it for that reason he felt a glimmer of protective concern?

'Miss Agres? What's the matter?' She was very pale,

he saw with alarm—could she be ill? The pallor served to highlight the rich darkness of her eyes, a fact that did not escape him. 'You seem unwell. Won't you please sit down and I—?'

'There's no time!' Selina burst out.

She was wringing her hands, and Edward had to fight the unwelcome urge to take them in his own and hold them still.

'Please, Mr Fulbrooke, come with me at once! You said you'd be a friend to me, and that your word was your law—I need you to prove it!'

Edward gazed down at her. He had been right; something truly terrible had occurred. There could be no other explanation for her coming to him, and in such a state of obvious distress.

'You must try to calm yourself.' He spoke with such firmness that Selina's agitation seemed to check a little. 'I will, of course, do anything within my power to help you, but first you must explain to me the particulars.'

Selina took a deep breath and clenched her hands into fists. Behind her, Edward caught sight of the below-stairs maids peeping from the servants' corridor, their eyes wide with curiosity.

'Evans. Would you please ensure the maids return to their beds and tell Greene to saddle my horse immediately? I have a feeling I'll be going out, and I'm not sure when I shall return.'

Chapter Three

Selina glanced across at Edward, riding next to her on his sleek thoroughbred mare. Even in the silvery moonlight she could see his sharp jaw was tightly clenched as he bent low over his horse's neck, urging her on at full speed. She swallowed. Even at this pace they might still be too late.

At that first cry Selina had vaulted from her bunk and thrown on her clothes. Something within her had known what was happening even before the woman had stumbled up the steps of her caravan and hammered on the door, shouting out what she had seen and moaning in fear.

'They're coming! They're coming for us! What will we do? How can we defend ourselves?'

'We can't.' Zillah had stumped the short length of the cabin, unbolted the split door of the *vardo* and taken the wailing woman outside firmly by the shoulders. 'The only hope we have of surviving this is to lock ourselves in and pray for a miracle.'

'Is that *all*?' The woman had stared at Zillah, and Selina had seen the horror in her eyes. 'Is that all we can do?'

'Yes. With the men away we have no protectors. We don't even have any tools with which to arm ourselves—curse our foolishness! We should have planned for this.'

In the dim light Zillah had looked haggard with fear, and for the first time in her life Selina realised her grandmother was afraid. The knowledge had shaken her to the core. If weathered, unflappable Zillah was frightened, their situation must be every bit as bad as Selina feared.

'We bolt our doors and we pray.'

'And if they break down our doors? What then?'

Zillah closed her eyes. 'Then we try to save the children. Whatever the cost.'

That was when they'd heard it: men's voices, perhaps ten in all, punctuated by the excited baying of a pack of hounds. The woman had paled and fled back to her caravan, to drive home the heavy bolt across her door and gather her children round her, as though there was something she could do to keep them safe.

'So this is where you're hiding, is it?'

'Did you think we wouldn't find you, child-stealer?'

Selina's blood had run cold. She had known those voices—Harris and Milton, Edward Fulbrooke had called them. She'd remembered their threats, and her stomach had begun to knot in animalistic terror.

'We've brought some friends with us. Why don't you come out and meet them? Such a shame you ran from us before—if you hadn't we wouldn't have needed to come and find you…'

Selina's heart slammed into her ribs now, as she and Edward rode onwards. They were so close. Was there a chance they would get there in time? She imagined the children, cowering behind their shaking mothers as the sound of the men's mocking laughter echoed around the camp and heavy clubs began to whistle towards shuttered windows—

She gasped for air. *No.* She couldn't allow herself to think like that. If she went to pieces how would Edward find the camp? She had to stay strong and do whatever it took to protect her people. She had already taken the biggest risk, in the name of salvation.

Zillah had stared at her, eyes wide with horror. 'What? What did you say?'

'You said yourself—we need a miracle!'

'That would be no miracle, girl, only madness!' Zillah had backed away from her. 'You would go to *them* for help? Our enemies?'

'What choice do we have?' Selina cried. 'He gave me his word; I mean to test it!'

'But, Lina—'

'This is all my doing. I'm the only one with even the smallest hope of getting us out of this unscathed.' Selina had grasped both of Zillah's hands in her own and felt them tremble. 'Do you think I would go if there was any other way? You know I would not. You know I don't make this decision lightly.'

From outside the caravan both women had heard a fresh scream, followed by a bray of boorish laughter.

'Grandmother, please. I have to try.'

Zillah had peered up at her, an unreadable expression in her ebony eyes, and given a shuddering sigh. 'Your mother wouldn't want this, Selina.'

'Perhaps. But I know she wouldn't want anyone getting hurt if I had a chance to protect them.'

She'd slipped from the caravan and out into the meadow. Keeping to the shadows, she'd called softly to

Djali and been up onto his back and gone from the camp before anybody could stop her.

She felt Edward's eyes upon her, although she didn't dare turn her head to look. She'd been grateful when he'd saddled up and followed her—more grateful than he would ever know—and amazed, too. She hadn't *really* expected him to keep his word, but to try had been her only option. What had been the real chances that an upper-class gentleman would honour his promise to a Roma?

She had obviously underestimated him in that moment, but that didn't mean she trusted him. The canker of suspicion ran too deep, and even now Selina had the unpleasant feeling of having jumped from the frying pan into the fire.

Even the horror of her current circumstances hadn't managed to completely obliterate her disloyal senses, however. A furtive glance towards him was like a swift punch in the guts. Once again she was assailed by the handsomeness of his face and the powerfully masculine frame of his body, and she felt her throat contract as she caught a glimpse of a tantalising expanse of toned chest: Edward's shirt had apparently been thrown on in great haste, with a few buttons left unfastened. There was a smattering of hair there, far darker than the gold on his head—*fascinatingly* so, in fact…

Selina wrenched her eyes away before he could turn and catch her looking. Even more mortifying than she ever would have believed was the realisation that she was *enjoying* the sight of him improperly dressed. It caused her great agitation, and her cheeks were flushed with both shame and guilt as she rode next to him in pained silence. Shame for appreciating such a trivial thing at such a time, and guilt at being appreciative of such a man at *any* time whatsoever.

Her instinctive attraction to Edward seemed to be tightening its grip on her, not loosening as she had hoped, and her grip on Djali's reins tightened likewise at the thought.

'Are we getting close?'

Selina swallowed hard, trying to force her voice into some semblance of normality. 'Yes. The camp is just beyond the line of trees up ahead.'

Edward nodded and spurred his horse onwards. Refusing to be outpaced, Djali surged forward too, and the horses flew neck and neck across the final stretch.

As they approached the screen of branches Edward began to slow. 'Miss Agres. Stop.' He pulled his mare up short.

Frowning, Selina did the same, and watched as Edward dismounted and hooked his reins over a branch. 'I want you to wait here.'

'What? No!' She slipped down from Djali's back and moved to stand at his head. 'Mr Fulbrooke, there's no way I'll be leaving my people to face this alone!'

'Be sensible.' Edward's voice was steady. 'If what you have told me is true, these men were drawn here by your presence. What effect do you think it will have if you suddenly appear in front of them?'

Selina opened her mouth, but her reply was quickly cut off by Edward's outstretched hand. He stood so close he could have touched her if he'd chosen to. His proximity made Selina's heart skip an unwilling beat and she quickly took a step backwards.

'The last thing either of us wants is to make things worse. I would consider it a personal favour if you would stay here until I come to find you.' He looked away. 'I would also like to know that you're safe.'

Selina blinked at him. He actually sounded concerned for her welfare. In all probability it was an affectation, born out of some misguided upper-class notion of honour, although she might have been fooled, had she been the foolish type, into believing he was genuine. And yet—to her shame—the notion that he might harbour some kind of regard for her wasn't unpleasant. Certainly some small part of her—a disloyal part, she thought crossly—hoped, against her better judgement, that he might be sincere.

Why, Lina? Because he's handsome? Selina scoffed at herself, irritated by her own brief weakness. *You should know better than that. Why should he feel any kind of concern for you? And why should you want it?*

'I'll stay here,' she said reluctantly. 'But only because I know you speak the truth. I can well imagine what would happen if those men laid eyes on me again.'

Edward nodded. 'I'm glad. Now I'll go and see what can be done to help your people.'

Selina stared at the ground. Edward's boots really were the best she had ever seen, and it was much easier to look at them than into the eyes of their owner. 'Thank you.'

'Don't thank me yet.'

There was an edge of grim humour to Edward's voice, and Selina chanced a glance up at his face. His firm jaw was fixed, and even in the pale light of the moon she could see the set of his expression. He looked determined, yet calm, and the combination only served to emphasise the handsome lines of his features. Selina twisted her fingers together beneath the cover of her cloak.

'We need to make sure I'm successful first. I intend to seek out every man who thinks he has the right to do this, and show him the error of his ways. Now, please, hide yourself. I hope to be back soon.'

Selina watched as he moved cautiously through the trees and vanished from her sight. *Well, I did what I could.* It was all up to Edward now, she supposed as she settled herself against the thick trunk of a spreading oak.

And what of Mama? Zillah's earlier rebuke echoed through Selina's mind. Would she really be so appalled? Or would she understand that family came first and must be protected even if at great personal cost?

Edward had taken her by surprise so far, she could not deny it. His conduct towards her had been far better than she would have expected from a gentleman—and a Fulbrooke, come to that. His face was undeniably pleasing, though his fair looks were in stark contrast to the dark Roma handsomeness, strange but not unappealing in their novelty.

Not that you should care for such pretty manners, or notice the colour of his eyes, she reminded herself sternly. It took more than such trivial things to impress her. It was just an observation, and one she would continue to strive to banish from her mind.

She shivered. A glance down at her hands showed that they still shook—with cold or fear? she wondered. She strained her ears, both hoping and dreading to catch a whisper of a clue as to what was happening beyond the trees, but there was nothing save the quiet breathing of the horses and the sigh of leaves stirring in the night air.

Selina squeezed her eyes shut. *Oh, Mama. What would you have done?*

* * *

Edward felt the brutal atmosphere change to one of shamefaced fear almost as soon as he stepped from the camp's shadows into the light of Harris's torch and swept it from his hand with rough force. One glance at Edward's flame-lit face—rigid with cold fury—was enough to make the group of men, frozen in the act of battering the spoked wheels of a caravan, decide that perhaps the Roma had learned their lesson, and Edward might almost have laughed at the instantaneous change of their voices from jeering to pleading.

'We were just trying to protect Miss Ophelia, sir,' Milton ventured meekly, attempting to hide a club behind his back as his friends shuffled from foot to foot, their eyes sliding past Edward to fix on the ground.

'Do you think me a simpleton, man?'

Edward turned to him, feeling the rage that bubbled within him course hotly through his veins. The Roma women inside their caravans must have been beside themselves, he thought disgustedly. What kind of man could take pleasure in such a thing?

'We both know this has nothing to do with my sister and everything to do with your need to bully those you feel beneath you. Am I wrong? Do you disagree? Answer me!'

The gamekeeper stared down at his boots, the ashen shade of his face visible even in the moonlight. 'I… I'm not…'

'Not a bully? Of course you are. You all are. What other possible explanation could there be for *ten men* to go to the effort of seeking out and then attacking a camp full of women and children?'

Edward glared down at the man from his great height.

The image of Selina's terrified expression and shaking body flashed before him and he felt his fury surge upwards. Even if the Romani woman hadn't been such an undeniable beauty—which, he had to admit to himself, was part of the reason he had extended the hand of friendship in the first place—he still would have interceded on her behalf. How dared these men take it upon themselves to behave so appallingly on *his* estate? And, to add insult to injury, to pretend they did so out of loyalty to his sister?

'You didn't do this for Ophelia.'

He gestured across the camp, catching glimpses of the damage as he turned. Cooking pots and blankets lay strewn across the ground, evidently kicked about by heavy boots, and more than one lantern had been hurled down to burst into shards of glass. The caravans had fared better than he had feared, at least. The half-hour it had taken for Selina to return with him hadn't left the men enough time to destroy any of them, although several now bore the marks of savage blows to their wooden walls.

'Not for her. You did it because *you* wanted to.'

It was an ugly truth, Edward knew, but a truth nonetheless. He'd heard tales of abuse before, from the Roma boys he had played with as a child, when their easy laughter and unselfconscious warmth had seemed poles apart from the stiff propriety of playmates in his own class and their welcome of him had left a permanent impression of their decency.

There was no basis for this mistreatment—no justification at all. But folk inherited their intolerances from their fathers, as had their fathers before them, and prejudice was passed down through generations to rest in the hearts of men such as Harris and Milton—men with little power of their own, whose low social standing fanned the flames of their desire to find someone, *anyone*, they perceived to be worth less than themselves to bear the brunt of their frustrations.

He surveyed the men surrounding him, taking in their various attempts at contrite expressions, and felt his rage renew its vigour. He could dismiss them—throw them off his land just as they had wanted to drive off the Romani—but they had wives who had committed no crime other than making a dubious choice of husband, and children, too, reliant on their fathers' employment for survival. To remove the men from his service would be to punish their families, some of whom had served the Blackwell estate for generations, and he felt a twinge of conscience at the thought of that.

Damn it all. These animals should count their blessings.

He looked down at them, his face set in an expression of grim dislike. 'I have decided on this occasion to let you off with a warning. Make no mistake, however,' Edward went on. 'I will not tolerate this kind of behaviour on my property. If I hear anything of this nature has happened again, next time I will not be so lenient.'

The light of their torches illuminated the men's faces, each sagging with relief.

Only Milton looked mutinous, and Edward raised a challenging eyebrow. 'Something troubles you?'

'No, sir.' Milton shook his head quickly, although resentment gleamed dully in his sunken eyes. 'Thank you for your kindness, sir.'

'Very well.' Edward nodded his head in the vague direction of where the estate workers' cottages lay.

'You may all return home now, to reflect upon what I have said.'

The men slunk off, dogs creeping at their heels. No doubt to tell their wives of Squire Fulbrooke's unfair and malicious treatment of his well-intentioned, faithful servants, Edward imagined. He snorted as he watched them go, slouching away between the trees. It was almost an anti-climax, how easily he had been able to intervene. They were cowards indeed.

Long grass knotted about his boots as he fought his way back up the bank and through the line of trees to where Selina waited, a silent shape at the base of an ancient tree.

'Mr Fulbrooke!' She leapt to her feet when she saw him coming, one hand at her throat and the other on the tree's trunk to steady herself. 'What happened? Is the camp—?'

'Do not fear.'

Edward could hardly keep himself from reaching out to touch her shaking hand. She looked as though she might faint, he noted in alarm. Not that he would blame her if she did. She'd had the most terrible experience, and if anything he was rather impressed by how well she'd handled it.

The notion almost made him frown. 'The men have gone and your camp is safe.'

'Gone? Safe?'

Edward looked at Selina a little more closely. Pale and beautiful in the soft light of the moon, she appeared to be swaying now. 'You look a little faint. Here, take my arm. We can walk together.'

'No.' Selina shook her head wildly. 'I'll ride—it'll be quicker. I have to get back *now*.'

'You're in no fit state to ride anywhere. Let me help you. You're no use to anybody unconscious.'

'But Djali—'

'Will follow us, I'm sure. Now, come. Take my arm.'

She hesitated, suspicion sparking in her eyes once more. Edward sighed, supressing a flicker of irritation. *Mistrustful as a feral cat.*

'Miss Agres. I have risen in the middle of the night, ridden for miles and dispersed a mob—all in the name of your safety. Do you really think it likely that I undertook all that only to lunge at you on the pretence of offering my arm?'

Selina's eyes flashed, and she opened her mouth to reply before evidently thinking better of it. She took a shaky step forward and, with the air of one with a gun to her head, slipped her hand beneath his arm and gripped tightly.

It was a warm little hand, Edward noted with a jolt of surprise. The night was chill, but the patch of forearm covered by her palm suddenly didn't seem cold at all. It was an unexpectedly pleasant sensation. Usually having a woman on his arm felt intrusive, but Selina's touch, although firm, was not invasive.

He wondered for a moment at how it was that her grasp was so much more bearable than anybody else's had ever been. If he were to be honest with himself, it was more than merely bearable… At the first touch of her fingers he'd felt a sharp pulse of something unexpected shoot through him—a bewilderingly quick nameless rush that had caused him to frown in surprise. He glanced down at Selina, searching her face for any indication that she had felt a similar sensation, but she studiously avoided his gaze, the faintest suggestion of a blush colouring her cheeks.

'Can we go now, please, Mr Fulbrooke?'

Edward smothered a smile at the careful politeness of her tone. 'Of course. Watch your step.'

The slight pressure of her hand on his arm was the only way Edward knew she walked beside him. Her steps were almost silent, graceful as any wild animal.

It was only a short distance to walk: down a small slope, through a band of trees and then out into the secluded meadow that Selina's Roma community had thought so safe.

Edward surveyed the scene in front of him. Fires had been lit in his absence, their orange tongues dancing in the night air, and a group of women stood to one side, conversing in low voices that flared with both sorrow and relief. Among them a young girl was singing softly in a tongue Edward didn't recognise, gently rocking a baby on her hip. An old man, bent almost double with age, seemed to be tending to an injured horse, while a small boy carefully swept up a heap of spilled oats from an upended sack. Another cluster of women were gathered around one of the caravans, its painted sides still gleaming cherry-red in the firelight but heavily dented by brute force.

He approached cautiously. Despite Selina's presence at his side he could almost feel the cold stares of the women upon him, their fear and uncertainty palpable.

'Grandmother!'

Selina slipped away from him and the place where her hand had rested on his arm felt suddenly cold. She had held it there for mere minutes, and yet he felt a curious sense of loss at the withdrawal of her touch. Ed-

ward pulled his coat closer about himself, shrugging off
the uncanny sensation. He must be getting tired… His
mind was beginning to play tricks on him.

Selina was in the arms of an old woman, being folded
into a fierce embrace. The woman was small and frail-
looking, but with a similarity around the cheekbones that
suggested a family connection. The embrace ended and
the two began to talk. He heard the rise and fall of their
voices, soft at first, but swelling to such a pitch that the
neighbouring Roma glanced across in concern.

He thought he saw the glint of tears on Selina's face,
shining like rubies in the light of the fire, and turned
away. *You shouldn't be here,* he warned himself. *You've
played your part.* Selina and her grandmother evidently
had much to discuss, and none of it his business. He
should enquire as to whether he could be of any further
assistance and then leave these people in peace.

'Mr Fulbrooke?' Selina stood close to him, her fingers working in apprehension. The fire lit up one side
of her face, making flames dance in one jet iris while
throwing the other into shadow. 'My grandmother told
me what happened, and what you did to help us. We are
so grateful.'

Edward smiled. 'It was a pleasure.' The tears had
gone, he saw: she'd rubbed them away with the back of
her hand when she'd seen him looking. There was softness under her tough facade, he was sure. Why was she
so determined that he not see it?

'We are forever in your debt.'

'There is no debt, Miss Agres.' He shook his head.
'You were kind to my sister when she was in need and
I've just shown the same kindness to you and yours.'

Selina nodded, although Edward saw unhappiness in

the lovely oval of her face. The sight niggled at him, creating an uncomfortable feeling of concern that took him by surprise. 'Has something else occurred?' he asked.

'Something else?'

'You were so relieved before we arrived in camp. Now you've spoken with your grandmother and you seem distressed again. What has she said to you?'

'It's nothing that need trouble you.' Selina's voice was quiet and she looked away from him across the camp.

Edward followed her gaze to where a little girl was attempting to coax her trembling dog out from beneath a caravan, the wheels of which were scarred by the blade of an axe.

'It's only—they said they'd be back.'

'What?'

Selina turned to him, her eyes huge with worry. 'As they were leaving Grandmother heard them. They said it was only on your land that you would feel obliged to protect us, and that as soon as we moved they would come to find me.'

Edward felt his pulse quicken. Those two-faced, disobedient rogues. How *dared* they make new threats? How dared they try to get around his express word? And yet...

There isn't much I can do to prevent it, he thought darkly. Edward couldn't control what they did outside his estate, and short of catching them in the act he would have no concrete proof of their involvement in any future incidents.

Selina's voice was hoarse. 'It's all my fault.'

'It is not.'

'Oh, but it is.'

She smiled then, a tight stretch of her lips filled with

such sadness and fear that Edward felt another sharp stab of that *something* lance through his chest, only to flicker and fade the next moment.

'Why do you say that?'

'Because it's me they want. And they'll continue to hound us, over and over, until they find me.'

He gazed down at her. Out of the corner of his eye he could see the group of women watching him, Selina's grandmother among them. Nobody seemed willing to come nearer, and the contrast between their wary distance and the way women of his own class clustered around him at any given opportunity was so absurd a part of him wanted to laugh.

The sight of Selina's rigid face stopped him. 'What is your plan?' he asked.

She sighed—a long drawn-out shudder of breath that seemed to come all the way up from her toes. 'I'll have to give myself up to them. There is no other way.'

'You cannot possibly!' Edward stared at her, hardly able to express his disbelief. 'You cannot mean that!'

'What choice do I have?' Selina stepped away from him, her face shuttered and blank. 'Apparently I've made fools of them—and they won't stop until they've proved they're the victors and I've lost.' She shook her head slowly. 'They'll continue to terrorise us when we leave here, and with the health of the babies and our menfolk's jobs we can't get far enough away to escape them. This is the only way.'

Edward passed a hand through the tousled thatch of his hair. Selina had given him a brief outline of the Roma's current situation as they had ridden out from Blackwell. To move the community now would indeed spell disaster.

'So, you see, it's what I must do. Grandmother forbids it, of course.' There was a ghost of that terrible smile again. 'But I won't allow a repeat of what happened tonight.'

It was unthinkable. Edward paced a few steps away from her, noting with perverse amusement the way the group of women standing nearby flinched backwards. She couldn't. The very idea that Selina would consider sacrificing herself for the good of her community was madness.

A commendable sentiment, Edward thought, *but utter madness.*

The fact that he couldn't see how to prevent it from happening pained him more than he cared to admit. He had no choice other than to acknowledge that she was a remarkable woman, quite unlike any he'd met before, and the notion of her in such danger was abhorrent to him. Of course she would face that danger bravely—there was that damned flicker of admiration again—but still…

If only there was a way he could reliably intervene… a set of circumstances that meant Harris and Milton could never touch her and she would be permanently out of their reach…

They would continue to hunt Selina, of that he was certain. Their lust for vengeance for her perceived victory and the pull of that generations-strong prejudice was too powerful. Neither common decency nor the pleas of their wives would prevent them from attempting to punish Selina and the other Roma. She had escaped them not once, but twice, and now their resolve would be firm.

No doubt it was the rumours of his family's mistreatment of the Roma that had made the men feel safe in persecuting them, Edward mused darkly. Charles had done something terrible, and Ambrose had all but chased the travellers off his land. Their prejudices had been clear to all—perhaps people suspected that Edward shared their sentiments.

The idea that he might so easily have followed their unthinking bigotry was uncomfortable. *Thank goodness I was taught better than that,* he thought, his eyes on Selina's silent face.

His childhood Romani friends had done him that favour, by including him in their play and allowing him to be himself in a way frowned upon at his austere home. *And that little Roma girl who showed me such rare kindness will never know the difference she particularly helped to make.*

Her tender care of him was something he hadn't experienced at Blackwell Hall; his mother had been only occasionally attentive, in a detached sort of way, and Ambrose had never so much as lain an affectionate hand on his shoulder.

The thought of his father caused a pain in his chest Edward could have done without, and resentment swelled within him once again as the contents of that enraging final letter ran through his head.

Having been temporarily replaced by the severity of Selina's situation, his own troubles now returned to the forefront of his mind with a vengeance, and Edward felt his insides twist with renewed anger at the late Squire's meddling. Time was running out for him to claim his inheritance—a needless pressure born out of one man's obsession with control.

But Edward was his own master and always had

been—that was what his father had hated so much. To *make* Edward obey him in death in a way he hadn't managed in life would have been Ambrose's final victory.

An idea exploded into Edward's consciousness with such vigour he could have sworn he heard it. *Of course.* It was so simple—and wouldn't it neatly solve Selina's problem at the same time as his own?

He would obey his father's will to the letter—right down to the final dot of the final 'i'. He would marry as instructed—but not to the kind of woman Ambrose would have so ardently desired, nor one in any way reminiscent of the lady who had taken his heart only to grind it into dust.

It was risky. People wouldn't like it. Certainly his father would have been beside himself with rage. But the opinion of society had never mattered much to Edward and, given the desperate circumstances of both parties involved, it now mattered even less. There was even some satisfaction to be taken in knowing he was, as always, acting according to his own wishes—dictated to by nobody but himself.

'Miss Agres?'

Selina had turned away from him. Standing before the fire, only her silhouette was visible to Edward's gaze, outlined in sparks and tongues of curling flame. He could see the tension in her back and knew it was only by sheer willpower that she was maintaining her composure.

'Yes.'

'I think I may have a solution to your current dilemma—depending on your answers to two questions.'

'Have you?' Her tone was flat and devoid of curiosity. 'And what would those questions be?'

Edward ignored how dull she sounded, feeling his hopes beginning to build. 'The first is: What is your age?'

She didn't turn to look at him, her eyes still fixed on the flames before her. 'How is that of any relevance?'

'Please. Humour me.'

She sighed, as though it was an effort to find the words to reply. 'Very well. I am recently turned twenty.' The fire crackled, sending sparks swirling into the night sky. 'Your second question?'

Edward reached for her. At the first touch of his hand on her shoulder Selina jumped and swung round to face him, a frown of distrust clouding her features. Edward smiled as the expression in her dark eyes, at first wary and fearful, turned to frozen astonishment as she watched him drop to one knee and take her small hand in his own.

'Selina Agres. Will you marry me?'

Chapter Four

'I— *What?* What did you say?'

Selina gaped at him, feeling her mouth drop open in shock. Had she misheard? Surely he could *never* have said what she thought he'd—

'I said, will you marry me?'

She stared downwards, first at Edward's intent face and then at their hands, joined together in a clasp uncomfortably like that of a pair of lovers. His hand was so much larger and yet it held hers so gently—*almost tenderly*, a disloyal voice in the back of her mind murmured.

To her horror, a sensation not unlike the warmth of a fledgling fire kindled beneath Edward's firm fingers, flickering against her skin and stealing upwards towards her arm. The feeling crept higher, warming her against her will, until it reached her chest and settled there, burning inside her with an inexplicable heat that sent her heart fluttering.

On the very edge of her field of vision she could just make out Zillah, watching them in uncharacteristically mute shock, for all the world as though she couldn't believe what she was seeing. Selina wasn't sure she believed it either. He couldn't be serious—of course he couldn't. Whatever had possessed him to make such a cruel joke at such a moment?

'Have you run *mad*?' The flickering embers of sensation sparked further, beginning to smoulder, and Selina snatched her hand from Edward's grasp, cradling it against her body with the other as though he had truly burnt her with his touch. 'Or do you think to mock me?'

'Neither, I hope.' Edward rose lightly to his feet again, and Selina took a step backwards, out of his long reach. He didn't attempt to come closer, but instead regarded her calmly as she glared at him. 'I asked in earnest.'

'No! Of *course* my answer is no—how could you have expected otherwise?'

'Because I think it would be helpful to both of us if you were to accept my offer.'

She stared at him, taking in the sincerity of his expression, and some private part of her regretted that such a face should be wasted on a madman. How on earth could he imagine his question to be *helpful*? Surely a proposal of marriage was the absolute opposite of a helpful suggestion? And yet there Edward stood, apparently entirely sober and set on his ridiculous request.

Selina's heart thrummed in her ears as she stood, silent, hearing the hostile muttering of the watching Romani women as they hovered a short distance away. Edward must have been able to hear them too, but he gave no sign as he waited for her reply, arms folded across his invitingly broad chest.

'How could that possibly be helpful?'

Edward glanced towards the nearby cluster of Roma and dropped his voice to a low murmur. 'It would solve problems for both of us.' He nodded engagingly, the light of the fire on his hair making it shine like burnished gold. 'I think we could both benefit if we were to come to an understanding.'

Selina narrowed her eyes, taking in the calm patience of his face. What problems could a pampered gentleman have that would reduce him to pinning his hopes on a Roma girl, of all people?

When she didn't reply he continued. 'I am in need of a wife in order to meet the terms of my father's will and retain my inheritance.'

Edward spoke lightly, but something in the set of his jaw increased Selina's suspicions.

'I thought if you were to help me navigate the issue I could do something for you in return.'

Navigate the issue? Selina opened her mouth to speak, but found she had no words. He must be a madman indeed; what other explanation could there be?

Her voice, when she finally trusted herself to speak, was strained. 'I see. Or rather, I don't see—not at all. Why me? What do you think you could do in return that would ever persuade me to accept you?'

His answer was not one she had anticipated.

'I am willing to extend an invitation for your people to stay on my land, under my protection, so your camp will not have to move during the winter months.'

Edward spoke quietly but with a conviction that made Selina pause.

'You, in turn, would be safe with me at Blackwell Hall until the spring, when we might annul our marriage, and then you would be free to leave with the rest of the Roma. By that time your menfolk will have completed their assignments, and your people will be able to travel far enough away to avoid any further trouble.'

Selina felt all the breath leave her body as she froze, pinned to the spot by his words. *No.* He couldn't offer her that. How could he?

'You jest. You can't promise me—'

'I can, and I do.'

Edward's face was grave, and Selina felt her heart check as his solemnity only served to enhance her appreciation of his sharp features.

'Without your help I will have to forfeit this entire estate. I ask for you to become my wife in name only, and not forever. My father's will specifies that I must marry, but it gives no indication of how long I must retain a wife after the fact.' A glint of something like wry humour passed over his face. 'Please believe I have explored every loophole in the legalities. An annulment can follow in the spring, so long as we admit you were under the age of twenty-one and did not have your father's permission to marry.'

Selina swallowed. He had played his cards well—he must have known that this was the one thing he could offer her that she would be tempted to accept. A whole winter without the worry of being moved on? The men would be able to keep their jobs, and the sick Roma babies would be safe—even the threat of the gamekeepers' mob would vanish. The only thing standing in the way was herself.

If she were to accept Edward's offer she would be ensuring the immediate future of the entire camp. Wouldn't that be worth the sacrifice? All their lives in exchange for living a lie for a few months?

But what would those few months cost her? To live with Edward, to *marry* him, would be to go against everything she had felt about the gentry ever since that fateful day twelve years before.

She could see, if all pretence to the contrary was abandoned, why a woman might be tempted by his offer, and even *she* might have considered it had he belonged to any other class. His physicality was compelling, and there was something in his look that seemed to call to her.

Even as he stood before her, awaiting her reply with quiet dignity, Selina felt drawn to him in a way that she couldn't explain. Never before had a man managed to affect her so powerfully, pulling her in even as she tried to dismiss him. It was beyond confusing, and a temptation like none she had ever known before.

But to marry him would be to forget almost an entire lifetime of suspicion and resentment and willingly enter into the lions' den of her worst enemy. And what of Mama? Selina's heart ached at that question.

Edward's a Fulbrooke, and it was a Fulbrooke who killed Mama—or as good as killed her.

That his face made her want to stare shouldn't matter one bit, and the fact that the urge to reach out and touch the scar that gleamed on his cheek still called to her wasn't something she should even consider.

'Selina—Miss Agres. It comes down to this: *you* don't want your people to come to any harm and *I* don't appreciate being forced to marry according to somebody else's wishes. If you accept my proposal both of us will be delivered from situations not of our choosing.'

'But why ask *me*?' Selina burst out, uncertainty and frustration boiling over into vexation. His effect on her was unnerving, and his request even more so: it just didn't make *sense*. 'There must be hundreds of women of your acquaintance. Why do you think *I'm* your best option?'

'Because you are. I have no desire to be bound to a wife. You don't *want* to be married to me. You place upon me no expectations and you will ask nothing of me other than that I honour our bargain. In turn, I will ask nothing of you other than that you marry me. You will have your own private bedchamber and I will not attempt to impose on you as a husband might expect to do. All I require is your help to allow me to keep my inheritance away from my uncle.'

If her fall from Djali had been painful, the mention of Charles Fulbrooke was like a drop from ten times the height. Selina felt her face freeze into a tight mask of horror and all words were stolen from her dry mouth as she stared up into Edward's face. An iron fist seemed to be squeezing her chest, and it felt like a lifetime before she was able to draw enough breath to answer him.

'Your uncle? Your *uncle* will inherit if you fail to marry?'

'That is correct.' Edward's speech was clipped, as though he was holding himself under control. 'He has been abroad these past twelve years, but I don't doubt he would be delighted to return here to take my place as Squire.'

Return here? Selina's blood was like ice and it froze her to every last bone. *The man responsible for Mama's death to return to a handsome inheritance? To a position of power?*

Surely it couldn't be allowed. Surely such good fortune could never come to such a monster as he?

And yet of course it could. Selina knew little of upper-class affairs, but even she couldn't fail to grasp the importance placed on the continuation of family names. They weren't so different from the Roma in that regard, in truth. The Agres family was ancient and respected, and Selina knew her mother had been proud to marry into it. Whatever past crimes Charles might be suspected of, the Fulbrooke inheritance would pass to him with ease should Edward somehow fall short of his father's expectations.

But I could prevent it.

The thought stole through Selina's mind like a cold wind, chilling her as she turned it over inside her head.

I could stop that man from returning here and from claiming the Fulbrooke fortune. Wouldn't that be the most perfect revenge? His inheritance blocked by the daughter of the woman his prejudice helped to kill?

The temptation glowed within Selina like a burning flame, chasing from her the chill of moments before. Perhaps some of its light showed on her face, for Edward peered down at her with something like confusion and she felt another powerful wave of that mysterious *something* engulf her from head to toe.

It would mean marrying a gentleman—a member of the same class she had been taught to fear for so long— but Edward had yet to show any sign of the cruel streak she had expected, and his physical effect on her was something she could not ignore. They had been almost friends once…could some shadow of the gentle lad he had once been still remain?

'What do you think, Miss Agres? Can you see—?'

A flurry of movement at her side caught Selina's attention a split-second before she felt the grip of a bony hand clench around her bicep.

'That's quite enough of that.' Zillah's words were

directed squarely at Edward, who looked down at her in surprise. The old woman glared at him as she jerked Selina by the arm. 'Come away now, Lina.'

'Grandmother—' Selina began to speak, but her words were abruptly silenced.

'No, girl. We're grateful for his help, but that doesn't mean he can take liberties.' Zillah thrust her chin towards Edward. 'You *know* what he is.'

'What I *am*?' Edward's brow creased in visible confusion, although his tone was courteous as ever. 'Perhaps you could explain what it is about me that troubles you, ma'am?'

Firelight glinted off Selina's dark hair as she tossed it back from her face, her cheeks slightly flushed. 'You're gentry, Mr Fulbrooke.' She spoke slowly, deliberately, as though explaining something to a child. One of her hands was attempting to prise the fingers from her arm, but the old woman held fast. 'Roma do not mix with gentry—for good reason. You must know this.'

'Exactly so,' Zillah rejoined firmly. 'I don't know what your designs on my granddaughter are, but I can tell you now they won't be successful.'

For a moment both generations of Roma women fixed Edward with black eyes: one pair filled with challenge, the other with uncertainty. It was the gaze of the latter that he returned.

Edward inclined his head politely. He would have to tread carefully, he thought, if he was to have a hope of achieving his aim. 'I understand your reluctance to engage with me, ma'am, under the circumstances. But I would very much appreciate it if you were to allow me to continue my address to Miss Agres.'

Zillah snorted. 'Continue your *address*? If there's something you wish to discuss with Selina, you can do it in my hearing. You may have done us a good turn tonight, and for that you have my thanks, but that doesn't give you leave to fill the girl's head with nonsense.'

Edward bit his tongue. *Remember your manners.* If he were to stand any chance of securing Selina's agreement to his plan he would need to find a way round her grandmother. She could hold the key to his inheriting. A wife was all the will required, and in Selina there was a chance for him to marry without the risk of forming any dangerous attachments that might end in disaster. He could see how she chafed under the grip of the old woman's hand, and how her brow was furrowed in thought. If he could just navigate her captor, all might not be lost.

He bowed. 'You're quite right. I've been exceptionally rude. I should, of course, have consulted you before I made an offer to your granddaughter. Perhaps I could have a moment of your time now, to discuss terms?'

Edward could see where Selina had inherited her spark from—he had no doubt her grandmother would have liked to give him a swift kick in the shins if she'd thought she'd get away with it. He wondered if Selina felt the same sentiment, and steeled himself against the smile that tried to curve his lips upwards.

'Now isn't convenient. You can see we have much to do before morning comes, and I have important things I need to discuss with Selina myself.'

'Grandmother.'

Selina's voice was firm, quite as resolute as Zillah's, and Edward marvelled at the world of determination he heard beneath the surface of that one word.

'I haven't finished my conversation with Mr Fulbrooke.'

'I don't see that he can have anything else to say. Our
troubles are no longer any of his concern.'

Edward seized his chance. 'I would like to *make* them
my concern.' He stepped a little closer and saw how the
old woman bridled but stubbornly stood her ground. 'I
offer your granddaughter sanctuary, Mrs Agres, and a
promise that by marrying me she will have the full protection of the Fulbrooke name, extending to everyone
living in this camp.'

'We are more than capable of solving our own problems, Mr Fulbrooke.' Zillah drew herself up to her full
height, still not reaching Edward's shoulder. 'We will
find a way to deal with this ourselves.'

'Grandmother!' With a final sharp tug Selina broke
free from the old woman's grasp and backed a few short
paces away from her. 'You're not *listening*. Think what
this could mean for you all.'

Edward saw how her chest rose and fell rapidly and
heard the edge of desperation in her voice. He nodded
at her, feeling a creeping glimmer of optimism. The fact
that Selina hadn't dismissed his proposal out of hand
was encouraging.

'I have no intention of trying to force Selina into
doing anything she doesn't want to do. Her wellbeing
is a large part of why I make this offer.'

The old woman looked from her granddaughter to
Edward and back again, taking in the girl's agonised
expression, and Edward saw her hesitation.

'I want to keep her safe. I will make sure she's treated
with every respect during her time with me, should she
choose to come.' He turned to Selina and saw a shadow

of doubt flicker across her beautiful face. 'I know you don't care for me, or for anything I stand for, but believe me—that is an advantage for both of us.'

Selina shook her head impatiently. 'That is what I do not understand. Why not choose a woman you *want* to marry? Why not find one you think you could love? And who could love you in return?'

It was the worst possible thing she could have asked, and it hit him squarely in the target of his heart. It was a fair question, he allowed ruefully, and he understood why she'd asked it. Perhaps he might have said the same in her position. But he couldn't...*wouldn't* bring himself to answer her boldness with the truth: that he no longer knew what it was to love anybody but his poor half-orphaned sister, and that even if he *could* open his heart to another it was not worth risking the pain of another rejection.

The only person he would ever admit that to was himself, he thought bitterly as he watched Selina's face turn from agitated to bemused at his silence. How could he ever put into words the damage his mother's abandonment and Letitia's later betrayal had done to him? And even if he managed to find a way, who could be trusted enough with the knowledge that between them they had irrevocably shattered his trust in the women of his own class—and perhaps women entirely?

The memory of the sickening swoop of his insides when he had learnt of Letitia's duplicity raked through his mind—and how the pain had gradually been replaced by a numb despair that was scarcely more bearable. There was no chance he would ever make himself vulnerable in that way ever again.

He forced a smile, but he knew his eyes must be cold

as he replied. 'As I said before, I don't wish to take a wife at all. If I must, I'd rather know the lady won't form an attachment to me that I can't return.'

'Well. You needn't fear for me there.'

Selina turned away from him, worrying at her lower lip with small white teeth. She seemed to be weighing his words. Edward waited with all the patience he could muster as she slowly paced back and forth, the firelight playing across her as she moved.

'If I were to take your offer—'

Zillah started, her face haggard with disbelief. 'You can't be thinking of *accepting* him, girl?'

Selina took the old woman by the arm, leading her the few paces towards what Edward assumed must be their caravan. She persuaded Zillah to sit on the wooden steps and squatted next to her on the ground, their heads close together in an age-old picture of intimacy.

Edward, taking a moment to pass a hand across his tired eyes, missed the fleeting glance Selina threw his way before she bent to whisper into her grandmother's ear. The old woman grew very still, listening intently. Edward could have sworn he caught the words 'inheritance' and 'uncle', and he saw Zillah flinch as though in pain. But in the next moment her face took on an expression of reluctant contemplation, and she clutched Selina's hand in her bony fingers.

'But what of you? What will become of you, Lina, up there in that big house?'

'I will manage.' Selina's face shone pale in the moonlight, her brow creased into a determined frown. 'My only other choice is to allow the mob to find me and to draw them away from the camp myself.'

'I won't allow it!'

'Then don't you see? Accepting Mr Fulbrooke is the lesser of two evils.'

Selina glanced at him entirely unapologetically and Edward attempted manfully to hide a small smile. Did she not know he was the most eligible bachelor in the county, or did she simply not care? *The latter, most likely*, he thought in wry amusement. *The lesser of two evils, indeed.* If it was a loveless marriage he desired— and desire it he did—Selina would certainly oblige him.

'So, do you have an answer for me, Miss Agres? Do we have a deal?'

Selina's eyes were huge in the firelight as she rose to her feet and came slowly towards him. Gazing down into them, Edward saw a world of reflected flames, leaping and tumbling in the ebony depths of her pupils, and he wondered for the first time if his offer was the solution to their problems or the start of another, far bigger than any before.

He frowned as a sudden twist of unease settled in his stomach as he looked down at the captivating woman who stood before him, her slender form still radiating a wariness that stirred him in a way he couldn't quite explain.

'You guarantee the safety of this camp?'

'I do.'

'You give me your solemn word that I can leave as soon as spring comes and the weather allows us to move on?'

'I give you my word.'

Selina sighed slowly, deeply, as though it pained her to breathe. Zillah watched from her perch a few steps away, and it was to her Selina turned with a face full of tender anguish.

How must it feel to be loved like that? Edward wondered as the old woman slowly nodded her head just once, unsmiling as a judge.

The gesture seemed to mean something to Selina— or perhaps everything; for he saw her blink rapidly, as though her eyes were suddenly sore, and when she fixed them on him he saw grim determination in their depths.

Chapter Five

Edward raked his hand through his hair and yet again turned his eyes to the door of the empty chapel. He half expected her not to come—wouldn't that serve him right for bribing her into marriage in the first place? He slipped his best silver pocket watch from his waistcoat and peered down at the ivory face for the tenth time in the space of a few minutes.

Exactly eight o' clock. Time to be married.

He had obtained the marriage licence as quickly as humanly possible after Selina's reluctant acceptance of his suit two days previously; there had been no time to be wasted in waiting three weeks to have the banns read. The common licence had been costly, but Edward was willing to pay almost anything to ensure his plans went ahead.

'Begging your pardon, sir.' Evans stood at Edward's elbow, dressed in his Sunday best and looking as though all his Christmases had come at once.

Perhaps it was an odd decision to ask his butler to stand as witness, Edward mused vaguely, his attention on other things, but Evans had served the Fulbrooke family faithfully for almost forty years and he could think of nobody more reliable to perform the task. Besides, Evans would do what was required, no questions asked—which was more than Edward could say of any of his gentry friends, who might pry a little too deeply into his choice of bride.

'I believe I hear footsteps outside.'

The sound of feet on wet stone grew louder. Edward fixed his eyes on the cross mounted to the wall above the reverend's head and determined there and then that, no matter what, he would not turn around. He didn't dare risk it. What if Selina took one look at him and decided she couldn't go through with their arrangement? If he could just wait until she reached the altar their fates would be fixed.

The church door creaked as it swung inwards on aged hinges and Edward felt the hairs on the back of his neck prickle. *Here she comes. My wife-to-be.*

At his side, Evans moved to gaze up the aisle towards where Selina had paused, presumably to gather her courage before making her approach.

The wait seemed to go on for half a lifetime. Edward shifted his weight from foot to foot, affecting restless excitement, although his heart raced with apprehension and, aggravatingly, with the tamped-down desire to once again lay eyes on the woman who had so piqued his interest, despite his efforts to the contrary.

What was taking her so long? If she could only keep her nerve for a few more moments… Wouldn't it be worth it? Wouldn't this gamble pay off and make her people safe from harm for the entirety of a cruel winter? And he from the threat of losing his inheritance?

Finally, *finally*, he heard Selina begin the long walk

down the length of the church and he exhaled involuntarily—he hadn't been aware he'd held his breath. He glanced sideways. Evans was staring in Selina's direction, his expression a mixture of curiosity and frank admiration. Edward shook his head to clear it. There was a buzzing in his ears, a whisper that tempted him to turn.

No. Look straight ahead. I mean it.

He turned around—and his breath seemed to catch in his throat.

Selina's face was ashen under a circlet of heather, her eyes ringed with shadows clearly the work of a broken night's sleep. She appeared to be gripping her grandmother's arm with the strength of a drowning man clutching a raft, and even from a distance Edward could see the rapid fluttering of her pulse beneath the thin skin of her throat.

But her steps were measured and steady, her hand perfectly still as she held her small posy against her chest, and her head was held up with a determination that was almost defiant. In the dim light of the votive-lit church the oval of her face was luminously pale, and her strained expression only served to highlight the fine lines of her jaw and cheekbones.

Edward swallowed. How could he have thought she wouldn't come? She was a warrior—she might be afraid, but she was damned if she would let him see it, and Edward felt a new respect for her flicker into being. His own nerves still thrummed within him, but Selina's resolve inspired a fresh sense of purpose that forced his lingering doubts into submission. If she could find the strength to honour their bargain there was no way he would fail her at the final hurdle.

What man wouldn't be proud to marry a woman such as that?

Even as he attempted to force his lips into some semblance of a smile the sudden shock of that thought reverberated through his mind. Of course he wasn't proud—that was entirely the wrong word, and he had been foolish to think it. The strength of Selina's will was no more to be admired by him than any other facet of her personality and he would do well to remember it. The fleeting thought that she looked positively angelic in her bridal gown would be likewise dismissed as entirely irrelevant—and dangerous.

Take that as a warning, Edward cautioned himself, a frown pinching his fair brows together. *Don't allow that nonsense into your head again; you know better than to be fooled by a pretty face.*

If Selina was pleasing to his eye—as was undeniable, he admitted reluctantly—it was not something to be encouraged. Their marriage was to be nothing more than a convenient lifeline for both of them, and he had no intention of feeling anything more for the woman who now approached him as though marching to war. Feelings led to nothing but pain, and not even his body's perturbing reaction to this Roma woman would convince him otherwise.

Selina swallowed hard as she saw Edward turn to look at her, her heart leaping within her and her throat as dry as if she'd thirsted for a week. *Only a few minutes and he will be my husband.*

How many women would give anything to be in her situation? she wondered as she moved down the aisle towards him, trying to ignore the rush of blood in her ears that obliterated all other sound but her own heart-beat. Rich *and* handsome. Perhaps she too would have considered herself lucky had they not shaken on their bargain like two hagglers at a market.

The unfamiliar sensation of lace against her legs only served to add to the strangeness of the moment. The dress had been Zillah's, made decades before by her own two hands for her wedding to Selina's long-dead grand-father. The lace had yellowed slightly with age, and Selina knew the cut was no longer fashionable, but it tied her to her people and to the Roma way of life; it gave her courage and she needed all the courage she could get.

She felt her legs tremble as she neared the altar and redoubled her grip on Zillah's arm. The older woman's hand came up immediately to cover her own, and she held it tight with the birdlike claws of her fingers.

'Steady, girl,' she murmured, too low for any of the three watching men to hear. 'You hold on to me. I've got you.'

Selina nodded, intent on reaching her goal. *Just put one foot in front of the other. You're almost there.*

Her eyes felt gritty with tiredness, the night before having been spent curled up with Zillah in wordless comfort in her bunk. There hadn't been much to say—both women knew what had to happen, and that no amount of talking would change what lay ahead. She would be leaving everything and everyone she loved and putting her trust in a man she barely knew.

At least he didn't expect her to consummate the marriage, she thought as she closed in on the altar, with Edward looming ever larger at her right-hand side. He'd intimated as much, and she recalled how her cheeks had flared hotly with girlish embarrassment. No Roma man had ever dared venture into such a conversation with her before, and she would have boxed his ears if he had.

A small voice in the back of her mind whispered that Edward looked well in his wedding suit. The pale blue of his waistcoat was paired well with his fair hair, and cream breeches emphasised the lean shape of his legs—a detail Selina couldn't help but notice with reluctant admiration.

Part of her—a very secret, apparently feral part, over which she had terrifyingly little control—had been anticipating seeing him again. Edward's broad frame and clean-cut jaw had robbed her of sleep the night before almost as much as her apprehension, and now he was before her Selina could feel the same ready blush he always seemed able to provoke in her simmering below the surface of her pallid cheeks.

The small smiles he insisted on shooting her were kindly meant, she imagined, and his mute expression upon first seeing her had been undeniably flattering—enjoyable, even. Not that any of that mattered, she reminded herself sternly as her stomach fluttered disloyally. What use did she have for flattery or for a handsome face? They both knew why they were doing this—it was a business transaction and nothing more. She was no blushing bride tripping happily to the altar, even if he *did* cut a figure most women would look twice at and be glad to get to know better—as she herself might have been, in truth, had the circumstances been different.

'I wasn't sure you'd come.'

Edward's voice was quiet, almost a whisper in her ear that stirred the hairs at the nape of her neck. He was standing so close Selina could have reached out and touched him, and the entirely too-tempting urge to do so was one she fought with every fibre of her being.

'Truth be told, neither was I.'

She felt the air shift as Zillah moved a few paces away and then she turned to Edward, both of them tense and silent before the clergyman, who cleared his throat with a dry cough and began to speak.

'Dearly beloved...'

Selina saw the man's lips move as though she were in a dream. He seemed to go on talking for a long time, although she knew it could only have been a few minutes before she heard Edward's voice and watched with blind eyes as he reached for her hand.

She hesitated. *Last chance, Lina.*

She could still turn and run, and there would be nothing Edward could do about it. He couldn't force her to marry him—what if she chose not to? What then?

Papa would be spared the pain of learning of her marriage when he next returned to the camp. There had been no question of sending him a letter to tell him of her situation—neither he nor Selina could read or write, and she hadn't been able to bear the shame of dispatching one of the children with a message.

Edward's gaze was warm as he looked down at her, although she thought she could detect a thread of uncertainty in his expression. *I doubt this is easy for him, either,* she realised, with a feeling uncomfortably close to sympathy growing inside her.

How was it that he actively sought a wife who would never love him? She knew he wasn't ignorant of the knowledge that he was everything she loathed, living his life of genteel idleness, with servants to pander to his every whim and enough money to feed a Roma camp for a full lifetime, let alone one winter. Heaven knew, he could surely have his pick of women, with his good looks and even better prospects. There was no doubt about that.

Selina felt another pang of that instinctive attraction Edward seemed able to inspire in her without even needing to try. Despite his explanations, it didn't make sense.

But she wouldn't run. The bait on the hook was too precious. With just a few months of worry she would buy a safer future for her people, and for that she would have done almost anything.

She placed her hand in Edward's and almost gasped aloud at the jolt of electricity that thrilled through her at the contact. His palm was warm and she could feel the steady beat of his pulse in the thumb that brushed her knuckles, a gentle caress of reassurance that took her by surprise. Even as her lips moved in the vows that would save them, all she was truly conscious of was that small movement of his skin on hers, lighting up her every nerve and inviting her to enjoy the sensations of that tiny comforting gesture—and then a ring was slipped onto her numb finger and the deal was done.

The sound of a tray being placed down somewhere close to her head roused Selina from her sleep. Dimly, as though muffled by something soft, she heard the trickle of liquid being poured, punctuated by metal clinking gently against china.

Selina raised her head slightly from her cloud-like pillow and slowly cracked open one eyelid. Blinding sunlight poured through the windows of the unfamiliar room she was in, and she instinctively brought a hand up across her face to shield her eyes—her left hand, where a slim gold band winked cheerfully at her from the third finger.

Blackwell Hall—Edward.

She had spent the rest of the previous day packing her admittedly meagre possessions into a trunk supplied by Edward—her *husband*—and saying tearful farewells to her family and friends. He'd come to claim her as night had fallen, and they had ridden together in silence up the long drive to his great home, Djali bearing her steadily onwards to meet her fate.

She'd fully expected to lie awake all night, with the events of the day running ceaselessly through her mind. Instead, however, it appeared that distress had sapped her energy and she'd been asleep as soon as her head had hit the pillow.

A young woman hovered at her bedside, holding a teacup and saucer in her hands. At Selina's questioning glance she held out the cup to her uncertainly. Selina noticed her hand trembled slightly.

'Who—who are you?'

'Dinah, ma'am.' The girl bobbed a neat curtsey. 'I'm to be your maid.'

'My *what*?'

Selina's eyes were still bleary from sleep, and she rubbed at them with a clenched fist. Looking at the girl clearly for the first time, she took in her short stature and round, honest face, sprinkled with a constellation of freckles. They must be around the same age, and she found she liked her immediately—although the deference in her tone made Selina wince. She hadn't been *ma'am*-ed in her entire life, and she would have been quite content to keep it that way.

'Your maid, ma'am…if you please.' Dinah peered at her nervously, apparently anxious for her reply.

My maid? Truly?

She stared blankly at the girl. Was it some kind of joke? Surely Edward knew she could fend for herself, for goodness' sake. Why had he sent her this poor creature, who now looked every bit as uncomfortable as Selina felt?

'But I'm not in need of a *maid*.'

The very idea of it—a Roma with a servant? It was almost an insult, and Selina bridled internally. Of course women born to upper-class life needed help: gentry ladies were more ornaments than functional beings. But surely Edward didn't dare lump her in with them?

'Oh, please, ma'am! Don't send me away!'

The girl seemed close to tears, and Selina regarded her with baffled horror.

'I'm a good worker, honest, and I've waited so long for a chance to wait on a real lady and not be in the kitchens anymore.' She whisked a handkerchief from the pocket of her drab dress and patted at her eyes.

Selina hesitated, unsure of what to do, then set her cup down on her bedside table with a sharp click of porcelain against varnished wood.

'Are you saying you *want* to be my—?' She couldn't finish that sentence; it was too ridiculous for words. Dinah nodded vigorously into the cloth folds that concealed her face, only increasing Selina's amazement. 'I see. Well…if it means that much to you… I would never want to—to—*deprive* you of—'

The girl whipped the hanky away and peered shortsightedly at her, her expression so absurdly hopeful that Selina had to fight the perverse desire to laugh.

If only the girls at home could see me now.

At Blackwell for less than twelve hours and already somebody's superior. 'But I've never had a maid before, and I'm certainly no real lady. I think you might be disappointed.'

'Never, ma'am! If you'll have me, I promise you won't ever regret being my mistress.' Dinah picked up the cup again and placed it back into Selina's hand, her homely face creased in determination.

Selina smiled ruefully. 'I'd really rather be your friend than your mistress, Dinah. I have a feeling I'll need all the friends I can get.'

The girl didn't understand—she could tell by her face—and it probably wouldn't be a good idea to elaborate further, Selina supposed. Instead, she slowly sipped her tea as she allowed her gaze to wander around the bedchamber she had slept in. It had been night when she'd arrived, and it was only now, in the cold light of day, that she was able to see her surroundings clearly.

She could barely believe how huge the blue-papered room was. The contrast between the cabin of a *vardo* and this vast cavern of a bedchamber was immense; Selina wasn't sure she liked it. She felt too exposed. Where was the cosy snugness of a caravan? Certainly nowhere in *this* room, for all its fine furnishings.

Admittedly, the huge oak-framed bed she had slept in was the most comfortable she had ever experienced—and, she realised with a jolt of shock, the first proper one, with luxurious pillows and a richly embroidered powder-blue coverlet, but it wasn't a patch on the familiar nest of her own bunk.

She traced the design worked on the borders of her blankets with one finger as Dinah fussed busily in the

Edward's thoughts? The idea of inspiring her new husband's admiration was a tempting one—would it *really* be so bad to want to make a good impression?—but reality flooded back to hit her.

She doubted he would notice if she were to come down to breakfast with no hair at all. Her presence in his house was a mere puzzle piece, part of a bigger picture and a necessary evil. He had made it clear he wouldn't have chosen her otherwise. What she looked like would matter less to Edward than a bonnet would to a horse, and she would be foolish to think otherwise, despite any confusing or borderline panic-inducing stirrings to the contrary.

She forced a smile at the waiting maid, aware of a curious sensation of something suspiciously close to disappointment circling inside her. 'I don't believe he minds one way or the other. You do as you see fit.'

Edward toyed with the silver salt shaker in front of him, wondering as he spun it exactly what feminine mysteries could possibly take so long as to delay breakfast by a full half-hour. Perhaps Selina hadn't slept well and was finding it difficult to rise from her bed in the great blue chamber he had picked out for her.

Arriving home in the darkness of the night with a mysterious new bride had caused a few whispers among the staff, as he had expected, but at least nobody had seemed surprised at Selina being given her own separate rooms. His father and Maria had never shared a marriage bed other than for the begetting of little Ophelia, and he supposed their chaste example had set the tone.

He was interested to see his new wife this morning—a little too interested, as he had silently chided his reflec-

background. *My own bunk.* How had Zillah slept last night without Selina lying there opposite? The two had shared a cabin ever since Diamanda had died, never missing a night in twelve years. Had she managed to snatch a few hours of rest after such an emotional day? Or had she lain there, staring up at the ceiling, wishing her granddaughter home, until the first light of a new day had crept beneath her shuttered windows?

Selina felt a lump rise in her throat and forced it back harshly. *No.* She had to be strong. It wasn't as though she would be away forever, and besides: it was because of Zillah she had to stay. Wasn't it for all the Roma? If she could just focus on the end goal, and keep her nerve despite the circumstances…

'Mr Edward has asked if you'd honour him with your company for breakfast, ma'am. I'm to do your hair and show you to the dining room.'

Dinah was waiting at a fine-looking dressing table—*her* dressing table, Selina realised with a start—in front of one floor-to-ceiling window, and the built-in looking glass reflected Selina's face back at her as she sat there in the great island of her bed.

'Has he?'

The maid was too busy rearranging a set of silver hairbrushes to notice Selina's frown. So it had begun already—Edward acting the husband, summoning her to him for…for what? *The pleasure of my company?* The notion made Selina's heart skip a little faster, before she dismissed it quickly. *Of course not. He's just being polite.*

A flicker of something suspiciously close to disappointment passed over her and she shook her head slightly against it. There was no reason to suppose Edward *wanted* to spend time with her, even if her own thoughts on the matter were confused at best.

The idea of seeing Edward filled her with an uncomfortable mixture of dread and, mortifyingly, an anticipation that only made her irritation at herself grow in strength. *You really must try harder to master this effect he has on you, Lina,* she chastised herself privately. It was already becoming an annoyance she could have done without, having to battle her rational mind against her apparent weakness for Edward's slow smile, or the way his hair curled delightfully at the base of his neck…

Oh, for heaven's sake, girl. She pinched the back of one hand—hard enough to snap herself out from her reverie. *Enough!* Aside from during the wedding ceremony she had barely exchanged two words with her new husband—what would they possibly find to talk about for the duration of a whole meal?

She thought back to their silent ride up the drive to Blackwell Hall, and how her heart had thumped within her chest as the grand old building loomed closer and closer. Edward had treated her kindly then. Even she had been able to recognise that his actions had been sympathetic as he rode near her, making no attempt to force her to talk but instead allowing her to wrap herself in quiet as fear and worry had risen up to twist her lips into a silent grimace.

She'd cursed herself for her weakness when she'd realised he'd seen, but other than the look of concern that had crossed his face he'd given no sign that he had noticed her distress. She'd been grateful for that at least—but not for the simultaneous realisation that the expression had made Edward look even more handsome than ever, if such a thing were possible.

Now, as she sat swathed in blankets that cost more than her entire wardrobe put together, she recalled how he had handed her down from Djali's wide back with more gentleness than she would have thought his strong frame capable of. The candlelight that had spilled from the windows had illuminated the striking lines of his face, and Selina had once again felt the curious sensation of flames licking at the base of her spine at the touch of his hand on her waist as he guided her, still in calm silence, upwards.

The memory was strong, and it made her shiver despite the fire that blazed merrily in her bedroom grate. How was she to manage a normal conversation with the man over breakfast? Selina wondered bleakly. Everything she had thought normal for twenty years had been taken from her overnight, and she could barely look at him without staring.

She took a deep breath and made to get up, approaching her dressing table cautiously, gingerly settling down on the seat like a wary cat. Her reflection in the looking glass gazed back at her sombrely, dark eyebrows drawn together above eyes clouded with doubt. What was she *doing*, allowing herself to be groomed like a doll? Pull ing a comb through her thick curls and then bindi them back from her face with a ribbon was as far as hairdressing skills stretched. Occasionally she ma braid for special occasions, but most often her hai left to its own devices, playing around her sho like a raven cloak.

Dinah brandished one of the silver-backed h 'How does Mr Edward prefer it? You'll be w look your best for your first full day as a marr

Selina screwed up her nose. How was sh

tion as he'd stood before his glass an hour earlier, waiting for his valet to make the vital decision as to which waistcoat would be most suitable for the day ahead. Some slight apprehension was to be expected, he'd thought; which was just as well, as he had felt a strange flicker in his stomach at the thought of Selina seated opposite him at the dining table.

He'd frowned to himself as the garment was buttoned around him—the cream today, Wellburn had resolved. It was only because he was anxious to be an attentive host, he had told himself, and in no way was he eager to see Selina for her own sake *per se*. It was merely good manners that had demanded he rise at a proper hour and invite his wife to take breakfast with him on the morning of what he recognised must be a very difficult day for her.

Difficult for me, too, in truth. His first day as a married man was an interesting thought, and one that gave him pause. Should he pretend to be pleased to see her? Should he remain a little cool and aloof? The knot of tension in his stomach tightened a fraction more as his uneasiness grew.

Bored now, with both his irritating trepidation and his wait, and getting more so by the minute, he glanced around the room, debating whether it would be a terrible display of bad manners to skim through his morning correspondence as he waited. There was another letter from his father's solicitor, and Edward almost smiled as he began to mentally compose his reply, stating his acquisition of one legal wife.

But any thoughts of his triumph were driven from his mind by a jolt of *something* in his chest as the door to the dining room finally opened and Selina stepped over the threshold.

His first thought as he rose to greet her was how different she looked, with her hair bound up away from her face. This was swiftly followed by a painful twist of his insides as he saw how much the style suited her.

Parted sharply down the middle, with a thick nest of curls pinned up at her crown and a bunch of ringlets hanging at each ear, the distinction between the elegant style and the wild mass of waves Edward had previously associated with Selina was stark. As was the contrast between her hair and her clothes: the dress she wore had seen better days, and was still half covered by a number of woollen shawls each more colourful than the last.

Edward wondered if a more unusual—or beautiful— woman had ever graced the dining table. The thought was a dangerous one, and yet again, to his alarm, Edward felt the same dart of attraction that managed to disturb him more and more each time he set eyes on her. It was getting stronger, if anything, and Edward felt his apprehension increase.

He would have to master these twinges of weakness. Nothing good could come of them, and there was no way he was willing to allow them to develop into anything worse.

'Good morning. I hope you slept well?'

'Like the dead, Mr Fulbrooke, would you believe?'

Her colour was better today. The shadows beneath her eyes had faded slightly and the bloom of her cheeks had chased away the pallor of the previous day. She certainly looked more well-rested than he had expected, and he felt his spirits lift imperceptibly as he pulled a chair out for her near his own place at the long white-swathed table.

'Please. Won't you call me Edward? I would very much like you to feel as comfortable as possible during your time here.'

He really *did* want her to feel at ease, he realised with a start. Seeing her there, so out of place in his world, gave him a sudden pang of sympathy that surprised him. She was like an exotic bird of paradise in an aviary of dowdy sparrows, and it was an uncomfortable feeling to think he had somehow forced her into a cage.

He pushed the thought away briskly. *She chose to agree to this, don't forget. She didn't have to marry you.*

Part of him had wondered what state she would be in upon waking in such unfamiliar surroundings, but she looked calm enough, despite the air of wariness that seemed to accompany her whenever he was near, and he couldn't help but feel pleased when she dropped into the proffered chair with only the smallest of hesitations.

He took his own seat again and nodded at the servant who hovered in the doorway. The man withdrew immediately, his footsteps swift and quiet, and Edward was left alone in the novel company of his distracted new wife.

She was squinting down at the array of cutlery laid out in front of her in obvious bemusement, touching each piece in turn, and Edward noticed her lips move as she counted to herself in a soundless murmur.

He watched her for a moment in silent amusement.

'Is everything to your satisfaction?'

Her head jerked up at the sound of his voice, a crease appearing between her dark eyebrows as she appraised him. 'I've got too many spoons.'

It was almost an accusation. Edward hid his smile behind the fingers of one hand. 'Ah. No. Each spoon is for a different part of your breakfast.'

'Why? Why not just use the same throughout?'

'I—I don't really know.' It didn't make a lot of sense now he thought about it, and he had to cast about for an answer. 'That's just how it is.'

He opened his linen napkin and laid it across his lap, more for something to do with his hands than for any other reason. He felt a vague unease now she was before him, a slight awkwardness in his own skin such as he had last experienced as an adolescent. It reminded him uncomfortably of how he had used to feel at that age when confronted with a pretty girl: a little ungainly, and more than usually aware of his movements. He'd grown out of that, of course. So there was no real reason he could think of for Selina to affect him so—or not one he was willing to admit.

When he looked up from his lap he saw she'd picked up one of the confusing array of spoons and was turning it this way and that, moving her head to catch the upside-down image of herself caught in its silver curve. He suppressed a smile. The magic the maid had worked on Selina's hair had evidently made quite an impact on her.

'That hairstyle suits you.'

The words left his lips before he could stop them, earning him a startled look and a clink of metal against wood as Selina dropped the spoon abruptly. Edward frowned to himself. He'd had no intention of speaking aloud, and now he had unnerved her.

Control yourself, man. What ails you?

She spoke more to the tablecloth than to him, her

dark brows drawn together. 'I've never worn it like this before. It feels a little strange.'

They lapsed into an awkward silence that lasted several moments. More for a way to break the tension than anything else, Edward cleared his throat. 'I've been meaning to ask you something.'

Selina looked up from her study of the table, one suspicious eyebrow cocked. 'Oh, yes?'

There was more than a touch of wariness in her tone, and Edward could have kicked himself for his mistake in allowing his inner thoughts to spill out of his mouth. Still, at least her silence allowed him the chance to ask a question that had been bothering him since they met.

'That first day, when you found Ophelia. You said that I owed you twice over—once for then, and once for before.' Edward leaned his chin on his hand, watching for her reaction. 'What did you mean?'

She held his gaze for a moment in a look so dark and penetrating that Edward felt the sensation she was attempting to read his mind. He couldn't quite tell whether or not he enjoyed being the object of her undivided attention. It felt a little like chess—both of them unsure as to the intentions of the other, each waiting to see what the other would do next.

He wondered idly if she knew how to play. If not, he felt sure he would enjoy trying to teach her. Her instinctive caution would make her a natural.

Selina's eyes were slightly narrowed when she finally answered. 'You truly don't recall me at all, do you?'

There was a ghost of amusement in the ebony darkness and Edward's heart rate picked up at the sight. Selina amused—that was certainly a new development, and one that served to soften the usual guardedness of her face. He couldn't deny it was a pleasant effect.

'I suppose I should be glad I look so different now. I'm less bruised and muddy than I was at eight, at least.'

It took a moment for Edward to understand Selina's answer, and when it hit him he could only stare, piecing together the fragments of memories only recently rediscovered.

'The little girl in the woods, all those years ago— that was you?' His hand flew to the scar on his cheek, a small raised island in the otherwise smooth skin of his face. 'You were the one who treated my wound? Who stopped the bleeding with moss?'

Selina nodded almost shyly. 'An old country trick. I learned it when I was very young.'

'I can't believe it.' Edward shook his head slowly, amazement plainly written across his handsome features. *That little wraith had been Selina?*

She was certainly more altered than he ever would have thought possible, with all traces of the tomboyish creature he remembered gone, to be replaced by distinctly feminine grace. It was uncanny.

'Why didn't you tell me before?'

She shrugged, her eyes slipping past his to fix again on her gleaming silverware. 'I didn't think it was important.'

'Not important?' Edward sat back in his chair, disbelief still running through him. 'How could you think so?'

He felt the temptation to revisit that day pulling at him, the desire to talk over fond memories strong.

Surely she should know how much her care then meant to me? How much I appreciated what she did?

It had been such a difficult time for him, those few

weeks after his mother's abandonment, and Edward was gripped with the sudden urge to tell Selina how much her kindness had soothed his troubled younger self— but then a renewed sense of caution crept over him and he closed his mouth with a snap.

A conversation like that would be too intimate, too friendly—it would invite Selina closer, and the odd sensations he felt whenever she was near warned him that they were quite close enough already. He couldn't take the risk, he thought as he glanced at her, taking in once again the gloss of her hair and the tawny perfection of her skin. To be polite was one thing, but to relive their shared past might foster a relationship that could all too easily stray into dangerous territory, and that he could *not* have.

The dining room door opened and a small procession of servants entered, each bearing a silver platter with the exception of one, who wielded a great teapot.

Under cover of the ensuing clattering and arranging, Edward lowered his voice and continued. 'Did you know me all along? When did you realise that I—that we—?'

'As soon as I saw you.'

Selina's voice was quiet too, and Edward could have sworn he caught a hint of colour flush across her cheeks.

'Your hair and eyes, both so light… I remembered you at once, and when I saw your scar I knew I hadn't been mistaken.'

Outwardly calm, Edward nodded. Inside, however, he felt a spark of satisfaction kindle. He dismissed it in alarm. That was exactly the kind of thing he should be trying to guard against—apparently with good reason. If he had made a lasting impression on Selina it was nothing to be proud of: no small number of upper-class women would have said the same thing, and the realisation was enough to pour cold water over any misplaced vanity.

The interest of women of his own class was something he never wanted to experience again, or to return. Selina should be no different.

It was an uncomfortable train of thought. Indeed, this entire meal was rapidly becoming even more uncomfortable than Edward had expected. With her new hairstyle and that gleam of humour, Selina was only growing more attractive by the moment, and Edward cast about for something, *anything*, to replace the disquieting direction of his thoughts.

Glancing at her as he poured out a cup of tea, Edward watched as Selina carefully buttered a freshly baked roll and spooned a little honey onto her plate. She was using entirely the wrong cutlery out of the range available to her, Edward noticed. If she was to successfully play the part of a squire's wife there was much for her to learn. He would definitely need to call in reinforcements—and he knew the perfect person to help him.

'I was hoping to reintroduce you to my sister today, if you've no objection.'

A large window directly behind Edward showcased the stunning grounds at the back of the Hall, and Selina toyed momentarily with the idea of leaping straight through it to escape into the green beyond.

Slightly dramatic, possibly? she debated as she crumbled the remnants of her bread roll into fragments, avoiding Edward's enquiring look. *But more appealing than the alternative?*

If only he'd stop staring at her with those blasted attractive hazel eyes she'd be much more able to think up some excuse. She didn't want to see Ophelia. It wasn't that she blamed the child for her current situation…it was more that she would serve as a reminder of things Selina would prefer to forget—including how she had got herself into this mess in the first place.

The way the little girl had called for her mama that day in the woods had struck uncomfortably close to the bone, conjuring memories that Selina had kept hidden for so long, and she was in no rush to repeat the experience.

Edward was still watching her, arms folded across his expansive chest, apparently in no hurry for her answer. She saw her uncertainty must be showing on her face, for one of his eyebrows was raised in the barest suggestion of a challenge.

'I realise she's a terrifying prospect, but she'll be very excited to see you again. You made quite an impression the last time.'

'I can imagine.'

'An impression' was probably something of an understatement. If Ophelia was anything like the young girls back at the camp, she had probably talked of little else since their dramatic first meeting mere days previously.

Had it really been less than a week since actions had swung into motion that would change her life forever? Selina spun the ring that gleamed on her left hand, feeling the unfamiliar sensation of metal against skin.

Silhouetted against the window, Edward's sharp profile was more striking than ever, and Selina quickly turned her attention back to her breakfast plate. Lounging in his natural habitat, Edward was a picture of masculine confidence, his every movement exasperatingly eye-catching and his every glance a physical touch to Selina's skin.

She groaned inwardly. This was *not* the plan. How was she to maintain a dignified distance from her new husband when everything he did was so damnably fascinating? Even the way he managed to juggle the bizarre number of spoons was more impressive than she would like.

Selina felt herself glowering down at her lap as heat snaked up from her neck to cross her face with burning fingers. There was an imposing fireplace directly at her back, and Selina found herself fervently hoping Edward would blame the crackling flames for her rosy cheeks and not his apparently swoon-inducing presence.

'Perhaps I could call for her now and she could help me give you a tour of the house? When you've finished eating, of course.'

She eyed him as he moved to the fireplace and tugged at a bell-pull hanging to the side of it, crossing the room in a handful of easy, long-legged strides. He really was very tall, and when standing next to the stocky servant who answered the summons he looked taller still.

The other man soon withdrew, and Edward turned back to her so quickly Selina had to scramble to avert her eyes in time. It wouldn't do for him to think she was looking. The fact that she had been, and had been undeniably pleased by what she had seen, made her shift uncomfortably in her chair.

She hadn't been prepared for his earlier compliment, and his praise had caused the aggravating embers that seemed to flicker in her stomach whenever he was near to glow brighter, their heat warming her insides. She'd quickly sought to dampen them, determined that some throwaway comment would not succeed in affecting her so worryingly, but the ashes remained, and Selina felt a nagging sense of unease that it would be all too easy for Edward to stoke them up again.

The idea rankled even as some distant part of her wondered how far his kind words were the truth, and how far they had been motivated by simple good manners. Her discomfort intensified as she realised she hoped it was the former.

'She'll be down directly. I hope you're prepared for lots of questions? I'm told she's been asking her governess when she can see you approximately every ten minutes ever since she woke this morning.'

A reluctant smile threatened to unfurl on Selina's lips. Perhaps seeing the little girl again would be better than she expected. It certainly sounded as though she was already Selina's most fervent admirer, and it could only be a good thing to have such a powerful ally. Besides, with Ophelia in the room she wouldn't be Edward's sole focus, and that would definitely be an improvement on the current way his gaze seemed to fix on her with unnerving regularity, with correspondingly unnerving results.

Chapter Six

Gravel crunched under her feet as Selina hurried away from the Hall, casting about her as she dipped her head down and pulled her worn cloak closer about her body. It was a grey day, the air oppressively still, and clouds brooded ominously overhead, threatening rain. A robin called from a tree as she passed through the grounds, its red breast vivid against withered leaves, but she knew she had no time to stop and listen.

She rounded a manicured hedge and ploughed on-ward. Shooting a fleeting glance over her shoulder in the direction of the Hall, she saw nobody had followed her. Only the huge old house was watching her go, its gleaming windows glinting like eyes in the stone walls. She wondered for a moment which of the windows was hers, where she'd stood that morning and gazed out at the green beyond before slipping down the creaking stairs and out through the heavy oak garden door.

The grounds were stunning—even Selina, whose preference was for the untamed beauty of the country-side, could appreciate the artistry that had gone into the well-laid beds and meticulously landscaped lawns. Trees and shrubs of all descriptions stood about in perfectly placed groups, and Selina knew the sight of the grounds in summer, when all the flowers were in full bloom and emerald leaves stirred in warm breezes, would be breathtaking. Not that she would be there to see it.

A sweet little stone arbour stood beyond an avenue of fruit trees, with classical statuettes set into alcoves on each wall. It was at one of these statues that she glanced out of the corner of her eye as she approached, and slowed her stride to a quiet, careful step. As she drew closer the mound of striped material she'd spied from a distance grew more distinct, nestled behind a Greek goddess she couldn't have named even if she'd wanted to.

Placing each foot with pinpoint precision, Selina inched forward. Her breathing was too loud. She forced herself to slow the rapid beat of her heart, fluttering against her ribs as she closed the final distance.

She pounced. 'Got you!'

With a high-pitched shriek of glee Ophelia struggled in Selina's arms, trying in vain to escape her sister-in-law's tickling fingers. 'Stop! Stop! Stop it!'

'Stop what? This?' Selina redoubled her efforts and the little girl's laughter gurgled in her ears, her skinny legs flailing.

'Yes! Stop it!'

'Do you admit I'm the Queen of Hide and Seek?'

'Yes!'

Setting the child back on her feet, Selina paused to get her breath back. A stray curl had escaped during their game, marring the fresh masterpiece of hairstyling Dinah had created for her that morning, and she swept it back behind her ear.

Ophelia was clutching the side of the arbour, still

breathless with laughter. She looked Selina up and down, frowning now, and her eyes grew round with innocent horror.

'You've torn your dress, Lina!'

'Have I?' Looking down at the cream muslin she wore beneath her old cloak, Selina saw the skirt was rent from hem to knee, displaying what she imagined would be considered a scandalous amount of bare leg among Edward's set.

'You'll have to change quickly, before anyone sees you!'

Just in time Selina managed to stop herself from reflexively rolling her eyes. During her first week at Blackwell Hall, Ophelia had taken it upon herself to begin educating her on exactly what it took to be a real upper-class lady. It didn't seem to matter how many times Selina tried to explain, as gently as possible, that she wouldn't be there for longer than a few months, and therefore didn't need such an in-depth knowledge of different types of spoons. It was a concept Ophelia seemed cheerfully determined to ignore.

Short of sitting down with the seven-year-old and outlining the terms of her marriage of convenience in brutal clarity, she couldn't think of a way to drive the point home without upsetting the little girl she had already begun to care for, despite her initial misgivings.

Perhaps it was because she reminded Selina of the Roma children she had left behind at the camp. All of her cousins had little ones, three of them girls, and she loved the way their hands would find their way into her own and the seriousness with which they confided in her their precious secrets.

Looking down at the girl in front of her, Selina felt

a sudden pang of loss at the thought of those she'd left behind and forced a smile to unwilling lips. She should be grateful they'd been able to form such a bond. Ophelia's sunny company brightened days that otherwise she didn't know how she would have managed, as well as providing a welcome distraction from the incessant thoughts of another certain somebody Selina seemed unable to master.

'Don't worry. I can mend it when we return to the house.'

The little girl's face expressed exactly what she thought of *that* statement. 'Why don't you just ask Ned to buy you some new ones? He buys me dresses all the time!'

Selina shook her head, feeling, as always, the same jolt in her stomach at the mention of Edward's name.

Damn it, Lina. Get a hold of yourself.

'Because N— *Edward* is your brother. He's allowed to buy you pretty things.'

'But you're his wife. Isn't he allowed to buy you things, too? I'd wager he would if you asked him. I don't think there's a kinder brother in the whole world!'

Selina raised an eyebrow but held her tongue.

His money is the last thing I want. Of course he had offered to purchase some gowns for her—beautiful things befitting her new station—but she'd refused. Her shawls and modest dresses had always been good enough for her, and would continue to be so within the privacy of Blackwell and its grounds, where the only eyes on her were those of Edward and his sister.

Perhaps the servants might gossip at her plain attire, but people would always find something to talk about, whatever one did, and it hardly seemed worth the effort to avoid it. Besides, spending her husband's money was what a *real* wife did, and there could be no gain in muddying the waters.

The time they spent together was tolerable enough, after a fashion, although heaven knew how much she didn't *want* to notice the strong shape of his thighs in his riding breeches, or how the green of his coat highlighted the rich colour of his eyes. She found things much less vexing when Edward left the Hall on business of his own, as he had that morning, and she was excused from spending time with him that always seemed to result in blushing confusion.

'It's—it isn't quite the same, Ophie. I don't want him to do that for me.'

The clouds were drawing in overhead. Selina could smell rain in the air—a scent she loved more than almost any other—and with her eyes closed and her nose turned towards the sky she prayed fervently for the weight she had carried these past two weeks to fall from her shoulders.

To be out in the open, free from the atmosphere of the brooding house, should be like a soothing balm to her troubled spirit. But thoughts of Edward still niggled at her, despite the cool breeze in her hair, and she felt no more able to force them back as the temptation to appreciate Edward's clear profile and impressive height became almost too uncomfortable to bear.

'What are you thinking about, Selina?'

Ophelia's little voice piped up beside her and Selina jumped a touch more guiltily than she was comfortable with. 'Oh. I—'

A deep rumble of thunder echoed suddenly through the grounds, just as the first drop of rain landed squarely on the toe of Selina's boot. Ophelia's fearful gasp at the sound rescued Selina from having to speak further, for which she was truly thankful. She would hardly have been able to tell the truth—*I'm thinking about your brother, Ophie. Again. Indeed, I can't seem to put him out of my mind.*

Selina's lips twisted into a wry smile that might have been mistaken for a grimace. *No.* That would never have done.

Even as she took the little girl's hand in her own and led their charge back in the direction of the Hall, Selina's mind whirled with unstoppable pictures of Edward as he'd looked that first morning in the woods, with no light of recognition sparking in his eye but still as courteous as though she'd been born a lady. There could never have been any mistake on that score, but that hadn't seemed to matter to him.

Once again Selina wondered *why* he had chosen *her*—a woman he truly hoped would never love him and whom he would never love in return—to take as his bride. She knew she shouldn't be flattered—he had made it plain it was nothing more than a business arrangement—but she still wasn't sure she trusted his bland explanation. There must be more to Edward than met the eye...

Rain pattered down upon their heads as they skirted a rapidly growing puddle and fled up the gravel path. Another boom of thunder sounded in their ears and Selina's attention was momentarily distracted from the jumble of Edward-shaped thoughts as Ophelia squeaked again at the loud noise.

'Almost there, Ophie. Don't be afraid!'

The two of them surged forward, the little girl clinging

tightly to Selina's hand as they rounded one hedge and then another, as quickly as their legs could carry them.

Selina collided with the broad male chest in front of her so hard she would have rebounded had its owner not reached out to catch her. She flung out a hand to steady herself, instinctively grabbing hold of the closest thing she could grasp—which unfortunately turned out to be Edward's firm and unyielding bicep, barely disguised by the damp fabric of his riding coat.

All the blood in her body felt as though it had rushed to her face as she gaped up at him, momentarily mute with surprise. His hand cradled the small of her back, holding her upright, and her own hand lay across the powerful muscle of his arm, feeling the strength beneath her cold fingertips.

Looking into his face, Selina saw how the rain had darkened the gold of Edward's hair. A stray lock curled across his forehead, and she was gripped with the sudden urge to reach up to brush it away. Her heart rate, already raised from running, sped up another notch as a slow glimmer of warmth unfurled itself from where Edward's hand held her close to him—a terrifyingly delicious feeling that would have robbed her of speech had she not already been rendered silent by his unexpected touch.

She blinked rapidly, forcing her body to respond to her orders. She should move her hand and step away, and she should do it *now*.

'Ned! I thought you'd gone into Warwick today?'

For the second time that morning Ophelia's voice interrupted the tension of Selina's thoughts. The moment broke and Selina stepped away from Edward smartly, shrugging out of his grasp with a low murmur of thanks.

'That was certainly my intention.'

Edward smiled down at his sister, although Selina was sure his lips looked a little fixed and she felt herself cringe. *Why did he have to see me being so clumsy?*

'Mr Lucas was called away on urgent business so I came back early. Miss Jenkins told me you ladies were out walking, so when the rain started I thought I'd better come to escort you back.'

He glanced across at Selina and she wondered with a jolt of dismay if he could somehow hear how rapidly her heart was beating in her chest. Her skin still tingled where Edward had touched her, and it was a monumental effort to pretend to be unfazed by the realisation that his arms had felt every bit as strong as they looked.

'We should hurry back—we'll catch our death, staying out in this weather.'

It was on the tip of Selina's tongue to reply that no Roma had ever died from a bit of rain, but at the last moment she thought better of it. She still wasn't sure she trusted herself to speak with any degree of normality, and her heart was still hammering with disloyal fury, so it was in silence that she joined the others in a dash back to the looming shadow of Blackwell Hall and in through the garden door.

Edward stood with his back to the roaring kitchen fire, all too aware of the slim figure of his wife crouching to one side of him, warming her hands by the hearth. He still hadn't got used to using that word—*wife*—despite Selina's now week-long residence at the Hall. Although she kept to only a few of the vast number of rooms the house boasted, and moved around them with a cat-like, almost silent step, the house felt more full, more lively, and it puzzled him how one extra person could make such a difference.

Her uncertainty at being caged within four walls was still plain to see, and he had noticed how much time she chose to spend out in the open air, going to visit her horse in the stable yard or walking in Blackwell's beautiful gardens. When he'd spied her from the window of the upstairs gallery that morning, however, something in her manner had piqued his interest.

At first the sight of Selina slipping down one of the paths away from the house had caused his brow to crease—what was she doing that made her movements so furtive? It was almost as though she didn't want to be seen… That alone had given him cause for concern. A quick glance up and down the long wood-panelled gallery had showed Edward he was on his own, apart from the painted portraits of his forebears that hung on every wall, and he had leaned closer to the lead-patterned window to get a better view of what Selina would do next.

She'd looked to be heading for the little stone arbour only just visible from the house. Edward had squinted slightly, following with his eyes as Selina slowed her pace to a stealthy creep, pausing for a moment before lunging downwards at something he hadn't quite been able to see. When she'd straightened up again everything had become clear—she held Ophelia in her arms, and even from a distance Edward had been able to make out his sister's familiar delight at being involved in a tickling contest.

He had drawn back from the window. A smile bloomed across his face, apparently without his permission, and he had carefully smoothed it away.

Selina's patience with the girl continued to impress him. Much as he loved his sister, he couldn't deny there were times when her mother Maria's influence was evident, and he feared she would eventually turn out to be a copy of her haughty mama. It was only little things—a forgotten thank-you to a servant here, a flash of temper at a trifle there—but Selina's firm but kind manner with the girl had already brought obvious improvements.

He found himself wondering again why Selina was so determined to keep that softness hidden from him. Given her revelation that she had been his mystery nurse all those years ago, he knew her heart was kind, but evidently something still held her back from allowing her to be her true self with him now.

Raindrops sparkled against the darkness of her hair as Selina brushed the moisture from the hem of her cloak and handed it to a waiting maid, who smiled shyly at Selina's use of her first name. Edward's brows twitched together briefly—at Blackwell a week, and already on Christian name terms with the servants? Apparently she had set out to make a friend of everybody except himself.

The thought was uncomfortable in a way he couldn't quite grasp.

'What shall we do now? We can't play outside anymore today.'

Ophelia peeped up at him earnestly, her hands held towards the fire glowing in the kitchen grate. Her hair had started to steam a little, he saw with interest, and her face was ruddy from exertion.

A swift glance towards his wife showed the same high colour in her complexion, and one ringlet slipping down to curl in front of her ear. She seemed to be holding the skirt of her dress together with one hand. It looked as though it had torn, and Edward caught a glimpse of an impressive expanse of bare leg before—with more than a shadow of reluctance—averting his eyes.

'*You* need to go back to Miss Jenkins, Ophie.' Leaning down, he gently pinched his sister's baby-soft cheek. 'You need to get into some dry clothes, and then you have to do your lessons.'

'Lessons?' Selina was leaning against a hulking dresser now, arms folded across her narrow chest. Her eyes were bright with interest. 'What is she learning?'

Edward shrugged. 'Drawing. How to read music, singing, how to dance—lots of things.'

Selina seemed about to speak when Ophelia dashed forward and took hold of her hands, her face alight with excitement. 'I can *show* you! I've learned a new step this week—come and dance with me and help me practise! Miss Jenkins will be so pleased with me if I've got better!'

'Oh…' Selina shook her head. 'I'm sorry. I don't think I can help much—I don't know any of the dances you learn.'

'Really?' The little girl's face creased in disappointment. 'Can't you dance? At *all*?'

'I can. Just not like you.'

Edward could have sworn he saw a glimmer of amusement in her eyes. *Pert thing.* He knew perfectly well what *her* style of dancing involved, and its passionate nature couldn't be further from the sedate steps beloved by the gentry. To watch her dance would be a rare treat, he imagined.

A sudden picture of Selina twisting in wild rhythm flitted through his mind, her hips swaying and her black hair falling about her like a curtain as she moved. He blinked it away distractedly. That was *not* an image he should dwell on—too enticing by half, and it strayed dangerously close to stirring thoughts within him that he was still trying his hardest to repress.

Selina continued, thankfully oblivious to the direction of his thoughts. 'Roma have a different way of going about dancing, and I don't think your brother would like me to teach you *that*.'

'Oh...'

The little girl still held Selina's hands, although her shoulders had slumped despondently. Edward was just about to console her when the blonde head snapped up again and the beam resurfaced like the sun appearing from behind a cloud.

'*Ned* could teach you!'

Selina started, the sudden movement causing the dresser she was leaning against to creak ominously. 'Ah, no... I really don't think—'

'Come along, now, Ophie.' Edward cut into Selina's stumbling excuse. He was only too aware of how distasteful she'd find the idea of dancing with him, and didn't feel it necessary, or flattering, to dwell on it. 'Don't embarrass Selina. She will never be able to dance like we can, and that's that.'

Out of the corner of his eye, Edward saw Selina frown.

'Now, it really is time for you to go back to Miss Jenkins. I'll look in on you later today and you can show me your new step.'

Ophelia sighed the sigh of a most dejected soul, but nodded obediently and left the kitchen, pausing only to receive a piece of freshly baked gingerbread from the indulgently smiling cook.

Edward watched her go, following the progress of her slippered feet as they pattered up the kitchen steps and disappeared from sight. Turning back towards his wife, Edward was surprised to find her wearing an expression of frank irritation.

'Is there a problem?'

The downturn of her lips deepened. 'You know, if there's one thing we Roma pride ourselves on it's our skill at dancing. If I chose to learn I could perform just as well as you or any of your upper-class ladies.'

Edward shrugged. What did it matter? 'If you say so. I just know you would never make that choice.'

'And how do you *know* that? Perhaps I might want to try!'

Edward eyed her narrowly. One of Selina's hands had come up to rest on her hip and her face was set in the same expression of determined challenge she had worn as she'd walked down the aisle towards him on their wedding day. The reluctant admiration he had felt for her ever since rose up within him once again, renewed in strength and mingled with a sense of frustration.

Wasn't the whole reason he had chosen Selina as his wife *because* she was the very opposite of everything he had previously admired in a woman? The spectre of Letitia flitted through his mind before he could banish her laughing ghost. He had no intention of allowing such feelings to unman him ever again, and yet at every encounter with the new Mrs Fulbrooke she somehow managed to get under his skin, to provoke in him a reaction he felt an aggravating inability to control.

It was unacceptable, and it troubled him more than he cared to admit.

Taking in the firm set of her jaw, Edward felt the beginning of an idea dawn upon him. Perhaps he could be the one to unnerve this proud Roma for once, taking the upper hand she always seemed to have without even trying.

'Oh? Well, if that's the case I'll teach you myself. We'll begin at once, shall we?' Without pausing for an answer Edward made for the kitchen stairs and began to climb. 'I'll let you go to change your dress. Meet me in the Great Hall.'

He heard her sharp intake of breath at his back and couldn't restrain a quiet laugh. Two could play at her game. If she insisted on turning such an insignificant thing into an argument he would call her bluff. Perhaps it was time for Selina to learn that she wasn't the only one who could be pig-headed.

She was hesitating near the door when Edward entered the Great Hall, having changed her gown and exchanged her muddy shoes for clean ones. Selina's previously damp hair had almost completely dried, he saw as he stepped close to her, and he noted with fresh admiration and discomfort just how much the new style suited the sharp lines of her bone structure.

'Shall we begin?'

'Yes. Let's.'

The defiant glint had returned. Whatever panic she had felt in the kitchen at his abrupt statement had evidently been squashed.

Edward smiled inwardly at her attitude. *Let's see how brave you are when we're actually touching. If you don't combust with horror on the spot I'll consider it a miracle.*

'Very good. We'll start with a simple waltz. It's a new dance, brought over from Europe and considered in some circles particularly scandalous.' He sketched a short bow, almost but not quite missing the cynical flicker of one dark Romani eyebrow. 'Take my hand and then place the other hand on my shoulder.'

Reaching towards her, Edward was barely able to

hide his smile at the fleeting look of mortification that flashed across her face. But then she grasped his hand, and suddenly it didn't feel amusing anymore.

With one palm in his, and the other lightly placed at his shoulder, the space between them was closed, and for the first time Edward was struck by the flawless fragility of her body. Supple and delicate, she felt light in his hold, but balanced with an underlying core of wiry strength that took him by surprise. It was a combination that momentarily robbed him of speech. Her waist was warm beneath his touch, and he was close enough to be able to count the dusting of freckles scattered across the bridge of her nose should he choose—an action he suddenly found quite unacceptably and quite unexpectedly impossibly tempting.

The immediacy of her effect on him was bewildering, as was the intensity of feeling that swept through his nerves, setting every sinew in Edward's entire body alight. He felt the way her body moved as she breathed, inhaling and exhaling in a steady rhythm his own wanted to copy, and he marvelled at how the curve of her waist fitted perfectly into his hand, as though they had been designed to meld together in seamless heat.

The urge to further explore the secret geography of her body came upon him in a rush of confusion and he forced it back, disturbed by the wayward direction of his disloyal thoughts.

'Like this?'

Edward felt the hair on the back of his neck prickle at the sensation of Selina's breath on his cheek. His own breath seemed to be coming more quickly than he could account for, and he had to swallow hard before answering. At such close range he could see each individual hair that shaped the lines of her brows, now pinched together slightly in concentration.

Why had his heart rate picked up to such a ridiculous degree, leaping within him like an animal in a trap? It wasn't as though it was the first time he had danced with a girl, and he had never experienced such a reaction before. Perhaps he had caught a chill during his cold morning ride across the fields—or perhaps it was something else entirely...something that he thought to guard so strongly against.

'Exactly like that. You're a natural.'

Looking down at her face, so close to his own, Edward saw Selina's uncertain expression. Her eyes had been averted while she considered the placement of her hands, but now she met his gaze full-on, with her head tilted back and lips slightly parted: lips, he realised at that moment, that were the prettiest he had ever seen.

Black eyes stared up into hazel, and for the longest moment of Edward's life neither of them moved. The silence was deafening, and the world seemed to halt on its axis as each of them drank in the sight of the other. But then Selina's long lashes came sweeping down, veiling her from his scrutiny, and Edward fixed his eyes on a spot on the opposite wall above Selina's head.

At a loss as to what to think, feel or do, he began to teach, all the while steeling himself against the whirl of new sensation that caused each nerve ending to stand to attention.

Selina moved, twirled and stepped as though in a dream, just as she was instructed—it was just as well she wasn't required to think independently, for her mind appeared to be playing tricks on her that she couldn't decipher. Her cheeks were suffused with inexplicable heat, and the place on her waist where Edward's hand lay felt as though it were smouldering under her gown.

It was entirely out of the question for her to peep up into her partner's face again. That one long look had shocked Selina to the core. She had been close enough to brush his face with her lips, and noticed for the first time how the deep hazel of his irises was flecked with tiny chips of gold. The intensity of his gaze had thrown her, and it had been all she could do to look away.

Now, as she turned gracefully in Edward's hold, following some dimly-heard instruction, she could scarcely breathe for inhaling the scent that seemed to emanate from him: a combination of soap, rain and spices from the kitchen that was horrifyingly, delightfully, extremely attractive.

Stop it.

Stop. It.

So what if his hand was large enough to almost span her entire waist? It meant nothing. The same went for the impressive musculature she could feel moving beneath the fabric at his shoulder. Nothing. It meant nothing. She would allow it no space in her mind. She would never allow herself to forget what he was—*who* he was: an unwilling husband, from a world so far removed from her own there could never be any real accord between them even if he had *wanted* a loving wife.

But the firm grip of his hand around hers sent a strange thrill down her spine, and her eyes *would* stray across the achingly impressive expanse of his chest, and there was precious little she could do to slow the hummingbird beat of her heart, pounding within her as the flames in her belly licked higher and higher and burned brighter with every step she took.

The whirl of confusion inside her mind held her attention for a moment too long and, distracted, Selina felt her breath catch as she missed a step, her foot coming down on the hem of her gown to make her stumble.

There was never any real danger of her falling, so quite why Edward seized her so firmly she couldn't say. But the next moment all such thoughts vanished as she found herself closer to him than ever before, and when she dared look up into his face it was all she could do to stay upright. His eyes found hers and she saw something flicker in them she had never seen before.

Edward's lips were gentle as they came down to slant across her own.

What? What's happening?

Selina's eyes flew wide in shock before drifting closed, as she was lost in a wave of sensation that threatened to overcome any rational thought she had ever had. His hands were warm as they held her close to the firm chest she had only allowed herself the briefest of moments to consider, so dangerously enticing had she found it, and Selina felt her own hands twitch with the desire to slide over Edward's coat, to delve inside and trace the hard planes of his body with wondering fingertips.

Her heart pounded in her ears as the flames inside her roared with approval, stoking themselves higher to burn her from within. She was sure she must have stopped breathing, and some tiny voice in the back of her mind screamed at her to pull away, but that suddenly seemed such a silly waste of time when she could be spending it exploring the fascinating terrain of Edward's lips. There was nothing she could do to stop herself from standing

on her tiptoes and reaching for Edward as ardently as
he reached for her.

Just when she was sure she would either pass out or
crumple into a heap on the floor, Edward released Selina's mouth and drew backwards, his breath coming
hard. He ran a hand through his hair and shook his head
slightly, his eyes fixed on Selina's flushed and dazed-
looking face.

Selina's vision was blurred, and she fought to pull
herself together. She had never experienced anything
like that before. Nobody had ever made her see stars
and feel as though her legs might fold beneath her. They
stared at each other, neither able to move or say a single
word to break the aching tension between them.

The sound of the dinner bell ringing made them both
jump.

Edward released Selina from his grasp and she immediately stumbled away from him, fanning herself with
one hand. She barely knew where to look—certainly
not directly at the man in front of her, who seemed as
much at a loss for words as she was. Edward's face was
flushed—and with more than the exertion of dancing,
Selina thought, mortified.

He was the first to speak in the beat of silence that
stretched between them—one Selina could no more have
filled than she could have snatched back the last few
minutes, never to be repeated.

'Well…' He cleared his throat distractedly. There was
another painful pause. 'So—what do you think of "gentry dancing"?'

Was he truly going to act as though nothing unto-
ward had just happened? she wondered in disbelief. As

though both of them hadn't just lost control and made their situation even more awkward than ever before?

She stared at him as icy fingers of shame snaked down into her stomach. *That was a mistake. Enormous. Unforgivable.* But if Edward could pretend nothing was amiss then, heaven help her, so could she.

'I like it well enough, I suppose.' She almost choked on the words, her mouth dry. A few more curls had escaped Selina's hairstyle, and in a passable show of nonchalance she reached up to twist them back into place. 'Will you want me to return the favour and teach you a few Romani steps?'

'I'm not sure I could keep up.' Edward had managed to muster a small smile, but Selina caught the impression of something hiding beneath the surface. 'I should go and change. Thank you for a very…interesting morning.'

He bowed to her and moved away, long strides taking him quickly from the room.

He had never behaved in such a way before. Usually he would allow her to go ahead of him, his good manners evident in his every action. Now it seemed as though he couldn't get away fast enough; hardly surprising, given the circumstances.

Selina watched him go, waiting for her breath to return as a feeling she couldn't identify gnawed at her. It was a new sensation, vaguely uncomfortable, and it circled in the pit of her stomach like nothing she had ever experienced before. Whatever it was—and however stupid she had been to cause it—she wasn't sure that she disliked it…

Chapter Seven

Edward lowered the correspondence he had been reading to the dining table and tapped his teeth absently with the end of his letter-opener.

Word of his marriage was spreading fast. The letter in front of him was the third he had received containing congratulations and a barely disguised hunger for information about his mysterious new lady, and he had no doubt that there would be many more to follow.

A sideways glance through the expansive window overlooking the Hall's grounds showed Selina crouching near one of the raised beds, gently patting Edward's favourite old dog on his grizzled head. The sight made his lips begin to curve upwards—a movement he quickly halted in vexation. Ever since their alarming kiss a few days previously Edward had found himself uncomfortably affected by small things Selina said and did—a glimpse of her being affectionate to old Tips should not be so pleasing to him, he was sure.

At least the ice between them had thawed slightly as a result of their impromptu dance lesson. Selina had been less chilly in her manner with him, and he had even caught her watching him on a couple of occasions without looking as though she was plotting his doom. The strange sensations he had suffered while they danced had been unfortunate, but surely only the natural result of holding so closely a pretty—very pretty...more than pretty—girl. He would not be so foolish as to allow it to mean anything more.

He would not be so foolish as to repeat his most catastrophic lapse in judgement either.

Edward pinched the bridge of his nose as the image of Selina's face appeared before him, scarlet with shock, kiss-swollen lips parted breathlessly. Once again it sent a shard of discomfort into his gut. What had he been *thinking*, allowing himself to lose control so unforgivably? It could never happen again.

The sensation of Selina's lips beneath his own had been achingly sweet, dangerously exciting. The last woman he had kissed had been Letitia, of course, and Edward felt himself grimace as the memory of blonde ringlets and sky-blue eyes rose up, an unwelcome reminder of a past he had no desire to revisit. Letitia's kiss had been chaste, though, and oddly cold. Selina's had been a burst of fire, and Edward felt the embers of that disconcerting *something* spark within him at the thought.

He should never have kissed her—that much was true—but he couldn't deny how much he had enjoyed it, and how even now he knew it would be a struggle to curb the desire to surrender to his urges again.

He suppressed a small sound of irritation and sat back in his chair, pushing away the letter in front of him. *You need to be more careful.* His mistake might so easily have led to something worse. His attraction to Selina might not be under his control, but how he chose to react

to it certainly was, and he had let himself stray peril-
ously close to the pain of a rejection he never wanted
to experience again just for the sake of a fleeting thrill.
Aside from his own determination never again to be
vulnerable to a woman's whims, Selina's Romani sen-
sibilities would never entertain a gentry suitor—and he
shouldn't forget that.

He heard footsteps on the boards outside the dining
room and moments later Selina entered, enveloped in
her customary shawls and with the elderly whippet trotting at her heels. She took her usual seat at the table and
nodded across at Edward, who passed her what he now
knew to be her favourite delicacy from the selection laid
out for luncheon—a little sugared bun topped with caraway seeds. It was far too sweet for Edward's taste, but
Selina could eat at least two at any given opportunity.

'Thank you.'

She laid the morsel neatly on her plate and hesitated
for the barest of moments before picking up her knife
and fork. Glancing at her out of the corner of his eye,
Edward saw she had selected exactly the correct cutlery.
Ophelia would be delighted that her seemingly relent-
less lessons had borne fruit.

Unaware of her audience, Selina took a fragment and
dropped it into the waiting jaws of the dog lying at her
feet. Edward raised an eyebrow. Apparently not *every*
etiquette lesson had hit its mark.

'I received another letter in the afternoon post. About
my very sudden, very private marriage.'

'Oh.'

'Oh, indeed.' Edward took another forkful from his
own plate and scanned the page once again.

Apparently yet another acquaintance of his father had

heard the news that young Master Fulbrooke had taken a wife—a wife nobody seemed to know much about. Was such talk true? There were rumours, he informed Edward darkly; hideous calumnies that the lady was not quite the *thing*.

Edward rolled his eyes. It was true that the only people officially informed of his marriage so far were his servants and, of course, his father's solicitor, for the purpose of the will. But it had been necessary to spread the news as soon as possible, to ensure Harris and Milton didn't get any ideas of new ways to attack the Roma camp and target Selina.

He could only imagine the looks on their faces when they had heard who the young Squire's new wife was. Edward would have paid a hundred guineas to have been there to witness it when they realised she was well and truly out of their reach.

He looked up. Selina had progressed to feeding Tips small morsels of bacon—rather brazenly, in Edward's opinion. The dog's skinny tail wagged and he peered up at the Roma girl with adoring eyes.

'I've been thinking. We're going to need to be seen together. People have started asking questions, and the only real way to answer them is to let people see you with their own eyes.'

Selina's hand stilled on its journey back to the meat platter. 'Seen together? Where?'

'Society venues, I'm afraid. I don't care for them any more than you do, I can assure you.'

'If you don't like them, must we go?'

'It would be a good idea. People are curious about you. I'd much rather we met them where we can leave if we like, rather than sit through hours of dull visits.'

He raised an eyebrow at her rigid face. What could be her objection? 'Unless, of course, you'd prefer to receive endless streams of visitors here, with no chance of escape until they leave?'

The notion of a host of nosy society busybodies descending on his house made Edward want to curl his lip. Unless he debuted Selina in public, however, he couldn't think how such a thing was to be avoided. It was customary in his circles to welcome a new bride, and there was little point in trying to avoid it, however much he might want to.

Her silence was more unnerving than any words she might have spoken. Edward allowed the quiet to stretch for a few moments before leaning a little closer to her chair. It had been raining again, and he just caught the appealing scent of damp earth and cut grass that clung to her, enticing him to lean closer still.

He sat back again smartly. 'Come along, Selina. It isn't the end of the world. You never know—you might even enjoy yourself.'

'Might I?' Her voice was quiet, restrained. 'Do you truly think I'm likely to find any enjoyment in meeting all your high-class acquaintances?'

Edward frowned. He understood her reluctance—given the choice he wouldn't venture out either—but certainly the prospect of a society outing wasn't *so* bad.

'Selina. This is part of our bargain. I have shielded you from your troublesome situation, and now you need to play the part of a squire's wife for me—only until you leave.'

'You don't know what you're asking.' A touch of something like a warning had crept into her tone, and the hands that lay on the table had balled into fists. 'Marrying you and taking your name is one thing. Your insisting on parading me about like one of your society ladies is quite another.' She lifted her chin and looked him directly in the eye. 'I don't want to go. I don't want to be around those people.'

Frustration broke over Edward like a wave, surprising him with its intensity. He'd allowed himself to believe they had managed to make some headway, to find at least some tiny shred of accord between them. Evidently he had been wrong, and he disliked the heavy feeling of disappointment that mixed with his annoyance.

'I'm afraid I must insist. We needn't stay very long, and you needn't enter into any deep conversations, but you must be seen with me as my wife until we have our annulment.'

He saw the anger that rose up in her face. It looked to Edward as though it was mingled with something else—something complex that was almost like anxiety. But what was there for her to be anxious about? What did she really have to fear from such a plan apart from a few hours of crushing boredom?

Selina stood up. An ingrained sense of etiquette dragged Edward to his feet likewise, and they faced each other across the expanse of table between them.

'I said I don't want to go.'

'Even if it will make our lives easier if you do?' Edward fought to keep the edge of frustration from his voice. 'Would you *really* rather half of society descends on this house to peer at you like a creature in a zoo?'

Both voices were tense. The old dog took one look at each of the set faces, tucked his tail between his legs and crept beneath the table.

'Of course I don't want that. I won't be seeing any-

body, anywhere. I'm not one of your kind, Edward.'
Selina shook her head, her eyes filled with that strange
emotion Edward couldn't seem to place. She looked almost haunted. 'I can't—I can't walk among them and
pretend I belong.'

Edward raked his hand through his hair, struggling
to restrain his exasperation with his determined wife.
There was high colour in her cheeks now, a dusky pink
that, despite the depths of his ire, Edward couldn't help
but note suited her.

The thought only fanned the flames of his irritation.
'Why are you doing this? Why must you make this simple thing so difficult?'

'You think me difficult because I won't be a good
wife and do as you demand? Don't forget you were the
one who never wanted a *good wife*.'

It was all he could do to bite back a growl. He was well
aware of the unsentimental terms of their marriage, despite his confusing stirrings to the contrary. Surely it was
Selina who needed a reminder of her part in their scheme.

'You didn't answer the question. Why are you so set
on denying me this request? Is it simple spite? What?'

She was moving away from him. One part of Edward's mind reeled at her poor manners—turning one's
back in the middle of a conversation?—while another
merely raged at her obstinacy. She couldn't possibly have
a real rationale for her actions; she simply wanted to
wound him.

The realisation stung.

Selina paused in the doorway, one hand resting on the
handle. She turned back to him, an expression of intense
feeling written upon her face. 'Nothing I do is ever born
out of spite. *I* was raised better than that.'

'Then what *is* your reason?'

Edward knew his voice was raised more loudly than a gentleman's should ever be, but the provocation was too much to bear. He flung the words at her back, but she had already thrown open the door and disappeared from his sight.

Selina's heart thudded in her ears as she swept down the cobbled path to the stable yard.

How could he?

Wasn't it enough that she'd sacrificed so much already? That she'd already swallowed her pride and tasted the bitterness of leaving her home, her family, her entire way of life to help Edward claim his precious inheritance? Certainly he had aided her in return, and for that she was grateful, but surely he was demanding more now than she could ever be expected to give.

The sound of her footsteps on damp cobbles rang out across the yard, and the two stable lads dipped their heads in respectful greeting as she strode past. Even that added fuel to the flames of her fire. All the servants were by now aware of her origins, she knew that for certain, and yet they still *'yes, ma'am-ed'* her as if she were a born lady. It was all so false. Everything of Edward's class was so insincere, so built on illusions and glamours. And now he wanted her to embrace it even more, to mingle with those but for whom she would still have a mother.

Djali flicked his ears at her as she approached, his huge grey head poking out over his stable door. Well used to his moods, Selina could tell just by looking that he was irritable at being cooped up. Roma horses were allowed much more freedom than gentry mounts, and

Djali didn't seem to be taking to the upper-class way of life any better than his mistress.

Selina unbolted the door and stepped inside, closing it behind her. The horse eyed her for a moment before turning to his trough, and Selina perched on the edge of it, her arms folded across the worn fabric at the bodice of her dress.

She hadn't seen Edward close to losing his temper before, and she would confess she hadn't enjoyed the experience. Following their dance lesson, and his wholly unexpected kiss, she had noticed his behaviour towards her undergo a subtle change. Whereas previously he had been polite but distant, he now seemed more inclined to seek her out during the day for innocuous conversation—conversation that, mortifyingly, Selina found she was beginning to enjoy.

Returning to her room after the events of that morning, Selina had seated herself in front of her looking glass and gazed long and hard at her reflection. Her mirror image had stared back unflinchingly, almost challenging her to voice the confusing array of thoughts that chased each other through her mind.

She had danced with Edward. And she had liked it.

Even worse: he had *kissed* her. And she had *liked* it.

Despite herself, her better judgement and all her attempts to squash it, her worrying attraction to Edward showed no signs of diminishing. Her thoughts of him *would not* cease to plague her day and night. The memories of how good his hand had felt on her waist, how his lips had moved on hers so urgently, were burned into her mind like a brand, and nothing could free her of their grip. It was an unexpected complication to feel her weakness for him increasing rather than the reverse, and the knowledge that Edward would be horrified by her fledgling feelings for him only made her feel worse.

Hadn't he made it plain that he wanted a wife who would form no attachment to him? His kiss must have been some strange lapse of thought—a thing of no importance that she ought to try to forget.

Tears pricked at her eyes. Sitting in the calm stillness of the stable, surrounded by the heady scent of hay and horse, Selina felt a sudden wave of powerful homesickness threaten to engulf her. The smells were of her childhood, when Papa would take her with him to market to look over some new pony, and for a moment she wondered if she should just take Djali and ride back home to Zillah. Hang Edward and everything he stood for—why should he be allowed to make her feel such confusion?

A shadow sliced across the cold sunlight filtering through the stable door.

'Selina?'

Edward's voice was quiet. Glancing up, she saw him looking over the split door, an unreadable expression on his infuriatingly handsome face. She said nothing as he entered the stable and leaned against one wall; his silence matched her own.

Tiny motes of dust danced in the shaft of light that streamed through the doorway and outside Selina could hear the stable lads sweeping the cobbles, one of them humming to himself as he worked. Djali stood close by, the grinding of his teeth against oats his only contribution to breaking the strained silence that neither Edward nor Selina seemed willing or able to end.

After what felt like half a lifetime Edward spoke. He wasn't looking at her. Instead his attention was fixed on the marked flanks of the steadily chewing horse.

'I keep meaning to ask you. How did Djali get his scars?'

Selina felt herself tense. She knew he was just trying to break the tension between them, but of all the questions he could have asked he *would* have to stumble across the one she would have given anything to avoid answering. Her heart rate, already raised at his entrance to the stable, picked up speed.

'It's not a story I like telling.'

Edward scuffed the toe of one immaculate boot through the straw strewn at his feet. 'Why is that? Was it an upsetting event for you?'

'Oh, yes.' Her voice was low and bitter. 'You might certainly say that.'

How could she tell Edward the truth of it?

She risked a glance in his direction—a quick sideways cut of her downturned eyes. He seemed to be waiting for her to elaborate, and Selina turned her face away. There was no way of explaining what had happened to Djali without revealing all: how the fate of her mother was tied to it, and the role his own family had played in the whole sorry business. To confess the full story to Edward would be to reveal his uncle's wickedness—surely he would not thank her for that.

'I'm not sure you would enjoy hearing about it.'

She stared down at the floor, noticing a new tear in the hem of her dress. *Another thing to repair.* If only her heart was as easy to mend.

The familiar dull ache she felt whenever her final day with Mama was recalled settled beneath her breastbone again, a weight in her chest she had grown used to carrying since childhood. Perhaps she *should* tell Edward exactly why the Roma hated his class, she thought, a sudden feeling of hopelessness stealing over her. It wouldn't change anything, but then he would know why she couldn't bring herself to walk among those responsible for causing so much pain to her people.

At least then he would understand—and besides, wasn't there some secret, shadowy part of her that wanted him to know she wasn't as heartless as he obviously thought her to be? She shouldn't care what he thought—she knew that—and yet that small part of her was undeniably there, and its whisper caused her to make up her mind.

'I'd like to think I could cope with whatever you have to say.'

Edward sounded far away, although he couldn't have been more than a few yards from where Selina sat stiffly, hunched slightly as though in pain. She forced herself to look up at him, watching her from across the stable floor. 'Would you truly like to know?'

'If you would be so good as to tell me.'

Selina could feel the jumping of her pulse at her throat, but her voice was calm and cold. 'Perhaps I should. I hope then you'll see why I can't bring myself to mix with the people you think of as friends. Only...' She tailed off for a moment as worry gnawed at her.

I hope he won't react too angrily. I can't imagine he'll like me calling his uncle a murderer, even if I suppose it was an accident.

'Only recall that I warned you first you wouldn't enjoy this tale.'

Edward opened his mouth to reply, a frown appearing between his brows, but Selina began to speak, forcing him into silence.

'Djali was a gift from my father to my mother. Mama

broke him in herself. Papa told me it took her weeks to get a saddle on him, but she was the only one who ever could have done it. Papa bought Djali cheaply, because of his bad temper, but Mama managed to see the best in him and he loved her, too.'

She swallowed, her mouth dry as she considered how to proceed. Edward watched her closely, the frown replaced by a look of wary concern.

'A good horse is worth its weight in gold to the Romani; it makes things a little easier as life on the road is hard. There are times when there's no food, no coal for our stoves. Winters are always the worst.'

The edge of the trough was digging into her thighs. Selina stood up and moved across to the doorway, standing with her back to her waiting husband.

'The winter when I was eight years old was the coldest I can remember. Papa was out trying to find work and Grandmother was sick with a fever, so it was just me and Mama who went hawking. We thought we'd test our luck at the nearest gentry house, see if anybody would buy our wares. We tied Djali up not far from the house.'

She swallowed hard. *Just say it.* There was no going back now.

'In fact, it was this very house. Blackwell Hall.'

Edward started, straightening up immediately from his position leaning against the stable wall, but Selina allowed him no time to speak.

'It was a freezing, iron day. We were so, so cold, and so, so hungry. I knew Mama was desperate. When the front door opened I swear to you I believe she thought our luck had changed.'

'But it hadn't.' It wasn't a question. Edward's voice held a world of grim foreboding.

'No. It hadn't. At the first sight of us standing on the doorstep your uncle bellowed at his men to release the dogs.'

Her chest was rising and falling faster than she could control as she saw Edward's mouth drop open, his face rigid with naked horror.

'So we ran. We ran as fast as we could away from those hounds and we heard your uncle Charles *laughing* as we went.'

Her voice was thick with emotion. How ugly it must sound to Edward, some distant part of her thought, but she couldn't stop now—not until the whole tale was told.

'We ran back down the drive and through the gates, and we were almost back safely with Djali when Mama slipped on the frost and fell down. The dogs were still coming. I could hear them barking as they got closer and closer, and Mama was still on the ground—'

It was as though she was living it all over again. The sounds, the sight of the pack of hounds almost upon her, and the worst, the very, *very* worst of it all: Mama lying among the sharp frosted blades of grass, so terribly, unnaturally still, her lifeless black eyes gazing upwards with no earthly way of knowing what they were seeing.

'I thought the dogs were going to tear us apart. I tried to help Mama up but she didn't move. I know now that she hit her head on a rock, killing her instantly, but at the time I just couldn't understand it.'

Tears were coming thick and fast now, falling from Selina's burning eyes. She could no longer see the stable yard beyond the door, her vision blurred and her mind fixed on the horror that consumed her.

'But then Djali leapt out in front of us. I still don't

know how he managed to break free from where he was hitched, but he put himself between me, my mother and the dogs and he took the savaging they would have given me onto himself. He saved my life. I remember every moment: how the dogs snarled and howled and lunged at him, over and over again, and how he fought them back, biting and kicking until they ran away—and then how he stood over Mama so quietly, touching her with his nose so gently. He must have known she was gone. From him. From me. From both of us. Forever.

'After a little while he came over to me. He was covered in blood and so many bites I don't know how he survived. I heard them tell Papa later, when they thought I was asleep, that I had followed Djali back to camp and then he had guided them to where my mother was lying. I don't have any memory of that. Only of what went before.'

The world seemed to have splintered into jagged fragments of light, shining in the flow of her tears. She leaned forward and grasped the stable door with both hands, overwhelmed by the grief and terror that threatened to fell her.

Selina felt Edward's arms come around her just as her legs gave way, all the breath escaping from her bursting lungs as he held her close to the firm column of his body. She knew she should push him away, force him to keep his distance, but the strength of his embrace was impossible to resist, and she allowed him to cradle her as sobs racked her body and grief overcame her powers of rational thought.

Don't let him, Lina! her subconscious screamed as she felt one of his hands come up to smooth the ebony silk of her hair away from her face, raising goosebumps on the sensitive skin of her neck with the power of one gentle touch.

But it just felt so good to be held. The unshakable circle of his arms held her swaying body firmly upright, and as her sobs quieted she became aware of the beating of his heart close to her ear, a steady rhythm she found unaccountably soothing.

'I am so sorry, Selina. More sorry than I can ever say.'

One of his hands stroked her back, gentling her in the same way she would calm a frightened foal, and she gave herself up to the comfort it brought. Of all people, how was it that this man should be the one whose arms felt the most secure? she marvelled, half dazed by grief and innocent wonder. Each movement of his hand down her back left sparks in its wake, drawing a tingling line of fire down the column of her spine, and she found herself speechless in the face of her uncontrollable desire to remain there, safe in the protection of his arms.

Some small part of her started at the realisation that she had never been held so close by a man before. Papa was the only male ever to have gathered her into his embrace, making her feel loved and protected from all who might wish to harm her. The sensation of utter security was the same now as it had been when Papa's strong arms had chased away all her childhood fears, so complete and unquestionable that all words were stolen from Selina's mouth.

Pressed up against the warm planes of Edward's body she could hardly move, but the horror of her last day with Diamanda felt more manageable now, the pain somehow more bearable, and the unlikely fact that it was Edward she had to thank left her stunned.

He was looking down at her with the same intent expression he had worn when they had begun to dance, his attention so completely fixed on her that she felt her cheeks begin to burn. The deep hazel of his eyes held a world of compassion, and she saw her own sorrow reflected back at her in the mirror of his face.

His lips were mere inches from hers. Selina felt something inside her will her to move, but to move towards him or away from him she couldn't quite tell.

The voice whispered louder. *You could be the one to lose control this time. Why not just try...?*

Seeing she had stopped crying, Edward gently put Selina from him. Delving into the pocket of his coat, he drew out another white handkerchief and passed it to her.

She took it with one unsteady hand. 'You won't have many of these left at this rate.'

'No. You're amassing quite a collection.'

Watching as Selina rubbed at her eyes in an unpolished movement took Edward straight back to the day she had found Ophelia. Then, standing in the gently stirring woods, he had been struck by her unrefined loveliness. His appreciation of her beauty had not diminished since. In fact, it seemed to be deepening—a fact that was becoming more and more difficult to fight.

No wonder she was reluctant to tell me her story.

Edward's head spun as he tried to make sense of Selina's words, their terrible meaning slotting into place like jigsaw pieces in his horrified mind.

The Roma woman Charles had been rumoured to have harmed was Selina's mother. It was *his* family's fault that she had been forced to grow up without her mama. It was a horrible twist of fate, almost unbelievable, and yet no part of him suspected her of telling anything but the truth. Her emotion, so real and unashamed, could never have been faked. His own feelings swelled with pity, and with a burning guilt that tasted like bile in his throat.

It had been a reflexive move to take her in his arms, driven by the sight of the tears that had torn at him in a way so unexpected it had almost caused him to gasp aloud. Selina's grief was raw and true, not constrained by any upper-class notions of respectability. She had given him a glimpse into the deepest secrets of her heart, quite unlike any true-born lady, and Edward couldn't help the way his own heart had leapt at this unfamiliar show of honesty.

He had never before felt such compulsion, or been so instinctively moved by a display of emotion. Urged into action by the depth of her distress, he had felt himself richly rewarded by Selina's surrender into his embrace.

She'd felt so small and soft in his arms, so unlike the fiery creature he had argued with earlier. Both versions of her were lovely in their own way, each so different from the other, but nothing could have prepared him for how protective he'd felt as she'd cried against the silk of his waistcoat. In truth, as much as her tears had caused him a deep and very real concern, he could not deny that the chance to take her in his arms once more had been too tempting to ignore.

'I came to tell you that I'm sorry. I shouldn't have raised my voice to you and I shouldn't have tried to force you into doing something you don't want to. I was so set on escaping my own problems that I didn't fully consider your feelings. I apologise.' He cleared his throat. 'Especially now, after what you've explained about your mother... For my uncle's part in your family's distress

I have no words to express my shame and sorrow. I had no idea he was responsible for such a thing.'

Selina was still playing with the damp handkerchief and she shook her head, avoiding his gaze as she spoke. 'I should apologise, too. You only wanted me to fulfil my part of our arrangement. You couldn't have known what happened to Mama.'

Edward rubbed the back of his neck, unsure of what to say. What *could* one say to a woman who had just poured out the worst experience of her entire life to a man who had, only minutes earlier, been cursing her for her apparent pig-headedness?

A fresh current of guilt coursed through him, alongside the intense pity. No wonder she had mistrusted him, had hesitated before accepting his hand. No wonder her entire camp had looked at him as though he were a monster prowling among them, related as he was to the one who had caused them such grief.

To undergo such an appalling ordeal at all was abhorrent; to be aged eight at the time was even worse. Another wave of sympathy for the devastated woman he had cradled in his arms crashed over him. Edward thought back to his own childhood, casting through his memories for pictures of himself at a similar age. His mother hadn't left yet; that had come later. Edward had only dim memories of flavoured ices in summer and candied fruits at Christmas, interspersed by a jumble of Roma playmates and fat, placid ponies. No tragedies at all.

'Even so. I should have behaved better.'

Selina had moved to stand at Djali's head and was blindly stroking his wiry forelock. She still looked so small, so fragile, and so unlike her usual self that Edward felt a powerful burst of protectiveness roar up inside him, rising to mix with the disgust for his uncle that circled in the pit of his stomach. It was close to nausea, what he felt for the man who had caused so much harm, and he could have growled in grim satisfaction at successfully keeping the Blackwell inheritance out of Charles' hands.

He will never be welcome here again, he resolved, even as he tried to swallow down the renewed urge to take his wife in his arms and hold her close once again. The moment had passed. There could be no excuse to allow himself such dangerous weakness now. He had indulged his secret desires too far already, and it was with an unpleasant jolt he feared his touch might have been unwelcome.

How could she bear for him to be near her after what she had just revealed?

'Where does this leave us?' she asked.

Edward wrenched his attention away from his unwanted thoughts. 'Leave us?'

'Yes. You wanted me to venture out with you. Publicly.'

Was that a blush he saw cross her cheekbones?

'Do you still?'

He shook his head with all the conviction he could muster. There was no way he would pursue his previous aim—not now he knew the reason for her reluctance. The sight of her face, still tearstained and slightly ruddy with distress, increased the guilt twisting in his gut.

'I would never expect you to accompany me to the assembly rooms now, in light of your revelation.'

'But it would make things easier for us if I did?'

Edward hesitated. There could be no pretence: Selina knew how set he had been on the idea, and he knew her

well enough by now to realise she wouldn't appreciate
being lied to. 'I can't deny that it would.'

'I see.' Half of Djali's forelock had been braided into
a neat plait by her careful fingers. 'So it truly would be
in our best interests to establish this connection in the
minds of others?'

She appeared to be considering something. Edward
waited.

'Perhaps I could propose a compromise.' She glanced
at him—a swift, cautious look, as though taking his
measure. 'In light of your apology.'

Edward's spirits rose just the tiniest fraction. A compromise? From the distinctly uncompromising Selina?
'What would you suggest?'

'I would be prepared to accompany you on a walk.
I don't want to visit anybody, and I won't be displayed
like a fairground attraction in any assembly rooms either.' She held up a warning hand. 'But a walk... That
I will do.'

Relief mingled with puzzlement surged within him.
A walk would be better than nothing; indeed, it might
even turn out to be better than his own original scheme.
They would see more people out walking than sitting in
some stuffy room, and Selina would be far more relaxed
out in the open air. It was an excellent suggestion. But
why had she changed her mind?

'I would appreciate that very much indeed.' He knew
the relief must have shown on his face.

Selina gave him the smallest of smiles before wiping it quickly from her lips with a touch of what struck
him as confusion.

'Very good. I shall leave it up to you to decide where
and when we shall have our outing.'

Edward bowed with all the courtesy he had been trained to show. The idea of half of society clustering at his home was unpleasant. Many of them were the same faces he had encountered on social calls with Letitia, and Selina's willingness to oblige him was as welcome as it was confusing.

'I didn't think you would change your mind.'

The look she gave him was strange. Not challenging, as had been her usual expression, and not anxious, either, as it had been earlier that afternoon. It was closer to thoughtful.

Edward felt the hairs on the back of his neck stir under her scrutiny, unable to read the expression in her dark Romani eyes.

'Neither did I. My only hope is that I won't live to regret it.'

Chapter Eight

Warwick was teeming with people, and Edward felt Selina's anxiety as they continued their stroll along the busy street.

He took in the sight of his wife, more demure than he had ever seen her before in the respectable navy cloak and prim bonnet rescued from Maria's expansive pile of cast-offs. Selina had raised an eyebrow when Dinah had helped her into them, but she had eventually accepted their necessity.

Gossiping servants were one thing, but Edward would not have Selina exposed to upper-class ridicule when a simple change of clothing could prevent it. Nobody glancing at her would guess she was anything other than a lady born and bred, and he felt a wry appreciation for the way the dark blue served to enhance the raven of her hair.

Of course you'd notice that. Why does that come as no surprise?

'Would you take my arm? I can see you're not enjoying this. We won't stay much longer.'

Edward caught the flash of gratitude in the glance Selina threw him, accompanied by a quick nod. Her small fingers reached up and slotted into the crook of his arm, sending a thrill of that unnamed *something* skittering beneath his skin, and he took a moment to marvel at how far their relationship had come.

On the night the Roma camp had been attacked, she had only touched him under the greatest duress; now she barely hesitated before entrusting him to guide her along the busy street. He wasn't sure whether to smile or frown that her trust in him had evidently increased so much, or that his chest swelled with something suspiciously close to pride at the thought. Ever since she had told him of her mother's fate he had tried harder still to repress his growing regard for her, more certain than ever that any hint of it would be unwelcome.

Selina was all eyes as they made their leisurely progress past shops and houses. Everywhere she looked there were new things to be seen, and her curiosity made Edward feel as though he too was surveying the scene with fresh eyes. Selina's head moved back and forth as she took in the carriages that trundled past, the enticing displays in shop windows, the costly fabrics of passing ladies' clothes—all things Edward had taken for granted for twenty-four years and rarely given a second glance.

Perhaps, although her almost childlike interest was tempered by the wariness he could feel radiating from her, he might dare to wonder if she might not be finding their outing such an unbearable ordeal after all…

'Good morning, Mr Fulbrooke!'

Edward felt Selina flinch as an older man and woman suddenly cut across them, the man's voice ringing out above the rattle of a passing barouche. He brought his hand up to cover her fingers, pressing them closer to the material of his coat, and felt them grasp tightly.

'Good morning, Mr Egerton… Mrs Egerton.'

Edward tipped his hat to the elderly couple, still feeling the vice-like grip of Selina's fingers on his arm. He saw how the woman's eyes widened in powerful curiosity, apparently absorbing every detail of Selina's face and clothes—in order to tell her friends about them later, Edward had no doubt—before they had passed by and moved out of sight.

Edward looked down at Selina, at her hand still gripping the material of his coat. 'That was Mr and Mrs Egerton. I was at school with their son Henry, the biggest blowhard you might ever have the misfortune to meet.'

He saw the corners of her lips twitch a little, the unease draining from her face, and felt relief wash over him. She had looked so startled by Mr Egerton's braying upper-class voice—not that he could blame her. The man was known in Edward's circle to be a human foghorn.

'Mrs Egerton is a determined gossip, so the news that she's seen my mysterious new wife will be all around town by nightfall.'

Selina gave a dry laugh. 'I'm glad to know it. The more people we see today, the fewer will come to call on us at Blackwell, I would hope.'

'That's certainly my desire.'

They walked on for a while in companionable silence, until Edward felt Selina give a small shiver. 'Are you cold?'

'A little.' She peeped up at him, eyes dark beneath the brim of her bonnet. 'I understand they would have seemed a little out of place, but no cloak is as warm as my own shawls.'

'I see.' Edward nodded, dismissing the smile that attempted to curve his lips upward.

He could just imagine the scandalised looks his wife would have attracted had she ventured out in her usual wardrobe, and Selina's indignant reaction was one he could all too easily picture.

'I think we should return to the carriage. You've indulged me quite enough.'

Selina's pert expression told Edward exactly what she thought of *that* notion, but she said nothing as he turned her gently and guided her back through the busy streets. She had more than upheld her end of their bargain, even going so far as to muster a passable attempt at a smile for some of the acquaintances they had passed during their walk. Edward couldn't fault her in that regard, and it was an enjoyable sensation to know that Selina had undertaken such a thing for his benefit when at one time the idea would have been unthinkable.

As they approached the place where the carriage awaited them Edward saw his coachman standing with hands on hips, looking over one of the pair of handsome black horses with a frown.

'Is something the matter?'

The coachman, a stout individual named Greene, looked round at Edward's voice and paced towards him, dipping a bow in Selina's direction. He nodded, a look of concern on his weathered face.

'Aye, sir. This one's gone lame.' He gestured at the nearest horse. 'I thought she was favouring her back right hoof on the way here, and now it's grown worse. She won't be able to pull the carriage back to the Hall in this state.' He patted the horse's flank with rough affection. 'I'm not sure what to make of it.'

Edward frowned, and was about to speak when Selina

stepped up to the horse and smoothed her hand along its gleaming back.

'May I look?'

Greene's eyebrows raised in surprise. 'If you'd like to, ma'am.'

He lifted his hat and rubbed the back of his head. Edward saw how doubtfully he eyed Selina as she moved to stand behind the horse.

'Be careful, ma'am—she might kick...'

The coachman's sentence died in his mouth as Selina flung her cloak out of the way and firmly seized the horse's back leg, bringing it up to clamp it between her knees. Edward started in shock. *What kind of woman did such a thing? And in public?*

He looked about him quickly. More than one passerby was looking askance at the otherwise respectable young woman who now bent to inspect the hoof, her practised fingers running across the shoe as she frowned in expert concentration.

'Hmm...' Oblivious to the mute disbelief of both watching men, Selina turned the hoof and pressed gently at the tender underside, searching for something. The horse gave a soft whinny, as though in pain, and Selina placed the foot back on the ground carefully. 'She's got an abscess.'

Selina straightened up, moving back to stand at the horse's head. She ran a hand down the animal's face, softly stroking the blaze of white splashed across jet-black.

'A mustard poultice will draw the heat out, and she'll be walking normally again quite soon.'

Greene blinked at her, obviously at a loss for words, and Edward felt himself scarcely less surprised than his coachman. Her complete lack of self-consciousness stirred his immense admiration—who else would throw quality propriety to the wind and, careless of anybody else's opinion, do such an unladylike thing in the middle of a heaving street?

Edward knew from the aghast faces of the well-dressed strangers walking by them that they were appalled at Selina's apparent lack of decorum, but Edward only felt an absurd glint of pride that his wife was so unbothered by their stares, intent only on helping the suffering horse.

That's the Selina I met in the woods all those years ago. Never one to ignore a poor wounded creature.

Selina brushed her hands together neatly. 'Do you know how to make up a poultice? I have a recipe, if you'd care for it?'

The coachman still stared at her with a combination of shock and no small degree of respect, and it was only when Edward audibly cleared his throat that the man seemed to find his tongue. 'My wife makes them when the children have toothache, ma'am. I'll ask her for one as soon as I return home.'

'Excellent. She'll be good as new directly.'

Edward clapped the man on the shoulder, seeing Selina's satisfied nod out of the corner of his eye. All that remained now was to work out how he and Selina would find their way back to Blackwell themselves, now the carriage was unavailable. Greene would walk the injured horse home slowly, and return with a fresh pair to retrieve the carriage in the morning, but how would they manage now?

Edward made up his mind. There was really only one option, and it was one that made his heart begin to beat quickly against his ribs. 'I think Mrs Fulbrooke and I will ride home on the other horse. Would you be so good as to see her saddled?'

'Of course, sir.'

Greene moved off in pursuit of his task, leaving Edward with the suddenly warily quiet Selina.

Selina watched with round eyes as Greene prepared the fit horse and brought her to stand at the mounting block. Edward climbed up at once, and it was all Selina could do to bite back a squeak of anxiety as she realised her first suspicion had been correct.

Heaven help me. Selina stared up at him, seated high above her with such natural elegance it was as though he'd been born into a saddle. *He wants me sit between—?*

She could hardly finish the thought, her breath catching in her throat and mortification stealing over her. He truly expected her to share his seat. It was so *intimate*, so *close*. She would be able to feel those strong legs she had admired for so long on either side of her, pinning her between them, while his arms would have to reach around her, drawing her close to that firm chest that she didn't dare allow herself to think about.

It wasn't proper to have such thoughts, but Selina couldn't help it as Edward looked down at her and raised a questioning eyebrow.

'Are you coming up or not?'

Greene was standing at her elbow. 'Allow me, ma'am.'

He extended a hand and Selina took it with a moment's hesitation. She didn't have much choice, but it was with no small amount of embarrassment that she allowed the coachman to help her up onto the waiting horse.

Selina swallowed down a rising sense of discomfort

as she settled herself between the warm spread of Edward's thighs. The feel of his legs touching hers through the material of her dress made her heart skip faster, and when his arms came around her to take hold of the reins she felt a furious blush come roaring up from her neck to burn the previously cold skin of her cheeks.

'Are you quite comfortable?'

Edward's lips were close to her ear. Selina steeled herself not to shiver as the feel of his breath stirred the hairs on the nape of her neck, deliciously sensitive. She nodded mutely and took hold of the pommel to anchor herself to the saddle.

'Very good.' Edward twitched the reins and gently touched the horse with his heels, raising a hand to Greene in farewell. 'Walk on.'

Selina held herself stiffly, determined not to allow herself to sink back against Edward's broad chest as they trotted through the town, Edward nodding politely to his left and right as they passed people he knew. It seemed to Selina he had an extraordinary number of acquaintances, and she thanked her lucky stars that he didn't pull the horse up short to speak to any of them.

A mile or so into their journey Edward leaned down to speak into her ear again, sending another delightful rush of sensation tingling through her nerves.

'Why are you sitting so oddly? You can't be at ease, holding yourself so unnaturally upright like that.'

Selina gritted her teeth on her alarm. *I can't very well tell you it's because I don't dare come any closer.*

The instinctive reaction of her body to Edward's proximity was hardly subtle, she feared, and her face grew warm again at the thought that Edward might notice the effect his all too enticing masculinity had on her.

'No, no, I'm quite well. This is how I always sit when I'm riding.'

She heard Edward's snort of amusement. 'I've watched you ride on a number of occasions, and I beg your leave to disagree that this is in any way normal.'

Selina opened her mouth to reply, but instead only a gasp escaped her lips as Edward took one hand from the reins to place it on her waist and draw her backwards, pulling her closer to the solid pillar of his body as easily as if she weighed nothing at all.

Shocked, Selina said nothing as sparks erupted in her stomach at the feel of his hand on the intimate curve of her waist, overcome by scandalised delight as Edward's very male heat warmed her back. She leaned against him, apparently powerless to move away.

'That's better. We have a fairly long ride ahead of us. I don't want you spending it looking so uncomfortable.'

Unseen by the satisfied man at her back, Selina shut her eyes tight in secret disagreement. If Edward thought nestling closer against him had decreased her discomfort, he was entirely wrong. Her shameful appreciation for the strength of the thighs that rubbed against her own with every movement of the horse was enough to make her blush all the more, and the place where his hand had gripped her waist felt as though it was on fire.

She was almost dazed by the whirl of sensation such proximity created inside her, and so she said nothing as they rode onwards, each footfall only increasing the delicious friction between her back and his chest that made her every nerve stand to attention.

'I was very impressed by how well you dealt with my poor horse.'

Selina felt the words vibrate through Edward's chest as he spoke.

'I've never seen a woman with such—ah—*skills* before.'

Selina could have sworn she heard a note of surprised admiration in his tone, and it pleased her more than she knew was entirely sensible. 'Thank you. I've been working horses since I was old enough to walk. My mother had just started teaching me her remedies before she passed away—' She broke off for a moment as a sudden wave of intense sadness washed over her. 'Her knowledge was my only inheritance when she died.'

She heard the note of curiosity in Edward's voice at her back. 'The only inheritance? Did she not leave anything else to you?'

Selina swallowed down a flicker of pain and shook her head. 'No. That is not our way.'

Flames had consumed Diamanda's body and all her worldly goods along with her, as was Romani custom. Everything that had remained of the woman who had shaped Selina's young life had been reduced to a towering column of smoke. Diamanda's dresses, her jewellery, even her hair combs had been piled around her slight body and set alight, while her family and all who loved her had stood with dancing flames reflected in the tears that rolled down their faces.

'We leave nothing behind.'

Edward was silent for a moment. When he replied his voice held genuine sympathy, its warmth so sincere that Selina felt something within her rise up to respond. It was almost a physical stirring, although nothing could quite force back the tide of grief that still welled inside her.

'It must be difficult, having no keepsakes. Was there nothing you would have liked to save?'

Selina sighed, her shoulders moving in a hopeless shrug. 'It hardly matters now.'

'But there was something?' he asked softly, interested but not imposing. 'A memento you would have liked to keep?'

A small smile twisted Selina's lips—a wistful thing that would have broken her mama's heart. 'There was a brooch she used to wear. Only gilt and paste stones, but she used to let me play with it and I was always the one to pin it to her dress.'

She held her fingers a couple of inches apart, seeing as she did so the memory of the brooch fixed firmly to her mother's chest. The picture made her smile stronger.

'It was about this big, and shaped like a flower. One big central stone surrounded by smaller ones like petals, and two metal leaves underneath. I'll never forget it.' She sighed again, so quietly this time that she knew Edward couldn't have caught the tiny sound. 'Never.'

There was another silence as Selina sifted through her memories, recalling all the times when her childish fingers had toyed with the brooch she ached to see just one more time. Her father had brought it back with him from some market or other, and slipped it beneath Diamanda's pillow for her to find...

Her papa's face when he and Selina had stood watching as his beloved's pyre sent sparks tumbling through the air was one she had never been able to forget. The thought of Papa gave Selina pause, and she felt a fresh knot of unhappiness rising to sit heavy in her chest. How was he faring, away working so hard? Had he heard the news of her marriage? Was he even now breaking a sweat while the pain of his daughter's actions weighed him down from within?

She felt her lips tighten and looked down at her hands, increasing their grip on the pommel until the knuckles gleamed white.

'You don't talk about your father.'

It was as though Edward had read her mind. His voice was quiet, hardly audible above the chill wind that rushed about them as they rode. They had long since left the town behind, and now all Selina could see in all directions was the patchwork green of fields.

'It's difficult for me.' Selina flexed the fingers of one hand, relieving the stiffness her iron grip had created. 'I miss him. I miss all my people.'

Edward said nothing for a moment. Selina was just beginning to wish she hadn't opened up at all when she felt a clumsy pat on her arm, and she twisted in surprise to look up into Edward's face.

'I understand.' Edward's expression looked a little strained and he gave Selina a tight smile. 'My relationship with my own father wasn't easy, but even so...' He tailed off, looking away from her across the open fields.

Selina waited for him to finish, but he didn't seem inclined to carry on. The look in his eye was almost sad, and Selina felt sympathy rise up inside her for the man she longed to comfort. Would he allow her such liberties? she wondered as she twisted back in the saddle to look over the horse's head. He had spared no time in soothing her when she grieved for her mother, and she felt another glimmer of that inexplicable comfort Edward's arms had given her.

But perhaps he would not appreciate her drawing attention to his moment of sorrow. Grief was a deeply personal thing—she knew that from bitter experience. He might rather she didn't say a word. Still, the glimpse of pain in his look had moved her, and it was by some unthinking instinct that Selina reached out to take Edward's hand in her own and squeeze it in wordless sympathy.

She felt rather than saw Edward's jolt of surprise, covered by a quick-thinking cough. *Perhaps I shouldn't have done that.* She turned her head slightly to the side, hoping to catch another glimpse of his face, but she could see nothing but a vague blur.

They rode on in silence, covering the few miles left to Blackwell Hall with neither one aware of the racing thoughts that swirled within the other.

Chapter Nine

Selina looked out at the frost delicately patterning the glass of the drawing room window. Winter was well and truly underway. The mornings were raw and uncompromising, and clouds moved across an iron sky. She could just make out the tiny forms of little birds huddling together for warmth in the skeletal branches of the grounds' trees.

She turned from the window and began to move in the direction of her bedchamber. Edward had expressed his intention of seeing his steward that morning, on estate business, stating that he wouldn't be returning until the evening, and he had left soon after breakfast, riding away down the long drive on his shining chestnut mare. It seemed to her the perfect time chance a visit to the Roma camp, without any accompanying questions.

She'd been relieved at his departure for other reasons, too.

There didn't seem to be much use in trying to hide from it anymore: her feelings for Edward had changed, and the knowledge chilled her to the bone.

She had always thought he was handsome. Even on the first day they had met, when he had coaxed her down from her hiding place and she had wanted to run from him, to be anywhere other than facing him across a carpet of fallen leaves, she had been struck by the knowledge that his face was the most comely she had ever seen. That initial attraction, a product of the most basic animal instinct, had been tempered by her utter contempt for his class, his way of life and everything he stood for.

His class hadn't changed, and neither had the life of privilege that was all he had ever known—but it seemed to matter less now, the gulf between them, and that was what frightened her. He'd given her glimpses of the real man behind the good manners and polite smiles, and she liked what she had seen. His grief for his father had shown her his vulnerability, and his care for her in the face of her own sorrow had left her in no doubt as to the kindness of his heart.

While she had felt nothing but mere physical attraction to him, she had been safe. Now she wasn't sure how close to danger she was straying.

Out in the yard she saddled Djali herself, with automatic swiftness, although the stable lads hovered a short distance away. Ever since she'd refused their offer of a side-saddle some weeks previously they had watched with undisguised fascination each time she'd mounted, half aghast and half admiring of her insistence on riding astride.

Passing them now, as she rode out from the yard, she raised a hand in greeting and saw their heads bob in reply.

Once out of their hearing she leaned forward to pat the horse's grey neck. 'Isn't this better, Djali? Out in the open air, just you and me?'

The horse flicked his ears at her voice and lengthened

his stride. He cantered easily down the long gravel drive, bearing Selina smoothly through the imposing wrought-iron gates and away from Blackwell Hall.

Try as she might to ignore him, Edward wouldn't leave her mind as she rode. He seemed to impose upon her more and more inescapably—both in real life and when she laid her head down on her luxurious pillow to dream—and it seemed even the freezing late-November air couldn't shock some sense into her.

I had hoped a day away from him would help me gather my wits. It seems I was wrong.

She didn't want to feel this way. No good could come of it. She was under no illusion that Edward felt anything for her other than a duty of care, and she shouldn't allow herself to think otherwise. A marriage of convenience was what he had wanted, specifically with no finer feelings involved—and that was what she must give him, despite any stupid, confusing, ridiculous thoughts to the contrary.

Her determination to disregard her feelings, however, hadn't stopped them from betraying her at every turn. Small, insignificant gestures from Edward insisted on taking on greater magnitude in her despairing mind. Each time his hand brushed hers as he helped her into the saddle her heart would skip a beat, and his smile as she played fetch with old Tips was endearing.

But he wouldn't want her affection, nor welcome it if she were foolish enough to let it show, and it was growing harder day by day to keep secret the stirrings she feared would so disturb her stoic husband.

The Roma camp looked just as it had the day she'd left it. The *vardos* still stood in a semi-circle around the cooking pits, their painted wooden sides gleaming in the wintry sunlight and their owners milling about busily, and the camp's horses still grazed in the makeshift paddock or were tethered to stakes driven into the ground.

At the sound of Djali's approaching hoofbeats one of the women—Selina's cousin Florentia—looked up sharply. Selina saw the apprehension in her kinswoman's face change to surprise as she registered who was riding into the camp, and she felt her spirits soar as surprise was in turn replaced by a wide beam of welcome.

'Cousin!' Florentia dropped the knife she had been using to peel vegetables and rushed towards her, arms outstretched.

Selina dismounted and reached out towards the other woman, who enveloped her in a tight embrace.

'Cousin. My poor cousin. You don't know how good it is to see you. We've all been so worried about you, all alone up there in that great house!'

'I am well.' Selina smiled as Florentia's daughters recognised the newcomer. They threw down their dolls at once and ran towards her as quickly as their little legs would carry them, and she bent to receive them into her arms.

'Lina! Lina!'

'Lina! Are you come back? Are you come to live with us again?'

'Not quite yet, dearest.' She hefted the youngest onto her hip and held out her hand for the other girl. 'But it won't be much longer.'

The other women had begun to crowd around her. The older ones touched the worn fabric of her dress, the wool of her shawls and even her hair in silent blessing, thankful for her return to them, while the younger rattled off questions more quickly than she could reply to them.

'I'll answer you all very soon.' Selina looked around at the rapt faces. 'First I would like to see my grandmother. Where is she?'

'The other end of the meadow. Another one of the babies has been ill, and Zillah went out to gather some herbs for medicine.'

All of the breath left Selina's body. 'Another one of the babies?'

Surely not. Their survival had been one of the most desperate reasons she had consented to become Edward's wife and thrown her entire existence into chaos. If a child had succumbed despite her actions all her struggle would have been in vain. The cruel irony was not lost on her.

'They have been unwell?'

'Yes. My son has been gravely ill, but he's a little stronger now.'

The child's mother, a young woman Selina knew had only been married a year, gave her a shy smile.

'He wouldn't have survived his fever if we'd been on the road. I have you to thank for saving my boy.'

'I can't take the credit for that.' She smiled back at the woman, relief coursing through her. So the children were safe? That was good news indeed. 'It was my fault we would have had to move in the first place.'

'Nonsense.' Florentia's look was stern. 'Those evil men would have found the camp eventually. If you hadn't sacrificed yourself for us we would have had to run anyway—and probably even faster.'

Selina shrugged off her cousin's words. Whatever they might tell her, Selina knew in her heart that she was responsible for the calamity that had almost befallen her people. It was good to know that they didn't blame her, but she could never allow herself any reprieve from the guilt that had haunted her ever since that night.

Zillah's back was to her as she approached, bent over to inspect what to most would have looked to be a clump of weeds, and the old woman spun round in alarm at the touch of Selina's hand on her shoulder.

'Selina? Oh, my Selina!'

Zillah's arms came around Selina in a hug that might have crushed bones had the old woman been a fraction stronger. Her grandmother held her for several long moments, gently rocking back and forth, before letting go to hold her at arm's length and peer up sharply into her face.

'Why are you here, child? Is aught amiss?'

'No, Grandmother. I simply missed you, that's all.'

'But is it not dangerous for you here? What of those men?'

'Peace, Grandmother.' Selina smiled down at the lined face and the old eyes that gazed into her own. 'They know I'm under Edward's protection—he has made sure they are aware of our marriage. While I am his acknowledged wife they won't dare harm me. If you have suspicions that they've returned I will tell Edward and he will deal with them, have no doubt. But I'm confident they won't risk their jobs by hunting me until they feel safe to do so.'

Selina realised her mistake as soon as the words left her lips. Using Edward's given name, and in a tone a shade too warm, had been a fatal error. She saw a shadow of suspicion flit across the old woman's countenance and felt her heart sink.

'I see. Well… Come to the *vardo*, girl. I'm sure you've much to tell me.'

Selina followed the slight form of her grandmother back to their caravan. Mounting the steps and crossing the threshold, she was at once assailed by the bittersweet familiarity of the compact space inside the cabin. It was only the size that surprised her. Had the cabin always been so *small*?

Her time at Blackwell must have affected her more than she'd realised, she thought, and her heart gave a lurch at the notion she had become adrift from her true way of life. She frowned to herself, feeling guilt in the pit of her stomach. Of course it wasn't the cabin that was too small. It was the fine rooms of the Hall that were too large.

She sat and waited as Zillah busied herself stoking up the fire to make tea. Cups in hand, granddaughter and grandmother regarded each other across the narrow space between their bunks.

'So.' Zillah's gaze was unwavering as ever. 'You are well?'

'As well as I can be. And yourself? How have you been faring?'

'Oh, you know me. I am as I always am.'

Selina sipped her tea, aware of a growing discomfort nagging at her. Zillah's careful scrutiny was nothing new, but the wary gleam in her eye was one Selina hadn't seen before. An unsettling feeling of being measured was creeping over her—but measured for what?

'And Papa? Have you seen him?'

'No.' Zillah looked away from her, instead watching the curling flames that flickered in the grate. 'He has had no time to visit. A few of the young men returned briefly, to see their wives, but your father has been promoted to foreman of a team and wasn't able to come with them.'

'He doesn't know—?'

'About your marriage?' Her grandmother still studied the fire. 'No. No—heaven forgive me—I couldn't bear to send word to him. I just couldn't do it.'

Selina stared down into her teacup. How was she to respond? Of course Zillah was right. Papa would be distraught at the knowledge of how his only daughter had wed. But it could only be a matter of time before he would have to be told, and the thought of his anguish made her tea turn to ashes in her mouth.

'But enough of that. I want to know everything that has befallen you since we last met. Have you been well treated?'

Zillah's voice was calm enough, but Selina knew her too well to be fooled. Worry had etched new wrinkles into the old woman's lined face since she had last set eyes on her.

'Yes, Grandmother.' Selina crossed the tiny gap between their bunks and took the frail body in her arms, feeling Zillah sag with relief at her words. 'I have been treated with nothing but respect and courtesy. You have no reason to worry.'

'That—that is good to know.'

Zillah patted her cheek with something like a smile, although Selina was sure she saw a shadow of unease still clouding her grandmother's eyes.

'I won't deny I have been concerned.'

'It's the truth.' Selina covered the bony hand with her own and squeezed gently. She wanted Zillah to think well of Edward, she realised with a rush of embarrassment. It mattered to her more now than she would have thought it could. 'Edward has been very good to me—better than I ever would have dreamed. In fact, he has been kind.'

Zillah was silent for a moment. She continued to hold her granddaughter close, but Selina could sense that the atmosphere had changed. Tension permeated the air of the cabin, replacing the tenderness of moments before.

Zillah was the first to draw away, and Selina saw immediately that she had not been wrong about the unease in her grandmother's expression.

'You speak as though you're fond of him. Of Edward.' Zillah's brow was pinched with wariness. 'Is that so?'

Selina felt her breath catch. Had she really been so transparent? She felt the slow tick of her pulse pick up speed. 'I didn't mean—' She stumbled for an answer, words evading her as she cast about for a way out of what she realised too late was a sprung trap.

'I know well enough what you mean.' Zillah passed a gnarled hand over her face, suddenly looking every one of her eighty-three years. 'It is as I feared.'

Selina's palms were damp as she clenched her hands into fists. *Keep your composure.* Her choice of words had been a mistake; she saw that now. How could she extricate herself from a situation that had already begun to spiral out of control?

'I don't know what you can be referring to. There's nothing for you to fear.'

There was another silence. Selina looked down at her balled fingers and forced them to straighten out, to relax on the worn fabric of her lap. The fire in the stove crackled quietly, casting an orange glow on the polished *vardo* floor.

Her grandmother's face was almost sad as she shook her head slowly, and in the silence her voice held a world of gruff pity. 'That's where you're wrong. I have a very real fear that you've made the same mistake as many a young girl and fallen for a man you cannot hope to have.'

Selina swallowed hard, panic rising within her. Her throat felt dry, tight, but she couldn't bring herself to take a drink from her cup. Her stomach fluttered with some unnamed emotion. How had this situation arisen? She should have guarded her tongue more carefully. Zillah was no fool. From a few hasty words she had guessed at the depth of feeling for Edward that burned within her granddaughter's heart, at her secret joy and pain rolled into one.

Selina forced herself to speak, all the while wary of betraying herself further. 'If by *fallen for* you mean developed a kind of friendship with—then, yes, I suppose I have. But—'

'Selina.' Zillah's voice cut across hers, halting her stuttering reply. 'Let us speak plainly to one another, as we always have. I believe that you have developed more than a friendly liking for this man, and I believe that if you continue on this path it will end badly for all concerned.'

Selina stared at her, her heart beginning to jump. *Too close. Far too close to the truth.* It was so like Zillah to get right the point of an issue, to see through Selina's protestations as though they were no more substantial than autumn mist. 'I— *No*— That is to say, he— I—'

Zillah sighed, long and deep, and when she peered into Selina's face there was a complex look of pain that sent a shard of ice through to Selina's soul.

'He is *gentry*, Selina. *Gentry*. I will not try to pretend he is as abhorrent as the rest of his kind—indeed, I will admit to you that I am grateful to him for his help in our time of need. But even so… You must know that our worlds are too separate, and always will be.'

Her grandmother's words stung.

'I don't say I have a special regard for him. I only say that he has treated me well.'

Selina tried to keep her tone indifferent, but all the same she could hear something beneath the surface and felt a lump rise up in her throat. Zillah was right. They *were* from different worlds, and all the wishing in the universe couldn't undo that. But that wasn't the reason she and Edward could never find happiness together.

The short laugh Zillah huffed out was entirely humourless. 'It isn't your words that betray you, girl. I see that look on your face so many young women have worn through countless generations. But, however handsome your Edward is, however kind, he is still gentry and you are still Roma, and the two are like oil and water. You cannot have forgotten that fact?'

Wordlessly Selina shook her head. Of course she had not forgotten the differences between them. The differences she had once thought it would be impossible to overcome. Now, however, they paled into insignificance in the face of Edward's desire for a cold marriage, his desire that they should annul it as soon as it had served its purpose. It whispered to her each time Edward pulled out a chair for her at the dining table, or laughed in genuine amusement at something she had said.

Each time he behaved towards her in a way that strengthened her esteem for him she would snap back with that knowledge: their marriage was on paper only and had no more depth than that. Zillah's words, misguided as they were, only served to bring home the truth to Selina in harsh black and white: *a man you cannot hope to have.*

'I am well aware of how things stand between us. There has been no impropriety, and for my part I can promise there will be none.'

The words almost choked her. It was all she could do to speak, with lips that did not want to move and a tongue that rebelled at the thought of naming the sadness that writhed inside her. Her grandmother was right, as she so often was. How much Selina would have given for her wisdom just once to be wrong.

'I think only of your happiness.'

The gentle way Zillah spoke almost brought tears to Selina's eyes, so different was it from her usual bluntness. She would never want to hurt her granddaughter; Selina knew that, but the words were like pinpricks to her heart nonetheless.

'It is far better for you to accept now that your marriage to Edward is based on convenience and nothing more. If you say he is a kind man I am willing to believe you—but never allow sentiment to cloud your eyes to the truth.'

For a long while neither woman spoke further.

What complex jumble of thoughts was twisting through Zillah's mind Selina didn't know. All she could be sure of was the turmoil inside her own. Staring down at the polished wooden floor, all she could do was surrender to the ceaseless procession of images that cycled through her head: Edward's intense face as he had taught her to waltz; the compassion in his look when she had cried for her mother; the closeness of his face to hers, tempting her to reach up and touch it with her lips.

Every single instance in which his goodness had been

displayed before her clamoured for attention, but she had to turn away. Because what Zillah said was true. She was a means to an end for Edward and nothing more, no matter how gently her grandmother had tried to phrase it. They had struck a bargain and he would fulfil his obligation to her. Anything further could only ever be a fanciful notion on her part, no matter how much she now wished, despairingly, that things could be different.

Edward rolled his aching shoulders as he cantered towards Blackwell. The day had been long and the estate business laborious and dull. He was looking forward to a good supper, a glass of port and his comfortable bed. He was just wondering if Selina would still be downstairs when he caught sight of the woman in question not far ahead of him, riding her distinctive grey horse around the side of the Hall toward the stable yard.

A smile crossed his face before he could stop it. There was a curious kind of pleasure to be found in returning home to a wife, and one he was increasingly powerless to resist. He had come to that conclusion the last time he had been away on business, and had subsequently spent the next hour studiously avoiding said wife by retreating to his library. It was getting exhausting, this persistent regard for the woman who haunted his thoughts despite his best efforts. He didn't seem able to master himself.

He hadn't been helping himself—that much he would have to own. He should not have instructed her to sit beside him at the pianoforte, for example, and attempted to teach her the notes, and he *definitely* shouldn't have felt a prickle of *something* shiver its way down his spine when he took her hand and placed each finger on the correct keys to play a simple tune.

He tapped his thigh lightly with his riding crop. It would have to stop. *He* would have to stop. He was getting carried away, and it was only a matter of time before somebody got hurt.

Edward knew it could only be himself.

Physically she stirred him in ways he fervently hoped she wasn't aware of. The image of her beautiful face and lithe figure taunted him at the most inappropriate times, but worse, much worse, was the reaction she caused in his heart and mind. There were flickerings there now—embers of feeling that her kindness and humour had crept in to ignite inside him—and it terrified him. However hard he tried to suppress them they would not be extinguished.

Her smile, so open and honest, in direct contrast to his mother's bland smirk, was becoming more and more contagious to him as the days went by. Her sweetness, hidden from him for so long, had begun to show itself—so different from Letitia's sharp cynicism. Everything about Selina was poles apart from the two quality ladies who had damaged his faith in women so completely, and it was so tempting to believe she could be trusted. But surely danger lurked behind the dark Romani eyes that watched him so closely, and the ability to wound him as he had been hurt before.

And besides, his own private thoughts were hardly relevant anyway. Selina would never reciprocate those feelings. She loathed the gentry, and with good reason. Certainly their relationship had blossomed of late, but surely on her side only into a brittle friendship, which might easily be broken by any hint of his esteem for her. She might have overcome the worst stirrings of her mistrust of him, but he wasn't naive enough to think she would ever forget his class, or forgive his kind for the loss of her mother.

It was this that would keep him safe and allow him to escape the perils of getting too close to a woman— just as he had always planned. He should be thankful to her for remaining so steadfast in sticking to their solely convenient marriage, for helping him to bolster his own defences when he felt them attempting to slip. To give in to his alarming weakness would be to invite the sting of rejection—something he never wanted to experience ever again.

She had already dismounted by the time he drew closer, and he called out to her as his mare's hooves clattered noisily across the cobbles. 'Good evening. Have you been out?'

Edward knew she must have heard him by the way her eyes flickered across to him before looking away again. Indeed, he could have sworn he saw her mouth twitch as though about to reply. Instead, however, she lowered her head and quickly left the stable yard, for all the world as though pretending she was ignorant of his presence—or that he was a stranger to whom she didn't wish to speak.

He watched her go, his face creased in surprise and more than a touch of confusion. *Have I managed to offend her somehow?* Surely there was no reason for such sudden and unexpected coldness.

Edward cast his mind back to their brief greeting that morning as he had passed her in the hall on his way out. There had been nothing out of the ordinary in their exchange and he frowned to himself as he dismounted and passed the reins to the waiting stable lad. What could have happened in the intervening few hours

between then and now to make her so apparently displeased with him?

The notion of having upset Selina, even uncon-
sciously, was uncomfortable—and the usual whisper that
it was unwise to care for her good opinion had grown
quieter of late. He found himself wanting to know what
could have transpired that was making it necessary for
him to swallow down a sharp disappointment at her
newfound reserve. He would have to find out what was
bothering her, and indeed where she had been.

A slow creep of suspicion began to steal over him,
and it was with heavy feet Edward climbed the stone
steps up to the Hall's front door—firmly closed only
moments before by the wife whom he suspected had just
had malice whispered into her ear by those with good
reason to dislike him.

Chapter Ten

Edward ran his eye over the small white rectangle of parchment covered in elegant script. To anyone else it would have looked like an invitation—*he* knew it was more of a summons.

Sir William Beaumont.

So his annual Twelfth Night ball was almost upon them again.

Edward had hoped rather than believed his father's death would excuse him from having to attend, but now, with the invitation in his hand, he had to face facts. His own aversion for high society parties made no difference: Ambrose Fulbrooke and Sir William had been boys together, and the presence of the Fulbrookes at each of the old knight's gatherings was considered essential to the occasion's success.

The real question, he mused as he moved from the hall towards his private study, was how to proceed with regard to Selina. She would have to accompany him—of that there was unfortunately no doubt. Word of his marriage had spread so far and so wide that for his wife not to attend the ball would register as a snub. It would also be a good opportunity for more of his acquaintances to see her, to see them together, so nobody would contest him having met the terms of his father's will.

Despite the potential benefits of the plan, the prospect of having to break the news to her almost made him groan out loud. She'd been acting so strangely of late, and his announcement would only make things worse. Any warmth between them seemed to have evaporated, and it was a source of constant frustration that she refused to tell him why.

I wonder what the old woman said to her to make her behave so oddly.

Edward had reached the safety of his study and he paced the floor with irritable strides. He could date the change in Selina from the day she had ventured out to visit the Romani camp, and the only explanation could be that her grandmother had filled her head with new doubts. Now she turned away when he greeted her with only the barest of acknowledgements, and she had taken to dining alone in her rooms.

Her avoidance of him stung. He knew he should be glad that she was making things easier for him in a way—wasn't that old saying 'out of sight, out of mind'? She would never feel the flicker of longing for him, coming as he did from the class who had done her people such wrong.

Instead of managing to withdraw his affections, however, Edward found they were intensifying day by day, apparently undeterred by their object's indifference. He had cursed his feelings, and himself, roundly and repeatedly. *Why* could he not break the spell of this madness? Even when she hurried away from him Edward was struck by the captivating shape of Selina's body, by the fine darkness of her eyes as she turned them from him. Was he to torment himself forever?

Of course not. She would be leaving as soon as spring arrived; that had been their bargain. The fact that he would be sorry to see her go only made her departure all the more necessary. He feared the power she had begun to hold over him. When a man cared for a woman he handed her the ability to wound him in ways too painful to imagine—as he knew all too well. Even if the prospect of her leaving was more unpleasant than he would have imagined, knowing she would be taking with her the fresh life she had brought to the brooding Hall, he knew there could be no alternative.

She would never choose to stay with him, and every one of the defences he had constructed around his battered heart reminded him that he should not desire it.

Selina was in her cosy drawing room when he managed to locate her, curled up in the depths of the most comfortable armchair and gazing into the fire that danced in the fireplace grate. She glanced up as he entered the room, and Edward saw her cheeks flush as she recognised her visitor.

'May I speak with you?'

'Of course.'

Selina gestured vaguely to another of the chairs that stood by the fire—the one furthest away from her, Edward noted in frustration. He settled into it, taking a moment to warm his hands before the flames as he considered how to proceed. The poker stood propped against the hearth and he seized it irritably. She was so difficult to talk to of late—how was he to know the best way to go about it?

'We've been invited to a Twelfth Night ball. My father's oldest friend has one every year, and I'm afraid my attendance is compulsory.'

Edward thrust the poker into the flames, stoking them higher. Out of the corner of his eye he could just make out Selina watching him, her face carefully expressionless beneath her raven nest of curls.

'Given your feelings on the landed gentry, I understand you might not be delighted at such a prospect. I would never try to force you into attending, but I should tell you that it would be considered an insult to the host if you didn't.'

She said nothing for a long while, instead looking down at her slender hands as they lay in her lap. The crackle of the fire and gentle ticking of an ornate clock on the mantle were the only sounds, the only movement the soft swirling of snowflakes against the windows.

Edward waited. It was her silence that bothered him the most, he'd come to realise. At least when she railed at him he knew what she was thinking. When she sat there so quietly, looking demurely down into her lap with her eyes veiled behind long lashes, he had no idea of what was happening inside her head.

How was it he found himself *wanting* to know? The ceaseless task of fighting against it was starting to wear him down, and the seductive temptation to give in to it and abandon his restraint whispered to him, its voice sweet in his ear. Edward shook his head quickly, to clear it, but an echo of that whisper still remained.

'How many people would be there? Is it a very grand occasion?'

Edward rubbed his jaw, hesitating before he answered. He couldn't lie to her, but he knew she wouldn't like his reply. 'Unfortunately, yes. Sir William extends an invitation to all the old families—there will be a good number of guests, all of them exactly the type of people you'd rather avoid.'

'I see.' The clock ticked in the quiet that settled between them for a few moments. Then, 'What would be required of me?'

'Required?' Edward had dropped his head into the cradle of his palms at her silence, but now he looked up from his hands. 'Why, nothing—aside from perhaps pretending my company isn't too distasteful to you. If such a thing can be managed.'

He realised as soon as they left his lips that his words had come out entirely wrong. He had meant for them to sound darkly comic; instead he'd heard an edge of bitterness, and he saw Selina's expression change as she too caught the dour note.

Perhaps it was too close to the truth for both of them? he wondered. He feeling slighted and she unwilling? He cursed internally at making such a mistake.

He saw her open her mouth to speak—to defend herself or upbraid him? he wondered—but she evidently thought better of it, for she closed it again and returned to staring into the flames.

He thought he saw tension in the way she held herself stiffly upright, but when she eventually turned to him her voice was restrained.

'If you think it would be for the best, you may accept the invitation. For both of us.'

'Oh?' Edward attempted what he hoped would turn out to be a normal smile, although a warm flood of relief washed over him. Perhaps he hadn't made such a grave error after all. 'Excellent. I shall reply to Sir William at once.'

Selina nodded, although Edward saw that the line of her jaw looked a little tight and a shadow of something like unease dimmed the usual sparkle of her black eyes.

'I'll look over my best dress. It isn't quite the height of fashion, but it might do with some fresh lace and a flower or two—if you can spare some from the hothouse.'

'I can do better than that.' Edward felt his smile become less fixed as an idea crept into his mind. 'I'd appreciate it if you'd allow me to buy you a gown for the occasion. I know you don't like the idea of me spending money on you, but I would consider it a favour if you were to oblige me in this.'

Selina's brows twitched together, but Edward could have sworn he saw her hesitate before she replied. 'We've talked about this before. I don't wish for you to waste money on me.'

'It wouldn't be a waste. It would be my way of thanking you for doing something I know you have little inclination for.'

He watched as Selina thinned her lips and fidgeted with the tasselled edge of her shawl, apparently wrestling with her thoughts. When she finally looked up her cheeks were tinged with the slightest hint of colour.

'Very well. If it means that much to you.' She toyed with the woolly trim again, her eyes hidden by the black sweep of her lashes. 'I can't pretend it wouldn't be a relief not to have to wear my shabby dress to a gentry ball. Thank you.'

In a sudden movement Selina uncurled her legs from beneath her and stood up. Spurred on by his usual good manners, Edward rose likewise, and watched as his graceful wife crossed the room, moving away from him. She was wearing the same outfit she'd worn when he had first ordered her down from that tree, he realised belatedly, and the contrast of scarlet against the black of her hair was just as striking now as it had been then.

He felt the now familiar stirrings of that *something* he still couldn't name move within him at the thought.

Selina had never seen such a stunning display in her entire life.

The inside of the dressmaker's shop was like something out of a picture book: shining rivers of silk gleamed in the wintry sunlight that streamed through large windows, and mirrors reflected the jewel tones back to dazzle her with their lustre. Long rolls of muslin, some plain and some printed with intricate patterns, were laid out carefully according to colour, demure next to the more flamboyant gloss of satin.

The shop assistants were far more welcoming than she had expected—but how much of that was due to Edward's presence on the other side of the painted willow screen was open to interpretation. He was seated in a fine chair, calmly perusing the morning's news sheets, and she could just about make out his silhouette against the barrier the ladies had so thoughtfully erected to save her modesty.

Apparently it wasn't usually the *done thing* for a man to invade such an exclusively feminine space, but the winning combination of Edward's handsome pocket book and even more handsome face had apparently been enough to overcome that particular obstacle.

Her own feelings at Edward being in such close proximity while she wore nothing but her slip were more complicated, and the thrill that crackled down her spine at the idea didn't bear thinking about. It wasn't decent, and it certainly wasn't proper, but some secret part of Selina wondered how warm his hands would feel with only one flimsy layer of material between them and her sensitive skin.

It was enough to make her breath come a little faster and that ever-ready blush to threaten to flood her cheeks once again. He was close enough to cross the room in a handful of those slow, long-legged strides. It would take him mere moments to reach her, to pull her into another heated embrace—

'And if you'd turn just a touch to the left, please, madam...'

The dressmaker knelt at Selina's hem, a measuring tape dangling from her practised fingers. Selina jumped guiltily, flushing scarlet as she hoped her train of thought hadn't shown on her face.

'Very good...thank you...almost finished...' The woman sketched a quick note on a piece of paper with a silver pencil and got to her feet. 'Excellent. Perhaps if madam is agreeable we could now pick out what fabrics might suit?'

Edward's voice issued suddenly from behind the screen, as firm and decided as ever. 'She'd like silk, if you'd be so good as to pull out your finest. Satin, too, and also lace—and perhaps some embroidered detail in places?'

Selina bit back a retort and instead arranged her face into an expression of calm interest as the girls fussed around her, leaping to do Edward's bidding and bring swatch after swatch of rich fabric for her consideration. She just *knew* he would be smiling that confident smile at having the last word, and it was with a twinge of irritation that she could picture just how much the upward curve of his lips suited him.

He seemed almost *pleased* to be indulging her. It was as though it wasn't merely a necessary evil for him to be spending the time and the money—enough to buy several weeks' worth of food for a Romani camp, she thought regretfully—needed for her to play what she knew was only a mummer's role.

For wasn't that all her wifely position amounted to?

She had been considering that very question when he had found her in her drawing room the previous day, striding in to interrupt her solitude with his all too alluring presence. Zillah's words had echoed in her ears as he had explained his reason for disturbing her, stoking the fire as he did so with such vigour that he had caused a shower of sparks to rain down upon the hearth rug.

He'd seemed distant, ill at ease, and Selina had wondered how much of his manner was her fault.

Don't be ridiculous, Lina. Her rational mind rejected the notion. *As if Edward cares two straws whether you've been avoiding him or not.*

But something about that immediate dismissal didn't ring true. Edward *had* sounded sour in his remark about her aversion to his company—surely she hadn't imagined it. His face had been set, too, in an expression of studied indifference—perhaps a little *too* set to be genuine. He had meant to sound comical, of that Selina had no doubt, but could it be that his real feelings on the matter had been laid bare instead?

She sighed internally. Was that why she now found herself here, pretending to have an opinion as to which of four almost identical shades of silk was the most fitting for a gown to wear to a landed gentry ball? Out of some misguided regard for Edward's feelings?

The very idea that she had agreed to his request was absurd. Sir William's ball would be everything she loathed: filled to the rafters with gentry folk, a pit of lavish excess and vain chatter that would make Selina sick to her stomach.

There were so many reasons for her to refuse to attend. But the bitterness of Edward's words had forced her to confront her own most secret thoughts, and after that how could she have resisted the powerful urge that had risen up within her, whispering in her ear that to grant him his request would please him? And—damn it all—wasn't that what she seemed to want these days, somewhere in the darkest recesses of her heart?

'I think perhaps this one? Would this be the best choice?' Quite a pile of swatches had built up before her. Selina hesitantly patted one of the fabrics, feeling its sheen beneath her fingers.

The dressmaker clapped her hands together softly. 'Perfection. Madam has a very fashionable eye.' She waved her assistants away and stepped a little closer to Selina. 'Now, if we were to move on to cut... As it happens, madam, we have a gown at the moment that was ordered but is no longer required. Perhaps trying it would give you an idea of the style you might prefer?'

'An excellent idea. She'd be delighted.'

Edward's voice drifted across the shop once again, and once again Selina bit down on her tongue to silence her reply.

The gown was brought forward from a gilded armoire—borne towards her with such reverence it might have been made of pure gold. Selina was forced to submit to the attentions of the army of assistants as they dressed her deftly, praising the slim shape of her waist and the slender length of her neck, until she was encased in the silky garment, complete with some gilt hair accessories that nestled within the softness of her curls.

'There, madam.' The dressmaker stepped back to admire the effect, satisfaction clearly written across her face. 'It's almost as though it were made with you in mind. Would you care to take a look in the glass?' She paused for a moment. 'Or perhaps you would prefer your husband to take the first look? He has been very…*involved* in the process, so far.'

Selina forced her lips into what she hoped would pass as a sweet smile. 'He most certainly has. Indeed, why would he stop now?'

She flicked her eyes towards Edward's silhouette. He had paused in the action of smoothing the page of his newspaper. She turned her back. He would have to see her in such ridiculous rig eventually—at least if she allowed him to observe her at this point he could tell her how far short of the image of a perfect lady she fell. He would likely be far more honest than the complimentary ladies who peered at her, good-natured but disturbingly unblinking.

'I suppose it's only fitting that he sees it through to a conclusion.'

'Very good, madam.'

Behind her, she heard the dressmaker instruct an assistant to bring Edward forward. When the heavy tread of a large pair of fine leather boots grew closer Selina sighed and turned around to face him. There was no going back now, and she could do nothing but wait for his verdict as she peeped into his face.

* * *

The sight in front of him was so wholly unexpected Edward found he couldn't speak.

The woman who peered up at him, half uncertain, half challenging, was the picture of a born lady. Her raven hair sparkled with golden accessories, the empire cut of her satin gown showcased the lissom lines of her figure and the square neck allowed the most tantalising glimpse of what lay beneath.

The cream of the fabric contrasted beautifully with the deep shade of her flawless skin and lent a radiance to her complexion—the finest that Edward had ever laid eyes on. Selina's back was straight and her chin held high, and it was only because he knew her, had studied her despite his every rational or sensible thought, that he could see the discomfort with which she wore what to her must only feel like a costume.

'You look—' Edward could almost feel the watching eyes of the delighted assistants boring into him as he struggled to form a coherent sentence. Even Selina's eyes were uncomfortably intent on his own, although for a very different reason. He roused himself with a small bow. 'You look wonderful.'

'Do I?' Selina's tone was doubtful, her insecurity plain. 'I feel…somewhat strange.'

'You don't look it. Here, see for yourself.'

Edward stepped to one side, revealing an elaborate mirror standing against a wall behind him. He watched as Selina approached it slowly, cautiously—and then couldn't hide his smile as her mouth dropped open in naked shock.

'That cannot be me!' She gaped at her reflection, standing stock-still in front of the glass. 'That doesn't look anything like me!' She stared, a combination of wonder and horror mingling in a vivid expression that lit up her face as though the sun shone behind it.

'Don't you like it?'

'I—I'm not sure.' Selina turned slowly, tracking her movement in the mirror. 'It's just so strange!'

She had never looked more beautiful. That was the only thought that rang through Edward's mind as he watched her turn this way and that, surrounded by a ring of entranced dressmaker's assistants. The loveliness of her face and the exquisite shape of her in the luminous cream gown eclipsed them all.

He could scarcely speak, and he certainly couldn't look away. Something in the back of his mind nagged at him, muttering some kind of warning—but against what? Falling for the charms of this Roma girl who had, quite accidentally, charmed him already? He was powerless to resist, and now he was powerless to deny it.

It happened before he could stop himself. One moment he was merely standing in front of Selina, having stepped forward to help her with the fastening of a gilt bracelet around one wrist, the next her hand had found its way into his own and he had lifted it to his lips. And then he had pressed a kiss to the smooth skin of her knuckles and she hadn't pulled away.

The rest of the room seemed to fall back as they gazed at each other. Selina's lips were parted on a tiny gasp that sang in Edward's ears and her eyes were round, the shock in them reflecting Edward's own. For a moment there was no other reaction, and then her cheeks were suffused with a rosy blush that crept up her neck and spread across her skin, stealing over her as he stared down into her face.

Get a hold of yourself, man!

That nagging warning growled again. His heart had begun to thump a rapid tattoo against his ribs and the warmth of her slender fingers beneath his own was scalding. He was on a dangerous path, and every second that he touched her was a second closer to the weakness he had always feared.

He released her hand. She drew it back to the safety of her body, holding it against herself with the other. But it hadn't been the lightning-fast movement of rejection, as it had been when he'd proposed and she had ripped her hand from his as though his touch were made of flame, and the horror of that night was missing from the complex expression he now saw dancing in her eyes.

There was no disgust there, he realised with a start; only the kind of half shy, half daring look any young woman might turn upon the face of her favourite, he having acted so boldly, and Edward felt his own eyes widen in surprise.

She was not displeased by his rash action?

Even as Selina was hustled away by the ring of delighted women Edward's mind raced with questions. He should not have kissed her, but never in his wildest dreams would it have occurred to him she would *like* it. The look on her face had imprinted itself into his mind, and the silks and satins of the dressmaker's shop dissolved into nothingness as he stood, dazed, with only the vision of Selina's open-mouthed expression in front of his eyes.

Why had she not flinched away from him? Wasn't his touch repulsive to her now, thanks to the intervention of her grandmother? There was no sense to be made of it, of her dizzying contrariness, and Edward cursed inwardly at his own lack of self-control. Had he not just made an already confusing situation a hundred times more unclear?

It was bad enough that he had lost his head and kissed her once before, in the quiet grandeur of Blackwell's ballroom. He'd reprimanded himself repeatedly since then, and used it as a lesson to guard himself against venturing any further. But now he had once again been foolish, and this time it was worse. His need for Selina to feel the same rush of desire for him as he felt for her had increased tenfold, and his confusion at the intensity of that need was almost breathtaking.

The rise and fall of too many excited voices grated on his ear, adding to the cacophony of thoughts that spun through his mind, and Edward felt a sudden need to escape into silence. He wanted to think, to process what in blazes had just passed between himself and his wife, and he could no more do that surrounded by birdlike chatter than he could join in with it himself.

A handful of blind strides took him to the door, and his last glimpse of Selina as he stepped through to take a deep lungful of crisp winter air was of her blank face, still mute with the shock of his thoughtless action.

Chapter Eleven

Sweeping boughs of winter greenery were spread across every available surface in Blackwell's entrance hall, and as Selina descended the curving staircase she saw balls of ivy hung in each of the doorways that led from it. A closer look at the little white berries that studded each one showed them to be mistletoe, and Selina felt the colour rise in her cheeks at the implication of what *that* implied.

Not that Edward needed one of these Christmas kissing balls to make his mark on her; that much she'd learnt already and it had been a damnably confusing lesson.

She allowed the thought to rise up in her mind for a moment as she reached the bottom of the stairs, before pushing it aside and moving through the huge front door into the snow-covered wonderland beyond. She and Edward had agreed she would spend part of the day with her people, before returning to Blackwell to take Christmas dinner with him and Ophelia, and Selina felt a curious sense of anticipation at the thought.

The weight of the small box in the pocket of her cloak acted as a constant reminder of its giver, gently knocking against her thigh as she rode in the direction of the Roma camp. With every movement her desire to know what lay within grew stronger, but she urged Djali on, watching the horse's breath blowing out in clouds that matched the white-covered ground.

Christmas Day had dawned bright and chill, the pale sunlight powerless to thaw the icy tendrils that had hung from Selina's window ledge as she'd looked out at the bleached beyond.

Edward had caught her just as she'd been leaving her rooms. She had clutched her gift for him under cover of her cloak and felt her palms prickle at the prospect of presenting it to him. Nerves coiling in her stomach, she avoided his gaze as they swapped parcels, hers looking so clumsily wrapped next to the neat blue box he'd deposited carefully in her hand. She had heard the note of surprise in his voice as he'd thanked her, and she had muttered a swift pleasantry of her own before escaping, feeling his eyes on her back all the way down the long corridor to the stairs.

She had decided to keep Edward's gift unopened until after her visit to the camp. That way she would be spared from being caught in an uncomfortable lie should Zillah ask—as she would, Selina knew—if Edward had presented her with anything for Christmas. She would be able to answer no with an almost clear conscience, for until one actually *opened* the box how could one say one had truly received a gift?

But he has already given you the gift you truly want, hasn't he, Lina? Another kiss. Only you would have preferred it to have been on your lips, rather than your hand...

The voice in her ear made her grimace, and she

gripped Djali's reins a little tighter. It was a low, mean thought, and she wouldn't entertain it. And yet...

Even now, with the cold December air stinging the tips of them, she could feel the warmth that had blossomed in her fingers at the first touch of Edward's lips, gently brushing them in a sensation so sweet it had taken her breath away. Selina could still see his head bent over her hand, low enough that she could have stroked the golden thatch of his hair, and feel the flames that had licked up her spine burst into a conflagration upon reaching her chest.

It had been as though somebody had dropped a lighted match into the bonfire of her heart.

Cantering through fields and past quaint workers' cottages, Selina felt it again, jumping against her breastbone as though trying to break free from the cage of her ribs, the memory of Edward's mouth against her skin the cause.

Edward's expression had reflected what she imagined her own had shown as she'd stood, speechless, staring up into his face. He had seemed entirely taken aback by his own actions, and Selina had been able to do nothing but watch as he released her hand quickly, as though suddenly coming to his senses, and shot her a hurried, uncertain smile before retreating outside, away from her and the cluster of captivated women who surrounded her.

Had her breathless wonder shown on her face? The very idea made her burn hot with mortification. Had Edward seen the effect his kiss had had on her? Perhaps heard the gasp he had dragged from her lips or felt her sway at the sensation of his mouth on her?

He couldn't know—he *mustn't*. It was one thing to confess the truth to herself...quite another for him to be party to the maelstrom of emotion he roused in her with his touch.

But why did he behave so? the voice whispered to her again.

Selina shook her head to dispel it. There was nothing to be gained in asking why. For all that Edward's gesture had shocked her, delighted her, robbed her of all rational thought, there could be no deeper meaning. It could not have signified so much to him as it had to her, and Selina knew it. It had surely been a spur-of-the-moment act, kindly meant, no doubt, to reassure her in what he must have known she found an uncomfortable situation.

If only she could persuade herself to listen to reason and cease replaying the moment in her mind time and time again. The pointless exercise made her chest ache with the knowledge that his kiss had meant so little to him, at the same time as it had meant so much to herself. It was a senseless torture, and one she knew she should not endure.

The line of trees that camouflaged the Roma camp hove into view and Selina took a deep breath in. She was almost there. Zillah would be waiting for her—although perhaps 'lying in wait' was a better phrase to describe the old woman's watchful welcome.

The air was so cold it burned her lungs as she inhaled, long and hard, but she held it there as she approached, narrowing the distance between herself and what had once been all she'd ever known.

Edward twitched a blanket across to cover Ophelia's sleeping form. She mumbled something he couldn't quite catch, her arm tightening its grip on her new woollen bear, but she slept on without interruption and he smiled to himself as he moved away from the sofa in front of the drawing room fire.

In truth, he'd been waiting for this moment ever since Selina had placed the parcel in his hands early that morning, with something like shyness in her eye as she had avoided his gaze. She'd left immediately afterwards, and the whirlwind that was his sister on Christmas Day had taken all his attention since.

Now she had finally collapsed into an over-excited stupor he could retrieve the intriguing bundle from his desk drawer and take a peep beneath the inelegantly wrapped paper.

He withdrew the parcel from the desk, wondering at the soft weight of it. Whatever was contained within seemed fluid, pliable, and he half frowned in puzzlement. *I didn't think she would give me a Christmas gift. How could she afford such a thing?* As far as he knew she hadn't come into any new riches—so what had she handed to him so uncertainly?

One of his many letter openers lay on the desk top, and he slit the twine that bound the paper with its sharp edge. The printed wrapping fell open and Edward stared down at the objects in his hand with brows raised in surprise.

Four crisp white handkerchiefs nestled among the paper folds. Each was edged with intricate embroidery of a kind he had never seen before, curling into a decoration of vines and leaves, and the sides were hemmed with a slim border of fine lace. Picking one up to hold it up to the light, Edward saw as it unfolded that his initials had been carefully worked in one corner, the letters picked out in scarlet thread to gleam against snowy fabric.

The embroidered leaves glinted in the light of the fire

as Edward stared at this most unexpected Christmas gift. When had Selina crafted these for him—and why?

Across the room Ophelia murmured in her sleep. Edward glanced at her, but she didn't wake, and he propped his elbows onto the leather top of the desk. A picture of Selina sitting in her little drawing room, her face pinched in concentration as she bent over her task, rose up in Edward's mind.

Had she worked by candlelight? he wondered. Or had she sat at the window, placing each stitch as snow had fallen the other side of the glass, her work serving to keep her slender fingers warm? Had she taken a secret pleasure in knowing she would take him by surprise with her gift? And was she even now smiling as she rode back to Blackwell in time to take Christmas dinner with him and Ophelia as they had agreed?

Edward passed a hand across his face. *I thought all the progress we'd made had been ruined. Perhaps I was wrong.*

He stared down at his initials, worked red on white, and traced the neat stitches with his fingers. A small bubble of hope, fragile but tentatively holding its own against the doubts that attempted to crowd it out, rose within him.

This would have taken her hours. Surely if she disliked me she wouldn't have taken the trouble?

A sudden desire to see her washed over him and he rose quickly to his feet. She would be back soon, freshfaced and windswept from her cold ride down to the Roma camp, and his mind buzzed with the questions he wanted her to answer.

What does this mean, Selina? Has your opinion of me changed?

Of his own feelings he was now sure. His reluctant wife had somehow, despite all the obstacles he had placed in her way, worked herself deep into the fortresses of his heart and mind, breaking down the walls he had constructed as though they were no more substantial than paper. Her face had been the head of the arrow that had first pierced his defences, but her wit, defiance and kindness had forced it through, and now he found himself vulnerable, unprotected by the armour of indifference he had cultivated for so long.

Another thought struck him and he sank back into his chair. *You know you can't really ask her any of those things.* The glimmer of hope within him dimmed a little, some of its sparkle fading to grey. *Even if this means she likes you a little more than before, that is still a far cry from the kind of feelings you would be a fool to believe she could ever have for you.*

Edward closed his eyes briefly. The little voice inside him could be right. Even if Selina *did* have some small regard for him, how could it ever match the depth of feeling he would only now truly accept burned within him?

It was a painful prospect, and one that made him grit his teeth—but it was true, nonetheless.

How long he sat, his head cradled in his hand and staring blindly down at Selina's gift, Edward couldn't tell. All he knew was that for a long while the only sounds were the crackling of the flames in the grate and Ophelia's gentle breathing, occasionally punctuated by the rustle of her new dress as she fidgeted in her sleep. His only company was his own confusing thoughts.

The little blue box had felt as though it was burning into Selina's skin like a brand the entire time she had spent with Zillah and the other Romani, and she could hardly bear it a second longer as she rode back up the sweeping drive to Blackwell Hall.

She'd been right not to open it before. Even as the rest of the Romani had surrounded Selina, blessing her safe return and exchanging the season's greetings, Zillah had hung back slightly, watching with all the keenness of a knowing old cat.

She had asked the question, exactly as Selina had known she would, and had looked thoughtful at the reply. Edward had not been mentioned again, although the atmosphere between the two generations of Agres women had been tense throughout their modest Christmas feast. Even now, as she cantered into the stable yard and dismounted from Djali's wide back with the ease of many years' practice, Selina was aware of the uncomfortable mixture of defiance and guilt that circled in the pit of her stomach at her deliberate deception.

She found Edward in his cosy drawing room, with Ophelia tucked up beneath a blanket in front of the hearth, still clutching the crimson bear Selina had knitted for her with wool unravelled from one of her own shawls. Diamanda had made Selina a similar creature when she was young, and it was a bittersweet memory that echoed now as Edward looked up from his desk at her entrance to the room.

'Ah, Selina. How was your visit?' He rose to greet her almost hurriedly, holding something in one large hand. 'I hope your grandmother is well and your people are enjoying the festivities?'

Selina was about to answer when she realised what it was that Edward held so carefully: one of her handkerchiefs, its lace edge peeping from between his fingers.

She felt a slow blush begin to climb up her neck. *He has opened my gift already, then.* Her heart quickened a fraction. *I wonder if he liked them?*

Seeing the direction of her gaze, Edward gave a small smile and opened his hand, spreading the little white square on his palm.

'I want to thank you for such a thoughtful gift.' He ran a finger over the red shapes of his initials. 'I've never known such craftsmanship—the lace alone is some of the finest I've ever seen.'

Selina glanced up at him. His face was sincere; he looked genuinely pleased. She couldn't help the glow that blossomed in her chest as a result. *That answers my question, I suppose.* He seemed truly to appreciate the lengths she had gone to in making his gift, and a tingle of satisfaction warmed her insides.

'I'm so glad you like them. Lacemaking has been passed down through my family for generations.'

Edward nodded, again running a fingertip across the delicate material. He seemed absorbed by the tiny details, his face intent, and Selina could have sighed aloud at the way the seriousness of his look enhanced the chiselled lines of his handsome features. They were more than handsome to her now. In all honesty beloved would have been closer to the truth, and the thought made Selina's throat contract in an involuntary swallow.

'I'm very grateful you took the time to make such things for me. Thank you.' He smiled down at her, with the barest suggestion of warmth in the rich hazel of his eyes.

'It was my pleasure. Besides, it was my fault you barely had a handkerchief left in the first place.'

Edward laughed—a short, low thing that seemed to

take him a little by surprise. 'I can't argue with you there. I had no idea taking you on as my wife would cost me so dearly.'

Ophelia mumbled something. She was still fast asleep before the fire, but all the same it saved Selina from having to reply. This was the most friendly conversation they had enjoyed since her unhappy visit to Zillah, when her dreams had been destroyed by the old woman's reminder of the truth—although not the way she had intended. To laugh with Edward was a wonderful thing, and she wished they could stay in this moment forever, with him smiling down at her and she feeling a glimmer of happiness that she would have given almost anything to be able to keep for the rest of her life.

'And have you opened my gift to you? I wasn't sure—I hope you like it?' Edward looked away from her, suddenly quiet in his uncertainty, his hands moving to clasp behind his back. 'You are a difficult woman to buy for.'

The little blue box that has caused me to be so secretive.

She'd momentarily forgotten it in the haze of delight created by Edward's praise of her skills, but now she blinked and patted at herself, feeling for the pocket in which she'd felt it necessary to hide her prize from Zillah's close scrutiny.

'I haven't yet had a chance. I'll open it now, of course.'

She drew the box from her cloak, glad to have an excuse to look somewhere other than up into Edward's face, so watchful and intent was his expression. A tiny gold clasp held it closed, and with her heart beating in her ears Selina flipped it up and lifted the lid.

For a moment her mind couldn't process what her eyes were seeing. Lying before her, cushioned within a bed of white tissue, was the brooch she had last seen pinned to the bosom of the dress her mother had worn on her funeral pyre.

Selina's hand shook as she lifted the brooch from its wrapping. She saw, once her brain had caught up with the rest of her senses, that of course it was not the same piece that had accompanied her mother on her final journey. This brooch was new—the gilt setting of the original was replaced with real gold, and what had been paste stones glittered in the firelight as only diamonds could—but the design was identical to the one she had touched countless times as a child. How had Edward—?

She gaped up at him, no words at all coming from her open mouth. *How? How has he done this?*

His eyes searched her face, his expression almost wary. 'Is it not to your liking?'

Dumbly she shook her head, still unable to find her tongue as realisation suddenly swept over her, mingled with doubt. Could it truly be that he had *remembered*?

She turned the brooch over, feeling with nerveless fingers the achingly familiar contours of metal and stone. Mama's brooch had featured a simple design of small oval paste crystals arranged around one central gem, fashioned to look like a flower with gilt leaves beneath. The sparkling copy Selina now held in her hand managed to replicate it exactly, and for some time her mind was silent in simple wonder at how Edward had managed such a feat.

He remembered every word I said.

The voice in her ear was filled with quiet amazement, and the same feeling ran over her like a shower of cool water, a complex tumult of emotion that would have taken any words from her mouth had she even been able to form them. She couldn't remember ever having felt so touched by a gesture in her entire life, and the overwhelming intensity of her wonder almost moved her to tears.

He had listened, and then he had used her words to commission a gift for her that tied Selina to the memories she had of Diamanda: a gift beyond price. The fact that Edward had gone to such lengths for her took her breath away. Why had he given her such a gift?

Some corner of her consciousness ventured an answer, and she swallowed hard at the notion. Could it be, against all her rational beliefs to the contrary, that he had developed some measure of fondness for her despite his initial intentions?

Selina didn't dare look at the idea directly. Worried that doing such a thing might cause it to flee, she instead considered it from a distance, watching it out of the corner of her eye.

He had given her such a thoughtful gift, one an indifferent man would never have dreamed of, and as for his behaviour towards her... Selina recalled how his first kiss had seemed so instinctive, so surprising to him even as he'd held her body close to his own, and how his arms had come around her so protectively when she'd cried.

A dozen tiny moments, each meaning nothing on its own, built up into a perfect montage of something deeper—something Selina could scarcely comprehend or dare to believe could be true.

'This is the most wonderful gift I've ever been given. I don't know how to thank you.'

Edward smiled, a shadow of something like relief passing over his face. 'I'm so glad you like it. I remembered how you described the piece belonging to your mother and thought a replica might please you.'

Selina nodded, her fingers still stroking the polished metal. The urge to rise onto her tiptoes and kiss Edward full on his upward-curving lips was almost overwhelming. There were no words strong enough to express her thoughts—only the touch of her mouth on his could hope to explain the depth of her appreciation.

Blinking back the tears that sparkled in the light of the fire, she instead settled for a light brush of her lips on the warm plane of his cheek, and watched as a look of surprise—but not displeasure—flooded Edward's face. Selina felt her pulse skip at her own daring, but the precious gift she held in her hand was worth any small embarrassment.

'I'll treasure it always. Thank you, Edward. Thank you a hundred times over.'

His eyes were warm with some unspoken thought as he smiled down into hers, black and hazel meeting in the orange light for one long, meaningful moment that stretched out between them, neither voicing what secret desires might be hidden within.

'You are most welcome. Merry Christmas...wife.'

passed, some looking with barely disguised curiosity at the woman who stood next to him, silently gazing up at the Beaumont ancestral home with an unreadable expression in her dark eyes.

Edward looked down at her and marvelled yet again at the miraculous powers of an expensive wardrobe to entirely transform the wearer.

It wasn't that she hadn't been beautiful before—far from it. It was more that now, swathed in the rose silk that ghosted the lush shape of her figure, falling in an empire cut from below her bosom in such a way as to emphasise the captivating curves pressed at the square neckline above, Selina radiated an almost ethereal femininity that had been previously hidden beneath layers of woollen shawls.

The soft colour that peeped out from beneath her cloak was the perfect complement to the tawny cast of her skin, and the ebony of her hair—braided and twisted into the most elaborate style Dinah had ever had free rein to create—was offset by ribbons intertwined with gilt flowers that gleamed in the light spilling forth from the house.

Her only other ornamentation was the brooch pinned to the centre of her chest, at which Edward glanced in secret satisfaction. She hadn't been lying, then, when she had said it was the most wonderful gift she had ever received. In turn he had carried one of Selina's handkerchiefs with him ever since that day—partly out of necessity, but largely for the feeling of confused delight he felt each time he looked down at the gifts she had given him.

He still didn't know what she had meant by it and had yet to muster up the courage to ask. There was still the possibility that he wouldn't like the answer.

She was silent as he guided her up the steps and al-

Chapter Twelve

Edward felt the tremor in Selina's fingers beneath his own as he handed her down from the carriage. In any other woman he might have suspected a chill, but Selina's rigid face throughout the duration of their journey to Sir William's estate had been an indication of determinedly suppressed anxiety, and he knew her hand's unsteadiness was not a result of the freezing January evening.

Candles blazed in every window of their host's grand house, bathing the guests who mounted the stone steps up to the front door in a soft orange light. The sound of musicians playing a lively tune floated through the night air towards them, carrying with it the buzz of a hundred conversations and the faint thud of footfalls as the guests within the manor moved in time with the music.

All around carriages rolled to a halt and streams of people stepped out into the cold, the men standing tall in their best knee breeches and stockings and the ladies glittering in the candlelight like birds of paradise, their gowns shining in jewel colours and feathers swaying in their headdresses.

No small number of them greeted Edward as they

lowed a servant to relieve her of her cloak, busy taking in her surroundings with eyes round with wonder.

'Are you well?' Edward murmured into Selina's ear, close enough to brush the delicate shell with his lips. The idea was tempting, and he swallowed hard.

What she needs tonight is a friend. Not you trying to find excuses to kiss her.

'Yes.' Selina's smile was small but determined. 'This is the grandest house I've ever set foot in. I don't think I could feel more out of place if I had arrived in my usual clothes.'

'You needn't worry about blending in.' Edward bowed to a passing acquaintance, noting how the man's eyes slid from him to Selina's face. 'You look quite the high-born lady.'

Stepping within the ballroom, Edward looked about him. People he had known his entire life were scattered in all directions—some seated at small tables dotted around the walls, some dancing, and still others standing in clusters, talking and watching the dancers with critical interest. Chatter and laughter rang throughout the room and the musicians' airs vibrated in his ears, their instruments clearly audible above the hum of conversation. Despite the wintry chill outside, the ballroom was extremely warm, and more than one lady was fanning herself with a little more enthusiasm than elegance.

'It's rather close in here. Would you like a glass of punch?'

Selina nodded, still looking this way and that in a combination of curiosity and distaste, and Edward moved away from her towards a table on which stood a bowl and several fine crystal glasses. On his return he saw a small group of ladies standing a short distance away, casting furtive glances at Selina's luxurious gown. Obviously they were wondering who such a fashionable stranger could be, and they dissolved into rapid whispers when Edward appeared and handed her the drink, their eyes shining with curiosity.

One of them, a young woman he vaguely recognised as a former friend of Letitia's, looked at him with particular interest, her gaze straying across him with a little more appreciation than was strictly polite. He was just about to turn away when he felt a jolt of surprised delight crackle through him at the sensation of Selina's fingers settling lightly on his forearm. It was a subtle movement, accompanied by a pleasant smile on her full lips, but there could be no mistaking it.

Selina's expression was serene, but Edward saw the determined angle of her chin, raised in the faintest suggestion of challenge, and his heart sang. She had staked her claim on him—out of injured pride, perhaps, but the notion was still absurdly pleasing. He had to fight back the urge to preen as the other woman's face fell and she pointedly turned her back on him and his quietly elegant wife.

There was a brief lull while the orchestra arranged their next piece, and when the music began again Edward leaned down to speak into Selina's ear.

'Is that the opening for a waltz I hear?'

'I believe it is. I sincerely hope I can remember the steps—I'm a little afraid for your toes.'

Edward took Selina's hand and steered her firmly in the direction of the dancers. Their progress was slowed by Edward's having to greet various acquaintances, bowing and smiling and introducing Selina to so many people he was sure he could see her anxiety increase. It was a relief to finally reach the dance floor and be able to hold her close to him once again.

She felt almost weightless in his arms, slight and instinctively graceful as she stepped to the music as though having had a hundred lessons, and Edward was powerless to resist as the memory of the first time he had held her so closely sent a flash of heat through his every nerve. She had been so stiff then, so patently uncomfortable with their proximity, but now, as they moved across the floor, it was as though they had been designed to be partners. Her small hand fitted perfectly into his grasp and her ear was close to his rapidly beating heart. Her awkwardness with him had entirely dissipated, Edward realised as she peeped up at him, a smile of genuine appreciation only enhancing the beauty of the face he now knew he held most dear.

'Thank you for rescuing me. I don't think I could have survived yet another introduction.'

Edward's laugh rumbled through his chest and Selina felt its vibrations against her cheek as she drew nearer still to the silk of his waistcoat. Perhaps it wasn't entirely proper to be *so* close to the broad chest that haunted her dreams, but the press of bodies around her and the braying of upper-class voices made her nervous, and nowhere felt so safe as being close to Edward.

Held in the unshakeable strength of his arms, Selina felt the knowledge that there was nowhere else she would rather be rise up in her again, and she made only the most half-hearted attempt to dispel it.

'No? But there's still—oh, I don't know—another two, maybe three hundred of my closest friends for you to meet.'

Selina shot him a narrow look that was entirely ruined by the wayward curve of her lips. 'I most certainly hope not. I couldn't stand the scrutiny.'

They danced a few steps closer to another couple, the male half of whom fixed Selina with an unnervingly bold stare.

She twitched her brows together and drew a little further into Edward's hold, murmuring up into his ear. 'Why do they stare so? Ever since we arrived I've felt too many eyes upon me. Is something about my appearance really so troubling?'

Edward glanced across at the other man, who dropped his gaze at once. 'They've been staring because you are, without doubt, the most beautiful woman in the room.' He turned her deftly, calmly continuing their dance as they began to sail back in the direction from which they had just come.

Any activity in Selina's mind stuttered and died and her eyes flickered up to meet Edward's before she could stop them.

He looked down at her with the most serious expression in his hazel eyes she had ever seen. There was no laughter now—no twinkle of humour in the greenish gaze that had settled on her more and more frequently over the past weeks and months, in a scrutiny she had tried in vain not to enjoy. Instead he was solemn, earnest, as though he had meant every one of the unspeakably delicious words he had just murmured in her ear, and Selina felt her breathing become ragged as she stared up into his face, robbed of the ability to recall any language in order to respond.

A slow creep of pleasure began to steal over her as she turned his words over inside her mind. He had called her beautiful, and now, with his hands holding her close to him, a thrill of something dangerous crackled beneath her heated skin. His touch was like a flame and her nerves the touchpaper, and the combination of the two called to the secret longing Selina had tried so hard to conceal.

She couldn't drag her eyes away from his. They were mere inches apart. If she were just to reach up onto her tiptoes she could rise high enough to claim him with her lips, and a powerful yearning to do just that swept over her as unrelentingly as a tidal wave.

Edward seemed to be bending down. His face was growing closer, the look in his eyes sharpening into an intensity that would have made it impossible for Selina to move away from him even if she hadn't been a willing captive in his arms. She could do nothing but wait breathlessly, dazedly, as his arm tightened on her waist and brought her closer still to the firm column of his body, for his mouth to meet her own. For surely that was his intention?

Their faces were almost touching as they danced, oblivious to any other people in the room. The vague notion that it might not be socially acceptable to explore Edward's mouth with her tongue crossed Selina's hazy mind, but there was nothing she could do to quell the burning she felt beneath her skin, or the desire for the man who held her so closely against him that blazed in her every sinew.

Etiquette be damned, Selina's subconscious whispered as she felt her eyes drift closed and Edward's lips finally meet her own, the heart-stopping culmination of all the hours she had spent dreaming of this very moment, hoping and yet fearing it would soon come to pass.

If their first kiss had been heated, this one was an

inferno. Selina felt herself set ablaze with the burning desire to hold Edward against her, to feel the touch of his hands on her skin as his lips moved over hers and she opened her mouth to receive him.

His grip on her waist tightened further, forcing her as close to the heat of his body as it was possible to be, and his other hand moved to cradle the back of her head— which was just as well, for Selina's bones seemed to have turned to water, and but for Edward's unshakable arms she might have collapsed entirely.

Her own hands twined into the fabric of his coat, trying to pull him closer still, and the whole world seemed to dissolve in the riot of sensation Edward's lips on hers were lighting up in every nerve in her trembling body.

Edward's breathing was coming hard and fast as his hand snaked down from her waist to splay over the small of her back, pinning her to the front of his towering frame. He deepened the kiss. Selina heard herself gasp as his tongue danced with her own in a movement so unspeakably sensual she could almost have stopped breathing had she any thought to spare for such a trivial thing as *that*. Her arms tightened around him, locked in an embrace that sent sparks of pure desire to writhe within her stomach—

'I say…is this really the place?'

Selina started violently at the sudden voice, too close to her for comfort. Eyes flying open, she saw an older gentleman looking at them with barely suppressed amusement, and stumbled backwards out of Edward's hold. All the breath had left her body and she felt winded by the blistering fire that seemed to have replaced it in her lungs.

She blinked rapidly, trying to bully her brain back

into action. 'Oh, I—I—I'm most terribly sorry.' Selina heard how breathlessly the words escaped her but had no power to make them sound stronger. 'I don't know—'

'Sir William.' Edward extended his hand and the other man shook it, a gleam of humour still clearly visible on his lined face.

If Selina hadn't known better, she might have suspected Edward felt as stunned by the unexpected turn of events as she. His own breath seemed to be coming fast, reminding her of Djali's after a long ride, and his cheeks were flushed with colour.

'So good of you to invite us. May I introduce my wife, Mrs Selina Fulbrooke?'

'Aha…' Sir William looked at her closely, dawning understanding filtering into his expression. 'Enchanted, I'm sure. A rare treat to meet such a beautiful lady. Madam…' He bowed over her hand, lightly holding her fingertips in a cool grasp.

Selina nodded mutely and attempted a smile, although her heart still pounded from Edward's touch and no words would come into her racing mind. Whatever must their host think of her, putting on such a shocking display? Edward was just as much to blame as herself, of course, but it was on her that every scandalised eye seemed to be fixed, and Selina's blush deepened as she heard loud whispers about their brazen behaviour from more than one direction.

'I'm so glad you and your lovely new bride could attend tonight. This is the first gathering I have had since your poor dear father left us, you know, and he is very sadly missed.' Sir William didn't seem to hear the muttering surrounding them as he sighed and patted Edward on the shoulder. 'He would be pleased, I think, that you came to honour us with your company. And I hope you won't think me too forward when I say you have grown into a fine young man, most worthy of your new position as Squire.'

'Thank you, sir.' There was a touch of something like emotion in Edward's voice, and Selina had to restrain herself from reaching out to touch him.

Sir William glanced about him and lowered his voice conspiratorially. 'You know, I never agreed with that condition old Ambrose included in his will, and I told him so. You're a grown man with a sensible head on your shoulders; you can be trusted to make your own way.' He nodded reassuringly. 'I'll be willing to say the same to your uncle when he arrives here, too, should that be necessary.'

A shard of ice shattered the warmth that mere moments before had burned in Selina's chest, slicing through to chill her to the bone.

What does he mean—when he arrives here?

Her eyes flew to Edward's face, and she saw his brows drawn tightly together in confusion.

'My uncle, sir?'

'Your Uncle Charles—has he not written to you of his forthcoming visit?' The older man was at once unsure, hesitant. 'I received a letter just last week, stating his intention to return to Blackwell and help you run the estate. Perhaps I was not to mention it…?'

'Indeed, I have received no such letter.' Edward's voice was quiet suddenly, seeming to come from far away. 'Did my uncle mention when he is intending to visit?'

Selina barely heard him speak, lost in the cold grip of dread that had begun to squeeze her in its fist.

'Within the month, as I understand it.'

Within the month. That could be any day...with no warning.

Selina backed away a little, narrowly avoiding a collision with another pair of dancers. Her head swam with sudden nausea and her hands felt clammy with horror, fear choking the air from her lungs.

Charles Fulbrooke, Mama's killer, is coming back to Blackwell.

It was every one of her worst nightmares come true, and panic rose up within her like an unstoppable flood. The room seemed as though it was spinning, and suddenly she could no longer breathe.

'I feel a little warm. Please excuse me while I go to take some air.' She managed to force out the words, only dimly aware of how raspy they sounded issuing from her dry mouth.

She felt Edward's eyes on her as she retreated through the crowd, but she knew better than to look back over her shoulder. He would see the blank terror on her pallid face.

Selina quickened her step on unsteady feet as she left the ballroom and tottered out into the hall. The light of the candles was suddenly too bright, throwing her into blind confusion as she fought her way towards the front door, dumb and unresponsive with images of unspeakable horror tumbling through her mind. The music that issued from the ballroom was suddenly too loud, and the press of bodies claustrophobic. And had it always been so *hot*?

A woman nearby laughed—a shrill, whinnying sound that made Selina shudder—and a gentleman's speculative look at her as he passed by made her skin crawl. She had to get out. *She had to get out.*

It was as though a dam had given way inside her— one that had been shielding her from the worst of her recollections. All the fear and disgust she had been struggling to quell since hearing Charles's name now threatened to pour forth, and image after image of the reason for her revulsion flickered through her mind in unstoppable cruelty. The man responsible for her pain would soon be closer to her than he had been in twelve years, and the memories spun faster.

She was surrounded. Gentry stood close on every side, and suddenly she couldn't *bear* it.

Selina knew she would have to fight to push her way through the crowds that thronged Sir William's Great Hall, but even the idea of touching them made her stomach turn. Perhaps she ought to go back to Edward, she thought as she felt her throat begin to close with anxiety and a fresh wave of nausea wash over her. He would surely escort her outside, help to guide her past the people who now sickened her with every glance.

But then Zillah's words echoed through her mind, mingling with the fear that squeezed her in its iron grip. *A marriage of convenience and nothing more.*

Selina's mind stubbornly replayed the image of his face, growing closer to her own as they danced, the look in his eye, determined yet tender, as he closed the distance between them and his lips sought her own. Edward was better than that, and her faith in him would not be so easily shaken.

And yet… Selina's shoulders slumped as the cold sting of reality turned her blood to ice. Charles was Edward's kin—almost the only relative left to him. Hadn't she seen the glint of sadness in his eye when he'd talked about his father and sensed that, despite all their differences, Edward regretted the late Squire's early passing?

Charles was Ambrose's brother, despite his cruel acts,

and tied to Edward by blood. Surely he would rather his uncle returned than hear Selina's tale of woe yet again. The tale of a wife he had taken only for their mutual advantage. After the death of his father Edward must want to draw nearer to the family he had left. Of course he regretted his uncle's behaviour, but wasn't blood thicker than water? Especially if that water had only been married out of cold necessity?

Shame, fear and regret washed over her, tumbling her in the maelstrom they created within her. She was tossed by the waves of her unhappiness, and supremely conscious of it being all her own doing.

A man you cannot hope to have.

Those had been Zillah's words—and they had been entirely right. Edward would never return her feelings now, despite the precious gift he had given her and the breathtaking passion of his kiss—not now Charles was returning to Blackwell, to undermine her at every turn.

What poison he would whisper in Edward's ear she didn't yet know, but there could be no chance of the happy future she had so foolishly hoped for, despite her better judgement.

'Ma'am? Ma'am, are you quite well?'

An elderly gentleman stood close to her, watching her breathless confusion with genuine alarm. His concern for her might have struck her as kind, once upon a time, but now all Selina desired was to be as far away as possible. With her heart hammering, and tears gathering at the corners of her eyes, she did the only thing she could think of to do.

Selina turned and ran.

Chapter Thirteen

'Any sign of her?'

'Not yet, sir.'

Edward cursed aloud as he scanned the frozen waste-
land of the Beaumont estate that surrounded him and
his coachman on all sides. Deep snowdrifts covered the
ground in every direction as far as the eye could see, and
Edward pulled his coat closer about his body, gritting
his teeth as another blast of freezing air tried to wend
its way beneath his clothes.

'Mrs Fulbrooke is out here somewhere, without a
cloak in this bitter cold. We must keep looking.'

'Aye, sir.'

Edward lowered his head against the biting wind and
ploughed onwards, sinking almost knee-deep into the
snow. His breeches were soaked and he could feel the
chill beginning to reach his bones. Each step was getting more and more difficult as the cold seeped into him
and squeezed his chest in its icy grip.

Where the hell are you, Selina?

He brought a hand up to shield his eyes from the
moonlit glare of snow all around him as he peered across

the great expanse of white, searching for any clue as to the direction in which she must have travelled.

An elderly gentleman in Sir William's hall had said he'd seen a woman matching Selina's description bolt past him and out into the freezing night, without even so much as a cloak to warm her. Her flimsy ball gown would give her no protection at all against the unrelenting cold. If he didn't find her soon, he shuddered to think what might become of her.

Edward tried to tamp down his rising panic. He thought back to her face, how it had looked when poor, well-meaning Sir William had given her the worst news she ever could have heard, and the picture made him grimace.

She looked like a hunted animal. I don't know when I've ever seen a person look more afraid.

Of course she feared Uncle Charles returning to the estate. The death of her mama might have been a tragic accident, but Selina would always hold him responsible for what had happened, and Edward didn't blame her. Charles Fulbrooke would stir memories within Selina she doubtless would have given anything to forget forever, and her horror at the news that she might risk seeing him again would have been too much to bear.

No wonder she had been spooked at the notion and had run into the night like a fox from a pack of hounds.

'Sir! Over here!'

The coachman's voice carried to Edward on the chill wind. Turning at once, he saw Greene crouching by a snow-laden hedge at the border of the field and stumbled towards him, his heart beating so fast it was almost painful. Whatever Greene was looking at was lying on the ground, and Edward felt a sharp twist of fear that they might be too late.

I'll never forgive myself if—if—

He couldn't bring himself to finish the thought as he reached a small shape stretched out in the snow, half covered by a soft sprinkle of white.

Selina's face was pale in the moonlight, and frost sparkled on the tips of her long eyelashes. Her hair had come undone from its elaborate style and fanned out around her, a dark splash on the pristine white of the snow, and as Edward swiftly wrapped her in his own coat he felt her skin was as cold as death.

Her chest still rose and fell with quiet breaths, but they were slow and shallow, and as Edward gathered her into his arms and lifted her from the ground she made no sound, her eyes still closed as though in the deepest sleep.

Edward carried her towards his carriage in pained silence. She weighed little more than a child, and under any other circumstances he knew he would feel a thrill at holding her so closely against him. Instead, however, he felt only dread as he reached the carriage and climbed inside, still bearing her as if she was made of glass. He sank down onto the richly upholstered seat and gathered her into his lap, feeling the jolt as Greene geed up the horses and turned their heads for home.

My stubborn, headstrong Selina.

He looked down at her silent face, her lips blue and cheeks paler than he had ever seen them before.

Couldn't she have waited? I would have taken her home myself. If she never wakes—

He swallowed—a painful convulsion of his burning throat. A complex mixture of despair and frustration churned inside him as he chafed at her hands, seeing how her fingers were blue at the tips.

Running off into the snow. Who would go running off into the snow without so much as a cloak—apart from Selina?

It was just his luck to have lost his heart to such a wild creature, he thought with grim acceptance. An upper-class woman would never have acted with such instinctive rashness. But it was her difference from those of his own class that had made him, despite his best efforts, her most devoted servant, and it was with worried eyes that he watched her unconscious face as the carriage swept him and his wife through the night, back to where Edward felt sure they both belonged.

He would have strong words with her when she awoke—*if* she awoke. The prospect of her never again opening her dark eyes was enough to twist his insides so hard he could have cried out in pain. She *had* to wake up: the alternative was simply unthinkable.

The pillow beneath her head was soft, and Selina enjoyed the delicious sensation of waking slowly from a deep sleep for several long minutes before attempting to open her eyes. She had been having the most wonderful dreams, and was in no hurry for them to end, but she surfaced gradually, feeling their sweetness linger until her eyelids flickered open and a grim face swam into focus before her.

'Edward?'

He was seated in a chair drawn up to the bedside, so close that the red coverlet she lay beneath touched his knees. But her own bed was always swathed in powder-blue, and Selina's brow furrowed as she took in the decor of a room she had never seen before. A swift glance down showed she was wearing her nightgown, and a furious blush roared hotly up from her neck at the question of who had dressed her in it.

'Where am I? What happened?'

There was no preamble to his anger.

'Selina. What in seven hells were you about, running off by yourself into the snow without even a cloak to warm you?'

Selina attempted to sit upright in the bed, but Edward checked her with one strong hand.

'Don't try to get up. The doctor said that when you awoke you would need to rest.'

'The doctor? Why has he been here? I am quite well.'

'*Quite well!* Are you indeed, madam?' Edward's eyebrows were raised so high they were almost lost in the flax of his hair. 'You must forgive me if the evidence to the contrary was quite compelling!'

Flames danced in the grate of a grand fireplace not far from where she lay, their light hurting Selina's eyes. A slight ache was beginning to niggle at the back of her head, and she sighed at Edward's angry words. What she wouldn't give to be allowed to drift back into the dreamland she had so recently visited, where she and Edward had existed in perfect harmony without his furious voice ringing in her ears.

She remembered now, as she took in the set of his expression, why she had been trudging through the snow. A sudden weight settled beneath her ribs and she attempted once again to sit up. Once again, however, she was stopped by a large hand.

She pressed her own hand to her chest, feeling the place where that knot now lay heavy over her heart. 'I'm sorry, Edward. I just—I had to get out. If I gave you cause to be worried—'

'Worried?' Edward stood up from the bed and paced the floor in front of the fire, the flames casting shadows on his hair as he moved. 'Do you have *any* idea what passed through my mind when I found you lying on the ground, covered in frost and with your lips completely blue? You didn't move for the entire journey home. I didn't know if each breath would be your last!'

Selina winced at his tone. It was unsettlingly similar to Zillah's when she delivered a scolding. The comparison only served to remind her of the words that had haunted her just before she had sunk down into the snow.

A man you cannot hope to have.

'I'm sorry. It was never my intention to get into such trouble when I left Sir William's house.' Edward glanced at her but didn't cease his fretful pacing to and fro. 'I just couldn't stay there a moment longer. I suppose I should have told you, but I didn't think you would mind my leaving.'

Zillah's words echoed louder in Selina's mind as she looked across at her tight-faced husband, and fresh sorrow began to ache in her chest. The dark shadows beneath his eyes touched her heart and made her want to reach out and pull him to her, to allow him to chase away the final vestiges of the winter's chill with his masculine warmth.

Zillah's words echoed louder still—*convenience and nothing more...a man you cannot hope to have*—and she forced the urge back. She could never now tell him how she longed for his touch, or how living without him would be daily torture. He had never sought her love, and with his uncle's return Selina's feelings could only grow more and more irrelevant.

It was time for her to voice the decision she had come to moments before the cold had overcome her and she had sunk into a heap on the ground, so icy and so still that Edward had mistaken her for dead. Selina knew there would never be a better moment, and yet the words fled from her as she struggled to speak.

'I had not the smallest idea of you being so moved.' She spoke quietly, her eyes fixed upwards on the red embroidered canopy of the unfamiliar bed in which she lay. 'I have no wish to be a further burden on you, and therefore I shall be leaving Blackwell as soon as I am able.'

Edward had moved to stand close to the fire, one arm leaning on the mantel as he waited for her to answer, and the expression Selina saw flit across his face as he turned sharply towards her was unreadable.

'You mean in the springtime, as we agreed?'

'No. I mean now—as soon as I'm able to leave this bed.'

Staring upwards, Selina missed the shadow that clouded Edward's features.

'That was not our agreement,' he said.

'I'm aware of that. Given the circumstances, however—you must understand why I can't stay?'

'If it is only on account of my uncle's return, I—'

She cut him off with a shake of her aching head. Intense unhappiness welled up inside her and she bit the inside of her cheek to prevent her mouth from trembling. 'It isn't *only* that.'

The terrible truth returned to pinch at her again and she was powerless to push it aside. The return of Charles Fulbrooke was indeed a horrible prospect, but so was the notion of how close she had come to allowing herself to believe her deepest, most secret wish could ever come true.

There was no room for both her *and* Charles at Blackwell Hall, and she was under no illusion that Edward would choose her—a necessary evil—over his own flesh and blood. She and Edward would never be together in any real way, and the knowledge made her want to weep. The fact that she couldn't tell him the real reason for her suffering only made it more painful. He must never know how truly she had fallen for him, and there was only one lie she could think of that would explain her sudden decision she knew he would believe.

Her eyes burning with supressed emotion, Selina forced herself to speak. 'I—I have realised the truth of my presence here.' That much was true at least, but the rest of her falsehood tasted bitter on her tongue. 'I have seen the reality of my situation and now I know I cannot stay.'

Edward's blood ran cold in his veins as his mind struggled to process Selina's words.

It was as though he had been suddenly doused in a bath of icy water, and his thoughts spun uncontrollably, unable to comprehend the dizzying turn of events that now unfolded before him.

She intended to leave him.

The image of Selina's rapt face staring up into his own as he bent towards her lips burst upon him, and he involuntarily tightened his grip on the mantel.

I pushed her too far. I frightened her, and now she wants to run from me as well as my uncle.

She was silent as she lay, unmoving, in the splendour

of the carved oak bed—the bed in which Edward had spent so many sleepless nights thinking of her, wondering if there was a way to break down the walls Selina seemed so determined to build between them.

His first thought upon seeing her raven hair fanned out across his own pillows had been how badly he wished he could see the same sight every night, and the realisation that such a thing could never come to pass sat in his stomach like a stone.

'What do you mean, the reality of your situation?' Edward crossed the room towards her and dropped unceremoniously into the chair at her side. The urge to seize one of her little hands, now tracing the embroidery at the edges of the blankets with tense fingers, almost took his breath away.

'I have been pretending to be something I'm not.'

Selina's fingers paused in their activity. Edward gripped his own in his lap to prevent himself from reaching out.

'I wore those clothes, and smiled, and danced—all the while denying who I truly am.'

Edward saw her throat move as she swallowed, his eyes tracking the movement of her slender neck even as he fought the desire to touch it. He passed a hand across his face, hiding the emotion he feared he could not contain.

'You have denied nothing. All your people know you married me only as part of a bargain to save them— surely anything else you have done has been in the same vein.'

When Selina raised her eyes to his Edward was surprised to find them dimmed, dulled by a look of hopelessness he couldn't understand.

'Yes. That was why we wed, was it not? There was no feeling there. If I recall, you thought our mutual indifference could work to our advantage.'

She smiled at him, a sad, thin thing that somehow managed to make her look much older than her years.

'That was the only reason you could possibly have welcomed me into your home.'

Edward frowned, his brows drawn tightly together as he forced himself to stem the automatic contradiction that rose to his lips. The urge to deny her words was strong.

How could she still think she mattered so little to him, even after all this time? After they had shared such a heated embrace and he had comforted her as she cried? After he had lifted her from what he had feared was her icy grave and laid her down in his own bedchamber, knowing it was the warmest in the house, and taken up a bedside vigil that had lasted long into the night? Did that strike her as meaning nothing? Despite these actions, she still attributed to him so little feeling... Perhaps to her he was still, deep down, the same as all the other faceless gentry she feared.

Her face was lovely in the firelight, despite the strange sadness that sought to undermine the beauty of her eyes. Edward looked away when she avoided his gaze, staring instead at his hands as they lay in the broad spread of his lap.

'I wish you would reconsider.'

Even as he spoke the words he feared they were worthless. The heaviness in his gut increased with every second that passed, and he cursed his inability to tell her honestly that he would be lost if she left him, his existence without her like a living death. But the fear of rejection roared up within him again, the mocking faces of his mother and Letitia sneering at his pain, and he lapsed into silence.

'I cannot. I realised this evening I have no place here, living among my betters.'

'Your *betters*?' Edward stared at her, incredulity creeping into his voice. What new nonsense was this? 'This cannot be. When have I ever treated you as anything other than my equal? Or given you the impression I think you are somehow beneath me?'

Selina still refused to meet his eye. Vexation beginning to pump through his veins, Edward abandoned his restraint and reached for her, circling one fragile wrist with the fingers of his right hand. He felt the rapid tick of her pulse beneath the thin skin, and marvelled at how warmth had returned to what had before been so cold— before she pulled away from him.

'Never in word, but I am not a fool. I see now how truly wide the chasm is between us. I am not and never will be a real lady, no matter how expensive a gown I am hidden beneath. Our worlds are poles apart and can never fit together. I do not belong here.'

Edward sat back in his chair. They had finally reached the crux of the matter, he thought in fierce frustration, and it was in no way flattering. The injustice of her words hit him with cruel severity, and he felt what tenuous control he held over his temper begin to slip.

So that was her opinion of him: that he was every bit as bad as the shallow society he took such pains to avoid, and that the only woman who could ever satisfy him was a vapid, fashionable, upper-class lady.

The spectres of his mother and Letitia rose up before him again, even as Edward stared at his stone-faced wife. The contrast between the three women had never been more stark than at that moment. How could Selina possibly imagine *she* was the one lacking? Her warmth and instinctive kindness might be a different kind of fortune, but Edward had never been so certain that such riches were the only ones truly worth having.

But what was the point in such idle thoughts? The treasure of Selina's goodness would never be his. That much was now painfully plain, Edward lamented as the shadows from his past loomed ever more largely. Letitia's presence in his mind disgusted him, and yet there was nothing he could do to banish her from stalking through his head, unlocking memories he had kept hidden for so long.

He balled his hands into fists, clenching them tightly as though faced with some physical assailant. 'Damn it all, Selina. Is this how you think of me? That I judge your value on how high you were born or how well you look in a silk gown?' Edward's voice was low as he struggled to maintain his composure. 'I value a good soul above all else, madam, which is one of the reasons I hold you in higher esteem than any woman I have ever met.'

Selina's eyes flew to his face and he saw the glimmer of uncertainty that flickered within them.

'You know you don't mean that. We both know a Romani has no place in your home—'

'Will you stop telling me the contents of my own mind?' The final thread by which Edward's temper hung snapped, and he turned to Selina in real anger. 'I and I alone am party to what I do and do not know, and I tell you this: I would rather a Romani in my home than any number of young ladies of my own class. Do you truly think it's the ability to tell one spoon from another or speak flawless French that impresses me? I once knew two women with those accomplishments and more—the epitome of perfect gentlewomen—and their conduct scarred me for life.'

He swallowed. Selina's gaze never left his own.

'I am in no rush to repeat the experience.'

A silence stretched out between them, filled only with the crackle of flames as they writhed in the grate. Edward flexed his fingers, uncurling them from the angry fists they had made, and out of the corner of his eye he saw his wife watching in wordless contemplation.

She would ask questions now—of course she would. Any woman would be curious, but Edward knew Selina well enough to understand the depths her curiosity could run to. His mind began to work, running over possible falsehoods and diversions from the truth. How could he ever find words to explain how between them his mother and Letitia had left him unable to love? To the one woman on earth he now felt he would love for the rest of his life?

'Who were they, Edward?'

Selina's voice broke the silence, quiet against the stirring of the fire. Edward glanced at her, and all thoughts of deception melted away at the genuine concern in her eyes.

He felt her gaze on him, warm as he shook his head. *You don't have to answer. She doesn't have to know.* But the look in her eye was so gentle, so sweetly concerned, that the dam within him broke and he muttered the words he had thought never to share with anyone.

He sighed. 'My mother and my former fiancée.'

The concern in her face softened further into an expression of such deep compassion Edward felt his breath catch in his throat.

'And what was it they did to scar you so terribly?'

Edward leaned his head back onto the top of his chair, staring up at the ceiling as he marshalled his thoughts.

Two paths lay ahead of him. The first one—to minimise the damage Mother and Letitia had wreaked upon his ability to trust in the constancy of women—was tempting. He could keep his demons hidden from Selina and offer her some fake tale. The other path was that of complete honesty. It would be to trust Selina with the knowledge of the pain he had kept buried deep down within himself for almost his entire life, to lay bare to her the inner workings of his heart and mind.

Could he take that step? Certainly she had shown him time and again that she possessed great empathy with the troubles of others—her devotion to her people was evidence enough of that—but could it be that her sympathy would extend to him, a member of the class that had done her such a terrible, life-shattering wrong?

A sudden burst of fire erupted in the fingers of his left hand. Edward started, looking down quickly for the cause, only to see Selina's fingers entwined with his own and her dark eyes watching him with silent understanding.

Sparks exploded in the pit of his stomach as he watched her small hand gently fold over his, and he released one ragged breath. How was it that she managed to unman him so? Even after the long months of their marriage his reaction to her still took him by surprise.

Edward began to speak, wondering even as the words passed his lips by what witchcraft Selina dragged them from him.

'I was twelve years old when my mother left my father for another man—only a week or so before I met you for the first time in the Blackwell woods. She was never the most attentive parent, but I loved her as fiercely as any boy loves his mother, and thought she felt the same.'

He frowned, a crease appearing between his fair brows. He should stop talking, he knew, but Selina's soundless encouragement gave him reason to continue.

'I realise now, of course, that I never mattered to her very much. She was proud of me as an extension of herself, and for what I would become: a rich country squire with a huge estate, once I inherited.'

Edward paused, looking down at Selina's hand held tightly in his own.

'I know now that it was her arrogance that prompted any affection she had for me, and it ceased as soon as she found another, more valuable prize. The man she left us for was a foreign nobleman, with a fortune ten times the size of my father's.'

Edward heard Selina's soft intake of breath and allowed a grim smile entirely devoid of humour to twist his lips.

'She left without even saying goodbye and I have never heard from her since.'

Selina's eyes were filled with wonder as she shook her head slowly, compassion radiating from her so strongly it was almost palpable. 'I am so, so sorry, Edward.' He saw her throat move as she swallowed, evidently at a loss for words. 'I had no idea. I assumed your mother must have died—I never dreamed…'

'No. You could never imagine such an unnatural mother when your own loved you so fiercely.' The light from the fire stung his eyes and he rubbed them roughly.

'And your fiancée? Did she—?'

'Leave for another man? Just as my mother left my father?' Edward's laugh was short and bitter. 'Your instinct is uncanny.'

Selina said nothing, apparently waiting for Edward to continue.

I might as well tell her everything. She already knew half of his shame—why not finish the sorry tale of why his heart had been so cold?

Edward gazed deeply into the fire, ignoring the burning in his eyes. 'Letitia was everything a man in my position could have wished for: beautiful and accomplished. When she set out to catch me I found her captivating, despite myself, and it wasn't long before I believed myself sincerely in love.'

He glanced towards Selina's intently listening face.

'I was lonely, I suppose. I was living in London to escape the daily wars with my father, and for a while Letitia seemed like the answer to my empty life. We were quickly engaged and my father was thrilled—until three days before the wedding, when I received word she had eloped with another man of our acquaintance and was lost to me forever, taking my faith in gentry women with her. You asked me once why I did not choose to marry a woman I could love. The truth is I feared it. Certainly love for a woman in any way reminiscent of my mother or Letitia.'

He traced his fingers down the back of Selina's hand, noting the contrast between the tone of his skin and hers.

'Do you see it now? I *value* your difference from the people with whom I was raised. Your kindness, your honesty and complete lack of guile… If you are unlike a gentry woman it is only to your credit. It's because of who you are that I—that I—'

That I love you, he concluded silently, knowing without question that he could no more voice his thoughts aloud than he could grow wings and fly.

She might be feeling some modicum of sympathy for him in that moment, but the knowledge that Selina's opinion of him had previously sunk so low stung. The fact that she had wanted to leave him could only be taken as proof that her feelings did not match his own.

Selina's brow furrowed slightly, but she did not pull her hand away as his fingers lightly sketched the network of veins at her wrist.

'Where are they now?' she asked.

'Both out of the country.' Edward shrugged. 'Mother moved abroad with her noble lover, although where I do not know. After their divorce Father banned any mention of her—even her name. All her portraits were removed, and now it's as though she was never here at all. As for Letitia—her new husband owned a fine chateau in France, and they settled there after their elopement.'

There was a short pause, during which Edward silently admired the slender shape of each of Selina's tanned fingers. She appeared to be thinking, but it was only when she began to speak that Edward realised the direction of her thoughts.

'We both mourn for our mothers, in a way...'

Selina's voice was soft, almost shy. Edward inclined his head slightly to look into her averted face and wondered at the rosy blush he saw spread across the smoothness of her cheeks. His heart rate picked up, beating quickly inside the prison of his ribs.

'I would never presume to put the manner of my mother's absence in the same category as yours,' he said.

'Even so.' Selina turned back to him and Edward saw new emotion dawning in her eyes. 'You know how it is to feel that pain.'

'I do. I felt it keenly.' He tried to smile, but his heart was hammering so fast it hurt him to breathe. 'In truth, I feel it even to this day.'

It happened too quickly for him to see—or perhaps it was more that it happened so gradually he didn't notice. All Edward knew was that Selina reached for him, and this time when their lips met there was nobody there to interrupt.

Chapter Fourteen

It was as though Edward's hands were made of flame as he touched Selina's skin, leaving behind trails of fire as they traced the slender length of her neck. A strangled cry was dragged from her lips as his fingers continued their steady progress downward, and Edward smiled unseen against the warmth of Selina's throat.

Her nightgown lay in a heap on the floor, entangled with the shirt she had helped remove from Edward's chest with fingers that trembled with desire. She gritted her teeth on a whimper, unable to stop the telltale roll of her hips at the sweet sensations that coursed through her.

'Edward…'

His name escaped her lips like a plea, although what she was pleading for Selina hardly knew. She had no awareness of anything other than the desperate need within herself that only *he* could satisfy: her husband— the aggravating, confusing, beautiful man who smiled at her whispering of his name and bent his head to kiss the shivering peak he had awakened, drawing from her another breathy sigh.

She reached for him with hands made clumsy by want

and pulled his face towards her own, her heart pounding in her ears as he captured her lips once more.

A nagging voice in the back of her mind needled her, whispering for restraint, but Selina could no longer understand the need for her to do anything other than slide her tongue past Edward's own and feel a rush of heady satisfaction as this time it was his turn to groan, to show her more clearly than words ever could how much his desire for her had grown. His arms wrapped tightly around her, melding her slight frame against the power of his own, and Selina held him to her and felt the muscles in his back shiver beneath her touch.

His physique was just as impressive as she had dared imagine, although the hair that roughened the broad expanse of his chest had taken her by surprise. It was so much darker than the flaxen thatch on his head, and she had wondered at it momentarily, as she'd pulled Edward's shirt from his body, leaving only his breeches intact. But then he had taken hold of the hem of her nightgown and begun to inch it higher, sliding his hands against her skin as he followed its progress upwards, and all sensible thought had been chased from her mind by animalistic craving.

She clung to him, feeling the final dregs of self-control leave her. *You shouldn't be doing this*, some distant corner of her mind insisted, its panicked voice sounding far-off and foggy. *What would Zillah think? Or Mama? How will you explain yourself?*

The questions were fair ones, Selina conceded with her last ounce of rationality as Edward's tongue found her ear and traced the lobe, creating splinters of want that lanced through her and turned her limbs to water; but she could no longer fight a losing battle. Her desire

for Edward's touch was too strong, and her newly discovered connection to him as a fellow hurt and frightened child too profound. They had at last found some
common ground on which something might be built—
something *real*.

Selina had found herself reaching for Edward before
she even knew what she was doing, spurred on by the
powerful sorrow in his face that she knew she so often
wore on her own.

Edward drew back a little, his eyes never leaving the
soft landscape of her curves, and ran one strong hand
down the length of Selina's leg. She bucked immediately, her fingers clutching at the sheets that lay tangled
beneath her, and when she gazed up at Edward his eyes
were burning.

'Have you ever—?'

Selina stared at him, her chest heaving. Sweat had
begun to gather on her skin, its sheen gleaming dimly
in the firelight, and she could have sworn she felt the
temperature of the room rise at his question. She shook
her head, and almost gasped at the intensity of Edward's
answering look.

'No. In my culture, too, that honour is reserved for a
woman's husband.'

'I see.'

Edward's voice was low with want; Selina felt herself stir in reply.

'In that case I shall endeavour to make it worth the
wait.'

His eyes devoured her as she lay before him, tawny
skin and raven hair laid bare to his hungry gaze. Selina
wondered if she ought to feel some sense of shame in
being so exposed, in allowing Edward's eyes and hands

free rein to wander where they pleased, but the notion died at the reverence with which he watched her rapt face and she gave herself up to the pleasure that glittered within her body, sparkling through her blood and turning her to pure gold.

His hands were skilled, urgent and yet gentle, and when they strayed to the secret part of her that nobody else had ever known she shuddered and gasped, her back arching against the pillows where Edward had lain sleepless for so many nights, his mind full of the woman who now writhed in his bed.

Selina's brows drew together in an expression of pained ecstasy as Edward's fingers moved against her sensitive flesh, her breath escaping in a staccato rhythm that matched the frenzied beating of her heart. Her eyes drifted closed and she felt rather than saw Edward lean down to scatter melting kisses across the cage of her ribs, working up from her navel until he reached her fragile collarbone.

She tried to lift her arms to pull him closer but found all strength had left her. She was rendered immobile by the heat of Edward's caress. A tiny thread of sound, somewhere between a moan and a sigh, fell from her lips as Edward delved a little deeper, pulling her further and further out to drift in the sea of sensation that he created within her.

Dimly, as though in a dream, she thought she heard him groan in reply, and she made another attempt to reach for him. This time her hands connected with the firm breadth of his chest, and her eyes opened to see him watching her with undisguised hunger written across his handsome features. The same glint of sweat that ghosted over Selina's skin seemed to gleam on Edward's, serving to highlight the contours of his defined muscles despite the snowflakes that swirled against the windows of the chamber and the wind they could hear whistling through the trees outside.

Splaying her trembling hands against the heated sheets beneath her, Selina pushed herself up, rising unsteadily to her knees. Edward's gaze never faltered from her face. 'I think you're being a little unfair,' she said.

'Unfair?' Edward's voice hitched, his breathing uneven as Selina's fingers moved to trace patterns across the smooth linen of his breeches.

There was so much to explore, so much to see, she thought as she stretched up to cover his willing mouth with her own. She didn't want to waste another moment.

'You seem to be wearing far more clothes than I am. Doesn't that strike you as a little unjust?'

She felt him smile against her lips. The deep ache he had awakened within her intensified as he rose from the bed and stood before her, hesitating for the briefest of moments before loosening the fastening at his waist and allowing Selina to see, for the first time other than in her most fevered dreams, the full marvel of his masculine form.

Some last remnant of propriety caused Selina's cheeks to burn with fierce heat, adding to the conflagration Edward had inspired inside her, and for several seconds she found herself speechless, unable to conjure up a single word with which to break the taut silence that stretched out between them. He gazed down at her from his great height, eyes molten with need, and Selina could do nothing but drink him in as he stood, tall and proud, with the proof of his desire for her evident for all to see.

He dropped down to kneel in front of her on the red

coverlet he had so carelessly torn from her, grasping her hips to hold her firmly to the hard planes of his body as once again he explored the cavern of her mouth with his clever tongue.

Selina was aware of the evidence of his longing pressing against her, and she felt the blush climb up from her neck again to suffuse the burning skin of her cheeks, even as she sifted her fingers through Edward's hair and clung to him, deepening the kiss and exulting to hear his growl of guttural delight.

Hands still firmly locked around Selina's waist, Edward gently tipped her backwards, following her as she fell and bracing himself above her on his forearms. The hardness of his belly against the soft skin of her own sent a thrill running through the entirety of Selina's being, and she swallowed hard at the overwhelming feelings that coursed unchecked within her.

'May I?'

Edward's words were quiet in her ear, but Selina heard the hoarse undertone of want and it made her shiver. She looked up into the face of the man above her, barely illuminated by the embers of the fire dying slowly in the grate. His gaze was locked on hers, hazel on black, and even in the depths of his intense need Selina saw how he waited for her signal.

Her heart was beating so hard and so fast it was almost painful, but she smiled, a slow upward curve of her voluptuous mouth that Edward's lips soon copied.

'Yes, husband. You may.'

Edward still slept.

One of his arms was beneath his head and the other rested across Selina's waist in a gesture so protective she felt a wave of pure contentment steal over her. She lay quietly, unmoving, and drank in the new knowledge of how he looked when those hazel eyes were closed in sleep and the muscles of his face had relaxed completely, with no trace of his usual carefully cultivated smile.

This was Edward as he truly was, Selina thought wonderingly. Only when he was sleeping could his guard be down entirely. His face was turned slightly away from her, giving her an uninterrupted view of his sharp profile and the scar that gleamed white on his cheek, and Selina had to lock her fingers together on the flat plane of her ribs to stop herself from reaching out to trace it softly, from reading the lines of his face with her hands.

He shifted slightly, still immersed in whatever dream was currently running through his subconscious, rolling from his side to rest on his back. The movement shifted the sheet he lay beneath, dragging its scanty cover downwards, making it close to being no cover at all, and Selina felt her eyes drift to follow it.

Whoever could have guessed that a pampered gentleman would have such an impressive physique? she contemplated as she surveyed the peaks and valleys of Edward's musculature, taut and toned beneath fair skin. His chest resembled that of a hard-working man's, and his biceps were almost as defined as those that belonged to Roma men with a lifetime of graft under their belts.

She laced her fingers together again, still fighting the urge to touch. The euphoria of the night still sang in her veins, and she was aware of a growing ache in the muscles of her limbs. It was a sweet ache, similar to the ache she felt the day after a long session breaking in a new horse: painful, but accompanied by such a sense of satisfaction that it made the discomfort bearable.

She stretched, feeling the tension in her arms as a vivid flashback of what had caused it burst upon her. *I wish he'd wake.* A thrilling mix of anticipation and anxiety pooled in her stomach. What would his reaction be, waking to find his wife lying beside him in the great red and white expanse of his bed? Pleased, she would hope.

The reverence with which Edward had touched her burning skin could not be faked, she thought as she drummed a rhythm on her ribs with impatient fingers. They had seemed to join together not just physically but emotionally, connecting in a way she could never have dreamed of. Even sleeping next to him felt natural.

Selina felt her faith in Edward surge upwards as she waited, nerves fizzing with delicious nervousness, for him to wake. Casting her eye yet again over the sleeping face so close to her own, she tried to pinpoint the moment she had fallen so completely and utterly under his spell. Had it been the first moment she saw him? Or perhaps later, upon finding there was more to him than a handsome face and an even more handsome inheritance?

Whenever the moment had been, Selina thanked her lucky stars for it—for without the realisation that Edward was everything she had been missing from her life, even without knowing it, she would have continued on as she always had, carrying the unhappy weight of her mother's death with her for the rest of her days with no one to help her bear it.

The thought of Diamanda wiped the smile abruptly from Selina's lips. The memory of Sir William's ball crashed through her rosy daydreams: Charles Fulbrooke was returning to Blackwell Hall, and if she stayed she would have to see him.

Selina felt her chest tighten with panic once again

as the spectre of the person she least wanted to meet in all the world rose up before her. To set eyes on Charles would be unthinkable, unbearable. Would she faint if he stood in front of her? Or would she simply run wild with fear?

Edward would never allow any physical harm to come to her, she tried to remind herself as her thoughts began to spiral downwards and her breath became short, but even his protective arms wouldn't be able shield her from the hatred with which Charles would look at her, and the heart-stopping terror she knew would drive her half-mad at the sight of him. Seeing her mother's killer would be more than she could bear—an all too real reminder of the nightmare he had forced her to live.

But what alternative was there? He was Edward's blood—the only kin he had aside from Ophelia. She couldn't ask him to refuse the uncle who had been a part of his life for far longer than she had herself. Even if their night together had somehow overcome Edward's reluctance to care for her, as she hoped so fervently it had, she still couldn't ask him to choose between his desires and his duty to his family.

Almost as though his mind had sensed the frenzied activity of her own, Edward's eyelashes flickered, and Selina watched as his eyes opened slowly, adjusting to the grey light that crept between hastily drawn curtains. Still lying on his back, Edward seemed to study the red canopy above his head for some moments, before rolling over onto his side and fixing Selina with the hazel gaze she had come to adore more than any other.

There was a genuine smile playing about his lips— an upward curve that made her heart swell painfully with love—but it slid abruptly from his face as he took in the anguished expression on her own.

Edward saw Selina's distress and wondered, as a tight fist of dismay squeezed the air from his lungs, what could have happened to cause it.

He had woken slowly, his mind still sluggish as he surfaced from the deepest sleep he had enjoyed in months. The feeble light of a new day assailed his still closed eyelids, and the only sound had been the gentle breathing of *someone* lying close to him on the rumpled sheets of his formerly lonely bed.

The breaths had been quiet and even—quite unlike the fevered panting of the night before—and Edward felt himself stir in response even as his brain shuffled his thoughts into some semblance of order. The uncomfortable feeling of wrinkled blankets under his back served as a reminder of how they had got into such a state, and Edward had felt the stirring grow a little more intense.

We spent the night together and she's still in my bed.

The realisation broke over Edward in a wave of amazed elation as his eyelids had finally struggled open and he'd taken in the red canopy above his head. *Whoever said miracles don't happen?*

Selina's cheeks were flushed with warmth, rosy against the untidy ebony tresses of hair that tumbled around her unhappy face. One tawny shoulder peeped out from beneath the sheet that shielded her from his gaze, smooth and perfect, and the urge to lean across to kiss it almost took Edward's breath away. *She is utterly beautiful*, he thought as his eyes roamed her face, and for the first time felt the true fathomless depth of his adoration for her mingle with his growing concern.

A powerful sense of vulnerability swept over him now as they stared at each other, neither uttering a word to break the silence. She had completely destroyed all his defences, forcing her way into the heart he had never intended to share with anyone. She had worked herself so irrevocably into his mind and soul that Edward would have nowhere to run if she were to leave him—nowhere to hide from the feelings he had declared to her so unmistakably.

If she carried on with her plan to leave with her people his heart would be ripped from his chest, but surely she would not abandon him now. They had shared the most profound experience a man and a woman could share, Edward thought dazedly, memorising the pattern of freckles across Selina's nose as he watched her lovely face intently. There was no way she would return to the Roma—not now she had confirmed, in action rather than words, how her fledgling regard for him had grown into something so precious.

I need to find out what's worrying her—I can never let her run from me again.

'Good morning, Selina. Are you well?'

Edward pushed himself up to lean back against the pillows, allowing himself a better view of her face. 'You look…troubled.' Apprehension crept into his voice and he watched her closely, as though searching for clues, some snippet of an idea as to why she looked almost on the brink of tears. Her apparent distress tore at him, his feelings still raw after their unexpected airing the night before. The urge to gather her into his arms was strong, but the unhappy set of her jaw gave him pause.

He saw her throat move as she swallowed, her slender neck seeming to cry out for him to kiss it as he had mere hours previously. Instead he tore his eyes away and waited for her to speak.

'I have been thinking about your uncle's return.' She spoke quietly, her gaze fixed on her fingers as she worried at a lock of her midnight hair. 'He could arrive any day and I— Forgive me.' She broke off for a moment, her emotion obvious. 'I do not have the strength to see him.'

Edward felt a sharp pang of relief burst in his chest and his spirits soared upwards once again. *Is that all that troubles her? Uncles Charles's return?*

It was almost an anti-climax after his dizzying despair that the cause of her haunted look could be so easily solved. It wasn't that she regretted their night together— it was something else entirely. He could have laughed aloud as the weight fell from his shoulders.

He turned to Selina, reaching out to take her small hand in his much larger grasp. He saw her almost flinch at his touch and knew the same crackle of sensation he felt flared within her too. His body reacted at the sight, but he forced himself to set the ungentlemanly train of thought to one side in favour of reassuring his unhappy-looking wife.

'Selina. Let me make you a promise: you will never have to set eyes on my uncle ever again.'

He traced his thumb over the ridges of her knuckles and felt her hand tremble at the feel of his skin on hers. He wanted to kiss her tawny skin, to give in to the hunger for her that was beginning to stir within him once again, and the dawning hope he saw in Selina's eyes only made his appetite grow.

'I will write to Charles this very morning and tell him not to leave the Continent. Would that set your mind at ease?'

He brought her hand up to his mouth, his gaze still locked on hers. He heard her tiny sigh at the touch of his lips and smiled down at her as her frame visibly relaxed, only moments before having been held so tightly he had wondered if it hurt.

'You would do that?'

Selina's voice held a world of amazement and her face was a picture of wonder, although Edward almost narrowed his eyes at the hint of disbelief.

'I—I would not want to be the cause of you missing the chance to see your family.'

There was more than a shadow of irritation in Edward's voice when he answered—though it was not directed at the woman in his bed. 'There is no reason I can think of for his return other than an attempt to impose upon the running of my estate. My father and I fought often as a result of his controlling nature. My uncle is cut from the same cloth.'

He looked down at Selina's fingers, so small inside his palm, and marvelled with a fresh burst of dazed wonder at this second chance of happiness he had been given.

'As the Squire of Blackwell I am more than capable of governing my own estate. I have no need of anybody to hold my hand as though I were a child.' He paused for a moment before a small smile curved his lips. *You romantic fool.* 'The only person whose hand I ever wish to hold is—'

'Sir? Sir, are you awake? Apologies, but I'm afraid I need to speak with you.'

Evans's discreet knock at the door made Edward curse softly and wrench his eyes from Selina's wide-eyed face. He snatched up his shirt from the tangle of clothes and linen on the floor next to the bed and pulled it over his head, at the same time swinging his legs over the side in search of his breeches.

'You might want to pull the curtains.'

He heard Selina's giggle as she shuffled forward to draw the rich hangings of the four-poster bed into place, shielding her from Edward's glowing gaze. He was just wondering if it would be terribly rude simply to ignore the servant at the door and rejoin his wife beneath the covers when the knock came again, this time a little more firmly, and so it was with his breeches held up by one hand and his shirt untucked that Edward finally opened the door.

'Good morning, Evans.'

'Good morning, sir. I'm very sorry to wake you.'

Edward bit down on a smile. He could hardly have looked less like a man who had been innocently sleeping. Trust the old butler to attempt to maintain his master's dignity.

'Think nothing of it. Is there something you need to speak to me about?'

'Yes, sir.' Evans nodded, his expression slightly disapproving. 'You have an unexpected visitor. We found him very early this morning, attempting to gain entry to the Hall.'

The butler cleared his throat and Edward felt a sudden creep of dread at the unhappiness on the older man's face.

'We have put Mr Charles in the West Wing guest suite, where—I *am* sorry, sir—he insists he would like to speak with you at your earliest convenience.'

Chapter Fifteen

Edward quickly stepped through the door and pulled it closed behind him. 'My uncle? He is here? In this house?'

The butler nodded apologetically and Edward drew in a harsh breath.

'Damn.'

He brought a hand up across his eyes. Charles must have left to return to Blackwell almost as soon as he had written of his intentions to Sir William, no doubt hoping to catch his nephew off-guard.

Edward felt a hot pulse of anger at Charles's presumption in arriving unannounced and lowered his voice to mutter in Evans's ear. 'I shall see to this at once. Don't mention his presence to Mrs Fulbrooke.' Edward looked the other man intently in the eye. 'Do you understand me? Mrs Fulbrooke is *not* to be told.'

'Yes, sir. I understand.'

It was evident by his face that the butler didn't *truly* understand, but he would do as Edward ordered despite his own politely concealed confusion, and Edward clapped him on the shoulder.

'You did right to tell me. I shall go to dress at once.

Please send Wellburn...' Edward hesitated, struck by
the sudden thought that he couldn't dress in his bedchamber as usual.

The presence of Selina in his bed made his lips want
to curve into a disbelieving smile, but he forced himself
to return to the matter at hand. *There will be plenty of
time to spend with Selina later—once you've dealt with
Uncle Charles.*

Edward set his face grimly. It was essential that Selina didn't catch wind of Charles's arrival at the Hall.
To say she would be distressed was something of an understatement, and he could hardly bear the thought of
her in such pain.

'Please tell Wellburn I shall dress in my drawing
room today. I will wait for him there.'

'Very good, sir.'

Evans moved off with his silent step and Edward
ducked back into the bedchamber. The curtains were
still drawn around the bed and, twitching them aside, he
saw Selina's eyes were closed and that her chest rose and
fell with gentle breaths. He watched her for a moment,
wondering yet again at the dizzying turn of events that
had brought them together so inseparably, and felt the
same grin he had fought back earlier tug at him again.

*I'll speak with Charles and then come to wake her. I
think the time may have come for me to tell her...*

He allowed the train of thought to tail off as a cold
veil of doubt clouded his mind. To tell Selina of his true
feelings for her would be to admit them out loud—something he had never even done alone in his rooms. There
would be no turning back, no more hiding behind the
walls he had built around his heart for so long, and the
thought of laying himself bare chilled him to the bone.

She might still reject him—might take his love and thrust it aside as had happened to him twice before. Her rejection would be kind, Edward didn't doubt that, but all the same it would wound him in a way with which his previous suffering would not compare.

He turned away, smoothing the curtains back into place and allowing Selina to sleep on, her raven hair fanned out across his pillows. An uncomfortable combination of apprehension over Selina's reaction and anger at his uncle's intrusion settled heavy in his stomach, and Edward drew his brows together in a frown as he left the bedchamber and made for his drawing room.

An audience with Charles was the last thing he wanted to deal with on this surprising morning, but it would at least postpone the hour when he had to look Selina square in the eye and tell her that, despite his fears, he couldn't live without her—and then hear her reply, either making his dreams come true or crushing them beneath her heel.

The snow lay in deep drifts as Selina wandered slowly down one of the recently cleared paths that meandered through Blackwell's gardens, but even the chill couldn't dampen the warmth she felt lighting up her insides. She pulled her shawls closer about her body and breathed in deeply, savouring the crisp air as she allowed a smile of perfect happiness to spread across her face.

The image of her husband as he had looked that morning, his hair rumpled from sleep and his eyes regaining their twinkle as he woke slowly, caused her heart to turn over in her chest. The memory of the heat of his body and the achingly masculine scent of his skin made her close her eyes briefly, recalling every detail of their un-believable experience together.

It hadn't been a dream. She truly had spent the night with Edward, and the delicious feel of his lips on her knuckles as he had assured her that she needn't fear his uncle's return still tingled on her skin.

He'd had to postpone their taking breakfast together while he dealt with some urgent business. Evans had murmured as much to her apologetically when she had emerged from Edward's chamber, respectable once again in a gown hurriedly brought in by a blushing Dinah, with her Christmas brooch pinned to it, and she had thought that while she waited for him to reappear a walk in the gardens might help to clear her head. It still ached a little from her snowy adventure, although the pleasure that sang in the rest of her nerves helped to soothe the slight niggle of pain.

Nothing could completely drown out the anxious flut-tering in her stomach, however, at the thought of what she would have to tell Edward on his return.

Selina ran a hand across the frosted leaves of one im-maculately kept hedge as she walked, feeling the chill beneath her fingertips. Her breath hung in the air in lit-tle clouds—a visible reminder of how her nerves had quickened it.

Surely you can be honest now? He must have guessed the truth of it.

If Edward was in any doubt as to her feelings for him now she could only shake her head in wonder at the blindness of men to female emotions. He *must* be aware of how her love for him had grown. Every touch of his hand, every kind word, every thoughtful gesture had increased her fondness for him until it had erupted into something far more powerful than the instinctive attraction any woman might feel for such an undeniably handsome man. It was deeper than that.

Selina swallowed as the sudden desire to see Edward seized her in its grip. She had to tell him—she couldn't bear the tension anymore. Even if he didn't feel the same way she had to stay true to her own heart—even if that meant risking the agony of rejection. He might have entered their marriage with the intention of mere convenience, but there was surely no way that could be his feeling now.

The sound of footsteps crunching through snow made her turn. 'Edward?'

They were definitely a man's steps: long strides made by large leather boots, unless she was very much mistaken, and they were coming from the other side of the hedge that bordered the path she had been following through the gardens.

'Edward? Is that you?'

A sudden vivid thrill of delicious anxiety flooded her and her heart began to pound. This could be the moment she had waited for, agonised over. The moment when she would finally know the answer to the question she had whispered in her sleep for months.

The footsteps grew louder, and Selina felt her mouth shape into an instinctive smile as a figure rounded the corner before her.

The smile dropped from her lips as a blindingly painful bolt of sheer horror punched through her chest, snatching the air from her lungs and winding her as though she had fallen from a great height. She could only stare with eyes huge and glassy with terror as Charles Fulbrooke came towards her, her every nightmare made flesh, and she was fixed to the spot by legs that suddenly felt as though they were made of water.

It was in mute, heart-stopping fear that she saw Charles's brow crease into a frown, before clearing to be replaced by a look of pure, arrogant contempt. His mouth twisted in a sneer, and the bow he swept Selina was so low it was clear even to her frozen mind that it was intended to mock her.

'Well, well… The new lady of Blackwell Hall, I assume?' He raised an eyebrow, elegantly amused. 'I've been so looking forward to meeting you. I am Edward's Uncle Charles—brother to his late father.'

Charles's eyes roamed across her and Selina felt herself shudder, her skin clammy with a sudden heat that made her palms prickle with sweat. He appraised her as though she was an animal at market, blatantly lingering over the shape of her figure in a way no gentleman would ever look at a respectable lady, and Selina almost gasped at the intense wave of nausea that swept through her.

He looked just as she remembered, his face imprinted onto her brain forever, and the memories he unleashed flashed before Selina's wide eyes, their unspeakable horror filling her with a dread she had hoped never to feel ever again.

She had no words with which to reply. Instead she felt the air choked from her burning throat and fire scalding hot within the prison of her ribs. A voice inside her screamed at her to *run*, in any direction as long as it was far and it was fast, but her legs wouldn't obey her churning mind and still she stood, staring at the man responsible for the death of her mother and for a lifetime of nightmares, with no way of escaping his cruel smile.

'I've yet to see my nephew. I had intended to wait for

him in my rooms, but he was taking such a long time to come to me I thought I'd look over the grounds while he roused himself. It's been so long since I was last here.'

Charles spoke idly, self-assured in the face of Selina's obvious panic. She swallowed painfully, bile acrid on her tongue.

He stepped closer to her—close enough for Selina to smell the tobacco on his breath and the expensive pomade on his hair.

'I heard some whispers about you. Rumours, stories... that sort of thing.'

Selina closed her eyes, attempting to blot out the face that had haunted her dreams. Perhaps she was asleep? Perhaps at any moment she would wake up, find herself back in the warmth of Edward's bed with his face smiling down at her?

'I heard that my foolish young nephew had taken a wife far below his station, but I hadn't imagined he had sunk *quite* so low in his search for a bride. I returned at once, to make sure he saw reason, but now, having met you here so fortuitously, perhaps I needn't speak with him at all.'

Selina's eyes flew open. Charles's chestnut hair and ruddy complexion were entirely unlike Edward's fair colouring, but the hazel eyes were similar enough to make her heart skip a painful beat. How one set of eyes could radiate such kindness while another the same shade could be so cold was a mystery, but Selina had no time to dwell on the question as Charles continued.

'No doubt my nephew has been good to you, but your time here has come to an end. He has always had the most peculiar regard for your kind—one his father and myself did *not* encourage.'

He paused to flick a scathing glance across her, and Selina flinched as though he had touched her skin.

'I see no reason to involve him further. He has already shown how badly he is in need of my guidance and my instruction on how to conduct himself. If you had any decency...' He trailed off, once again eyeing her from head to toe with unconcealed contempt. 'Well... The less said about that the better. Still, even one such as *you* can surely see there is no place for you here?'

Selina backed away from him, never taking her eyes from his hateful face. There was such venom in his voice it made her want to shrink into the hedge at her back, but some tiny part of her spirit, small but stubborn, crept from behind her blind terror and defiantly raised its head.

They were no louder than a whisper, but Selina somehow managed to force words from her bloodless lips. 'Edward wants me here.' She almost choked on the sounds. 'He was going to write to tell you not to come.'

Cold anger flooded Charles's face and he took a step towards her, closing the gap between them. Selina pressed herself against the frosted leaves behind her and felt an icy shard of fear pierce her like a knife to her chest.

Where is Edward?

She didn't dare look away from the furious man in front of her and cast a desperate glance back in the direction of the Hall. All she could do was offer up a silent prayer that he would somehow sense her distress and appear to rescue her, as he had all those months before.

'Audacious lies!'

Charles's nose was mere inches from Selina's own and she shrank a fraction further.

'You wish to drive me off, do you? To isolate the boy from his family so you can have him and his fortune all to yourself? You think to ruin his life with your self-ishness!'

Selina's heart leapt within her as though it was trying to escape her chest. Acute fear and nausea had robbed her of her senses, leaving her deaf and blind to everything other than this dangerous man who looked as though he might try to grab her at any moment, crowding into her space and making every muscle in her body stiffen in terror.

She swallowed down another hot pulse of panic, balling her hands into fists that were damp with sweat. She *wasn't* selfish. Edward had said himself that he hadn't wished for his uncle's return, and had implied he had chosen her happiness instead.

Some trace of her thoughts must have shown on her face, as with a sudden whip-like flick of his hand Charles seized Selina's wrist and dragged her towards him, his face twisted into a sneer. Selina felt her eyes grow huge with wordless panic and her breath short-ened into shallow pants, as if all the air was being expelled from her lungs in tiny painful bursts as her heart hammered harder than she had ever known it to do before.

'Listen to me.' Charles tightened his grip on her arm, fingers biting into the skin. 'My nephew has no father and his own mother abandoned him. His own *mother*! I am almost the only family he has left. Now, thanks to you, people are whispering about him, shunning him. He will find himself friendless and alone, and it will all be *your* fault. If you cared about him at all you would leave and return to where you belong. You have no place here—ruining my nephew's reputation and that of this great house.'

Selina wrenched her wrist from his hand, cradling it against her chest. The skin was red and sore, but it was the pain in her chest that made searing tears rise up behind her horrified eyes.

Edward's face as it had looked the night before, when he was telling her his most secret sorrows in a voice so low and pained it had hurt her to hear it, flashed through her mind. He had felt the agony of rejection twice already and it had made him turn away from the world, even to go so far as to choose a wife he had hoped would never love him. The idea of being the cause for him to be cut off again from those he might care about was like a fist in her gut, and Selina felt herself wince as a shard of burning realisation cut through her.

'Surely you can see the truth of your situation? Edward only married you to secure his inheritance—an unfortunate circumstance forced on him by his father. Do you truly wish for him to pay so dearly for something he couldn't avoid? To see him humiliated and alone because of your selfishness? Besides...' He tossed the words at her with casual malice. 'There has only ever been one woman for whom Edward cared—a beautiful, accomplished, high-born woman—and she betrayed him with another. What makes you think he would risk his heart again for a low creature like you?'

It was the confirmation of all her previous doubts and insecurities, laid out before her in brutal clarity. Edward might have some measure of fondness for her, but would that survive if she was the reason for his downfall and disgrace in the eyes of his people? All her plans for their future lay in ruins at her feet, and as she looked up into

Charles's face through the starburst of her tears Selina thought her heart might break in two.

There was a glimmer of triumph in Charles's smirk as he sighed and shook his head. 'Poor, silly creature. Save yourself the grief. Go now—you needn't see my nephew. He might try to persuade you to stay out of some misguided attempt at gallantry, and it would be pointless to delay the inevitable.'

He reached out a hand and a powerful wave of intense loathing broke over Selina's trembling body as he placed a finger beneath her chin and jerked her head upwards to meet his cold gaze.

'Let there be no misunderstanding. Whatever pretty words he may have spoken to you, and whatever hopes you may have had, I have returned to guide Edward in a position that should by all rights be mine, and I have no wish to set eyes on a Roma peasant girl in *my* home ever again.'

Selina pushed his hand away from her, terror and revulsion clouding the ebony of her eyes. Her legs felt weak with distress and she longed to sink to the ground, but the fear of being unable to get to her feet again held her upright, although she swayed slightly beneath the weight of her horror. Bile rose up in her throat again and she forced it down, the taste burning her tongue.

A person could live without a fortune and be happy— the Romani were proof enough of that. It was the lack of *people* that led to real misery, and Selina almost flinched at the thought of Edward alone, without anybody to surround him. Would society's disgust at his actions extend to little Ophelia? Would she be tainted by association and grow to resent her brother for his choice?

The notion of Edward being deprived of the only

warmth in his life pained her more than she had ever thought possible, and she knew in that moment what she must do.

To turn her back on the man she mistrusted more than anybody else in the entire world took all of Selina's willpower, but on unsteady legs she forced herself to push up from the hedge against which she leaned and to stumble away, her feet slipping over the wet gravel with each wavering step. She was sure she heard a satisfied grunt from behind her but didn't turn to look, instead focusing all her energy on reaching the garden border and the stable yard beyond.

Each one of Charles's cruel words rang in her ears—spoken proof of her every insecurity and secret fear. He had dragged her lingering doubts from the darkest recesses of her mind and flung them into the light, naming them out loud with harsh triumph. With every word he had shattered the foolish dreams she had clung to, confronting her with the truth.

Ever since she had learned about his mother's abandonment Selina had not been able to wipe from her mind the image of the young Edward, sitting alone, wondering when his beloved mama would return. It was enough to make her heart ache with sorrow and a lump rise in her throat. He had already suffered abandonment twice at the hands of those supposed to love him. Selina would not allow herself to be the cause of history repeating itself and inflict such suffering on the man she loved: in leaving she would save Edward from himself and his misplaced regard for her.

That was the most she could hope for, and she clung to the thought like a lifeline.

To leave Blackwell never to return, never to see Edward again, was more than Selina thought she could bear. Her chest felt as though it would burst with the ocean of grief she felt welling up within her as she lost her footing and almost fell, but she forced herself onward, down another path and towards the stable gate.

She was only dimly thankful that nobody lingered to witness the anguish she knew must be present on her face, to see her lips twisting in distress with every agonised step she took towards a future she no longer wanted.

Chapter Sixteen

'Edward, my boy!'

Charles opened the door to the guest suite with a confidence Edward could only wonder at. How was it possible for him to arrive at another man's home without so much as an invitation and walk around it as though he owned the place?

Edward felt his lips set in a grim line, but he rose from the armchair in which he had waited with growing annoyance for a full hour and extended his hand to his uncle out of ingrained politeness. 'I was wondering where you had gone, sir. I understood you were waiting for me here, but I found the rooms empty.'

'Aha.' Charles moved towards the crystal decanter of port standing on a nearby table and poured himself a generous measure. The fact that the sun was barely up was apparently unimportant, as he drank it down with relish and flashed Edward an expansive smile. 'You kept me waiting too long. I thought I'd entertain myself with a jaunt about the grounds.'

Edward nodded shortly, knowing his face was rigid with dislike but unable to unlock the tension of his jaw.

Seeing his uncle strolling about as though he was a welcome visitor now that Edward knew the consequences of
his despicable actions made his pulse skip a little faster,
and his disgust and irritation with his unwanted guest
were plain to see. Edward could even feel a slight tic in
the tight muscle of his jaw—an outward sign of the rising temper he sought to quell beneath icy good manners.

'An unexpected pleasure, Uncle. How long had you
intended to stay?'

Edward's voice was as polite as ever, but his mind
was full of Selina as he waited for his uncle's reply. He
would have to get rid of him quickly; Selina must never
be allowed to feel the overwhelming horror that would
surely consume her should she stumble across their unfortunate visitor.

I will not risk her running again. After how far they
had come together, and how close they now were to
the potential of finding real happiness, Edward felt a
sharp dart of anxiety at the notion that anything should
threaten their future. It hung in the balance, by the finest
of threads—and Charles *would not* be allowed to ruin
this chance of a real future for both him and his wholly
opposite wife, to spoil the connection they had forged
between them despite all the odds.

'How long?' Charles poured himself another drink, a
frown of good-humoured confusion on his ruddy face.
'My dear boy, I'm not here for a short stay. I'm here permanently, of course.' He tossed back the port, missing
the tightening of Edward's face.

'I'm afraid that won't be possible.' Edward heard the
note of barely concealed dislike in his voice but was
powerless to restrain it.

I think not, Uncle. This is not your home. There was

no chance in hell that he was allowing Charles to stay indefinitely, and even his uncle seemed to realise his nephew's feelings as he turned to him with a challenging scowl.

'Come now. Don't be absurd. I have every right to be here. Why, if you hadn't so rashly taken a wife the estate would have fallen to me anyway—and quite rightfully so.'

The mention of Selina made the hairs on the back of Edward's neck stand up like the hackles on an angry cat. The memory of what Charles had done to her and her mother rose up before him, and he shook his head with cold firmness.

'No, Uncle. You do *not* have the right. As you said yourself, I have taken a wife—she and I will live here together with no interference from anybody else.'

He saw his uncle's face flush with temper, his good humour of minutes before evaporating in his indignation.

'Oh, your *wife*. I had the pleasure of meeting her only an hour ago in the gardens, while I was waiting for you to finish dressing and attend me.'

His look was scathing, but Edward hardly noticed as the sensation of his heart dropping into his boots hit him hard.

Selina has seen Charles?

It was enough to make his mouth open in horror, but his uncle ploughed on, regardless of his nephew's blank dismay.

'That was a shocking and disappointing lapse in judgement on your part, which it fell to *me* to rectify, and it only serves to prove to me that I am right in returning to guide your hand in the estate. Evidently you cannot be trusted to behave properly.'

Edward's eyes narrowed in cold suspicion. His pulse had begun to jump in apprehension, and worry loomed ever larger in his mind. 'What do you mean by *rectify*?'

The words were almost a growl, quiet with menace. A dawning sense of dread crept over him; he knew instinctively what answer he was about to receive, at the same time hoping—without hope—that he might be wrong.

'Well, I told her the truth, of course.'

Charles picked at a cuticle, affecting idle unconcern, but Edward caught the flash of hesitation that flickered over the older man's face.

'I reminded her that she had no place here and insisted that she leave at once. I'm pleased to say she listened to reason—at least one of you has.'

Edward felt his face freeze into an expression of pure horror. His worst nightmare—the one he had dreaded, that had robbed him of sleep and surely some part of his sanity—had come true. Selina had gone.

The blood in Edward's veins turned to ice. His uncle's harsh words had surely obliterated any understanding he and Selina might have reached, and she had run from him just as she had tried to flee on the first day they had met, when he had watched her ride like the wind in front of him and felt admiration for her skill grow with each beat of her horse's hooves.

That admiration had blossomed into so much more during the strange months of their marriage, and the idea of anyone seeking to destroy it made Edward's hands ball into fists. That his uncle had been successful in driving Selina away before Edward had been able to speak to her of his true feelings was more than he could stand. He heard his knuckles crack from the pressure of being so tightly clenched, and when he raised his eyes to meet Charles's he knew they must be burning.

'She has *left*?' Edward lurched towards him, feeling the rage that throbbed inside him begin to beat like a drum. 'You have driven my wife from her rightful home?'

His uncle's cheeks flushed puce and he took a small step backwards. '*Rightful home?* If she has left then she has behaved as she ought—eventually. She knows she is not wanted here and has acted accordingly.'

Edward felt his face twist into a grimace of anger, and his voice, when he managed to find a reply, was a low rumble of barely controlled fury. 'Who do you think you are to decide whether she is wanted?'

A shadow of something dark and wild was growing steadily in Edward's chest, gripping him with rising rage.

'Who are you to arrive in *our* home—hers and mine—and make her feel as though *she* is the one who is unwelcome?'

It was his father all over again. Charles was trying to assert his control over not only Edward's estate but also his heart. How *dare* he try to destroy the tender shoots of Edward's blossoming happiness? The very idea of it made Edward want to roar.

Instead, he fixed his uncle with an eye so devoid of warmth he could have sworn he saw the other man shudder. 'You will excuse me, sir. I must beg you to postpone the rest of this discussion until after my return.'

Edward turned away, his mind already swirling with activity. There was nowhere else she would have gone other than back to the Roma camp. If they were going to move on he would have to leave quickly… Talking with his uncle had taken up too much of his time already, and the idea of wasting a single moment more on this man who disgusted him so deeply was enough to make him sick to his stomach.

'Your return? Where can you mean to go?' Charles seized his arm, clinging to him like a bad-tempered child. 'I *know* you cannot mean to chase after that gypsy woman!'

Edward wrenched himself free and bit down on a snarl. 'That *gypsy woman* is my wife. Of course I will go to look for her.' He gazed down at his uncle, into the hazel eyes that matched his own, and felt the final pieces of his life fall into place like those in a jigsaw puzzle.

He had never sought to love Selina. That had grown inside him slowly, day after day, putting down roots in his heart until it had bloomed in all its beautiful colours, chasing away the sadness he had carried within him since he was a child. Nobody would stand in his way now—he would make sure of it.

'I expect you to be gone by the time I return. You are not welcome in my home and I never wish to see or hear from you again. You have no place here. Leave.'

Edward's heart thumped within the cage of his ribs, and his face when he turned towards the door was set. Without another word to his uncle, who watched him with his mouth slack with disbelief, Edward left the suite and marched with long strides from the top of the house to the bottom, into the entrance hall and out through the front doors.

The stable lads scrambled to ready his chestnut mare as Edward stood in the yard, bare-headed and clear-eyed, and inhaled great lungsful of the damp Blackwell air. The scent of snow and wet soil assailed his senses and he almost smiled in bittersweet determination. If there was still a chance for him to win Selina he would take it with both hands. His mind felt clear, like a lake of crystal water. All doubt was washed away, leaving only the true path he knew he must now take.

It would be hard for him to leave the safety of the fortress he had built around himself for all these years—desperately hard, and nothing would ever be the same again. But against all his efforts this Roma woman had forced him to examine the true wishes of his heart, and there could only be but one way ahead.

Selina heard the buzz of conversation beyond the shuttered doors of her *vardo*, but she lay still in the nest of her bunk and continued to gaze up at the curved ceiling. The chatter was occasionally punctuated by the sharp staccato of Zillah's voice as she warned away those who strayed too close to the porch on which she sat guard. She had taken one look at her granddaughter upon her unexpected arrival and waved her into the caravan without a word, the agony of Selina's expression telling her all she needed to know.

At any other time Selina would have been grateful to the old woman for protecting her from the Roma's endless questions, but now her mind was blank with grief and her head empty of anything other than the image of Edward's face.

I will never see him again.

The same six words echoed in her ears as she lay immobile, the only movement her fingers blindly stroking the brooch pinned to her chest. She touched the metal and stone as though it were a talisman, the last thread connecting her to Edward, and felt the slow thud of her heart beneath it.

Had the death of her mother not so cruelly taught her otherwise, Selina might have wondered if it were possible to die from the pain that gripped her chest, squeezing the life out of her with every wretched breath. A broken heart couldn't kill a person—Diamanda's passing had shown her that—but its agony made her wish it could.

Her eyes were dry now—no tears left to fall. They had coursed down her face in an unrelenting stream to patter onto Djali's neck as she had ridden from Blackwell to the camp, the ache in her core deepening with each of the horse's long strides. But sorrow still welled violently within her, and only the undeniable fact that she had helped Edward secure his inheritance, and that by leaving she would spare him future pain, kept her from galloping back in the direction from which she had come.

Her life would never be the same again, she acknowledged dully as her fingers traced the brooch's golden setting. She would have to continue on, knowing that the man she loved could never be hers, his name the only part of him hers to keep.

The hum of voices from outside suddenly halted abruptly, but Selina heard it cease with blank indifference. Her world had shrunk to fit within the four walls of her *vardo*, closed in on itself in a mixture of hopelessness and pain, and she felt as if nothing beyond would ever move her again. She couldn't stay shuttered away forever, of course—but for this one day at least she would hide and give herself up to the anguish of having found love only to allow it to wither and die.

Zillah's voice sliced through the silence, her words

muffled by the crochet blankets Selina lay burrowed beneath. Whatever words her grandmother had spoken were answered by a deeper tone—one that vibrated through the wooden walls of the *vardo*—and with only a half-second of disbelief it sent Selina flying from her bunk to tear open the caravan's door.

A very tall man stood a few yards from the *vardo*'s steps, surrounded by a ring of stunned Roma and looking warily at Zillah. Hearing the door open behind her she turned to address her granddaughter, but Selina was deaf and blind to anything other than the sound of Edward's sigh of relief and the sight of his achingly handsome, painfully familiar face.

His eyes found hers and it was as though the sun had come out from behind the clouds to shine through Edward's face from within. His smile reached all the way up to illuminate the hazel of his gaze, and Selina felt the breath leave her body as she was pinned to the spot by the upward curve of his mouth.

'Edward…?'

His name dropped from her lips as though murmured in a dream. She could hardly believe he stood before her, brightening the dull winter day by the power of his smile. Even a few of the Roma women looked a little dazed by his good looks, although from the way Edward's eyes never left Selina's face it was clear that to him there were no other women in the world.

'Selina. I'm so glad you're still here.' He gestured at the camp around them—a small, somewhat uncertain movement.

Selina gazed at him in mute wonder, the frenzied jumping of her heart robbing her of speech. Why had he come? There could be no reason for him to seek her. The combination of confusion and overwhelming pleasure at the sight of his face rendered her speechless.

When she did not reply, Edward cleared his throat. 'I know that I have no right to ask anything of you, but please—let me speak just once.' His voice was a fraction less steady than before. 'Then, if you wish it, I will leave and you need never see me again.'

Selina hesitated, overcome with bewilderment, all too aware of the small figure of Zillah at her elbow. Her grandmother was studying her face as intently as a scholar with a new book, scouring her features from top to bottom as though searching for some hidden clue. Selina saw how the old eyes narrowed, just for a moment, and then she caught the minute shake of her head in wordless resignation.

'Speak, boy.' Zillah tossed the words at Edward, her eyes never leaving her granddaughter's face. 'My Lina might be lost for words, but I know what is in her heart and what I suspect lives in yours. Speak, I say.'

Selina saw the surprise in Edward's expression, but he offered the old woman a courteous bow. Selina's brows rose almost into her hair when she saw it returned with a short nod from Zillah that was almost bordering on civil.

The crowd of silently watching Roma moved a half-pace closer as Edward laced together his fingers and looked down at his palms, apparently arranging his thoughts. Selina felt a lump rise up in her throat at the sight of him so quiet, so unsure, and every one of her sinews burned to slip down the steps and run into his arms. But then he started to speak, and with only the rush of blood in her ears accompanying his words Selina gripped the *vardo*'s door to anchor her where she stood.

'I have spent so many years caring for scarcely anyone but myself. Ever since my mother and Letitia left my heart had been closed, so determined was I never to let myself be broken again. I had thought I would never love, would never allow myself to feel the things other people felt, leaving themselves vulnerable—and then out of nowhere you came into my life.'

The words tumbled from Edward's dry lips and hung in the frozen air between him and Selina, who watched in silence, the rapid flicker of a pulse at her throat the only sign she was not carved from stone. Her face gave nothing away, but her black eyes, fixed on him so unblinkingly, seemingly gave Edward the courage to continue.

'I remember as though it were yesterday. You stood in front of me that day with mud on your face and your hair so wild, and I remember thinking you were the most beautiful thing I'd ever seen. It frightened me to discover I could think such thoughts, and when you disappeared through the trees I was determined to put you from my mind.'

Selina felt her breath come more quickly, escaping her in a shallow rhythm she couldn't control. A curious warmth began to unfurl in her stomach, reaching up with golden fingers in the direction of her chest, and she almost gasped at the sensation. The warmth seemed to curl around her heart, and suddenly she felt as though she was aflame with a fierce hope she didn't dare express.

The feeling lingered there, hot against the cage of her ribs, inviting her to accept the truth: Edward had sought her out, and he had told her she was beautiful, and still he stood in front of her with apparently more to say. She tightened her grip on the *vardo* door as her head swam with the assault on her senses, almost robbing her of the ability to stand.

'I tried to deny what I felt for you. I tried to convince myself that when you returned to ask me for help I behaved towards you the way I would have behaved to anyone in need. Later, I tried to convince myself that our marriage meant nothing to me, and that it was no more than a convenient arrangement. I failed both times.'

He took a step towards the caravan, mere paces from the wooden steps on which Selina stood. She was just out of his reach.

'It was never just that. In fact, it was precisely the opposite: it was very *in*convenient when I finally allowed myself to admit my feelings for you, knowing you would never return them.'

He must have seen how Selina's taut frame had flinched a little as she started, she thought. Her nerves were responding to him of their own accord, and now her lips had parted as though she wished to speak. She could force no words to emerge, however, and she merely tightened her fingers on the shawls she clutched to her chest.

With another step forward he spoke to her again. 'I do not come to you as gentry. I come as a simple man who has lost his heart to you and who has to tell you how he feels—how he *truly* feels.'

The ground beneath his feet was cold and wet, but Edward paid it no mind as he dropped to his knees in front of Selina's disbelieving gaze. All around her she heard the Romani women break out into low whispers of shock, looking from Edward, kneeling in the mud, to Selina, who stood on the back porch of her caravan with her eyes as round as saucers at his sudden move.

The damp and chill must have seized him immediately, but Edward ignored the unpleasant sensation as he smiled up at the woman he adored. 'Whatever my uncle said to make you run was a lie. He will never speak for me, or know the first thing about my feelings. I swear to you, if you consent to take me as your true husband I will spend the rest of my life trying to win your heart. I can't—'

He ran a hand through the thatch of his hair and gave a short, resigned laugh.

'The simple truth is I cannot live without you. Whatever the circumstances, whatever cruel falsehoods you have been told, you are all that I want and all I will *ever* want.' Edward shrugged, the final vestiges of the weight he had borne for so long falling from his shoulders as he laid his soul bare. 'I love you.'

The entire camp was silent. Every eye swivelled to fix on Selina, who stood like a statue and then felt her limbs turn to water as the full weight of Edward's words hit her like a lightning bolt.

Edward stayed likewise as still as a rock, looking up at her from the mire in which he knelt, with mud spattering breeches that had cost almost as much as a horse and caring not one single iota that they were ruined beyond saving.

The cold winter breeze stirred Selina's raven curls, moving past her to drag the skeletal branches of trees against the dour sky. The smell of snow still hung in the air, and the chill of the evening had begun to wend its way beneath the wool of Selina's shawls. In the silence of the Romani camp she took in the scene before her, her racing mind slowing and slowing until finally, *finally*, it ceased its swirling and allowed her to act as her heart longed for her to.

There was no sound but that of her own footsteps as

Selina stepped down from the caravan, crossed the barren stretch of ground between them, and flung herself into Edward's waiting arms. Every last trace of fear and uncertainty fell away as she reached down to draw his face up to her own, leaving the raw truth exposed as his mouth met hers and she felt him smile against her trembling lips.

Rising up, his arms closed around her in an embrace so tight it almost took her breath away, and then Selina felt her feet leave the ground as he lifted her as gently and as easily as he would a child and held her against the warm column of his body, one hand supporting her weight while the other blindly stroked her hair back from her face.

Edward covered her skin with breathless kisses time and time again—her closed eyelids, her cheek, even the end of her freckled nose. Each kiss set her nerves alight and culminated in him capturing her lips once more in a kiss so powerful Selina felt herself swoon, sagging in Edward's arms as she allowed feelings too wonderful to name to course through her body and set her ablaze.

The Romani's ragged cheers echoed around them, and Selina broke the kiss to look up into Edward's face and feel the delicious sensation of his tender expression warming her to her very toes. He gazed down at her, his eyes filled with the vibrant life she had once feared she might never see again, and she buried her face in the silk of his waistcoat.

It was all too much, suddenly, and the knowledge that her suffering was over was almost overwhelming. Edward was all she wanted, would ever want, and now, as he held her in his arms, it was as though every secret wish she had ever made, every whispered prayer she had uttered in the darkness of her lonely bedchamber, had come true. He loved her—truly loved her—and Selina knew her breathless happiness to be complete.

He lowered her, still holding her firmly against him as her feet hit the ground. She staggered a little and Edward's grip tightened immediately to steady her, gathering her to him more closely than ever before.

'May I take that as a yes to my request?' The smile lines at the corners of his eyes stretched as his lips curved upwards.

Selina felt her own lips twitch in reply. 'I suppose I shall allow it.'

Edward's laugh rang in Selina's ears as her friends and family closed in on them, too many hands to count reaching out to touch her, to touch Edward. Selina saw their joy for her, saw it even in the ancient lines of Zillah's face, and she felt her heart swell with pride at the warmth of her people. They welcomed Edward now as though he were one of their own. His love for her had shattered the barriers between his world and hers, and now they abandoned their pride to pat his back and pinch his cheeks and blush in scandalised delight as he bowed to the women as low as if they were the highest-born ladies.

Selina reached up onto her tiptoes to murmur into Edward's ear. 'What about your uncle?'

The prospect of meeting Charles again was enough to dim the perfect happiness that glowed within her, casting a cold shadow over the warmth of her joy. Edward would always be there to shield her, she knew, but the notion of encountering his uncle made her heart check.

Edward's expression was bordering on triumphant as he pulled her close again. His hand caressed the small of Selina's back, the movement making her toes curl in catlike pleasure despite her sudden worry. She saw the sly amusement in his face, and glanced up at him suspiciously.

'He is no longer welcome in our home. *You* are the mistress of Blackwell Hall, and my beloved wife—and nobody will ever make you doubt that ever again.'

He smiled at her rosy blush, and that slow upward curve of his lips Selina now knew so well enhanced the handsome lines of his face.

'And, with that in mind, I would like to extend my affection to the rest of your people and invite them to stay on our estate for as long as they wish. Forever, if they choose.'

Selina gasped, hardly able to take in his words as a bubble of intense relief mingled with gratitude rose up inside her. Edward had neatly taken care of the only obstacle that could have got in the way of their happiness: now her people would have a safe haven for the rest of their days.

No Roma baby would ever gasp its last breath on a pitted and frosty road; no mother would have to choose between food or coal. Zillah could grow frail without the worry of where their next camp would be, and without the constant fear of persecution that had followed her like a shadow her entire life.

The pain of her mother's passing would never truly heal, Selina knew, and she felt the smallest pang of sorrow tinge her joy as she felt Edward take her hand in his far larger palm and squeeze tightly. But she knew, too, that Diamanda would be proud of the sacrifices her daughter had made, and glad that they had, against all the odds, led her to find real happiness. There would always be a gap in Selina's life that only her mother could fill, but with Edward by her side Selina felt a hope rise within her for the first time, and knew that he could help her feel almost whole again.

He was looking down at her and, as black eyes gazed up into hazel, Selina could have sworn she felt the love radiating from him.

'May I take you home now, wife?'

Selina swept into a deep curtsey any gentry lady would have been proud of and came up smiling. 'Yes, husband. You may.'

* * * * *

LOOK AHEAD, LOOK BACK

For Abby —

LOOK AHEAD, LOOK BACK

By
Annette Laing

Cheers!

Annette Laing (2012)

**CONFUSION
PRESS**

For my husband, Bryan, and our son, Alec: my boys
And in memory of Dr. Doris Pearce,
a force for good in South Georgia.

Library of Congress Control Number: 2012901398
ISBN-13: 978-0-9848101-0-9

Proudly Printed in the USA by King Printing Co., Lowell, MA

Cover design: Deborah Harvey
Inside Design: Kelley Callaway

AnnetteLaing.com

Contents

Acknowledgements

LOOK AHEAD, LOOK BACK

Chapter 1:
STARTLING DISCOVERIES

Digging a ditch in Braithwaite Park wasn't Alex Dias's idea of a fun time on a hot September morning in Snipesville, Georgia. But his friend Brandon had promised him a burger and Coke if he would do some shoveling, and it wasn't like there was anything else to do on a weekend in Snipesville, anyway. Alex sometimes missed San Francisco, and this was one of those times.

"So what are you making a movie for, again?" he asked, puffing heavily as he heaved yet another shovelful of soil over the top.

"History Day," Brandon wheezed, stopping to mop his forehead on his sleeve. "It's, like, this competition for social studies projects. I'm entering the video contest. Javarius and me, we're going to play World War One soldiers. That's why I need this trench. The armies fought that war with machine guns, so the soldiers spent most of their time hiding in holes in the ground . . ."

"Yes, I know about trenches," snapped Alex. The heat and hard work were making him grouchy. At least, that was what he told himself.

"Okay," said Brandon carefully. "But did you know there was a whole company of black American soldiers who got medals from France for distinguished bravery? That's who we're going to play. The lady in the college's theater department loaned us the costumes, but I'm going to have to duct-tape Javarius' pants because they're too long."

Alex smiled at the thought of Javarius' duct-taped pants, and then thrust his shovel at the dry, hard soil. The blade clanged as it hit a large rock, and he let out a long sigh. "This is getting hard," he said wearily. "How much farther we gotta dig?"

Brandon wished Alex wouldn't complain so much, because he was making him feel guilty. Looking past Alex at the elegant old house that was the Clark family's funeral home, Brandon felt even guiltier. His dad had asked him to help at the home with organizing some files, but Brandon had made the excuse that he absolutely had to get on with his History Day project this weekend, which wasn't entirely truthful.

"Almost there," he grunted. "Anyway, look on the good side. At least this isn't solid clay we're dealing with, like it is up where my Uncle Bob lives." He lifted his shovel again, and, as he did so, a corner of the blade lightly scraped the wall of the trench.

The sandy soil crumbled away, revealing the end of a small bone.

Alex pointed at it, his eyes narrowed. "Whoa, what is that?" he said.

"Don't let your imagination run off with you," Brandon warned him. "Look, it's just trash from somebody's chicken dinner." With two fingers, he began to excavate the bone.

But as more soil fell away from it, he stepped back with a gasp, collapsing against the other side of the trench.

Alex leaned forward to get a closer look. Now he could see why Brandon was in shock: The bone was not from a chicken. It belonged to a skeletal human hand, and a gold ring hung loosely from one of its fingers.

Within an hour, the park was crawling with police cars and police officers, and a straggling line of bystanders had formed to watch the spectacle.

A young Snipesville Online reporter in jeans and sweatshirt was interviewing Brandon and Alex, while acting as his own cameraman. "So why were y'all digging in the park?" he asked, squinting from behind the lens.

Brandon took a deep breath. "Well, sir, I was making a World War One trench for my History Day project, and Alex here was helping me. . . ." As he talked, a heavyset middle-aged woman in pigtails and a bandanna ducked under the yellow police tape, and marched up to them, wiping her hands on her overalls. Ignoring the reporter, she tapped Alex on the arm and asked in a heavy northern accent, "So, which one of you found the remains?"

Before either of the boys could reply, the reporter swiveled around and pointed the camera at her. "Dr. Barrett, good to see you!" he cried. He adjusted his lens, and then said into the microphone. "This lady is Dr. Sonya Barrett, professor of anthropology at Snipesville State College. I'm told she is leading the excavation. Dr. Barrett, I'm guessing from your presence here that this body that's been discovered is pretty old?"

Meanwhile, Alex nudged Brandon. "Hey, isn't that your Aunt Marcia?" he whispered. He nodded to a sour-faced middle-aged black woman standing behind the police tape, her arms folded. Aunt Marcia was the business manager at Clark and Sons Home of Eternal Rest, Inc., Brandon's family's funeral home.

"Yeah, that's Aunt Morticia," joked Brandon. "She can always tell when there's a corpse around. She's looking for business. She never lets up."

Meanwhile, the reporter was asking Professor Barrett, "Are the remains from the War Between the States?"

"You mean the Civil War? No, they're not," she said brusquely. "The skeleton's even older than that. Eighteenth century, I'd say, and not Indian."

The reporter whistled. "Wow. So there were white folks in Snipes County that far back?"

She answered his question impatiently. "Not many, but yes, there were. And Africans."

"So this was a long time before Snipesville was built," said the reporter. "What was this place called back then? Do you know?"

"Actually, yes, I do . . ." she began.

Alex was so excited by the question, he butted in. "Me too! I know what it was . . . Ow!"

Brandon had kicked him.

Dr. Barrett glanced at the boys, and then cleared her throat. "By the early 1750s," she said slowly, "this park was part of what was called Kintyre Plantation. My students and I plan to do a full excavation."

The reporter eagerly leaned toward her. "Think we'll find a secret hoard of Confederate gold?"

Dr. Barrett smiled tightly and ran a grimy hand over her bandanna. "I'm an anthropologist, not a treasure hunter. Anyway, I don't think . . ." she hesitated. Then she said, "I can't imagine we'll find a secret hoard, but we did find this with the remains."

She held up a small plastic pouch. Inside, clearly visible, was the gold ring from the skeleton's finger.

"Could you hold that still for me, please?" the reporter muttered, focusing his camera and zooming in. "That's pretty, all those little circles."

"Tiny whorls, yes," said Dr. Barrett, dangling the bag next to her head. "It is a very strange design she was wearing for the . . ."

The reporter interrupted her. "So the deceased was a woman. Was she murdered?"

To Brandon's surprise, Dr. Barrett seemed intrigued by the suggestion. "Possibly. Yes, it's possible. It was a shallow grave, I think. But it's too early to be sure."

At that moment, a bearded student trotted over. "Dr. Barrett?" he said in a hushed voice. "We want you to take a look at something."

The boys traipsed back up the hill on East Main Street to the center of downtown Snipesville, past the row of early twentieth-century shops, the pool hall, and the drugstore. Alex turned to Brandon. "What do you think?" he asked apprehensively. "Has this got anything to do with us?"

"Nah," said Brandon. He knew what Alex had meant, but he kept on walking, avoiding his friend's earnest gaze. He did wonder, all the same. Were they about to travel in time again? Was this discovery some kind of sign? He found the thought strangely exciting as well as scary. Brandon had never imagined that the arrival of Alex and his sister Hannah from San Francisco would totally change his life, that it would turn him into a time-traveler. He had always loved history, and he had thought over the years how cool it would be to travel in time. He had never seriously thought it would happen, of course. He still couldn't quite believe it.

With a screech of brakes, a small blue car pulled up next to them, and the middle-aged woman behind the wheel lowered her window. "Hey, guys!" she called out, giving them a cheery wave.

"Hi, Dr. Harrower," said Brandon cautiously. Alex gave her a shy, silent wave.

Dr. Kate Harrower was a history professor at Snipesville State College. She was also the kids' occasional companion on their travels in time. She was not an easy person to know: Whenever the kids asked her why the time travel was happening, she became evasive, avoiding any direct answers to their questions. But she clearly knew more than she was saying, and she showed up at random times and places on their adventures to offer them help and advice.

Running into the Professor now, Brandon thought, was definitely another sign that something was up. They only ever saw her before the time travel started. In fact, Alex's sister Hannah was convinced that the Professor was responsible for all their adventures.

"Listen, I don't have time to chat," the Professor said urgently, as a line of cars waited patiently behind her. It was normal in Snipesville for people to stop their cars in the middle of the road and chat, even when that meant holding up the traffic. "Meet me at the County Health Department at two. Call Hannah and tell her she has to be there. It's important."

The boys nodded dumbly. Brandon opened his mouth to ask what was going on, but the Professor was already pulling away from the curb. As she reached the traffic lights at the courthouse, she turned onto South Main Street just a little too fast, and then vanished from sight.

"I guess we're going on another adventure," Brandon said, after a small pause.

"Why do you think that?" Alex asked him.

Brandon gaped at his friend. "What? You don't think it means something that we saw her?"

"No, I don't think so," said Alex, matter-of-factly. "That's kind of superstitious of you. This is a small town. I'm surprised we don't run into her more often."

"I'm not superstitious," said Brandon defensively.

"Yes, you are," Alex said. "Nothing personal, but you're pretty religious, so you always think everything has a reason."

"Of course it does," said Brandon. "We don't always know what the reason is, but there always is one."

"No, there isn't," Alex said quietly, reluctant to get into an argument with his friend. "A lot of things are pretty random."

A hostile silence fell between them as they walked. Brandon didn't appreciate being called superstitious. Religion isn't superstition, he thought angrily. Christianity and superstition are two totally different things, he insisted to himself.

While Brandon seethed, Alex texted his sister to pass along the Professor's message. A few seconds later, he got Hannah's reply in capital letters: NO WAY.

He showed Brandon her reply, and they both shrugged.

The Snipes County Health Department was a grim, whitewashed, cement-block, single-story building. Only a derelict old farmhouse and a cotton field kept it company on the very edge of Snipesville. Beyond were fields. At two in the afternoon on a Saturday, one car waited in the parking lot, and it was the Professor's.

As soon as the boys approached, she anxiously waved them over, and they ran to her open window.

"I'm sorry, but I have to leave," she said. "I've told the receptionist that I'm your guardian and we're going to Senegal. So make sure you stick with the story."

"Senny where?" said Alex. At the same time, Brandon asked, "Ma'am? What story? What are you talking about?"

"Senegal's in Africa," she explained breathlessly to Alex, turning the key in the ignition. "But we're not going there. I just think some precautions might be necessary for the future. Just in case. So I'm getting you guys a course of malaria pills, and since there's lots of malaria in Africa, I figured it was best to tell the clinic that's why you're getting the meds. Where's Hannah? Well, fill her in when she arrives."

"I don't think Hannah's going to . . ." Alex started to say, but the car was already pulling away.

"Man, doesn't she ever slow down?" Brandon exploded. "What was that about?"

"I guess we better find out," said Alex, heading for the clinic door.

The nurse was not happy. "I told her you'll need yellow fever shots if you're going to Africa, but she didn't listen," she complained. Then she looked Brandon square in the eye. "That lady is your guardian?" she said skeptically. "Both of you?"

"Yes, ma'am," he said, a little too quickly. "She's great. She's always taking us places. She took us to England this summer. It was awesome, wasn't it, Alex?"

"It was awesome," Alex agreed. "We went to London to see the Crystal Palace . . . ."

Brandon groaned. The Crystal Palace had burned down in 1936, so it was going to be hard to explain how they could have visited it.

Fortunately, the nurse didn't know anything about the Crystal Palace, London, or England, and she wasn't interested, either. "That must have been nice," she said absently, as she made a note on her computer. "I'll be right back. Wait here."

Brandon and Alex exchanged glum looks, expecting the worst. But when the nurse returned, she handed each boy a slip of blue paper. "Here's your prescriptions," she said. "The doctor says to be sure to start taking them two weeks before you leave, and to read all the instructions. Have a blessed day." She shooed them toward the door.

As they walked out into the stifling heat, Brandon said, "We better get these filled at SpeedyDrug. I don't think I know anyone who works there. I don't want someone asking questions. You know anyone in the pharmacy there?"

"No," said Alex. Truth was, he really didn't know very many people in Snipesville at all.

The gray-haired pharmacist in the white coat grimaced when he examined their prescriptions, holding one in each hand. "Malaria pills, huh? We don't get much call for those around here. You boys going on a mission trip?"

"No," Alex said, at the exact same moment that Brandon said, "Yes, sir."

Alex tried very hard not to look nervous. Then, to his horror, he heard himself asking, "Do we need our parents' permission?"

Brandon glared at him angrily.

The pharmacist gave him an odd look, but then he shrugged. "No, I guess not, not unless your prescription is for a controlled substance." He entered something into the computer. "Ready in fifteen minutes," he said.

Alex's dad dropped him off at home in their large house in the subdivision in rural Snipes County, then went back to his office at the bank downtown. Alex found his sister in the living room. She was listening to music, munching on an apple, and playing on her new phone.

Hannah pulled out the earbuds when Alex walked in. In a bored voice, she said, "So what did That Woman want?"

Alex ignored the question, and flopped into the recliner, flipping up the footrest. "Why didn't you get back to me?" he said reproachfully.

"Oh, did you text me again?" Hannah said innocently.

Alex scowled. "You know I did. I texted, I called. I bet that phone hasn't been out of your hands the whole time. You should have come."

"Why?" said Hannah, returning her gaze to her game. "I don't owe that witch anything. She's not the boss of me. What did she want, anyway?"

"She got us malaria pills."

Hannah sat up straight, and tossed her phone aside. It bounced on the sofa. "She did what?" she hissed. "Does Dad know?"

Alex made a face. "Of course he doesn't know. You want her to get arrested?"

"No skin off my nose," Hannah huffed.

Her brother scowled at her. "That's just stupid. Anyway, you should get some pills too. Maybe it's not too late."

"No chance," Hannah said. "Maybe if I refuse to get vaccinated for weird diseases, she won't kidnap me for her stupid adventures."

"Don't count on it, sis. And you don't get vaccinated for malaria, anyway: You have to take these pills we got. Anyhow, you're wrong about her. She doesn't want to go time traveling any more than we do."

Hannah groaned, and shook her head in disbelief. "Man, your Professor buddy has totally brainwashed you. You and Brandon are such total wusses, always doing what she tells you to. Did you even ask her why you need the pills?"

"No," Alex admitted. When Hannah rolled her eyes at him, he decided it was time to change the subject. "Oh, but that wasn't the most exciting thing you missed. Brandon and me, you won't believe what we found . . . ."

At school on Monday, Hannah was still thinking about her brother's news. Two adventures in time had been more than enough for her, but she was starting to think the unthinkable: The time travel wasn't over. She frowned. Would it go on forever? Not for the first time since she had arrived from San Francisco, she sighed heavily at the unfairness of it all. Moving to remote South Georgia was bad enough, without her life being turned into a sci-fi movie.

She snapped back to the more pressing problem of the moment: She did not fit in at Snipes Academy. School was not going well.

While summer had lasted, it was hard enough for Hannah to live in Snipesville. She was constantly reminded that she was a long way from California—in fact, she was a long way from anywhere. Her new house was surrounded by pine trees and fields, and it was miles from the center of town. Not that downtown Snipesville was exciting, exactly.

Hannah had kind of hoped that starting school would help her make friends. Truly, though, she had always doubted it. It wasn't like she had a lot of friends in San Francisco, either. And as soon as she started classes at Snipes Academy, things went wrong.

At lunchtime on the first day, a giggly group of girls in the cafeteria had stared openly at her. She tried to look cool and confident, and finally, the girls cautiously approached her. She recognized one of them as Natalie Marshburn, her dad's boss's daughter.

While Natalie stayed in the background, a tall blonde with long straight hair said to Hannah, "Hey, you're new, right?" She spoke through a mouthful of gum.

Hannah nodded to her. "Yeah, I'm Hannah. From San Francisco."

The girls giggled in unison.

"Wow, how'd you wind up in Snipesville?" asked the blonde. Before Hannah could answer, she extended a willowy hand and gave Hannah a limp handshake. She said, "I'm Ashlee Bragg. Natalie says we should welcome you to SA."

More giggles.

"My mom told me to say that," Natalie grumbled from the edge of the group, staring at her red-painted fingernails.

Ashlee smiled brilliantly at Hannah. "So, have you got family in Snipes County? What's your last name?"

"No, my family's in California," Hannah said. "My last name's Dias."

"Huh?" Ashlee said loudly, her jaw hanging open.

"Dias," Hannah repeated uncertainly. "D-I-A-S."

Hannah had noticed a slight chill fall between her and the girls. The bell rang.

"Nice meeting you, Hannah, er, Dias," Ashlee said with a fake smile, and she flapped her hand delicately in a goodbye as she and the others drifted off.

What was that about, Hannah wondered?

Hannah wasn't the only new student. Her homeroom teacher ordered her to sit next to the other newbie, a girl called Tara Thompson.

Straightaway, Hannah recognized that Tara Thompson was not one of the popular kids: She frowned, slumped in her seat, and wore glasses with black frames and thick lenses that magnified her heavily outlined eyes. One hank of her lank hair was dyed bright purple, the rest was dyed black, and she had three piercings in one ear. If Tara had been old enough for tattoos, Hannah was sure that she would have had several. She never said a word to Hannah, but when she first spoke in class, she talked with the thickest southern accent Hannah had ever heard. The other kids laughed and nudged each other.

On this particular day, Hannah and Tara were paired up for a project in science class. As Hannah arranged glass test tubes in a rack, Tara nodded toward Natalie Marshburn. Leaning forward, she drawled to Hannah in a barely audible voice, "Just look at her acting like she knows what she's doing. You wouldn't guess that she don't have two brain cells to rub together."

Startled, Hannah almost dropped a test tube. "You talking to me?" she said.

"Yeah," said Tara. "I am. That Natalie, she's my cousin. But I live in a trailer, so I ain't good enough for her, and she don't speak to me." She added slyly, "Praise the Lord."

Hannah giggled, and the teacher threw her a sharp look. Tara continued in a low voice, "So how's it going for you? I hear you're from San Francisco. That's pretty cool. Too bad you got stuck here in the Ville. I like to call this place the Vile. Fits, don't it? So why did your parents dump you at SA?"

Hannah shrugged. "I've always gone to private school," she said. "And this is the only one in town, except for the Baptist academy."

Tara smiled grimly. "I got a scholarship to go here. Unfortunately. Only reason I'm stuck here is Daddy won't hear of me going to school with black kids."

"Wow, that's seriously racist," Hannah muttered, pouring the contents of one test tube into another. "Hey, aren't you supposed to be helping me?"

But Tara wasn't done. "Racist? You ain't seen the half of it. You watch what happens. Nobody's going to talk to you because you're a Mexican."

"Mexican? I'm not Mexican," said Hannah. "And so what if I was?"

Tara shrugged. "You got a Mexican name."

"As a matter of fact," Hannah said haughtily, "It's Portuguese. You have a problem with that?"

"Not me," said Tara, wrinkling her nose. "But there's only one thing worse than being white trash or Yankee at this school, and that's being a Mexican. Well, the worst thing would be being black, if they ever had black kids here, which they don't, except for the African doctor's kid, and he won't stay long. . . . No, come to think of it, Mexican's worse. If they think you're Mexican, ain't nobody gonna talk to you."

Hannah frowned and returned her attention to the test tubes. "But you're talking to me, right?"

"Oh, sure," said Tara, lifting a test tube and waggling it. "But I'm nobody. My folks don't belong to the Country Club. Heck, we don't even go to First Baptist."

Hannah lifted an eyebrow. "First Baptist Church? We don't go there either. So what?"

Tara sighed. "Hannah, you got a lot to learn about living in a little bitty town in the South. Now, what am I supposed to be doing with this tube thingy?"

Hannah gave her a sour look. "You can stop messing with it, for a start."

In the cafeteria, Hannah was standing with her tray at the end of the lunch line when she spied the stony gazes of Natalie Marshburn and her friends, and felt the hairs stand up on the back of her neck.

As she hovered awkwardly, she saw Tara make room for her at a table and beckon to her.

Hannah hesitated. Sitting with Tara would forever label her a freak. Then again, why did she care what Natalie Marshburn and her slimy friends thought?

Impulsively, Hannah made a decision she knew would be fateful. Dumping her tray next to Tara's, she said, "Move up, so I don't fall off the end." Out of the corner of her eye, Hannah saw Natalie Marshburn grinning behind her hand, and she cringed a little.

Tara finished chewing a mouthful of pizza. "So. You never said. Why did y'all move to Snipesville?"

"My dad's job," Hannah said. "He's with GrandeStates Bank downtown. He got transferred."

Tara puffed out her cheeks. "Wow, that sucks. What did your mama have to say about moving to this dump?"

Hannah hunched lower over her burger, and mumbled, "She's dead."

Her eyes widening, Tara looked away. "Sorry," she muttered.

Hannah shrugged. She hated how people acted when she told them. "S'okay. I'm used to it."

Tara glanced sideways at her. "Do you miss her?"

"Well, duh," Hannah said, but not angrily. "Sometimes."

Tara didn't hide her amazement. "Sometimes? If my mama passed, I'd miss her all the time."

Hannah felt herself go hot with embarrassment. She didn't want to explain. She didn't want to talk about what had happened with her mother to anyone, least of all this girl she had just met. But she knew that she must seem weird. She tried to act cool. "Yeah, of course," she said, "but life goes on, yeah?"

"Hey, that's cold," Tara said in a low voice.

Suddenly, Hannah felt fury rising in her face. "What do you know? You didn't know her. You don't even know me. Excuse me." With that, she jumped to her feet, and moved her tray to an empty table nearby.

To Hannah's horror, Tara followed her, and plunked herself down next to her. "Look, I'm sorry, okay?" Tara said. "My bad. You're right. I don't know what it's like."

There was an awkward silence while Hannah ate her burger.

And then, out of the blue, Tara said, "Hey, you know Brandon Clark, right?"

Hannah was so taken aback, she forgot to be mad. Tara knows Brandon? "Yeah, he's my brother's friend. How'd you know? Is he a friend of yours?"

Tara smiled slyly, and whispered, "He's my cousin."

Hannah's mouth fell open. "What? How?"

Tara's relationship to Brandon was complicated, and Tara explained the family tree in excruciating detail. Hannah learned that Tara and Brandon shared a set of great-great-great-grandparents. They were a black man and a white woman who had two kids: Their son, Brandon's ancestor, was black; The daughter, from whom Tara was descended, was light-skinned, and had decided to 'pass' for white.

Listening to Tara, Hannah couldn't help staring at her, looking for some hint of African ancestry, but only her brown eyes suggested it.

"So if part of your family is black," Hannah said slowly, "how come you say your dad is a racist?"

Tara gave a rueful smile. "Because he is. I'm kin to Brandon through my mama's family, and even then, nobody on that side talks about it much. It's kind of embarrassing for most of them."

"I think it's cool," Hannah said. "I didn't know black people and white people in the South were ever related to each other. Hey, has Brandon told you . . ." She almost asked if Tara knew about the time-travel adventures, but she let it go. Tara would never believe her.

Hannah had made a friend. Alex had not.

At lunch on the first day of school, he sat next to Trey Marshburn, the only boy he recognized, who grudgingly allowed Alex to join him. Trey and his buddies pointedly shut him out of the conversation as they talked about football. Alex knew nothing about football, or any sport, and they did nothing to teach him.

He learned his lesson. The next day, he sat at another table, alone, well away from Trey and his friends. But this somehow made things worse. Trey and his little gang kept stealing glances at him, then laughing among themselves. Finally, one of them, a stocky kid with curly black hair, strolled over and sat next to Alex. Trey and the others tailed him, and gloated as they saw Alex's nervousness.

"Hey, ain't you the boy who found the skeleton?" asked Curly Hair with a sneer. "The one with the black friend who was on the tee-vee? The one who sat next to us yesterday? What's your name?"

"Alex," said Alex, fighting a lump in his throat, his insides seizing up. "My name's Alex Dias."

"So, Di-as," the boy said slowly. "What kind of name is that? You Mexican? You from old Meh-hee-co?"

"No," said Alex quietly. "I'm not Mexican. I'm . . ."

"Sure sounds like a Mexican name to me," the boy laughed to his friends. He turned back to Alex, and said, "You don't look Mexican."

Before Alex could stop himself, he snapped, "You mean I'm not brown and holding a leaf blower? Is that what Mexicans look like?"

But, to his dismay, the boys thought he was making a joke. Curly Hair slapped him on the back, a little too hard.

"Funny guy!" he said patronizingly. "So you're not Mexican, huh?"

"No," Alex said, his temper cooling. "My family's Portuguese," he added lamely.

"Say what?" said the boy.

"Nothing," said Alex. "So where are you from?"

"Let me tell you something, Di-as," the boy said with a creepy smile. "I'm from right here. Snipes County native, just like my daddy, and my granddaddy. My name's Clifton Hunslow. You got that? Hunslow. You already know Trey, right?" He jerked his head toward Trey Marshburn, who smiled awkwardly. "His family started Snipesville."

Clifton could not have imagined for one moment that Alex had actually met Trey's ancestors. But he had, in the year 1851.

"Oh, yeah," Alex said without thinking. "The drunk guy who started the inn, right?"

Trey stepped forward, clenching his fists. "Are you calling my family drunks?" he demanded.

"No," Alex said, suddenly and painfully aware that he had said too much.

"You better not be," Trey growled, staring at him.

Great, thought Alex. I'm bully bait.

Apart from the Professor, Dr. George Braithwaite was the only adult in Snipesville who believed, or even had heard, that three local kids traveled in time.

George Braithwaite didn't just believe. He knew. He had first met Hannah, Brandon, and Alex in England in 1940, when he was just a boy. Now that he was a respected retired doctor—he was the first black doctor who had settled in Snipesville—Dr. Braithwaite had become the kids' most important friend and ally.

Now, however, he had bad news for them. Very bad news indeed. He sighed as he picked up the phone and dialed Hannah's number.

When Hannah got out of her last class, she switched on her cell phone and saw that Dr. Braithwaite had called. She called him back while she waited for the school bus.

"Thank you for getting back to me so quickly, Hannah," he said. His accent was a little American, but, despite decades in the States, he still sounded very English. "I just had a call from Verity."

"Cool, how is she?" Hannah asked eagerly. "How's Eric?" When Hannah, Alex and Brandon were transported to World War II England, Verity and Eric became their best friends.

Now, Verity and Eric Powell were an elderly married couple, living in the house that had once belonged to Verity's grandmother, Mrs. Devenish. For Hannah, their childhood friendship was a recent memory. But for Verity and Eric, it was a lifetime ago.

There was a pause on the line. "Hannah, I'm afraid I have something rather sad to tell you," said Dr. Braithwaite. "I'm afraid that . . . well . . . Eric died yesterday."

Hannah gasped, "Oh, no!" Her knees felt weak, and she felt blood rush to her face.

Soothingly, Dr. Braithwaite explained, "It happened very quickly. He had a massive heart attack. Verity says he didn't suffer."

All Hannah could see in her mind's eye was Eric as she had known him: a mischievous and funny little boy in short pants, with a heavy Cockney accent. Her eyes welled up. "Poor Verity . . . How is she doing?" she said.

"Well, as you would expect, she's very upset," said Dr. Braithwaite. "But I think she's glad to have had him around as long as she did. His health hasn't been very good in recent years. Look, why don't you send her a card, then wait a week or so until the dust settles, and then give her a ring? She would be thrilled to hear from you."

"Yeah, I will . . . It's just so hard to think that Eric's dead," Hannah said wistfully.

"Yes, it is," agreed Dr. Braithwaite. "But, perhaps, you know, what with the, er, time travel, perhaps you will meet him again."

I hope not, thought Hannah, but she had the presence of mind not to say it aloud. It wasn't that she hadn't liked Eric, of course. She was just tired of being a time-traveling freak.

The color drained from Alex's face when Hannah told him the news, and he felt his eyes go moist. But he didn't say anything. Eric had been his best friend in 1940. More than that, he was his best friend ever. Most kids thought Alex was a dork, but Eric didn't even know the meaning of the word. Literally, since the word "dork" didn't exist in 1940. He had liked Alex for who he was, and never, ever criticized him for it.

Alex calmly went upstairs, lay down on his bed, and sobbed quietly.

Hannah wasn't fooled by his bravado. Climbing the stairs after him, she slipped silently into her brother's room and sat on the bed, holding his hand.

"No kid should ever have to go through this," she said bitterly. "I can't believe our friends get old and die. Time travel sucks."

"It shouldn't," said Alex, wiping his eyes. "We should get to choose when we go. Then we could visit Eric when he was our age."

"I guess," said Hannah. "Trouble is, we don't. That Woman does the choosing for us. We're just victims."

Alex knew he should argue with his sister, but he didn't feel like it. Not today.

Two weeks passed after the boys' visit to the clinic and Eric's death, and in all that time, the kids nervously expected to be swept without warning into another journey in time. But it didn't happen, and the school routine gradually distracted Hannah and Alex.

Brandon, however, could not forget. He thought about it constantly. He prayed fervently for that magical moment when he would lift his head, and find himself in another place and time. Of the three kids, Brandon alone secretly looked forward to time travel: He would do anything to free himself from the suffocating boredom of life in Snipesville.

It was Brandon, then, who plucked up the courage to call the Professor, to ask her if she thought that another adventure was coming soon—not that he truly expected her to answer his questions honestly. He also wanted to know what she had learned about the skeleton, and whether the gold ring would become his property when the excavation was complete.

The first time he called the Professor, she didn't answer her phone. He tried her again several times over the next few days, but despite all his messages, she never returned his calls.

Finally, one day after school, Brandon made the long trek through town to Snipesville State College. But when he finally arrived at the history building, he found the Professor's office door firmly closed. He knocked hopefully, but heard only silence in reply. Despondent, he trudged away, dodging through a rowdy crowd of students who were leaving classes. It was then that he spotted the history department office.

"Can I help you, young man?" A bespectacled and plump middle-aged black woman, the department secretary, smiled at Brandon as he hesitated in the open doorway.

He smiled back shyly. "Yes, ma'am, I was looking for Professor Harrower?"

The secretary frowned, and Brandon wondered nervously if he had said the wrong thing.

When she spoke again, however, her tone wasn't angry, but worried. "We haven't heard from her in weeks," she said. "Professor Harrower is on sabbatical—that means she's taken a semester off from teaching. But she usually tells me if she's going to be out of town. I'm a little worried about her. Are you a friend of hers, honey?"

Brandon's mouth dropped into his stomach. He looked off to the window, avoiding the secretary's gaze. "No, ma'am. Well, kind of. I mean, I wouldn't exactly call her a friend, but . . ."

The secretary interrupted him impatiently. "But you know her? What's your name?"

"Brandon Clark," he said reluctantly.

The secretary put a finger to her lips in thought, and then said, "She mentions you sometimes, Brandon. I'm Miss Arlene. Oh, and hey, I'm from Augusta, so I don't know too many people down here, but I believe I've met your momma. She's a nurse, right? And your family keeps a funeral home? You stay near there?"

Brandon nodded, and Miss Arlene smiled. "It's nice to meet you. Look, if Dr. Harrower contacts you, sugar, would you ask her to get in touch with me? I just want to know she's okay."

Brandon smiled weakly. "Me too, ma'am," he said. "Are you sure she didn't say where she was headed?"

Miss Arlene sniffed. "No, baby. Like I said, she didn't even say she was leaving."

Brandon said quietly, "Are you going to call the police?"

"I'm thinking about it, to be honest with you, sweetheart," Miss Arlene said somberly. "Now remember, the moment you hear from her, you ask her to call me. I'll give you my number."

As Brandon walked back across the campus, he felt like punching something. He wasn't sure if he was upset, furious, or both. He was tired of waiting for stuff to happen to him. He wanted to make things happen, to have control over his life. The Professor had never explained how she traveled in time. She had never told him, or Alex, or Hannah why they were involved in her adventures. In fact, she dodged all their questions. She just dragged them through her weird life without their permission. Brandon was suddenly aware that he had screwed up his fists so tightly, his nails were digging into his palms.

All he could ever do, he thought angrily, was to wait for her to return and feed him a little hint about what would happen next. In frustration, he kicked a pinecone as hard as he could. Being a pinecone, it didn't soar into the air as it should have, but rolled lamely a few feet in front of him. Brandon was too mad to laugh about it.

Verity Powell's message was the first email Hannah saw when she opened her inbox after school.

> *Dear Hannah and Alex,*
> *Thank you for your card, and for your kind words about Eric. It was a shock, of course, but he died the way he would have wanted, without a fuss. I want you to know that he so enjoyed your visit last summer . . .*

Hannah had to think about that for a moment, because her entire friendship with Eric and Verity had taken place since the beginning of the past summer, when the time travel had begun. She guessed, however, that Verity was referring to her visit to England with Alex and Brandon in what she thought of as "real time," the twenty-first century. She read on.

...He said it brought his life full circle to meet you again in his old age. And how delighted we were to find out that you three are time-travelers! For you, of course, it has only been a few months since you first met us. But for Eric and me, decades have passed. How wonderful it was for us to have had you rekindle those happy memories, of living with Granny (Mrs. D., as you called her) in Balesworth during the War, and of all our adventures together.

Hannah paused and blinked back tears. How she had loved Verity's grandmother, Elizabeth Devenish. Her beloved "Mrs. D." had fostered her, Alex, and Brandon in 1940. Hannah could just picture her now: a tall and imposing woman with gray hair, wearing an apron, and puffing on a cigarette. She smiled at the memory of those awful cigarettes. At first, she and Mrs. Devenish had battled furiously. Mrs. D. railed against Hannah's twenty-first century American manners and attitude, while Hannah failed to recognize that the formidable but kindly 'Mrs. D.' was stressed out by day-to-day life, juggling war work with care of her granddaughter and several evacuated children. But Hannah and Mrs. D. had come to understand and grow fond of each other. How Hannah missed her.

She snapped out of her reverie, and reminded herself what a comfort it was that Verity had grown old looking like Mrs. D., and that she was still on the planet. Hannah returned to Verity's email.

I've been taking computer classes, Verity continued. All very basic compared to what you kids know, I'm sure, but as you see, I am making progress, and can now use email. The best thing about my newfound knowledge, however, is that it allows me to research my family's history. Now, my dear, this brings me to the picture that I have attached to this email.

Hannah noticed the attachment icon. She clicked on it. It was a huge file, and while it was downloading, she continued to read.

I have discovered that, long ago, my family owned an inn on Balesworth High Street. So many pubs have closed in recent years, but this one is still alive and well, so I paid a visit. It's a very interesting place, very large, because like many of the old pubs in Balesworth, it was once an eighteenth-century coaching inn. The current landlord is a Mr. Tarrant. His great-grandfather was the first in his family to own the pub, but the portrait in the picture I've attached dates back to the eighteenth century, and it hangs in Mr. Tarrant's living room. Mr. Tarrant says that the portrait belongs to the pub, and cannot be sold, no matter who owns the building, which I thought delightful!

Take a look at the painting. Pretty staggering, isn't it? Will it be all right for you to ring me? Hopefully, it's not too expensive to phone from America. Don't forget that England is five hours ahead of Georgia. My number is . . .

Hannah was confused, to say the least. But now the picture finally finished loading, and it popped up. It was far too large for the screen, and she shrank it down to see it.

"Whoa!" she exclaimed.

It was indeed a portrait: a proper painted portrait, of a man in his thirties, an old woman, and a young woman, all of them dressed like they belonged in Colonial Williamsburg. The man was wearing a white wig, just like George Washington. But what startled Hannah was that the older woman looked just like Verity and Mrs. Devenish. And the young woman—a girl, really–looked just like Hannah.

Chapter 2:
ANOTHER BALESWORTH

On Saturday morning, it took Hannah several minutes of Googling to figure out how to phone England. Soon, however, she was listening to the unfamiliar double-purr of a British ringtone.

"Hello?" said a familiar English voice.

Hannah took a deep breath. "Verity? It's me . . . Hannah. I just saw the picture. It's wild."

Verity laughed. "She certainly looks like you, doesn't she, dear?"

"Verity, she is me. I'm sure of it."

There was a silence on the other end of the line. "Yes," Verity said quietly. "I was rather afraid you would say that." She paused. "Do you have any idea who. . .?"

"No," said Hannah. "I have no clue who the others are. I guess it just hasn't happened yet. Maybe it never will . . . . I don't know."

Verity tried to sound cheerful. "You know, I do think that we could be wrong. The girl might not be you at all. As a dear friend of mine used to say, the Good Lord only made so many molds. Lots of people look like each other, even though they aren't related at all."

Hannah studied the picture on her computer. "I hope you're right," she said uncertainly. "You know, there is something wrong about her mouth and her eyes."

"Well, you would know," said Verity. "And, of course, the artist wasn't exactly Leonardo Da Vinci, was he? It's a terrible painting. So we can't be sure either way."

Hannah laughed. "No, the painting kinda sucks," she agreed. Then a thought occurred to her. "Hey, have you found anything out about these people?"

"Not yet," said Verity. "Lizzie, my daughter, works at the V and A. That is, she works at the Victoria and Albert Museum. She tells me it can be very difficult to identify sitters in a portrait. But she did say that the more I know of the painting's provenance, the better."

Hannah frowned. "The prov . . . What? What does that mean?"

"The provenance means the painting's history," said Verity. "Where it came from, who's owned it in the past, all that sort of thing. Unfortunately, Mr. Tarrant at the pub doesn't know anything about it, except that, as I told you, it's been hanging there at least as long as his family has owned the place. Still, I'm going to burrow through the archives at the Balesworth Museum, and see if I can come up with anything. I'll let you know if I do."

At that instant, Hannah thought to herself, *I hope you find out before I disappear.* It was a weird thought, and she shivered. Why had that popped into her head? What did it mean? Then she got a grip. *It doesn't mean anything,* she told herself sternly. *It's just a passing thought.*

In the early evening, Brandon called Hannah, and told her the news that the Professor had vanished.

Her reaction shocked him.

"Well, what am I supposed to do about it?" she said peevishly.

Brandon scowled. Hannah was probably the most annoying person he knew. "Look, I don't know," he said, "but we should look for clues."

"This is life, not Scooby Doo," grumped Hannah. "Anyway, she's probably fine. She's an adult. She can take care of herself. I don't feel like helping her, anyway. What has she ever done for me?"

But Hannah wasn't being entirely honest, even to herself. As soon as she hung up on Brandon, she felt remorse. In her gut, she knew that helping the Professor was exactly what she should be doing. But how?

It was then, for the very first time, that Hannah found herself needing to go back in time.

She didn't want to. She needed to. It was such a bizarre feeling. It was physical, and it was sudden, like a hunger or a thirst. It was beyond her understanding or control, but it was real, a sensation both powerful and frightening, as though she were being dragged by her center to somewhere she didn't want to go. For one terrifying moment, she fought for breath, and leaned on the wall for support.

After he got home from church on Sunday, Brandon called to ask if Alex and Hannah would accompany him to Snipesville State College that afternoon. Alex was enthusiastic. Hannah was not, and agreed to come only after Alex promised to buy her a Frappuccino from the college Starbucks.

Mr. Dias dropped off Hannah and her brother next to the main campus entrance. The moment he drove away, Hannah confronted Brandon. "What's the point of coming here?" she demanded angrily. "You told us she's disappeared. We're not going to find her here, are we?"

Hannah had dreaded visiting the college campus: This was where the first time-travel journey had begun, and to return here seemed like tempting fate.

"I don't know what the point is," Brandon admitted. "But I think this is where we should be. Don't you?"

"I do!" Alex piped up.

So do I, Hannah thought silently. *But I don't know why, and I really wish I didn't have to be here.* What she said was, "So where are we going, exactly?"

"We're going to meet a woman about a corpse," Brandon replied with a lopsided smile. "I made an appointment to talk to Professor Barrett, the lady who dug up the skeleton. Anyway, Hannah, don't tell me you have anything else to do on a Sunday afternoon."

"Uh-huh," Hannah said in a tone that was both resigned and skeptical. She followed Brandon and Alex along a twisting dirt path through a large grove of tall pine trees. "Hey, wait," she complained. "Why are we going this way?"

"It's fastest to go through the forest preserve," Brandon called back to her, stepping over a fallen tree with Alex following right behind him.

"Great," griped Hannah, glancing at her bare legs and flipflops. "I always wanted my own pet tick."

"Wrong time of year for ticks," Brandon yelled back. He was getting really fed up with Hannah's whining. Wickedly, he added, "But you still gotta watch out for snakes."

Hannah jumped slightly, and hurried to catch up with the boys, watching her feet as she did so.

But Alex had already halted to examine a massive and lumpy brown growth on the side of a dead tree trunk. "Look at this, guys," he said. "It's the biggest fungus ever!"

Hannah was unimpressed. "You are such a nerd," she said scathingly. "Come on, nobody else cares . . . Hey, which way did Brandon go?" She peered through the undergrowth, but she couldn't see him.

"That way, I guess," said Alex, gesturing into the woods without looking up.

"Come on, let's go," Hannah said impatiently, grabbing her brother's sleeve and tugging at it.

Ignoring her, he shook her off.

"Okay," she said, pouting. "Please yourself. Just don't blame me if you get lost."

"This isn't exactly a huge forest," Alex muttered, not looking at her. "I'll catch you up in a bit."

Tutting irritably to herself, Hannah carried on traipsing along the dirt pathway. She caught up with Brandon just as the path petered out, leaving them standing in a clearing in the woods.

"Where's Alex got to now?" Hannah said, scratching her nose and turning to glance behind her. All around her were trees, although not just the usual pines. There was an oak, a maple, and a beech, all of which she recognized from her adventures. Do beeches grow in Snipesville? she wondered vaguely.

When she turned back to Brandon, he was gone. She had looked away from him for less than one second.

"Brandon? Brandon?" Hannah called frantically, as she took a few panicked steps, first one way, and then another. She stopped in her tracks, stunned by what had happened. He could not possibly have walked off so quickly. Terrified now, Hannah screamed out his name again, and then started calling for her brother.

But there was no reply from either of them. Only the birdsong broke the silence, and even the birds did not sound the same as they had just moments before. Through the rustling of the leaves in the suddenly chill breeze arose the mournful song of an English wood pigeon, so close in sound to its American cousin the mourning dove, and yet so distinctive. To Hannah, its song could mean only one thing: She was no longer in America.

She started to run. As she stumbled through the woods, she called out desperately for Brandon and Alex, again and again.

Brandon knew he was in England: The trees and the stinging nettles told him that much. Thorns and twigs tore at his legs, but the undergrowth became much sparser as he ran, so he kept pushing forward, hoping to find his way clear, and, with sick heaviness in his stomach, knowing that there was only one explanation, which was no explanation at all.

Alex couldn't help looking in horror at his hands, crying harder all the time. Splashing knee-deep through the swamp, his bare feet sinking into the muck, he was too freaked out by what had happened to him to be afraid of alligators and snakes.

Hannah's clothes weighed her down, and putting her hand to her head, she tore off a ruffled white cap, just as someone crashed through the bushes right in front of her. Screaming, she staggered backwards, and held up her arms to protect herself . . . .

But it was only Brandon, dressed in a white linen shirt, a black cravat, blue knee breeches, and a red vest.

Relieved, Hannah threw her arms around him. "It's happened, hasn't it?" she said, her voice muffled by his shoulder. "Oh my God, I thought I was here by myself. Where's Alex?" She stepped back, and looked around in panic for her brother.

"I don't know," Brandon said despondently. "I've been running around here for about an hour now, and there's no sign of him. I'm just relieved to find you."

Hannah was floored. "An hour? You've already been here an hour? But I just got here! We must have arrived at different times. Alex could be anywhere. And where are we? Is this . . . ?" She didn't want to say it.

"England, probably," Brandon said for her. "Eighteenth century, I'd guess, judging from the clothes. I have no idea exactly where or when, though. Weird."

Hannah gave an exasperated sigh. "Brandon, it's always weird."

"No . . ." he said hesitantly. "I just mean it's weird that we found each other so easily when we arrived an hour apart.

"This is all your fault!" Hannah cried. "I knew we should never have gone to the college. You went there on purpose, trying to make this happen."

"Don't get mad at me, Hannah," said Brandon. "I'm just trying to figure it all out. Like what triggers the time travel, how it happens."

He bit his lip. Then he said slowly, "Honestly? I don't think it made any difference where we were. I think all the signs were there, like the skeleton and the Professor taking us for malaria pills . . . . Anyhow, there's no sense in pointing fingers. Look, Hannah, I hate to say it, and I know you're worried about Alex, but I think we better look after ourselves for now, you and me. It's getting dark, so we need someplace to stay, or else we'll be camping in the woods, and unless there's a full moon, we won't be able to see anything. But Alex will survive. He'll be okay."

Hannah looked at him doubtfully. She was desperately worried about her brother, but with a sinking feeling, she realized that Brandon was right. Daylight was fading, and if they didn't want to spend a cold, damp night in the woods, they had to find shelter soon.

"Do you think the Professor will show up?" she asked quietly.

"Of course," Brandon said with a confidence he didn't feel. "That's probably why she went missing. I bet she's already here."

Hannah said nothing. That wasn't really how time-travel worked: They always arrived back at the same time they had left, so they weren't missed. But she wanted so much to believe what Brandon was saying. Now another thought struck her. "Have we got any money?"

Brandon searched his pocket and, with relief, drew out a small leather pouch filled with coins. Meanwhile, Hannah slipped her hand into a slit in her outer skirt, and felt through several layers of clothing in search of her pocket, before realizing that her pocket was a separate garment. It was strung around her waist between her skirt and petticoat, and from it, she pulled out a purse identical to Brandon's.

"Well, good. Money's always helpful," said Brandon with a grin.

The forest wasn't nearly as deep as they had feared, and within minutes, they had emerged into a field next to a church. "That's a good sign," Brandon said, pointing up to the dark shadow of the steeple. "If there's a church, there's people. There must be a town or village near here."

But there was no town, or even a village, only a miniscule hamlet of five mean cottages clustered at the entrance to the churchyard. A small, bearded old man, wearing a rumpled and dirty white smock and a broad-brimmed black hat, was lolling on a bench outside one of the dwellings, smoking contentedly on a short white clay pipe.

Hannah waved away his smoke with a peevish look, and said, "Excuse me, what year is this?"

Well, that gets to the point, Brandon thought.

The man stared at them, and Brandon worried for a moment that he believed them to be supernatural creatures. But then he cackled and said, "Maid, you are a confused 'un! This here is the year of our Lord seventeen hundred and fifty-two."

Brandon cringed inwardly now that his hunch was confirmed. This was the farthest back in time they had ever traveled.

"Great," Hannah said sarcastically. "And where are we, exactly?"

"This here's the estate belonging to Lord Chatsfield," the man said patiently. Brandon and Hannah exchanged excited looks.

"We're close to Balesworth, then?" Brandon asked, wanting to be sure. If the old man was surprised to meet a strange black kid asking directions, he didn't show it. Instead, with an amused smile, he pointed the way with his pipe, along a dirt track. "T'ain't far. Just follow the path."

Before they set off, Hannah described Alex to the old man, and asked him to direct her brother to Balesworth if he should pass by.

Walking toward the town, Hannah glanced back at the church, which was now silhouetted against the fast-setting sun. "I know that church," she said quietly, with a satisfied smile. "It's St. Swithin's. Mrs. D. and me, we climbed the tower in 1940. That seems like a long time ago now."

"Funny you should say that," said Brandon with a bitter smile. "Because, technically, your climb with Mrs. D. hasn't even happened yet."

The kids had known Balesworth in several incarnations across time. In 1940, it was a small market town. In 1851, it was a rural backwater. And twenty-first century Balesworth was something else again, a bustling medium-sized city.

But Brandon and Hannah were truly astonished by what they saw in 1752. Hannah could only say "Wow . . ." when she clapped eyes on the High Street, the main road that ran through the town.

As night fell, the High Street was thick with coaches and wagons, men on horseback, and heavily-laden people on foot, some tending flocks of sheep and herds of cattle. Traffic trickled off to either side of the road as travelers sought rest for the night. Hannah and Brandon joined the river of people and vehicles, just as a lumbering coach, pulled by a team of horses and packed inside and on top with passengers and luggage, took a sharp left through the great archway of an inn's courtyard.

"Balesworth is a happening place!" Brandon laughed over the noise. "Who'd have guessed it?"

"I know, right?" Hannah agreed with a grin.

She watched in fascination as coaches turned this way and that, left and right, up and down the street, into the courtyards of the various inns. "I guess this explains why Balesworth has so many pubs," she said excitedly. "You know what this means? They didn't start out as pubs! They're, like, hotels."

Brandon sighed heavily and gritted his teeth. "Yay, you. Ten thousand points. I know that. I told you before. Balesworth High Street used to be part of the Great North Road. That's like the freeway is today . . . . I mean, like the freeway in our time." Suddenly, a thought struck him. "Actually, it kind of reminds me of Snipesville. You know, all those old rundown motels we have on Main Street? Snipesville used to be where people stopped on their way to Florida, on the old Highway 301, before the I-95 freeway got built."

Hannah had been proud of figuring out why Balesworth had so many pubs, and she resented Brandon's patronizing tone. "Too much information," she sniffed. "Come on. Let's go check in before they all get full."

As Brandon rushed to keep up with her, Hannah made a beeline for the most brightly lit and grandest inn of all. Candles guttered in every window, and the light drew her like a moth to a flame. She boldly shoved open the heavy wooden door and stepped inside, holding it open for Brandon. But then she halted in the entrance to the bar, feeling very out of place: The room was full of men. The only woman was a barmaid wielding an earthenware beer jug. A few men looked up from their tankards and card games, but nobody seemed surprised to see two young people enter the bar. A cluster of customers sloshed around their drinks as they laughed uproariously at a joke, while an elderly man slowly ambled across the room toward the staircase. A large man sat down heavily in the corner by the fire, then, taking up a paper spill from a container by the fireplace, lit a foot-long white clay pipe.

"This place looks like the Leaky Cauldron," Brandon muttered.

"You got that right," said Hannah. "Except no witches. Only wizards. Hey, where's reception?"

A male servant with a dishtowel slung over his shoulder caught Hannah's eye and hurried over. However, he did not give them a welcoming smile. Instead, he scowled at them, and held up both hands to stop the two of them from coming any farther inside. "Can I help you?" he asked guardedly.

"Yeah, we want to check in," said Hannah.

Abruptly, the servant said, "We don't lodge passengers who arrive on foot." Then he added in a mocking tone, "We cater only to the coach and carriage trade. Did you arrive by coach or private carriage? No? Then get yourselves to the Woolpack Inn, just up the High Street. They cater to those of your rank."

Hannah bridled at him. "We've got money, if that's what's worrying you."

But Brandon put a hand on her arm and said quietly, "Leave it, Hannah. Come on, let's go check out this Woolpack place."

The servant gave them both a haughty stare as Brandon returned outside, reluctantly followed by Hannah.

The Woolpack was not appealing. For one thing, it was obviously filthy: It smelled very, very bad, like unwashed bodies. Cobwebs, dead flies and dirt were scattered about the windowsills and floor. For another, the men in the bar looked rough, and a few of them stared openly at Hannah, making both her and Brandon feel deeply uncomfortable. The kids had no sooner entered the door than they were out again, gulping down fresh air.

"No," Hannah said firmly. "No way are we staying there. That place is scary."

"Fair enough," Brandon said, relieved. "But if the other inns won't take us unless we arrive by coach, what do we do?"

Hannah exhaled noisily. "So we gotta arrive by coach, I guess. Come on, I've got an idea."

She led Brandon by the arm toward a whitewashed pub bearing a sign that announced its name as The Balesworth Arms. Brandon smiled. He already knew this establishment, having visited it in two other centuries. The kids halted a safe distance away, close to the large arched gate to the left of the building.

"Next slow coach that comes along," Hannah muttered, "Let's get right behind it. They're so busy, they won't even see us walk in."

Brandon wasn't so sure, but since he didn't have a better plan, he nodded. He tried not to look conspicuous as he anxiously gazed south along the highway toward London, while Hannah looked northward. Both of them awaited the telltale lurching silhouette of a coach.

They had several false alarms when fast post chaise carriages thundered through town, but within minutes, a slow coach lumbered up the street. Fortunately for Hannah and Brandon, the passenger seating on the roof was empty, and so no one spotted the two of them speed walking right behind the coach as it trundled into the Balesworth Arms' courtyard.

The moment after vehicle and kids passed through the gates, the big black-painted doors slowly swung closed, pushed by two young stable lads wearing smocks. With their backs to Hannah and Brandon, the boys busied themselves latching and bolting the doors for the night, while the coachman supervised the ostlers as they unharnessed the horses. The coach's passengers, meanwhile, gathered their hand luggage and disembarked, looking as relieved to be on the ground as any air traveler in the twenty-first century.

Brandon and Hannah tried hard to look like they fit in while they hovered on the edges of the activity. Nobody paid them any attention.

At the side courtyard entrance to the Balesworth Arms, a very fat and tall man in his late fifties was standing with legs planted firmly apart. From beneath his slightly-askew white wig, he smiled genially at the newly-arrived passengers, all of whom were respectably-dressed men.

"Welcome to Balesworth, gentlemen," the innkeeper boomed cheerfully, stretching his arms wide in greeting. "My name is Jenkins, and as landlord of this house, I bid you a warm welcome to the Balesworth Arms. Be so good as to step this way. My servants will direct you to your quarters, and then serve you a fine dinner of choicest steak."

Nervous, and expecting to be busted at any minute, Hannah and Brandon followed the passengers inside, while the servants continued to unpack luggage from the coach. As the guests passed through the doorway, a maidservant stationed in the hall glanced at their feet, then handed each of them a pair of slippers from a large basket.

Hannah and Brandon accepted the slippers offered them, and then sat on a wooden bench in the hall, and fiddled with removing their street shoes. Both struggled with the unfamiliar buckles, and with fitting into the slippers, which were too small in Brandon's case, and too large in Hannah's. While the maid helped them find better-suited footwear from her basket, they heard a woman's voice greeting the guests.

"Good evening, gentlemen," said the voice. "I am Mrs. Jenkins, and I am gratified to be of service to you. Our servants will deliver your luggage to your respective rooms, and I invite you all to inspect our accommodations before dinner, should you wish to do so."

When Hannah and Brandon finally found and put on satisfactory slippers, they stood up to get a look at Mrs. Jenkins. She was a tall, dignified woman in her mid-fifties, wearing a long blue dress, a white bonnet, and a plain white apron tied around her waist. She was also the spitting image of Mrs. Devenish, their foster mother in World War Two Balesworth. Their mouths fell open.

Hannah loudly blurted out, "Mrs. D!"

The room instantly fell silent, and at that moment, everyone also clearly heard Brandon's angry whisper of "Shut up, Hannah!"

Mrs. Jenkins shot the kids a startled look, but she quickly gathered her wits, cleared her throat, and continued with her welcome speech.

Hannah, meanwhile, was gazing at her in fascination. As the guests began to shuffle toward the staircase behind Mrs. Jenkins, Hannah turned excitedly to Brandon. "Oh, my God, Brandon. That's the woman in the picture Verity sent me! I'm sure of it!"

"Either that," said Brandon, "Or a lot of Brits look alike, and it's one big fat coincidence. But I think you're right. You know," he added with a grin, "it's very helpful that she's here. This must be where we're supposed to be. We always seem to end up with a member of Verity's family."

"Hmm," said Hannah absentmindedly. "But how can we afford to live in a hotel? I'm not even sure we can stay for one night."

As the passengers tromped upstairs, Hannah and Brandon followed. At the landing, Mrs. Jenkins directed Brandon to a room, which he was discomfited to realize that he would be sharing with strangers. To Hannah, she said kindly, "Since you are the only female traveler, you shall have a room all to yourself." Then she opened a door, and bid Hannah enter.

As Hannah stepped forward, Mrs. Jenkins lightly laid a hand on her arm. "You do remind me of someone, my dear," she said with a kindly smile.

Hannah was unnerved. "I don't really think we know each other," she replied awkwardly.

"No," sighed Mrs. Jenkins. "I suppose 'tis just a curious happenstance. Please accept my apologies."

Their tour of the Balesworth Arms complete, Brandon, Hannah, and the other guests returned to the dining room, at the center of which sat a large oak table. At the head of the table stood Mr. Jenkins, who smiled heartily at the guests. "You arrive in good time for a fine repast," he announced. "For recompense of only two shillings, I am pleased to offer you steaks of your choosing from the fireplace, with carrots and roasted potatoes, to be followed by plum pudding and choicest Cheddar cheese. Mrs. Jenkins will now show you to the kitchen, there to select your steaks."

Two shillings seemed reasonable to Brandon, but he overheard a pair of passengers grousing about the outrageous cost of the meal. One of them asked Mr. Jenkins whether there was a tavern in Balesworth where he might seek a cheaper supper. Mr. Jenkins's reply was a stony-faced "No."

Most of the passengers, however, were too hungry to argue over the price, and the kitchen smelled temptingly delicious. Slabs of meat sizzled on racks over the coal fire. Some steaks were barely browned, some had turned to shoe leather, but still others looked perfectly done. The would-be diners jostled each other as they lined up, craning their necks to spot the best-looking steaks. Once they were handed plates and cutlery, they took turns spearing steaks and lifting them from the fire, using their two-pronged forks. When Brandon reached the front of the line, he chose a filet with heavy grid marks on it, and he prodded it to be sure it was done before spearing it and lifting it onto his pewter plate.

While the guests trickled back to the table, two servants stood by to offer steaming bowls of vegetables. Hannah sat down, and the maid immediately leaned over her shoulder, and deposited a heap of piping-hot golden-brown roasted potatoes on her plate. They smelled wonderful. However, the carrots which the young waiter served her were not so appealing: They were so over-cooked and waterlogged that they were practically liquid. But when she turned to complain, the boy had moved on to another guest.

Shrugging, she cut into her steak. It was rare and bloody, and she recoiled. She turned to Brandon and whined about it until, to shut her up, he finally offered to swap meats with her, an offer she happily accepted.

Brandon, rolling his eyes at Hannah's pickiness, tasted the coffee, and grimaced. He decided that it was not coffee at all. It was a sort of warm brown liquid, and that was where its resemblance to coffee ended. He pushed it aside, and asked the manservant for a glass of water. When he got only an incredulous look in return, he pulled the coffee back in front of him.

A man sitting opposite took a large bite of potato, and chased it down with a gulp of alleged coffee. Then he turned his attention to Hannah and Brandon. "You weren't on our coach," he said firmly through a mouthful of food, looking Hannah in the eye. Shocked, Hannah silently appealed to Brandon for help.

Unlike Hannah, Brandon had presence of mind. He said casually, "No, I don't think we met you before. We arrived on a coach about an hour ago. We went to have a look at the horses in the stables, so we missed our time for supper." The man seemed satisfied with that explanation, and returned his attention to his food.

The meal otherwise passed without incident. Toward the end, as some guests cleaned their plates with chunks of white bread, others started to drift toward the bar, or upstairs to their rooms. Soon, Hannah and Brandon were alone. They tucked into their desserts, sweet and hot plum pudding, darkly thick with dried fruit and spicy with cinnamon and nutmeg.

Just as they scraped the last crumbs from their pewter bowls, Mrs. Jenkins stalked out of the kitchen, making straight for the kids. She put her hands on the table, and leaned over them threateningly. "Whence came you?" she demanded loudly.

Brandon, shocked, gulped as he instinctively shrank back from the angry old woman. "About an hour ago," he said.

Mrs. Jenkins shook her head impatiently. "I asked you whence, not when. From where did you enter this inn?"

He tried to look truthful while Hannah stared at the floor. "On a coach," he said.

"You did not," the landlady snapped, thumping the table with her fist. "None of my other guests saw you."

"Not the same coach as the others," Hannah said quickly. "An earlier one."

The landlady arched an eyebrow at her. "One of the gentlemen said that he saw you join their company on foot after they disembarked. Now, give me good reason why I ought not to take a broom and chase you from my premises."

"We've got money," Brandon said, holding up his purse. "We can pay."

Mrs. Jenkins took the pouch from his outstretched hand, peered inside, then shook out a couple of silver coins and held them up. "I will take two florins for your dinner. Now be off with you."

Hannah burst into tears. She was so tired, and so frightened of having nowhere to stay except the scary, smelly inn down the street.

Mrs. Jenkins was a tough woman, but she was not cruel, and Hannah's breakdown softened her. She took in their anxious faces, looked once again into Brandon's purse, and removed more money, and showed it to them. "You may remain tonight," she said firmly. "And be gone on the morrow."

They nodded. Hannah wiped her eyes, but she still looked as miserable as she felt.

Brandon and Alex had always argued that the Professor would protect them from serious harm while they traveled in time.

Hannah had always thought that they were both seriously naive. And where, she thought, was their precious Professor now? But she was not glad to have been proved right.

On this night, Hannah lay on her bed, fretting in the dark. Mrs. Jenkins had made a big deal about giving her a single room, but the room had turned out to be the size of a closet. Hannah, having lived in crowded conditions on other adventures, wasn't too surprised. Regardless of the room size, she was depressed.

Random thoughts flitted by: her misery at Snipes Academy . . . how much she hated Snipesville . . . how much she missed San Francisco . . . her mother . . . her mother's death . . . her mother again, ignoring Hannah . . . how much she hated San Francisco . . . The thoughts were becoming more and more painful, and Hannah rubbed at her face, as though she were trying to rub clean her mind.

She tried to recall happy memories: shopping with her grandma in London . . . going with Grandma to Starbucks in Sacramento . . . baking scones with Mrs. Devenish in 1940 . . . watching movies with Verity . . . The terrible sadness of saying goodbye to Mrs. Devenish . . . The Professor has disappeared, and so has Alex. *What am I going to do?*

Hannah angrily rearranged her feather pillow, and tried to settle, but all she could think about was Alex, the Professor, her mother, and losing Mrs. D. Finally, she could stand it no longer, and burst into tears.

The night stretched out before her, full of visions, nightmares, dread, and phantoms. Curling up in the cold bed, she sobbed in despair.

Hannah awoke the next morning to the raucous sound of a young woman's angry shouts, followed by a slamming door. Bleary-eyed, she opened the heavy drape, and peeked outside, just in time to catch sight of a girl storming out of the building, then turning back only to hurl more insults at someone standing in the doorway.

Curious about this drama, and hungry for breakfast, she dressed quickly and ran downstairs. Brandon sat alone at the table eating a simple meal of bread and butter with the inn's awful coffee. Hannah took the seat across from him.

"What was that about?" she asked, reaching for a cut slice of bread. "All that yelling?"

After taking a swig of coffee then wiping his mouth on his hand, Brandon explained. "The maid had a big falling-out with Mrs. Jenkins. She just quit, said she was going home to her parents' farm. From what she said, Mrs. Jenkins kind of nags a lot." He grinned. "Sound familiar?"

"Oh, yeah," said Hannah, smiling. "Reminds me of Mrs. D., of course. I guess being a naggy old bat runs in the family." She felt better now. At least she had Brandon for company. She picked up the breadknife and began to saw herself another slice.

But then she stopped, furrowed her brow, and laid down the knife. She had an idea. Scraping back her chair on the flagstone floor, she jumped up and slipped into the kitchen, where Mrs. Jenkins was supervising preparation of the midday meal.

"Excuse me? Mrs. Jenkins?" Hannah said brightly. "I hear you need a new maid?"

Mrs. Jenkins looked at her skeptically. "You?"

"Yeah, me," said Hannah, feeling slightly insulted. Talking quickly, she went on, "I've got experience, okay? I worked as a chambermaid."

Mrs. Jenkins looked carefully at Hannah. There was a long pause. Finally she said decisively, "You may work on trial. If your work is pleasing, you may stay on. What is your name?"

"Hannah," she replied. "Hannah Dias . . . I mean, Hannah Day."

Hannah Day, the closest thing in English to her Portuguese last name, was always what she went by in the England of the past, a much less diverse place than the England of the present. Using an English name saved awkward questions.

"Very well, Hannah Day," said Mrs. Jenkins. "You will take the maidservant's room upstairs." Her eyes twinkled. "Only be sure to watch out for Jack Platt."

Hannah was puzzled by the warning. "Jack who?"

"Our ghost," said Mrs. Jenkins, putting her hands on her hips. "They say he was murdered in his bed by his traveling companion, and on occasion he appears in the maidservant's room, wringing his hands and begging for help. Sometimes, he only shakes the maid awake, and then disappears."

Hannah rolled her eyes. "Whatever. Hey, do you have a job for my friend Brandon, too?"

"No, I do not," Mrs. Jenkins barked, irritated by Hannah's lack of gratitude. "I require only the services of a maid."

When Hannah's face fell, the landlady relented a little. She sighed. "But I will allow your friend to remain on the premises until he finds a new master. However, he must sleep in the hayloft, above the stables. Balesworth is very busy at this time of year, and a position may present itself at one of the inns, if he does but enquire about town."

Hannah grinned, and almost hugged Mrs. Jenkins. But then she thought better of it, and instead she dashed off to tell Brandon the good news. Life was looking up again.

In the bleak small hours of the next morning, Hannah was dragged from bed by a powerful force. But her assailant wasn't the ghostly Jack Platt. It was Mrs. Jenkins who ripped away the blanket in which Hannah had wrapped herself, and who pulled her upright by the arm.

"Rise, you lazy little miss," the landlady cried cheerfully, her gray hair flying from beneath her cap as she yanked Hannah to her feet. "Robert knocked on your door a quarter of an hour ago. See and you be downstairs in the next two minutes, or I shall come and fetch you." She left the tiny room, and Hannah heard her shoes on the stairs.

Groggily, Hannah pulled her petticoat, pocket, and skirt over her shift, and crammed her feet into her leather shoes. Glancing outside through a gap in the curtains, she saw that it was barely dawn, and she shuddered.

Hannah found Mrs. Jenkins in the kitchen, expertly slicing a huge hunk of raw ham with an enormous knife. She nodded to Hannah and said, "Know you how to cook?"

There was no point in lying. Hannah shook her head.

Mrs. Jenkins didn't seem at all surprised. She laid down her knife and wiped her greasy hands on her apron. "Very well, you shall learn from me," she said, in a tone that did not invite argument. "You can help me make the breakfast."

First, Mrs. Jenkins had Hannah collect bread dough from a cupboard next to the fireplace, where it was rising under a towel. They set about making rolls. Mrs. Jenkins demonstrated how to squeeze a fistful of dough between thumb and forefinger to produce a perfect bubble of bread. But when Hannah tried to make all the rolls exactly the same size, her mistress accused her of wasting time. Hannah couldn't help wondering where she had got the idea that all rolls should be exactly the same? Then again, she didn't think she had ever eaten a homemade roll. Maybe she was just too used to the ones from the supermarket.

Over the next hour Hannah cooked goopy oatmeal in a massive black cauldron, and carved a large chunk of boiled beef. It made her nervous to wield a huge knife, even though she followed Mrs. Jenkins' instructions precisely.

Still, when breakfast was ready for the serving boy to carry into the dining room, Hannah felt strangely proud. This job, she thought, was shaping up to be pretty cool. And working with Mrs. Jenkins was wonderful: Her mistress knew so much about cooking, and she was a patient tutor. Best of all, she was warm and attentive toward Hannah, and that made Hannah happy.

And then Hannah remembered that nothing made sense, nothing at all.

Why were she and Brandon here? Why was Mrs. Jenkins acting so kindly to a pair of strangers? Brandon had already asked that question. "We're lucky," he had told her. "This is a brutal time in English history. There are lots of desperate unemployed people wandering around, lots of crime, and people don't trust strangers. Mrs. Jenkins is a pretty special lady."

Why, Hannah wondered, would Mrs. Jenkins trust her?

Despite Mrs. Jenkins's prediction, Brandon did not find work that day, even though he visited every business in Balesworth. When Hannah visited him in the stables that evening, she found him exhausted and discouraged.

"No luck?" she asked, plopping herself next to him on a pile of dry and crunchy straw.

He shook his head, drew his knees up to his chin, and grunted, "Nah."

Hannah looked at him with sympathy. "Are people being racist at you?"

He shrugged. "Probably. Maybe. Thing is, nobody who sees me seems surprised to see a black person, even though everyone in this town is white. They all say they don't have any jobs going right now, but it doesn't seem personal." He felt uneasy, but he wasn't sure why. People had acted so normally toward him this time around, it was bizarre. In his past time-travels to England, his skin color had made him a novelty.

Hannah changed the subject, and told him about her day, and how she and Mrs. Jenkins had got along so well. Then, suddenly, she slapped her forehead.

"Oh my gosh, I almost forgot to tell you. Mrs. Jenkins says the . . . what did she call him? . . . like, the vicar . . . anyway, the guy up at the church, whatever you call him, he's looking for a servant. It's worth checking out. Except . . ."

"Yeah," Brandon interrupted wearily. "I'll stop by tomorrow."

Hannah shook her head. "No, let me tell you something first. Listen to this. He's interviewed almost every servant in town, and they all turned him down."

"Maybe they're pickier than me," said Brandon, running his fingers through the straw.

"Not exactly," she said. "They just don't want to go to America with him."

At the mention of America, Brandon abruptly sat up straight, and his eyes connected with Hannah's.

"Hannah, don't you see?" he said excitedly. "This is my sign to go. This is always how it seems to happen. When we're supposed to do something in the past, we just know. Maybe we don't even need the Professor to tell us what to do. Don't you get a funny feeling inside when you have to make a big decision while we're time-traveling?"

"Yes . . ." she said reluctantly. "Yes, I do. But what will happen to me if you leave, Brandon?"

He beamed an encouraging smile at her. "You'll be fine," he said. "We'll both be fine."

"Says you," said Hannah crossly.

The church was a typically English stone building, beautiful and ancient, but it was oddly situated on the far outskirts of town. Standing in the drafty stone porch, Brandon gingerly pushed at the great wooden door, opening it with a very loud creak.

Inside, it was profoundly silent. It had a musty smell. But the church was well lit, for this was a sunny day, and bright rays poured into the interior through the plain glass windows. It did not look like it had in 1940. Now, in 1752, most of the pews were enclosed on four sides by low wooden walls, forming boxes in which the congregation would sit.

Brandon crept into the aisle, nervously looking about him. Suddenly, a booming voice rang out from on high, saying "Is it me whom you seek?"

Brandon's first thought was that God was speaking to him, and he squeaked in fright. But the voice actually came from a man in his twenties who was stationed high up in the wineglass-shaped pulpit. He wore a black academic gown, a short white wig, and a very serious expression on his face.

"Hi, Vicar, sorry to bother you," said Brandon breezily, relieved to see the very mortal young man who was descending the steps.

"I am not the vicar," the man replied haughtily, "And I am certainly not the rector. I am merely the curate, and my name is Mr. Osborn. Now, how may I be of service?"

"You're the preacher, right, sir?" Brandon wondered why Mr. Osborn had made a big deal out of his job title: Whatever he was called, he was obviously a pastor.

Mr. Osborn nodded. "I preach from the pulpit here at St. Swithin's, yes," he said.

"Great," said Brandon. "Well, I hear you need a servant. I'm Brandon Clark, and I want to apply for the job."

Mr. Osborn brightened. "I do, I do indeed need a servant. Come, let us repair to the vestry, and we shall talk. Your name is Brandon, did you say?"

In the tiny office, Mr. Osborn pushed back on his gown with a great billowing flourish, as he took his place at a small desk. He did not invite Brandon to sit down.

As the curate shuffled a few papers laid out in front of him, looking for something, Brandon glanced around the room. High on the wall, he could see graffiti: deeply scratched writing in some language he didn't understand, and a crude drawing of a man's face, framed with leaves.

Mr. Osborn exclaimed in satisfaction as he picked up a folded letter with a broken blob of red sealing wax on the back. He flourished the letter at Brandon. "I have recently received this license from His Grace the Bishop of London. It authorizes me to bring the word of Christ to His Majesty's Colony in Georgia. Brandon, this is a high honor, and I flatter myself that His Grace was impressed by the book I wrote, an inscribed copy of which I had the honor of presenting to him some months ago . . ."

Just as Brandon started to wonder why Mr. Osborn was telling him all this, he realized he had just heard the magic word: Georgia.

Then a terrible thought struck him, and his hopes deflated.

"I'm sorry, Reverend, but I can't go to Georgia," he said apologetically. "They would make me a slave."

Mr. Osborn laughed. "No, no, foolish boy. Of course they would not. Only negroes are slaves."

Brandon was baffled. "But, sir, beg pardon, I'm a, um, negro." It felt weird using that old-fashioned word, almost like he was insulting himself.

Mr. Osborn smiled indulgently, shaking his head at Brandon's foolishness. He stood, and opened a closet in which his vestments hung, to reveal a small mirror. He beckoned to Brandon to stand before it, and then stood behind him with his hands on Brandon's shoulders. Brandon gasped at the reflection of his face. A strange pale boy stared back at him. A white boy.

Chapter 3:
CHANGING COLORS

A boy with blond hair, blue eyes, and freckles gazed out from the mirror. Brandon was so freaked out, he thought it was a trick. He touched the boy's face to see if it really was a reflection. As his hand slid across the hard glass, he saw that his fingers were still black, while the mirror showed white skin. He felt his guts dissolve.

Meanwhile, Mr. Osborn was rambling on, although Brandon could scarcely begin to take in what he was saying. "So, you comprehend, those poor unfortunate creatures known by the name of 'negro' are former inhabitants of Africa, and it is their lot in life to be enslaved on the plantations of America. However, their souls are as eternal as yours and mine, and it is within our power to lead them to Christ. And so I intend to minister to those unfortunate creatures in my parish in America."

Mr. Osborn continued to hold forth on his plans to bring Christianity to slaves while Brandon, shaking, stared at the mirror. Finally, the curate realized that his sermon was falling on deaf ears. "Come away from the looking glass," he said irritably. "I offer you a great opportunity, Brandon. The Government will pay your passage, for they are desirous of white settlers, lest Georgia become a place of slaves only. You see, the Board of Trustees of Georgia first declared slavery to be against the law, but they rescinded their decision two years ago. Now that slavery is legal, slaves have poured into the colony. Therefore the Government has agreed to offer recompense to any who bring white servants with them to restore the balance. I will use that compensation to pay your passage. In return, you will work on my land for five years thereafter, and thenceforth you would be in good stead to become a landowner yourself in the colony. What say you?"

Brandon was not listening at all. He was staring at his new face. "Yeah, um, great," he muttered faintly. "I'll take it."

Mr. Osborn's eyebrows shot up. He had not expected the boy to agree so readily. Every other young person he had interviewed had politely refused him, or even laughed at his plans. They had told him that while the free land sounded good, America was a savage country, only reachable by a perilous sea voyage. Yet this boy made no objections. Perhaps he was an idiot? Or perhaps he had some reason to wish to flee the country?

Mr. Osborn plowed on. "I shall need to speak with a man who will attest to your good character. Will your former master be pleased to speak with me if I should correspond with him?"

"Huh?" Brandon said. He could not take his eyes off the mirror, and the stranger's face that stared back at him.

Mr. Osborn sighed heavily. Apparently, the boy *was* an idiot. He stepped forward, and firmly turned Brandon around to face him. "One would think that you had never cast eyes upon a looking-glass before."

Now, Brandon came to his senses. "That's . . . That's right, sir," he stammered. "I've never seen a mirror before. I've only seen my reflection in ponds and things."

"Come," said Mr. Osborn impatiently, moving back to the desk. "We must attend to your employment ere the day is ended. Let us make haste." He picked up a sheet of paper and a stubby quill pen with all its feathering stripped away, and pulled the cork stopper from a tiny glass ink bottle.

While Mr. Osborn wrote, Brandon remembered Hannah. "The thing is," he said tentatively, "I have this cousin, and she has to come with me. She would be a lot of help to you. She's got a bunch of experience as a maid, and she's working at the Balesworth Arms right now. I can't go to America without her."

Mr. Osborn looked conflicted. "It would be very expensive for me to bring another servant to Georgia . . . . But I suppose my wife could make use of a girl to help her. Does your cousin know anything of cookery?"

Brandon nodded frantically and said, "She's an awesome cook, and she loves kids." This was a total lie. So far as Brandon was aware, Hannah hated babies and barely knew how to make toast.

Despite Brandon's enthusiasm, Mr. Osborn hesitated. "I must needs think this over. As I said, it would be expensive. Now, to the present. You will return on the morrow to begin work. Do you know where to find my house? No? Then meet me here at the church at ten of the clock, and I shall lead you there."

When Brandon arrived back at the Balesworth Arms, he found Hannah in the kitchen, squatting on a three-legged wooden stool, and clumsily peeling a potato over a large wooden tub half-filled with dirty brown water. Muddy potatoes were piled next to her. As she finished peeling the spud, she dropped it into the tub with a splash.

"Well, peeling potatoes sucks," she said by way of greeting. She held up her knife and potato to show Brandon the filthy rag tied around her thumb.

He smiled. "Good to see you too, Hannah. What happened to your hand?"

"Cut myself," she said matter-of-factly. "No big."

Brandon was astonished that, for once, she didn't try to milk sympathy from him. He wondered if the real Hannah had been kidnapped by space aliens, and he smiled.

"You look tired," he said conversationally.

"Yeah, I am," Hannah sighed. "I'm not sleeping too well. Mrs. Jenkins keeps going on about this ghost in my room, and it's creeping me out."

"Ghost?" Brandon repeated, alarmed.

Hannah smiled at his reaction, mistaking it for mockery. "Yeah, I know it's kind of silly, but she has me totally freaked. I guess this ghost likes to wake up the maid and tell her his problems."

"Oh, I get it. A ghost with issues," Brandon said. "At least he's not dangerous. Have you seen him yet?"

Hannah looked at him crossly. "'Course not. No such thing as ghosts, right?"

"Oh, there aren't, huh?" said Brandon. "Then why are you so freaked out?"

She scooped up a handful of dirty potato water and hurled it at him. "Shut UP," she cried, laughing. "Anyway, what's up with you?"

He took a seat on the chair next to her. "A lot. Listen to this."

By the time Brandon finished telling Hannah about the white boy in the mirror, she was shocked. "That's bizarre . . . ." she said.

"No more bizarre than anything else that happens to us," said Brandon. "It's still weird to me that we talk normally, but *they* hear us talking like them, with British accents and all."

"Yeah," Hannah said slowly. "You know, I've been thinking . . . ."

"There's a first time for everything," Brandon said with a sly grin.

"Oh, *ha ha*, Mr. Thinks-He's-A-Comedian," said Hannah. "No, listen. I don't know if it's the Professor, though I think it is, but *somebody* is *so* controlling what happens to us."

Brandon's face fell. "Maybe it's the Lord," he said solemnly.

Hannah tutted at him, and rolled her eyes. "It's all Jesus with you Southerners, isn't it?" she said peevishly.

"That's offensive," muttered Brandon.

"Whatever," said Hannah, scraping at a potato to hide her embarrassment at what she had said. "Look, Brandon, whether it's the Professor, or God, or whoever, someone's making these things happen to us, like, pulling the strings."

"You're not saying anything we haven't said a million times," said Brandon sharply. "What about it?"

"I don't know," Hannah said, throwing the peeled potato into the water. "It just bothers me. I have so many questions, but there's nobody to ask, not even That Woman."

Brandon sighed heavily. "Have you got any leads on what's happened to her and Alex?"

She frowned and shook her head. "What, you seriously think I wouldn't have told you the moment you walked in? Honestly? I haven't asked anyone about That Woman, and there's no sign of my brother. Every time Mrs. Jenkins sends me out shopping, I look for Alex, and I ask people, but nothing. I hope he's okay."

"We all survived on our own before," Brandon said gently.

"I guess so," said Hannah. "But I'm starting to feel like we're not going to get out of this one alive."

"Come on, cheer up," Brandon said. "You're just being superstitious. Tell me how things are going here." As soon as he said that, he regretted it. What was there to like about the dirty work in an inn, he asked himself?

But Hannah surprised him again. "It's cool," she said perkily. "I mean, the work's pretty heavy sometimes, but I've been learning loads from Mrs. Jenkins about cooking and stuff."

"You're enjoying *cooking lessons*?" Brandon was incredulous.

"Yeah, why not?" Hannah said defensively. "Mrs. Jenkins is a great teacher, and she's pretty nice in a grumpy kind of way."

Brandon grinned. "She reminds you of Mrs. Devenish, doesn't she?" he said slyly. "She pays attention to you like Mrs. D. did."

Hannah scowled and looked away, but Brandon continued to scrutinize her with a knowing smile. Embarrassed, she muttered, "Nothing wrong with that," then scraped furiously at a potato with her knife.

Now it was Brandon's turn to feel a pang of conscience for having given his friend a hard time. It was unlike Hannah to admit that she desperately craved attention from adults, and he knew that this was the closest she had ever come to confiding in him. He also knew it was only fair to change the subject. "Hannah, there's something else you need to know," he said. "My new boss, Mr. Osborn? He's not just planning to move to America. He's planning to move to *Georgia*, and he's taking me with him."

With a sharp intake of breath, Hannah dropped her potato knife in the water. "What? Can I go with you?"

"I don't know," Brandon said uncomfortably, idly scratching at his palm. "I already asked, and he's thinking about it. If he won't take you, we need to find a way to raise the cash so we can buy you a ticket. I bet it costs a lot."

But Hannah had another concern. "What about Alex? We can't just leave him here."

Brandon bit his lip. "Hannah, face it, he's not here," he said. "He could be anywhere. He might never have left Snipesville. We just have to hope for the best."

"I guess," Hannah said uncertainly.

Brandon leaned over and touched her hand. Immediately, she drew away from him, and he was mortified. "Sorry," he said quickly, "I just wanted to . . ."

"It's okay," she said, pushing up her sleeve and reaching into the tub to pull out her paring knife.

"So," Brandon said, speaking quickly, "How much does Mrs. Jenkins pay you?"

"Not enough," Hannah replied, throwing aside a potato peel. "Looks like we're gonna have to win the lottery to pay for my ticket to Georgia. If there is a lottery in 1752."

The next morning, Brandon showed up at St. Swithin's Church promptly. Mr. Osborn put on his long black coat, and crammed a broad-brimmed hat over his wig. Then the two of them started the journey to his house. They strolled briskly toward Balesworth along a dirt trail through the fields. Soon after they left the church, horse chestnut trees lined their path on either side. Brandon felt a pleasant shock of recognition. He had traveled along this footpath in three other centuries, and it brought back very fond memories.

As they walked, Mr. Osborn prattled about religion, about life at Cambridge University, and about his frustrated ambitions for a career in the Church of England. Occasionally, he paused to draw breath, or to ask Brandon a question. But when Brandon tried to answer, the curate simply carried on speaking over him.

Suddenly, Brandon noticed that Mr. Osborn had lapsed into silence, and that he was nodding toward a cottage that lay ahead of them. With a quiver of excitement, Brandon recognized it. He had known this house in other centuries, and as Verity Powell's home in his own time.

Eagerly, he followed his new boss up the short garden path. But then he came to a sudden halt, and Mr. Osborn turned to see what the matter was.

"I just thought of something, sir," Brandon said anxiously. "Do you have any kids?"

Mr. Osborn shook his head. "Not yet," he replied with a puzzled look. "Why do you ask, pray?"

"No reason," Brandon said, a little too quickly. He found it hard to disguise his relief that, for the first time in all his adventures, he wouldn't be playing babysitter to anyone.

The cottage wasn't large, but its lack of furnishings made it seem spacious inside. Mrs. Osborn, a lean, dark-haired, and pretty but serious-looking young woman, entered the hall from the kitchen, lugging a wicker basket of apples. She set it down on the floor and rubbed her aching back, while nodding to Mr. Osborn. He smiled in greeting, and then introduced her to Brandon. Brandon stared openly at her slightly swollen belly. Was she pregnant? He got a sinking feeling that his babysitting days were not over, after all.

"Brandon will work in the house and garden, carry messages, and prepare for our removal," Mr. Osborn told his wife. "Perhaps he may begin now by assisting you."

Mrs. Osborn didn't hesitate. She gave a curt nod, and heaving up the apple basket, she shoved it at her new servant. "Here, Brandon," she said. "I intended to take these to Mrs. Reynolds. You will find her on the High Street at the sign of the green man. Tell her that these are the fruit I promised her from our trees."

The errand took Brandon the rest of the morning, because he couldn't figure out where he was supposed to go. It was a while before he realized that "the sign of the green man" referred to a pub called the Green Man. But at last, he found it: A crudely-painted human face surrounded by branches and leaves painted on a sign swung over his head outside a tavern on the High Street.

Mrs. Reynolds was a jolly-faced stout woman who was evidently pleased to receive her gift of small red-tinged green apples. She offered one to Brandon, along with a glass of milk, and he gladly accepted them both. A thin layer of cream floated on top of the milk. When he tasted it, he found it was slightly warm, but not unpleasant. He wondered whether the milk had come directly from the cow, then decided it would be better not to think about that.

As Mrs. Reynolds busied herself peeling carrots, Brandon remembered now where he had seen an image of the Green Man before. It was scratched into the wall of the vestry in St. Swithin's Church. "Mrs. Reynolds? What is a Green Man?" he asked.

She looked up at him. "Oh, now, he's what we used to call Jack o' the Green. My grandmother always said that the Green Man lived in the woods, and that it was best not to disturb him."

"Creepy," muttered Brandon, sipping his milk.

"You might say that," said Mrs. Reynolds, tossing a peeled carrot into a basin of water. "I have always thought so. Indeed, I have never cared to walk through the woods since I was but a girl. A strange place it is, away from the company of men. An unholy place."

Something about the way she said that made Brandon shiver.

Brandon returned to the Osborns' house just before noon, and right in time for dinner, the main meal of the day. Mr. and Mrs. Osborn were already seated in the kitchen, at a large table that Brandon knew well. He almost laughed when he first saw it, because it was the very same table that Verity was still using in the house in the twenty-first century.

He did not, however, recognize the huge fireplace: He supposed that it must have been bricked up sometime in the future. Now, however, in 1752, it was very much in use. A small coal fire burned in the hearth, over which was hanging a black cauldron on a chain, and a long horizontal metal spit that shone with blackened grease. The air was richly perfumed with the tantalizing smell of cooked meat, rising from a golden pork roast that sat temptingly on the table.

Mr. Osborn carved the roast, and Mrs. Osborn served each of them a small portion of pork. Brandon noticed that his own portion was *very* small. They all helped themselves to boiled potatoes, stewed apples, and thick slices of white bread. Brandon took up a small knife, and cut off some butter from the rough-pat yellow round, then slathered it on his bread slice. He had loved real farm-made butter since he had first encountered it on his adventures: Unlike the stuff his mom bought at the supermarket in the twenty-first century, it actually had flavor. He was about to sink his teeth into his lavishly buttered bread, when Mr. Osborn caught his eye and frowned at him.

Sheepishly, Brandon set down his bread, folded his hands, and bowed his head. He was ashamed to have been caught by surprise: His family in Snipesville always said a blessing before meals. In his own defense, he thought, he had rarely heard anyone say grace during his travels in time.

When the prayer ended, Brandon picked up his clay mug and sipped his juice. Except that it wasn't juice. It was beer. Hurriedly, he put it down again. Watching Mr. Osborn take a drink from his own tankard, Brandon marveled yet again at how even religious Brits had no problem with alcohol. He smiled as he thought of his preacher at First African Baptist Church of Snipesville, and what he would say if he saw a clergyman supping booze.

Mr. Osborn mistook Brandon's sly grin for an interest in hearing him talk. "You arrive in good time," he said in his usual self-important fashion. "We must prepare for our departure. On Friday, we make our way to Gravesend, and wait upon the ship that will carry us to Georgia. I am told that a splendid parish awaits me there. It lies upon the frontiers of English settlement, and some miles inland from the town of Savannah. But a fine church has already been built by the subscription of numerous godly men of the parish. They are English planters who are impatient to hear the word of God. I am certain that they will welcome me into their midst as a man of the Church of England, the one true faith. You see, Brandon, the need for clergy is great in a land where our countrymen are surrounded by nonconformists, papists, heathen, infidels, and all manner of godlessness."

Listening to this rant, Brandon wondered silently whether Baptists like himself were considered nonconformists, papists, heathens or infidels, whatever any of those words meant. He wasn't entirely sure about any of them, but it was pretty obvious that Mr. Osborn considered them all bad.

"But what I most look forward to," Mr. Osborn continued as he speared a chunk of pork on his fork, "is bringing the word of God to the piteous negro slaves, who are in greatest need of His divine grace. I hear that the poor creatures are used most grievously by their masters, and I shall bring all my authority as rector to bear in their defense."

Brandon was pleased and impressed to hear that Mr. Osborn was opposed to slavery. Until now, he had found the curate self-obsessed and totally annoying, so this was a welcome glimpse of another side of his character.

But Mr. Osborn spoiled the moment by returning to his favorite subject: Himself. Between bites of food, he told his life story, in a tone of hurt self-pity. "I am from a great family of genteel clergymen," he said to Brandon in subdued tones. "My father is a gentleman, as was my grandfather. And so I naturally expected that, upon my graduation from Christ's College, Cambridge University, His Grace the Bishop would bestow a living upon me, and appoint me as rector of a generous parish."

Brandon was now confused, and he interrupted. "Sir, what do you mean by a living?"

Mr. Osborn bestowed a patronizing smile upon his servant. "The men of every parish give their rector a handsome income, which we call a living," he said. "However, rectors are gentlemen and so, of course, they do not labor. They employ lesser clergy to do the church's work in the parish."

A light went on in Brandon's head. He remembered reading somewhere that the original meaning of "gentleman" was a man who was rich enough not to need to work.

Mr. Osborn continued, "My father, the Reverend Edward Osborn, had hoped to find me a living as a rector. Alas, it was not to be."

"So that's why you're a curate?" Brandon asked, "That's why you have to work?" He was trying to make sure he had understood correctly.

Mr. Osborn nodded. "Alas. There is something of a shortage of livings in England. My father did what he could on my behalf. He sought the patronage, the support I mean, of numerous eminent clergy, while I myself wrote untold numbers of letters of application. But nothing availed. After all our trouble, the only employment I could find was as a tutor in the household of Sir Richard Peploe. I taught his sons the rudiments of Latin and Greek, but he, ah, dispensed with my services when he disagreed with my views on religion. Fortunately, I obtained this curacy here at St. Swithin's after my father wrote to the Bishop, and that great man took pity on my state. However, my income here is not sufficient to maintain a family." Here his tone grew bitter. "I have been repeatedly passed over for livings, for there are far too many gentlemen's sons who aspire to be clergymen."

Brandon looked at him doubtfully. "So the Bishop appoints some rich guy as the rector," he said, "but then the rector turns around and hires other preachers to do his work for him, while taking all the profits?"

"You do not put it daintily," Mr. Osborn said, "but you have grasped the substance of my remarks."

"Well, that stinks," Brandon muttered.

Mrs. Osborn said hotly, "Mr. Osborn has *not* received the honors that should be his."

Mr. Osborn hushed his wife. "No, no, madam, I am now quite content with my provision. I look forward to a new life in His Majesty's colony."

"What about you, ma'am?" Brandon politely asked Mrs. Osborn. "Are you excited about living in Georgia?"

He was surprised and embarrassed to see Mrs. Osborn's eyes brim with tears, but she choked them back. "To be sure, Brandon," she said carefully, "it will be no small sacrifice for us to leave behind our family, and travel so far across a howling ocean to a strange wilderness . . ."

"But I must do as the Lord commands," Mr. Osborn interrupted, looking reproachfully at his wife, "and a wife must do as her husband bids."

Mrs. Osborn looked like she thought of arguing with him, but then decided against it. She contented herself with a sour look in her husband's direction.

Brandon's days with the Osborns were filled with chores and errands. He helped Mr. Osborn repair a fence, learned from Mrs. Osborn how to milk a cow, and weeded the garden. He also packed up some of Mr. Osborn's belongings into a wooden trunk, ready for the Atlantic voyage.

But he was a little bored, and not just because of the lack of TV and video games. Brandon, who had found books to enjoy in every century he had visited, had nothing to read. There was no public library or bookstore in Balesworth in 1752. He looked in vain for an enjoyable read in Mr. Osborn's tiny library. The few books that the minister owned were beautiful, it was true. They were printed on heavy and crisp white paper, and bound in colorful marbled covers, with embossed leather spines. But every single one of them was totally boring.

Actually, if Brandon was to be honest with himself, the books weren't just boring: He couldn't even understand them. All were about religion, and they were very hard to follow. They reminded him of browsing through one of Dr. Braithwaite's medical textbooks in Snipesville. Then, to his chagrin, he had only understood the bit at the beginning where the author thanked his wife.

Brandon wished he had brought a book with him to 1752. He giggled at the very idea, but then grew solemn as he remembered that, during his previous adventures, the Professor had always presented him with modern history books. When would she show up? Or would she never appear again, leaving him stuck in the eighteenth century? A spasm of pain crossed his face.

Hannah's life, like Brandon's, revolved around chores, but, unlike Brandon, who was bored, Hannah found her work enjoyable and strangely calming.

At the factory where she had worked on her last adventure, she had sometimes thought she would go mad. Her work there had been tedious and exhausting. She had longed for the sound of the factory bell that signaled her meal breaks and the end of the day.

But there were no bells in the inn, only hungry travelers needing to be fed. Their needs, unlike those of the cotton spinning machines, were very real, and their appreciation was worth working for. Hannah's work was hard, but it was rewarding. There were also periods, especially in the afternoons, when everyone could take it easy.

On one of those afternoon rest breaks, Hannah and Mrs. Jenkins sat by the fireplace. Mrs. Jenkins was teaching Hannah how to knit, and they were both busy with wooden needles. Although Hannah's progress was slow, she was surprised to find out how much she enjoyed knitting, just as she enjoyed learning how to cook. It was, she decided, fun to make things, a lot more fun than she would have ever imagined. Well, maybe fun wasn't quite the right word, she thought. It was more of a warm happy glow.

"Only five guests last night!" exclaimed Mrs. Jenkins. "We have seldom seen so few at this time of year, but I'm not complaining. It is good to have some peace and quiet. I believe I shall visit my grandchildren tomorrow."

"That should be the end of the peace and quiet," joked Hannah. At the same time, she felt a pang of jealousy toward Mrs. Jenkins' grandchildren. "How many grandkids have you got?"

"Oh, but three," said Mrs. Jenkins, knitting furiously. "Stephen had five children, but two of the poor infants succumbed to measles last year."

"Wow, that's really sad," Hannah said. "Is Stephen your only kid?"

"No," Mrs. Jenkins said, as she set her knitting in her lap, and stared into the fire. "We did have two living children, but our daughter was taken from us many years ago, while we lived in London."

Seeing the pain in Mrs. Jenkins's face, Hannah didn't think she could imagine what it was like to have a kid, much less for her child to die. But it had to be hard. There was an uncomfortable silence.

Suddenly, Mrs. Jenkins laid down her knitting, rose to her feet, and said to herself, "I must use up the last of the cider." She fetched an earthenware jug from the pantry and filled two pewter mugs, handing one of them to Hannah. The cloudy liquid looked more like orange juice than apple juice, but Hannah took it gratefully.

She had no sooner put the mug to her lips than she made a face. "This has got liquor in it!" she said.

Mrs. Jenkins looked puzzled by her reaction. "Of course it will have fermented. It is last year's cider, after all."

Hannah sipped at it cautiously. The drink was sweet and apple-y, but it was also powerfully alcoholic. She sipped it again. This time, strong though it was, it didn't taste so bad. In fact, it was delicious.

When Mrs. Jenkins left the room to fetch her sewing, Hannah swiftly drank off her cider. She immediately felt like another glass. Listening out for her mistress's return, she slipped into the larder, found the jug on a shelf, and helped herself. Still standing in the larder, she downed the drink quickly, and poured out a third serving. Then she hurried back to her seat before Mrs. Jenkins could return and guess what she was up to.

But Mrs. Jenkins, who had misplaced her sewing basket, was away from the kitchen for almost half an hour.

By the time she finally returned, Hannah was thoroughly woozy, and she lolled in her chair. Mrs. Jenkins sat across from her, setting down her sewing basket. "What ails you, Hannah?" she asked with concern.

Hannah groaned in reply. Puzzled, Mrs. Jenkins noticed that the girl's glass of cider was still half full. She stepped across to feel Hannah's forehead for fever.

At that moment, Hannah leaned forward and threw up on her mistress's shoes.

That same day, Mr. Osborn gave Brandon his first wages, a couple of coins, and awarded him the afternoon off. Brandon's first excited thought was to visit Hannah, but he decided to treat himself first. When he reached the High Street, he stopped in at a small pub, and ordered bread and cheese, hoping he had enough money to pay for it. He asked the barmaid for water to go with his snack, but she laughed at him. "You wouldn't want no water," she scoffed, "not less'n you wants gripes in your belly. Hold but a moment."

She poured out a pint of ale from an earthenware jug, and handed it to a doubtful Brandon, saying kindly, "Here, take this for your health, on the house."

Being thirsty, Brandon reckoned he had no choice but to drink it. Standing at the bar, he sipped the ale cautiously and made a disgusted face. But he didn't want to insult the barmaid by not drinking her gift and, anyway, although the beer was bitter, it was also weak, so he figured he would be able to choke it down. He pulled off a piece of bread, plucked a morsel of pale yellow cheese, and popped them both in his mouth. He was relieved to find that eating them made the ale taste better. And the cheese was wonderful, nothing like the orange stuff from the supermarket at home.

By the time Brandon polished off his snack, the ale was making him feel fuzzy, although not drunk. At least he didn't think he was drunk. He wondered vaguely if beer might be healthier than the coffee at the Balesworth Arms.

Despite his fuzziness, he worried. Two weeks had passed, yet the Professor hadn't appeared at all. But maybe Hannah had seen her? Popping the last fragment of cheddar into his mouth, he waved to the barmaid, walked uncertainly to the exit, and pushed open the heavy wooden door to the street.

It was only a short walk down the High Street to the Balesworth Arms, and Brandon was still feeling lightheaded as he knocked on the side door of the pub. But the sound of Hannah shrieking struck him stone cold sober. Shoving open the side door, he dashed into the dining room, where at once he collided with Mr. Jenkins, who spilled ale from the tankard he was carrying.

"Oy, where are you going, boy?" Mr. Jenkins spluttered, his wig askew as usual.

"I heard Hannah screaming," Brandon yelled, trying to push past him.

Mr. Jenkins laid an arm across Brandon's chest, slopping the rest of his ale on the floor as he did so. "Now, now, it is of no consequence," he said reassuringly. "My wife is chastising the maid for drunkenness."

"What? Where are they?" Brandon demanded, grabbing Mr. Jenkins's arm. But Mr. Jenkins had had enough of Brandon. He slammed down his now-empty tankard on a table, and seized Brandon by the shoulders. Roughly, he pushed him out the door, and kicked him hard up the backside for good measure. Brandon found himself sprawled in the dirt of the courtyard, his hand wrapped around a lump of horse poo.

Several times that week, Brandon visited Balesworth High Street on various errands from Mrs. Osborn. He stopped by the Balesworth Arms at least once on every trip, hoping to check on Hannah. But each time, he was turned away by one of the Jenkinses or the staff, all of whom claimed that Hannah was too busy to see him. He was running out of excuses to go to town.

On Saturday, he begged Mrs. Osborn to let him go into Balesworth once again, this time to the market to buy produce. She happily agreed. "I do not feel altogether well for going myself," she told Brandon gratefully. "Just mind and be sure that they sell you no rotten vegetables."

When Brandon arrived at the inn door with a loaded basket of potatoes and cabbages on his arm, it was Mrs. Jenkins who greeted him with a smile, and she called for Hannah. "It is her day off," she told Brandon, putting a finger on his arm. "I'm sure she will be glad to see you."

Sure enough, Hannah soon rushed to the door and gave Brandon a huge hug. "Come on, let's go shopping!" she said.

She looked pretty cheerful for an abused servant, but Brandon didn't want to trust appearances. He was careful not to say anything within earshot of Mrs. Jenkins, but as soon as he and Hannah were walking down the High Street, he told her how he had overheard her hysterical screams. "What happened to you?" he asked earnestly. "Is everything really okay?"

Hannah was touched by Brandon's concern, although she didn't plan to tell him that. She gave him a weak smile. "Yeah, I'm okay. Mrs. Jenkins is usually nice, but she totally wigged out on me. I drank too much of her cider, and I didn't realize it's pretty strong alcohol. Then I barfed on her shoes. So she whipped me." She looked embarrassed.

Brandon was deeply relieved, and tried not to laugh at Hannah's latest misfortune. Hannah had a habit of getting herself into trouble with adults on their adventures, and he had a hard time feeling sorry for her.

"Belt?" he deadpanned, thinking of the whipping Mrs. Devenish had given her in 1940.

"No," she grimaced. "She tied together a bunch of little switches. You wouldn't believe how much *that* hurt, Brandon. There was *blood*." Even she seemed stunned by what she had said.

Brandon whistled in awe. "Wow. I've, like, read about that, so I don't think it's weird for this time period, but . . . Ow." For once, he sympathized with Hannah. He furrowed his brow. "Do you need to see a doctor?"

Sniffing, Hannah said, "No, I think I'm okay now. But I have scabs on my butt. I think I might have *scars*. Brandon, you know stuff about history: What is it with Verity's ancestors that they go around whipping people?"

"Not people. Just you," Brandon laughed despite himself. "Alex and me, we never get whipped. No, seriously, Hannah, believe it or not, it's not about you. There's a lot of whipping in history. You're not the only one."

She scowled at him. "Thank you for your support, jerk. Man, I'm so glad I live in the twenty-first century."

"Which we do," Brandon conceded, "most of the time, anyway. Look, are you going to keep your job?"

"Of course," Hannah said matter-of-factly. "Mrs. Jenkins has kind of taken me under her wing, you know? I'm glad to hear you say she's probably not a psychopath. But she was really mad at me for taking all that cider, and she said it was the stealing that ticked her off more than me being drunk. The thing is, I don't think it *was* stealing. I mean, when we have drinks in the fridge at home, Dad doesn't mind if we have more than one glass."

Brandon thought for a second, and then said slowly, "Yeah, but in our time, food's made in factories, so it's cheap, and it's no big deal to buy more of it. But I bet Mrs. Jenkins made the cider herself, right? She was probably angry because it took her a long time, and you took more than your fair share."

"Oh, that makes sense," Hannah said thoughtfully.

Brandon preened. It wasn't often that Hannah admitted he was right.

What she said next threw him completely.

"Brandon . . ." she said hesitantly, "I kind of think we need to steal something."

Shocked, Brandon angrily shushed her, hoping that passing people in the street hadn't heard what she said. "This is 1752, and that's dangerous talk, Hannah. What are you talking about?"

Hannah stopped, and rubbed her shoe in the dirt of the High Street. "I need money for my ticket to Georgia," she said. "I have to come with you, I just know it . . . . It's hard to explain. It's like we talked about. I have this weird feeling I get in my head whenever this time travel junk starts, I just know there's something I have to do . . . I mean, my mom always laughed at me for being superstitious, but. . ."

"Me too," said Brandon solemnly. "I know exactly what you mean. I get that feeling too."

She took him aside and began to whisper urgently. "Then you know I have to go with you. Trouble is, I don't know how to get the money. I feel like we both need to steal something from these people we're living with, and then catch a plane . . . . I mean, ship."

"Hannah," Brandon whispered back angrily, "That's a bad idea for all kinds of reasons, but the number one reason is that stealing is wrong."

Hannah did not back down. "No, you're wrong," she hissed. "This is so not a big deal. Brandon, these people are dead in our time. Long dead. They're dust. It's hard to feel guilty about stealing from dead people. Okay, I do feel kind of guilty even *trying* to get my head around stealing from Mrs. Jenkins. But suppose stealing is what I'm *supposed* to do?"

"No," Brandon said levelly. "I don't believe that. You can't just imagine that you're allowed to do something so wrong, hurting other people, because of a feeling. We'll figure something out, but that isn't it. Look, you better go shopping without me. I have to get home, or Mrs. Osborn will think I'm a slacker. I'll be in touch."

He turned on his heel, and left her standing in the High Street. Hannah, mad at him, tried to make herself feel better with a little retail therapy. She went shopping. She never did find anything worth buying on Balesworth High Street. The few shops sold only everyday products that people needed, like food and hardware, not fancy clothes or gifts. She made this discovery only by walking the entire length of the street and stopping in almost every shop.

But later, after she returned home to the Balesworth Arms, Hannah found a different kind of pleasure. It was something that felt much more rewarding than shopping. She made pastry.

As she wiped the flour from her hands on a kitchen rag, she gazed proudly at a giant ball of dough resting in an oval wooden trencher on the kitchen table.

Hannah had amazed herself: Not only could she now make pastry, but she could do it without measuring the ingredients. She had grabbed handfuls of flour, and then, just as Mrs. Jenkins had taught her, rubbed soft white lard into it with her fingers, until all the big lumps were gone.

Now a thought struck her, and she said, "Mrs. Jenkins, do you have any cookbooks in the house?"

Laying down her stirring stick, Mrs. Jenkins turned to Hannah in surprise. "A book, Hannah?" she said. "I did not know you could read. Besides, you can learn more from me than ever you could from a book. Although I must admit that I possess a copy of *The Art of Cookery*, which Mr. Jenkins bought me. I told him I was curious about the idea of a book of receipts, and he brought it back with him from London. I confess, I have learned a trick or two from it. Would you like to try a receipt with me?"

"Sure," Hannah said, her eyes lighting up, even as she smiled at Mrs. Jenkins calling a recipe a "receipt."

"Very well," Mrs. Jenkins said, fetching a small hardbound book from a cupboard. She began flipping through the pages. "Just remind me that we must stir the soup that's on the fire so it does not burn, and meanwhile we will make a cake. Hmm. . .Let's see. . .I rather fancy this one." She pointed to a recipe, and held open the book on the table, so they could both read it together:

To make a fine feed or faffron-cake.

You must take a quarter of a peck of fine flour, a pound and a half of butter, three ounces of carraway seeds, six eggs beat well, a quarter of an ounce of cloves and mace beat together very fine, a pennyworth of cinnamon beat, a pound of sugar, a pennyworth of rose-water, a pennyworth of saffron, a pint and a half of yeast, and a quart of milk; mix it all together lightly with your hands thus: first boil your milk and butter, then skim off the butter, and mix with your flour, and a little of the milk and stir the yeast into the rest and strain it, mix it with the flour, put in your feed and spice, rose-water, tincture of saffron, sugar, and eggs; beat it all up well with your hands lightly, and bake it in a hoop or pan, but be sure to butter the pan well. It will take an hour and a half in a quick oven. You may leave out the seed if you chuse it, and I think it rather better without it, but that you may do as you like.

"What's a feed or faffron-cake?" Hannah asked, pointing to the words with a grin.

Mrs. Jenkins turned to her and tutted in mock shock. "Silly girl! That's *seed* or *saffron* cake. I thought you said you could read?"

"I can!" Hannah protested, "I just don't understand why it says *f* instead of *s*."

"Well," Mrs. Jenkins said, "for one thing, that is not an *f*, you see. It is a long *s*. Observe the difference."

Hannah looked closely, and at first she could see no difference at all. But then she noticed that the crossbar in the middle of an *f* struck right through it: On the long *s* it went only halfway. Suddenly, it was much easier to read the recipe, and she beamed with pride.

"It will be an expensive cake," Mrs. Jenkins said, "but I think quite delicious, and since Mr. Osborn the curate is to come to tea with me tomorrow, it will prove useful. Hannah, run to the apothecary's for a pennyworth of rosewater and a pennyworth of saffron. Ask the grocer for the caraway seeds, and if he lacks them, we shall do without. Now, don't fret about finishing your pastry for the pies. I will roll them out for you."

After Mrs. Jenkins handed her three large bronze pennies, Hannah grabbed the shopping basket from the corner of the kitchen. With a pang of guilt, she remembered that she was planning to steal from Mrs. Jenkins. She wondered if she could bring herself to do it.

The cake was hard work: Hannah had never baked a cake from scratch before, but doing without a boxed mix wasn't the hard part. The hard part was making up the batter without an electric mixer. Mrs. Jenkins supervised, as Hannah flailed at the mixture with a wooden spoon. Within seconds, she stopped, and grimaced.

"What ails you?" asked Mrs. Jenkins sharply.

"My arm's cramping," Hannah whined. "Can I rest for a bit?"

The look on Mrs. Jenkins' face told her that no, she could not. With a sigh, Hannah switched to her left hand. Within seconds, she discovered she couldn't stir the mixture very well with that arm, and switched back again. Gritting her teeth, she beat the batter so hard, some of it splashed on the table. Mrs. Jenkins snapped at her, then snatched the bowl away, and quickly finished the job, her arm moving so fast that Hannah could barely follow it.

"Wow," said Hannah admiringly. "How do you do that?"

"Practice," said Mrs. Jenkins. "You will learn, too."

"Hmm," Hannah said, unconvinced. "You know a lot about baking, that's all I can say."

As she watched Mrs. Jenkins scrape the batter into a greased pan, Hannah wondered what else her mistress knew. Drumming her fingers lightly on the table, she asked, "Have you ever heard of a man called George Washington?"

"Who?" said Mrs. Jenkins, picking up the cake pan with a folded cloth.

"George Washington," Hannah said, less confidently now. "He's famous in the American Revolution."

Mrs. Jenkins looked at her blankly. Just then, her husband came into the kitchen and grabbed the end of a loaf of bread, which he proceeded to slather with butter.

"Mr. Jenkins," she said, as she placed the cake in the oven and closed the door. "Hannah here asks me if I have heard tell of a gentleman by the name of George Washington in the American colonies. Know you of him?"

Mr. Jenkins looked like a perplexed hamster, his cheeks stuffed with bread. He shook his head, and looked around for something else to eat.

"A strange, savage place, America," said Mrs. Jenkins to Hannah. "Good Englishmen become like the heathen Indians, dressed in furs, or so I do hear tell. This George Washington, is he kin to you?"

"Uh, no," said Hannah, grinning at the very idea. "He's kind of famous. But maybe not yet."

Mrs. Jenkins shrugged, and handed Hannah the batter bowl and spoon to wash.

One afternoon a few days later, Hannah sat in the dining room, sewing a patch onto a torn bed sheet, when the first coach-load of overnight guests pulled into the courtyard. She watched through the window as the stable lads took charge of the horses, and Mr. Jenkins ambled out to greet the passengers, as usual.

Hannah realized that she, too, needed to be on duty, and she hastily stuffed her needle, thread, and sheet into the sewing basket, and then hurried into the hall to offer house slippers to the guests.

This was not her favorite chore. Feet were smelly, and it was hard to estimate shoe sizes at a glance. The next several minutes went by in a flurry of gross stinks and wild guesses. Finally, only one gentleman still waited for his slippers. This last guest had been picky about Hannah's slipper selections. He had tried on and rejected several pairs of footwear. Now, he and Hannah were alone, as Mrs. Jenkins and the other guests headed upstairs to view the rooms.

"I think this will suffice," said the difficult guest, as he pulled on yet another slipper. "Hand me the other of the pair."

He was, Hannah guessed, in his thirties, and he had taken off his tricorn hat to reveal a white wig with tight curls. As she rifled through the slipper basket with ill-concealed irritation, Hannah wondered why on earth gentlemen in 1752 wore wigs that made them look old and ugly. When she looked up again, she found the man staring openly at her. "Are you the landlady's daughter?" he asked casually.

"No, sir," Hannah said curtly. She hated having to call men "sir", but Mrs. Jenkins insisted on it.

"And have you worked here long?" he asked in a haughty voice.

Hannah thought he was creepy, and she wanted the conversation to end. "Only a few weeks," she muttered.

The gentleman was not easily deterred. "You are local then?"

"No, sir," she said, and immediately wished she hadn't told him so much already. He sat silently, waiting for more information, but Hannah changed the subject. "If you go upstairs, sir," she said briskly, "Mrs. Jenkins will show you where you sleep."

He gave her an oily smile. "Very well. Perhaps I shall see you later . . . . What is your name, girl?"

Before she could stop herself, she told him.

The encounter with the creepy guest left Hannah unnerved. That night, she used the lock on her door, and shoved the low wooden chest against it before she settled down to sleep.

Over the past week, the nighttime temperatures had dipped, and even the extra blanket she had begged from Mrs. Jenkins did little to fend off the cold. Hannah wrapped herself tightly in her two blankets and imagined that she was a burrito. A frozen burrito.

Realizing that she had not extinguished the stubby candle Mrs. Jenkins had given her to see her way to bed, she reluctantly brought out two fingers from under the blankets, licked them, and snuffed it out.

Hannah was startled awake by the sensation of being violently shaken. Wide-eyed, she desperately tried to get to her feet, but, still wrapped in her blankets, she only managed to tip herself onto the floor with a loud thump. She writhed around, whimpering to herself in fear, until she was finally free. Clambering to her feet, she felt the wall around the door for several seconds before recalling that there was no electric light switch.

As her eyes became accustomed to the darkness, however, Hannah saw that nobody was in the room with her. To be sure, she checked under the bed, and then nervously lifted the lid of the chest that she had shoved against the door. But she was alone.

She let out a huge sigh of relief. Almost immediately, however, she had a new and terrifying thought. Had the ghostly Jack Platt played one of his tricks on her? Hannah could hear her own breathing quicken. *Of course not*, she thought. *It was a stupid dream. That's all.*

All the same, she kept a wakeful vigil for the remaining nighttime hours.

The next morning, a drowsy Hannah helped to serve breakfast. While she stumbled around under the displeased eye of Mrs. Jenkins, the guests ate and drank heartily. Breakfast consisted of bowls of oatmeal, bread and butter, tankards of dark beer, and steaming mugs of bad coffee. Hannah was relieved when the guest she thought of as Creepy Guy ignored her as she served him. But, to her dismay, he was soon the only person still at table.

Now Mr. Jenkins sauntered in, and greeted him enthusiastically. "Mr. Evans! It was a pleasure to make your acquaintance over a pot of ale last evening," he said. "I trust you rested well, sir?"

"I did indeed, sir," Mr. Evans replied smoothly. "Might I avail myself of your hospitality for one more night?"

"Of course! Of course!" Mr. Jenkins cried. "I am delighted to have you as a guest, sir! However, I must, with great regret, leave you in the capable hands of my wife, for I am bound for the City today." He puffed himself up proudly.

Mr. Evans smiled. "To London, eh? And what, might I enquire, draws you there, sir?"

"Business!" exclaimed Mr. Jenkins eagerly. "I am to attend a dinner in the city, by the invitation of an old friend and fellow inn-keeper."

"Business, sir? You will forgive me for saying so," said Mr. Evans with a wink, "but that sounds more like pleasure to me. I trust you will enjoy yourself."

Amused, Mr. Jenkins held a finger to his lips, then said in a loud stage whisper, "Sir, I beg of you, do not let my wife overhear you! For she believes that my trip is purely for business!"

"I will pledge to keep your secret, if you will do me but one favor, sir," said Mr. Evans.

"And what would that be, pray?" Mr. Jenkins asked jovially.

"In private, sir, if you please," Mr. Evans said, glancing meaningfully at Hannah, who was scraping plates at table. Waving his fingers at her in a dismissive gesture, Mr. Jenkins ordered her to leave the room.

Hannah rolled her eyes as she went back to the kitchen. Adults could be so annoying.

The following morning, Mr. Evans was not at breakfast. Hannah was relieved, although not entirely surprised by his absence. Not all of those who stayed at the inn ate breakfast, because many coaches departed before dawn. And anyway, guests of the Balesworth Arms came and went: That was what made it an interesting place.

Hannah was in the kitchen, rinsing out the breakfast tankards to give to the potboy, the young man who cleaned the pewterware, when Mrs. Jenkins stuck her head around the door. "Hannah?" she said sharply, "Come with me."

Mrs. Jenkins didn't sound very happy, and Hannah wondered desperately what she could possibly have done wrong. Anxiously, she followed her mistress through the dining room and into the empty bar. And there she saw Mr. Evans. He was perched on the edge of a table, his arms crossed, and he was tapping one foot on the ground.

"Is this the girl?" Mrs. Jenkins asked him, shoving Hannah firmly in his direction.

"Yes, madam, she is," he said without batting an eye.

Confused and alarmed, Hannah said, "Hey, what's going on?"

"Return to your duties, Hannah," Mrs. Jenkins replied sternly. As Hannah reluctantly left the room, she thought she overheard Mr. Evans say to Mrs. Jenkins, "You see how she avoids my gaze?"

Why would he say that? She had done nothing of the kind or, at least, she hadn't avoided looking at Creepy Guy any more than she normally avoided looking adults in the face.

Then she heard Mrs. Jenkins speak. "I shall search her bedchamber forthwith, sir."

Hannah didn't like the sound of that, either.

Ten minutes later, Mrs. Jenkins stormed into the kitchen, and yanked Hannah by the arm, almost knocking her down. She then proceeded to cuff her about the head as she half-dragged her through the house.

Hannah tried to shield herself from the blows. "What is it? Ow!"

Suddenly, she found her nose shoved against a silver plate on a table in the bar.

"Do you recognize this?" Mrs. Jenkins shouted, shaking her by the shoulder.

"No, I don't," Hannah protested. "Let go of me!"

"A liar as well as a thief, eh?" Mrs. Jenkins cried. "Well, my girl, I found this in your bedchamber, and it belongs to Mr. Evans, as well you know."

"No, I don't. . ." Hannah cried, tearing up. "I don't know anything about it."

Mrs. Jenkins wasn't impressed by her tears. "What did you do?" she demanded. "Did you hide your stolen treasure in the woods until cover of nightfall, and then bring it into my establishment? Did you not think that you would bring ill-repute to the Balesworth Arms when you asked me for a position? Or did you care not?"

Hannah was now in floods of tears. "I don't know what you're talking about."

"Thief! Liar!" screamed Mrs. Jenkins, slapping Hannah so hard across the cheek that she fell to the floor. As Hannah lay groaning and weeping, the grim-faced landlady seemed to collect herself.

"Mr. Evans has gone to fetch the constable," said Mrs. Jenkins in a calm voice. "We shall see what you say then."

But as Hannah lay on the floorboards, weeping and rubbing her aching head and face, Mrs. Jenkins suddenly burst into tears, threw her apron over her face, and fell to her knees next to her.

When Brandon, on his day off, returned to the Balesworth Arms, a pale and drawn Mrs. Jenkins answered the door. She took one look at him, and grabbed the broomstick that was leaning against the hall wall. She pointed it threateningly at him, saying, "She's gone. And I want you gone from my premises, too."

Brandon's eyes widened in shock. "Gone? Hannah's gone? Where?"

Mrs. Jenkins advanced on him. "What care I? She has been dismissed. Now be gone with you."

Brandon was furious, but not with Mrs. Jenkins. All he could think was that Hannah must have done something pretty stupid to get herself fired. *Typical,* he thought. *She messed up again.* Still, at least now she would have to come to Georgia with him. It made sense. Sort of.

As Brandon stood silently on her doorstep, Mrs. Jenkins said, "The girl was arrested by the parish constable for thieving, not but an hour ago. Before you two arrived in Balesworth, she stole silver plate from a London gentleman named Mr. Evans. After she began to work for me, she smuggled it into her room." Now her voice rose. "And I'll wager you know all about it, Brandon, since you are doubtless in league with her. Now be gone, ere I take this broom to you!" She jabbed the broom handle at his midriff.

Brandon jumped backward to avoid being poked, but then he stood his ground. "I don't know what you're talking about, ma'am," he said levelly. "Hannah wouldn't steal anything, I'm sure of it. This is some kind of mistake. I'll go if you insist, but this theft is nothing to do with me or Hannah, Mrs. Jenkins."

He spoke so bravely and certainly that Mrs. Jenkins let the broomstick drop, and her kindly nature reasserted itself. "You swear upon the Bible?"

"I do," Brandon said firmly, shocking himself by the ease with which he was telling lies. He honestly had no idea whether Hannah had stolen or not.

Mrs. Jenkins looked askance at him, and then asked sharply, "Why was the silver plate in her bedchamber?"

Good question, Brandon thought. "I don't know," he said, "but I know Hannah, and she's no thief." *At least,* he thought to himself, *I hope she isn't.*

Mrs. Jenkins pointed a finger up the road. "Look for her in the constable's lock-up house on the High Street. I would venture that she is in there."

"Thank you," Brandon said politely, wondering what a "lock-up house" was, but not wishing to seem ignorant by asking.

"Wait here for the moment," Mrs. Jenkins said. Setting the broomstick against the wall, she headed for the kitchen. Moments later, she emerged with a half-loaf of bread, and a hunk of cheese. She shoved them at him. "Here," she said. "Give these to Hannah."

Brandon saw the landlady's mouth quiver. She said sadly, "I had high hopes for that girl. I treated her as my own daughter. Ask her why she stole, will you?"

Chapter 4:
THE FORTUNES AND MISFORTUNES OF HANNAH DIAS

The little stone hut was a very gloomy place. Dark patches of damp crept down the walls, fed by tiny rivulets of rainwater. A slatted wooden pallet served as a bed, and it was on this that Hannah was sitting. Her breath appeared as puffs of fog, her teeth chattered from the cold, and she shook uncontrollably. Trying to get warm, she stood up once again to take a few steps around her tiny cell, stopping to peer through the barred unglazed window to look for passers-by. She hoped that someone—anyone—would come to her rescue.

Suddenly, as if by magic, Brandon's face appeared on the other side of the bars. "Hannah, we've got to get you out of here!" he cried. In his arms were the bread and cheese Mrs. Jenkins had given him, with a flagon of weak beer he had purchased.

Hannah had never been so happy to see Brandon, but she was also scared. "Brandon," she said without taking breath, "the constable said I have to see the magistrate tomorrow, and then they'll probably take me to London for trial. Can you tell the magistrate it wasn't me who stole the plate? You heard about the plate, right?"

"Yes, I heard about the plate," Brandon said evenly. "And did you? Steal it, I mean?"

Hannah burst into tears. "I'm sorry . . . I'm sorry. . ." she hiccupped. "I have to tell you what happened. I just . . . I didn't. . . I didn't want you to go to Georgia without me . . . and I couldn't think how else to get the money . . . ."

Brandon felt sick with fury. "You did it? You stole from Mrs. Jenkins? Hannah, how could you? I defended you!"

But Hannah, waving her hands, interrupted him, her face horrorstruck. "No! No, I didn't. Would you please listen, Brandon?" she yelled. "Listen, Brandon. I didn't do it. I *was* going to steal something, I was thinking about it, but I decided not to. Then Mrs. Jenkins found the plate in my room. But I never took it."

Brandon shook his head in bewilderment. "So why was it in your room?"

By now, Hannah was almost hysterical. "I don't KNOW," she cried, and then collapsed on the bed. The dramatic gesture was spoiled when she said "Ow"as she landed on the hard "bed."

"This is bad," Brandon said quietly. "I mean, really, really bad. Do you know what they do to thieves in the year 1752? They get whipped, and that's not the worst thing that can happen . . . ."

"What's the worst thing?" Hannah asked piteously, lifting her head to look at him. Her hair, wet with rainwater, hung in rats' tails across her face.

Brandon solemnly drew his finger across his throat. Then he said, "Well, actually, more like this." He pretended to hang himself, his tongue lolling. Hannah flinched, before bursting into a fit of weeping.

Brandon felt ashamed. His gestures had been totally tactless, and he knew it. But part of him thought that Hannah had stolen the plate, and he was furious at her.

"I've got to go," he said awkwardly. "I'll be at the magistrate's hearing, don't worry. And take this, it's food from Mrs. Jenkins." He pushed the bread and cheese through the bars, and Hannah grabbed them. But the flagon of ale wouldn't fit, however much he wiggled it. "What do you want me to do with it?" he asked.

"Leave it outside," she said miserably. "The constable said he'll be back to check on me. He can give it to me then."

As he walked away, Hannah called after him, her hands wrapped around the bars of her prison. She tried to sound brave. "Brandon? The Professor won't let anything happen. When we go to the court tomorrow, I bet she's pretending to be the magistrate. You'll see."

Brandon wasn't so optimistic. "Don't count on it," he warned her. But then he felt bad for scaring her again. He added quickly, "I'll try to get you out somehow. I'll ask Mr. Osborn for help. And I'll pray for you."

"I'd prefer a sledgehammer," she said. "Or a hacksaw."

Walking back along the High Street, Brandon felt as though someone had poured cold water through his veins. Was Hannah lying to him about stealing? He didn't think so, but what if she was? Stealing was a terrible sin, but she certainly didn't deserve a cruel punishment. There was no question in Brandon's mind about what he had to do: He could not stand by and see something horrible happen to Hannah. He would have to take her side, no matter what.

He found Mr. Osborn in the church vestry, busily composing a sermon with quill pen and ink. The young curate looked up impatiently when Brandon entered. "Speak," he commanded.

Brandon was nervous, but he explained what had happened, editing his story to take out all his doubts about Hannah's innocence. Finally, he said with passion, "She didn't do it, sir. I'm sure she didn't." As he spoke, he wondered if there was a special place in hell for kids who lie to preachers.

Mr. Osborn looked worried. "It is unfortunate that tomorrow is the day that the petty sessions will be heard, for that gives us no time to prepare a defense. If the magistrates find cause, and I am sure they will, then your friend will be committed to the county jail in Hertford to await trial." He pronounced the town's name "Hartford", and for one moment, Brandon had the muddled thought that Hannah was going to Connecticut.

Now he furrowed his brow. "She thinks they're going to take her to London."

"How very odd," said Mr. Osborn, laying down his pen. "I wonder why. Tell me, has the girl ever been to London?"

Not in this century, Brandon thought. What he said was, "No, never."

"If I were you," Mr. Osborn said patiently, "I would speak again with your friend. Make haste to her now, Brandon. Find out what you can about the incident before nightfall."

Brandon didn't see what good this would do. Hannah had seemed as baffled as he was. "But can you help her, sir?" he asked.

Mr. Osborn shook his head sorrowfully. "You invest me with greater power than is rightfully mine," he said. "I can advise, but that is all. Now go into town, and learn what you can."

With a heavy heart, Brandon thanked his boss, and left immediately to retrace his steps back to Balesworth High Street.

Hannah was lying on the rough bed, curled up miserably.

"Hannah, wake up!" Brandon hissed. "Mr. Osborn says I have to get some information from you before we can help."

Abruptly, she sat up and wiped her eyes. "Information? Like what?"

"Tell me why you're going to London for trial," he said. "Mr. Osborn says you should have gone to Hertford."

Hannah pouted. "How would I know? I have no idea." But then she thought about it, her face screwed up in concentration. "I guess it has something to do with this guy who's accusing me, this Mr. Evans. He said I stole the silver plate from him in London . . . ." But now she felt rising panic. "I don't understand. Why did Mrs. Jenkins call the constable? I thought she cared about me."

Hannah was crying again, and Brandon watched silently, his mind reeling. She was clearly exhausted, confused, and depressed. He would have to hold things together. *As usual*, he thought bitterly, and then he dismissed the thought as unkind. At least now, he reflected with relief, he knew that Hannah had not stolen the plate: She could not possibly have visited London since their arrival.

But he also realized that nobody would investigate and find out what really happened. With a sinking feeling, he recalled reading that there were no detectives in England in 1752. There weren't even any police officers, except for the parish constable, and he would be no professional.

Brandon decided his only choice was to be his own policeman. What would a detective do? He thought about the mystery dramas he had watched on TV.

And that was when he understood that his course of action was really pretty simple, at least in theory. He would interview people, starting with the Jenkinses and Mr. Evans.

It was dark when Mrs. Jenkins opened the side door to Brandon, and she was reluctant to allow him in. However, she agreed to meet with him in the bar, and sent him round to the front entrance of the Balesworth Arms. Even then, she watched him like a hawk as he stood uncomfortably before her in the noisy barroom. She did not invite him to sit.

"Tell me why you wish to speak with me," she said impatiently. "And make haste."

Talking quickly, Brandon explained that he hoped to find out the truth before Hannah appeared in court. As Mrs. Jenkins listened attentively, he stressed that he was worried that there had been an injustice done. Finally, the landlady seemed to make up her mind that he was serious, and agreed to answer his questions. She led him into the kitchen, where she began kneading a large batch of dough on an oval wooden trencher.

"Ask, then," she said to Brandon as the flour puffed into the air around her fists.

Brandon took a deep breath. "Why do you think Hannah took the plate?"

"I know not," said Mrs. Jenkins, "I came upon it in her bedchamber." She looked at him severely, as though he had asked a really stupid question.

He persevered. "Who does it belong to?"

"It is the property of one Mr. Evans," she said curtly. "I do not know the gentleman. He was a stranger who lodged with us last night. As soon as he saw Hannah, he knew her as the wench who had vanished from his service in London, taking the plate with her."

Brandon was thinking. Why would this guy claim that Hannah was his maid? It could be a fault in time, of course, so that perhaps, in some other reality, she really *had* been his servant . . . Unless . . . unless Evans was lying.

Brandon had watched enough old TV detective shows to know what to ask Mrs. Jenkins next. "Did he ask you anything about her before he accused her?" he said.

"No, he did not," said Mrs. Jenkins. Then she stopped kneading, and looked at him keenly. "But he spoke with Mr. Jenkins also, and my husband may have told Mr. Evans about her."

Politely, Brandon said, "Thank you for your time, Mrs. Jenkins. May I now speak with your husband?"

She dusted off her hands. "No, you may not," she said briskly. "He has business in London. But he is to return late this week, and if he desires it, you may speak with him then."

Brandon didn't want to leave without more evidence. "What about Mr. Evans? Is he around?"

Mrs. Jenkins nodded. "Mr. Evans is still here, for I have offered him accommodations until the hearing tomorrow," she said. "I shall ask him if he would speak with you." Wiping her hands on her apron once more, she headed through the dining room, and up the stairs.

Brandon waited with bated breath. He wondered nervously what he would ask Hannah's mysterious accuser when they met.

But Mrs. Jenkins returned alone, shaking her head. "On no account will he speak with you, Brandon. I am sorry. You may return to speak with my husband on Saturday . . ."

"But Hannah will have gone to London by then!" Brandon cried desperately.

"Yes, she will have," Mrs. Jenkins said softly. "I am sorry for it, but I can do no more for you. I would talk of the matter with Mr. Evans myself, but he seems bound and determined to speak only in court, and he gave me to understand that he did not appreciate your prying into his affairs."

"His affairs!" Brandon yelled. "What about Hannah?" He was almost in tears. Mrs. Jenkins looked at him sympathetically. Then she surprised him by taking him in a warm embrace. "There, there," she clucked. As she let him go, she took his hand and said, "Perhaps my husband can deal with this when he returns."

Brandon wanted to believe her, but from what he had seen of Mr. Jenkins, he rather doubted it.

Mrs. Jenkins now looked very troubled. "You and Hannah are almost strangers to me," she said hesitantly, still holding his hand. "But I admire your loyalty to the girl, and I agree that there is something most peculiar about what has happened . . . . I cannot help but wonder if there is more to the affair than I at first believed."

Brandon thanked Mrs. Jenkins for her concern, and promised to return to interview her husband. As he walked forlornly up the High Street toward Mr. Osborn's house, he thought with dread of the magistrates' hearing the next morning.

A small audience of onlookers gathered for the court in the back room of the Balesworth Arms. The audience was composed of a few curious and sour-faced local women, an elderly man who rested his grizzled chin on his walking stick, and Brandon. As they waited for the proceedings to begin, Brandon occasionally spotted Mrs. Jenkins' anxious face peeping around the door to the kitchen.

Everyone got to their feet when the magistrates finally made their entrance. Brandon was disappointed, but not surprised, to note that neither of them was

Professor Harrower in disguise, as Hannah had hopefully predicted. In muttered conversation with the woman next to him, he had already learned that they were two important local men, a merchant named Mr. Rivers, and Mr. Fox, a wealthy landowning gentleman.

When the constable escorted Hannah into the room, Brandon was dismayed by her appearance. She was a mess. Her clothes were filthy, her hair was tangled, and there was a big patch of dirt smeared across her cheek. What Brandon noticed most of all, however, was that her eyes were wide with fear.

Mrs. Jenkins was called as the first witness, and she reluctantly described how she had found the plate in Hannah's room. Brandon saw her trying to avoid Hannah's anguished gaze. As she finished speaking, however, she turned to face Hannah, giving her a tender look, and sadly shook her head before taking a seat.

When Mr. Rivers called for Mr. Evans to testify, a tall, handsome, and smartly-wigged man rose to his feet. He told the hearing that Hannah had been his maid, and that she had absconded with his silver plate. He spoke so confidently, even Brandon would have believed him if he didn't know better. Could Hannah really have been this man's maid in another adventure yet to come? Stranger things had happened to them.

Suddenly, Mr. Evans was interrupted by the defendant. "Liar!" yelled Hannah, and Brandon cringed, silently willing her to keep her mouth shut. Mr. Fox sharply ordered her to be quiet, and she hung her head.

Next, it was Brandon's turn to be called as a witness. He described Hannah as honest and hardworking, and he glanced over at her to see her eyes shining with tears of gratitude. He hoped nobody in the room could tell that he was exaggerating.

But then Mr. Rivers asked him a question. "You say, Brandon, that you and the defendant did not come to Balesworth from London. In that case, where did you come from?"

Brandon hesitated, and he saw that his silence spoke volumes to the magistrates. He knew then that they did not find him believable. And why would they? He was a mere servant, a stranger to the town.

Worse yet, there was no way he could tell the court the truth. All the same, he desperately tried to make up something. "We traveled from the Black Country, near Birmingham . . ." he said. Then his voice trailed away. To his horror, he had remembered that Hannah could not possibly back up this story: Unlike him, she had never even been to the Black Country. And, he realized with a shudder, the area probably wasn't even called "the Black Country" in 1752, a hunch that was confirmed by one look at the obviously skeptical magistrates.

Abruptly, Mr. Fox told Brandon that no further testimony was required from him. Brandon fled back to his place in the audience, pausing only to give Hannah an apologetic look.

The two magistrates conferred in whispers, and then nodded to each other. Mr. Rivers cleared his throat, and in a ringing voice, ordered the parish constable to deliver Hannah immediately for trial at the next Quarter Sessions of the Old Bailey, London's criminal court.

While they waited for the constable to fetch a wagon, Brandon took the chance to slip over to Hannah and comfort her. "I'll meet you in London," he said. "I'll be there for you." She nodded tearfully and squeezed his hand.

But what she said next took him completely by surprise. "Brandon, don't. You can't do anything for me. And I'll be okay. The Professor will show up and make sure. You'll see. We'll get back together somehow."

Brandon looked doubtful, but Hannah insisted.

As she was hustled from the inn, Hannah felt deeply afraid. Truthfully, she had wanted Brandon with her. But she had a feeling that he was supposed to go to Georgia, and that she needed to be in London.

It wasn't an ordinary feeling, either. It was a milder version of that weird experience she had had before she time-traveled. Or was she just imagining things? Since when, she wondered, did she trust feelings, even her own?

Brandon, unaware of Hannah's inner struggle, gazed at her with admiration as he stood with the small crowd that watched her board the wagon. She was, he thought, tougher than he had given her credit for.

Hannah's long and bumpy journey from Balesworth took her along the Great North Road, and then through the filthy streets of the eighteenth-century city of London. She saw people using gutters as toilets, and dead animals lying in the streets. She saw two brightly-dressed and heavily made-up women fighting viciously, cheered by onlookers. She saw a workman precariously balanced on a tall ladder as he painted an elaborate shop sign, a spare paintbrush clenched between his teeth. Everywhere, she saw people and horses. Fascinating though these sights were, Hannah's attention was mostly on the rope tying her hands together. It was chafing her wrists.

Her travels ended at the entrance of Newgate Prison, which faced the Old Bailey. "Here's where I leave you," said the constable shortly. "You'll be locked up in there until your trial." Hannah looked up in fear at this forbidding stone fortress. What terrors awaited her behind these walls?

The jailer met her at the entrance door. He was a balding small man with bulging eyes, a snub nose, and a scraggly beard, and he waved off the constable, then escorted Hannah into the jail. Roughly, he untied her hands, and she rubbed her sore wrists. "Right," he said, "I require a fee of six shillings and sixpence for myself, and ten shillings for the steward."

Hannah was agog. "This is a prison," she said, looking around her in disbelief. "I have to pay to get in?"

"Only if you want to be treated right, girl," he said unpleasantly.

But Hannah knew that if she gave away her money now she would be in trouble later: She had already learned from the constable that prison food did not come free, and she would need money to eat.

"Who's the steward?" she asked, to buy time.

"She's the chief prisoner of your ward, that's what we calls the women's cell," the man said. "Now are you going to pay up, or aren't you?"

Hannah decided to take a gamble. She could always change her mind. "I haven't got any money," she told the jailer.

He sneered at her. "You got no other ways to pay me, then?"

She shuddered at his tone. "No," she said, her voice wobbling.

The man drew himself up. "Then I don't think you'll like where I'm putting you. I got a particular place for them that can't pay, or won't pay." Roughly, he pushed her down a hallway, and thrust her into an enormous dark cell. Then he slammed the door behind her.

Hannah's nose was hit with an unimaginably foul stench that almost made her throw up. At first, she could hardly see anything in the dim light. But as her eyes became used to the darkness, she saw them: women, girls, even babies, mingled together in the filthy, stinking cell. Running down the middle of the room was a shallow watery trench, with poo floating in it. Some of the prisoners were dressed only in rags, and all of them were filthy and unwashed, with dirty faces and matted hair.

Yet there was life in this unlikely setting. A huddle of women laughed raucously as one finished telling a rude joke. Another group sat on the floor, tossing dice from a small cup, while naked toddlers ran around them giggling. Curses filled the air, so that even Hannah (who had heard plenty of bad language before) was embarrassed.

Remembering TV shows about prisons, she tried to look tough so that nobody would bother her. She found a place to sit, as far from the others as she could get, against the wall on a relatively clean bit of floor. She tucked her knees under her chin.

"Oi! That's my place, that is," said a girl with tangled and dirty blond hair who suddenly stood over Hannah, her hands on her hips. Hannah shrugged in reply, so the girl collapsed on the ground next to her and started pushing at her to move. She smelled terrible, and Hannah shrank away from her, as the girl kept shoving against her arm.

"Okay, okay!" Hannah protested. "Stop pushing me! Where am I supposed to sit?"

"There," said the girl, and she pointed to a spot on the floor two feet away. Hannah moved three feet. The girl noticed. "What's wrong? Why won't you sit close to me?"

Hannah glared at her through narrowed eyes, her nostrils flaring. "I thought you said you didn't want me to! Anyway, to be honest? You stink."

The girl laughed. "'Course I do! Tell you the truth, girly, so do you."

"My name's not 'girly'," Hannah said, miffed at being told that she smelled bad. "I'm Hannah. Who are you?"

"Jane," said the girl, hugging her knees tightly. "What you in 'ere for, then?"

Hannah frowned. "Nothing. I never did anything."

Jane smirked. "That's what we all says, innit? We're all innocent in 'ere, until we're proved guilty."

Hannah wondered if Jane was making fun of her, but she decided not to get into an argument. She needed a friend in a place like this. "So," she said, "why are you here?"

"Now 'ere's the story," said Jane. "I was down at Clare Market after I went to see the 'anging in Hyde Park, and this woman comes . . ."

"You went to what?" Hannah interrupted, aghast. "Wait, did you just say a *hanging*? Like, someone getting executed?"

Jane stared at her blankly. "Yes, of course. Ain't you never seen an 'anging before? It was a good 'un, too. Two men, and one of 'em sang an 'ymn before he got turned off. Danced a merry dance on the gallows, he did."

Hannah had no answer for that. She nodded dumbly, and Jane resumed her story.

"So, like I said, I wanders down by Clare Market, and this woman comes up to me, and offers me to buy an apron, a straw hat, stockings, a cloak and an 'andkerchief off of 'er. 'ow much you want, says I? Three shillings, says she. I says to her, I ain't got but two shillings and this 'ere bottle of gin. . ."

Hannah stopped her again. "You had a bottle of gin with you? You look like you're my age."

"So?" Jane said, irritated by Hannah's repeated interruptions. "Anyway, as I was saying, she took the money and gin off me, and I gets the clothes from 'er, and I go 'ome, and put them on. Next thing, this servant wench stops me in the street, and she says, 'Oi, those clothes belong to my mistress, what you do-ing wearing them?' *And* she says 'You must go along with me, and if you won't come by fair means, you'll come by foul.' Then she drags me by my 'air to her mistress's house, and I end up 'ere.'

But Hannah was already thinking ahead. "What will they do to us if we're found guilty?"

"Dunno," said Jane, picking a bug off her knee. "Might get a whipping. Might get 'anged."

The color drained from Hannah's face. She felt faint.

"But I doubt it," Jane added, and Hannah grabbed on to this hope.

Oblivious to Hannah's shifting emotions, Jane continued, "Most likely, I'll get transported, this being my first time before the court, and me being young. Mind you, I think I'd rather 'ang than get transported, myself."

"What do you mean, transported?" Hannah asked. She imagined being tortured in a dungeon.

"It means they send you across the sea to America for seven or fourteen years," said Jane, "and you get used like a slave all that time."

"Well, that's better than hanging," Hannah said with relief.

"So you say," Jane shot back. "But I 'ear America is a terrible place."

Hannah kept quiet, and listened to the sounds of heavy wooden doors banging, and the bitter sobs of a nearby woman. What would happen to her? And where was the Professor? Had she abandoned them? Hannah dismissed these thoughts. They were too frightening to contemplate.

Jane snapped her out of her reverie. "Well, least you ain't got long to dally in Newgate," she said, scratching her leg. "Quarter Sessions is tomorrow."

"And what's that?" Hannah asked anxiously.

"That's when we'll start 'aving trials, tomorrow or later this week," Jane said. "We'll know our fate soon enough, one way or another. And they say the next convict ship to Virginia departs on the tide this Saturday morn."

Virginia? Hannah thought. *That can't be right.*

When, on the Thursday, Hannah finally made the short walk from Newgate prison through the underground passage to the Old Bailey, her heart was in her mouth.

Now, as she stood in the dock, the small enclosure for accused criminals in the courtroom, she felt very small and very vulnerable. She felt as though she had already been convicted, especially when she realized that "the prisoner" whom the judge and lawyers were discussing was *her*.

The courtroom was filled with bizarrely-dressed people. The judge wore what looked like a red bathrobe, and a long flowing white wig covered his head like a marshmallow blanket. His seat was a sort of high throne with a desk that was strewn with fresh flowers. Hannah vaguely wondered why. She didn't know it, but they were there as air fresheners, since the prisoners brought to court, including her, smelled awful. At the judge's feet sat another desk at which several men in black robes and short wigs scribbled with featherless quill pens. Off to one side sat the jury, made up of twelve plainly-dressed men, all of whom looked very bored.

Hannah had a hard time understanding what was going on in court, and her attention wandered. Her eyes scanned the public galleries, which were packed with spectators, but there were no familiar faces. She had half-hoped that Brandon would ignore her instructions and come to the trial to offer moral support, but he had not.

When the first witness was called, Hannah returned her attention to the proceedings. Mr. Evans walked gravely to the witness box. The judge asked him to identify "the prisoner in the dock," and he glanced at Hannah.

"I have no doubt, my lord," he said gravely, "that the prisoner in the dock is the thief who stole my silver plate."

Even though she was intimidated by the court, Hannah couldn't stop herself. She shouted, "It's not me! You're lying!" The judge banged his gavel on his desk, and called for her to remain silent, while the guard in the dock with Hannah roughly shook her shoulder and growled at her to shut up.

Her shoulders slumped. It was hopeless. Mr. Evans was a thoroughly believable gentleman, while she, Hannah, was just a filthy criminal.

Now things took an unexpected turn.

"What is the prisoner's name?" the judge asked Mr. Evans.

"Elizabeth Strachan, my lord. She was formerly my servant . . . ."

As Hannah sat in shock and confusion, the judge interrupted Mr. Evans. "You say then, sir, that the prisoner in the dock, this girl who calls herself Hannah Day, has given a pretended name to this court?"

"I do, your lordship," Mr. Evans said smoothly.

The judge gave Hannah a hard stare. Hannah was panicking now, and she looked away from him.

Now it was Hannah's turn to answer questions. A man in a wig (she couldn't tell if he was her lawyer or not) asked her to explain, in her own words, her version of events. Hannah tried, but the right words wouldn't come to her. She stumbled over her speech, and said things that made no sense, even to her.

The judge asked sternly if she could produce any witnesses in her own defense. Hannah now realized that she should have brought Brandon to speak on her behalf, but it was too late for that. She silently cursed herself for having trusted in a superstitious feeling, rather than thinking things through.

The jury did not go outside to decide on a verdict, but simply huddled together on their benches. Within seconds, they declared Hannah guilty. The entire trial had lasted no more than ten minutes.

But, Hannah wondered, as she was hustled away downstairs, *what about the sentence?*

There were several girls and women in the holding cell below the court, Jane among them. She was sitting on the floor, twiddling her thumbs, and she looked up and smiled when she saw Hannah.

"You got guilty, then?" she asked eagerly.

Hannah nodded, her eyes brimming with tears.

"Most of us did," Jane said. "T'won't be long for sentencing," she added somberly. "They bring all of us up together at the end of the session."

Hannah nodded, and crouched down next to her friend.

"I wish I 'ad some money," Jane said. "If we get sentenced to transportation, we get branded on the thumb, and that's going to 'urt. I hear tell that if you pay the executioner, 'ee'll use a cold iron."

Hannah silently thanked her lucky stars that she had held on to her cash. "How much for the two of us?" she quietly asked Jane, as she felt for the money in her pocket.

Jane looked at her keenly. "A shilling apiece should do it," she muttered from the side of her mouth.

With an enormous key and a loud clang, a jailer opened the cell door a few hours later. "All right, my *ladies*," he bellowed in a cheerily sarcastic voice. "It's time."

The small group of women and girls, including Hannah and Jane, huddled together as they walked upstairs and entered the dock.

Hannah trembled as, with a terrible air of doom, the judge sat up straight, while one of his clerks laid a black handkerchief on top of his wig. He looked straight at her, and said, "You have all been found guilty of felony crimes. The law is, thou shalt return from hence, to the place whenst thou camest, and from thence to the place of execution, where thou shalt hang by the neck until the body be dead! Dead! Dead! And the Lord have mercy upon thy soul."

Hannah staggered. She felt hot and sick, and she looked around desperately for the Professor to help, but there were no friendly faces in the crowd. And then she collapsed in a faint, into the arms of the other prisoners.

When Hannah awoke, she was back in Newgate Prison, with Jane at her side.

Jane saw her eyes flutter, and shook her arm gently. "'annah? You all right then?"

Hannah nodded, and then her face crumpled in despair. "When are they going to kill me?" she cried miserably.

"Oh, they ain't going to kill you," Jane said with a sigh. "Me neither."

Hannah looked at her skeptically, but her hopes rose. "What?"

Jane gave her a sly grin. "While you was asleep, the King 'imself granted us a pardon, and so we get transported to Virginia instead."

Hannah gave a half-laugh, half-sob in relief. She would live after all. "That's amazing! What made him do that?"

But Jane wasn't at all surprised. "Oh, 'ee does it all the time," she said, "'specially if you're young, or it's your first offense. I got transportation, too."

"That's great!" Hannah said.

But Jane didn't share her happiness. "That's what you fink," she said, scratching away a bug from between her bare toes. "But I know a man what's come back from Virginia, and 'ee said 'ee was lucky to be alive, much less come 'ome. 'Ee said it was 'orrible."

Hannah wasn't too worried. What would an urchin like Jane know about America, anyway? And the Professor was sure to save her. But a voice in the back of Hannah's head whispered, *Will she?*

An elderly woman in rags shuffled up to the girls. "Your sister all right, is she?" she asked Jane kindly.

"My sister? She ain't my sister," Jane said. "She's a pal of mine. Yeah, she's all right. Ain't you, 'annah?"

Looking at Jane's dirty, scabby face, Hannah thought that, obviously, the old woman who had called them sisters was a blind old bat.

The very next day, Hannah and Jane were among the prisoners returned to the courtroom to be branded on the thumb. Hannah shook with fear as she heard the screams of the men and women undergoing the punishment, and she gripped her leather money pouch tightly in her pocket. "Why do they do this to us?" she asked Jane plaintively.

"So's we cannot return early from America wivout people knowing," Jane said glumly. "I 'ope you still intends to pay 'im."

Hannah was now at the front of the line, watching the executioner apply the red hot end of a long branding iron to the hand of man who was being held by guards against a low wooden wall. The man did not cry out, but he grimaced and whimpered as the smoke rose from his thumb. A crowd of onlookers watched the spectacle from the gallery behind him, clearing enjoying themselves. When the man was released, he begged for water to dip his injured hand.

Now the executioner beckoned to Hannah. As discreetly as she could, she slipped him two coins. "Two shillings," she whispered, "for me and my friend." She pointedly glanced at Jane, and the executioner's eyes followed.

"Four," he mumbled.

Hannah sighed heavily, and brought out two more shillings. It was a lot of money. She passed the coins to him as she stepped toward the low wall.

The executioner returned the long brand to the fire, then picked up another from the floor, and dipped it into the flames. Hannah watched nervously as a guard seized her hand and held it against the wooden partition, while another guard gripped her shoulders. Deftly, the executioner took the brand from the fire, and pressed it briefly against the pad of her thumb. She screamed as it burned her skin. "You lied!" she cried, but she was quickly shoved away toward a waiting guard.

Yet when she looked at her thumb, even though it smarted, there wasn't a mark on it. The iron hadn't been hot enough to burn through the skin. The executioner had not cheated her after all.

Brandon had considered ignoring Hannah's wishes, and following her to London. In fact, he was on the verge of asking permission from Mr. Osborn to do just that when he realized that they would both be better off if he stayed in Balesworth. He decided he would try to learn more about Hannah's alleged crime. And at least he knew where he could find Hannah later.

Every day that week, he knocked on the side door of the Balesworth Arms, and asked if Mr. Jenkins had returned, only to be disappointed. But on the following Monday, when Mrs. Jenkins answered the door, he saw her look over his shoulder, just as he heard horses' hooves behind him.

"Here he is!" she cried.

Brandon turned to see Mr. Jenkins dismounting from his horse, with no small difficulty, onto a wooden block that one of the stable lads had swiftly placed for him on the cobbles of the yard.

"Good morrow, Mrs. Jenkins!" he called out heartily to his wife.

Mrs. Jenkins nodded and beamed in reply. "And to you also, Mr. Jenkins. Sir, I know that you must be tired from your journey, but could you speak with this lad here? It is a grave and urgent matter indeed that brings him to our door."

Mr. Jenkins looked puzzled, but he followed his wife and Brandon into the kitchen, where he sat down wearily on a wooden chair. "What has happened?" he asked as Mrs. Jenkins pulled off his boots. "You both appear most solemn."

Rising to her feet, Mrs. Jenkins told him the whole story, while Brandon listened quietly. Mr. Jenkins looked horrified, and he tried to interrupt his wife several times, but she wouldn't let him, for she was determined to finish her tale.

Finally, he could stand it no longer, and jumped to his feet. "There is not a moment to lose!" he exclaimed. "There has been a gross miscarriage of justice." He turned to his astonished wife, and demanded, "Is Evans still here?"

"No," she said nervously. "He had urgent business to attend, and he has gone. Why ask you, pray?"

"And did he take the silver plate with him?" Mr. Jenkins said, as if he already knew the answer.

"Yes," Mrs. Jenkins said, baffled. "Of course. It was his . . . ."

"Damn it!" Mr. Jenkins roared, stamping his foot hard on the floorboards. "It is my fault, madam, entirely my fault. This Evans, if that indeed be his name, came to me on the very day he arrived, and asked to speak with me in confidence. He had no ready money to pay for his lodging, he told me, for he had been robbed on the highway. Would I accept this plate in pawn for his room? 'Of course', said I. 'It will be more than ample for a week's lodging, or you may redeem it with interest on modest terms.' What a fool I have been."

Mrs. Jenkins looked aghast as it dawned on her what had happened. "He pawned it to you? But how came it to be under Hannah's bed?"

"I reckon he placed it there," Mr. Jenkins said. "Or perhaps the girl stole it from where I had secreted it . . ."

"No," Brandon interrupted. "She never touched it."

"I am inclined to believe that," said Mr. Jenkins gravely, "since this Evans has proved himself a charlatan by claiming to you that the plate was still his property, and not mine. He must have planted it in her bedchamber to incriminate her, and to deflect the attention from his own crime. And now I know why he was so curious to converse with me about Hannah. I thought he had merely taken a fancy to the girl. Where do you think he has gone?"

"He told me he was abandoning his journey to York, and going back to London to testify in court," said Mrs. Jenkins weakly.

"Of course," Mr. Jenkins said in disgust. "He must ensure that she is unable to return to Balesworth and implicate him in his crime. Brandon, fetch the magistrates here at once. We must all act quickly in the interests of the girl. I don't doubt but that this "Evans", whose name is surely otherwise, will vanish once Hannah has been transported . . . or hanged."

Mrs. Jenkins was already weeping as Brandon ran from the room. He ran all the way to Mr. Fox's house as if his life depended on it, because he was afraid that Hannah's life almost certainly did.

Once he finally figured out what a frantic Brandon was trying to tell him, Mr. Fox decided that the only course of action was to go to London to meet with the judge. To Brandon's relief, Mr. Osborn not only allowed him the day off to accompany the magistrate, but also gave him the stagecoach fare to London. Brandon knew that Mr. Osborn could ill-afford the money. But the curate was insistent that he go, and Brandon was touched by his generosity.

At the Old Bailey, Brandon waited apprehensively with Mr. Fox outside the judge's office until a clerk called them in. It was late in the evening, and the judge slumped in his seat in the grand wood-paneled chamber: He had spent a long day hearing cases. However, he listened patiently to Brandon's testimony, pursing his lips and asking occasional questions.

Finally, he gave his verdict. "It appears that an injustice has been committed," he told Brandon and Mr. Fox. "I will issue a warrant for this man Evans' arrest. I fear, however, that he will prove difficult to apprehend. As to the unfortunate case of the prisoner . . ." It took Brandon a moment to realize that he was talking about Hannah. "Regrettably, she has already been transported to Virginia, this past Saturday. I will request an investigation into her whereabouts by the office of the Board of Trade, for it is they who handle American affairs. But since, in their purview, this is but a minor matter, I'm afraid my request may be of no consequence."

Brandon sagged in his chair. He felt so alone. He had read enough about history to know what transportation meant, and to understand the grave danger that Hannah was in. Perhaps he would catch up with her in America, assuming she survived the voyage, but he could not imagine how far a distance it would be between Georgia and Virginia by horse, by water, or on foot.

Screams and cries arose from the hold as the ship lurched violently to starboard, but the sailors on deck couldn't hear the wails over the roar of waves and wind, as they struggled against the storm for control of the ship.

Down below, the suffering convicts whose pitiful cries went unheard were packed together in two cages, one for men, the other for women. The shock of the sudden movement of the vessel had been too much for Hannah. Crouching in a corner of the cage, she was throwing up into an earthenware pot.

When she had first boarded and her shackles had been removed, she had been afraid of her fellow convicts, and she had clung closely to Jane. But there was camaraderie in the women's misery, and she grew to trust the other convicts as they tended to each other. When the ship started to pitch and roll a few days into the voyage, as it plowed through the English Channel, Jane was especially kindly to the seasick Hannah, even though she was almost as sick herself.

Now, in the second week of the voyage, Hannah's nausea had been improving, or at least it had until the storm hit. But she had been deeply depressed. She had nothing to think about on board ship except her own misery, and the misery of her fellow convicts. As the days passed at sea, she withdrew into herself. The more she pretended that her soul was separate from her body, and the more she daydreamed, the more the horror around her went out of focus.

Now that she had stopped heaving wretchedly, she spat, slumped back against the bars of the cage, and returned to her fantasies to distract herself from the terror around her. She dreamed she was in San Francisco with her mother . . . no, not there . . . . She was in Balesworth with Mrs. Jenkins . . . no, that was too painful . . . . She was in Balesworth in 1940, with Verity and Mrs. D., and it was a beautiful day, and they were going on a picnic . . . .

Brandon owned no spare clothes to take with him to America, and so Mrs. Osborn escorted him down Balesworth High Street, and bought him a set of used garments from a street trader. "We must be prepared that even if cloth may be had in Georgia, it will be very expensive," she told him briskly. Even on this nippy September morning, Brandon thought, it would still feel good to take a shivery wash from a wooden tub of cold water, and to put on clean clothes.

Mr. and Mrs. Osborn's furniture had all been sold, except for the massive kitchen table that was too large to move. The Osborns and Brandon took lodgings at the Balesworth Arms for their last few days in town, before they were due to travel south to the county of Kent to meet their ship. Brandon was impatient to begin the voyage.

He felt relieved, though, that he would be going as a white person to Georgia. That would mean he was not in any danger of being mistaken for a slave. People treated him differently when they saw him as white. They treated him better. No more tiresome stares from passersby. No more racist remarks. No white people acting weird around him. It made him feel strange, even a little guilty for thinking this way, but, he reflected, it hadn't been his choice to become white, and there was nothing he could do about it.

Would he feel the same way about his transformation once he reached Georgia, he wondered? He imagined how black people would react to him if they thought he was white. Sadly, he wasn't optimistic about making friends with them. That thought made him feel very lonely.

By the time the Osborns were ready to board ship at Gravesend, the port in Kent, Brandon was fed up to the back teeth. He had listened for hours now to Mr. Osborn boasting about his abilities, and complaining about the lack of respect he got in England.

Now, however, Mr. Osborn was in a more cheery mood. He was talking about his prediction that his stay in Georgia would change his fortunes. Even as he waited with Mrs. Osborn and Brandon to board ship, he was off on a self-congratulatory ramble: "Just think . . . A parish full of lost souls, thirsty for the comfort that only the true Church can provide. Once I have regained hundreds of people for the Church, who knows what reward will await me in England? Certainly my own living, to be sure, but perhaps, too, dare I say it, preferment to a higher sphere?"

Brandon looked sideways at him. "Okay, I'll bite . . . ." he muttered, and then more loudly, he asked, "What do you mean, sir, by higher sphere? Like heaven?"

Mr. Osborn puffed out his chest and looked annoyed. "Of course not. I speak of this world, not the next. I have always thought that the Lord intended great things for me, perhaps even elevation to the office of bishop."

Bishop Osborn, Brandon thought, and suppressed a smirk. But now, Mr. Osborn and his family were already halfway to the ship's deck, and Brandon hurried to follow them up the narrow gangplank.

As he stepped down onto the deck, Brandon turned to help Mrs. Osborn. He took her bag and offered a hand to steady her. As she thanked him, he saw she was crying.

"You all right, Mrs. Osborn?" he asked.

"Yes, Brandon," she said with a watery smile. "It is hard to bid farewell to England, is it not? Do you think that we shall ever see her again?"

"Of course we will," Brandon said kindly. But he knew that it was very likely to be a one-way trip for the Osborns. And perhaps for him, too. Would he ever see England again? Or twenty-first century America?

When Hannah awoke, she instantly remembered where she was. But she felt numb, as though the whole horrible experience were happening to somebody else. She was wretchedly filthy, and she didn't care. Her stomach was empty, and she didn't care. In fact, she didn't really care if she fell asleep and never woke up again. For once, Hannah felt at peace.

"It's melancholy she has," an old woman said softly to Jane, nodding at Hannah, who was staring into space with glassy eyes. "She won't live long."

Hannah wondered vaguely what the woman meant by "melancholy." Didn't it mean sadness? How could sadness kill you? And then Hannah thought, *She means I'm depressed. Is this what being really depressed feels like? It feels like nothing.*

Jane meanwhile was looking worriedly at Hannah. "She ain't been drinking nuffing today," she said.

"More water for the rest of us, then," said a hard-faced young woman sitting in the opposite corner of the cage.

"Shut up, you," spat Jane, turning threateningly on her. The young woman shrank away from her. Taking Hannah's hand, Jane whispered, "Bo'sun says we'll be there sooner than we thought. Ship's got a bit of damage, so we're putting in at port early. Come on, 'annah, whatever it's like in America, it won't be as bad as this."

"You said you wanted to be hanged instead," Hannah said sleepily.

Jane gave her a brave smile. "Oh, that was just me talking foolishness, wasn't it? I dunno what it's like in America, I ain't never been there, and I don't know no one that has, neither. That was a bit of a fib. Maybe it's better there than I think. Now, 'ere's some water. Try to drink a bit."

But Hannah turned her head away, clamping her lips shut.

"'annah, you got to drink," said Jane firmly. "You won't be around much longer if you don't."

Hannah's eyes welled up, but she took a tiny sip as Jane watched over her.

Once the ship dropped anchor, the bo'sun came down to the hold to tell the transported convicts that they were not to be allowed on shore just yet. "We're not in Virginia," he told them. "The ship needs repairs, so we put in at Savannah, and the master needs permission for you to land here. If he gets permission, he'll send word through the country that you're here and for sale, so planters in South Carolina and Georgia can come and bid on you. Wherever we land, you're all to be quarantined, to make certain that you won't bring your nasty diseases to America."

"So this is where they will sell us," said the old woman whom Jane had befriended. "I don't know that Georgia is any better than Virginia."

Only Hannah felt gladdened by the news.

Life on board did improve a little with the ship's arrival in port, for the prisoners were provided fresh water and fresh food. Jane continued to make sure that Hannah drank water, and fed her small pieces of bread by hand, until Hannah one day took a chunk of bread from her, and began to gnaw on it herself.

"It's okay," Hannah said weakly, when Jane looked at her with concern. "I'm okay, I think. I guess I was seriously dehydrated, but I just couldn't stand drinking that nasty slimy water they gave us. I'm okay now. I'm gonna make it."

Jane playfully slapped her arm. "Well done, 'annah."

Hannah, struggling not to cry, looked into Jane's eyes, and grabbed her hand. "Thank you," she croaked, her voice quavering. "Thank you for saving my life."

"Weren't nuffing," Jane said modestly. "You'da done the same if you was me."

Hannah doubted it. And that bothered her. She looked at Jane, this urchin from the London streets, and saw a better person than she was. Jane took satisfaction from giving to others, something Hannah found hard to understand, but admired all the same.

She tried to get to her feet, and Jane jumped up to help her. As Hannah's legs gave way, Jane caught her in her arms. Hannah apologized, but Jane would have none of it. "You're sick, you are," she said. "You ought to relax yourself while you can. Now sit down, and rest."

More than four long and harrowing weeks on the open seas had passed when the sailor in the crow's nest of Brandon's ship spotted the mouth of the Savannah River. Brandon, the Osborns, and all the other passengers rushed up to the deck to see land. Of course, it wasn't Brandon's first sight of America, although he had never approached Savannah by sea, or, for that matter, in 1752.

He had never guessed that he would be so glad to see Georgia, but his heart warmed as the ship approached Tybee Island. He knew it had to be Tybee, because it was next to the river, but otherwise he would never have recognized it. No houses or pier adorned the beach, and the lighthouse ahead of them was a simple wooden structure.

It had been a tough voyage, no question. One night, a brutal storm had hit, tossing around the little ship and everyone in it. To Brandon, even worse than the seasickness was the realization that he might die.

As the crew had struggled against the storm for control of the ship, he gathered the terrified passengers together, and led prayers as he struggled to remain upright. Despite the doomed atmosphere, Brandon could see that the clergyman was in his element: Until that moment, few of the passengers and even fewer of the crew had attended Mr. Osborn's services. Indeed, the crew had generally treated him as a nuisance, because he constantly complained to the ship's master about their swearing and card-playing.

But thanks to Mr. Osborn's bravery during the storm, the passengers now treated Mr. Osborn with greater respect for the remainder of the voyage. The crew was still rude, but the passengers' new attitude had put him in a very good mood for their arrival in the colony.

When the ship finally weighed anchor in Savannah, Brandon didn't recognize the dock at all, although he supposed they had landed at what would eventually be River Street. The tall and elegant Victorian warehouses and cobbled street that would one day grace the waterside were yet to be built. In their place was only a narrow strip of beach, short cliffs rising up to the town, and two stairways leading up the cliffs.

Rowboats carried the passengers to the beach, and from there, they climbed the steep steps. As Brandon and the Osborns reached the summit of the bluffs, they saw Savannah for the first time. Brandon was astonished to see that it was a little village of small houses, which he supposed, from his knowledge of Georgia history, were already laid out in the famous city squares, although it was hard to tell from where he was standing.

While Mr. Osborn negotiated the cost of the next stage of their journey with a man who owned a wagon, Brandon idly messed up the sand with his foot, and watched a small gathering of men who stood expectantly at the top of the cliff.

At first Brandon wondered if they were friends and relatives waiting for passengers from his ship, just like at an airport. He immediately realized that this was very unlikely: Nobody would have had any idea of when the ship was due to arrive. The Atlantic, not the ship's master, set the timetable.

Mr. Osborn's return snapped him back to reality. "Come, Brandon. While we wait for the baggage, let us escort Mrs. Osborn to a place of shade. It is devilishly hot here."

THE FORTUNES AND MISFORTUNES OF HANNAH DIAS

By English standards, it was indeed very hot for September. But Brandon was used to early fall in Georgia, and as soon as he joined Mrs. Osborn under the branches of a small tree, he stripped to the least clothing he could get away with without offending the English people around him. He was still wearing too much: shirt, breeches, stockings, and a neck stock, a sort of tie. He felt sorry for Mrs. Osborn in her heavy skirts and petticoats, and Mr. Osborn in his long black overcoat and itchy wig.

Mrs. Osborn was looking around her fearfully, and Brandon didn't blame her. It was all unfamiliar to him, too. He couldn't help noticing that there were only a few black people about. Savannah in 1752 was very much whiter than the Savannah he knew. Then, suddenly, he remembered: Slavery was banned in colonial Georgia. That explained it.

He gave a sigh of relief—he had no desire to see slavery in action. But, in that case, he wondered, why did Mr. Osborn think that he could preach to slaves in Georgia? And if there were no slaves, who were the black folks working on the riverfront? Brandon did not remember Mr. Osborn's lecture on the recent introduction of slavery to Georgia, for the simple reason that he hadn't listened to a word of it.

Suddenly, the white men who were waiting at the dockside perked up. Moving forward to the edge of the bluffs and craning their necks, they jostled for a better view of the river below. Soon, Brandon saw what they were looking at, when a line of white women in chains stumbled up to street level from the steps on the cliff.

The waiting men gathered around the exhausted and wary-looking prisoners. As though shopping for cattle or horses, the men inspected the convicts. A sandy-haired man in his fifties, with a weather-beaten face and a sour expression, halted in front of a bedraggled girl with matted hair, and spoke to her. When he gestured toward her face, she opened her mouth and he began examining her teeth.

Brandon almost looked away in distaste from the peculiar scene. It looked too much like a slave sale, except with white people as the slaves. But as he kept on looking, he realized with a shock that the girl being examined was Hannah. What was she doing here?

He was excited, but worried. He had never seen Hannah look so frail.

Finding his voice, Brandon called her name. Hannah looked up. But as she stared in his direction, she looked so dazed and shaky, he wasn't even sure she recognized him.

The man who had inspected her was now arguing over Hannah's price with the ship's master.

"I stand to lose the cost of bringing her if I accept so little money from you," the master protested. "Better I take my chances at auction."

"Nonsense," said the sandy-haired man in a Scottish accent, holding out a handful of gold coins. "In case you haven't heard, negro slavery in Georgia is now legal, and the price of servants has fallen as a consequence. And these servants you have transported are only a sorry group of convict ruffians who will be of little use to any of us. Here, don't be a fool. Take this ready money." He jangled the coins in his hand.

The ship's master reluctantly took his payment, shoving the coins into his pocket. He jerked his head at a sailor to tell him to remove Hannah's chains. Then he pulled a piece of paper from his vest, and gave it to Hannah's new owner.

Hannah, meanwhile, was weakly pointing toward Brandon. In a hoarse voice she said to nobody in particular, "There . . . that boy . . . He's my friend . . . ."

Brandon made to rush toward her. But suddenly he was seized by the shoulders.

A furious Mr. Osborn swung him around and yelled at him, "I distinctly remember telling you to escort Mrs. Osborn. Why were you associating with that wench?"

Brandon shook him off, and said urgently, "I'm sorry, Mr. Osborn, really I am, but she's my cousin. You know, the one who was arrested in Balesworth?"

"Good Lord," Mr. Osborn said, astonished. "She's here? Let me see what I can do."

Even before they had time to turn back, they heard Hannah cry out, "Brandon!" They watched helplessly as the heavily-laden wagon in which she sat turned a corner of the street, and was gone.

As Brandon stood open-mouthed in dismay, Mr. Osborn had the presence of mind to dash over to the ship's master. "That girl, who did you send her with?" he demanded.

The master squinted at the minister. "Begging your pardon, reverend," he asked carefully, "But is it any business of yours who bought her time? I'm not meaning no disrespect."

"Yes, it is my business," Mr. Osborn said firmly, raising his chin. "The girl hails from the same town in England as me. She has been wrongfully convicted, and on appeal she was found not guilty of the crime she was alleged to have committed. There is a warrant being drawn up in London to have her returned home."

The sailor shrugged. "That's as maybe, reverend, but Mr. Robert Gordon paid me for her passage. She is no longer my charge. You'll need to take up the matter wi' him."

Brandon had followed Mr. Osborn, and he was now standing behind him, his mouth agape. "Mr. Robert Gordon, did you say?" Robert Gordon was the name of the Scottish dentist who had employed Brandon during his first time-traveling adventure. It couldn't possibly be a coincidence, he thought excitedly. Not that they were the same man, but the Gordon family kept popping up through history.

"Be quiet, Brandon," Mr. Osborn hissed, gently pushing him aside. He returned his attention to the ship's master. "Know you this Mr. Gordon's whereabouts?"

The master scratched at his beard. "Sir, I know not, but there's people in Savannah who'll be acquainted with him, of that I don't doubt."

Mr. Osborn thanked him, and then led Brandon to rejoin an increasingly irritated Mrs. Osborn, who was trying to shade herself from the blazing heat under the skinny branches of the tree.

Chapter 5:
INTO THE WOODS

Brandon had always reckoned that the most boring road trip ever was the car journey on the freeway between Savannah and Snipesville. But the same journey by horse and wagon along a dirt trail was even worse. *At least the freeway takes you past the pine forests, marshes and swamps,* he thought, *not through them.*

Now, in 1752, he gazed glumly at the woodlands as the wagon bumped its way at an agonizingly slow pace along the track.

Mr. Osborn noticed Brandon's dismay, and assumed that he was pining for England. He tried to put a positive spin on things. "It is impressive that after a mere fifteen years of settlement in Georgia," he said, "Englishmen should have already built roads into the wilderness."

" 'Tain't our doing," said the cart driver abruptly. He was an Englishman called Mr. Plummer, and he apparently took special pleasure in squashing any happiness among his passengers. "This were the Indians' trail through the woods. We just follows it." He spat a black stream of chewing tobacco onto the ground. Mr. Osborn visibly cringed.

"How do you know where you're going, sir?" Brandon asked Mr. Plummer. The trail wasn't always obvious.

Mr. Plummer pointed to a nearby tree. "See them hatchet chops?"

Brandon peered, and he saw three axe marks come into focus on the tree trunk.

"That there's the sign I follow," Mr. Plummer said, "and that is why it's called Three Chop Road."

Brandon thought for a moment, and then asked the driver if he knew a planter called Mr. Gordon. "I knows the gentleman planter Mr. Robert Gordon, sir," Mr. Plummer said, and Brandon's spirits soared. "He's not been long in Georgia, just a year or so. He came down from South Carolina to get more land. Brought a few slaves with him, he did, and he lives on the farthest eastward part of your parish. Not sure he will stay. He's found out that Georgia isn't as prosperous as South Carolina. Sometimes think of going to Charleston myself."

But Brandon was not listening to the cart-driver's lament. He was thinking excitedly. Finding Hannah, it seemed, was going to be a piece of cake.

He snapped out of his daydream when Mrs. Osborn slapped loudly at a mosquito. She looked miserable, and Brandon wondered what it was like to be pregnant, especially in Georgia without air conditioning. At that moment, the rain started. It was a typical Georgia thunderstorm, so within seconds it turned from a few drops into a torrential downpour. Mr. Plummer pulled a blanket over his head, while all of his passengers hunkered down in the wagon as best they could. Brandon soon felt water soaking through his woolen clothes, and within less than a minute, he was drenched.

Shortly, the rain ended, but the excitement wasn't over. Arriving at a narrow and shallow river, Mr. Plummer brought the horse to a halt at the edge and inspected the slow-moving brown water. "The ferry isn't running," he said glumly. "We can ford this river, sir, but you and your family must get out."

One by one, as Mr. Plummer waited, the passengers climbed from the cart. Mr. Osborn helped Mrs. Osborn down, but Brandon was left to his own devices. Eventually, he managed to clamber onto the riverbank, lowering himself from the end of the cart. As soon as he was off, the driver coaxed the horse into the water, and drove to the other side.

"Okay," Brandon said slowly, looking across the river at their transport. "Does anyone see a problem here?"

Mr. Osborn nodded unhappily. "We must make our way across. Do you know how to swim?" he asked.

"Yes, but I'm not that great at it," Brandon said. "I don't think it's that deep, though."

"My wife does not swim," said Mr. Osborn with a sigh. "We must support her in case the wading becomes too difficult for her."

Fortunately, the river was as shallow as it looked, and Brandon and Mr. Osborn were able to help Mrs. Osborn across without much difficulty. Now, however, they were all soaked from head to toe. Mr. Plummer waited patiently for them, smoking his clay pipe. As the bedraggled passengers wearily climbed aboard, he said, "The river marks the bounds to St. Swithin Parish. But still got a ways to go to your house, sir."

This was the first time Brandon had heard that Mr. Osborn's new parish had the same name as his last, in Balesworth. Another coincidence. Or not.

The storm clouds soon disappeared as though they had never been, and the sun shone brightly as the dark woods opened into grassy fields in which cattle grazed. Steam rose from the pastures, forming an eerie mist across the trail.

Mr. Osborn, soaked though he was, perked up noticeably. "Are we near to the end of our journey?" he asked eagerly. Mr. Plummer nodded, and gestured ahead of him with the whip. "The church be just yonder, sir," he said.

On the dusty edge of a field sat a brown wooden hut, very small and plain. Brandon thought it looked fine, but Mr. Osborn blanched. "Are you sure?" he said to the driver. Mr. Plummer gave a taciturn nod.

Mr. Osborn's eyebrows shot up. "Surely it ought to be built from stone?" he said desperately.

"Not in America, sir," Mr. Plummer assured him. "None of our churches is built but from wood, not even them back in Savannah. It's not home, sir."

Mr. Osborn continued to lean forward and peer at the church as the cart rattled forward. "Where is my rectory?" he asked anxiously. There was no reply. As they passed the church, and rounded a bend, they saw a barn surrounded by fields carved from the pine forest. "There," pointed Mr. Plummer.

"I spy a barn," Mr. Osborn said falteringly, "but where, I say again, where is the house?"

"'Tis the house," the driver said smugly. "'Twas once a barn, but the parish has made it fit for the use of you and your family, sir. Or so I heard."

Mrs. Osborn burst into tears. Mr. Osborn was dumbfounded. He opened his mouth as if to say something, but then closed it again, speechless.

Hannah understood that Mr. Gordon had paid money for her, but she had no idea why he had bought her, and that was very worrying. She wasn't the only purchase he had made that day: The wagon was loaded down with wooden boxes, barrels of various sizes, and what looked like furniture wrapped in sacks and brown paper. As the cart trundled jerkily along the rutted track, Hannah examined her new master from the corner of her eye. He was very finely dressed, in a gentleman's attire. His clothes looked brand new. Rough though his face was, he certainly didn't look like a farmer.

Hannah began to feel optimistic that she would be living in a grand colonial mansion, like the ones she had seen in Colonial Williamsburg. She had gone there with Alex and their grandparents for an educational vacation two years earlier. Bored though she was there, she had enjoyed imagining herself living in colonial days, except with TV, a hairdryer, and other modern conveniences.

She wanted to know more about Mr. Gordon, scary though he looked. Even in her exhausted state, she had not missed the coincidence that he had the same name as people she and Brandon had known at other times in the past. Was he connected with the Gordons she had known in Scotland? With the Gordons of Balesworth? It seemed too much of a coincidence to be, well, a coincidence.

Finally, she plucked up the courage to ask him a question. "Where are you from, sir?"

"Scotland," he said curtly, looking slightly surprised to be spoken to. He didn't seem in the mood for conversation.

But Hannah persisted. "Where in Scotland?"

"You're English, lass," he snapped. "You willna know the place I belong."

But Hannah was too curious to be put off so easily. "Try me," she said.

Mr. Gordon sighed. "It's ca'ed Dundee," he said dismissively. Hannah's ears perked up. She had lived in Dundee during another adventure, but she decided it was probably best not to mention that to her new master.

"And where do you belong?" Mr. Gordon asked Hannah, without enthusiasm.

"London," she said, just to have something to say. But then she corrected herself. "Well, it's near London. It's called Balesworth. My parents . . . My parents own an inn. It's called the Balesworth Arms, and I helped my mother in the kitchen."

"Did you now?" Mr. Gordon sounded intrigued. "Your mother and father must be sore grieved by your wickedness."

Hannah at first wondered what he meant. "My wickedness? Oh, you mean the stealing? No. No, I never stole anything. The whole thing was totally unfair."

"I see," Mr. Gordon said evenly. He was clearly not ready to give Hannah the benefit of the doubt. "So you can cook? That is as well. My wife was not brought up to cook. She can only manage cornmeal mush." He gave a short mirthless laugh, and then pointed ahead of them with his whip. "Here is my plantation," he said. Among the trees appeared a small field in which a dozen cattle were grazing, and tucked in its nearest corner was a large wooden shed, with another hut next to it. Seeing Hannah stare at them, Mr. Gordon explained, "That is where my negroes live."

Hannah stared. *Negroes? He owns slaves? That's so weird*, she thought.

As if on cue, a young black boy dressed only in torn, dirty knee-breeches scrambled barefoot from the small hut. He suddenly stopped in his tracks, staring open-mouthed at Mr. Gordon and Hannah.

The cart kept on rolling, bumping along the trail. Hannah watched the kid, who was waving his arms and yelling. Mr. Gordon waved to him, and grunted. To Hannah, he said in an ominous tone, "You had best stay clear of the blacks. You will work in the house. From this time forth, we leave the field work to the negroes."

Alex watched the cart roll past. He was too far away to see Mr. Gordon's passenger clearly, but she looked a lot like Hannah from a distance. Was it too much to believe that his sister had actually found him? Yet here she was, apparently. He was too afraid to get any closer to be sure. But what a shame, he thought, that Hannah was white.

The cart rolled on, past woods, swamp, and more fields on which brown cattle were grazing, until Mr. Gordon pointed out his house. He had described himself as a planter and his farm as a plantation, and so Hannah had imagined that he owned a majestic two-story mansion, with white columns. She was not prepared for the reality of a backcountry Georgia property in 1752.

The Gordons' house could most charitably be described as a cottage. Truthfully, it was a wooden hut with a brick chimney. Its tiny windows were unglazed and open to the outdoors: Only rough wooden storm shutters protected the interior against bad weather.

Nearby, two shanties, both wide open to the air, housed hay and farm tools. There was also a barn in which tobacco hung to dry. A scrawny dairy cow was tethered near the barn, while chickens pecked in the dirt yard, and a huge hog roamed freely. The smell of wood smoke that Hannah had noticed all through the countryside was even stronger close to the house.

As Mr. Gordon drew up, a thin woman shyly appeared in the house's open doorway, her arms folded across her chest. Hannah wondered if she was another servant. She was very young, but very plain, with a nose and chin that almost met in the middle of her face, and large milky-blue eyes. Her dress looked old and worn, and so did she. "Sukey is sick again," she said to Mr. Gordon. Her accent was sort of English, sort of American.

Mr. Gordon was climbing down from the wagon, but on hearing this news, he heaved himself back into the driver's seat, while signaling to Hannah that she should climb off. "Sukey's a lazy wench," he said angrily. "I will tell her she had better get back to work before I take a whip to her. And you are a fool for believing her. These negroes will dodge any work they can."

As an afterthought, he said, "This girl is called Hannah. She grew up in an inn near London. You can see she is the worse for her voyage. Have her bathe, and let her regain her health a day or two before you put her to work."

With that, he turned the cart in the direction of the slave quarters. Hannah smiled at the woman, who gave her a slight smile back, and gestured her inside. "I am Mrs. Gordon," she said, to Hannah's surprise. She seemed young enough to be Mr. Gordon's daughter.

"What do you know how to do, Hannah?" Mrs. Gordon asked, leading her into the house.

"I can cook some, I guess," Hannah said. "I can do cleaning. I can read and write."

Mrs. Gordon looked surprised. "You have an education? Then what brought you to Georgia?"

Hannah looked awkward. "I was convicted of stealing, but I was framed. I never did it."

Mrs. Gordon regarded her skeptically. It was obvious she didn't believe Hannah's protest of innocence any more than her husband had.

"There's precious little to steal here," she said dryly. "I hope you will be of great help to me. My father was a planter in South Carolina and I was brought up a lady. We had slaves and servants to cook and clean for us, and I know little of domestic work."

Hannah didn't like the sound of that. She also wondered if it was true. The Gordons were so obviously poor, how could Mrs. Gordon have come from a rich family?

Alex was seized with apprehension as he saw the cart return toward the slave quarters. This time, Mr. Gordon came alone, without Hannah, if indeed it had been her. As he approached, Alex ducked back inside Sukey's hut, hoping to stay well away from the master.

"What is the matter?" Sukey mumbled. She was lying on a deerskin-covered pallet, shivering. From what she told Alex, he reckoned she had malaria. He had always thought that slaves didn't get malaria, because of the sickle-cell trait they inherited from their African ancestors, but apparently it wasn't that simple, because Tony and Cuffee told him that they got it, too. "It afflicts us again and again," Tony had said to him. "You mean to say you never had it?"

Alex again offered up a silent prayer of thanks for the Professor's malaria pills, just as he heard the cart grind to a halt outside, and Mr. Gordon jump down from the driver's seat. To Alex's horror, the master appeared in the doorway, clutching his horsewhip, and looked right at him.

"Why aren't you in the fields?" he growled.

"I came to check on Sukey," Alex said, his voice quivering. Quickly, he added "sir."

Mr. Gordon took a few paces toward the bed, where Sukey lay trembling and groaning. Frowning at her, he tapped her on the shoulder with his whip.

"What ails you?" he demanded gruffly.

"Ague, Master," she said weakly.

Mr. Gordon made a disparaging sound, as though he didn't believe her, but he could not argue with the evidence before his eyes. Sukey was not a malingerer. She was sick.

Stiffly, he said, "Tomorrow, I expect to see you back at work. Luckily for you, I have purchased a white servant to work in the house. But you will carry on doing our laundry, as well as the domestic work for the men."

He seemed suddenly to remember Alex. "And didn't I tell you to get to work?" He raised the whip threateningly, and Alex ran from the hut, grateful to get away from him.

The moment he had arrived in 1752, Alex had realized that he was in trouble. He had stared aghast at his newly-acquired black skin as he stumbled through the swamp, too freaked out to wonder how he could have acquired a different body. And before he had time to think too deeply about his predicament, Mr. Gordon had spotted him from the trail, and taken him captive.

At first, he was held in a tiny jail, no more than a hut, while Mr. Gordon investigated his identity. The Scotsman was convinced that Alex was an escaped slave and, after all, what else would he have been? Predictably, however, no owner was found, and a relieved Alex was released from his cold prison. On the principle of "finders, keepers", however, Mr. Gordon told Alex that he was now his property, and that his name was Cato, pronounced "cay-to".

"Cato" was delivered into the care of Sukey, the only female slave. She was an older woman, in her fifties as near as Alex could tell, who did the laundry for both slaves and the Gordons, and cooked everyone's meals. Sukey was kindly to Alex, but she complained constantly that she had too much to do, especially when the other slaves needed her to help in the fields at busy times. Once, Alex overheard her telling Tony, her grown son, that she had deliberately dropped a dish of food at the Gordons' house, claiming it as an accident, in hopes that the Gordons would find someone else to help her.

A few days after Alex's arrival, Mr. Gordon had called together all the slaves to witness the flogging of a man called Quashee, who had slaughtered and cooked one of the chickens he tended, and which were only supposed to be eaten by the Gordons unless the slaves had permission to consume one. Mr. Gordon ordered the other slaves to strip off Quashee's clothes and bind his wrists with a rope, and then hoist him into the air. As the slave struggled and cried out, Mr. Gordon had beaten him with a long whip until he had passed out. Alex, horrified and afraid, had sat on the ground with his knees up to his chest, his head in his hands. He was now absolutely terrified of Mr. Gordon, along with everyone else. He didn't guess that this had been the whole point of the punishment of Quashee.

Within a few days of her own arrival at Kintyre Plantation, Hannah came to realize that her duties, while tiring at times, were not so hard as she had feared they would be. For one thing, she had very few people to look after: The Gordons had no children at home, they lived very simply, and Mr. Gordon was sometimes away. Hannah's mornings began with fetching water from the well and milking the cow. In fact, milking the cow was at first the hardest thing she had to do, since she didn't have a clue how to do it.

Mrs. Gordon had to teach her. Hannah was initially shocked by how awful the cow shed smelled, and she held her nose until her mistress told her to stop being so silly. Hannah watched as Mrs. Osborn lowered herself onto a milking stool and wrapped her hands lightly around the cow's teats. Soon milk was squirting from the udders into the wooden pail. When it was Hannah's turn, she jerked on a teat and the cow, mooing loudly, aimed a kick that hit her squarely in the thigh. With a yell, she fell from the milking stool, knocking the bucket sideways as she landed in the dirt. Mrs. Gordon made a jump for the bucket, but she didn't reach it in time. The milk quickly soaked into the sandy soil.

"Foolish girl," said Mrs. Gordon, not unkindly, as Hannah rubbed the painful hoof-shaped bruise that was forming on her leg. "Here, I shall help you."

She put her hand over Hannah's and guided her. Soon Hannah was sending great shoots of milk into the bucket. "Hey, look, Mrs. Gordon, I'm doing it! I'm milking a cow!"

Mrs. Gordon gave her a knowing smile. "Then it will be your job from this day forth. Every morning and every evening, mind."

This wasn't the only animal experience for Hannah. She was to feed the hens their ground corn, put out fresh water for them, and collect their eggs from the coop. Hannah thought it would be fun to collect eggs, but when she leaned inside the dark henhouse, every perch was occupied by a live hen. Mrs. Gordon told her to reach under each bird and collect any eggs she felt there.

Nervously, Hannah wiggled a hand under the first hen, and felt the smooth cozy feathers against her fingers. Just as she wrapped her hand around the hard, warm egg, the hen squawked and pecked her. It didn't really hurt, but Hannah was so shocked, she squeezed the egg, breaking it. She grimaced, and held up her hand, dripping egg, for Mrs. Gordon to see.

"Quickly, take the hen out and muck out her place," Mrs. Gordon scolded. "Elsewise, she will eat her own egg, and acquire a taste for them."

"Ugh, cannibal chickens," Hannah groaned, wincing as she scraped out the straw and chicken muck with her dirtiest hand.

And then there were the pigs.

Hannah wasn't expected to be in charge of tending the pigs, because a slave called Tony had that responsibility, but she did have to feed them kitchen scraps. It didn't sound too hard: She only had to tip the kitchen swill into a wooden trough.

When she came to the trough, however, the pigs were already waiting for her. Tony saw her hesitation, and laughed. "Pigs are friendly, Hannah," he said. "Don't be afraid of them."

She looked suspiciously at the enormous creatures, then as quickly as she could, she dumped the wooden bucket full of leftovers and kitchen peelings into the trough and hurriedly stepped away.

Behind her, one huge pig with a large scar running along his back, trotted up to Hannah, nipped at her skirt, and then leaned against her, almost knocking her off her feet.

"He's just being a friendly pig, now," Tony laughed as Hannah staggered in the mud. "Scratch him. He likes that."

As the pig continued to press against her with what felt like all his weight, Hannah nervously leaned down with her free arm and scratched his back. It felt scaly, coarse and hairy. The pig responded by snuggling closer to her. She stepped aside a little to avoid being squashed, and then rubbed his back more enthusiastically. The pig flopped onto his side at Hannah's feet, awaiting more attention. She burst out laughing.

"He likes you!" Tony said with a grin. "See, Hannah, I told you he's friendly. Look at him."

Hannah did as she was told, and the pig indeed appeared to be smiling contentedly. "I just wish," she said, "he wasn't so dirty."

"Pigs ain't dirty!" Tony exclaimed. "Have you been listening to Quashee? He's one of those Moslems from Africa, and he don't eat pig. But pigs ain't dirty. Take a look around their trough, you see that?"

Hannah looked at where he was pointing. "There's nothing there," she said.

"Exactly!" Tony cried. "They don't like their muck to be near their food. Now, that's cleaner than a dog, ain't it?"

"So where do they, um, use the bathroom?" she asked.

"Out in the woods. That's where they spend most of their time. They like to run around, eating what they can, but they come back to us because we feed them."

Hannah bent down and scratched the scarred pig. "Does he have a name?"

"No, no name, just Pig," said Tony. "What do you want to call him?"

"Bacon," Hannah said with a mischievous smile.

Hannah prepared three meals a day, but since most of them were ham and corn mush, they didn't take much effort. Sukey came from the slave quarters one day a week to fetch the laundry to be washed, but Hannah found it hard to start a conversation with this grim-faced older woman. She, in turn, said very little to Hannah.

One rainy afternoon, Mrs. Gordon invited Hannah to sit and chat with her at the fireplace.

Handing her mistress a rough earthenware cup of hot water, Hannah said, "You don't look much older than me. How long have you guys been married?"

Mrs. Gordon hesitated, and then she admitted, "I am seventeen, and we married but eighteen months ago. I am not Mr. Gordon's first wife."

"Did he get divorced or what?" Hannah said.

"Divorced? Of course not," Mrs. Gordon said, offended. "His first wife died in childbed."

Hannah, feeling awkward, quickly changed the subject. "So, how did you guys meet?"

Visibly relaxing, Mrs. Gordon smiled. "He came a-courting me in Charleston, at our town house. My mother had always said I would forever remain under her roof, for I am not the prettiest of girls, nor was my father the wealthiest of planters, and my mother is now a widow with only a small dowry to give my husband. But when I met Mr. Gordon, he was a widower all alone, and a rising man, and desirous of another wife."

"So do you have any kids?" said Hannah, taking a sip of water.

Mrs. Gordon looked sadly into the middle distance. "I do not. Mr. Gordon has a son and a daughter. Robert, his son, manages Sidlaw, Mr. Gordon's plantation in South Carolina, and his daughter, Betty, lives there also. Mr. Gordon had many more children with his wife Mary, but they are all dead and buried in South Carolina. My baby, Jonathan, is buried outside. He did not live but three days." She pointed through the open door to a massive live oak tree, hung with trails of spindly pale green Spanish moss. Through the rain, Hannah spied the tiny stone marker under the shade of the sprawling branches.

She didn't know what to say. Mrs. Gordon sighed again. "Jonathan died of the ague. It kills so many of us, the fever, and especially our babies. Oh, how I long for the day when we may return to Charleston. We have fever there too, of course, but the climate is healthier."

Hannah wondered anxiously what this mysterious fever was, and she resolved to ask about it. Meanwhile, she decided to keep her hands washed and to avoid anyone sick.

"So Mr. Gordon is pretty rich, huh?" said Hannah, prying further. "I'm kind of surprised, because you guys don't exactly live like kings, know what I'm saying?"

Mrs. Gordon frowned, and Hannah realized that she had overstepped the mark.

"Mr. Gordon is ambitious and wealthy," Mrs. Gordon said firmly. "You are fortunate indeed that it was he who purchased your time, for little is expected of you. We do not spin our own thread, and the slaves provide most of our needs. What they do not provide, we purchase from England."

This little speech seemed to remind Mrs. Gordon that Hannah was supposed to be doing some work. She stood and, with difficulty, lifted a bucket, wanly handing it to Hannah. Hannah, taking it, was surprised to find it wasn't heavy at all. Mrs. Gordon was not a strong person.

"Now go fill it," Mrs. Gordon said, pointing to the well, "and set the water to boil." She gestured to a small black cauldron that squatted in the fireplace. "Then you may make the cornmeal mush."

As Hannah waited for the water to heat over the fire, she thought about what Mrs. Gordon had told her about the family. If Mr. Gordon was rich as his wife claimed, she wondered again, why did they live like poor people? And how could Mr. Gordon have got rich if he was a poor boy from Dundee, Scotland?

Once the water was bubbling, Hannah threw in a couple of handfuls of cornmeal, took the wooden spoon that was hanging next to the fireplace, and stirred the mixture. Mrs. Gordon, who was sitting behind her, said gently, "You'll need more." Hannah added a couple of handfuls, and her mistress nodded, satisfied. "Now stir it again. I know you don't eat cornmeal mush in England, for my husband has told me so. But it is not difficult to make, as you now know."

But it's bland and boring, Hannah thought as she stirred and Mrs. Gordon sat. There was an awkward silence, and Hannah was relieved to hear the sound of Mr. Gordon's return. She half-expected Mrs. Gordon to leap up and try to look busy, but she remained seated, staring into space.

Mr. Gordon walked in, hung up his black tricornered hat on a hook, and looked at his wife approvingly. He smiled for the first time Hannah had seen, and the smile transformed his face from forbidding and stern to cheerful and kindly. Hannah wished he looked like this all the time. "You need not tax yourself further," he said sweetly to his wife, "now that Hannah is here. You are a lady, Mrs. Gordon, married to a gentleman. Never forget it. Now, what say you we have a look at what I have brought from Savannah?"

Mrs. Gordon beamed. Going outside, Mr. Gordon soon returned with a large wooden box from the wagon, and set it on the floor of the house. Grabbing a poker from the fireplace, he kneeled on the floor and easily jimmied open the box, breaking the lid as he did so. He pulled out great wads of straw, and then reached inside and carefully removed two small objects wrapped in brown paper and string. He handed them to his wife. Eagerly, she unwrapped a china teacup and saucer.

"It is a tea service," Mr. Gordon said. "I ordered it from London with the profits from our last shipment. I do believe that all the contents of this box, at least, arrived safely, but there is more in the back of the wagon. I shall have Cuffee remove them to the house in due course. Best of all is what I have ordered for you in the next shipment." His eyes twinkled. "It is a new carriage."

In wonder, Mrs. Gordon examined the delicate cup and saucer, a huge smile spreading across her careworn face.

Next, Mr. Gordon pulled another two brown paper packages from his pockets, and held them up. "Here is tea, and here a loaf of sugar. You will find a teapot and all the necessary equipment for tea-making in the boxes. Mrs. Gordon, you will soon make tea. Once the carriage arrives from London, God willing, you may call on other ladies in the parish. I promise you, we shall join Charleston society ere long. My son Bobby told me in his letter that our rice crop this year shall be beyond all expectations." His eyes grew moist, and Mrs. Gordon's chin trembled.

Why were the Gordons getting emotional over a tea set? Hannah was confused, but she kept on stirring her corn porridge, saying nothing. The Gordons' affairs had nothing to do with her, after all. Suddenly she felt very lonely, and she glanced over at Mrs. Gordon. But Mrs. Gordon was paying her no attention. She was still sitting proudly, turning her tea cup this way and that.

As she did so, Hannah noticed a gold ring gleaming on her finger. The design was very curious, and it rang a bell in her memory. Could it be the ring that Brandon and Alex had found on the skeleton in Snipesville?

And if it was the same ring, was Mrs. Gordon the skeleton?

The Osborn household in St. Swithin's Parish, Georgia, was not a happy place. Brandon worried constantly about Hannah. He also heard Mrs. Osborn weeping every night, and during the day, saw an ashen-faced Mr. Osborn walking around in a daze.

The house really was nothing more than a barn. At night, the Osborns climbed a stepladder into the loft, where a desk in the corner served as Mr. Osborn's study during the day. The "house" had come supplied with very little other furniture, and Brandon slept on the ground floor, on a sack stuffed with straw.

Working alongside Brandon, Mrs. Osborn made a desultory effort to clean the barn, which was coated in dust and cobwebs. She didn't seem at all bothered by spiders, but the first time she saw a huge cockroach, she almost screamed the place down.

Brandon had rushed to her when he heard the commotion, and he smiled when he saw its cause. "It's just a palmetto bug," he said, before realizing that it was most unlikely that an eighteenth century English boy would know the name for a Georgia cockroach. "Er, someone told me about them," he added hurriedly. "They're harmless. They don't bite or anything."

Mrs. Osborn seemed only a little mollified by this news, and she had more wildlife worries. "My husband tells me that there are many, many snakes here in the summer," she told Brandon anxiously. "He advised me that I should learn which are harmless, and which deadly."

"I can help you with that," Brandon said. "I read about them."

Mrs. Osborn smiled at him gratefully, just as they heard a rap at the door. Brandon opened it, to find their first visitor waiting on the doorstep.

Mr. Jones, they quickly learned, was their closest neighbor. He was a ruddy-faced man with long thinning hair, a bulbous nose, and a southern English accent. He had brought presents: a large sack of corn and another of beans, along with a large and rather moldy-looking ham. Nobody but Brandon seemed at all worried by the mold on the ham, so he reckoned it had to be normal.

The Osborns peppered Mr. Jones with questions about the Georgia colony. Mrs. Osborn was especially anxious to learn about life alongside slaves, and Mr. Jones was happy to advise.

"They are savages, ma'am, Africans and Indians alike," he proclaimed, and then spat into the fireplace. "But I daresay we have them under control. We took great vengeance against the Yamasee Indians when they attacked us in 1715, and against the rebel negroes in South Carolina some years ago. That scared them all into submission. Not, I say, that we ever lessen our vigilance, Mr. Osborn, especially here on the frontier."

Mr. Osborn was clearly disturbed by this information. "What was this slave rebellion of which you speak? I'm afraid I have no recollection . . . ."

"The rebellion at Stono, called Cato's Conspiracy," said Mr. Jones. "Of course, it was some dozen or so years ago, and I know not whether much news spread of it in England. The rebels were Africans, new-arrived slaves from Angola, and they killed dozens of whites before our men halted them."

Mr. Osborn looked rattled, and Mrs. Osborn was blinking back tears. Mr. Jones clearly realized he had stuck his foot in his mouth, and he added hurriedly, "Of course, the Negro Act that followed the uprising created strict rules to control the slaves' behavior, although I daresay its provisions are not so strictly enforced as they ought to be. The law here in Georgia says that white men must always carry a pistol, but . . . His voice trailed away as he saw the aghast looks on the Osborns' faces. Boy, Brandon thought, this guy doesn't know when to shut up. He's scared the heck out of everyone.

"Now, Mr. Osborn," Mr. Jones said after an embarrassed pause. "I come not purely on a social call. I come also as my duty, for it is my honor to serve as the chairman of the vestry of St. Swithin's Parish."

"Excuse me, sir," Brandon said, lifting up a finger to interrupt, "but I thought a vestry was a little office?"

Mr. Osborn patiently explained that the vestry was also the name of a committee of important men who attended the church. They not only ran the church, but also the entire parish. As far as Brandon could tell, they were basically what would one day be called the county government.

Mr. Jones, who hadn't so much as glanced at Brandon before now, looked at him appraisingly. "Begging your pardon, Mr. Osborn," he said. "Would this bright lad be your son?" He looked expectantly at Brandon.

Mr. Osborn shook his head. "No, sir, he is not. The boy Brandon is my servant. I brought him to assist me in farming the glebe land."

Mr. Jones glanced at Brandon again, and then addressed Mr. Osborn. "But, begging your pardon, sir, field work is increasingly reserved for negroes. The lad is literate, yes? A boy like Brandon here will want to rise in society as soon as he is able, and he may already be able to command a decent wage in Savannah. No, a gentleman such as yourself should consider buying a slave or two for domestic work."

Mr. Osborn anxiously bit his lip, and then, to Brandon's shock, he said, "I see your point, sir, and I should be glad to purchase slaves." Brandon thought, *He's just saying that to make nice to Mr. Jones. Isn't he?*

"However," Mr. Osborn continued, "my means are limited, sir. I must know what salary the vestry intends to settle upon me."

Here Mr. Jones became uncomfortable. "Mr. Osborn, we were given to understand that since you are a missionary, you will receive a salary from London, from the honorable Society for the Propagation of the Gospel . . . ."

"I will indeed sir," said Mr. Osborn, "but my salary from London is modest. The Society expects this parish to assist in my support."

Mr. Jones was now clearly embarrassed. "But, Mr. Osborn, St. Swithin's is a frontier parish, and it is sparsely inhabited. We were led to believe that you would make up your salary by serving as an itinerant, ministering to the surrounding parishes as well as to ours . . . ."

"I was given no such instruction," Mr. Osborn sputtered.

"That is as may be, sir," said Mr. Jones, shaking his head, "but we have so few settlers in this parish, indeed in any parish outwith Savannah and Augusta. You will find that one parish cannot by itself support you."

But Mr. and Mrs. Osborn appeared so upset by the news that Mr. Jones softened a little. He sighed, and spread his hands. "Sir, I shall raise the matter of your salary with the vestry. In the meantime, I urge you to ride to our neighboring parishes of St. Matthew and St. John, and ask for their support, although I warn you that they are even less prosperous than we."

"I am sorry, sir," said Mr. Osborn firmly, "but I do not consider this a satisfactory alternative. I must urge you for more support from this vestry. And I must protest also that this house is not sufficient for one of my position. If I may be so bold, I am shocked that my office as a clergyman, my gentlemanly status, and my education do not command greater respect from you."

Mr. Jones did not answer, but stood up to leave, and he and Mr. Osborn shook hands. Mr. Jones gave him a stern look. "I shall see what I can do," he said abruptly. "I daresay the three other gentlemen of the vestry will call upon you within a few days. It would be wise not to discuss your salary with them, and to leave the matter in my hands."

"Thank you," Mr. Osborn said simply. "Oh, and, by the by, know you a gentleman called Mr. Robert Gordon? I need to speak with him."

Mr. Jones looked surprised. "Mr. Gordon? Why, sir, indeed I do."

"And what know you of him?" Mr. Osborn asked cautiously.

"Why, sir," said Mr. Jones, "he is a vestryman, and a leading man in our parish. A Scotsman, I say, but he has lived in the colonies for many a year. He holds a plantation in South Carolina. It is a flourishing place by all accounts. But now that slavery is legal in Georgia, he moved south a year or so ago with his slaves in search of even greater opportunity. He has acquired a large number of acres, with high hopes of speculating on the value of the land, and meanwhile he raises tobacco and cattle, as well as cutting timber. I believe he also trades for deerskins with the Indians. I suspect he had hopes of raising a great fortune in growing rice, as he has in South Carolina, but if so, he has made a regrettable error. If I may say so, the land he has purchased here is greatly unsuited to the cultivation of rice. But Mr. Gordon's industriousness is nonetheless admirable, if rather dizzying."

Mr. Osborn listened to this account of Mr. Gordon's success with a peculiar look on his face. Only later did Brandon wonder whether it had been envy.

Within moments of the door closing behind Mr. Jones, Mrs. Osborn cried out, "But Mr. Osborn, how are we to manage?"

"My salary is insufficient," Mr. Osborn confessed, holding up his hands in a hopeless gesture. "I am astounded that Mr. Jones seriously expects me to ride through the country begging for a living. Perhaps I may make up the difference by charging higher perquisites for performing baptisms, marriages, and burials."

Oh, like a tip, I guess, Brandon thought to himself, as he pretended to read a book he had borrowed from Mr. Osborn. *A perk! That must be where that word comes from.*

Mr. Osborn said, "It is fortunate that my father settled a modest sum of capital upon me before our departure, especially since it seems that I am expected to purchase slaves."

Brandon was shocked. "But I thought you were promising to buy slaves because you wanted to please Mr. Jones? I thought you were poor? And I thought you were against slavery, Mr. Osborn?"

Mr. Osborn looked surprised and slightly amused. "I am not wealthy, but I am hardly poor. And oppose slavery? Good Lord, no, Brandon. One feels compassion for the poor negroes, and objects to their mistreatment, of course. They must be brought to God by our best means. But their lowly station is as He intended."

Brandon did his best to hide his disappointment in Mr. Osborn. But the respect that he had been building for his boss was seriously damaged.

"This brings me to what I intended to say," said the minister, oblivious to Brandon's dismay. He nodded to the book in Brandon's hands, which he had been trying (and failing) to read. "I see that you are reading the book of sermons. Your interest in religion encourages me to think of your future. What Mr. Jones said is true: You are fitted for a less lowly occupation in America than that of a servant. And Mr. Jones is also right that now slavery is legal in Georgia, a young white man should look to a less modest ambition than servitude, because most servants here are negro slaves. If you are willing to work hard, I can speak with the vestry about appointing you as schoolmaster to the children of the parish when you are of age. Perhaps, later, you may take holy orders in the Church and join me as a member of the clergy. For now, however, I wish to appoint you as catechist to the negroes."

Brandon was perplexed and a bit alarmed to hear all these plans on his behalf. "Sir?" he squawked.

Mr. Osborn laughed. "You appear befuddled. I shall explain. A catechist is one who catechizes his pupils. In other words, he teaches them the rudiments, the basic knowledge, of the Christian faith."

This was something Brandon could do. He suddenly saw a very practical use for all the long hours he had spent in Sunday School and at Wednesday night Bible studies at First African Baptist Church in Snipesville. He quite liked the idea of talking about his faith. And it would be very interesting to meet slaves.

The next day was Sunday, and Mr. Osborn led his first service in the tiny wooden church. The pews were full, because people were curious to meet the new minister. Everyone who sat in the church was white, but a crowd of slaves had gathered outside to listen through the open windows. At least, Brandon was told they were slaves, but he was surprised to see Indian as well as African faces among them.

He also noticed a pecking order in the pews. Mr. Jones sat in the most honored pew at the front left, facing the pulpit. Brandon and Mrs. Osborn sat behind him. The farther back the congregants sat, the more worn-out their clothes were. There were only about half a dozen families altogether, as far as Brandon could see.

One family arrived just as Mr. Osborn was climbing the steps to his pulpit. The latecomers, led by a grim-faced man in his fifties, marched to the front right pew, and as they did so, Brandon caught sight of Hannah in the group. Although she didn't notice him, he was relieved to see that she was alive and well. He sat up straight with a big grin.

Mr. Osborn shuffled his notes and then launched into his sermon, reading it in a dry monotone. Brandon quickly lost track of what he was saying, and was soon bored out of his mind. This was even more dull than attending St. Swithin's Church in Balesworth in 1940. Why, he wondered, was white people's church always so boring? Then he admitted to himself that he didn't really know if all white churches were as subdued as the ones in the Church of England, or if all black churches were lively. After all, he thought, Dr. Braithwaite was black and he seemed pretty happy with the Episcopal Church, which was what the Church of England called itself in modern America.

It was strange, he thought, that the slaves who stood at the open windows listened to Mr. Osborn with rapt attention. How could they understand what he was talking about? And yet, they hung on his every word. Meanwhile, the slumped bodies he saw in the pews suggested that the rest of the congregation felt the same way as Brandon. Brandon suddenly found himself having an interesting thought: Did everyone get out of religion what they wanted to?

He would soon learn what some of the congregation wanted from their church experience. Halfway through the sermon, a man seated in a middle pew got up and ambled back down the aisle, throwing glances, nods, and winks to other men in the congregation, who rose to follow him. Hannah's master was among those who turned to see what was going on. He then motioned to his wife to allow him out of the pew. Soon, every adult man had filed out of the body of the church.

Curious, Brandon mustered the courage to get to his feet and follow them, a decision he regretted as soon as he glanced at the pulpit. Mr. Osborn, who had soldiered on with his sermon through the noisy interruption, was now shooting a look like thunder in Brandon's direction. But Brandon was too far gone to turn back. He reasoned that he could always tell Mr. Osborn later that he was checking out the disturbance. What he really wanted was to get some idea of what this Robert Gordon guy was like.

He didn't have to go far to solve the puzzle. Outside, next to the water trough where the congregation's horses were tethered to trees, the men had congregated around a watering trough of their own. A large bowl was set on the back of a wagon, and the men were laughing and ladling out a brown liquid into cups. Brandon's jaw dropped when he realized that they were drinking alcohol. They were having a tailgate party during church.

"Join us, lad," said Mr. Gordon with a cheerful smile that greatly softened his rough features. He clapped Brandon on the back, and handed him a cup of the mystery brew. Brandon tried to give it back, but Mr. Gordon looked offended and brushed it away with the back of his hand. One sniff of the drink confirmed Brandon in his intention to not drink the stuff: It smelled extremely strong, and he began looking about for someplace to dump it. But all the men were now looking at him expectantly.

"Drink up, laddie," the Scotsman said in a threatening voice. A smile still played around his lips, but his pale blue eyes had grown hard. The others urged him on, too. Brandon took a sip, grimaced, and gasped. The liquid tasted revolting, and it burned his throat. The men were still watching him intently, and he realized to his horror that they were waiting for him to drain the cup. Taking a deep breath, he held his nose, and drank it down.

"What is the meaning of this?" were the first words Brandon heard when he awoke. Mr. Osborn was angrily shaking his shoulder. Brandon slowly turned his head this way and that, to find himself flat on his back on the grass behind the church. Confused, he sat up. The men and horses had vanished. And he didn't feel good. Not at all.

He suddenly leaned to one side and threw up on the grass. Mr. Osborn gave an outraged shout, and grabbing him by the scruff of the neck, pulled him upright, and half-dragged him toward the house. Brandon staggered along as best he could.

Back at the Gordon plantation, the fields were empty of people. "Where is everyone?" Alex asked Sukey. She was feeling much better, and was eating a bowl of corn meal porridge.

"Some of them, they gone to church," she said, slurping her food. She made a face. "I don't like to go. They make us slaves stand outside, and I'm too short, so I can't hear what the reverend say, or see him neither. But Tony tells me about it, and that does me."

Alex didn't know what to say. He didn't go to church much, and didn't care either way what Sukey did on a Sunday morning.

"Anyhow," Sukey said, wiping her mouth, "I don't like to be around the master on a Sunday. I see enough of him as it is."

"Yeah, he's scary," Alex said with a shiver.

"So, who are you?" Sukey finally asked him. "How come you to be here?"

Alex considered how to reply to that. Could he trust Sukey with a made-up story about running away? Would she believe the truth?

But she had taken his silence to mean that he didn't want to talk about it. "That's okay," she said. "You don't have to tell me, and you're here now. I reckon your last master is pretty bad if you rather be with Mr. Gordon."

Alex nodded. It was easier this way.

"Have you, um, worked for him long?" he asked.

"A long time," said Sukey. "He buy me when I was a girl, and bring me to Sidlaw."

"You mean here?" asked Alex.

"Naw," said Sukey, "Sidlaw. It's what he calls his big plantation in Carolina. It belong to his uncle, and when his uncle die, he leave it in his will to Mr. Gordon, along with his slaves. So Mr. Gordon come from Scotland. He have a good rice crop the first year, and that's when he buys me. The next year, he do well too, and the next. He keep on buying slaves, and land. He's soon a rich man."

"Why doesn't he seem rich, then?" Alex wondered aloud, but Sukey seemed confused by the question. He supposed that anyone who owned other people must seem rich to a slave, but why didn't Mr. Gordon own a big house, or other signs that he was a wealthy man? And what was he doing in Georgia?

Sukey seemed to read his mind then. "He come here for more land," she said. "Sidlaw is surrounded by other big plantations, so he can't expand too easy. Mr. Gordon tell me he needs more land, more slaves. I don't know why. Seems to me, he has plenty already."

"So you have known him a long time," said Alex thoughtfully. "Has he always been a psycho?"

Somehow Sukey understood what he meant, and she frowned. "I think sometimes that evil spirits possess him. When I come to the plantation, he is already a bad man. But the other slaves at Sidlaw, they tell me that he was not like that when first he come from Scotland. He is a sweet young man, no more than a boy. He does not know at first how to make his slaves work for him. Then the Carolina white men got ahold of him . . . ." Her voice trailed off, and tears sprang to her eyes. "And the slaves say then he change."

So, Alex thought, somehow Mr. Gordon had changed from a nice Scottish boy who had innocently come to America to claim his inheritance, to an angry, grasping, and violent old man. Maybe he was possessed by demons, just as Sukey had said.

Now he had a chilling thought. Just how safe could Hannah be in his company? Suddenly, he found himself asking the same question aloud.

"Hannah?" laughed Sukey, who had no idea that Hannah was "Cato"'s sister, of course. "Don't you worry about her none. She is a white girl, and she will soon find out that she is safe. He never troubles white folk if he can help it." She patted Alex's hand.

Alex looked at her doubtfully. Then he said, "When you go to the house to fetch the laundry, please will you tell her that Alex is safe?"

Sukey's eyes widened. "She knows you? How can that be? And your name, it is Alex?"

Alex nodded.

"Then I call you Alex," said Sukey decisively, "except when other people are around. Then you are Cato. Don't let Mr. Gordon hear your true name."

Alex smiled gratefully. "And you will speak with Hannah?"

"When I can," said Sukey, and gave him a tense smile back. "When it is safe."

That night, Brandon lay miserably on his makeshift bed, on his stomach. He could not lie on his back, because an outraged Mr. Osborn had whipped him with a bundle of switches. It was excruciatingly painful, and now Brandon knew that Hannah hadn't exaggerated. His whipping, too, had drawn blood. He couldn't help thinking that if this was what eighteenth-century people did to white servant kids, kids they lived with and cared about, what did they do to slaves?

He tried to take his mind off the pain, focusing on the good things that had happened that day. He had seen Hannah and she seemed healthy. After the beating, he had at least persuaded Mr. Osborn not to fire him from his new job as a catechist. He had also managed to explain why he had left the church during the service, and what had happened outside.

Now, as he lay on the bed, Brandon strained to listen to Mr. Osborn's muttered conversation with his wife.

"I cannot understand this place," Mr. Osborn said. "I will write to His Grace the Bishop of London, and ask his advice about today's disgraceful episode at church. Truly, we ought to have a bishop here in America to resolve disputes between missionaries and parishioners. Here, I cannot even consult easily with my brother clergy for advice in matters of this sort, for they are too far distant from me."

There was a pause, and Brandon heard Mrs. Osborn weeping softly. Then Mr. Osborn said tenderly to his wife, "I am so very sorry I brought you here, Caroline. But I promise that our circumstances will improve. I will speak with Mr. Jones and the vestry, and demand that they make provision for us. Perhaps I will even buy a negro house servant."

"No!" Mrs. Osborn whispered fiercely. "I will not have one of those strange savage creatures under my roof."

If only she knew about me, Brandon thought with a bitter smile.

Mr. Osborn replied gently, "The negroes are God's children, Caroline, perhaps of a lesser sort, but they are immortal souls nonetheless. And I feel sure that the Lord has sent us here in part to minister to them. Once I have purchased slaves, we may do them good by bringing them into the Church. Indeed, I hope that Brandon will soon help me bring all the slaves of our parish to Christ. Judging from the crowd outside the church today, they do not lack interest in Christianity."

Brandon had read a lot of history, and in American history, he had already moved on to adult books, thanks to the Professor. He knew that the "kindly slaveowner" was a Southern fairytale, meant to make people feel better that their ancestors had owned slaves. He knew that even people with good intentions allowed the power of owning slaves to go to their heads. And he worried how slave ownership would work out for Mr. Osborn. For all his faults, the minister was a good and decent man. Would he stay that way once he had the power of life and death over another human being?

The next day, the Osborns set out early to visit neighbors, and so Brandon was home alone when the rain started. Within minutes, water had trickled through the roof in a dozen places, one of them directly above Mr. Osborn's desk. Fortunately, Brandon's first thought was to look for leaks over the bed, and so he was upstairs in the loft, gazing anxiously at the roof when the leak began. He hurriedly packed the minister's books in a trunk to keep them dry. But one book was already soaked before he could rescue it. Carefully, Brandon carried it downstairs, fanned open its pages, and stood it up to dry on the kitchen table, facing the fireplace.

As he did so, he heard a hesitant knock at the door. He opened it a crack, and broke into a delighted smile when he saw a dripping wet Hannah on the doorstep. Flinging open the door, he hugged her awkwardly.

The very first thing Hannah said was, "Have you seen Alex?"

Brandon shook his head sadly. "No, I'm sorry. I ask about him every chance I get."

Hannah's face fell, and she sat down on one of the upright wooden chairs by the fire, warming her hands by holding them up toward the burning logs.

Anxious to cheer her up, Brandon said, "Hey, it's great to see you. I hear your boss is called Mr. Gordon. Mr. Osborn says he's going to talk with him about freeing you."

Hannah puffed out her cheeks in a sigh. "Oh, yeah, my boss . . . my master, like they say here. It makes me feel like a dog."

She hesitated for a moment, and then she said, "Mr. Osborn shouldn't try to get me free. I think I'm where I'm supposed to be. I'm pretty sure that this Mr. Gordon is related to the Gordon family I lived with in Dundee, and your Mr. Gordon in 1915, but there's no way to know for sure. Anyway, I don't want to leave you here and have to go off to find work to support myself. I have no idea where I would find work, anyway."

"So what have you found out about him?" Brandon said. "Mr. Gordon, I mean?"

Hannah sat up. "Okay, the plantation I'm living on? It's called Kintyre. That was the name of the plantation that Alex went to in 1851. Mr. Gordon told me he named it after where his mother was born in Scotland. He's from Dundee . . . ." Brandon's eyebrows rose, and Hannah continued. "I know, right? Well, he has another plantation in South Carolina, called Sidlaw, and I know that's the name of some hills near Dundee."

"So that's pretty much connected to our adventures . . . but it's complicated," said Brandon with a frown. "What do you think it all means?"

Hannah smiled ruefully. "No clue. You got any ideas?"

"Not yet," Brandon smiled back. "How's life going, anyway? You sound pretty happy, which is weird, if you don't mind me saying."

Hannah waved her hand dismissively. "Whatever. It's okay. The work could be worse. At least I get some downtime, like now. And I think a big part of my job is to keep Mrs. Gordon company, which isn't, like, hard. Mr. Gordon's kind of gruff, but they're both okay."

Out of the blue, her mouth crumpled, and she started to sob. She didn't even try to cover her face. The sobs turned into wails, and Brandon anxiously came to stand next to her, taking her hand. Had she been putting a brave face on life in St. Swithin's Parish? Was she really miserable?

"Is it that bad?" he asked gently. "Do you want me to help you get away?"

She wiped first one eye and then the other with the heel of her hand, and then she broke down again.

Brandon was really worried now. "Hannah, it's okay, no matter what it is, you can tell me."

Finally, she could speak, but she spoke in a rush, punctuated by hiccups. "Brandon, it's not the Gordons," she said. "They're fine. It's . . . It's Mrs. Jenkins . . . . I thought she cared about me, but she called the police. I could have died. I was sentenced to death. And that awful prison . . . and then the ship . . . ."

Brandon was relieved that what was troubling Hannah was now in the past. He thought of his own trip across the Atlantic. "Yeah, that was a lousy journey, wasn't it?"

Hannah sniffed and wiped her nose on the back of her hand. "I nearly died. I'm still not sure I'm okay. I'm worried about my health. And Mrs. Gordon says I'm lucky, I could have arrived in August, when all the mosquitoes are out . . . ."

"They're still hanging around," Brandon groaned. "I got bitten yesterday."

Hannah winced. "I know, I'm just hoping they'll all be gone soon. Oh, and Mrs. Gordon says everyone new goes through 'seasoning,' and everyone catches fever. What is it, this fever?"

Brandon bit his lip. "It's malaria. People used to catch malaria in Georgia from mosquitoes. But we're good, remember? The Professor got us pills . . . ." His voice trailed off. Even as he said it, he remembered that Hannah had not gotten pills. He looked at her in horror.

"What? What is it?" Hannah said irritably.

Brandon cringed a little. "Look, just try not to get bitten, okay?"

"Is malaria really that bad?" She looked concerned.

Brandon dodged the question, and tried to reassure her. "You know, African-American people have some resistance to malaria, because our ancestors got exposed to it in Africa. Maybe your Portuguese ancestors had resistance too. Then you might not catch the disease." But he added, "Still, though, try not to get bitten."

Hannah nodded dumbly, and stared into the distance. After a long pause, she said in a small voice, "I have nightmares now. Every night. I dream I'm going to die in the eighteenth century. Sometimes I dream I'm hanged, or I drown in a swamp, or I die in a slave rebellion . . . . I am so scared."

Brandon shook his head, and said soothingly, "Hannah, they're just bad dreams, that's all. You had a rough time in England and on the ship, but things don't seem so bad for you here. Look, let's just focus on figuring out why we are here. There's always a reason, right? And I think ours is pretty obvious: We need to find out who the skeleton in the park was."

Hannah suddenly sat up, eyes wide . "I forgot! I totally forgot! Mrs. Gordon wears this weird ring. I need you to see if it's the same ring you guys found on the skeleton."

Brandon said excitedly, "Then maybe she's the skeleton!"

"That's what I was wondering," Hannah said. "And guess what? Her health isn't too great."

Brandon's face fell. "So we're on death watch?"

Hannah gave a mischievous grin. "Maybe I should put some poison in her cornmeal to speed things along."

But Brandon was scandalized. "Hannah!"

Hannah looked at him pityingly. "Joke, Brandon? Honestly, you can be so sad. Why do you always have to be so super-mature?"

It was more of a back-handed compliment than an insult, but either way, Brandon ignored her. He had a more pressing concern. "I have to tell you something. I called Dr. Barrett, the anthropologist. That was why I made an appointment at the college, and that was where I was taking you when we time-traveled. I wanted you to meet her. She said she thought the skeleton was a murder victim. And she said something else, but her cell phone crapped out and I never bothered to call back, because it didn't seem that important, and I figured she would explain to me when we met. She said something about the teeth being all wrong. What do you think she means? Does Mrs. Gordon have strange teeth?"

Hannah thought about it for a moment. "No. Not that I've seen. How bizarre. I wonder what she means?"

Chapter 6:
SHOPPING AND SLAVERY

Sleeping on a straw-filled mattress on the wooden floor was really uncomfortable. More than once, Hannah thought she felt a cockroach run over her legs. But her sleeping arrangements didn't bother her that much, which surprised her. She was less and less troubled by things that once would have sent her up the wall, like sleeping on a straw mattress and being trampled by roaches. One of her grandma's favorite sayings was "don't sweat the small stuff," and now Hannah knew what she meant.

Meanwhile, she fretted about the big stuff. Worrying about the disappearance of her brother kept her awake tonight, as it did most nights. And there was something else that troubled her: Mr. Osborn looked familiar. She didn't think she had seen him in Balesworth, because the afternoon he came for tea with Mrs. Jenkins, she was upstairs cleaning. So why did she recognize him? She must have seen him out walking on Balesworth High Street, she thought. Yes, that had to be it.

One problem solved, she turned over yet again and tried to sleep.

The next morning, Hannah felt exhausted. As she halfheartedly scrubbed the floor, she daydreamed. As time went on, cleaning was a larger and larger part of her day. Now that a second and third set of purchases had arrived from England, the tiny house was stuffed with chests, armoires, a tea table, chairs, and all manner of knick-knacks. Hannah again asked herself why the Gordons were bothering to buy all these nice things, when their house was nothing but a shack.

She didn't have long to wait for an answer. While she was scrubbing, Mr. Gordon returned from another three-day trip to Savannah, bringing with him a huge rolled-up document that he spread on the table to show to his wife. Now was one of the few times that Hannah had seen Mrs. Gordon smile.

Hannah wasn't invited to look at the document, but it wasn't difficult to overhear that Mr. Gordon was showing his wife the plans for their house in Charleston. Getting up on her knees and craning her neck, Hannah could just see the drawings. The house didn't appear all that impressive by modern standards, but compared to everything she had seen in Georgia in 1752, it looked awesome. In fact, with its three stories and windows, it looked much like it would belong in Colonial Williamsburg.

Mr. Gordon smiled fondly at his wife and said, "I spoke with John Harvey, the builder, and he tells me that work has begun also on our new house at Sidlaw."

Mrs. Gordon clapped her hands together in glee. "Not one house, but two? Oh, Robert, we are fortunate indeed."

Mr. Gordon beamed as he went to pour himself a glass of whisky. "Fortune has nothing to do with it, Mrs. Gordon," he said, uncorking the bottle. "With God's blessing, I am master of my own destiny. We have lived simply here in Georgia, and I have managed my business prudently, and now we shall reap the rewards."

"No doubt, Mr. Gordon, your good sense has much to do with it," Mrs. Gordon said, her eyes downcast. "But there was good fortune, surely, in how we obtained the land?"

Hannah looked up, surprised that Mrs. Gordon would challenge her husband's version of events. She was clearly daring him to take all the credit for their wealth, when she, it seemed, knew better.

Mr. Gordon frowned, but did not reply, knocking back a swig of whisky instead.

Hannah had a question of her own. She figured that now was as good a time as any to ask, although it made her nervous to do so. She coughed. "Mr. Gordon, Mrs. Gordon, this is kind of a personal question, but . . . If you're so rich, how come you guys live like you're poor?"

Mr. Gordon laughed loudly. Evidently, he was in a good mood. "Hannah, your insolence is endearing," he said, flecks of whisky and spittle flying from his mouth. "Let me see if I can help you to understand. When first I came to America, I intended to make my fortune here, and then return home to Scotland. Therefore, like many of my fellow planters, I lived frugally as I built my wealth in land and slaves. But, Hannah, I have found that a man's fortune goes much further living in America than in Britain, and here lies the certainty of making more and more profit. Now that Charleston society has risen to one suitable for respectable ladies and gentlemen, I am drawn to stay in America, where I can become a leading citizen. My family's fortunes are assured, and my property continues to increase. Now is the time for me to spend some of my income on showing that I am worthy to take my place with ladies and gentlemen in Charleston society."

Hannah was still puzzled, and looked around her. "But Kintyre Plantation . . ."

" . . . is not nearly so profitable as Sidlaw," Mr. Gordon admitted. "I was misled about the potential for prosperity in Georgia. But still. Kintyre makes a small profit from cattle and lumber, not to mention tobacco, and the value of this land continues to increase now that slavery is permitted. By next spring, I shall decide whether to sell this place, or else I will find an overseer to manage it. Then Mrs. Gordon and I shall return to South Carolina, and you will accompany us."

Hannah was fascinated. She had assumed that the Gordons were struggling to get by. But she now understood that they hadn't spent lots of money on the house at Kintyre because Mr. Gordon was too busy making money, buying up land and slaves. Now, however, he was ready to show off how much money he had made, but he wanted to do it somewhere lots of other rich people could see him showing off. Finally, she thought, this explained the new furniture and the tea set.

Hannah's job hadn't seemed at all arduous when she arrived. But now that Hannah was trained, Mrs. Gordon had settled readily into her new role as a lady of leisure. As far as Hannah could see, this mostly involved sitting around and doing embroidery. Clearly, this was not much fun, for a restless Mrs. Gordon often entertained herself by finding fault with Hannah's work around the house.

Hannah escaped outside as often as she could, since Mrs. Gordon seldom left her home, often complaining of feeling unwell. Luckily, Hannah had a lot to do around the yard: gardening, milking cows, feeding chickens and pigs, collecting eggs, and cooking over the outdoor fire whenever the weather allowed, which Mr. Gordon preferred her to do because of the fire risk indoors. Even outside, though, Hannah was not safe from her master's and mistress's nagging.

"The turnips are not coming along well," Mr. Gordon complained to his wife one evening. "Has the lass been picking off the worms?"

More and more, he referred to Hannah as "the lass", or "the lassie" or "the girl," much more often than he used her name.

"Yes, I have," Hannah said, tired of being spoken of as though she weren't in the room. "Sir," she added hurriedly.

Mr. Gordon glared at her. "I did not address you, girl. Kindly mind your tongue."

Embarrassed, Hannah put her head down, and carried on sweeping the floor. Was it her imagination, or was Mr. Gordon becoming more snobby?

Mr. Gordon turned back to his wife and said, "I met Mr. Jones on the road, and he tells me yon new minister is calling upon members of the vestry. If he should show his face here, I will tell him to return at my convenience. I do not want that black-coated rascal assuming he can call upon me at any hour he pleases."

"Yes, Mr. Gordon," his wife said meekly, and then returned to her embroidery.

As predicted, Mr. Osborn came calling the next afternoon. He was accompanied by Brandon. Mr. Gordon answered the door, since Hannah was cutting up a greasy roasted chicken she had just pulled from the spit over the fire.

"Good day, sir," said Mr. Osborn cheerfully. "You would be Mr. Gordon, sir?"

"I would," Mr. Gordon snapped, not making a move to invite him in.

Mr. Osborn shifted uncomfortably on the doorstep. "Sir, I have had not the opportunity to meet you after Sunday services, and I thought . . . Well . . . May I come in?"

"If you wish, but this must needs be a short visit, for we shall soon be at our victuals," Mr. Gordon said ungraciously. He reluctantly opened the door to admit the minister. Brandon, who clearly had not merited an introduction, meekly followed Mr. Osborn inside.

"This is my wife," Mr. Gordon said offhandedly, indicating Mrs. Gordon. Mr. Osborn nodded politely to her, and she quickly returned to her needlework, pretending to take no interest in the men's conversation. Hannah, meanwhile, had finished hacking up the chicken. She resumed her own sewing, mending a ripped hem on her petticoat, although she exchanged the briefest of smiles with Brandon. Mr. Osborn took one of the two remaining chairs, and Mr. Gordon the other. Brandon stood awkwardly against the wall.

"I am come to introduce myself to you, Mr. Gordon," said Mr. Osborn, trying too hard to sound friendly. "I understand that you are a member of my vestry."

"I am a member of the vestry, sir," said Mr. Gordon, folding his arms.

"There are a number of matters I wish to discuss with you, sir," Mr. Osborn said. "Some of them are of a difficult nature."

"Is that so?" said Mr. Gordon in a voice that did not encourage the minister to continue. He picked up his long white clay pipe and lit it.

"I am given to understand that you own a number of slaves," Mr. Osborn said.

"What of it, sir?" Mr. Gordon said suspiciously.

"I am considering the purchase of a slave," replied Mr. Osborn.

Mr. Gordon brightened at this news. "As a matter of fact, sir, I have a slave who may be of interest to you. He is a mere boy, and too young to work as well as a full field hand, but he can help you, and he will grow, of course. I will have him brought here when our discussion is done."

Mr. Osborn looked flustered. "That is very kind of you, but I do not think that, at present, I quite have the necessary funds in ready money . . . ."

"You may pay me back in time," said Mr. Gordon, clearly relishing the prospect of the new minister being in debt to him.

But Mr. Osborn wasn't so easily taken in. "Perhaps," he said curtly. "Now, in the matter of slaves, I have learned that you, sir, do not permit your slaves to be catechized in the Christian faith."

Mr. Gordon frowned. "No, sir, I do not," he said stoutly, as if daring Mr. Osborn to make something out of it. "I have no need for my slaves to learn self-regard and insolence."

Mr. Osborn shook his head at that last comment. "I must persuade you to fulfill your Christian duty to the poor negroes," he said, gesturing to Brandon to step forward. "My servant's name is Brandon Clark, and I am training him up to be a catechist to the negroes. He will teach them the one true faith of the Church of England."

Mr. Gordon ignored Brandon. "I would dispute that assertion, sir. The Church of England is certainly not the one true faith, as you put it. I am a Presbyterian, myself."

Mr. Osborn utterly failed to hide his shock. "A Presbyterian? How can you be a Presbyterian when you are a member of my church's vestry?"

Mr. Gordon did not seem apologetic. "We handle matters differently in Georgia than at home. It is only right that an eminent planter such as myself should sit upon the vestry, regardless of my Christian denomination. Anyhow, your idea of catechizing the slaves is foolishness, Mr. Osborn. You are a young man, a newcomer, and you do not understand the negroes. They will take any interest in their spiritual welfare as a sign that we accept them as the equals of white men. Truthfully, they are savages at heart, and they have some very strange ideas, all magic and superstition."

Brandon's eyebrows practically shot through the ceiling. It was all he could do not to run forward and stomp Mr. Gordon's foot.

"Precisely," Mr. Osborn said with a smile, to Brandon's consternation. "And that is why they must be brought to a full understanding of God's grace, and that is the responsibility of their masters, and of the clergy."

Brandon put his head down and gritted his teeth. This conversation was making him very angry. It was taking all his self-control not to say or do anything.

Mr. Gordon abruptly changed the subject. "What other matters wish you to discuss with me?"

Mr. Osborn, nervous again, cleared his throat. "I, um, wish to discuss my parsonage. The building is, I am afraid, rather unsuited to the needs of a growing family . . . ."

He trailed off. Mr. Gordon was glowering at him. Fixing the minister with an angry stare, he said, "Look around you, Mr. Osborn. There are but few families in your parish, and we all subscribed to the cost of your house according to our abilities. If it is not to your satisfaction, then I am afraid you must fund your own house."

Mr. Osborn gulped. "I see. Well, I . . . I shall consider what you say."

"That is just as well," Mr. Gordon said with a satisfied nod. "Now, was there anything else you wished to bring to my attention?"

"No, no, that will be all," said Mr. Osborn lamely.

Brandon couldn't help smirking at the silly thought that he had just witnessed a battle between Godzilla and Bambi. It was pretty clear that "Godzilla" Gordon was the winner, and that Mr. Osborn had been squashed.

Then a more sobering thought occurred to Brandon: What did any of this conflict mean for him? He was loyal to Mr. Osborn, but was that wise? Shouldn't he look out for himself in this tough colony? The moment he thought this, Brandon felt treacherous and mean. And realizing he had this ruthless and self-seeking side of him, he thought, meant he had begun to understand Georgia for the very first time.

Now, Hannah caught Brandon's eye, and she stole meaningful glances toward Mrs. Gordon. Brandon followed her stare, and soon he was looking openmouthed at the gold ring gleaming on Mrs. Gordon's hand. Hannah had been right. It was the same ring that the skeleton had worn, he had no doubt about it.

He plucked up the courage to ask about the ring, and leaned forward to get Mrs. Gordon's attention. "Excuse me, ma'am, but where did you get that ring? It's, er, beautiful."

"This?" Mrs. Gordon smiled as she held up her hand and wiggled her fingers. "It was a present given me by my mother. It crossed the Atlantic Ocean with her when she came from England to South Carolina some thirty years ago."

Brandon didn't know what made him ask the next question. "Where is your mom from, originally?"

Mr. Osborn interrupted to apologize for Brandon's nosiness, but Mrs. Gordon waved aside his concern. "No, sir, I am pleased to answer your servant's question. My mother was from the county of Hertfordshire, from the town of Balesworth, if it is of any consequence."

Brandon glanced across at Hannah, who was looking as fascinated as he felt. Even Mr. Osborn smiled at the coincidence, although, of course, he had no idea that it was important.

Balesworth, thought Brandon. *Everything always comes back to Balesworth.*

Early the next morning, after breakfast, Mr. Gordon rode off to a session of the magistrates' court, which was held in the church. He returned some hours later with unexpected company: A filthy young white girl in a torn skirt. She stood next to him with shoulders rounded and head down.

"We decided to remove this girl from her master," Mr. Gordon said to his wife as he took off his hat. "As you can see, he used her abominably. I will keep her here for the time being, until she is recovered, and then I will find a new master for her. Meantimes, the parish will pay her keep. Lass, help her to bathe."

Hannah hurried to the well. She fetched water in a wooden bucket, and then set a fire outside to heat it in the cauldron. When she returned, lugging hot water in the bucket, the girl was sitting against the wall, with her chin resting on her knees.

Now that Hannah got a good look at her, she had a shock. The abused servant girl was Jane, her friend from London.

Hannah dropped to her knees and took Jane's dirty hands. Surprised, Jane looked up at her, and then a smile spread across her face.

"'annah!" she said softly. Then, she started to cry in huge, convulsive sobs.

"You know the girl?" Mr. Gordon asked Hannah.

Hannah simply nodded, and handed Jane a none-too-clean rag from her pocket with which to wipe her nose.

"She has been horribly ill-used," said Mr. Gordon quietly, shaking his head. "Her master has fled the parish, and good riddance to him. His indifference to the suffering of this poor girl has shocked us all."

Hannah looked up at him admiringly. Mr. Gordon really was kinder than she had first thought. She had always assumed that slave owners were mean, and since Mr. Gordon was hardly what you would call friendly, she had been a little afraid of him. But, she thought, he really wasn't all that bad.

Over the next few days, even as Jane assisted Hannah with the lighter tasks like butter-making and stirring cornmeal mush, she hardly said anything at all. Despite Hannah's prodding, she wouldn't talk about her old master and mistress, except to say once that they were "terrible cruel."

Hannah guessed that Jane was suffering from depression and maybe PTSD, but she had no idea what to do about it. So she just tried to be as kind to her as she could be, sensing that this was exactly what Jane needed.

"It is peculiar, Mrs. Jones," Mrs. Gordon said to her visitor one afternoon, over tea, "I have two white servant girls in the house, and hardly enough work for one. Neither, of course, may be allowed to work alongside the negroes in the fields. And so I find I must invent tasks for them both. As you can see, my floors are cleanly swept."

"But, my dear," Mrs. Jones said, "why don't Mr. Gordon auction off the other girl's time?"

Jane and Hannah heard this, because they were sitting outside the open window, eavesdropping. They looked at each other in alarm.

"Mr. Gordon intends to find a buyer for her at the earliest opportunity, I assure you," Mrs. Gordon continued. "He proposed to me that we take Jane to South Carolina to work in our new house, but I don't care much for the girl. She lacks good manners and she is dirty. Hannah is much more suited to serve in a genteel household."

Hannah looked at Jane to see that her eyes were brimming with tears. Silently, she took her friend's hand, and led her toward the woods, where they sat together on a fallen tree, far from the prying ears of their mistress.

"I can't go to another place . . . . I won't," Jane sobbed. "I want to go 'ome to London."

Hannah exhaled loudly through her nose. It was so frustrating. What could Jane do? Even if she ran away, how would she ever get to England?

For one unnerving moment, Hannah wondered if she was supposed to run away with Jane, but truthfully, she wanted to stay where she was. Life with the Gordons wasn't too bad, Brandon was nearby, and even if a way could be found across the Atlantic, she shuddered at the thought of repeating the horrific voyage.

She desperately racked her brains for a solution. "Why don't we write to your parents," she asked her friend, "and see if we can get them to bring you home?"

Jane rubbed her eyes and said in a flat voice, "I don't know where they are. I ain't seen them since I was a little kid. They worked in an inn just south of the river in London, but when I got old enough to go a-looking for them, they was gone."

"They abandoned you?" Hannah was furious on Jane's behalf. What kind of people abandoned their children?

But Jane was shaking her head. "Nah, they didn't abandon me. There was this woman, see? She sees me playing in the street one day, and she says to me she would buy me sweet cakes if I came with her. But it turns out that she was stealing me away. I wasn't the first kid she had spirited away, neither. She lived with this fellow—fine gentleman he seemed to be—and they made us kids steal for them.

"I wasn't a pickpocket or nothing, though. They dressed me up fine, like, and they would 'ave me cry and wail in the marketplace, so people would take pity on me, and 'elp me look for my parents. I would lead them down an alley, and my master and the older lads would rob them there. Or the people would take me 'ome to their 'ouse, and I would nick off them what I could, and then fly off back to my master. Oh, yes, I had a fine training as a thief, make no mistake."

Hannah idly scratched her own name in the dirt as she listened in horror to Jane's story. How, she wondered, could she help make Jane's life better?

"You can write, eh?" Jane said wistfully. "I wish I could. I started to learn writing when I was little, but I don't remember it now."

"Here, I'll show you," Hannah said. This was something she could do for her friend. Taking a stick of wood, she cleared away pine straw and leaves on the ground, and scratched "JANE" into a patch of sandy soil.

Jane smiled. "Oh, I can read my name, but I ain't wrote it in such a long time," she said. She took the stick from Hannah and painstakingly copied out her name.

"So you can read?" Hannah asked.

"Not much," Jane admitted. "Words 'ere and there."

"I'll teach you," Hannah said, and surprised herself with the decision in her own voice. "Let's start with the alphabet, yeah?"

Jane had saved Hannah's life. Teaching her to read and write, Hannah thought proudly, was the least she could do to repay her friend. But how was she going to save her from being sold? That was another matter altogether.

Later that afternoon, Mrs. Gordon ordered Hannah to walk to the slave quarters and fetch a slave named Cato. As Hannah trudged through the drizzling rain, she was nervous but also curious. She had never been to the slaves' huts, and the only slaves she had met were the old lady called Sukey, who came for the laundry, and Tony, Sukey's grown son, who tended the pigs. He had been born in America, and he was very chatty, unlike his mother, who seldom spoke in the presence of whites.

Sukey had looked like she wanted to speak to Hannah on her last visit to the house, but Mrs. Gordon was there, and so it never happened, to Hannah's guilty relief. She found Sukey a bit scary, honestly. She always looked so fierce, kind of like Brandon's Aunt Morticia.

Hannah knew that most of the slaves were men from Africa, and that many spoke little English. She only saw them in passing, as they tended the cattle, corn, and tobacco, or cut down trees, and none had tried to talk to her. Hannah didn't blame them for keeping their distance from white people. If she had a choice, she wouldn't want to chat with the Gordons either.

The men ignored her as usual as she passed them by in the pasture, pretending not to see her as they herded the cattle and wiped away the rain that dripped down their faces. Ahead of her, a stream of fragrant wood smoke issued from the roof of one of the huts, and she hoped she could find Sukey or Tony to tell her where Cato was.

Sukey was stooped over the cooking pot that hung by a chain from the ceiling in the smoky hut, her back to the door. Not for the first time, Hannah wondered to herself why Sukey had long straight hair. Nobody had invented hair relaxers yet, had they? She stood at the open doorway, hoping that Sukey would acknowledge her, but her arrival went unnoticed until she loudly cleared her throat.

Sukey twirled around, and she stiffened when she saw the white girl standing on her threshold. "What do you want?" she asked tersely.

Hannah gave her an anxious smile. "Hi, I'm Hannah. Remember me? I, like, work at the house? I'm looking for Cato?"

Sukey sighed heavily. "I know who you are, Hannah. What do you want with him?"

Hannah frowned. "I don't. Mrs. Gordon needs him to do some work, I guess."

Sukey sniffed. "I take you to him, but first I finish boiling the corn." She carried on stirring the pot. Hannah coughed, and peered through the smoky air for somewhere to sit. Apart from a couple of ragged and stained straw mattresses (if they could be called mattresses) she saw only a tree stump. After a moment's hesitation, she sat on it, and was relieved to find that the air was clearer now that she was closer to the ground.

There was a silence while Sukey stirred. Finally, Hannah decided to make conversation.

"So, where are you from?" she asked.

Sukey looked askance at her. "Here."

Hannah tutted. "No, I mean originally? Where are your parents from?"

"My mother was Yamasee," Sukey said reluctantly, "and my father from Angola."

Hannah had no idea what Yamasee meant, or where Angola was. So she asked, "Was it nice where they came from?"

"I don't know," Sukey said grumpily, and Hannah decided not to push things further. The room fell silent again.

Finally, Sukey threw some dirt on the fire to extinguish it, and wiped her hands on her tattered skirt.

"We go find Cato now," she said firmly, and she walked outside without waiting for Hannah. Hannah rose and followed her, feeling awkward and forlorn. The Gordons didn't treat her as an equal, but they had made it clear that she was supposed to be better than the slaves. She had already figured out that the slaves wouldn't want anything to do with her, because she was white and a house servant, and because she might report what they said to the Gordons. If it weren't for Jane and Brandon, she thought, she would live a very lonely life.

"There he is," Sukey said, pointing toward a black boy who was hoeing in the field. Hannah followed as Sukey, her long skirt flapping as she walked, called "Cato!"

The boy turned and straightened up, breaking into a broad grin when he saw them. Dropping his hoe, he threw off his hat, and ran. Then, to Hannah's stunned surprise, he threw himself at her, wrapping his arms around her waist.

"Hannah!" he cried.

Immediately, Hannah's eyes grew wide as saucers, and she held the kid out at arm's length to look at him. There was only one possible explanation. "Alex? Is that you?"

He nodded, his chin trembled, and he teared up. Hannah hugged the strange boy tightly, kissing his head. But she couldn't help blurting out the obvious. "Oh, my God," she mumbled into his wiry hair, "you're black."

Alex wiped his eyes. "Yes, I know that. It's freaking me out."

Hannah rushed to reassure him. "Brandon's white, and he's pretty freaked out, too. But . . . But I don't see him as white. He looks normal to me. You don't."

Sukey had been listening to this conversation in disbelief. "What is this?" she demanded suspiciously.

Alex said quickly, "Hannah's a friend of mine, remember? I knew her at my old place, and this is our joke."

Sukey looked at them both in confusion. To Alex, she said, "I must go do my work. You go with her," she jerked her head at Hannah. "*They* want to see you."

Alex was frightened, and he looked it. "It's okay," Hannah muttered, grabbing his arm and giving it a comforting shake, "Mrs. Gordon always looks hungry, but I promise she won't eat you."

But her brother was not amused.

When they arrived back at the house, Mrs. Gordon studied Alex carefully.

"Cato, I have spoken with Sukey," she said, "and she has praised your cleanliness and your manners. Would you like to work indoors?"

Hannah was mystified. There wasn't enough work for her and Jane, but Mrs. Gordon wanted Alex as a servant, too?

However, Mrs. Gordon explained. "We don't need you in this house, Cato, but Mr. Osborn, the missionary, has expressed an interest in purchasing you. I shall teach you, and perhaps, if you learn well, you will be suited as a house servant. Let us begin with how you set a table. Go and fetch the knives, forks, and spoons to start with. Hannah, show Cato where to find the cutlery."

Hannah thought Alex should be pleased, and yet still he looked very scared. Why?

Not surprisingly, Alex's first lesson was a remarkable success. He had no problem, of course, setting a table and serving food. "You must have worked as a footman before," Mrs. Gordon said admiringly, when Alex served her at the noon meal. "It is impossible for me to believe otherwise."

He smiled and nodded. Hannah, watching him from the corner of her eye, saw his smile vanish as soon as Mrs. Gordon looked away from him. But as soon as she looked at him again, he switched the smile back on.

As she finished her meal, Mrs. Gordon delicately dabbed the corners of her mouth with a napkin. "I will discuss your work with Mr. Gordon," she said to Alex, "You may return to the quarters."

Alex gave his sister a small wave as he left. Hannah decided to catch up with him as soon as she could. Something was wrong.

Later that night, Hannah waited until Mr. and Mrs. Gordon and Jane were all asleep. As usual, everyone went to bed as soon as it was dark. Some evenings, when he wanted to read, Mr. Gordon would direct Hannah or Jane to light a rush light, a reed dipped in animal fat.

More rarely, he would light a candle, which Hannah had learned was a very expensive thing to do. Mostly, however, everyone turned in as soon as the light fell.

Tonight, Hannah thanked her good fortune: There was a full moon, and its light would help her find her way through the woods and fields.

As Jane snored, Hannah quietly crept from the house, opening and closing the door quickly so that it wouldn't creak too long. She waited outside for a few moments, holding her breath and listening for sounds of movement from the house. If the Gordons awoke and asked where she was going, she planned to tell them that she had stepped out for fresh air, as if she didn't get enough of that already. Living with them was like camping, and she spent most of her day outside. Without sunscreen, she had quite a tan, unlike Mrs. Gordon, who was pale from spending most of her time indoors.

Satisfied that the Gordons hadn't heard her, Hannah decided to walk through the woods to be sure that no one saw her as she made her way to the slave quarters. Fortunately, the path though the woodland was well-worn, but she trod carefully for fear of startling a snake or twisting her ankle in a pothole.

Hannah stepped in from the darkness to find Alex, Sukey, and the other slaves sitting around the bright fire.

Everyone except Sukey and Alex jumped to their feet, their smiles vanishing, and their merrymaking descending into silence.

"Hi," she said nervously. "There was, like, no way for me to knock. Wow, is the party over already?" She knew why they were quiet: They didn't trust her. She wondered if they had ever met a white person they could trust.

Alex, meanwhile, was glad to see his sister, and he now clambered to his feet and hugged her. Clearing his throat, he announced to the group, "This is the girl I told you about." Hannah noticed that Sukey was smiling cautiously at her as though recognizing at last that she was a real person.

Now Sukey addressed the men. "This is Hannah, and she is fine. Hannah, come sit at the fire." The men finally relaxed, and sat down again. Sukey's word clearly commanded a lot of respect from them.

Sukey turned to Hannah, "Do they," and here she jerked her head in the direction of the house, "They know you here?"

Hannah shook her head. "No. So I can't stay long."

Sukey seemed satisfied with her answer, and she soon handed Hannah a hot drink, some sort of herbal tea. Her son Tony, the pigkeeper, began singing a song that he said was taught to him by an old African man he once knew.

After he had sung just one verse, another slave, who Alex whispered to Hannah was named Quashee, interrupted him, grumbling that the song was in the language of enemies of his own people. Tony made a face and looked ready for an argument, but then Quashee offered to sing a song he had learned from an Irishman in Savannah.

As he sang, Quashee played a small hand-drum, while Cuffee accompanied him on a stringed instrument made from a gourd, and Tony kept time by thumping on the ground with a large stick. As the energy of the music picked up, Sukey leapt to her feet, and to the shouts and cheers of the others, started to dance energetically.

Extending an encouraging hand toward Alex, she brought him to his feet. "You dance, too, Cato!" she cried, and Alex was so overwhelmed with her joy, he forgot to be shy about performing in public. As the others clapped along, he danced wildly, throwing his limbs in all directions. Suddenly, he dropped onto his belly and did the worm, his head and bottom bopping up and down as he propelled himself across the dirt floor. The others laughed and applauded, Hannah most loudly of all.

When the song ended and Alex scrambled to his feet, Sukey hugged him around the shoulders, laughing. "You dance good, Cato!"

"Way to go, bro!" Hannah agreed. She felt a little weird to be partying with slaves while sitting on a dirt floor in 1752, but she was mostly happy to be out from under the constant scrutiny of the Gordons.

Now the musicians laid down their instruments, and the atmosphere became more subdued. Tony and Cuffee took up small white clay pipes, stuffed them with tobacco, and lit them from straws dipped into the fire. Alex sat down by the fire and rested his head in Sukey's lap. Hannah felt a pang of jealousy, although she wasn't sure who she was jealous of.

"Tell us a story, Tony," Alex pleaded. "The one about the white witch . . . ."

Tony laughed. "No, I've told that one too many a time. Here, I tell you another one. There was this man called, uh, Pompey walking through the swamp, see, and he hears another man calling behind of him. So he calls back to him, 'Hey, brother, who are you?' But the other man don't answer.

"Now he starts to worry that this man means to rob him, and he starts walking faster. But the other man walks faster too.

"Soon he is running for his life, and the man is chasing him through the woods. Pompey is jumping over stumps, and getting torn by thorns as he pushes through the trees, but that man behind him never gives up.

"Now, Pompey sees the sinkhole in front of him, and quickly, he slides in, under the water, and holds his breath. But then he realizes he's out of his depth, and he can't swim, and he has a vine wrapped around his foot. He's going to drown. He splashes and thrashes, and just then, the man who was following him catches up with him, and Pompey sees that he's an old man. He's huffing and puffing, and he tries to throw Pompey a branch to save him, but Pompey can't reach it.

"And just as his head comes above the water again, he gets a look at the man, and he is shocked to see that the man is him, only old. The old man on the bank calls out, 'I try to save you, but I still can't swim.' The very last thing that Pompey sees is the old man vanishing before his eyes."

"Is that true?" Alex asked, his eyes huge.

"So says the man who told it to me," Tony said impassively.

Alex shuddered, but Hannah was not impressed. "Come on, it can't be true. Like, if Pompey did drown, how would anyone know the story?"

Tony laughed at that, as if to say "Good point!"

Alex yawned, and that set off everyone else. Soon, all the merrymakers except Hannah, Alex, and Sukey had melted into the night with goodbyes. Then Sukey rubbed at her forehead.

"I got a terrible headache," she muttered. "Maybe tomorrow I go into the swamp, see the white witch, and she give me some medicine."

"There really is a white witch?" Hannah asked, curious. "She's not just a story? Like Glinda, the Good Witch from the Wizard of Oz?"

Alex turned to his sister. "This witch is like a sort of African doctor who lives in the woods," he said. "People think she has great powers, and she gives them, like, herbal supplements so they feel better. Don't mention her to the Gordons, though. Nobody tells the white people about her. I think she must be a runaway, and they might try to capture her."

"They don't try," Sukey murmured sleepily. "She's not a runaway, and anyway, they afraid of her. She might put a curse on them." Then, abruptly, she said, "It's late. I'm going to sleep now." She lay down on the straw, and pulled a thin blanket over herself. "Cato, you put out the fire when Hannah leaves."

Hannah whispered to Alex, "Is Sukey African? I asked her where she was from, but I didn't understand what she said."

Alex drew a stick through the smoldering remains of the fire, sending up tiny ash clouds. "Not exactly," he said. "She's half-Indian, half-African. I'm not really sure what that means—she was a bit confused herself. But it seems like her entire tribe was on the run for a long time, trying to get away from being enslaved, and a lot of different people joined them on the way. When she was young, she was captured by Creek Indians, and they sold her to Mr. Gordon."

Hannah was puzzled. "That's strange. I didn't know that Indians sold slaves. Heck, I didn't know that Indians could be slaves."

"Yeah, I thought that was weird, too," sighed Alex, "but there are definitely Indians who are slaves, and some of the slaves I've heard about are Mustees. That means they're half-black, half-Indian, like Sukey. I guess it doesn't happen so often any more, Indians selling slaves, but it still happens."

"Freaky," Hannah said, intrigued. "Has Sukey got any family?"

"Just Tony, I think. He's her son. A couple of her other kids escaped years ago, and the youngest one here died last year," Alex said. "She has a couple of grandkids at Mr. Gordon's plantation in South Carolina, but she never sees them. She asked Mr. Gordon to take her with him when he visits his son, but he's not done it." He added with a smile, "She says she wants to adopt me."

They heard Sukey's quiet snores from behind them. "She must be pretty lonely," Hannah said quietly. "She's the only woman here, right?"

"Yeah," Alex whispered. "Unless you count Mrs. Gordon, but they never really talk to each other, and Sukey likes it that way. We're all scared of the Gordons."

"I was thinking about that," Hannah said. "Here we all are, stuck out in the middle of nowhere, everyone just trying to get by, and nobody wants to know anybody else. There's no communication. Nobody trusts anybody here. Has anybody tried talking to each other?"

"That's not true," Alex objected. "All the slaves here trust Sukey. But it's hard for us to want to know white people like the Gordons when they want to get rich off of everyone else, and they don't care who gets hurt."

"That's not fair," Hannah said. "I mean, they're not my favorite people ever, but they're not so bad when you get to know them. I've never seen Mr. Gordon be really mean to anyone."

"That's what you think, Hannah," Alex said sharply. "But you're white. What do you know about what he does to black people?"

"What do you mean, I'm white?" Hannah said. "So are you. Most of the time."

Alex sniffed contemptuously. "Not right now, though. Hannah, you don't know what you're talking about. Just watch out for Mr. Gordon, that's all I'm saying."

There was a pained silence. Then Hannah said, "Man, I thought Georgia was kinda strange in the twenty-first century. But this is just . . . beyond."

Alex exhaled sharply. "Yeah. It's too bad, because Georgia's much prettier now than it is in our time. I love looking around. I can't get over all the wildlife. I went downriver with Sukey one day, and you should see the size of some of the trees. They're huge, like California redwoods."

Hannah rolled her eyes. "I dunno, that just doesn't do much for me . . . . I can see why the Gordons are more interested in moving to Charleston. At least there's good shopping there, I guess."

"There's something else strange here . . ." Alex said. But then he lapsed into silence.

"What?" asked Hannah

"Nothing. Forget it."

But his sister wasn't so easily put off. "Oh, come on Alex, what?"

He looked embarrassed, but reluctantly he said, "There are the spirits."

"The what?"

Alex felt himself blush. "See, I knew you would say that. Never mind."

Hannah smirked at him. "Okay, you can tell me. I promise not to laugh."

Alex fidgeted awkwardly. "Everything has a spirit, Hannah," he said. "The animals, the trees, the rocks."

Hannah couldn't help herself. She laughed so loudly at him, Sukey stirred in her sleep.

Alex made a face at his sister and said defensively, "It's true. You'll see."

"Uh-huh," said Hannah, folding her arms. "Right."

Embarrassed, Alex changed the subject. "What's happened to the Professor?" he asked Hannah. "Do you think she got lost?"

"I have no idea," she replied, staring blankly into the fire. "But . . . hey, wait a minute . . . You know how that skeleton you guys found was wearing a ring? Mrs. Gordon is wearing it. The exact same ring they showed on TV."

Alex sat up straight. "No! For real? I didn't notice! Are you sure?"

She nodded. "Yeah, positive. Brandon said it was, too."

"Then I guess we found the dead person," said Alex. "Do you think Mrs. Gordon will die soon?"

"Don't get too excited," Hannah said. "I hope not. Brandon said that the skeleton might have been murdered."

Alex frowned. "Wow. I hope that doesn't have anything to do with us."

"Of course not," said Hannah crossly. "It's not like any of us are psycho."

"True," Alex said. "But you're a convicted criminal, right? They might suspect you."

Hannah's brow puckered. That was a scary thought. "Anyhow," she said, glancing over at Sukey, who was snoring gently, "there's no point in worrying about that. The big question now is if we should run away."

Alex looked at her with concern. "Didn't you notice Cuffee?"

"No, can't say I did," Hannah said, poking with a stick at the remains of the dying fire. "Why? What does he have to do with anything?"

"Most of his left foot is missing," Alex said solemnly. "And his back is covered in scars, like it's made from rope or something. When he ran away after he got here from Africa, they caught him and beat him half to death and then they cut off his foot with an axe to make an example of him."

Hannah shuddered, and then had a thought that made her cringe inwardly. Hesitantly, she said, "When you say they, Alex, who exactly are we talking about?"

Alex looked into her eyes. "Mr. Gordon, Hannah. It's what I've been trying to tell you. Mr. Gordon whipped him and cut off his foot. If anyone is a psycho around here, it's him."

His sister gasped.

Chapter 7:
WORK AND WONDERS

As the dawn's light crept around the rough wooden shutters, Hannah rubbed her eyes, rolled over, and stumbled to her feet. Dressed only in a shift, the long shapeless garment she wore night and day, she grabbed a pot to fetch water for the morning coffee and cornmeal mush. But then she realized she should dress before going outside: Even though her shift covered her from neck to toes, it was still considered underwear. So she would have to dress properly before she went outside to pee and fetch water, or risk scandalizing everyone.

With a sigh, she returned the pot to the floor, and struggled into her petticoat and shortgown. The shortgown was held together at the front with straight pins, and she had to insert them carefully to avoid pricking herself as she worked. The shawl she pulled around her shoulders wasn't really necessary for warmth: It was for modesty, and it had the added advantage of draping over the pins, reducing her risk of hurting herself. Hannah had asked Mrs. Gordon for buttons, but buttons cost money, and Mr. Gordon wouldn't consider buying them for his convict servant.

Hannah decided not to wear stockings because she only had one pair, and she had stopped wearing shoes except for church on Sundays. Mr. Gordon had told her that if her shoes wore out, he would not replace them. They cost more money than he wished to spend. So Hannah decided to wear them only when she absolutely had to. She went barefoot the rest of the time.

After she lit the fire and drew the water from the well and poured it into the outdoor cauldron, Hannah sat down close by the tripod on which the cauldron hung over the fire. Waiting for the water to boil, she chewed thoughtfully on a piece of wiregrass. In modern-day Georgia, she never sat on the grass because of the fire ants, which seemed to be everywhere, and which ganged up to bite people in lots of places at once. But she hadn't yet seen fire ants in 1752, and she had wondered why. She had asked Alex about them last night, and he told her that they were accidentally brought into the South on a ship from Brazil in the 1930s. Which was an Alex kind of thing to know.

Outdoors had always seemed incredibly pointless and boring to Hannah. If she was to be honest with herself, she thought, she hadn't liked to go outside in California either, not even on the most beautiful day. Hannah's grandmother liked to drag her and Alex down to Aquatic Park on San Francisco Bay for a scenic walk by the tiny beach. Soon after they arrived, Hannah would always get bored and drift off to look at the jewelry sold in the little booths on Beach Street. Why would she want to admire the view anyway? The bay was nice, but all around them were cars and pylons, and people inline skating and riding on Segways. What was so scenic about that? Even Alex always quickly lost interest, and persuaded Grandma to take them to Ghirardelli Square for ice cream instead. So much for the Great Outdoors.

But in her travels in time, Hannah started to feel differently about being outside. Now, she craved the outdoors when she wanted to be away from work, and noise, and people, and confinement within four walls. Outside, her problems felt less overwhelming.

A chilly breeze told Hannah that fall was arriving. She hugged her knees tighter, and gazed into the distance, wondering calmly what on earth she and the boys were supposed to do to get home. There was always some purpose to their travels. It was never easy to spot, but on their previous trips, the Professor had shown up and offered hints and advice. Vague though her guidance was, at least it was something. But she wasn't here. Not this time.

Now, in the still quiet of the morning, Hannah decided that Brandon was right: To get home, they had to solve the mystery of the skeleton's identity. *The skeleton is obviously Mrs. Gordon,* Hannah thought, *so all we have to do is wait for her to die, right? She never looks healthy, so how long can that be?* But then Hannah remembered that Mrs. Gordon was probably going to be murdered. And she felt guilty for wishing her dead. With a sudden chill, she wondered whether Mr. Gordon was to be her killer.

The blade of wiregrass Hannah had been chewing fell from her mouth. She reached down and wrapped another around her finger, and yanked it from the ground. Tugging at the wiregrass from both ends, she thought to herself that it *was* like wire: round, not flat, and so tough it could almost be used to mend things. Now, that was a practical idea . . . . She was a practical person, she decided. Not, she thought smugly, like her silly brother, always with his head in the clouds, believing that junk about spirits.

Hannah shook her head. Alex would believe anything he was told, she thought condescendingly. Maybe what people had told him about Mr. Gordon being violent wasn't true, she thought. She was certainly having a hard time believing it herself. The other slaves were probably just pulling Alex's leg. He was so naïve.

She was glad that Sukey was looking after her brother. And his work wasn't too bad, either. At least he didn't have to pick cotton, probably because nobody in 1752 seemed to grow it. Anyway, he was fine. If anything, it was she, Hannah, who had the tough job. But what else was new?

Even before the vestry meeting began, Brandon could tell that Mr. Osborn was very nervous. Over and over, he checked the inkwells and quills, as if somehow the ink would dry up and the quills wear out all by themselves.

Finally, he asked Brandon to take over the note-taking while he spoke during the vestry meeting. Brandon agreed, although the prospect made him almost as nervous as Mr. Osborn.

"Of course, the gentlemen of the vestry will need to approve you in that task," said Mr. Osborn, mopping his brow with a cloth handkerchief for the third time. He flinched at the sound of hooves, and a horse whinnied outside. Mr. Jones had arrived, and Mr. Gordon's horse followed moments later. The other men trickled in during the next half hour or so. Brandon couldn't help but notice how hard it was to measure the passage of time when he didn't have a watch.

Once the gentlemen of the vestry were all seated, Mr. Osborn formally proposed that Brandon take notes.

Mr. Jones, the chairman, gave him a benign look. "I should have no objection, sir," he said, "since we approve the minutes and may make corrections if our recollections differ from the account the boy gives us. Provided he proves competent, his acting in that capacity should prove no obstacle to our business."

The others nodded.

Brandon supposed that they would not have given their permission if they had known he was black. In fact, the question would never have been raised in the first place. He was fascinated to see how differently he was treated as a white boy. But he also felt a sting of resentment because of it. It wasn't fair, he thought, that as a black kid, he spent his life always trying to prove himself. All he had to do as a white boy was just exist and do nothing bad, and everyone assumed the best for him.

Early in the meeting, Brandon figured out why Mr. Osborn was so nervous. The vestrymen were a seriously scary bunch. All the men wore wigs and severe expressions, so that their gathering looked like an English law court.

After reading the minutes of the previous meeting, Mr. Jones turned to Mr. Gordon. "I wonder, sir, if you would report to us on the convict girl who was removed from the household of James Burton?"

Mr. Gordon rose to his feet. "I have little to report, but it is promising," he said. "My wife is teaching Jane to be a tolerable house servant, and if she proves suitable, I will send her to my house in South Carolina, if that would prove agreeable to the vestry. I would, of course, pay the parish for her."

There was a murmur of agreement, and Mr. Gordon acknowledged it with a curt nod. "Thank you, gentlemen. The girl will remain on trial in my household for the next few months."

Mr. Jones coughed. "There is one item that I am embarrassed to say that I forgot as we began business today," he said. "Gentlemen, I trust that you will join me in making a formal welcome to our new missionary, Mr. Osborn, who, as you know, recently arrived in St. Swithin's Parish."

There was a general cry of "aye" and stamping of feet from everyone except Mr. Gordon, who stared dolefully at the minister.

Undeterred by Mr. Gordon's coldness, Mr. Osborn got to his feet and gratefully thanked the committee. Mr. Jones then picked up some papers and shuffled them, as though he was about to move on to other business. But Mr. Osborn had something to say.

"Gentlemen, I would beg your indulgence for a few minutes," he said. "I come before you as a humble servant, but not, if you will pardon me for my directness, as a servant of this vestry. No, gentlemen, I come not as your servant, but as a clerk in holy orders, and as a servant of God. If you have had occasion to see the great seal of the Society for the Propagation of the Gospel, that august organization that sent me hither, you will know that it depicts a rector reading God's word to the eager masses on America's foreign shore."

The men looked at him expectantly, but they also seemed puzzled, except for Mr. Jones, who appeared worried, and Mr. Gordon, who looked hostile.

Mr. Osborn faltered, paused, and then seemed to regain his courage. "Moreover, I come not only to minister to the white inhabitants of this far-off land. Although your spiritual welfare is certainly an important part of my mission, I am also bound to bring the Holy Gospel to those poor, pitiful souls we know as slaves."

Brandon could see that Mr. Osborn was startled by the range of reactions to what he had said. Mr. Jones looked peeved. Mr. Gordon looked furious. And the other men laughed.

It took a moment for Mr. Jones to regain control of the meeting.

"What do you propose, exactly?" one man asked with a cynical smile.

"I propose," said Mr. Osborn, desperately seizing on the question, "that Brandon here becomes a catechist to the slaves. He can read and write, and he is learned for a boy of his years and station. I have examined him at length on his religious knowledge, and found that his Biblical understanding is sound. I fear that his grasp of Church principles shows the pernicious influence of dissenters, but I have been instructing him in the one true faith of our most holy church . . . ."

Brandon had not mentioned to Mr. Osborn that he was a Baptist, but he had learned that anyone in 1752 who belonged to a Protestant Christian church that wasn't the Church of England was known as a dissenter.

Meanwhile, Mr. Gordon scowled even harder. Finally, he leaned forward in his chair. "Mr. Osborn, what mean you by slandering my faith? I am what you call a 'dissenter.'"

Mr. Osborn blinked, but he was not put off by Mr. Gordon's hostility. He lifted his chin. "I am aware, sir, that you are a Scottish Presbyterian, and thus may be offended by my remarks. However, I am a clergyman of the Church of England, and I cannot pretend that your faith is the equal of mine. Furthermore," and here he turned to the other vestrymen, "I must protest the presence of a dissenter on a Church of England vestry."

There was an embarrassed silence, and all eyes were on Mr. Gordon, who looked ready to explode.

Mr. Jones saved the day. In a soothing voice he said, "As a newcomer, Mr. Osborn is as yet unschooled in the ways of America." The vestrymen nodded, with the exception of Mr. Gordon, who slumped in his chair and seethed.

Turning back to Mr. Osborn, Mr. Jones reproached him. "I must remind you, Mr. Osborn, that the vestry is the governing body of the entire parish, and not merely of the established church. We have developed a tradition here by which the vestry has greater powers than in England, and for all our sakes we must include our foremost citizens on this body, even when, like Mr. Gordon, they are not formally members of our church. In any case, Mr. Gordon takes communion at St. Swithin's, and regularly attends our services. His religious opinions notwithstanding, he does conform to the Church of England."

Brandon cringed on Mr. Osborn's behalf, sinking low in his seat. Mr. Gordon said nothing, but he continued to glare at Mr. Osborn. Mr. Osborn, it seemed, had made an enemy.

But Mr. Osborn was nothing if not proud. And he did not know when to shut up.

He gave the vestrymen a stern look. "There is another matter I must raise. I must express my grave disappointment with the vestry's accommodations for me and my family. My house, sirs, is entirely unsuitable. The roof leaks, and the wind blows through the walls. By winter, our situation will have become intolerable. I demand that you provide me with a suitable house."

There was another stunned silence. Everyone was uncomfortable, especially Brandon, who wasn't used to being around a bunch of scary white guys in wigs fighting a battle of wills.

Mr. Jones said icily, "I believe that you and I have already discussed this matter . . . ."

Sitting forward, Mr. Gordon waved at the chairman to hold his tongue. "It seems that we have done very little to please you, Mr. Osborn," he said in a dangerously quiet voice. "Is there anything else your parishioners have done to offend you?"

"Yes, there is," Mr. Osborn said stoutly, looking him in the eye. "I refer to the unseemly, indeed, the *disgraceful* behavior of several men outside my church during services. I believe that you, Mr. Gordon, are among those who go to drink punch when you should be attending to my sermons. I expect better of a member of my vestry, and I trust that you will show repentance. Perhaps such behavior is acceptable among the Presbyterians, but I assure you that it has no place in the one true Church."

Mr. Gordon gave him what Brandon could only think of as the Evil Eye. Finally, Mr. Osborn lost his nerve and looked away.

Brandon had scribbled down what he could, which wasn't much, since he had very little experience with quill pens. He had also had a hard time following everything that was said, although the men's body language was clear enough: The entire vestry, and especially Mr. Gordon, with the exception of Mr. Jones, had it in for Mr. Osborn.

Mr. Jones now cleared his throat. "Perhaps," he said, "we ought to adjourn, and reserve our discussion for a time when tempers have cooled."

As Brandon corked the ink and wiped off his quill with a rag, he worried. The meeting had not boded well for Mr. Osborn. Not at all. But then he wondered why he was worrying. At that moment, the answer came to him: He liked Mr. Osborn more than he had realized. The guy at least stood up for what he believed in.

First thing in the morning, Mrs. Gordon ordered the girls to bring her tea. Hannah was about to head outside when she realized that she had never seen Jane prepare hot water. "Hey, Jane?" she called, "Could you go boil the water?"

Jane shrugged and examined her fingernails. "Dunno 'ow to light the fire, do I?"

Hannah's eyebrows rose. "Seriously? I thought everyone in the olden days . . . I mean, I thought everyone could do that?"

Jane shook her head, looking bored.

Digging in her pocket, Hannah fished out the metal tinder box, flint, and striker. "Okay, let's go," she said with a sigh, picking up the water bucket. "I'll teach you."

She was a little irked. She seemed to spend a lot of time teaching Jane. Reading and writing she didn't mind—quite enjoyed, in fact—but housework lessons were always a chore, especially because Jane looked put upon every time Hannah asked her to do anything.

Outside, Hannah carefully built a fire with kindling and logs from the woodpile, as Jane watched. She pulled a tiny piece of blackened cloth from the tinder box, and put it on the ground. Taking some shreds of kindling, she rubbed them between her hands to make tinder, and carefully placed it on the charred rag. Then she held the flint and striker over the tinder. But despite repeated efforts, she could not get a light. As she struggled with the flint, Jane smirked.

Finally, Hannah looked up at her, annoyed. "You're so smart, why don't you try?"

Jane took the striker and flint from Hannah. On her first attempt, sparks flew from the flint, and a tiny glow appeared in the pile of tinder. She gathered up the tinder in her cupped hands and blew on it. Smoke began to appear between her fingers. Carefully, just as flames erupted from the handful of smoking tinder, she nestled it among the kindling, then blew on it again. Soon, flames were leaping up.

Hannah looked at Jane suspiciously. "I thought you said you never did this before?"

"Fortune smiled on me," said Jane in a sing-song voice.

"Liar," Hannah said irritably. "I'm going to get the water."

"Nah, I'll do it," said Jane, putting a hand on Hannah's arm. "Sorry, 'annah. I meant well. I was showing you a lesson I learned from them slaves at my last place. I saw one man pretending not to understand 'ow to use a wheelbarrow, no matter 'ow many times 'ee was shown how to do it. I thought 'ee was simple, until one of them slave girls tells me that if you don't want to do all the work, you ought to make the master fink you're foolish. If the master sees it's too much trouble to teach you, he might even do it 'imself. 'annah, you do as you're told too much."

Hannah couldn't help smiling at that. "Nobody ever said that to me before," she laughed.

"Well, you do," Jane insisted. "But mind, now, arguing too much does no good, neither. Best to agree with the masters, and then do as you will, yes? Now, as a sign of good faith and friendship, I will fetch the water. You sit down and watch the fire."

She took the bucket from Hannah, who sat down gratefully next to the fire, thinking again to herself how funny it was that Jane had told her she was too obedient. Soon Jane returned from the well and poured water into the cauldron, watching eagerly as flames leaped into the air.

That evening, Hannah, Jane, and the Gordons sat down to their supper of cornbread and sliced ham by the flickering light of a single candle in a hurricane lamp. No sooner had Hannah settled on her stool, but Mrs. Gordon commanded her to fetch a glass of shrub, a drink made from a vinegar and sugar syrup mixed with water.

As Hannah resentfully uncorked the bottle of shrub syrup, she remembered Jane's advice that morning, and decided not to rush.

Mrs. Gordon said, "Mr. Gordon, I have been wondering whether it is proper to continue to permit our serving girls to eat at table with us?"

"Should I not permit it?" Mr. Gordon asked with concern, through a mouthful of cornbread.

His wife replied, "In Charleston, we wouldn't have dreamed of it."

"Aye well," said Mr. Gordon, taking a drink of rum and water, "This isnae Charleston. This is the frontier, and things are less genteel here than in the city. But at least we have a white servant, nay, even two white servants, and I doubt they have many of those in Charleston."

"But don't you plan to sell Jane?" asked Mrs. Gordon, her face creased in concern.

"No, I do not," Mr. Gordon said firmly. "I had thought to send her up to Sidlaw, but I have changed my mind. Unlike Hannah, she is proving a fine seamstress. Hannah's skills in sewing are poor, but she is a competent cook, unlike Jane. Between the two of them, they ensure that you, my dear wife, need not lift a finger. Since you are concerned with the gentility of this household, I suggest that you use some of your time in polishing your learning for those conversational arts so necessary to a lady of Charleston. That way, you will find your re-entry into Charleston society takes a smooth course. I will order some books for you, and I hope that we may discuss them together."

Hannah and Jane had exchanged delighted looks on hearing the news that they wouldn't soon be parted. But after the discussion, Hannah couldn't help but feel that it was creepy for a stranger like Mr. Gordon to have so much power over her life.

While Hannah was milking the cow, she heard the front door of the house open and close, and the creaking sounds of someone walking down the wooden steps. Soon Jane was at her elbow in the cattle shed.

"Nasty stinky fings," she grumbled, her arms akimbo.

"She's kind of nice, actually," Hannah said, turning to address the cow. "Aren't you, Bessie? Anyway, Jane, it's not your job to do this, so don't sweat it."

Suddenly, Hannah found herself sitting on a pile of straw. In one swift motion, Jane had shoved her off the milking stool and wrapped her hands around the cow's teats, even as she giggled at Hannah.

Hannah was flabbergasted. "What . . . What did you do *that* for?"

Jane giggled again as the warm milk squirted into the wooden bucket. "Just jesting. You didn't think I could do this either, did you? What with me being a London girl. But my mum and dad used to work in an inn, remember? My mum used to let me help with milking the cow."

Hannah looked at her disbelievingly. "You had a cow in London?"

"Yeah, 'course. 'Ow else would an inn get fresh milk?" Jane rolled her eyes at Hannah, and then smiled. "You are a country girl, be not mistaken."

Hannah smirked at the very idea. If only Jane knew she was from San Francisco. Of course, San Francisco probably didn't exist yet.

"So what amusements shall we find here?" Jane asked, wiping her hands on her skirt. "I am city born and bred, and this place is so quiet, it is eerie."

"I know, right?" Hannah said with a smile.

"I have a notion," Jane said decisively. "What say you we go down to the river?"

Hannah was doubtful. "I dunno. I'm kind of late with the milking, and we're supposed to make supper . . . ."

But Jane gently cajoled her. "Come, 'annah. Mrs. Gordon's taking a nap, and she won't be up to eat, I would venture. We have some ham and cornmeal anyway, and so supper need not be a great labor. Come on, won't you? You must learn to take your pleasures when chance warrants." She stood and held out her hand to Hannah.

"Okay," Hannah said. Then she smiled as she clambered to her feet. "Sure, why not? Where do you want to go?"

Jane shrugged. "I don't know. Let us see what there is to see. Just so long as we don't go deep into the woods."

"Exploring shouldn't take too long, then," Hannah muttered to herself. "This place is all woods."

Jane ran ahead of Hannah under a huge oak tree, picked up something, and threw it back at her friend. Hannah caught it, and saw it was an acorn. "Hey!" she yelled, and picking up a handful of acorns, flung them back at Jane, who laughed and dodged the tiny missiles, then ran ahead of her friend across the cow pasture, nimbly dodging the huge cow pies.

"Hey, don't get us lost!" Hannah yelled.

"I won't," Jane yelled back. "I can see the slave quarters from 'ere. Come, let us go and see who's there."

Hannah jumped at the chance to go see Alex. She hadn't seen him in a couple of days, and she missed him.

With relief, she spotted her brother standing by the door of Sukey's hut, feeding chickens from a pot of grain. He waved happily to her, and then nodded shyly to Jane.

"Hi, uh . . . Cato," Hannah stammered. "This is Jane. I met her in London."

Alex said nothing, but he looked at Jane with suspicion, and Hannah wondered why. Was it because she was white?

Jane ignored him. "Is the river near here?" she asked Hannah. Hannah pointed to it in reply. They could see Sukey washing the laundry at the water's edge, slapping wet clothes against an old log. Jane clapped her hands together in glee and sprinted toward the riverbank.

Alex turned to his sister. "Where did *she* come from?"

"She's cool," Hannah reassured him. "I met her in prison." Alex's eyebrows went skyward, but Hannah explained. "She's not a scary criminal, seriously. She was nice to me on the ship and everything. I would have died without her."

"Where does she live now?" Alex asked, flinging another handful of meal to the chickens.

"Here. Her master was beating up on her, so Mr. Gordon and the other magistrates took her away from him. He's decided she's going to work with me. I guess it's kind of a coincidence she ended up here, right? Wonder if she's got anything to do with the time travel thing?"

Alex shrugged. "Who knows? I guess we'll find out. Must be nice being white, though. None of us slaves have ever been rescued from Mr. Gordon because he's cruel to us."

Hannah looked curiously at her brother. "You're not black, remember?"

Alex looked determinedly back at her. "Yes, I am. Look at me."

Hannah scowled. "Yeah, but you're *not* black, not like Brandon's black, you know?"

Alex bristled. "What's that supposed to mean? I mean, Brandon's African-American, and I'm not, and that hasn't changed because he's turned white and I've turned black. It's a . . . I don't know what to call it . . . . I guess it's a culture thing. But we're still the same inside. What's different now is how people treat us. White people are scary to me now, except for you of course. And they're a whole lot nicer to Brandon."

Hannah couldn't really argue with that. After an awkward pause, Alex said lightly, "By the way, Mr. Gordon wants me and Sukey to go upriver to trade with the Indians for him."

"Why you?" Hannah was incredulous. "That sounds dangerous. How would you protect Sukey if you guys got attacked?"

Alex shrugged, and said, "Well, we don't trade directly with the Indians. We go see some Scottish guy who trades with everyone. He buys from the Indians and sells to us. I'm going to keep Sukey company, I guess. Gordon trusts her, because she always gets a good deal from the trader. We're taking some things to sell that he got sent from England, and we're gonna bring back deerskins, then he'll ship them to London. It's not how he makes most of his money, but I guess he makes a profit. Anyway, it's something he's been doing for years, since he got to South Carolina. His uncle made the money to buy Sidlaw Plantation from trading with Indians under the noses of the rich men who tried to keep the trade for themselves. When Gordon inherited Sidlaw he took up trading, too."

"How do you know all this about him?" said Hannah.

"Oh, from Sukey," Alex said knowingly. "Old Gordon bought her years ago, so she knows tons of stuff about him. Anyhow, she wants me to go with her.

She says it's fun, and she needs someone to help her paddle upriver. Gordon doesn't like her taking any of the guys with her, 'cause he's always afraid they'll run away, or at least, that he won't get as much work done when they're gone."

Hannah grinned. "So that's why he wants you to go. Because you're pretty useless here."

Alex aimed a mock kick at his sister. But then he said modestly, "Actually, I am kind of useless when you compare me to the guys. I do my best, but I'm still learning how to herd cattle and that kind of thing. Gordon doesn't mind too much, 'cause he thinks he got me as a freebie. I just walked out of the woods one day. He thinks I'm a runaway, but he's not seen any ads for me in the newspaper. He probably still hopes he can claim a reward for me when someone figures out who I am. Of course, I guess he also reckons that if he sells me to Mr. Osborn as a house servant he'll make some money, and if someone else claims me as their slave, poor Mr. Osborn will be left holding the bill."

"Wow, I hope nobody does try to claim you," Hannah frowned. "Anyhow, I think he's working you light because you're a puny little guy."

"Thanks a lot, sis," Alex said, scowling. "I appreciate your support. Useless? Puny? I think you spend too much time around Brits."

Hannah laughed, and admitted he might have a point.

Alex said, "So, how are you doing?"

His sister sighed, and flopped down on the grass. "Okay, I guess. Kind of bored. Jane is livening things up a bit. Before she got here, I was just working and waiting for Mrs. Gordon to die. Oh, and hey, sounds like you saw Brandon?"

Alex nodded. "He came by yesterday. He's trying to persuade slaves to become Christians. Even me."

Hannah rolled her eyes. "He's totally lost it, then. Alex, did you remind Brandon that you're already a Christian?"

Alex made a face. "Yeah, sure I did, but he said Catholics don't count."

Hannah put a hand on her hip. "Next time he shows up with his little Bible, tell him to shove it," she said irritably. "Like things aren't bad enough, Brandon turns into Ned Flanders."

"S'ok," Alex said, "I didn't pick a fight with him. I just smiled and nodded and talked about other stuff."

"Hmm," Hannah said. "That's what Jane says I should do more. Don't fight with people, she says, just kind of do my own thing."

Alex smiled to himself. "Not a bad idea, sis. It works for me."

Jane rejoined them then, breathless from her run to and from the river. "'annah, Sukey wants to talk to you," she said, wheezing.

"What about?" said Hannah.

"I dunno, do I?" said Jane goodnaturedly. "Ask 'er yourself."

As Hannah left, there was an awkward silence between Jane and Alex.

Alex couldn't believe his sister had made friends with a thief and jailbird. Worse, he couldn't help wondering if Jane was to be trusted. The only white people he knew he could trust were his sister and (weird though it was to think of him as white) Brandon. Alex had learned well from the other slaves: He saw how they were open and honest to each other and to him, but how differently they spoke to whites, and especially to Mr. Robert Gordon. They were always very careful about what they said, seeming to be friendly enough, but revealing nothing about what they really thought. Alex had met slaves before in his travels in time, and he had learned then that this was what people did to survive in slavery. But now he understood, fully and completely.

Jane interrupted his thoughts by looking past his head and pointing upward.

"What are them fings in the trees?" she asked, looking upward just as another pecan popped from its husk and plopped onto the bed of leaves below it.

"Pecans," said Alex. "They're a kind of nut. They don't grow in England."

Jane never asked how "Cato" would know whether pecans grew in England. She put a finger to her chin. "Tasty, are they?"

"Yes, very," said Alex. "Here, I'll show you."

She followed him to the tree, where he picked up two pecans from the ground. Holding them in one hand, he squeezed them together, just as Tony had showed him how to do. The shells cracked loudly. Alex pried out some of the meat, and handed it to Jane, who cautiously sniffed at it, then popped it in her mouth.

She chewed thoughtfully. "Tastes like walnuts," she pronounced. "Only not so bitter. Show me 'ow you opened 'em."

Alex showed her, just as Tony had shown him. "Sukey cooks with them," he said. "She made a kind of stew last night with pecans, cornmeal, and bits of venison jerky. You know, dried deer meat."

Jane looked blank.

"It's actually pretty good," said Alex, chewing on a buttery morsel of pecan. "Well, better than most of the stuff we get to eat. I've hardly had any meat since I got here. I'm hungry most of the time, what with . . ."

And then he lapsed into silence, and looked downward. Would Jane report him to the Gordons for complaining? He didn't want to take the risk.

But Jane was thinking of something else. Picking up a large stick, she aimed it at the tree, and then, with all her might, hurled it high into the branches. A small shower of pecans tumbled down, and she grinned at Alex. "'Ere's somefing to eat," she said. "Go on, get some."

Alex couldn't help but smile at Jane's inventiveness. "I thought you were a city girl?" he said.

"I am," said Jane. "That's why I'm so quick-witted." She winked at him.

They both turned at the sound of hoof beats, in time to see their master riding toward them. Jane looked unfazed, but Alex cringed inwardly. Anxiety washed over him as Mr. Gordon stopped his horse right in front of them, and giving them both a dirty look, pointed his whip at Jane. "Do not steal my pecans," he said sharply. "They are my property, and they fetch a good price. They are not food for slaves and servants. And Jane, you should not be associating with the negroes. Go back to the house at once. My wife feels unwell and needs attending."

Sukey and Hannah caught the end of this speech as they returned from the river, each hauling armloads of wet laundry.

"Sukey," rumbled Mr. Gordon. "Remind the other slaves that they are not to eat the pecans."

"We need something more to eat than pig fat and corn," Sukey said sullenly. "We get weak and sick, then we can't work."

Mr. Gordon looked taken aback. He clearly hadn't expected an argument. "Yes . . . Well, maybe you, Sukey, can gather some for the slaves' meals and for the house," he said uncertainly. "But the rest of the nuts are to be prepared for sale."

With that, he turned the horse and set off back toward the house, passing Jane as he did so.

"What an old cheapskate," said Hannah, frowning. "Like he doesn't have enough money?"

But she did wonder how Sukey had gotten away with ordering the master around.

"Hey, where are you going?" she called to Jane's retreating back.

"Mr. Gordon told her to go back to the house," Alex replied, "to look after Mrs. Gordon. I guess she's sick."

Hannah groaned. "Oh, man. She's always sick. She seems to get every illness going. I guess I better go help. Sukey, can I leave these clothes with you?"

"Put them inside," said Sukey, with a resigned air. "On the log. I take care of them."

When Hannah was gone, Sukey asked Alex to help her hang out the laundry on a rope strung from two trees. Alex was happy to help, but he was still shaking from his encounter with Mr. Gordon. "I didn't know the pecans were his," he said apologetically to Sukey. "But I guess everything here is his. Even us."

"Not everything," said Sukey, shaking her head. "See that ground over there? That is where I grow my tobacco and my vegetables and beans. Mr. Gordon give it to me as my own ground, and I keep what I raise there."

"But you're a slave," said Alex, confused. "Why would he do that?"

Sukey looked at him calmly, and gave a bitter smile. "He remembers Cato's

Rebellion. Not you, of course, Alex, but another slave called Cato. He was an African who fight the white people in South Carolina. His men kill Mr. Gordon's first wife."

Alex was shocked. "Whoa, why did he call *me* Cato, then?"

Sukey shrugged, throwing another shirt over the washing line. "Maybe he thinks it's a joke, giving a little boy like you the same name. Anyhow, Mr. Gordon and his son are lucky to escape from the angry slaves. The white people make new laws, say slaves can't learn to read, or travel without a pass, or lots of us gather together. They say we can't grow food, or make money for ourselves. They also say that masters can't treat slaves cruelly, because they afraid we rebel again. Of course," she chuckled ruefully, "It's one thing to make laws, and it's another thing to carry them out."

"So," Alex said, his brow furrowed. "Why does Mr. Gordon let you grow tobacco and sell it, when that's against the law?"

Sukey was lifting a pair of trousers up to the line, but she stopped and looked at him, puzzled. "Alex, you don't know?"

Alex solemnly shook his head.

She looked self-satisfied. "Because he's afraid," she said. "He's afraid that if he don't give us poor slaves anything, we take everything from him. That's why he pretends not to notice when one of the pigs disappears, because he reckons that's a price he has to pay for us. He give me my land when I say that Tony and them were complaining they were hungry. Mr. Gordon got the idea they are threatening him."

Suddenly, a lightbulb went on in Alex's head. "You made him think that, didn't you?"

"I don't know," said Sukey, shrugging, a coy smile playing about her lips. "Mr. Gordon worries I put a curse on him, maybe, unless he do as I bid."

Alex had noticed how frosty Sukey was in her dealings with Mr. Gordon. It was weird, because he had so much power over her, but she acted as though he didn't. He couldn't help thinking that it was a very dangerous game that she was forced to play with her master.

"I don't get something, though," said Alex, standing on tiptoe to hang up a wet shirt. "I don't understand why he was so angry about the stupid pecans."

Sukey slung the last shirt over the line, and said, "Maybe he is worried about Mrs. Gordon. Beware of him, Alex. When he's unhappy, he is a dangerous man."

Alex shivered again. *That's weird*, he thought. *Even when I'm afraid, I don't normally shiver.*

Alex was a subject of discussion at the Gordons' breakfast the next morning. Mr. Gordon said, "Since nobody has claimed Cato, and we see that he has the makings of an excellent footman, I suggest we send him to Sidlaw. I'm sure Bobby can use the help."

Hannah almost choked on her bacon. "Wait, you're sending Cato to South Carolina? What happened to selling him to Mr. Osborn?"

Mr. Gordon looked at her through narrowed eyes. "What business is that of yours, Hannah? Hold your tongue."

She blurted out, "He's my . . ." and then she stopped.

"Yes?" Mr. Gordon asked sharply, chewing on his bacon. "He is your what?"

"Nothing," Hannah whispered, looking downward. "Sir."

"He is *nothing* to do with you, girl," Mr. Gordon warned. "He is my property."

As he finished speaking, there came a knock on the door.

The caller was a slave named Gideon, and he brought news from Sukey. "Cato," it seemed, would not accompany her upriver that day, because he was sick.

Alarmed, Hannah listened closely to Gideon's conversation with Mr. Gordon. She hesitated to ask Gideon what was wrong with Alex, because she didn't want to make Mr. Gordon angry again.

Then she had an idea.

"Mr. Gordon," she said. "Can I go with Sukey instead of Cato?"

Mr. Gordon thought about it for only a second. "Very well. Jane can perform your chores. You may accompany Sukey on her journey. It will be good for you to learn from her about trade."

Hannah didn't need to be told twice. She tore off after Gideon.

Hannah didn't know that she could run as fast as this, and by the time she reached the slave quarters, her chest was bursting from the effort, and her stomach felt queasy from running on her greasy breakfast. She leaped into the men's hut, where Alex was lying on a deerskin-covered wooden pallet. A rough and worn blanket covered him, and a roaring fire burned in the hearth at the center of the smoky room. After being outside in the nippy air, and already warm from her run, Hannah had trouble breathing in the hut's stifling atmosphere.

Alex smiled wanly at his sister. "You okay, Hannah?"

Hannah panted, "Yeah, but . . . what . . . about . . . you?"

Alex sniffed. "Not too great. Don't worry, though, I got pills for malaria, remember? But I think I might have the flu."

Hannah's mind reeled at this news. How would Alex fare with flu in the middle of the eighteenth century? No antibiotics . . . oh, wait, they didn't help the flu anyway . . . . No modern medicine, anyhow. What could she do to help her brother? She felt helpless, and she was terrified of losing him.

Alex knew Hannah was worried, and he spoke reassuringly. "It's okay. I'm drinking lots of boiled water. Oh, and Sukey got me some medicine from the white witch in the woods."

Now Hannah noticed Sukey in a corner of the hut, stripping leaves from twigs.

Alarm bells went off in Hannah's head. Medicine? In the eighteenth century? When she tried to imagine what that would be like, she drew a blank. "Alex, be careful, okay?" she hissed. "You don't know what kind of weird stuff she's giving you."

Nodding to Hannah, Sukey set a small skillet to heat over the fire. "The witch, she say nothing much does good for this fever," she explained to Alex. "But she says to keep drinking water, and when I urge her to give me a cure, she tells me she thinks this medicine might help. Hannah, can you bring me a brown paper bag from the house?"

Hannah was baffled. "Brown paper? What for?"

Sukey shooed her. "Just go for some. And fetch a nightcap. Hurry, I must leave upriver soon."

Hannah looked at her doubtfully. "Yeah, Mr. Gordon says I'm supposed to go with you. But who will look after Alex . . . I mean, Cato?"

"Oh, the men will keep watch on him," Sukey said dismissively. "Now hurry, for we are already late. We must prepare medicine for Cato, and then we must leave."

Hannah knew that Mrs. Gordon had carefully saved all the brown paper that wrapped the products from England, but she felt silly trying to explain to her mistress why she needed it.

However, as soon as Hannah mentioned that Sukey had sent her, Mrs. Gordon rummaged in a drawer, and then handed over a crumpled bag, along with a worn lace cap. "I have no men's nightcap," she said, "but this will suffice."

Hannah looked anxiously at the brown bag. She had assumed that she would be handed a grocery sack, not a tiny bag, and she hoped it would be big enough. Seeing her concern, Mrs. Gordon assured her that it would suit the purpose.

"Tell Sukey to advise me and Mr. Gordon of Cato's condition," she added kindly. Hannah was touched, and smiled gratefully at her.

When she heard about Mrs. Gordon's concern for Alex, Sukey was not impressed.

"She just worried that he die," she grumbled, "and then Mr. Gordon lose money. But don't you worry, Hannah. He won't die."

Sukey quickly dry-fried the leaves from the plants she had brought from the woods, shaking the pan to stir them. Then she beckoned to Hannah. "Open the bag to catch them," she said, wrapping a thick rag around the handle of the frying pan, and lifting it from the fire.

Hannah held open the brown paper bag, and Sukey tipped the hot and wilted leaves into it, gingerly scraping in the last few with her bare finger. Setting down the skillet, she took the bag from Hannah, and folded over the end to close it. Placing it flat on her palm, she quickly smoothed it out. Then she took Mrs. Gordon's nightcap from Hannah, and told Alex to sit up.

Without warning, Sukey plopped the paper bag onto Alex's head, then tied on Mrs. Gordon's cap to hold it in place. "Now," she said, standing back to admire her handiwork, "you don't take that off for three days, hear?"

Alex looked astonished, and Hannah burst into peals of laughter, pointing at her brother. "Oh, my God," she shrieked, her hand to her mouth, "you look hilarious! Do you want a pacifier with that?"

Alex stared at her, his lips pursed. Hannah felt a little guilty for mocking him while he was sick. But not very guilty.

Never in her life had Hannah paddled a canoe, and this particular canoe was quite a sight. Twenty feet long, made from birch bark, it was laden down with barrels of tobacco and sugar, burlap bags of cornmeal, and iron kettles that Mr. Gordon had imported from England.

In short, it was absolutely groaning under the weight of stuff.

Hannah wondered if the canoe could handle any more weight, or if it would sink like a rock as soon as she and Sukey climbed on board. Sukey, however, did not seem at all worried. In fact, she said to Hannah, "Not much to carry this time of year. We only need this one canoe."

Hannah stammered that she didn't know how to drive a canoe.

"There is naught to the thing," Sukey said with a laugh. "I tell you what to do. You get in first."

She pointed to a tiny plank on which Hannah was to sit. A paddle was propped against it. The canoe sat mostly on dry land, but the far end on which Hannah was to travel dipped into the water. Unsteadily, Hannah clambered onto a rock in the river, then gingerly, she stepped onto the plank.

For a moment, she feared she would lose her balance, but the canoe held still, and awkwardly she dumped herself down onto her bottom, her knees crammed against barrels. She reached under her seat and pulled out her paddle from where it had fallen.

Sukey grabbed the end of the canoe with both hands, then leaned forward and shoved the craft most of the way into the water before hopping in, sitting down, and pushing off, all in one easy motion. To Hannah's astonishment, they were afloat.

Sukey commanded, "You paddle now, Hannah."

Hannah paddled.

An hour after Hannah and Sukey departed, Tony brought Alex a gourd dipper full of water. He had to work to persuade Alex even to sip at it.

"I feel lousy," Alex moaned. "I can't get warm. I keep getting shivers up my spine. Tony, can you get me a thermometer? So I can see what my temperature is?"

Tony tilted his head in puzzlement, and Alex, in his fevered state, couldn't understand why. After a moment, he ceased to care. With Tony still watching him, he drifted off to sleep.

When Alex awoke, he was alone. He was lonely and depressed, not just about being sick, but about his whole situation. He had the appearance of a stranger, and he was constantly on edge, afraid of the white people who had so much control over his life. Tony and Sukey had assured him that kids were rarely whipped. Both of them told him that Mr. Gordon's brutal punishments of Cuffee and Quashee were unusual: He meant them as cruel warnings to the other slaves, to keep them afraid of him. Tony said that Mr. Gordon always made sure that they heard of horrible things that happened to slaves who stepped out of line.

But Alex couldn't help worrying that he would somehow offend the Gordons, and that something horrible would happen to *him*. So he had followed how the others behaved: He tried not to look white people in the eye, and in fact, he had resolved not to have anything to do with any of them except, of course, Hannah and Brandon. And possibly Jane.

Alex thought he saw something out of the corner of his eye. The room seemed strangely bare, as though something were missing, although he couldn't imagine what it would be. On impulse, he turned his head toward the doorway.

A miniature face stared back at him. Not just small, but impossibly tiny. A perfect, miniature human face.

The face suddenly disappeared, and Alex thought vaguely that he must have imagined it.

But here was the face again, and this time, it came with a body, stepping out from behind the door post. His visitor was a miniscule but perfectly-proportioned Indian warrior. He was barely more than a foot tall. He had bronzed skin, very long black hair, almost down to his ankles, and he wore only a loin cloth. He carried a tiny bow and arrow. He returned Alex's stare with a curious look.

Alex knew he must be seeing things, and he desperately looked around the room to get his mind off this live action figure. But when he looked back at the doorway, the tiny man was still standing there, and still staring at him.

"What do you want?" Alex blurted out. The man replied in a string of words in another language. It meant nothing to Alex, who shook his head to show the tiny man that he didn't understand. The man said nothing more, but smiled kindly. Then he turned, stepped back through the doorway, and disappeared from Alex's sight.

Chapter 8:
GOING UPRIVER

Hannah had crossed rivers in Georgia in the twenty-first century, but she only knew that she had because the green signs on the freeway had told her so, and because of a split-second's glimpse of brown water as she glanced out the car window.

Nobody had ever suggested to Hannah that she might want to take a boat or a canoe on a river, and she wouldn't have been interested if they had. But now was different, not only because paddling was the only efficient way to travel, but also because she was enjoying herself.

"This is pretty cool," she said breathlessly to Sukey as she slid her paddle into the water. Sukey smiled, but did not reply.

The journey upriver was strangely peaceful. Only birdsong, breezes rustling through the trees, and the gentle splash of the paddles in the water broke the silence. Hannah had had a tricky start with the paddle, finding steering difficult, but Sukey soon taught her. To Hannah's own astonishment, she took to canoeing as though it was something she had been doing all her life. Going upriver wasn't entirely easy work, but the river was flat and gentle, and so it wasn't too arduous, either.

All the same, Hannah worried about wild creatures.

She knew alligators lived in southeast Georgia, of course, but she had never actually seen one. Now, on the river in 1752, she saw them everywhere: floating in the shallows with only their creepy eyes peeking out of the water, or resting on the riverbank, watching the passing canoe with mild interest. When the canoe skimmed close to a floating log, Hannah gave a small shriek and practically jumped out of her skin.

"I thought it was a 'gator," she explained sheepishly to Sukey, who had spun around to see what the matter was. Sukey laughed at her.

"Well, it looked like one," Hannah grumbled.

"They do not harm you if you leave them be," Sukey said kindly. "They are clever. Like the snakes, they see all we do. And some snakes are once people. Perhaps that one."

She nodded toward a water moccasin that was sunning itself on the riverbank.

Hannah remained silent, wondering what on earth Sukey was talking about.

Sukey took up the story. "Once, there are two hunters who come from a people who never eat squirrel. All day the two men hunt, but the only animal they ever catch is squirrel, which they do not eat. At night, the two men build a fire near the riverbank, and begin to prepare their meal. The first takes some cornmeal from his pocket, scoops up river water, and makes a bread to bake. But the other hunter, he decides to eat a squirrel. 'Don't do that!' his friend says. 'We are forbidden to eat squirrel! If you eat that squirrel, something terrible will happen!'

But the second hunter is starving, and so he says to his companion, 'Oh, that is nonsense. It is the story of a witch.' And then he prepares the squirrel, and cooks it over the fire."

Sukey paused for what felt to Hannah like a very long time. "So," Hannah said, "Is that it? Is that the whole story?"

"No, of course not," Sukey said. "I am just watching the snake over there." She pointed to another water moccasin. "He is listening to my story."

Hannah looked over at the snake. It did appear to be paying close attention to the canoe.

Sukey continued. "The squirrel that the hunter cooks, it looks like any other squirrel. It is delicious, and the second hunter eats every scrap of meat, but his friend refuses to touch it. Soon after, they lay down to sleep. Late that night, as the fire burns down, the first hunter awakes suddenly, hearing a terrible noise. He who eat the squirrel is screaming for help and rolling around on the ground in pain. His friend is shocked to see that his legs are gone."

"Somebody cut his legs off?" Hannah was shocked.

"No," Sukey said, "His legs are vanished. In their place, the second hunter has a snake's tail. His friend cannot help. As the hunter screams and writhes, his friend keeps watch, but he cannot do anything for him. It takes hours and hours, and the hunter is screaming almost to the end. His arms slowly draw into his body, his skin grows scales, his body shrinks, and finally, he becomes silent as his head becomes the head of a snake."

"And what happened then?" Hannah asked breathlessly.

"He slithers down the riverbank, and into the water. And for all we know, he is there still."

A horrible thought struck Hannah. "Wait, did you know this guy?"

Sukey shook her head. "No, but my mother say he was well-known among her people."

Hannah was disturbed. She tried not believing the story, but the way Sukey told it, it seemed so real. Afterward, she peered nervously at every snake they passed, trying to glimpse any human spark in its glassy stare.

As Hannah surveyed the riverbank, she occasionally spied a gap in the densely packed trees and shrubs. Through these gaps, she could see what looked like teeny dirt trails into the woods, with miniature trees lining the ways. She pointed out the next one to Sukey. "That looks like a freeway for elves, or something," she laughed.

Abruptly, Sukey shushed her.

"What's the matter?" Hannah asked, alarmed. Had Sukey seen somebody watching them from the forest?

When Sukey didn't reply, Hannah turned and looked back at her, and was astonished to see her companion appearing tightlipped and anxious. Nervously, Hannah paddled harder.

Only when they were well past the "elves' freeway" did Sukey speak. In a loud whisper, she said, "That path you see, it belongs to the Yunwi."

Hannah repeated, "It belongs to the . . . What?"

"The Yunwi," Sukey hissed, "the Little People. You are most like to see them after dark. But if you do meet them on a trail, never tell another living soul that you seen them, or the Yunwi find you and they kill you."

Hannah was creeped out. To lighten the atmosphere, she tried to make fun of what Sukey had said.

"Are you seriously telling me to watch out for killer gnomes?" she giggled.

"This is no jest," Sukey said sharply. "The Little People are dangerous if you trifle with them. They appear especially to children, but . . ."

Hannah interrupted, "Have you seen one?" She couldn't believe what she was hearing.

Sukey said solemnly, "I cannot say. Do not ask me again."

The way she said it sent a shiver down Hannah's spine.

Hours later, the canoe glided toward a wooded hill rising from the riverbank. It was the steepest hill Hannah had ever seen in South Georgia, which wasn't saying much, but still. About halfway up sat a cleared plateau, on which was built a log cabin that looked like any other hut in the Georgia backwoods, except for the metal bars on every window.

Sukey steered the canoe toward the shore. A spry man in his fifties emerged from the open door of the house and ran down the dirt trail to the riverbank. Without a word, he grabbed the rope that Sukey threw and helped pull the canoe fully onto shore. Hannah, her legs stiff, climbed out.

The man clearly knew Sukey, and he greeted her with a smile, a kiss, and a warm embrace. "How's Mr. Gordon?" he puffed in a fluting accent that Hannah couldn't place, although she thought he might be Irish. "I haven't seen him for a long time."

"He's a busy gentleman, Mr. MacKenzie," said Sukey, brushing dirt from her skirt. She lifted a sack from the canoe.

"Yes, I'm sure he is," Mr. MacKenzie said, wiping his hands on his pants.

"Wait, don't unload. You have had a long journey. I will summon John to help me." He turned and yelled a long stream of words in a language that Hannah didn't recognize. She thought it might be German, because its sounds were guttural, with lots of throaty "ch" noises, but unlike German, it was also soft and gentle. A young black man came running from the woods and began to unpack the canoe.

To Hannah's amazement, the slave now spoke to MacKenzie in his own peculiar language. Hannah couldn't help asking, "What language are you guys speaking?"

"Gaelic," said Mr. MacKenzie with a smile, pronouncing it "Gallic." "It is the language of Scotland."

Hannah had lived in Scotland during her last adventure. But she had never heard anyone speaking like that, and she said so.

Mr. MacKenzie chuckled. "You lived in the Lowlands, did you?" he asked teasingly.

"No," Hannah said crossly, not entirely sure what he meant. "I lived in Dundee, and it had mountains. It wasn't low."

"Dundee?" Mr. MacKenzie said. "That's in the Lowlands. They have hills, not mountains."

Hannah sneered at him. "How would you know? I bet you never went there."

"I did that," Mr. MacKenzie laughed. "I traveled the Lowlands with Prince Charlie's army in the Forty-Five Rebellion. I fought Johnnie Cope's men at Prestonpans, I'll have you know. And in the Lowlands, the people are English."

Hannah was now thoroughly confused. "I don't know what you're talking about," she said. "Everyone I met in Scotland was Scottish. They weren't English."

Mr. MacKenzie drew himself up and tutted at her ignorance. "We in the Highlands call them the English, those people who dwell in Dundee and Edinburgh. They are not like us, for they know not the Gaelic. I am a Highlander, from an t-Eilean Sgitheanach." The words he said sounded like "an Tellen Shkee-a-nach." He added, "the English call my birthplace the Island of Skye."

"Whatever," Hannah muttered, although she silently resolved to look up Skye on a map someday. She stomped off up the trail as Mr. MacKenzie chuckled.

When she got to the trading post, she found Sukey already inside, sifting through the goods on offer. Hannah stood awkwardly just inside the doorway of the cramped hut, where she soon found herself forced to make more conversation with Mr. MacKenzie. "So what are you doing here?" she asked him reluctantly.

Mr. MacKenzie said slowly, "You have heard of the great Highland rebellion of forty-five?"

Hannah hadn't, but she nodded. Mr. MacKenzie shook his head sadly. "Prince Charlie's army was destroyed at the battle of Culloden. Two of my brothers and my father were killed. I was lucky to escape with my life. I was taken captive, and I was luckier yet that I was banished from Scotland, and not executed. My other brothers were not so fortunate as me: They were banished too, but they died in the ship on the way across the ocean."

Hannah had no idea which war this was, but she felt bad for Mr. MacKenzie. The tough rugged Scotsman looked bowed down by his losses.

"So you were transported, like me?" Hannah asked carefully.

"Aye, to Barbados," said Mr. MacKenzie.

"So how did you wind up here?" Hannah asked.

He didn't answer, but instead looked over to Sukey. Hannah wondered if he had run off from Barbados, and stowed away on a ship to Georgia. She supposed he must have.

Sukey, meanwhile, was pawing through a large heap of animal skins, building a pile of those she had chosen, and another pile of those she had discarded. Mr. MacKenzie picked up one of her rejects, and ran his hand down the fur. "Good quality, I tell you, Sukey," he said. "You should take it."

"Uh-huh," she said skeptically. "These are not so good as last time."

Mr. MacKenzie laughed. "Come now, do you think I would be a fool, and lose Mr. Gordon's business? I only trade the best."

She looked sideways at him, as if to say, "Give me a break," and carried on sorting through the deerskins. Finally, giving a firm pat to the pile she had selected, she said, "I take these for Mr. Gordon."

"Not so many, I'm afraid," tutted Mr. MacKenzie, shaking his head morosely. "Your trade goods won't fetch so much with the Cherokee as once they did."

Sukey opened her mouth to protest, but then changed her mind, took one skin off her pile, and stood with her arms crossed, daring Mr. MacKenzie to insist on more concessions.

Mr. MacKenzie sighed heavily. "Very well. You drive a hard bargain for Mr. Gordon, indeed you do. Now, would you like a bit of supper?"

"I would," Hannah interrupted. "I'm totally starving."

Mr. MacKenzie laughed and spread his arms wide. "Then let us eat!"

Hannah should have guessed what would be on the menu. She gazed balefully at her unappetizing wooden bowl of corn mush. Scooping up the gloppy white paste on her wooden spoon, she scowled at it.

"It's only porridge," Mr. MacKenzie laughed.

Hannah looked up sharply. "No, it's so not. Porridge is made from oatmeal. This is more like grits."

Mr. MacKenzie shook his head. "We can't get oats here, girl, you must know that. So like everyone else, I make my porridge with Indian meal."

Hannah took a taste and made a face. She had learned to truly hate cornmeal mush and all other bland combinations of corn and water. "Got anything to put in it?" she asked grumpily.

"Only this," he said with a grin, passing her some salt. She mistook it for sugar, and had added about half a tablespoon before she realized her mistake. But she was so hungry, she ate most of it anyway.

Mr. MacKenzie was still chortling at Hannah's pickiness when John dashed in, agitated. Signalling frantically, he rattled off a long string of Gaelic to Mr. MacKenzie, who immediately lost his smile, and leaping forward, grabbed his musket from next to the door. Alarmed, Sukey dropped her spoon, while Hannah felt panic grabbing her insides.

"What is it?" she breathed .

"Wheest! Someone is in the woods," grunted Mr. MacKenzie, aiming his musket from the window toward the rocky bluffs across the river. Loudly, he yelled, "Show yourself!"

There was a tense moment. Then a young Indian woman rose slowly from a crouch in the bushes on the opposing riverbank, her hands in the air.

Mr. MacKenzie lowered his gun, and gave a nervous chuckle. "Och, it's only Indian Mary," he said. "She fairly gave me a fright." He waved to her, and she waved back limply.

The entire room let out a sigh of relief.

"So who did you think she was?" Hannah asked.

"I know not," Mr. MacKenzie said, replacing his musket by the door. "There are thieves and beggars who pass this way. I have many riches here that they would gladly take. And one day maybe the Creeks will turn on us. Begging your pardon, Sukey."

Sukey shrugged and said, "I care not, for I am not Creek."

For some reason, Hannah thought, Mr. MacKenzie seemed more approachable and normal than anyone else she had met so far.

"So," she snickered, figuring he would appreciate the humor, "did you hear about the little people who live in the woods?"

There was a long silence before he replied. "You speak of the fairies?" he said slowly. His face was deeply serious.

"No," Hannah said awkwardly, aware that both he and Sukey were now staring at her. "Not fairies, no wings or anything, just . . . um . . . little, you know, people . . . Really small . . ." She leaned down and gestured with a hand about a foot off the floor.

"Aye," Mr. MacKenzie said slowly. "Where I am from, we call them na Sìthichean."

What he had said sounded like "na- shee-uh." Hannah looked quizzically at him, and he explained. "The English, you call them fairies. Fairies are very powerful, and you should never, never cross them, or they will take revenge. Treat them always with respect."

Hannah looked hopefully for signs that he was joking. He wasn't.

She continued to pick at her mush without enthusiasm. *Obviously*, she silently told herself, *all these people have lost their marbles.*

That evening, while Sukey sang quietly in a language Hannah didn't understand, Mr. MacKenzie worked at his desk by candlelight, writing in a huge leather-bound book.

Hannah peeked over his shoulder and saw that the pages were filled not with writing, but with tiny doodles and scratch marks. "What's that mean?" she asked, pointing.

"My accounts," he said with a smile. "I can neither read nor write, so here is how I keep a note of what I have bought and sold."

Hannah looked closer, and saw little drawings of pots, pans, guns, furniture, and, most of all, animals, each representing a skin. Most were deer.

"That's cool," said Hannah, although she wondered what it would be like not to know how to read. There was a silence, until she thought of another topic of conversation. "Why do you keep a horseshoe over your front door?"

Mr. MacKenzie put down his quill, and looked sideways at her. "You don't know? It protects my house from the evil eye, and brings good luck. All the evil that approaches the house is caught in the horseshoe. At least, I hope it is."

"So," Hannah said, "You really believe that stuff about fairies, don't you?"

Mr. MacKenzie looked crossly at her. "Why would I not believe in that which is?"

"I don't know," Hannah said with a shrug. "Have you ever seen them? The fairies, I mean?"

"Here in America, no," Mr. MacKenzie said. "But when I was a boy, I came upon them as they danced in their glen. I was not supposed to travel that road unless I left a gift for the fairies. But I had no gift to give. I was sore afraid to walk through the glen. It was a fair day, but the wind began to blow hard as I walked, and there was a ghostly wail in the wind. I walked faster.

"And suddenly clouds appeared from nowhere, and I began to run, as fast as I could. There is a loch, what you English call a lake, in the glen, and that was where I saw them. Men, women and children were they, the little people, and they danced a merry tune in the pouring rain. I did not wait about, but climbed the side of the glen to get away. I fell as I climbed, and gashed open my legs on the rocks, but I did not stop. I stole away before they could see me and carry me off forever."

For once, Mr. MacKenzie didn't laugh. Neither did Hannah. She shuddered.

Looking over at Sukey, who was still singing with her eyes closed, Hannah wondered what it was like to be her: a slave, separated from the family and friends she had grown up with, and then from her own children and grandchildren. Sukey said so little, and she said almost nothing that wasn't necessary. Hannah had wondered if she was shy, or if she was silent because she didn't trust whites, or if there was something else; the huge gap between her life and Hannah's. Whatever the reason, she was jealous that Alex had somehow developed a close relationship with this strange and quiet woman. Hannah felt frustrated that she had a hard time connecting with Sukey, or any of these people. Except for Jane.

As Sukey and Hannah were making straw beds for themselves in the loft of Mr. MacKenzie's shop, Alex had another unexpected visitor in the slave hut. Mr. Gordon arrived, carrying a brown leather satchel. The other slaves fell silent and jumped to their feet when they saw him, but he ignored them.

Kneeling down by Alex's bed, he opened his bag and began to pull out an odd assortment of items, including a small knife and what looked like a drinking glass, along with a metal box that rattled when he picked it up. Peering bleary-eyed at him, Alex croaked, "What are you doing, Mr. Gordon?"

"I've come to administer physic to you," he said matter-of-factly. "We must cure you of this ague." Pulling out a bottle of water and a small stone block, he laid them on the tree stump that served as a table in the hut. He poured water on the stone and, to Alex's alarm, began to sharpen the knife on it.

Alex gulped, then said, "So, what's the knife for?"

"Never you mind," growled Mr. Gordon.

But Alex, looking over Mr. Gordon's equipment, minded a lot. He was interested in the history of science, and he knew enough about the history of medicine to know he was right to be concerned. He realized that Mr. Gordon was preparing to "cup" him: to cut his arm, and then apply a vacuum seal to remove blood.

Alex said desperately, "Sir, that won't cure me. It'll just make me sicker."

Mr. Gordon looked at him in astonishment. "How say you?"

Alex took a deep breath. He knew that saying what he was about to say probably wasn't a good idea, but the alternative was risking his health by allowing Mr. Gordon to slice him open with an unsterilized knife.

He took a deep breath. "You think we get sick because of, um, an imbalance of humors, right? Blood, urine, no, wait, not urine, um, phlegm, and, hey, what was the other one?"

"Bile," Mr. Gordon said helpfully, astonished by his slave's knowledge. "Good God, boy, how do you know this? Were you formerly the property of a physician?"

Alex ignored him. He was struggling to think and speak, and the effort was wearing him out. "That theory, it's not true. Diseases are caused by germs. They're microscopic . . . . I mean, they're too small to see without a special eyeglass."

"I know what microscopic means," Mr. Gordon said officiously, rolling up Alex's left sleeve, "but you're talking nonsense."

"No, Mr. Gordon. It's true." Alex yanked back his arm with all the strength he could muster. "What you're doing might give me blood poisoning. Fevers are caused by tiny, um, creatures that invade the body. The best thing you can do is bring me fresh water to drink and leave me alone."

For a moment, Mr. Gordon was dumbstruck. He looked at Alex with growing concern. "What is this? The fever has made you rebellious, and you have taken leave of your senses."

Now he roughly grabbed Alex's arm. Alex struggled for a moment, but he was too weak to stop him. Seizing the knife, Mr. Gordon slashed Alex's upper arm, and he yelled in pain.

While Alex tearfully examined his wound, which bled profusely, Mr. Gordon quickly heated a small glass in the fire. Picking it up with a rag, he flipped over the glass, and applied the open end to Alex's wound.

The glass's rim was boiling hot, and Alex howled miserably as he felt his skin burn. Blood soon flowed freely into the glass.

Mrs. Osborn was having a difficult pregnancy, and now spent much of her time in bed. On Mr. Osborn's orders, Brandon had taken over from her responsibility for the vegetable garden that the parishioners had planted in anticipation of the Osborns' arrival. Today, Mr. Osborn was helping him to weed it, and, dressed in shirtsleeves, he energetically wielded a hoe.

When Mr. Gordon came riding across the cow pasture toward them, Mr. Osborn self-consciously put down his hoe. "I wonder what the matter could be?" he muttered nervously. "Perhaps he comes to advise me that a gentleman ought not to labor in his field alongside his servant."

But Mr. Gordon had something else on his mind, and it was urgent. He didn't even dismount to share his news. "My youngest slave, Cato, is suffering from ague and from sickness of the mind," he said breathlessly. "Sir, I wish you to conduct an examination of him."

"Certainly, I shall," Mr. Osborn said happily, clearly flattered that his erst-while enemy had come to him for help. "I will fetch my apparatus and come to your slave quarters forthwith."

Brandon was worried to hear that Alex needed medical attention. And he could not imagine how Mr. Osborn was qualified to administer it.

Calmly, Mr. Osborn rode his horse at a leisurely pace. Riding on the saddle behind him, clutching the minister's medical bag, Brandon asked him why on earth Mr. Gordon had asked a pastor to attend to "Cato."

"Like many clergymen, I have some medical training," Mr. Osborn said self-importantly. "We men of God are frequently expected to care for the bodies as well as the souls of our flocks, and so I studied medicine some two years in Edinburgh."

"In Scotland?" Brandon asked.

"Indeed," Mr. Osborn said. "Edinburgh University is the home of the finest medical school in the world. You know, it is good for you to accompany me on this visit, Brandon, for you may learn a great deal about medicine. Physic is a useful skill for any gentleman, but especially for a man of the cloth."

Brandon, unfortunately, already knew quite a bit about eighteenth century medicine, and he was desperately thinking how he might persuade Mr. Osborn and Mr. Gordon not to inflict it on poor Alex.

As Brandon stepped into the slave hut, Alex greeted him with a wan smile. Brandon was encouraged to see that his friend didn't look as though he was at death's door. But he was seriously bothered by the sight of a bloody rag tied around Alex's arm.

Mr. Gordon was standing by Alex's bed, and he politely welcomed Mr. Osborn. "Thank you for attending so promptly, sir. The boy resisted my treating him, and he blethered some nonsense about the cause of his sickness. I would like you to bleed him again, for I fear his humors are still imbalanced."

"What nonsense did he speak, may I ask?" said Mr. Osborn, as he kneeled on the dirt floor, and began to unpack his black bag.

Alex groaned, and addressed Brandon: "He did bleeding on me, and I tried to tell him it won't work . . ."

"Quiet," snapped Mr. Gordon, turning on him.

But Brandon stepped forward, leaned down, and tapped Mr. Osborn on the shoulder. "Sir? I'm sorry, but he's right. Bleeding doesn't work."

Mr. Osborn looked up at him crossly. "And you are a doctor, are you?"

"No," Brandon reluctantly admitted. "But I do know that too much blood doesn't cause diseases. They're caused by germs. They're too small for the eye to see."

Both men stared at him now. Mr. Gordon looked positively afraid. After a moment's pause, he turned to Mr. Osborn. "That is exactly what the boy Cato said to me earlier."

"Where are they learning such foolishness?" Mr. Osborn asked.

"I know not, sir," Mr. Gordon muttered sourly, shaking his head slowly. "But it is superstition. Perhaps even witchcraft."

Mr. Osborn smiled condescendingly. "Surely an educated man such as yourself does not believe in witchcraft, sir? That is a superstition in itself."

Mr. Gordon glared at his adversary. "Of course I do not," he sputtered. "But the slaves believe in it, and it carries great power with them."

"All the more reason," Mr. Osborn said pointedly, "why we should attend to the slaves' souls, and bring them to the Truth of the Church."

Mr. Gordon scowled furiously.

Brandon raised a hand for permission to speak. "Sirs? Maybe the best thing would be to pray over Al . . . Cato. Prayer is the strongest thing we have, right? And, anyway, he seems to be on the mend."

On cue, Alex sat up on his elbows, trying to seem as healthy as possible.

Mr. Osborn glanced at Mr. Gordon, who nodded, then he instructed everyone to bow their heads. He said a very long prayer, but Brandon wouldn't have minded if it had lasted all day, so long as Alex wasn't subjected to any more medical treatments.

As the minister intoned "Amen," Mr. Gordon asked to meet with him outside. The two men left Brandon and Alex.

"Wow," exclaimed Alex. "Thanks for saving me. I thought Mr. Gordon was going to insist."

"Me, too," said Brandon with a relieved smile. "And hopefully God will answer us, and make you better soon. What do you think you've got? Is it malaria?"

Alex shook his head. "Doubt it, 'cause of the pills. I think it's the flu. I do feel better than I did yesterday, but I don't think it was the bleeding that did it."

"I'm sure it wasn't," Brandon agreed. "Hey, have you washed that wound on your arm?"

"Good idea," Alex said. "I'll do it as soon as he's gone."

"Do it," Brandon urged him. "And put a clean rag on it if you can find one. You have to keep everything super-clean."

Alex nodded, just as Brandon turned at the sound of Mr. Osborn calling his name.

"Brandon," Alex said quickly. "Have you ever heard of such a thing as tiny people? . . ."

"Huh? Tiny people? Sorry, Alex, no," Brandon said, giving him an odd look as he stepped through the doorway. "What makes you ask that? Look, just tell me later. I gotta go."

Hannah and Sukey were almost home in their canoe, which was piled high with deerskins. But even though they were still a quarter-mile shy of the river landing at Mr. Gordon's property, Sukey steered the craft into the riverbank and leaped ashore, beckoning to Hannah to join her.

Walking along a narrow trail through the thick woods, Hannah glimpsed shimmering water ahead. Finally, after climbing over a huge fallen tree, she reached the edge of a large, round pond. Jagged dead tree stumps thrust up from the water close to where it lapped the edge, and three sparse tupelo trees clung to the pond's banks, which sloped gently into the murky depths. Hannah watched as a few tiny fish darted about in the shallows.

"This is the sinkhole," Sukey said quietly. "It has no end. If you drown, you sink forever."

"That's so wrong," Hannah muttered uncertainly. "Give me a break."

But now she felt the hairs stand up on the back of her neck. It did feel very creepy here. When neither she nor Sukey spoke, there was absolute silence, not even birdsong. Hannah stared into the depths of the water, but she could see nothing. The water was so black, the pond looked like a giant pot of ink.

Suddenly Sukey said, "A young man was murdered, because he cheats another man out of money. His body is falling through the water."

Hannah wondered why Sukey was speaking in present tense. She normally spoke mostly in present tense because, Hannah assumed, English was not her first language. But this time was different.

And then, staring out over the pond, Sukey said matter-of-factly in a voice that chilled Hannah to the bone, "His spirit is here with us. He is here."

She said it as though the dead man were standing next to them. Hannah felt adrenalin rising through her, and her breathing quickened. Her head involuntarily swiveled, as she looked around for a ghost. A gentle breeze played through the trees around the pond, rustling the leaves, and Sukey flinched.

From her pocket, Sukey extracted a tiny bottle, and uncorked it. Extending her arm over the pond edge, she poured the liquid into the water.

"What is that stuff?" Hannah asked.

"Whisky from Mr. MacKenzie," Sukey said. "My father tells me I should share liquor with the spirits of the dead. I bring whisky to the spirit of the bottomless pond after every journey, so he will rest content, and not trouble us."

Hannah wasn't sure what was freaking her out the most: the strange, utterly still pond, or Sukey's weird behavior. Either way, she wanted to escape as soon as she could.

When they got back to the quarters, Sukey called Tony and Cuffee to unload the canoe and take the deerskins to Mr. Gordon's house. Hannah said goodbye to her, but before returning to the Gordons', she visited Alex. With relief, she saw him greet her with clear eyes: His glassy stare had disappeared.

"How was the trip?" he said weakly. "Wish I could have gone."

Excitedly, Hannah told him about the trading post, Mr. MacKenzie and his Gaelic-speaking slave, and the long journey by canoe. She didn't mention the bottomless pond, or the legend of the Little People.

In return, Alex described his medical misadventures, explaining how Brandon had saved him. His sister was grossed out.

"There was something else," Alex said hesitantly. And then he told her about his tiny visitor.

Hannah was agog. The chills she had felt before were nothing compared with what she felt now. Alex was still telling his story when she held up her hand. "Stop! Sukey says that if you tell anyone about a visit from the Little People, they'll come back and kill you."

Alex was shocked. "You think he was real?"

Hannah shook her head, bewildered. "All of these people, they think he's real. They believe in the Little People. And you actually saw one. What am I supposed to think?"

Alex looked dazed. "I was kind of hoping you would say it was my imagination. I thought that was what you would think."

"I don't know what to think anymore," Hannah muttered. "Not about anything."

Chapter 9:
IDENTITIES REVEALED

Hannah returned to find Mr. Gordon working at his desk, and Mrs. Gordon sitting by the fire, wrapped in a shawl, halfheartedly attempting to do a little embroidery. Jane was sitting across from her, bored and staring into the fireplace. She alone greeted Hannah with enthusiasm.

Hannah sighed. "Jane, I'm so tired, and I still have to make supper."

"No need," Mr. Gordon said without turning around. "We have eaten already, and there is enough cornmeal mush left for you."

Hannah looked, and sure enough, congealed corn porridge puddled in the bottom of the pot. She scooped the mush into a wooden bowl, where it landed with an unappetizing "glop." Hungry though she was, it was hard to get excited about cornmeal mush. *This*, she thought, *is what keeps me alive. That's about the best I can say.*

While she ate at the table, Jane came and sat with her. "'annah, pray tell, 'ave you 'eard anything of the white witch in the woods?" she asked quietly.

"Yeah," Hannah muttered, swallowing a mouthful of mush. To herself, she said under her breath, "Fairies, ghosts, witches. What next?"

"What did you say?" Mr. Gordon said sharply, and Hannah jumped, thinking that he had spoken to her. Turning around, however, she saw that he was looking at Jane.

"The white witch . . ." Jane said slowly. "The slaves speak of 'er, sir."

"I will thank you, lassie, not to bring their ignorant, unchristian superstitions into this house," Mr. Gordon said angrily. "I have just this day witnessed Cato's refusal to be treated with physic because he holds that ill health is caused by invisible evil creatures in the blood. Mr. Osborn's servant believes the same. We are Christians, not heathen, and you will remember that in your conversations with the negroes."

"Yes, sir," Jane said quietly. "But, you see, the white witch is . . ."

"Enough!" Mr. Gordon shouted, startling everyone. "Do not speak of this again. Not to Hannah, not to the negroes, and certainly not to me."

Jane looked frightened by his outburst and she fell into silence. But now Hannah was curious. She resolved that as soon as they were alone, she would ask Jane what she knew about this witch.

Mrs. Osborn had ventured outside for the first time in three weeks, saying that she was feeling a little better. Brandon was glad to have her working alongside him, tending the garden. She still huffed and puffed whenever she lifted all but the lightest things, but the color had returned to her cheeks. He stared at her enormous belly, and tried to guess how long it would be until her baby was born. She saw him looking, and gave him a friendly smile. He turned away, embarrassed.

As he returned to his hoeing, Brandon saw three young black men, one of them with a limp, walking purposefully in his direction. They looked so determined, they made him anxious. He was ashamed to find himself reacting in this way to black men. Had he listened to too many horror stories about slave rebellions? More than ever, he felt self-conscious that he appeared white.

"Can I help you?" he called out, leaning on his hoe. He sensed Mrs. Osborn tensing up in fear next to him.

"Sir, it is Mr. Osborn we come to see," replied the man with the limp in heavily accented English.

Brandon thought he recognized him. He said, "Hey, don't you work for Mr. Gordon?"

The man reluctantly nodded. "We are his slaves, sir," he said. Then he looked around impatiently. "Is Mr. Osborn here?"

"Not at the moment," Brandon said nervously. "Can I tell him you stopped by?"

The leader of the group looked at the other two, and they agreed with nods to leave a message. He said, "Tell him that Cuffee and two friends wish to speak with him."

"Any particular subject?" Brandon asked.

"Yes, sir," said Cuffee. "We wish to take communion."

Brandon would never have guessed that any slaves were Christians. He had assumed that they were Muslims, or people with no religious beliefs that he would even recognize. Now that he knew better, he hated to disappoint them. But he had learned from his boss that communion was an infrequent ceremony in the eighteenth century, not a daily or even weekly event. He cleared his throat and said, "Next communion won't be until Christmas, Mr. Osborn says."

Cuffee gave a curt nod in reply.

Brandon suggested that they stop by again tomorrow afternoon, when he expected Mr. Osborn to be home, and the men agreed that they would.

When he heard the news of the slaves' visit, Mr. Osborn was no less surprised than Brandon had been, but he took this unexpected development in his stride, and when the group returned the following day, he received them warmly.

"So, you wish to take catechism, and become Christians?" he said, stepping out of the house to greet them. With a smile, his hat in his hands, Cuffee replied on the group's behalf. "No, sir, we are already Christians, except for Tony here. My Christian name is Mark. I am from Angola, and so is John, here. "

"Angola?" Mr. Osborn asked, puzzled. "Angola in Africa? Surely Africa is a heathen land."

"No, sir," John said. "Not Angola. The Portuguese brought Christianity, through our holy mother church."

Mr. Osborn looked puzzled at him for a long time, and then the lights went on. He frowned. "Oh, so you are Papists."

Everyone including Brandon now looked at him in confusion. Mr. Osborn hurriedly explained. "By that, I mean you are Catholics, and you owe your loyalty to the Pope in Rome. This presents something of a problem. You must all first take instruction. John and, er, Mark, I'm afraid that, as Papists, you hold some very peculiar ideas about Christianity that we must first address. Will you willingly meet with me after church on Sundays?"

The three men looked worried. "We are willing," Tony said. "But Mr. Gordon does not wish us to learn about Christianity."

Mr. Osborn gave a small smile. "Well, since it is obviously too late to prevent you from learning about it, perhaps he will consent in your case? Brandon, will you catechize these men? You may visit them in their quarters on Sunday."

Brandon greeted this command with a nervous nod. What had he got himself into? How could he teach three adult men anything?

As soon as the slaves had bid farewell and set off across the fields, Mr. Osborn said to Brandon, "Mayhaps, I needs must teach these men myself, for they will surely have fallen into serious errors as members of the Popish church."

Brandon let out a silent sigh of relief. But Mr. Osborn hadn't let him off the hook. He added, "Let us first see how your presence on Mr. Gordon's plantation is received before I attend there myself. Brandon, you will go on Sunday as I directed."

Brandon felt a bit like an untrained dog being sent into a minefield.

Taking the back trail through the woods to the quarters, Brandon trod nervously for fear of stepping on snakes. He had never seen so many snakes in his life as he had in 1752. Deadly cottonmouths hung out by the river, copperheads hid in the woodpile, and massive black king snakes (which were fairly harmless but didn't look it) crawled through the fields. Brandon had also spotted more than a few rattlesnakes. In fact, he had seen more snakes than he had known existed: Some were small and bright green, others were red and orange, still others were long and brown. He was relieved to see fewer of them now that the cold had set in, but to be on the safe side, he stomped heavily everywhere he walked, making as much noise as he could to scare them away.

Now, emerging from the woods, he felt more than ever like a trespasser in the slave quarters.

To make matters worse, he really wasn't sure he could teach the slaves as Mr. Osborn wanted. He didn't exactly feel confident about his understanding of the Church of England's complicated beliefs. True, Mr. Osborn had coached him in the Thirty-Nine Articles, the basic points on which Anglicans agreed. But Brandon had a problem with the article about baptizing adults. However, he was reluctant to ask too many questions, afraid that Mr. Osborn would somehow figure out his secret, that he was a Baptist. Otherwise, he didn't have any deep personal objections to anything Mr. Osborn taught him.

All the same, he wasn't sure he was competent to teach the Church of England's beliefs to other people. So, without consulting Mr. Osborn, he decided to hold a Bible study as an icebreaker for his catechist group. After years of Sunday school and Church youth camps, he felt more comfortable starting out this way. He didn't think that Anglicans were much into Bible studies, but he couldn't see the harm.

Bashfully, he silently approached the small group of slaves who were sitting outside their barracks, singing. Tony was playing a drum, while Cuffee was bashing a stick on the ground, and the others, including Sukey, sang their mournful song. The words of the song were in English, but Brandon didn't recognize it at all.

When the music faded to a close, Brandon coughed to make his presence known, and the men who had been sitting on the ground scrambled to their feet and snatched off their hats.

Brandon turned to look behind him, to see who had provoked this show of respect, and realized with a start that the fuss was directed at him. He coughed again, and raised a hand in greeting.

"Er, hi? I'm Brandon?" he said nervously. "You wanted to talk about the Bible? And church stuff?"

Tony nodded. One man made a disapproving face and drifted away, but the others stayed, and Sukey brought out a low rough wooden stool for Brandon. He squatted on it, feeling smaller than ever, and opened his Bible. It was a little hard to read because of the long s's that Mr. Osborn had explained to him, and the italic script that seemed to have no particular rhyme or reason. Still, he was ready. He was familiar with the ancient language of the King James version of the Bible, since that was the one used at his church in Snipesville.

He flipped through the pages until he found the chapter and verse he wanted-ed.

"I thought we could discuss what Jesus means in the Sermon on the Mount," he said quietly. "You know."

They didn't know, but they listened politely as Brandon read it to them. ". . . Blessed are the meek, for they shall inherit the earth . . ."

He put down his Bible. "What do you think that means?"

Nobody wanted to say anything, but they all looked approvingly at Brandon. So after an awkward silence, he read the chapter to the end. When he was finished, he waited for comments. But none came. "Anyone want to say something?" he asked.

Cuffee's hand shot up, and Brandon gratefully pointed to him. "Yes?"

"Can we take communion now?" said Cuffee.

"Uh, no," Brandon said. "That is, Mr. Osborn wants to meet with you first, to, um, prepare you."

"Oh," Cuffee said. But something was clearly troubling him, so Brandon waited for him to say more.

Now Cuffee took a deep breath. "I know more about Christianity than Hannah does," he said, "and she's allowed to take communion. And she is also in the church of Rome."

There was no denying it. Hannah was a Catholic, and a pretty clueless one. Cuffee had made a good point. Why should he have to jump through a hoop when Hannah didn't?

Brandon was about to change the subject when Tony raised his hand.

"I dreamed of Jesus," he said.

"Hush," Cuffee chastised him. "You are not a baptized Christian!"

"What of it?" Tony said. "I had a powerful dream, as though it was real."

Cuffee continued to look skeptical, but the others paid close attention to Tony. He spread his arms dramatically. "I dreamed that the swamp turned into a pool of blood, a whirling pool, and fire lit up the sky. At first, we were all afraid, but then, as we watched, a man came out of the center of the pool. He told us he was Jesus, and he told us not to be afraid. Then he handed each of us a burning torch, and he bid us light a way for him, which we did. And he made us powerful, kings of our own countries."

There was a rapt silence, and then Tony added, "He told me, clear as I tell you now, that this will all happen soon in the daytime world. We must pray to him."

Brandon's jaw had dropped, and it took him a moment to gather his wits. "Yes, well," he said, "Yes, well, I, uh, I agree with the last part. About praying to him. Great idea. Now, if we turn back to the Bible . . ."

"I knew an Indian conjuror who made a prophecy like that," said Sukey.

"What, about the Bible?" Brandon asked desperately.

"No, about the end of this world coming in a pool of blood," she said. She turned to Tony and said, "You have been given a prophecy."

Tony beamed. Brandon couldn't help wondering if Tony got the story from Sukey, and had just sort of made it Christian.

But now Sukey was speaking again. "I listen to Mr. Osborn's sermons whenever I am able," she said to Brandon. "I cannot always understand his words, but I learn from him that Jesus is great and powerful."

Brandon nodded frantically. This was a line of discussion he wished to encourage. Sukey continued, "Brandon, Jesus says that the meek inherit the earth, and you say we are the meek, yes?"

Brandon continued to nod enthusiastically.

"Then," Sukey said, leaning back and slapping her thighs, "thanks to Tony, we know what to look for when deliverance comes, the time when we are kings. We look for fire and blood."

Brandon had stopped nodding. He had a very bad feeling about this.

As soon as he returned home, Brandon reported to Mr. Osborn, who was not pleased to learn of his decision to lead a Bible class.

"You must understand that it takes years of study to be qualified to discourse upon the Bible!" he said angrily. "I was a Cambridge scholar, and I learned from the greatest theologians of this age. You cannot ask the miserable negroes to decide for themselves what is meant by the subtle language of God's word. I suspect, Brandon, that you are a New Light, who has fallen prey to George Whitefield's peculiar ideas of religion."

Brandon had no idea what his master was talking about. He wished that he could look up things that Mr. Osborn said on Wikipedia.

For now, he needed to settle a question that was bothering him. "I just think," he said carefully, "that people have a right to get to know Jesus better through His Word. I mean, we pray to Him about all our little problems, right? And He answers."

Mr. Osborn sighed heavily. "No, Brandon, He does not, not in the way you seem to think. I believe, Brandon, that God is a reasonable God. The age of miracles has passed. He does not expect to follow us around, intervening willy-nilly in human affairs, as though we were incapable of decision. We are not merely blades of grass in the wind, who allow ourselves to be buffeted by fortune, or to act only at His divine whim."

"Blades of grass? No," Brandon said. "He blesses people, and we do nothing to deserve that."

Mr. Osborn gave him a stern look. "Brandon, what you say is a perfect example of why it is too dangerous to permit slaves and others of low standing, such as you, to decide for yourselves the meaning of your faith. You have great intelligence but you are not educated."

Brandon was pretty sure that he and the Baptist faith had just been insulted, but he held his tongue. In the silence that followed, Mr. Osborn calmed down.

"I must confess, however," he said, scratching his head, "it was always thus. Whenever heathens are introduced to Christianity, no matter how carefully we try to mold their beliefs, they attempt to combine Truth with their superstitions."

Brandon looked at him quizzically, and Mr. Osborn sat back with his hands steepled together at the fingertips, almost as though he were at prayer. He gave a small smile. "Brandon, allow me to explain. You remember St. Swithin's church in Balesworth?"

"Yes, of course," said Brandon.

"Did you ever see the Green Man?"

Brandon frowned. "You mean the pub on Balesworth High Street?"

Mr. Osborn shook his head impatiently. "No, no. I mean the image of the Green Man in the church, scratched high on the wall of the vestry . . . ."

"Hey, I did see that!" Brandon exclaimed. "And there was a bunch of writing too, but I couldn't see to read it. I just thought it was graffiti anyway."

Mr. Osborn leaned forward. "Balesworth folk say that their ancestors drew on the church walls while they took sanctuary from the ravages of a plague, a very long time ago. The Green Man was a pagan god, and I suppose the poor people looked to him as a sign of life, of renewal. Even in this year of 1752, the people still speak of him, especially in the spring. Of course, they also believe in Christ, but I suppose we in the Church find it easier to accept the old beliefs alongside the new, rather than to try to argue with the common folk."

"Hmm, that makes sense," said Brandon. "It's easier to get people on board if you don't make them give up the fun stuff."

"Quite," said Mr. Osborn. "And the same is true of the negroes. I am sure they hold all sorts of heathenish beliefs, but it would not be wise to wage war on those. Rather, we should endeavor to use gentle persuasion to bring them from the wilderness of superstition to the light of Christian truth. As our friendship grows, they will surely see the error of their ways, and our kindnesses will be repaid."

"Great," Brandon said. But then he remembered something. "I just hope Mr. Gordon sees it that way."

"I think Mr. Gordon's concerns are altogether different from mine," Mr. Osborn said thoughtfully. "Mr. Gordon is a Presbyterian, and so he ought to think as other Presbyterians do, which is to be greatly intolerant of pagan beliefs. Yet, where his negroes are concerned, he is instead intolerant of Christianity. Now why do you think that is?"

Brandon said hesitantly, "Have you asked him what his problem is?"

"No," Mr. Osborn said, smiling slyly. "What I just asked you is a question to which I suspect I already know the answer. I would venture that his love of

God has largely succumbed to his love of gold. He is a slave-owning planter first, and a Christian second."

Brandon smiled back. "I think you pretty much nailed it, sir," he said.

It was Sunday evening, and Hannah had agreed to go for a walk with Jane. It was everyone's alleged day off, but even so, Jane and Hannah spent much of the day doing chores. They ended up in the evening visiting with Sukey and Alex at the slave quarters, arriving just after sunset to find Sukey and Alex outside with a large newly-lit bonfire.

It was Sukey who first greeted the two girls, but the very first thing that Hannah noticed was that Alex looked healthy: He was now fully recovered from his illness and its treatment. Mr. Gordon was happy to take credit for this, Alex told Hannah.

"Nonsense," tutted Sukey. "Cato is alive because of the magic of the white witch."

"How so?" asked Hannah with a frown.

Alex explained, "Sukey went to see her a second time, and fetched me another herbal medicine. It was a hot drink, and it was really good."

"And you were dumb enough to drink it?" Hannah hissed at her brother. "That stuff could be really bad for you."

"It was fine," Alex protested. "It was actually pretty good. It even had honey in it."

Sukey looked reproachfully at Hannah. "You think I would give him poison?"

"No," Hannah said quickly. "Of course not." Still, she muttered to Alex, "Don't do it again, okay?"

Alex ignored his sister. "Sukey, can you tell us my favorite story?" he said. "The one about the ghost and the man on the horse?"

Sukey drew a deep breath and then exhaled noisily. "Again? I tell it so many times to you."

"Please, Sukey!" begged Jane.

Sukey relented, and Hannah could see that she was really flattered to be asked to retell a story. "Oh, very well. But Jane, first you bring another log for the fire."

Alex watched Sukey expectantly, and drew up his knees to his chin. Jane carefully added a log to the flames.

Although the night was cold, the bonfire's glow kept Hannah warm. Sitting around the leaping flames made her long for hot dogs and s'mores. But she had to content herself with hoe cakes, pancakes from cornmeal and water, and cooked over the fire on the blades of hoes that were normally used in the fields.

As the flames snapped and crackled, they lit up Sukey's face, and she began to speak. "This is a true story, from Sidlaw, the master's plantation in Carolina. When I live at Sidlaw, I once know a gentleman on another plantation, a man called Master Smith. When he was a young man, Master Smith sometimes pay a visit on an old gentleman he know, a man called Master Cooper.

"Now one day, old Master Cooper say to him, 'I die soon, but when I do, I return and visit you, to repay your kindness to me.' But Master Smith does not believe in h'ants . . . ."

"Ghosts," Alex whispered to Hannah.

"Yeah, I guessed that," his sister whispered back impatiently.

Sukey continued, " . . . and so he laughs about it all the way home. A few weeks later, the old gentleman, Master Cooper, he dies. But no h'ant appears, and so Master Smith forgets his friend's promise. Over the years, Master Cooper's old house begins to molder and to crumble, and the weeds grow tall, and the woods take back what belongs to them.

"Master Smith grows grey, and prosperous, and he builds a fine house on his plantation. Sometimes, for old times' sake, he rides his horse by where his friend's house had been.

"One night he is riding by, when, to his astonishment, he sees Master Cooper's house as though it is new! He reckons somebody has rebuilt it, but when he turns back to look again, it is a ruin."

"Was he on his way home from a party?" Hannah asked, smirking.

Sukey pretended not to hear her. "When he is almost home," she said in an ominous voice, "he suddenly feels warm, and he fears he is afflicted by sickness. But now he sees his friend Master Cooper appear in the road ahead of him. The h'ant is as real as Master Cooper was in life. But it says nought. It just stares at him."

She paused, and the kids continued to watch her, rapt.

"So, Master Smith starts a-shaking and a-sweating, for he knows, this must be a h'ant," she said, and then paused again.

"Pray, what did 'ee do?" Jane asked breathlessly.

Sukey stared at her, and said slowly, "He looks the h'ant in the eye, and says, trembling, 'Good evening to you, neighbor . . .' And the h'ant smiles . . .and then it vanishes, right afore his eyes."

Hannah felt a cold shiver running down her back, and she glanced behind her involuntarily. Alex shuffled closer to his sister.

Jane picked up a short, narrow, fallen branch from behind her, and thrust it into the fire.

"I'm making a big torch, now that it is dark," she said. "I want to scare away ghosts."

The end of the branch caught light, and Jane held it up. In the darkness, the glow from the end of her stick reflected in everyone's eyes, and the effect, Hannah thought, was very sinister. Jane stared at the torch in fascination.

Tremulously, Alex said, "Sukey, do you have any stories that aren't so scary?"

Sukey laughed, and Alex turned to Jane. "Why don't you tell us about your life, Jane?"

Hannah wondered where her brother was going with this. If she and Alex took turns telling their life stories, what on earth would they say?

But Jane was thrilled to be asked about herself. "I was born in London, and I lived there all my life," she said dramatically. "My parents, they worked in an inn. My dad was the barman, and my mum ran the kitchens. I was 'appy, I suppose, but when I was nine, this woman and man, that man what accused you, 'annah, they steals me away, and makes me work for them. Eventually, I got sick of that, and I ran off."

"Did you find your parents again?" Alex asked.

"Nah," Jane said, shaking her head sadly. "They'd gone, 'adn't they? The pub had a new landlord, and he threw me out when I came a-calling. But the maid what works there, she comes out to the street and calls after me, to tell me what happened to them. She says my dad inherited some money, like, and they'd gone. That was all she knew, she said."

To Hannah's embarrassment, tears began to pour down Jane's cheeks.

Sukey looked at her sympathetically. "It is hard," she said. "I miss Sidlaw. I miss my children, and my grandchildren. Maybe Master Gordon take me to visit Sidlaw one day, and I see them."

She didn't sound hopeful.

Alex encouraged Jane to continue her story.

"Ain't much to tell," Jane sighed. "I took up a little pocket-picking and 'ouse-breaking. I got caught once, and I spent a few months in prison, but they found me not guilty. The court never knew I'd 'ad a conviction, because at that time I called myself Elizabeth Strachan."

Hannah was dumbfounded. "Wait, that's the name they called me, in court in London!"

Jane was surprised. "Is that so? Do you suppose you was mistaken for me?"

Alex turned from one girl to the other. "You guys look like each other, for real."

Hannah looked at him skeptically, but when she returned her attention to Jane, she had to admit that there was a resemblance. True, Jane was blonde, while Hannah was not, but there was something about her eyes and nose that seemed very familiar. Hannah suddenly put two and two together. "So your name is really Elizabeth Strachan?"

"Not anymore," said Jane. "Not since a year or more past."

Hannah was excited now. "They did, they mistook you for me in court! I mean, me for you! No, wait . . .That man who kidnapped you, was his name Evans?"

"That was what he sometimes called 'imself, yes," Jane said.

Hannah's brow furrowed. "So he must have seen that I looked like you," she said slowly, "and . . . look, according to Brandon, this Evans guy came to Balesworth, to the inn where I was working, and he kept looking at me funny, like he knew me. Then he accused me of stealing his silver plate. Turns out, he had pawned the plate to my boss, and this was his way of stealing it back."

"That sounds like 'im," Jane nodded with a sigh.

"What a scumbag," Hannah said angrily.

Alex asked Jane, "What's your real name? Is it Elizabeth Strachan?"

"Oh, no. My name is Jane," she said earnestly. "My true name is Jane Jenkins."

Hannah blanked for a second, then gave a delighted gasp, and cried, "I think I know your parents! I mean, it's a pretty common name and all, but . . ." She described Mr. and Mrs. Jenkins.

As Hannah spoke, Jane's face grew bright and happy. But suddenly, her eyes filled with tears, and she turned away from Hannah. "Don't matter anymore, does it?" she muttered. "I'll never clap eyes on them again so long as I live, no matter where they are, because they are in England, and I'm here."

Hannah was about to say something optimistic to Jane, when what she had learned hit her with full force. Stopping only to pat Jane's hand, she turned to Alex excitedly. "Mrs. Jenkins was one of Mrs. D.'s ancestors, so do you think that means . . ."

Alex interrupted her. "Yeah, and you look like Jane, so do you think . . ."

They said it together: "We're related."

Hannah repeated it in wonderment. "We must be related. To all of them."

But now Alex had doubts, and his face fell. "Wait a minute," he said. "How?"

Hannah's shoulders sagged. "Oh, right. I have no clue. I mean, we're Portuguese, right?"

"Right. It's just a coincidence, then," said Alex. He was disappointed. It would have been so great for everything to start to make sense.

Just then, Sukey asked, "What is a coincidence?"

Alex had to think about how to explain. He wished he had a dictionary. "It means that even though Hannah and Jane could be sisters, it's just an accident."

"Nothing is an accident," said Sukey. "Everything happens for a reason."

Hannah and Alex smiled politely at her. *She's so superstitious,* Hannah thought. *But suppose she's right?*

Chapter 10:
UP IN FLAMES

Every time Hannah emptied scraps into the trough, the scarred old pig she called Bacon gave her a gentle nuzzle that almost knocked her off her feet.

"Hey, you're too big to do that!" she protested yet again. She laughed, and tried to shove him away with her knee. He didn't move. But after she scratched his rough back, he obediently tottered away.

"You are way too smart," Hannah groused. It was then that she noticed that the pig was limping. "What's the matter, Bacon?" she murmured. She followed him, and then crouched down for a better look at his legs.

Bacon's back right leg was badly gashed, and even against his dark skin, she could see rivulets of dried blood. She called over to Tony. "Hey, you need to take Bacon to the vet. He's hurt."

Tony gave her a puzzled frown, then leaned down to take a look. Immediately, he stood up straight, ran his hand over his head, and smiled ruefully. "Yes, it's his time. I'll tell the master."

What time, Hannah wondered? But Mrs. Gordon called for her, and so distracted, she never asked.

Early the next morning, Sukey shook Hannah awake.

"What's wrong?" Hannah mumbled.

"You got to get up," Sukey whispered. "I need you and Jane to help me."

"Help with what?" Hannah moaned, reluctantly swinging her legs out of bed and rubbing her eyes. "What time is it?"

Before Sukey could answer, an unearthly screech rent the air. Terrified, Hannah lurched out of bed. "What was that?"

"That's why you got to help me," Sukey said insistently, tugging on the sleeve of Hannah's shift. "Come."

Hannah felt rising panic. What was going on? Why was Sukey acting so strangely? Was there a slave rebellion? Was Sukey luring her to her death?

Hannah glanced at Jane, who groaned as she awoke on their shared bed, but she didn't seem at all alarmed.

When Sukey left the hut, Hannah pulled her crumpled petticoat and skirt over her head, tied the strings that held them around her waist, and rushed to the door. What greeted her outside was a horrifying sight.

Tony and three other slaves, all stripped to the waist, were standing around Bacon. Hannah recognized the pig immediately from his scar. And the next thing she noticed was that he wasn't moving.

Cuffee was standing behind Bacon's head, pulling on a rope hooked over his snout, while Tony was holding up a knife. Bacon was lying on his back on a pile of straw, and a stream of red water was pouring from him. Only it wasn't water. It was blood.

Hannah screamed, dashed back inside, and threw herself face down on her bed with her hands over her ears.

It took Jane and Sukey a few minutes to calm Hannah down. Shaking and in floods of tears, she swore she would never eat meat again. "It's supposed to come in little plastic trays from the supermarket, not all this blood and stuff," she whimpered. Jane and Sukey glanced at each other in confusion.

"Now then," Sukey said sternly, "You talk foolishness. That pig, he has a good life, and it is time for him to go. He die quick when Tony cut his throat, and now he is at peace."

Hannah sobbed even harder, and Sukey lost patience, tutting at her. "Come, now. Pig doesn't mind. He offer himself to us for our vittles. Now, come, you help me. Fetch water to boil, so we can singe the bristles. Later, the men start butchering, and we make the sausages."

Hannah gagged at the thought. Bacon had been her pet. *I am so going vegetarian*, she thought.

While Hannah learned where meat really came from, Brandon and the Osborns were eating a breakfast of bacon and eggs. "I am concerned," said Mr. Osborn to nobody in particular, "that if Mr. Gordon learns that Brandon is catechizing his slaves, he will no longer be willing to sell me a slave at a reasonable cost."

There was a silence at the breakfast table, because it wasn't clear that Mr. Osborn wanted anyone to reply to him. Finally, Mrs. Osborn said, "Perhaps, Mr. Osborn, if you are determined to do so, you ought to arrange the purchase with him at the earliest opportunity?"

"Before he discovers the truth, you mean?" Mr. Osborn said, chewing on a piece of meat. It seems dishonest and dishonorable . . . . But it also seems the wisest course of action."

"Sir, I think you should offer to buy Cato from him," Brandon said quickly. "Why so?" asked Mr. Osborn.

Brandon folded his arms. "Because he's young, so he'll be cheap. But I also happen to know that he's honest. And he's a Christian."

"Is he, indeed?" Mr. Osborn perked up with a smile. "In that case, I shall approach Mr. Gordon at the first suitable opportunity."

Brandon liked the sound of that, and he also looked forward to having Alex's company.

By the time Brandon returned to the house from his morning chores, he was famished. Shoving the door open, however, he was disappointed to find no noontime meal awaiting him on the table. Instead, Mrs. Osborn called weakly from her upstairs bed, "Brandon? Go for . . . my husband . . . . Tell him it is my time. The baby is coming."

Forgetting his hunger, Brandon yelped an acknowledgment, slammed through the door, and tore across the fields. He was breathless by the time he reached Mr. Osborn, who immediately dropped his hoe on hearing the news, and ran back to the house. There, he checked on his wife, and then hurriedly hooked up his horse to the wagon, instructing Brandon to stay with Mrs. Osborn while he fetched help.

To Brandon's shame, he couldn't muster the courage to sit by Mrs. Osborn's bedside. She screamed and cried during her contractions, while he helplessly paced the floor downstairs, hating himself for his cowardice.

It felt to Brandon like an eternity before Mr. Osborn returned, although he was gone for less than an hour. He did not come back alone: Mrs. Gordon and Mrs. Jones clambered down from the wagon and quickly took over. He surely heard his wife's distressed cries as she had another contraction, but this time, he did not go to her. Instead, he turned pale and slumped in a chair at the table, next to Brandon. However, Mrs. Jones, taking charge, would not allow them to remain there, but shooed both of them from the house. "This is no place for men or boys," she fussed.

Actually, Brandon was relieved to be banished back to the fields, far from the unsettling sound of Mrs. Osborn's wails. He knew there was no point in asking whether there were any drugs to ease her pain: He already knew the answer.

Later that morning, Brandon laid down his hoe to give his sore hands a brief break from weeding the winter garden. Never in his life had he imagined that he would miss sticky bandages, he thought, but now he did as he examined his blisters. Looking up he saw a small black figure approach, and it took him a few moments to figure out who it was. He still couldn't get over Alex's new appearance.

"Mr. Gordon is loaning me to you," Alex said. "He thought maybe you guys might need help today."

At that moment Mr. Osborn's voice echoed across the field, calling Brandon's name. Brandon, followed by Alex, hurried to see what he wanted.

When they found him outside the house, Mr. Osborn looked pale and drawn.

"The women need more help. The infant died . . . and my wife is losing much blood," he said desperately.

Brandon didn't know what to say, but Alex glanced at him and then said, "I bet Sukey can help. Shall I go get her?"

Mr. Osborn nodded rapidly, and Alex took off at a run.

By the time he arrived at the Gordons' place, Sukey was pouring more boiling water over the dead pig, while a glum Hannah watched, waiting to scrape off more of the bristles.

Alex explained why he had come back, and he asked Sukey to go to the Osborns with him. Sukey said quietly, "I will go to Mrs. Osborn, but first I go to the witch."

She handed her bucket to Hannah, saying, "Hannah, you finish this task." Without further explanation, she hurried in the direction of the woods. Alex remained behind, unsure of whether he was supposed to go or stay. He worried, too, whether he had followed his instructions by allowing Sukey to make a detour to see the witch. Hannah, meanwhile, was scraping bristles off Bacon's corpse, with an air of boredom and resignation. Alex couldn't help being impressed by this sight: These days, it seemed, his sister could turn her hand to practically anything.

Two hours later Sukey approached the Osborns' house, bearing an armful of herbs. Watching her walk across the fields, Brandon knew that her arrival would bring only dismay, not relief. She was too late: Mrs. Osborn had died.

Alex returned to the plantation in mid-afternoon and found his sister pulling up greens for supper. "What a rotten day," Hannah said. "Mrs. Osborn and her baby died, which is awful. And I saw Bacon get killed, and I have to make him into meat. It's gross. I'm going to be a vegetarian."

"But then all you can eat is cornmeal and greens," Alex warned. "Anyway, you knew they would kill and eat the pig someday."

Hannah rubbed her nose with the back of her hand, before she renewed her assault on the turnip root. "Someday, sure, but not yet," she said. "And he was really sweet, more like a dog than a dumb old chicken."

"Well, never mind," Alex said, "He gave his life for a good cause." He rubbed his stomach.

"You're so weird," Hannah said. "I thought you liked animals?"

"I do," Alex conceded with a shrug. "But I like meat, too. I don't think the pig cares much what happens to it when it's dead. And anyway, pigs are not pets, especially these pigs. They're more like wild boars than the pigs we know."

Hannah grunted as she finally wrenched the turnip from the ground. She stood up and looked at her prize. "Huh, smaller than I thought. I'll need another one. Hey, that is totally sad about Mrs. Osborn, though. I feel really bad for them. How's Brandon doing?"

"You can ask him yourself," Alex said, pointing to an exhausted-looking Brandon as he emerged from the woods.

"Hey, is Mr. Gordon around?" he asked wearily.

Alex nodded, and jerked his head toward the house.

Hannah was already pulling on another bunch of turnip greens, but she looked up and greeted Brandon. "How's it going over there? How's Mr. Osborn taking it?" she asked. Brandon twitched slightly, but did not reply.

Hannah could tell he didn't want to talk about it, but she said, "I kind of thought it was stupid of Sukey to go to that witch doctor they all keep talking about. Maybe she could have helped if she got there sooner. And what good would some stupid magic do?"

Brandon shrugged. "It's 1752. That's about as good as medicine gets. At least the witch's medicine wouldn't have done any harm, not like what Mr. Gordon and Mr. Osborn do. Anyway, I don't think anyone could have done anything for Mrs. Osborn. My mom's a nurse, and she says it's pretty rare in our time for anyone to die giving birth. But it was pretty common back in the day. I mean, like, now."

Alex asked hopefully, "So Mr. Osborn wasn't shocked that his wife died?" But Brandon just gave him an exasperated look, and shook his head.

"Alex, don't be dumb. Of course he's shocked. Nothing prepares a man for losing his wife. I learned that in the funeral home. Sometimes, you would get these old men in, who were like eighty years old, and they were still stunned that their wife had passed."

"What is Mr. Osborn going to do now, Brandon?" Hannah asked gently.

"First thing," Brandon said grimly, "is he needs help to bury his wife. Matter of fact, that's why I'm here. Mr. Osborn wants one of the guys to help us dig the grave."

The neighbors gathered to witness the burial of Mrs. Osborn and her baby. The two bodies were not placed in coffins, but rather wrapped in shrouds, which Hannah found rather creepy. Mr. Osborn led the service, speaking in a wobbly voice, and with tears streaming down his cheeks.

Brandon thought guiltily that he hadn't really known Mrs. Osborn at all. She had been so quiet, and so often ill in bed. He wondered whether, if she had lived in the twenty-first century, she would have been diagnosed with serious depression. Whenever he had spoken to her, she had seemed kindly, but distant. But now the house felt empty without her presence.

He was proud of how Mr. Osborn was coping with the tragedy, even as he felt sorry for him. At night, he heard his master weeping quietly, but during the day, the minister carried on his usual schedule at his desk and in the fields. Even on Sunday, Mr. Osborn was in his pulpit as usual, giving his uncomfortable and irritated audience of planters yet another of what Brandon thought of as his "hinty-hint" sermons about the religious conversion of the slaves.

Two weeks after his wife's death, Mr. Osborn called on Mr. Gordon. Hannah watched as the two men had a quiet conversation. She only caught scraps of what was said, but she learned that Mr. Osborn needed more help around the house and in the fields, and that he hoped to replace Brandon with a slave one day. Mr. Gordon was clearly touched by the minister's plight, despite the differences between them. The two men shook hands, and Mr. Osborn then handed over some gold coins from a leather pouch. In return, Mr. Gordon wrote out a receipt. With that, Alex was sold.

As November wore on, there was less to do on the farm, except to feed the chickens and the cattle, and tend the tobacco and winter greens. Alex kept house, which mostly involved learning to cook, with Brandon's help. He was boiling a ham donated by a neighbor, when he hesitantly asked Mr. Osborn about the arrangements for Thanksgiving. His questions were met with a blank stare.

He assumed he had offended his boss, but Brandon explained that Thanksgiving wasn't celebrated in 1752, or at least, it wasn't celebrated in Britain or Georgia. He was hugely disappointed: He hated being stuck in a rut, sitting around the house with Mr. Osborn brooding, as he complained to Brandon when the minister was away.

Brandon agreed that he also needed something to look forward to, and he reckoned that Mr. Osborn did, too. Living in backwoods Georgia in 1752 could be a pretty joyless experience, Brandon thought: At least the slaves knew how to enjoy themselves when they got the chance. But the white people he had met seemed reluctant to let their hair down. He admitted to Alex that he thought much the same way about black and white people in modern Snipesville. Alex thought he had a point.

So when, one Sunday at the slaves' catechism lesson, Tony invited Brandon to join Cuffee and him on a hunting expedition, Brandon happily accepted. But then he paused, thinking about it. "Wait, hunting? You mean with guns?"

"Certainly!" Tony said.

Slaves with guns? Was that possible? Brandon tried to remember if he had ever read of such a thing. Not for the first time, he wished he could ask the Professor.

As if reading Brandon's mind, Tony explained, "Mr. Gordon lets us borrow guns to hunt, so long as a white man accompanies us."

Brandon was once again reminded that he was living in strange times. Even though he was a kid, he was supposed to chaperone gun-toting guys just because he was white and they were black? Now he wondered nervously if he had been wise to accept Tony's invitation. Would Tony try to kill him?

On the morning of the hunt, Brandon rose when the cockerel crowed shortly before dawn, dressed, and walked briskly to Mr. Gordon's slave quarters. Tony and Cuffee were already waiting for him, smoking short clay pipes while squatting on the ground outside their hut, their hunting guns lying on the grass alongside them.

Brandon eyed the two men nervously as they scrambled to their feet and picked up their guns. He was comforted to notice that if they had any designs on murdering him, they seemed very relaxed about it.

When, Brandon wondered, had he started being afraid of black people? He was beginning to understand why white people in 1752 were so paranoid. They were surrounded by people who had every reason to hate them.

But Brandon also knew that if Tony and Cuffee had decided to run away, or start a rebellion, he wouldn't try to stop them. He just hoped they wouldn't kill him in the process.

As they tramped through the woods, Brandon plucked up the courage to ask the most obvious question he could think of. "So why don't you guys just run away from slavery?" he said quietly. "Like right now?"

There was a pained silence, and Brandon was reminded once again that, in this world, he was white. But he plowed on regardless. "I mean, what's to stop you?"

Finally, Tony answered with a forced laugh. "Run away? Where would we go? The Indians would find us and sell us as slaves. We would always be running, all our lives. And if Mr. Gordon catches us . . ." He glanced pointedly at Cuffee's half foot, and said, "Cuffee can never run away again. That is what happened when he tried."

Cuffee gave a sardonic smile. Brandon already knew that Mr. Gordon had cut off Cuffee's foot, but he still shuddered when he thought about it.

"You could go back to Africa," he suggested. "Maybe you could stow away on a ship."

Tony looked at Brandon as though he were nuts. "Africa? Why would I go to Africa? I am not from Africa. My father was an African, from the country of Angola, and he was banished by his own king. He sold my father into slavery because he fought in the rebellion of Dona Beatriz Kimpa Vita. She was Saint Anthony, returned to earth in a woman's body, and my father was proud to have fought for her. But he could never return to his homeland."

Brandon remained silent, but he was fascinated by this fantastic story. Could it be true? He made a mental note to ask the Professor about this Donna Beatrice person, whoever she was.

Tony continued his story. "I was born in South Carolina, and I would never want to go back there, either. Terrible, terrible place. Here is better than working on the rice plantation in Carolina. Anyway, wherever we live, we are slaves. We will never be happy in this world, only the next."

"I am from Africa," Cuffee chimed in. "From Angola, like Tony's father. If I ever get back there, I will be slave trader."

Brandon was shocked. "What? Why?" he sputtered in horror.

"Because it is better than being slave," Cuffee said with a smile. "What else will I be? If I am a slave trader, I will be wealthy and powerful man in my country."

Brandon shook his head in amazement. He walked in silence for several minutes. Then he had an idea. "Hey," he said, stopping on the trail. "How about I help you guys get to England? You could be free there." Did slavery exist in England, Brandon asked himself? He had no clue.

Tony looked at him suspiciously. "Tell me, Master Brandon. Why do you want us to be free?"

Now Brandon realized that he had gone too far. Tony didn't trust him at all. And that made sense. Why would some random white kid encourage slaves to run away, unless he wanted to get them in trouble? And if a miracle happened, and Cuffee and Tony made it across the Atlantic, would England be friendly to them? Or was there slavery there, too?

Brandon felt frustrated and useless. He knew now that he could do nothing to end slavery in 1752. Nobody could. It was not the time. Maybe the people here were right. Maybe they were all innocent victims of "fortune's wheel," as Jane put it. And when God blesses people, Brandon thought angrily, why does He never bless slaves with freedom?

Suppose these guys never got off the plantation? Suppose they met women, and had kids, and doomed their children and grandchildren to lifetimes of slavery?

As Brandon thought and walked, he found himself keeping pace with Tony. Glancing up, he looked at Tony's face in profile for the first time.

How could he not have seen this before?

The resemblance to his father was faint, but it was there.

Was it possible?

Were Tony and Sukey his ancestors?

Suddenly, Tony stopped Brandon in his tracks with a hand on his chest. Something was moving in the trees ahead of them. Tony and Cuffee lifted their guns and pointed them. In the still of the forest, Brandon could hear the sound of his own breathing.

Just as suddenly as he had raised his gun, Cuffee lowered it, and reaching out, slapped the barrel of Tony's weapon toward the ground. Tony looked questioningly at him, but Cuffee put a finger to his lips and then pointed.

Their prey wasn't a deer, but a human. Through the trees Brandon could just glimpse a tall black man, who was concentrating on wrenching something out of the ground.

Tony signaled to Brandon to turn around and return the way they came. Brandon didn't know why, but he obeyed.

But as he turned, he tripped over his own feet and fell flat on his face. By the time he sat up, the man was vanishing through the trees.

"What was that about?" Brandon exclaimed, brushing pine straw and dirt from himself. "Who was that guy?"

"Nothing and no one," Tony muttered. "Come hither, and we will follow this other trail instead."

But Brandon didn't move. "Wait a minute," he said. "Do you think he was a runaway slave or something?"

Neither Tony nor Cuffee looked back at him, but he could sense them both tensing.

"No," Tony barked without turning his head. "I never saw nothing. Did you, Cuffee?"

"Me neither," Cuffee growled. "I saw nothing."

Once again, Brandon was forcefully reminded that he was not part of the men's brotherhood of trust. But he couldn't help wondering, who was the man in the woods?

It all happened in seconds.

Hannah awoke to the acrid smell of burning. It wasn't the usual aroma of firewood, or even overcooked food, but something altogether more pungent and repellent. It smelled like cigarettes. She knew that it was not yet dawn because no light seeped through the cracks and holes in the shutters.

At that moment, Mrs. Gordon was walking downstairs, with Mr. Gordon right behind her, holding her hand. Mr. Gordon escorted his wife outside, but returned almost immediately afterward, running upstairs past Hannah and Jane, who rubbed her eyes and sat up. "What's going on?" she asked Hannah.

In his haste, Mr. Gordon had left the door open, and with horror, Hannah could see flames outside. Before she could say anything, Mr. Gordon had reappeared on the stairs, yelling, "Hurry! The tobacco barn is ablaze! Jane, assist my wife. Hannah, go and draw water from the well while I collect important papers."

Hannah grabbed the bucket and darted for the door. As soon as she stepped outside, she started coughing from the thick black smoke. Quickly she began to pump water from the well. Slaves were arriving from the quarters, some bringing buckets of river water, but the barn was now completely ablaze, orange and yellow flames leaping into the air at twice the height of the building, and the water evaporated as soon as they hurled it on the flames. Sparks drifted lazily through the air, many flying dangerously close to the house. Instinctively, Hannah glanced up at the house roof, and, in the light of the blaze, she saw how much pine straw had collected up there. She bet that Mr. Gordon would regret not having removed it.

When Mr. Gordon arrived outside and saw that the barn was completely ablaze, he ordered everyone to redirect their efforts, and throw water on the house, to keep it damp.

Shivering in the night air, Mrs. Gordon was standing barefoot in her shift, wrapped only in a blanket. She was in tears, but Mr. Gordon rushed to console her, clasping her arms. "My dear, this is a loss, certainly," he said, "but do not forget that the greatest part of my fortune remains at Sidlaw, and if we can stop the fire from spreading, we may yet save this house. If not, it is but a minor loss to our fortunes, I promise you."

He called over to Hannah. "Fetch a lantern from the house, and take Mrs. Gordon to Mr. Jones's house," he said. "Remain with her there until you are both sent for. Ask Mr. Jones if he can spare any slaves to help us extinguish the flames."

But the smell of smoke drifting through the pine forest had already brought Mr. Jones, Mr. Osborn, Brandon, and several of Mr. Jones's slaves, all of them carrying buckets. As Hannah put her arm around Mrs. Gordon and began to lead her away, she couldn't help thinking that this motley crew was a pretty poor excuse for a fire brigade.

On the way to Mrs. Jones's house, Mrs. Gordon began to shiver uncontrollably. Alarmed, Hannah half-dragged, half-carried her mistress for the last hundred yards. As soon as they reached the house, Mrs. Jones and Juba, her silent and grim-faced young slave woman, helped Hannah to get her to bed.

"Do you think she's going into shock?" Hannah asked Mrs. Jones, a bustling, practical sort of woman, who didn't answer except to tell Hannah to fetch water and heat it over the fire. When Hannah returned to Mrs. Gordon's bedside with the boiled water, Mrs. Jones said, "Go tell Mr. Gordon that his wife has been afflicted with ague once more, and that he ought to administer physic to her. Hurry now."

Hannah had hoped for a hot drink, but there was no chance of that now. Cold and exhausted, she grabbed her lantern, and set off.

Thirty minutes later, Hannah arrived home to find Mr. Gordon still supervising the effort to save his house. She struggled to remember Mrs. Jones's message to Mr. Gordon. Finding her master, she tapped him on the shoulder. He whirled around. "What is the matter?" he barked. "Don't touch me."

Hannah shifted from foot to foot. "Mrs. Jones says that Mrs. Gordon is, um, affected by a glue, and that she needs some physics."

Mr. Gordon somehow figured it out. "A glue? You mean ague, surely. A fever, yes? I will go to her as soon as I am able."

But Mr. Osborn, standing nearby, overheard the conversation, and he put a hand on Mr. Gordon's arm. "Sir, with your permission, I will do what I can for your wife." He hesitated before adding kindly, "So soon after losing my own dear wife, I would do all I could to spare you the same loss."

Mr. Gordon nodded in gratitude, and Mr. Osborn hurried off toward his own house to get his medical equipment. Hannah started back toward the Jones' house. She didn't want to miss the drama. And it wasn't as though she had a bed to go to at the Gordons'.

Hannah reached the Jones' house ahead of Mr. Osborn, and it was she who opened the door for him when he arrived with his black bag. She offered him a seat but, soon afterward, Mrs. Jones came downstairs to greet him. Mr. Osborn got to his feet.

"Madam, I am here to examine Mrs. Gordon," he said gravely. "I am informed that she suffers from the ague."

"She is very bad, sir," said Mrs. Jones in somber tones. "But I do not think it is the ague, after all."

"You would know better than I the symptoms, madam," Mr. Osborn replied, "for although I have read of this disease and its treatment, I never have encountered it before."

Mrs. Jones nodded primly. "Let me show you to her, sir," she said, then turned to Hannah and gestured toward the stairs. "Girl, come up with us. Mrs. Gordon wishes to speak with you." Without further ado, she led the way.

Upstairs, Mr. Osborn kneeled down on the wooden floor next to where Mrs. Gordon lay sleeping on the bed. Hannah, behind him, was shocked at how pale she looked.

"So, like, what is the ague, Mr. Osborn?" Hannah whispered to the minister as he unpacked his instruments.

Mr. Osborn turned to explain. "It is a disease that is sadly common in America. My professors in Edinburgh referred to it as 'malaria,' and it is caused by bad air from the swamps."

"Uh-uh, no, it's not," Hannah said, shaking her head emphatically. "I know what malaria is. You catch it from mosquito bites."

"Foolish girl," Mr. Osborn muttered. "What would you know of medicine? You have listened to the slaves' superstitious nonsense. Be off with you."

"No," said a feeble voice. It was Mrs. Gordon. Her eyes were open. "Let her stay awhile. Mr. Osborn, would you kindly allow me a moment alone with the girl?"

Mr. Osborn nodded, and bowed to Mrs. Gordon before taking his leave. Hannah was taken aback that Mrs. Gordon had anything to say to her at all, much less in private.

Nervously, she glanced down at Mrs. Gordon's pale hand lying on the blanket. The ring was still on her finger. Mrs. Gordon closed her eyes again, and Hannah thought she was going back to sleep. But she opened her eyes once more, and focused on Hannah. Noticing that Hannah was staring at her ring, she smiled at her. "I have not long left on this earth," she said weakly. "Here, take my ring as a keepsake by which to remember me." She lifted her hand slightly.

Hannah was horrified. She wanted nothing to do with it. "No, you're going to get well," she said desperately. "Anyway, your family should have that ring. Not me." *Why does Mrs. Gordon want to give it to me, anyway?* Hannah thought. *She doesn't even know me.*

Mrs. Gordon smiled sadly. "My family are dead, Hannah. Mr. Gordon has no need of this ring. I should like you to have it. I think it is meant that I give it to you. Here." With effort, she pulled the ring from her finger, and signaled to Hannah to come closer and put out her right hand.

Hannah reluctantly held out her hand, and Mrs. Gordon wiggled the ring onto her finger. It felt like a good fit, if a little tight, and it was undeniably pretty. But Hannah couldn't stop thinking about the skeleton. If she wore the ring, would she be the skeleton?

She decided she would take it off as soon as she was out of Mrs. Gordon's sight. And since there was nothing left for her to do at the Jones' house, she had a good excuse to leave now. She didn't know what to say to the dying woman, anyway.

"Thanks, Mrs. Gordon. I'd better get back and help with the fire. Take care," she said quickly. Without waiting for a reply, she tore off downstairs. "Hey, can I have another candle for my lantern?" she asked Juba, but she got no answer. "I guess I'll help myself," she muttered, grabbing her lantern from beside the hearth. Taking a candle stub from the table, she lit it in the fireplace and rushed from the house.

Long before Hannah arrived home, she could see the flames through the trees as she walked. The air was thick with black smoke, carried by the breeze. It was no longer just the barn that was ablaze. When she got to the Gordons' plantation, she found everyone looking on helplessly while the house burned. Hannah had lost very little—just a very few clothes she owned—but she couldn't help thinking of all the nice new furniture and Mrs. Gordon's tea set.

Even the slaves, on Mr. Gordon's orders, had given up trying to put out the fire. They stood silently, watching the flames.

Alex sidled up to Hannah. "That was weird," he muttered.

"What was?" Hannah said, puzzled. She was tugging at Mrs. Gordon's ring, and she screwed up her face from pain as it chafed against her swelling finger.

Her brother said quietly, "Hannah, I saw what happened here. The house started burning from the inside, not from the roof. I guess a spark must have flown in the window. But I can't figure out why the upstairs shutters were open when it's this cold."

"Whatever," said Hannah, grunting as she continued pulling on the ring. She held out her hand to her brother. "Check this out."

When he caught sight of the ring, he gasped. "What? How did you get Mrs. Gordon's ring?"

"She gave it to me," Hannah said, holding up her hand to show him.

"Take it off," Alex said, panicking. "I don't want you to be the skeleton."

"Duh. I already thought of that," Hannah snapped. "Why do you think my finger is all swollen? I've been trying to get the stupid thing off, and it won't move."

"Let's go ask Sukey. She'll help us," Alex said, grabbing his sister's hand and leading her away. But Mr. Gordon had spotted the unusual sight of a slave taking his white servant by the hand, and he approached them.

"What is the matter here?" he demanded.

Hannah made the mistake of quickly hiding her right hand behind her back, and Mr. Gordon saw her do it. He leaned forward, seized her arm and jerked on it. As soon as he saw her hand, he saw the ring. "What are you doing with my wife's property?" he asked angrily.

"She gave it to me," Hannah said, as calmly as she could.

"You are lying, girl!" Mr. Gordon roared, roughly throwing aside her hand. "Take it off at once. It doesn't belong to you."

"I can't get it off," Hannah cried, tugging at the ring on her finger to demonstrate. "That's why we're going to ask Sukey to help us."

"Sukey!" Mr. Gordon exclaimed. "Is that why you're going to her? Is she part of your thieving plot?"

Hannah gasped in outrage. "Yes! No! I mean, there is no plot. Look, Mrs.

Gordon gave me this ring, and now it's stuck. End of story. We just figured Sukey might know how to get it off."

"You had better find a way to remove the ring, and return it to me forthwith. I will punish you later," he hissed, giving her one last vehement look, before turning to Mr. Jones. "May I visit your house, sir, to attend to my wife?"

Mr. Jones nodded. "But, of course, sir," he said. "With your permission in turn, I shall remain here to supervise."

Mr. Gordon inclined his head toward his neighbor, and set off.

Brandon, meanwhile, had shown up at Mr. Jones's house, in search of Mr. Osborn. Hesitantly, he rapped on the door, and hearing no reply, he stepped inside.

Upstairs, he found an anxious-looking Mr. Osborn standing over Mrs. Gordon, his cupping equipment attached to her left arm.

Brandon cleared his throat, but Mr. Osborn didn't turn around. "What is it, Brandon?" he asked testily as he peered into the cupping glass.

"I just came to ask if you want me to bring you some food, sir," Brandon said meekly.

Mr. Osborn waved him away. "No, no, thank you, that will not be . . . Oh, no!"

Brandon was alarmed by Mr. Osborn's sudden exclamation, and even more so to see him lean down to listen to Mrs. Gordon's breathing, which had suddenly grown deep and rapid. Then, just as suddenly, her breathing stopped altogether. The minister straightened up, and taking Mrs. Gordon's wrist, felt for a pulse. He sighed heavily, gently placed her arm across her body, and stepped back.

"She is no more," he said somberly.

"Hey, aren't you even going to try CPR?" Brandon said in panic, realizing as soon as he had said it that nobody knew how to resuscitate a patient in the eighteenth century. And he didn't have a clue how to do it himself.

Except . . . maybe . . . maybe he could just try to do CPR like they did it on TV? It was worth a shot.

Hesitantly, he stepped forward to Mrs. Gordon's bedside, put one hand over the other, and placed both hands on her chest. Mr. Osborn's puzzlement turned to alarm when Brandon started pushing against the corpse.

"What are you doing?" The cry came not from Mr. Osborn, but from Mr. Gordon, who was now standing behind him, aghast.

Embarrassed, Mr. Osborn grabbed Brandon by the shoulders, and shoved him hard across the room, before turning back to Mr. Gordon.

"Mr. Gordon, I must apologize," he said earnestly, wringing his hands. "I do not know what possessed the boy, but I think he was trying to help. Alas, your wife is already beyond help. I regret that she died a few moments ago, despite my most urgent ministrations. May I extend my condolences to you, sir?"

Mr. Gordon ignored him, and leaned over Mrs. Gordon's body, running a hand across her forehead.

"I must beg you to excuse me," he growled quietly. "I wish to be alone."

As Mr. Osborn and Brandon retreated toward the stairs, Mr. Gordon suddenly turned on Mr. Osborn. "I hold you responsible, sir," he barked. "You allowed your servant boy to practice superstitious nonsense on my poor wife, some rubbish he has surely learned from the negroes, and in doing so, you have hastened her demise. And how dare you, sir, how dare you permit my servant girl to steal a valuable ring from my poor addled wife?"

Mr. Osborn tried to explain, but Mr. Gordon advanced on him threateningly, roaring at him to get out. Brandon and his boss beat a hasty retreat.

Sukey had never come across a ring stuck on a finger before, and she examined Hannah's hand uncertainly.

"Use somefing slippery," Jane suggested. "Somefing like butter."

Sukey thought for a moment. Then she fetched a small clay jar from the corner of her hut, and removed its deerskin covering. Inside was a bright white ointment. She scooped a little onto her index finger, while Hannah, sitting on the ground near the fire, watched nervously.

"What is that stuff?" Hannah asked.

"Lard," Sukey said, massaging the fat onto the ring and the skin around it.

"What's that?" Hannah asked.

"You know, pig fat," said Jane with a cheeky smile. "Bacon the pig 'as done you a favor."

Hannah winced at this news, but Jane was right. Thanks to Bacon's final sacrifice, the ring now slipped off easily. Hannah held it up to show Sukey and Jane, and then carefully set it beside her on the ground. "Thank you," she said with a relieved smile. "I was getting worried that old Gordon would cut off my finger." But she was still worried. He would get his ring back, but she was afraid that her reward would be a whipping.

"Now, since the house is soon ashes, where do you sleep?" Sukey asked the girls, wiping her fingers on a rag, then handing it to Hannah to do the same. "Sleep here if you wish it."

"It's okay," Hannah said. "We're good. Mr. and Mrs. Gordon are staying with the Joneses, and Jane and me are going to Mr. Osborn's house."

"You had something to eat?" Sukey asked.

"Not yet," Hannah said. "Actually, I'm starving."

Jane nodded in assent, and the girls looked hopefully at Sukey.

"Make yourself some hoe cakes," Sukey said grumpily. "I'm going back to sleep."

As dawn rose, it was still cold, and the exhausted and shivering girls finally arrived at Mr. Osborn's house. Brandon opened the door, and quietly broke the news to them about Mrs. Gordon's death.

Hannah gasped and stumbled inside. "What? She's gone? No way!"

"Shh," Brandon hushed her. "Mr. Osborn's asleep upstairs, and he's beat. I don't want to wake him."

He sat on one of the rickety wooden chairs by the fire, and Jane sat across from him, while Hannah stood, waiting for an explanation. "She passed last night," Brandon confirmed. "I tried to do CPR, but it didn't work."

Jane looked blank. But Hannah said, "You did what? Are you crazy? Do you even know how to do . . ."

And then she surprised herself by bursting into tears. She hadn't felt at all close to Mrs. Gordon, hadn't even liked her much, really. She just felt sorry for her. It was too strange to think of her as gone forever. And it was just bizarre, she thought, that Mrs. Gordon should die so soon after Mrs. Osborn.

Thinking of Mrs. Gordon, Hannah looked at her ring finger. The ring. Where was the ring? She panicked. She didn't dare tell Alex and Brandon she had lost it. They would never forgive her. "Guys," she said, trying to sound calm. "I have to go back to Sukey's place, right now. I forgot . . . I forgot to tell her something."

But nobody was listening to her. "I'm starving," Jane was saying. "You got any food, Brandon? Real food, I mean. I hate them 'oe cake things."

"Sure, we can fix you some ham and eggs if you like," said Brandon. "Alex, can you fetch the pan?"

"I'll save you some ham," Alex called to his sister as he saw the door close behind her.

"Where's she gone then?" asked Jane.

"Beats me," Brandon said, handing her a basket. "Here, go grab some eggs."

Hannah slumped miserably on her way back from the quarters. Sukey was nowhere to be found. Hannah had searched the empty hut on her hands and knees, but found no trace of the ring. *I must have dropped it somewhere,* she thought. *Oh, man, when Mr. Gordon finds out, I am so toast.* She knew she would have to tell him, but she hoped that tonight of all nights, the ring would be the least of his worries.

She knocked tentatively at the Jones' door, and Juba admitted her with the usual sour look. A haggard Mr. Gordon was sitting at the table with Mr. Jones, slumped over a cup of coffee. He was unshaven, and his clothes were covered with splotches of soot and dirt from the night before. He seemed to be half-listening to Mr. Jones, who was speaking rapidly.

"Thompson in Savannah will, I am certain, be more than happy to advance you the sum required to replace your furnishings," he said, "and I shall be pleased to loan you the assistance of my slaves in buiding a new house for you."

Mr. Gordon cleared his throat. "I am much obliged to you, sir, but that will not be necessary. I have decided to offer the plantation for sale, and to return to my lands in South Carolina."

"If I may be so bold, sir," Mr. Jones said carefully, "perhaps it would be better to hesitate before acting upon such a decision. Meanwhile, let us attend to our most pressing matter. Let us go together and place the culprit under arrest."

Mr. Gordon said nothing, but stared into his coffee. Hannah thought he hadn't even noticed that she was in the room, and so she was startled when he looked up at her abruptly and said, "Where is my wife's ring?"

She swallowed hard. "I don't know, sir. I'm sorry. Sukey helped me get it off, but then I put it down, and I don't know where . . . ."

She stopped speaking when Mr. Gordon jumped to his feet, and advanced on her threateningly. Intimidated, Hannah shrank away from him.

"What have you done?" he screamed at her. "Does Sukey not have possession of it?"

"I don't think so . . . ." Hannah said nervously. Mr. Gordon suddenly turned and slammed his fist on the table. Even Mr. Jones jumped.

"Was it not sufficient that Sukey left the slave quarters in the night, and set the fire? Now she intends to rob me of even the smallest trinket?"

Hannah gaped at him open-mouthed. "What?" she gasped. "No! Sukey wouldn't do that!"

"SILENCE!" Mr. Gordon roared at her. More calmly, he turned back to Mr. Jones. "Negroes are never to be trusted, sir. Never."

"Why do you think Sukey started the fire?" Hannah asked desperately. She began to babble, forgetting who she was supposed to be, and when in time she was. "I mean wasn't it just an accident? You guys use fire all the time, and you live in wooden houses, and you don't have smoke detectors or anything . . . ."

Mr. Gordon had stopped listening. As he threw on his cape and tricorn hat, he gave her a murderous look.

But Hannah was on a roll now. She finished, "And how come you never took the pine straw off the roof?"

With lightning speed, Mr. Gordon stepped across the room and slapped Hannah so hard across the cheek, he knocked her to the floor. She lay crumpled in a stupor at his feet.

Meanwhile, Mr. Jones acted as though nothing had happened. As Hannah groaned, he said calmly to Mr. Gordon, "If you wish it, sir, perhaps we could assemble the magistrates later this week for a special session."

"An excellent idea, sir," Mr. Gordon replied, as he stepped over Hannah and followed Mr. Jones out the door. "And the execution should be carried out forthwith. I regret the loss of my property in Sukey, but it is vital that the negroes see that punishment is immediate and terrible. You will recall, sir, that the penalty for arson by a slave is burning at the stake."

At that moment, Hannah clearly heard Mrs. Gordon's voice in her ear, saying, "Why should the negro live when I am dead?"

Stunned and frightened, she burst into tears.

Chapter 11:
BRANDON AND ALEX INVESTIGATE

A livid red mark lay across Hannah's face, and her head was still buzzing when she got back to Mr. Osborn's house. Alex, Brandon, and Jane rushed to her when they saw her stagger in.

"I heard her!" she cried. "Mrs. Gordon was speaking to me! I heard a ghost! And Mr. Gordon wants to kill Sukey. Come on, we gotta go. We have to stop this."

The noise had awoken Mr. Osborn, and he came downstairs wigless in his nightgown and cap, holding a candle and rubbing his eyes. Alex thought he looked like Wee Willie Winkie.

"What is the matter?" he said irritably. But then he saw that Hannah was distraught, and his mood grew solicitous. "What has happened? Surely there are no more ill tidings this night."

Brandon, Alex, Jane, and Mr. Osborn all listened solemnly as Hannah told them about the loss of the ring, her encounter with Mr. Gordon, and his threats against Sukey.

Hearing that Mr. Gordon wanted Sukey burned at the stake, Alex began to sob, and Hannah put her arm around him. As she did so, Brandon noticed that her hands were shaking.

"I don't understand," Brandon said in disbelief. "I remember one of my teachers saying that slaves must have been treated well, because they were valuable property, and that never made much sense to me. But why would Mr. Gordon want to kill Sukey? He depends on her to do the laundry and stuff, right?"

Hannah rubbed her eyes. "Yeah, but he could get me and Jane to do that," she said. "Oh, wait . . . he does need her for something. He sends Sukey to do business with Mr. MacKenzie, the trader upriver, and she's really good at it. I saw her . . . Oh, no." Hannah's face fell.

"What's wrong?" asked Brandon.

She sighed. "Last time, Mr. Gordon was going to send Alex to Mr. MacKenzie's with Sukey, and then, when Alex was sick, he sent me instead. I couldn't figure out why she would need me or him. It's not like we could help much if she was attacked, and she didn't need us to help lift stuff. Now I'm thinking he wanted us to learn, so we could replace her. Brandon, I thought he totally depended on her. But now I'm not so sure."

Mr. Osborn had been listening quietly, but now he cleared his throat. "I rather think the situation is more complicated than you understand. Mr. Gordon owns a highly profitable plantation in South Carolina, and I hear that he has contemplated selling Kintyre, which profits him very little. The difficulty is that land here in Georgia is very cheap. Indeed, Mr. Gordon was able to acquire this particular land gratis, that is to say, for no payment at all."

"Just a minute," Brandon sputtered, raising a hand. "Mr. Osborn, sir, I'm sorry to interrupt, but are you saying that Mr. Gordon got his plantation for free? How?"

Mr. Osborn drew breath. "His Majesty the King allows British subjects to claim free land in South Carolina and Georgia. Regrettably, land speculators have taken most of the land in South Carolina, either through connections in the government, or by purchasing it cheaply from the men who originally claimed it. Most men who acquire land free, you see, cannot afford to buy slaves, and they quickly find that their farms cannot compete with slave-run plantations. And so they sell the land to speculators, often for very little ready money. Speculators hold the property in hopes that fortune's wheel will turn toward higher land prices in time."

"Kind of like people who flip houses," Hannah said, intrigued. "I heard Dad talking about that one time."

Mr. Osborn gave her an odd look, and continued, "In Georgia, there is still free land to be won, but the same problem has begun to emerge here as it did in South Carolina, now that slavery is permitted. Once again, men who can afford slaves and land on the coast will make great fortunes, while others will struggle to make a living, or be forced to sell."

"But Mr. Gordon isn't struggling," Alex piped up. "He owns slaves. I'm one of them."

Mr. Osborn looked uncertainly at Alex for a moment, unsure of how a slave like "Cato" could understand the conversation. He decided to forge ahead.

"He does indeed," he said. "But I imagine that he has concluded, as have we all, that the land in St. Swithin's Parish is of a very poor sort. Unlike the rest of us, however, Mr. Gordon has other prospects."

"That's right," said Hannah. "He's building two houses in South Carolina: one on his plantation, and one in Charleston."

"Is that so?" said Mr. Osborn, lifting an eyebrow. "How very interesting, when he has pleaded poverty every time I have asked for a decent house to be provided for me."

"Isn't there anything we can do for Sukey, sir?" Hannah pleaded.

Mr. Osborn fidgeted uneasily. "I shall appeal to Mr. Jones and Mr. Gordon in the strongest possible terms. Even if Sukey were guilty of this dreadful crime,

such a vicious punishment should be unconscionable to all Christians. But..."
and here he sighed heavily, "I do not think that Mr. Gordon is much interested
in my opinion. What happens, I am afraid, will depend on the other magistrates. Meanwhile, Brandon, we shall visit Sukey tomorrow morning, and offer
her our spiritual counsel."

"Can I go with you to see Sukey?" Alex begged. "Please?"

"If you wish, Cato," Mr. Osborn said. "Now, I suggest that Hannah and
Jane go forth to Mr. Jones's house, and wait upon Mr. Gordon. He may need
your assistance. He is your master, after all."

"Don't remind me," muttered Hannah.

An hour later, Brandon, Alex, and Mr. Osborn found Sukey in the wooden
lock-up near the church. It was even more miserable than the tiny jail in which
Hannah had been imprisoned in Balesworth.

Pressing his eye to a chink in the wood, it took Alex a moment to adjust his
vision to the gloom. The first thing he noticed was that there was barely room
on the dirt floor to lie down. Then he saw Sukey. She was hunched miserably
in the corner of the tiny shack, shivering violently. Her hair was wet and water
was dripping onto her from leaks in the roof.

"Sukey, it's me," he called. "It's Cato. Are you okay?"

At first, there was no reply. Sukey said nothing, and Alex was alarmed.

"Sukey? Are you okay?" he repeated.

He saw her pull her tattered shawl over her shoulders. "They will burn me,"
she said faintly. "But I never do nothing."

Unlike Alex, Mr. Osborn was tall enough to look through the bars in the
lock-up door. "Sukey, confess your sins to God," he intoned, "and you will
receive His divine mercy."

She raised her head, and looked Mr. Osborn in the eye. "I swear by God, sir,
I never do nothing. I do not steal that ring, and I do not make that fire. Cuffee
tells lies to Mr. Gordon."

Brandon looked perplexed. "Did Cuffee set the fire?"

Sukey shrugged. "I don't know, Mr. Brandon. Maybe he is scared. Slaves say
things we don't mean when we are scared."

Brandon nodded, and turned to Mr. Osborn. "She's right," he said gravely.
"I read about this. Slaves sometimes betray other slaves when they're planning
rebellions, because they're scared they'll get blamed and tortured."

Mr. Osborn was staring at him now. "What are you talking about, that you
read such a thing? Were you reading about the ancient Romans?"

"No, Mr. Osborn, I wasn't," Brandon said calmly. "I'm talking about American history. I read it in the twenty-first century, which is where I'm from."

Mr. Osborn shook his head in bewilderment, and said aloud to himself, "As though I were not besieged by difficulties, my servant reveals himself as a lunatic."

"No, I'm not, sir," Brandon retorted angrily. "I'm from the future, and so is Alex, I mean, Cato. That's Cato's real name, by the way. Alex. We're both from Snipesville. It's a town that will be right here one day, right on this spot. We travel in time, and we don't know why, but I do know it isn't so we can stand by and allow an innocent person to burn to death. It's true, sir, I swear it on the Bible. In our time, carriages are known as cars, and they work with mechanical engines, not horses. We've sent flying machines into the air, and into space. And we could have saved your wife from dying in childbirth."

"What is this madness? If that were true," Mr. Osborn said angrily, "Then why did you not save my wife's life? And that of Mrs. Gordon?"

"We couldn't do it ourselves," Alex snapped. "We're just kids. But our doctors can. They know much more about medicine than anyone in your time."

"This is absurd. Am I to believe that a slave is also a traveler in time?" Mr. Osborn said in evident disbelief, looking at Alex.

"He's not really a slave," Brandon said. "He's . . ." He stopped, and sighed, then said calmly, "Look, it's like religion, sir. There's more truth than we can prove. Sometimes you just have to take a leap of faith."

Mr. Osborn looked from Brandon to Alex, and back again. Neither of them avoided his gaze. Stunned, the minister put a hand to his head. "Why do you tell me this?" he whispered. "What have you to gain?"

Brandon said stoutly, "I'm telling you because it's true, and because we'd like you to help us. We need to find Mrs. Gordon's ring, and we need to know who really set the fire. I don't think it's Sukey. Do you?"

"I believe you may be right about Sukey, even if nothing else you say makes the slightest sense," Mr. Osborn said weakly. "But what in the name of creation do you expect me to do to help?"

To everyone's surprise, Sukey spoke up from behind the door. "Sir, you must go to the witch. She will know what to do."

"Um, no," Brandon said sadly, "Sorry, Sukey, but that's actually not helpful. Look, Alex, maybe we can start interviewing people. We can just ask around. I'm a fan of mysteries, so maybe I can think up some questions."

"And I? What shall I do in this madness?" Mr. Osborn asked, still bewildered by the strange turn of events.

"We'll let you know," Alex said brightly.

But if the kids thought that the minister had accepted their story of who they were and where they were from, they were about to be disappointed.

Mr. Osborn looked deeply troubled. "I will assist as best I can to prevent an appalling miscarriage of justice," he said. "But, Brandon, we will talk later about what you claim. If, as I believe, you are lying, then I shall hold you responsible for misleading Cato with this fantasy of yours. If you are suffering from some disorder of the mind . . . I know not what I shall do with you."

With that, he turned and headed back in the direction of his house.

For a few seconds, Brandon watched him go. He was troubled by how the discussion had ended. Then he snapped out of his frozen state. "Okay, let's make a plan," he said to Alex. "First, we need a notebook. Or something like a notebook."

Alex raised an eyebrow. "And when have you seen a notebook around here? Or is there a Walmart that I don't know about?"

Brandon bit his lip. It was true. The only notebook he knew of belonged to Mr. Osborn, and it was one of the minister's most prized possessions. Paper, Brandon remembered, was very expensive. A notebook was out of the question.

He shrugged dismissively. "Okay, no notebook. We'll just have to try to remember stuff."

Over the next few hours, the boys interviewed almost all of the slaves. But by the time they were done, Brandon was hopelessly confused about who had said what. He really wished he had thought harder about where he could find paper.

But it was Alex who called time out to unravel their findings, and who smugly announced that he knew where they could take notes. He led Brandon down to the river, to a tiny sandy beach that jutted into the water. Grabbing a stick, he began to write names in the sand, starting with Sukey, then Tony, and so on.

"That's brilliant!" Brandon exclaimed. "Way to go, Alex. Why didn't I think of that?"

"Because you're not perfect?" Alex smiled. "Right, the number one problem is that Sukey says she was home the entire evening before the fire. But nobody can confirm her alibi."

"On the other hand," Brandon said, "nobody says they saw her outside."

"Hmm," said Alex, waving his stick. "And nobody says they saw anyone else, either. So that leaves us . . ."

"Up a creek?" Brandon suggested.

Alex shook his head. "No. That leaves us Cuffee. He's our next witness. Let's go see what he has to say."

Cuffee was helping Tony to saw down a tree, and he smiled when he spotted Alex. His smile faltered a little when he saw that Alex was with Brandon.

"Good day, Master Brandon," he said with forced cheerfulness. Brandon immediately wondered if Cuffee had something to hide, but then he remembered that the slaves were never exactly relaxed around white people. And he was, at least for now, a white person.

"Brandon and me," Alex said, "we're just wondering if you saw anything last night?"

"Saw anything?" Cuffee asked, looking confused.

"Well, actually," Brandon said in his most self-important voice, "we mean anyone. We're asking if you saw anyone leaving the quarters around the time of the fire, or hanging out near the house and the outbuildings."

Cuffee looked away. "I saw someone."

"Was it Sukey?" Alex asked nervously.

"I can't say," Cuffee whispered, shrugging. He clearly was afraid that Tony would overhear the conversation about his mother.

"Where were you when you saw her?" Brandon asked sharply.

Cuffee thought for a moment. "I was in the barracks," he said finally. "I was lying abed, but the door was open, and I see someone through the door, walking by."

Brandon leaned forward eagerly. "Did you see her come back in her hut? Was it Sukey you saw?"

Cuffee shook his head. "Master Brandon, sir, Tony waits for me to cut down the tree. I best go back to work."

But as he left, Brandon called to him. "Cuffee, Sukey will die if you don't help us. They will burn her to death. Can you call yourself a Christian with that on your conscience?"

Cuffee turned back toward the boys and hesitated. Then he walked up to Brandon. "Master Brandon, I don't know that I saw Sukey. Might have been someone else. Might have been Jane."

Then he looked scared, as though he had said too much.

"Do you think it was?" Brandon pressed him. Cuffee just shook his head, and returned to his work. But now Tony was looking at him inquisitively, and as the boys left, Brandon noticed him cornering Cuffee.

"I think we have our culprit," Brandon muttered to Alex. "I think Jane did it. She was a criminal in London, a thief and who knows what else. But why would Cuffee cover for her?"

And then Cuffee and Tony surprised them.

Tony dragged Cuffee by the arm, back to the boys, and shook his shoulder. "Master Brandon," he said slowly, "We have something to tell you."

Hannah and Jane found themselves in an awkward situation.

Mrs. Jones had told them that it would not be seemly for two white girls to work under Juba's direction, and it was clear that Juba didn't want them around anyway.

"What's her problem?" Hannah whispered to Jane, after Juba threw them yet another dirty look. "Does she think we're lazy? Why won't she let us do anything?"

Jane looked thoughtful. "I reckon she's worried that we will take her job in the house, and she'll 'ave to work outside."

"Huh, I hadn't thought of that," Hannah muttered. "So what do we do?"

"I dunno," Jane said, biting her nails. "Wait until the missus gives us something to do, I suppose. I'm in no 'urry to work, are you?"

As though reading their minds, Mr. Gordon returned to the house, closing the door behind him.

"Jane, Hannah, come here," he said.

Alarmed by his tone, the two girls reluctantly approached him. Hannah now had a bruise on her face where he had hit her, and she found herself shaking as she stepped toward him.

He looked squarely at the girls. "It will be some time before my new house is completed here. In the meantime, I have decided to return to my home at Sidlaw. So the time has come for me to find a new master for Jane, and since I have no further use for your service, Hannah, in light of your ill-behavior, you will both have your remaining time auctioned in Savannah on Saturday."

Hannah was appalled. "You're selling us?" she blurted out. "Both of us? But that's just two days from now!"

"Indeed it is," Mr. Gordon said. And then he swept out of the house.

Hannah stared after him.

"Well," Jane said miserably. "That's that, then. We just have to hope we don't get cruel new masters."

But it wasn't, because Brandon and Alex chose that moment to arrive. And the news they brought was more shocking than Hannah could possibly have imagined.

The boys beckoned Jane and Hannah outside, then led them into the woods, out of earshot of the people in the house. Brandon did not waste time. Immediately, he turned to Jane. "I have to ask you a question. Did you go back to the quarters before the fire?"

Jane grew visibly nervous. "Why do you ask me that, pray?" she said.

Brandon shook his head. "Never mind why I'm asking you. Did you?"

But the answer was written all over her face. The other three kids looked at her curiously.

Finally, it was Hannah who asked the most pressing question in a shocked whisper. "Jane, did you start the fire?"

"No!" Jane exclaimed in horror. "T'weren't me. But yes, I went back to the quarters. And I found this."

She reached into her pocket and pulled out something. It was Mrs. Gordon's ring. Hannah's eyes grew wide, and anger flashed across her face. "Why didn't you tell me? Why did you lie to me?" She grabbed Jane and shook her hard. Alex and Brandon had to pull Hannah off her friend.

Jane was unrepentant. "Because if I give it to you, you'd 'ave given it back to old Gordon, and he don't need it, does he? Anyway, Mrs. Gordon gave it to you, fair and square, not 'im. It's yours, 'annah. I reckoned I'd just hold on to it for you until it was safe to give it back. He didn't suspect me."

"You're lying!" Hannah cried. "Did Sukey know you did this?"

"Yeah, of course she did," said Jane matter-of-factly. "You can ask 'er. And I ain't lying. Sukey thought it was a good idea too, although she wanted me to 'ide it somewhere in the woods. 'Course, I didn't do that because I was afraid I'd forget where I put it. All them trees look the same to me. Oh, blimey!"

In her nervousness, Jane had slipped the ring onto her finger. Now, when she tried to pull it off, she found it was stuck.

Hannah was beside herself. "This is a disaster. Brandon, Mr. Gordon is planning to sell me and Jane two days from now. What are we gonna do?"

"I don't have a clue," said Brandon miserably. "But there's something else I have to tell you both."

"What?" Hannah asked, glancing around for fear that Mr. Gordon would turn up and spot the ring on Jane's finger.

Brandon took a deep breath. "We do know who set the fire. Cuffee saw everything, and he told us about it. He even saw you, Jane, going into Sukey's hut."

"And?" Hannah said impatiently, glancing at Jane, who had gone pale.

"Don't worry, Jane," Brandon said, seeing her fear. "We know you didn't do it."

In a solemn voice, Alex said, "It was Mr. Gordon."

"Oh, come on!" Hannah yelped. "That's the best you can do, Sherlock? Why would he burn down his own house? Duh!"

"To collect the insurance," Brandon said bluntly.

There was a stunned silence. Then Hannah said, "Brandon, are you sure about that?"

"Not one hundred percent, no," said Brandon. "I don't have any history books here, and I can't ask the Professor, so I can't find out for sure if they had insurance in 1752. I'm just guessing that's why. But we do know he did it, and that's the only reason I can think of."

"But why would Cuffee cover for Mr. Gordon?" Hannah asked irritably. "Why wouldn't he just report him to Mr. Jones or someone?"

"Yeah, we wondered about that, too," Alex said. "I think it was fear, All of us slaves are afraid of him. And do you really think Mr. Jones, or Mr. Osborn, or any of them would take a black man's word over the word of a white man?"

"I don't know." Hannah shook her head. "I just can't imagine Mr. Gordon would stand there and watch Sukey burn to death when he knew he was responsible."

"Try," Alex said firmly to his sister. "He cut off Cuffee's foot, and Sukey said that didn't bother him at all. He doesn't care about slaves, Hannah, or white servants, either. Do you know that Mr. Gordon is Tony's father?"

Hannah didn't know that. "Seriously?" she said. "Sukey was his girlfriend? He enslaved his girlfriend? His son?"

Alex pressed on. "Look what he did to you, when he hit you. Look how he's selling you. He just uses all of us to make money."

"But isn't Sukey valuable?" Hannah was still struggling with the idea of Mr. Gordon as a murderer.

"Not really," Brandon said. "She's getting old, and he doesn't need her at all up in South Carolina."

"Well . . . whatever. We have to save her," Hannah said firmly. "Come on. Let's go to the lock-up. Then I think it's time we all hightailed it out of here."

"Not so fast," Brandon said, putting a restraining hand on her arm. "Where will we go? There's no point in me running away from Mr. Osborn."

"Let's not argue, okay?" Alex said. "First, let's go see if we can get Sukey out of jail. Then we can worry about what to do next."

He ran to the side of the house and yanked a hatchet out of an old log where it was used for splitting firewood. Lifting it up, he yelled, "Come on, you guys."

When they arrived at the tiny jail, Brandon suggested that it would be wise to let Sukey know that they were about to smash the lock. But when Hannah peeked through the bars, the tiny prison was empty.

"Do you think they already took her away for trial?" Alex asked anxiously, putting down the hatchet.

Brandon shook his head. "Mr. Osborn would have told me. I guess she escaped. Look, the lock is open."

Alex examined the heavy black padlock. "That's weird," he said. "It doesn't look like someone opened it by force."

"Maybe they picked it," said Jane. "All them locks use the same key."

"Well, you would know about picking locks, Jane," Hannah spat. She was still annoyed that Jane hadn't told her about the ring. "Whatever. We have to find Sukey. I bet she's taken the canoe and gone to Mr. MacKenzie's."

"Doubt it," Brandon said. "MacKenzie's a white guy, right? No, she will be looking for black people to help her."

"How do you know?" Hannah asked crossly, but then she backed down as Brandon aimed a level gaze at her.

"Oh . . . right," she said, chagrined. "Yeah. You would know. I guess."

"Maybe she's gone to see the white witch," Alex said.

Brandon and Hannah exchanged looks.

"Good point. There's only one problem," Brandon said. "Does anyone know where to find her?"

"I do," Alex said. "Sukey pointed out her house to me just last week."

"Could you find it again?" Brandon asked.

He nodded. "I think so."

Alex got lost several times along the way, and an hour later, the four kids still hadn't reached their destination.

As they walked along the trail, Hannah began to shiver. "Is it just me, or is it cold?" she griped.

"It's cold," her brother said, kicking up leaves and pine straw.

"No," Hannah said, "I mean really, really cold."

Nobody replied. Hannah pulled her cloak more tightly around her shoulders as a shiver ran up her back. As she did so, she felt the first pangs of a headache.

They finally found the hut almost by accident, when Alex spotted it deep in the woods. It was surrounded by trees and tangled undergrowth, and it was as well hidden as anything could be in a place as flat as southeastern Georgia. Only a stream of smoke issuing from the chimney gave it away.

"This is weird," Hannah said, as the kids spied on the back of the hut. "I wonder if she'll mind a bunch of white people showing up on her doorstep? Maybe you should go first, Alex, and tell her what's going on. She won't mind you, I'm sure."

Alex didn't look much like he fancied that idea, but reluctantly he agreed.

While he disappeared around the corner to the front of the house, the kids remained in the bushes. But very soon, to their surprise, Alex returned with a stranger, a black man. Brandon thought the man looked familiar, but he couldn't think why.

"We have Sukey with us," the man said in what sounded like a West Indian accent. He spoke with authority, which surprised Brandon. He had expected the man to be much more subdued around whites. The man continued, "My wife says you can leave the two girls here with us for now. But you boys must say nothing at all, or all our lives will be in danger. Do you swear?"

Brandon wondered why the witch and her husband would trust them. He said carefully, "There's one person I do have to tell about Sukey. It's Mr. Osborn, the minister. But it's all right. He's on our side. He won't betray us. I got to tell you, though, the other white men will search for Sukey. Don't be surprised if they come here."

The man looked troubled by this news. He said, "I will ask my wife what she thinks. Wait here."

He walked back into the house, leaving puzzled faces behind him.

But he soon came back with a reply. "She says she trusts you to do what you think is best."

"Okay, that's just strange," Brandon muttered to the other kids. "She doesn't even know us, or Mr. Osborn."

"Maybe she's using her psychic powers?" Hannah smirked. In truth, she was very nervous about entrusting her fate to this unknown woman. Was she really a witch? Or just crazy?

With some trepidation, Hannah and Jane bid farewell to Alex and Brandon, and followed the old man toward the house.

As the door swung open, the old man called out, "Annie, here are the two girls."

From the upstairs loft, someone slowly stepped down the creaking stairs. Hannah first saw skirts and shoes. And as the woman carefully picked her way to the ground floor, Hannah got a shock.

Now she knew why this woman was called the "white witch."

It wasn't because she practiced good spells. It was because she was white.

The old woman was short, and slightly stooped, with flyaway white hair and masses of wrinkles. She looked to be at least eighty, and very stern in appearance. But her eyes were kindly and somehow familiar. She greeted Hannah and Jane with a big smile.

"Fred," she said to her husband, "please could you make us all tea?"

Fred smiled back at his wife as he returned outside. Hannah could see that he was quite a few years younger than she was, and that he adored her.

"Now then," the witch said to Hannah. "I am delighted to see you at long last."

Her greeting was warm, but Hannah looked at her suspiciously. "I know you're supposed to be a witch. Are you psychic or something? Did you know we were coming?"

The old woman smiled and said nothing.

Just then, Hannah's head swam and she felt slightly nauseated. "I think I've got the start of the flu," she said weakly. "Can I please lie down?"

"There is a bed in here," said a familiar voice from the other room. Sukey appeared in the doorway, and Hannah gave her a hug.

Watching them, the witch said, "By all means, settle in, Hannah. But Sukey, we must make haste. It is not safe for you to remain here long. I have sent word to a friend of ours who has agreed to help us, and I am sure he will spirit you away. I expect him in two or three days."

"But if it's not safe for Sukey, are we in danger too?" Hannah asked.

"Of course," said the witch calmly. "But not straightaway. I am thinking of what would be best for you two girls, too."

For a moment, Hannah wondered if the old woman planned to make them into a stew, sort of like Hansel and Gretel.

As they walked back through the woods toward Mr. Osborn's house, Brandon turned to Alex. "We have to tell Mr. Osborn what's going on," he said. "Right now."

"What makes you think he'll want to help?" Alex asked skeptically.

"I understand what you mean," Brandon sighed. "He's not exactly Mr. Popularity with the white guys around here, and getting involved in this could be seriously dangerous for him. So I'm just going to have to appeal to him as a Christian, you know, to do the right thing."

Alex was not sure that this would work, but he said nothing.

As the boys crossed the pasture, they spotted Mr. Osborn riding up to the house. Dismounting, he tied up his horse and then stomped inside, glowering.

"Maybe this isn't the right time," Alex said tremulously. "He looks seriously mad. Maybe he's been looking for us."

Brandon frowned. "Man, I hope not. We have to talk to him right now, or it might be too late."

Alex stopped and kicked at the soil with his bare toes. "Look, are you sure about that? The witch's house is pretty well hidden. Maybe we do have time to wait for him to be in a good mood."

"That's true," said Brandon slowly. "I don't think the white people have ever gone looking for her. They don't even know Fred exists, and they don't see the witch as a threat. But if they suspect she's hiding Sukey, that might change. Fast."

"Good point," said Alex. "Okay, let's talk to him now. Should we ask him to help Hannah and Jane, too?"

"I think," Brandon said, "it would be best not to mention Hannah and Jane, at least not for now. Let's just focus on getting him to help Sukey. Okay?"

In silence, the boys walked the last few hundred yards to the house.

Mr. Osborn had removed his wig and coat, and poured himself a glass of Madeira wine. He was slumped in a chair, staring into the fireplace. He no longer looked angry, but deeply depressed. He barely glanced up when the boys entered.

"The vestry has informed me," he said slowly, gazing into the smoldering embers, "that they no longer require my services, and that they have already written to the Bishop to ask for my replacement. In their letter, they tell me, they have told His Grace that I am a drunkard."

The boys began to protest this outrage, but Mr. Osborn held up a hand to silence them. "You know as well as I that this is a shameful lie, and a grotesque slur upon my good character. Indeed, as you probably know, some of the accusers themselves are guilty of the sin of which they accuse me. They are well-known for their familiarity with the bottle." He stopped, looking at the glass of wine in his hand almost in amusement.

"You know, before I left England," he said quietly, "I met with some of my brother clergy in London. They took me to supper, and they warned me that ministers who go to America are often falsely accused of drunkenness and other sins. Because there is no bishop in America, they said, the Bishop of London must determine the truth or falsehood of such accusations. His Grace has begun to suspect that many of these accusations indeed are false, they said, but it was difficult to make judgments across a vast span of ocean, and so . . ." He trailed off. "I was warned," he added unhappily.

"What do you plan to do now?" Brandon asked quietly, fighting down his rising panic.

"I know not," Mr. Osborn said, biting his lip and glancing downward. "I came here to do good, and also, I will confess it, I came here because I so very much wanted to have my own parish, to support myself as a gentleman ought to be supported. To confess failure is difficult for me. Nonetheless, I have failed."

"I don't think you've failed," Brandon said hesitantly. He was really moved by Mr. Osborn's honesty about his own weaknesses, and he was determined to make his master feel better. "They failed you. And you can still do good, sir."

Mr. Osborn looked at him sharply. "How so?"

Brandon took a deep breath, and said, "You can help us."

After Brandon and Alex had explained the results of their investigation, and their belief that Mr. Gordon himself had set the fire, Mr. Osborn, in silence, searched their faces. Brandon was suddenly afraid that he and Alex had made a terrible mistake by confiding in the minister.

But now Mr. Osborn rose to his feet. "The men of the parish are meeting this very minute to divide up the search among them," he said. "I shall volunteer to search due west of the plantation."

Brandon thought quickly. This wasn't quite what he had had in mind. If Mr. Osborn visited the witch's house, he would also find Hannah and Jane. If they told him about the girls now, he would wonder why they had not told him the whole truth before. And the less he knew, the better for everyone. Maybe Alex could go and warn the girls, so they could get out of sight before Mr. Osborn arrived?

But now Brandon wondered if he was just panicking and jumping the gun. He said, "Are we actually going into the witch's house, sir? I just thought maybe we should warn her."

Mr. Osborn was already halfway out the door, but he turned back. "Well put, Brandon. Indeed, it would be best if we did not trouble her, or confirm our suspicion that she is sheltering Sukey. The less we know for certain, the less we will need to bear false witness to Mr. Jones and Mr. Gordon. We need make only a brief investigation of the area, so that we can report to them that we have found nothing amiss, and thereby discourage further searches. Now, wait here. I shall return for you shortly."

With that, he left. Brandon and Alex turned to each other, and gave huge sighs of relief. They had an adult ally, and a good one at that.

Mr. Osborn was indeed as good as his word. He was the first man to arrive when the searchers gathered. In front of Mr. Gordon, Mr. Jones, and the others, he made a great show of walking his horse along a trail into the forest, with Brandon and Alex trotting alongside him.

As they went deeper into the woods, Brandon puffed to Alex, "Never been along here before. Where do you think we're going?"

Alex was worried. "I think we're headed straight at the witch's house," he whispered to Brandon. "Do you think he's taking us there? I thought he didn't know where it is, and he didn't want to meet her? What's going on?"

Brandon raised his eyebrows. He had no idea. He crossed his fingers and hoped for the best.

But Mr. Osborn never left the main trail. He passed the hidden trail that led to the witch's house, and took the boys up a gentle, densely-forested hill, which was practically a mountain by the standards of the flat lands of southeastern Georgia.

At the summit was a tiny log house, with deer antlers mounted over its front doorway.

Alex grinned. "I know where we are," he said to Brandon. "This is downtown Snipesville! I don't think it's called that yet, but it sure looks familiar."

Then he paused doubtfully, and turned his head. "That's a tavern, I'm sure it is. Check out the antlers. But I thought Mr. and Mrs. Marshburn were the first people to own a tavern here? The tavern I visited in 1851?"

"What makes you think they were first?" asked Brandon.

"Oh, my dad's boss is descended from the Marshburns," Alex said, "and that's what he told me. I guess it wasn't true."

"He probably didn't know what was true," Brandon said. "Look at all the stuff I don't know about my ancestors."

"Come along boys," called Mr. Osborn. He had tied up his horse, and was beckoning to them. "As the vestry have already styled me a drunkard," he said cheerily, "I don't suppose that a visit to a tavern will do my reputation any harm."

They sat at a table inside, and the tavern-keeper brought over tankards. Alex accepted a beer at Mr. Osborn's insistence. He sipped politely from the clay mug, stuck out his tongue at the bitter taste, and didn't touch it again.

When Mr. Osborn stepped outside to relieve himself, Brandon and Alex called over the serving girl to remove their unwanted drinks.

"I've been thinking, Brandon," Alex murmured. "You know where the witch's house is, at the bottom of the hill? When I was here in 1851, that land was part of Kintyre Plantation, Mr. Gordon's place. And in the twenty-first century . . ."

Brandon, excited, finished the sentence for him. "It's in Braithwaite Park. It's where we found the skeleton. Wow."

"So who is it?" Alex asked him, worry written across his face. "Is it Sukey, or Jane, or the witch or . . . ?"

A silence fell between them. Brandon didn't want to say Hannah's name either. So was this how their adventures would end? With Hannah dead?

Chapter 12:
THE WHITE WITCH

The very next day, Mr. Osborn started to pack up his stuff for the return to England. When Brandon and Alex found him in the loft, he was carefully placing each leather-bound book in his battered old trunk.

"Can we help, sir?" Brandon asked awkwardly, gesturing helplessly toward the last two books on the desk.

Mr. Osborn shook his head sadly. "No, Brandon, there is no need. I have so very few belongings with which to return."

"Where will you go, sir?" Alex asked.

"I doubt you would know the place, Cato," Mr. Osborn said in a patronizing tone.

"Try him," said Brandon with a sly smile.

Mr. Osborn sighed lightly. "I have written to the Bishop of London, and I have asked that he return me to Balesworth, or elsewhere in Hertfordshire. Now that I am a widower, I will be able to live on a small curate's salary. And if no suitable curacy can be found in England, I have suggested that I be dispatched as a missionary once more, this time to the West Indies. But regardless of His Grace's decision, I must return to London to hear his verdict. As I have informed His Grace, my circumstances do not permit me to wait in Georgia for months while a letter with his reply makes its way across the Atlantic. I have told the Bishop that I shall wait upon him in person at Lambeth Palace to hear his decision."

"So you're going to see him in London?" Brandon said. "May I ask you another huge favor?"

Lifting the last book, Mr. Osborn sighed again. "You may ask, but whether I grant your request will very much depend on its nature."

Brandon explained what had happened to Hannah and Jane. "We'll take care of Hannah," he said. "She's a time-traveler too, like us. But will you take Jane home to England with you and deliver her to her parents in Balesworth? I mean, even if you don't get your job at St. Swithin's, Balesworth's not far from London, is it?"

Mr. Osborn shook his head sadly. "Why would I risk my life and Jane's by breaking the law? She was sentenced to a fixed term of transportation, was she not? And she committed the crime of which she was accused, did she not?"

"True," Brandon admitted. "But she's Mr. and Mrs. Jenkins' daughter. You know, the couple who run the Balesworth Arms?"

Mr. Osborn looked incredulously at him. "Surely you jest?"

"It's true," Alex chimed in. "She was abducted when she was a kid, and the people who kidnapped her taught her to steal. But Brandon and Hannah figured out who she was when she talked about her parents."

Mr. Osborn said falteringly. "I lived in Balesworth only for a short time. Mrs. Jenkins once made mention in my presence of having lost a daughter, but I assumed that the child was dead."

"No," Alex said stoutly, "She's not dead. She's Jane."

Mr. Osborn looked at both of them. "But what you ask of me is quite impossible. To repeat, there is the problem that she has been sentenced to a fixed term of transportation. If she is caught returning before her time is up, she will be hanged."

Brandon thought about this for a moment. Then his eyes lit up. "Nobody carries ID here, right?" he said eagerly.

Mr. Osborn looked at him in confusion, so Brandon answered his own question, speaking rapidly. "Right. Nobody does. No ID. No passports. And Hannah said Jane told her she was convicted under another name in court. And neither of them got branded, because Hannah bribed the guy who does the branding. So as long as Jane stays out of London, and keeps quiet in Balesworth about what happened, and uses her real name, which is Jane Jenkins, there should be no problem. If anyone asks, you can tell people she's your cousin."

Alex nodded frantically in agreement.

Mr. Osborn smiled despite himself. But then his face grew serious again. "And you swear that my part in all this will remain a secret?"

"For the rest of your life, and so long as you wish it, yes," Brandon said.

Mr. Osborn breathed out heavily through his nose. "Very well. I believe that what you ask is right and just. But I do foresee one insurmountable difficulty."

"And what is that?" said Brandon.

Mr. Osborn raised an eyebrow. "How do you propose that Jane will pay for her passage to England?"

Alex looked quizzically at him. "Couldn't you just pay it, and ask her parents to give you the money when you get there?"

Mr. Osborn shook his head emphatically. "You are asking me to gamble no small amount of my own money. Should Mr. and Mrs. Jenkins refuse to reimburse me, or should the girl, God forbid, die upon the voyage, I should be out of pocket a considerable sum."

Alex screwed up his face in thought, and then suddenly, he exclaimed, "The ring! We could sell it. That would raise a lot of money, I bet."

But Brandon threw him a warning look, and changed tactics. It was time for an appeal to Mr. Osborn's conscience. "Mr. Osborn, please put your trust in the Lord," he said. "I promise, I swear, your goodness will be repaid. And without your help, the wrong will never be put right."

"By rights," the minister said slowly, "it should be the girl Hannah whom I return to England. It was she who was wrongfully convicted. I was unable to persuade Mr. Gordon of that miscarriage of justice, however."

But Brandon was already shaking a finger. "Don't worry about Hannah, Mr. Osborn. It's Jane who needs your help. You could tell people in Balesworth that it was mistaken identity. I mean, Jane and Hannah look a lot like each other. And you could say it was a miracle that you discovered on board the ship that the girl you were bringing back wasn't Hannah at all, but Jane Jenkins, who had been abducted away to America. That's not unheard of, right, kids being abducted and spirited away to America?"

Mr. Osborn licked his lips nervously. "So I believe . . . . Brandon, your ability to weave such a tangled story is remarkable, but I admit that what you say is plausible. Very well. I shall do as you ask. And may God in his infinite mercy protect us all."

"Amen to that," said Brandon with relief.

When they were alone, Alex asked Brandon why he didn't want to sell the gold ring to pay for Jane's ticket.

"Simple," said Brandon. "That ring is supposed to be here. It's supposed to be found here. If it leaves St. Swithin's Parish, how can I find it in Snipesville in the twenty-first century?"

"But don't you see?" Alex said anxiously, "Maybe you're not meant to find the ring. All you're doing by keeping it here is making sure that someone we know dies, maybe even Hannah."

Brandon blanched. "Do you really think so? Man. So what do we do? Mr. Osborn will leave before we have a chance to sell it in Savannah, and there's no way I want to give it to him. It's cursed. Maybe we can sell it after he's gone, and use the money to live on."

"Hold on," said Alex, thoughtful now. "Now I think about it, selling it is kind of a mean thing to do. Would you want to be responsible for selling somebody the Ring of Death? Shouldn't we just bury it somewhere instead?"

Brandon said nothing, but he looked somber. "This is hurting my brain. Look, I know we think we can control what happens. But one thing I've learned here is that, well, a lot of things happen that we can't do anything about. You were right when you said that, sometimes, things are just meant to happen. Maybe it would be better just to let whatever is going to happen, happen. And right now, what's happening is that Jane is wearing the ring."

Gingerly, the boys called out as they approached the witch's house, trying to alert but not alarm the occupants. There was no reply, so they tapped gently on the door.

"Who goes there?" asked a gruff voice. It was Fred.

"It's Cato and Brandon," Alex replied. The door opened a crack. When Fred had satisfied himself as to the boys' identity, he opened it wider.

"Come in, quickly," he urged them.

The boys did as they were told.

"What's wrong?" Brandon asked.

"We had a visit from Tony, Sukey's son," said Fred, as the witch and Sukey stood behind him. "He says that Gordon has now ordered a search for the girls also, but all the slaves are doing their best to distract the searchers from this place."

Jane stepped forward now, and she looked panicky. "You won't let 'em take us, will you, missis?" she pleaded with the witch.

The witch smiled and patted her shoulder. "Of course we won't, my dear. Over my dead body."

"I think you'll be okay," Brandon said uncertainly. "Mr. Osborn has told the gentlemen that he searched this whole area, and didn't find anyone. You should just lay low for now."

As quickly as he could, he explained the plan for Mr. Osborn to take Jane to England.

The witch seemed impressed. "That was very enterprising of you boys. Well done. Now, I have news for you, but not so good. Hannah is sick. I think she has malaria. I have no cinchona with which to treat her, and no means to obtain some. You see, I'm afraid it is too dangerous now for us to travel to the nearest apothecary, which is in Savannah."

Alex teared up and stole an anxious glance at his sister, who was sleeping in the other room.

"I could go," Brandon said quickly. "Nobody would suspect me. I bet Mr. Osborn would take me. What's the stuff you want? Does it work?"

The witch wrote the name with a finger in the dust of the cabin floor. "Cinchona. It is the bark of a tree from Peru, and it will heal her."

Brandon's heart sank. Tree bark? That was the best she could offer? The witch saw his dismay, and said firmly, "It is a proven cure for her fever."

"And you're sure I can get it in Savannah?" Brandon asked worriedly.

"No," she sighed. "There are often shortages. But it is our only chance."

"Will she die without it?" Alex asked tearfully. He was reeling from the news. Why did his sister have to be so stubborn? Why hadn't she taken the malaria pills when she had the chance?

"It is possible she will die," said the witch sadly, "but many people survive malaria. I have had it myself. Fred and I met when he found me lying in the swamp, lost and fevered, so many years ago."

Fred smiled at the memory and squeezed her hand.

In the other room, Hannah stirred in her sleep and groaned, her face knotted in pain. Hearing her, Sukey took a rag from a clay pot filled with water, wrung it out, and squatted on a stool next to her patient. Gently she mopped Hannah's forehead, then ran her hand across the girl's hair, murmuring to her. Alex, standing alongside, leaned down and stroked his sister's hand.

"We'd better get going," Brandon muttered. "Maybe I can persuade Mr. Osborn to give me a ride to Savannah. Come on, Alex."

"No," Alex said faintly. "You go. I'll stay with Hannah."

"Go with him," the witch urged Alex in a gentle tone.

"No," said Alex determinedly. "I'm staying here."

But the witch regarded him sternly. "I have enough work to do without you getting in the way. Sukey and I will care for your sister. You go with Brandon."

Only when he was well along the road to Savannah with Brandon and Mr. Osborn did Alex wonder how on earth the witch knew that he and Hannah were brother and sister.

The three of them arrived late in Savannah, and spent an uncomfortable night at a crowded and filthy inn. Only in the morning did they discover that they had lodged right next door to an apothecary's shop.

Outside, the shop was advertised by a sign bearing the image of a mortar and pestle. Inside, it was very basic: A wooden counter ran the length of the room, and behind it, shelves reached to the ceiling. Each shelf held large glass bottles and white china jars. Although they came in various sizes, the jars otherwise matched each other. All were illustrated in pale blue wash, with leaves, flowers, fruit, and mysterious abbreviations and numbers.

As Brandon stood at the counter with Alex and Mr. Osborn, he became fascinated by the wooden drawers below the shelves, which bore mysterious labels such as *Caryophylla* and *Rad. Cal. Ar.* He wondered what strange concoctions lurked behind these exotic names.

Mr. Osborn cleared his throat loudly, and the apothecary came bustling into the shop from a back room. He was a thin and balding young man.

"May I be of assistance, sir?" he asked Mr. Osborn cheerfully in a Scottish accent.

For once, Mr. Osborn got straight to the point. "I am looking for a preparation of Jesuit's bark, to treat ague."

Brandon whispered to Alex, "Aren't we supposed to get chinchilla or whatever it's called?"

"Er, that's cinchona, Brandon," Alex whispered with a smile. "Same thing, I guess. I mean, the Jesuit's bark is the same thing. A chinchilla, on the other hand, is a small, furry animal."

"Just like a marmite," said Brandon, and both boys got the giggles. It was an old joke of theirs.

Meanwhile, the apothecary looked concerned. "Where is the patient?" he asked. "Have I visited him?"

A pharmacist who makes house calls? Brandon thought. Now he had heard it all.

"No, you have not seen her," said Mr. Osborn. "The girl is in St. Swithin's parish, some miles distant hence."

"Ah," said the apothecary with a knowing smile. "Then it is fortunate that you arrived today. Had you called upon me last week, I should, regretfully, have had to turn you away. The most recent shipment arrived last Tuesday, you see, and it was the first supply I have had in some months. It is exceedingly difficult to obtain cinchona bark."

He trotted into the back room and returned with a step ladder, which he climbed to reach the top shelf. Carefully lifting a jar in one hand, he returned to ground, and put it on the counter. He produced a small hand-held brass scale from under the counter, and placed a tiny, coin-sized weight on one side of it. On the other side, he placed a piece of paper, and uncorking the jar, removed a stick of the brown, crumbly bark, and carefully laid it on the scale. When he was satisfied that he had weighed it properly, he used the paper to tip the bark into a mortar, and began expertly crushing it with a pestle.

"So where did you learn to be an apothecary, sir?" Brandon asked, watching him work.

"I was educated in Edinburgh," said the apothecary. Mr. Osborn smiled, and opened his mouth to say something, but the apothecary continued, "Why do you ask? Do you think to make a living in my profession, lad?"

"I might," Brandon smiled, thinking of his work with another Mr. Gordon, the dentist who had employed him on an earlier adventure. "I'd like to know what all those names on your jars mean."

The apothecary laid down his pestle. "The s," he said, pointing to a jar overhead, "stands for syrupus, the English meaning for which is 'syrup,' while the u stands for unguentum, or ointment."

"So the jars are labeled in Latin?" Brandon said. "I thought so."

The apothecary gave him a smile. "You understand Latin? I did not take you for a gentleman, young sir."

"I'm not, I'm a servant," Brandon said, "and I don't really know Latin. But I am interested."

The apothecary clearly approved of his enthusiasm. "You are evidently keen. A pity you are already indentured to this gentleman here, for you would make a fine apprentice to me. Having said that, I should warn you that I am now one of three medical men in this town, and there is not sufficient business for all of us. I have thought to purchase myself land and a slave, not too far distant from Savannah, while the land is affordable, and make my living that way. Or, perhaps, I shall return to Scotland."

The apothecary made a cone-shaped package from a piece of paper, and poured the now-powdered bark into it. Handing the package to Mr. Osborn, he instructed, "In this moist weather, it is of particular importance that the patient be kept cool and dry. Make sure, also, that as she recovers, she takes exercise daily by walking to increase her strength. The sum, sir, is two shillings."

Mr. Osborn gave a sharp intake of breath at the price, but he fumbled in his leather coin purse and handed over two silver coins.

As they turned to leave, Brandon said to the apothecary, "Thanks, Mr . . . I'm sorry, sir, I don't know your name."

"Gordon," said the apothecary proudly. "Robert Gordon, at your service."

"Sir," stammered Brandon, "are you by any chance related to Mr. Robert Gordon of Kintyre plantation?"

The apothecary smiled. "No, my lad, I am not, at least not that I am aware. I have heard tell of the gentleman in question. There are many Robert Gordons from Scotland, of course."

"Of course," Brandon said, although this was news to him.

As soon as they were outside, Alex said, "What do you think it means, about him being called Mr. Gordon?"

"I don't know," Brandon said, climbing into the back of Mr. Osborn's wagon. "It probably means nothing." He whispered, so Mr. Osborn wouldn't hear, "But I sure like the Mr. Gordon in Savannah a lot more than I like the one in Snipes County."

"That wouldn't be hard," muttered Alex.

While she was awake, Hannah felt worse than she had ever felt in her entire life. The freezing cold and shivering had given way to a violent fever. Her body felt hot and clammy, and she had thrown up more times than she thought possible.

She was afraid of dying. Was her life going to end here, in the backwoods of Georgia in the middle of the eighteenth century? Was her time up so soon?

While Hannah tossed and turned, wept and whimpered, the witch seldom left her side. She had taken charge from Sukey, and she now watched her patient from a chair near the bed. Occasionally she squatted on a stool next to

Hannah, and softly wiped her forehead with a rag. While Hannah threw up, the witch put an arm around her shoulders and held a bowl under her mouth.

After six hours of high fever, Hannah started to revive. She struggled to sit up, but the witch gently pushed her back onto the bed. "You must rest," she chided.

"But I feel better," Hannah protested. "I mean, I'm still really weak, but the fever . . ."

"You have malaria," said the witch decisively. "And it will soon return. Until Brandon and your brother come with the medicine, you will continue to cycle in and out of chills and fevers."

Hannah felt a chill then, but not because of her illness. "Wait, how do you know Alex is my brother?" she asked in a small voice. "Who are you?" Once again, she was shaking, and this time, it was not because of the malaria.

The old woman looked at her appraisingly. Then she said, "Hannah, you don't know?"

Hannah stared at the old woman's face, and with a spasm of shock, she recognized her and gasped. "You can't be . . . ."

The old woman threw back her head and laughed. "Oh, but I am. Hannah, I'm the woman you knew as Professor Kate Harrower. Now, I think you and I had better talk, don't you?"

Hannah was too tired, too cold, and too sick to talk, but she still wanted to listen to the Professor's story. She struggled to concentrate on the old woman's words.

"I came here about fifteen years ago," said the Professor, settling back on her rickety rocking chair. "When I was in my late sixties. That's a long time after you and I first met. I never planned to be here, of course, and I had never found myself thrown so far back in time before. When Fred discovered me lying in the woods, I was delirious with malaria. He was a runaway slave, you see. He was born in Barbados, but after he was shipped to South Carolina, he ran off. He lived among the Cherokee for a short time. But then they decided to sell him as a slave. He got wind of their plans and ran off again. Naturally, he didn't trust other people for a long time after that, and he decided to hide out in the woods. That's when he built this place. But around the time he got tired of living like a hermit, he found me.

"He was afraid to take in a white woman, but I was different, you see. For one thing, I was dressed so strangely. I arrived in modern clothes, which had never happened to me before. He assumed from my strange dress that I was an outcast just like him, which I suppose I was.

"After a few years here, I realized that I would probably never return home. So I resigned myself to making a life here. It wasn't easy, you know. Not at all. But Fred and I got married. Or, rather, we married ourselves.

"When the local Indians got wind of our presence, I persuaded them that I was a healer. I know quite a bit about eighteenth-century herbal medicine, what works and what doesn't. And of course, I have a little bit of modern medical know-how.

"So the Indians have protected us, and Mr. MacKenzie befriended us. He's a bit of an outsider himself. When slaves started to arrive here a couple of years ago, they also heard about us and started consulting with me, so they protect us, too. Everyone pays me with food. A bit of chicken or corn makes a nice supplement to what Fred is able to hunt and fish. But now more and more settlers are coming from Savannah, now that slavery is legal in Georgia. I'm afraid we'll have to move on. Slaveowners are very much afraid of people like us, people who live free in the woods. They consider us troublemakers."

Hannah struggled to take in what she was hearing. Her brain felt as though it were in a fog. "I don't understand," she moaned, "If you're the Professor, why do you look so old?"

"Oh, because I *am* old," the professor said patiently. "I'm much older than I was when you knew me. I'm eighty-four years old, Hannah. You last saw me when I was in my fifties." Suddenly, her eyes grew wide. "Hannah, the 'me' that you know, is she here? Is she with you? Have you seen her?"

Hannah struggled to think through the brain fog. There was something about what the Professor had said that didn't make sense. She tried to concentrate. And then it came to her.

"Don't you know if she's here?" she asked the Professor. "You're saying you're the same person, yes? So wouldn't you remember if you had been here before?"

The old woman smiled. "Yes and no," she said. "Yes, I am the same person, but no, I don't recall having been here before. I don't claim to understand this, so I'm not sure I can explain . . . .

"Look, each of us is faced with a series of possibilities every single day. And you will recall that things don't always happen as we expect. It is a peculiar life we lead, traveling in time. Nothing is inevitable for us. At least, I don't think it is. Except perhaps," and here she gave a wry chuckle, "that the child is always father to the man, as the saying goes."

Hannah was completely confused. But one thing she did know. "You aren't with us," she said. "You kind of disappeared. And there was this skeleton in Snipesville . . . . Alex and Brandon dug it up, and it was wearing a ring . . . . It's the same ring that Jane's wearing now."

"How very odd," said the Professor, frowning. "I have no recollection of that happening. I wonder why?"

Hannah continued. "But when we came back from 1851, you returned with us to the twenty-first century. Was that the last time you remember seeing us?"

The Professor crinkled her brow. "So you discovered the skeleton after you returned from 1851?"

Hannah nodded.

"I suppose I must have come with you again after that," said the Professor. But then she grew thoughtful. "Hmm . . . oh, I see. Yes . . ." she said to herself. But she did not explain.

Hannah groaned. She was hopelessly befuddled by the conversation, but she no longer cared. "I'm too sick to talk now," she whispered. "My head hurts so bad, and I think I'm gonna puke again."

When Hannah next awoke, she found herself lying on a bed. She was in a place she recognized, a palatial wood-panelled room in Chatsfield Hall in Hertfordshire, England, in the mid-nineteenth century. Trying to sit up, she found she couldn't move a muscle. How had she got here?

She tried to call her brother's name, but to her horror, she couldn't move her lips. She fought the panic rising in her, and took a couple of deep breaths. At least she could still breathe. She looked up at the wood paneling, and hesitantly tried to move the fingers of her left hand. When they responded, she reached up and touched the wall, running her fingers down the smooth surface. It was real. This was no dream. She studied the furniture and drapes, which certainly looked solid. But slowly, a patch of fog began to appear in the middle of the room, and she vaguely wondered what it could be. The fog began to take shape. It was her father.

"Where have you been?" he demanded.

Hannah tried to answer, but she couldn't.

"I've been looking for you everywhere!" he yelled. His voice sounded wet, that was the only word for it. Perhaps, Hannah thought vaguely, that was because he was made of fog.

Now another foggy figure started to shimmer into shape next to him, this time a woman, and her voice joined that of Hannah's father. "Hannah Day, I have had quite enough of your nonsense. For once, would you do as you are told?"

It was Mrs. Devenish from 1940 . . . . Didn't she know how strange this was? Didn't it bother her that she was in 1851?

"I've been looking for you everywhere!" her father shouted, again and again, while Mrs. Devenish said, over and over, "For once, would you do as you are told?"

Are you ghosts? Hannah thought desperately, as she tried to speak. *What are you?*

Now there was a third apparition. Hannah couldn't recognize it, and she struggled to hear what it was saying over the voices of her father and Mrs. Devenish.

And then, with a chill, she heard a familiar voice. It said, "I just can't deal with you anymore. I have to go."

It was her mother. Hannah tried to put her hands over her ears, tried to scream, but she could no longer move at all. The voices grew louder. She whimpered in fear.

Then Hannah felt a woman's hand gently lifting her head into her lap and stroking her hair, while murmuring to her in a soothing voice that gradually drowned out the voices. She felt the fear vanishing, and at the same time, the smooth wooden paneling and grand furniture of Chatsworth Hall vanished, and she was looking at the rough log walls and homemade chairs of an eighteenth-century cabin. At first, Hannah thought that it was Mrs. Devenish who had come to her rescue. But when she looked up, she saw the face of the Professor.

That evening, Brandon and Alex delivered the medicine. They were shocked to find Hannah writhing on the bed, bathed in sweat, and muttering incoherently. The witch was mopping Hannah's forehead with a damp rag.

Brandon handed over the small packet to the witch.

"Will this stuff really help?" Alex asked anxiously.

She tore open the top, and examined the contents. "Yes, this should help. The poor girl is delirious, although that's normal, I'm afraid. Here, help me make a decoction. Could you fetch me that dipper over there?"

Alex grabbed the gourd dipper and handed it to the old woman, who dipped it carefully into the steaming cauldron of water bubbling over the fire.

Carefully she took a small clay pot and set it on the ground, where she filled it half full of hot water. She tipped a little of the powdered bark into the jar. Finally, picking up a small bundle of twigs tied with wiregrass and pinestraw, she whisked the mixture together. "Oh, this stuff never blends well," she sighed, giving the water one last stir. "And I had best let it cool a little before I give any to Hannah. Thank you for bringing it, boys. You had better go home now."

As Alex and Brandon stepped outside, she took up the jar of medicine she had made, then lowered herself down onto the stool next to Hannah, who was moaning softly.

Lifting her patient's head, she held the cup to her lips. "Come on, Hannah, drink this. It will help what ails you."

Hannah sipped at the drink, and made an anguished face. "It's disgusting," she croaked. "It's bitter! I can't drink it, I'll puke."

"You must, dear," said the witch soothingly. "It is the only thing that will work."

"It's poison," Hannah groaned. "You're trying to kill me."

"No, I'm not," the witch said firmly. "Don't be stupid. Of course I'm not trying to kill you. This is medicine. Now drink."

Hannah pinched her nose and drank it down, ending with a grimace and a shudder. Then she smacked her lips together a couple of times, turned over, and fell asleep.

When Hannah awoke once more, the orange light from the window told her it was evening. The pain in her head had vanished, and so had her fever. She still felt very weak, but no longer did she think she was dying. The old woman was stirring something on the stove, but she glanced over at Hannah and saw that she was conscious.

"Feeling better?" she asked cheerfully.

"Yes," Hannah croaked. "Thanks."

The witch nodded, satisfied.

Hannah lay back on her pillow, feeling exhausted but happy. She would live. She wasn't going to die today.

And she had questions. Quietly, she asked, "So why don't you call yourself Kate Harrower anymore?"

"I don't know your meaning," the witch said. "What nonsense is this?"

So, Hannah thought, her fevered brain had tricked her into hallucinating that the witch was really the Professor. She had imagined their conversation.

Just then, Jane rushed up to her.

"'ow do you fare, 'annah?" she said excitedly. "You look much better. I've been out 'unting with Fred. 'Ee caught a deer, and we're outside butchering it. 'Ee's cutting strips of meat off the carcass and drying them on the fire. 'Ee says it tastes good, and it does smell very fine, but I don't . . ."

Hannah held up a hand to silence her. "Not now, Jane. I gotta sleep. I do feel better, but I've had a rough day."

Hannah looked past Jane, and saw the witch watching her keenly.

"Yes, I know you 'ave," Jane said impatiently, "And I am well pleased to see you come to your senses. But I must tell you something. Brandon told me that Mr. Osborn will come to fetch me on Friday night. 'Ee's taking me with 'im, 'annah. 'Ee's taking me to England! And just to be safe, so we don't stir up suspicion, I'm to leave something behind. I want you to 'ave it. But keep it well 'idden, just in case Mr. Gordon comes a-calling, yes?"

She held up the ring.

Hannah took it with trembling fingers, and then, with all her remaining strength, hurled it across the room.

"Why won't it leave me alone?" she cried, to Jane's amazement.

The old woman murmured, almost to herself, "Sir Isaac Newton said that every object in the universe attracts every other object. But I don't know that he understood how particular the attraction could be."

With that, she put down her stirring stick, bent down, and plucked the ring from the dirt floor. Then she slipped it onto her own finger.

Chapter 13:
GOING QUIETLY

"How do you feel now, Hannah?" the witch asked quietly, as she wove pine straw, her wrinkled old fingers working nimbly on a half-finished small basket. Hannah had been napping again. She awoke to the sounds of Sukey's gentle snores from the loft.

"Better," said Hannah weakly. "Kinda tired, but not sick."

The witch nodded, satisfied. "Good, I am glad to hear of it."

"I had some really weird dreams while I was sick," Hannah said. "More like hallucinations, I guess. I know I wasn't asleep, and even now it seems so real, what I saw, much more than dreams."

"That is usual with ague," the old woman said, tugging on a thin brown sliver of pine straw. "What kinds of dreams had you?"

Hannah laughed self-consciously. "I thought I was in a mansion in England, and the walls were made of wood panels. And my mom showed up, which was very weird, because she's dead. But the most bizarre thing was that you told me you were really this woman I know, the Professor."

Without looking up from her work, the witch said, "Oh, but that did happen. I am the Professor."

Hannah gasped. "It is you. Why did you act like it never happened? I thought I was going crazy."

The Professor smiled. "I didn't want to say anything in front of Jane. It would have confused her. But we're alone now."

Hannah wanted to get mad, but she was too tired, and it was just too hard to be angry at a sweet-looking old lady who had just cured her of malaria.

"Have some more to drink," said the Professor, lifting Hannah's head from the pillow, and holding a cup of water to her lips. Hannah sipped from it.

When she was done, she wiped her mouth with the back of her hand. Then she asked the question to which she most dreaded the answer. "Are we stuck in the past too, just like you? Me and the boys?"

"No, I don't think so," said the Professor thoughtfully. "And no matter what, I will look after you, I promise."

For the first time, Hannah didn't feel like saying something sarcastic. The Professor was a victim of the time travel, perhaps as much as she was. Hannah now understood.

"Thanks," she said quietly, and then she began to cry.

The Professor handed her a clean rag, and gently patted Hannah's arm as she wept.

"I do understand, my dear," she said soothingly. "More than you can possibly imagine. You have been through so much in such a short life, and I think you have done very well. I am very proud of you."

"I wish my mom had said that," Hannah said suddenly, sniffing. "But she never did. It was like she didn't get me at all. And then . . .What happened, happened. She left us. And then she died. I tried to be good, I really did . . . ." She dissolved into tears again.

"I know," the Professor said emphatically. "I know you did. But there was nothing you could do, Hannah, because it wasn't about you. Really, it wasn't. She was so busy worrying about your 'issues,' but her problems were so much greater than yours. And I must tell you that you are so much stronger than she was."

"But how can you know that?" Hannah asked in puzzlement. "I mean, that's the kind of thing my Grandma tells me to make me feel better, but she was my mom's mom. You never even met my mom."

"Oh, yes I did," the Professor said. "I can't say how, but I did. She was angry at the world, Hannah, not at you. You were just a convenient target for all her frustration. You are not her, and you won't be her, either, not if you play your cards right. Listen to my advice, Hannah. I have found that one of the great compensations of old age is that it can indeed give wisdom. And what your grandma and I are saying is wise. Listen to us old ladies. You have always been tougher and braver than your mother was. And this may surprise you, you are also a kinder person than she was. Your kindness has been deeply buried within you, but it is there. Don't be afraid to love people, Hannah. You are loved, even by people who are under no obligation to love you, people like Verity and Mrs. D., and even Mrs. Gordon. She was very fond of you, although she never really showed it."

Hannah didn't know what to say. But the old woman was looking at her intently, and with love of her own. Hannah had never felt so loved as she did at this moment, and she wanted so much to hug the old woman, but she was too weak, and so she contented herself with smiling back.

Suddenly, she had another moment of revelation. "You know me in my future, too, don't you?" she asked. "How does my life turn out?"

"How very astute of you to guess that," said the old woman wryly. "We do come to know each other very well indeed. And unless the future changes, which I warn you it can, you will have a wonderful life. But more than that, I cannot say."

Hannah thought about begging her for information, but something determined in the Professor's face steered her away from the subject.

"I like you more now you're old," Hannah said brightly.

The Professor chuckled at her tactlessness. "I suppose that is a compliment of sorts. I imagine I have mellowed somewhat. But I am sorry to say that the best part of my old age is behind me. I find it harder than once I did to remember things. My body aches, and I think I have cancer, and there is nothing in my bag of tricks or the apothecary's shop that will fix that. I no longer hold out hope that I will return to my own time, but Fred will take care of me while he still lives. I have had a great life, and I really can't feel sorry for myself."

Hannah looked around the room, seeing only Sukey, who was napping in a corner. "Hey, where's Jane got to?" she said.

The Professor laid down her basket, and took Hannah's hand. "I am sorry, dear. I should have told you straightaway. Brandon came to collect her while you were asleep. He has taken her to hide in Mr. Osborn's house, because they are leaving tonight. She told me to say farewell to you. She is your friend, and she is as fond of you as you are of her."

Hannah's mouth turned down, and the Professor patted her hand.

A knock at the door startled them both. But the face that appeared in the doorway in the fading evening light was friendly and familiar. It was Mr. MacKenzie. For once, he looked very serious.

"Good day to you, Annie," he said. "I have come for Sukey."

Hearing Mr. MacKenzie's voice, Sukey came downstairs, her hair disheveled from her nap.

"Come, lass, we must be gone from here," said Mr. MacKenzie, extending a hand to her. He turned to the Professor. "Annie, you and Fred must leave this place. I have known Robert Gordon for many a year, and that man is dangerous, I tell you. Lord knows, I am risking my life to help Sukey. I will hide her at my house until I can decide what must be done next."

The Professor nodded. "We will depart as soon as we can, but, as you see, Hannah is still too sick to travel through the woods. Thank you for your advice, Murdo, and for your help. You're a good man. God speed."

Just then, Fred popped his head around the door. "Annie, will you mind if I go with Murdo to fetch supplies? Will you be all right?"

"I'll manage," said the Professor, with a dismissive wave. "Take care, though, and hurry back."

"Don't worry, I will," Fred said. "I can pretend as usual to be Murdo's slave, and then we may both vouch for Sukey if anyone comes asking."

Sukey bade Hannah and the Professor a warm farewell, and then slipped out behind Mr. MacKenzie and Fred.

As soon as they were all gone, Hannah turned to the Professor. "How can you trust MacKenzie? He's white. He owns slaves, right?"

"We know him well," said the Professor calmly. "And he knows us. Mr. MacKenzie has had a hard life, and he is one of the rare white people here who have turned their own misery into kindness and compassion, rather than into greed and violence and selfishness. There's something else: He owns a slave, yes, but he doesn't depend on slavery for his livelihood, which makes it less tempting for him to treat his slave John as less than human. He has built a relationship with John, one that is not entirely about exploitation. Don't get me wrong: Slavery is slavery. Mr. MacKenzie holds unimaginable power over John, and of course John would rather be free than belong to another man. But his situation is better than most. Slavery is never a good thing, but people's experience of it is not always the same everywhere.

"Now," she said to Hannah, who was thinking grimly to herself that the Professor still knew in her old age how to deliver a long and pointless lecture, "Would you like a cup of tea?"

Mr. Osborn slapped the side of the last box after he loaded it onto the back of the wagon. "This miserable and paltry collection is all my worldly goods," he said ruefully. But then he smiled. "I confess, though, that I am also returning with a shipment of Carolina rice I bought with the proceeds from selling my animals. I hope to make a small profit."

Brandon said sadly, "I hope you do. Thanks for all your help, Mr. Osborn." He had come to like and respect his master. For all Mr. Osborn's puffed-up pronouncements of self-importance, he was a decent man.

Mr. Osborn put a hand on Brandon's arm, looked him in the eye, and asked him, "Are you quite sure you will not return with me to England?"

"Quite sure," Brandon said firmly. "Somebody has to look after Cato. And it was really generous of you to sign him over to me."

Alex gave a wan smile. He wasn't sure how he felt about being Brandon's slave, even if it was just for appearance's sake.

"I could not, in all good conscience, sell Cato to another master," Mr. Osborn said stiffly. "Knowing as I do from whence you both claim that you hail. And after witnessing the effects of slavery on white men, I can no longer condone it. It corrupts the souls of the slaveowners."

"And it's brutal to black people," Brandon said quietly. "Yes, well, even so, I know what a huge sacrifice you're making for all of us. You're a true servant of the Lord, Mr. Osborn."

Mr. Osborn inclined his head toward Brandon, and then shook his hand. "And you, sir, are a true Christian, and a true gentleman. Pray God, we shall meet again, and under better circumstances."

He squeezed Alex's shoulder, and then climbed up on the wagon, next to Jane. "I must make haste to Savannah," he cried, "for our ship departs early on the morn. Farewell, Brandon and Cato! God be with you!"

"And also with you!" Brandon called, his voice catching in his throat, as the horse jangled to a start. Jane and Alex waved frantically to each other until the wagon was out of sight.

"Do you think they'll be okay?" Alex asked Brandon.

"We can look it up when we get home," Brandon said, still fighting tears. "See if we can find out about them in a history book or something."

Alex bit his lip. "So do you think we will get home? Without the Professor?"

Brandon paused. Will we? he wondered. "I don't know. Let's head back to the witch's house. We have to see how Hannah's doing, and figure out our next move."

Stepping into the little cabin in the woods, they found Hannah taking tea with the witch. Proudly, she said, "Guys, I want you to meet someone."

Alex and Brandon were puzzled. There was nobody in the room they didn't recognize.

Hannah smiled at their confusion. "Alex? Brandon?" she said, "Meet the Professor."

They stared at Hannah for what felt like forever, until first Alex and then Brandon turned to look at the Professor, who was smiling broadly.

"Oh, awesome! It's you! It's really you!" Alex cried out, leaning down and throwing his arms around the old woman. But Brandon held back. Alarmed, he had noticed that the Professor was wearing the fatal ring.

With one arm around Alex, the Professor clutched at her heart with the other hand, in mock exhaustion. "My goodness, all this excitement has quite worn me out," she said. "Now, Fred doesn't know who I really am, and it would just confuse him if you said anything, so don't, all right? Oh, and by the way, I don't expect him back for some time. He has gone upriver with Sukey and Mr. MacKenzie, so I'm glad you boys are here. Now, let us talk. I am sure you have questions."

Alex piped up, "Why are you so old?" Brandon cringed at his lack of tact, but the Professor laughed happily.

"Because I am old," she said. "I shall be eighty-five next birthday, best as I can remember. I haven't suddenly aged, dear. It's just that I am a time traveler, and I arrived here many years after you first met me. Does that explain?"

Alex nodded, although he was still confused. "Is Sukey going to be okay?" he asked forlornly. He was sad that she hadn't asked him to go with her, even though he knew that going with her would have been very dangerous.

The Professor gave him a wistful look. "Alas, I have no idea. She disappears from the records, you see."

Alex looked crestfallen, but Hannah perked up. "So you do finally leave here! Otherwise, you wouldn't know that, would you?"

The Professor smiled at Hannah briefly and ignored her question. She returned her attention to Alex. "It's not a surprise that there's no record of her. Most people in this period vanish from history. Perhaps, if you are lucky, you or I will one day find mention of Sukey in an archive. But I wouldn't hold my breath if I were you."

Alex looked away, sadder than ever.

Brandon asked, "What about Mr. Osborn?"

" . . .and Jane?" added Hannah.

The Professor leaned back and began tapping the arm of her chair. "Let me see . . . . Well, they made the voyage safely. When they landed in London, nobody knew that Jane was a returning criminal. Thanks to Hannah, she had not been branded on the thumb, as many criminals were in the eighteenth century. If she had the brand, her return might have raised awkward questions. Mr. and Mrs. Jenkins must have recognized her as their daughter, for she returned to live with them. She . . ."

Here Hannah interrupted. "But did she get along with them? I mean, I love Jane, but she's, like, a street urchin. Did she start stealing again when she got back?"

"Not so far as I know," the Professor said. "Her story seems to have ended happily enough. She . . ."

It was Brandon's turn to interrupt. "But what happened to Mr. Osborn? Did he take her to Balesworth?"

"I assume so," the Professor said. "But listen, Brandon, because I will tell you something very interesting."

She shifted slightly in her chair, smoothing out her skirt. "The Bishop of London kept an excellent archive," she said. "We do know from those records that Mr. Osborn failed to convince the Bishop to appoint him to a new living as a rector. Like most young Church of England ministers at this time, he had very few job opportunities, and I don't suppose it helped that Mr. Jones and Mr. Gordon wrote some very nasty letters about him to the Bishop. But the Bishop was getting wise to the complaints of Americans by this time, and so he ignored them, and offered Mr. Osborn a curacy in Yorkshire. However, Mr. Osborn turned it down."

"Why?" gasped Hannah.

"Ah," said the Professor, waving her index finger. "You need to know that to a man like Mr. Osborn, from the south of England in the eighteenth century, moving to Yorkshire was like moving to North Dakota would be for most of us. It wasn't very appealing. He had had enough of living in the back of beyond, but he took a terrible risk in refusing the Bishop's offer. He might never have found another job in the Church.

"Fortunately, after leaving London I suppose, he stopped in to see the rector at St. Swithin's in Balesworth. Now, it turns out, the rector despised the curate who had replaced Mr. Osborn, and so when Mr. Osborn returned, he got offered his old job.

"I imagine Mr. Osborn was a little nervous about explaining to Balesworth people why he had returned with Jane and without Hannah, but perhaps he didn't deliver Jane in person. Perhaps Jane had made her own way home from London while Mr. Osborn was discussing his case with the Bishop of London? Or perhaps he used the excuse of mistaken identity that you suggested to him, Brandon? Who knows, because he never wrote about it, so far as we know. And neither the magistrates nor Mr. and Mrs. Jenkins left behind any letters or diaries."

All those lives, Hannah thought, disappearing without trace. It was heartbreaking.

Brandon was thinking about Mr. Osborn, and his crushed dreams and ruined life. His wife dead, his career destroyed. It was so unfair.

"I've been saving the good news for last," the Professor said cheerfully. "Jane seems to have been welcomed back into the family. But by the time she turned eighteen, her father had died, and I imagine her widowed mother was getting older, and finding it hard to run the inn alone. So Jane married the widowed curate, Mr. Osborn, and he gave up holy orders to become the innkeeper of the Balesworth Arms."

Hannah looked more excited than she had since her illness began. "But that means . . . Mr. Osborn was one of Mrs. Devenish's ancestors, too! And the couple in the portrait Verity found, it's them! It's Mr. Osborn, Jane, and Mrs. Jenkins!"

The Professor nodded. "Jane and Mr. Osborn produced a very interesting family," she said. "It has been a long time since I researched this, but I seem to remember that among their descendants were quite a few clergymen and teachers, all the way to the present day. The family also included a famous Victorian poet called Joshua Palmer-Osborn, and several actors. In fact, one of their multiple-great-grandsons in the early twenty-first century is a very famous actor. Let me see . . . . What was his name now?" She paused, thinking.

"Harry Osborn?" suggested Hannah excitedly.

"Yes, that's it!" exclaimed the Professor, pointing a finger at her. "Well done, Hannah!"

"Oh, he is so cute!" Hannah gushed. "I've got a poster of him up in my room. He's adorable."

The two boys made fingers down throat gestures to each other.

"What?" Hannah snapped, glaring at them both. "What's your problem?"

"Makes sense that all these actors are descended from Jane," Brandon muttered. "She's a total drama queen."

"Now, as for Mr. Gordon," said the Professor, folding her hands in her lap. "I expect you want to know about him, too."

There was a silence. Nobody really cared much what happened to Mr. Gordon.

"Mr. Robert Gordon," the Professor said with a mischievous twinkle in her eyes, "closed his apothecary shop and sold off everything he could, including his house . . . ."

It took a moment to sink in. "Oh, that Mr. Gordon!" cried Brandon.

"Wait, are you saying there are two Mr. Robert Gordons?" said Hannah in disbelief.

"Yeah," said Brandon, "I couldn't tell you because you were sick, but the pharmacist who gave us the meds for your malaria had the same name as your Mr. Gordon, the planter."

"No way," exclaimed Hannah.

"AND," the Professor continued in a loud voice over the kids' chattering, "That Mr. Gordon, the apothecary, bought Kintyre Plantation from your Mr. Robert Gordon. Your Mr. Gordon made very little money from the sale, because land here at this time is pretty cheap. But he returned to South Carolina, where he finished his house in Charleston, married again to another young woman, and became a fabulously wealthy gentleman of the city. His house is open to the public if you care to visit, so you can see exactly how filthy rich he got from slavery."

"That stinks," Alex said, wrinkling his nose.

Brandon was speechless. He looked disgusted.

"Believe me," said the Professor gently, "I share your feelings. But history is seldom nice or fair, my dears. And when we try to pretend that it is, we lie to ourselves."

"What about nice Mr. Gordon from the apothecary shop, then?" Brandon asked. "He seems like a good guy."

The Professor said slowly, "Well . . . Of course, he must have soon discovered that he had bought some pretty lousy real estate. I understand that he gave up his apothecary shop to raise cattle there, and that he scraped out a small living. He couldn't afford slaves. But his great-grandson began raising cotton at Kintyre in the late eighteenth century, soon after the cotton gin was developed. He plowed all his profits back into buying slaves and land. By 1820, the great-grandson also bought what was once Mr. Jones's land, and he cleared the trees all the way to the foot of the hill on which Snipesville was built, so he could grow more cotton. And then it was his grandson who, in 1851 . . ."

" . . . gambled away the plantation in a poker game," Alex concluded for her.

"In a nutshell," said the Professor, grinning.

"But I don't get this," Brandon said slowly. "You're the Professor from a later point in your life, right? And if you've been stuck here, as you claim, how could you have found out about all these people?"

The Professor looked at him, serious now, and said, "I know all about them because you told me."

The kids stared at her.

"Okay," Hannah said gravely, "You finally lost your marbles."

"Less of your cheek, young lady," warned the old woman. "I'm absolutely serious. When you get home, you must tell me—the other me—what I just said, and she—that is, I– will help you look it all up. I can tell you where to start: The family papers of the apothecary Mr. Robert Gordon are in the Savannah Historical Society archive."

"But how will we find the rest?" Brandon asked, perplexed.

The Professor replied impatiently, "I told you, I will help. Just tell me . . . That is, the 'me' you know in the future, and I will help you. And then she—that is, I—will know."

"So do we get to go home?" Alex asked. "Man, this is making my brain hurt."

"Yes, you do go home," said the Professor.

"When?" said Hannah eagerly.

The Professor smiled, "Ahh, you see, I know the answer to that question because you told me that, too."

"But how can we tell you something that hasn't happened yet?" said Alex in a confused whine.

"A very good question," said the Professor, getting stiffly to her feet. "That's one of many mind-blowing questions about time travel."

She gazed at the ring on her finger. "I think it looks rather good on me, kids, don't you?" There was a stunned silence.

"No," cried Hannah suddenly. "Don't keep wearing it, please. Don't you get it? It means that you're the dead woman in the grave. It's you."

The Professor gave her arm a gentle squeeze. "Don't concern yourself so, Hannah. I told you, I'm eighty-four years old. What makes you think that I'm not ready for death? Death has no fear for me now. As I told you, I probably have cancer, and in any case, I am ready. I admit, I should like to have seen my . . ." She stopped herself, as though she thought she had already said too much. "But no, there's no sense in wishing. I am content. I am tired. And I have had an astonishing life. It is time."

She smiled at Hannah. Hannah jumped up, threw her arms around the Professor, and began to sob. "Thank you f-for looking after me," she managed to say.

The Professor patted her back with one crooked and wrinkled hand. When Hannah broke away from her, she took Hannah's hand, and looked into her eyes. "Be brave, Hannah. I'm almost finished here, but there is so much required of you yet. You must be up to the task. And you will be."

Hannah's heart sank. She had thought they were about to go home, but obviously that was not to be. What else was left for them to do?

"Why can't we go home now?" Hannah asked desperately.

But the Professor didn't answer.

"Come outside with me, all of you," she said with a sigh, leading the way to the clearing outside the house.

Looking upward, she said, "What a beautiful sky," almost as though she were saying a line in a play.

Tilting their heads back, the kids gazed through the tops of the pine trees at the pink evening Georgia sunset, where light, puffy trails of clouds fell one upon another, layer after layer.

"Now," said the Professor, "I need you to leave here. Things are very dangerous, I'm afraid."

"But how will we get home without you?" Alex asked, his lip trembling.

"I don't know," said the Professor. "Honestly, I just don't. But you will, I do know that much. Now, be gone with you, and good luck."

With that she abruptly returned to the house, and closed the door.

"That's it?" Hannah said, on the verge of tears. "We just have to take off?"

"I guess," Brandon said uncertainly. He felt like crying himself. "Where do we go? Who will we go to? Mr. Gordon?"

"No!" Hannah spat. The boys shrank back from her, and she struggled not to panic. "Okay, I know where we can go. Let's follow Sukey to Mr. MacKenzie's. He's nice. Maybe he can shelter us until we figure out what to do next."

"But I'm black," Alex said, crying now. "He'll know I'm a runaway. He won't want anything to do with me, or he'll sell me to the Indians."

"No, he won't," said Hannah, although she really wasn't sure. "He'll help . . . ."

And then she heard the sounds of approaching men on horseback.

"Quick," she whispered. "We gotta hide. There's no time to run." She pointed to the thick undergrowth in which they had hidden when they first found the hut in the woods, and the three of them hurried toward it.

The two men chatted nervously as they rode side-by-side along the trail through the woods. "I suppose she is herself a runaway slave," said Mr. Gordon, pistols hanging from his side.

"That's not what I've heard," replied Mr. Jones, shifting his hands on the reins. "Didn't you know? The slaves tell me she is a white woman."

Mr. Gordon looked askance at his companion. "Good Lord. Are you sure?"

For a moment, he seemed lost for words. But then he seemed to gather his wits. "Regardless, she has cost me my slave and my servants, and she is a disruptive and dangerous presence. It is our duty as vestrymen and magistrates to suppress her."

"By which you mean . . . ?" Mr. Jones said anxiously.

"I think you know what I mean," Mr. Gordon growled from between gritted teeth. "For God's sake, man, who will miss her? But we must never mention this again, do you understand me? Dealing with her is a matter for the law, but you and I are the law in St. Swithin's Parish. There are others, of course, who may not understand the difficult position we occupy. We are engaged in a war for our very survival."

Mr. Jones gulped and nodded.

As the kids watched from their hiding place, the two men dismounted and tied their horses to trees at the trail's edge. They walked silently through the woods the rest of the way to the hut.

Hannah looked at Brandon, raising her eyebrows in a question: What are they going to do? Brandon shrugged, and grimaced.

"There is the place," whispered Mr. Jones, staring at the tiny house through the trees.

"Follow me," whispered Mr. Gordon, as he led the way to the front of the hut, pulling out both of his pistols and cocking them. The guns clicked sharply.

As Mr. Jones kept a safe distance behind him, Mr. Gordon stepped forward, lifted his right leg, and kicked the door open.

Cautiously, he entered the darkened hut, calling out, "Reveal yourselves."

"Only me," said the Professor calmly. She was sitting in her accustomed rocking chair by the smoldering fireplace. "But I expect it's me you've come for. I wondered when you would get here."

Without a word, Mr. Gordon stepped forward, raised a pistol, and fired.

Alex jumped up to scream, and Hannah slapped a hand over his mouth just in time. Her heart was pounding, and her breathing quickened. Brandon's knees gave way, and he slumped to the ground, his head in his hands.

Hannah watched in horror from the undergrowth as Mr. Gordon brought a flaming stick from the house, and tossed it in the front door as he left, closing the door behind him. In silent agony, she watched as the two men waited for smoke to seep from the unglazed windows. When it did, they ran back to their horses, still unaware of the kids' presence.

As soon as the men had galloped off, the kids ran to the house. Hannah threw herself at the door. It opened, but she was driven back by the thick smoke.

"Don't go in," screamed Brandon, dragging her away from the hut. "It's too dangerous. She's already dead, Hannah. If you go in there, you won't make it out."

Hannah threw herself on the ground, and pounded her fists in the dirt in frustration. Alex fell to his knees beside her, and threw his arm around her as he cried helplessly. Brandon wept quietly, his hand cupped around his mouth in shock.

Suddenly, Fred emerged from the woods at a run. Before the kids could stop him, he dashed into the house, pulling his shirt up over his nose and mouth as he did so, and immediately dropped to his knees to crawl through the cleaner air near the floor.

Seconds later, he staggered outside with the Professor in his arms, and after he made it a safe distance, he gently laid her on the forest floor. Her face was covered in soot from the smoke. Worse, a huge blot of blood seeped through the cloth of her shortgown.

Lying on the ground with her head nestled in Fred's lap, the Professor opened her eyes. "A pity eighteenth-century guns never quite shoot straight," she murmured. "I think he was aiming for my head, but he seems to have got me in the chest instead."

Hannah, Brandon, and Alex sobbed, clinging to each other, and tears flowed down Fred's cheeks, but the Professor smiled. "Don't cry on my account, kids. Fred, take care of yourself, darling. And thank you for looking after me."

Still smiling gently, she closed her eyes, and was gone.

The kids looked up. They were in the park in Snipesville.

They were home. And Fred and the Professor were nowhere to be seen.

When Hannah, Brandon, and Alex vanished before his eyes, Fred was frightened. He knew that there were spirits in the woods, of course, but he would never have guessed that the two young white servants and the slave boy were among them. He had little time to waste worrying about it, though, for the thick smoke was rising in a steady column above the trees, and would surely draw attention. Fortunately, it would not take long to bury his dear wife. The loamy soil in the woods was easily shifted.

Fred used his old shovel to dig the grave as fast as he could. It wasn't very deep, but he hoped it was deep enough that animals would not disturb her. When he was done, he laid the Professor's body in the hole. He quickly covered her with pine straw and sandy soil, trying not to look at her face, and then pulled out his flask from his pocket. Sobbing helplessly, he poured the last of his whiskey onto the grave, and silently commended the woman he knew as Annie to the spirits of her ancestors.

Moments later, with one last grieving look at his wife's resting place, he stole away toward the river bank, where his canoe was hidden, and toward his next life, wherever fortune would lead him.

The boys hugged, tears still wet on their faces, but their grief was now mixed with joy at being home.

"You're white!" Brandon said, pointing to Alex.

"You're black again!" Alex said, jabbing a finger in Brandon's chest.

There was an awkward silence. "We better get home," Alex said in a subdued voice. "It's getting dark."

Hannah was still sitting on the ground, and her brother looked at her with concern. "You okay, sis?"

"Yes, I think so," she said, rubbing her head. "Coming back just made me a little dizzy, that's all. But I feel better than I did. Now it's like I never had malaria."

"The usual, then," said Brandon. "Whatever happens to our bodies in the past, stays in the past. I hate it, because I get really fit and healthy with all that work, and then when I get home, my gut comes back. But it's just as well you didn't come back with malaria. I have no idea how we would have explained that."

Still, Hannah didn't move. "Give me a second, guys," she said in a subdued voice. "I'm not ready to go home yet."

Nobody wanted to talk about what had happened to the Professor.

Brandon crouched down next to Hannah. "Do you think you have what they call shock? Are you sure you're okay?"

Hannah said nothing, but continued to stare at what once had been the clearing around the Professor's house in the woods. The area was cordoned off with police tape, and two archeology students were still poking around with trowels.

Without a word, the boys sat down next to Hannah and waited for her, watching the pink sky on layered clouds of a Georgia sunset.

Across the street, a police car pulled to a stop. The young cop gave the kids a long hard look, and opened his door.

"Where have you been?" Mr. Dias yelled. Alex had never seen his father so angry. "I don't see the point in giving you guys cell phones if you don't use them. I had to call the police to go look for you. I had to skip an important meeting. My boss isn't happy, and neither am I."

Unlike her brother, Hannah wasn't concerned or nervous. She didn't really care. His anger seemed so small, so unimportant after all that she had been through. That was why she remained strangely calm as she stood in the living room, listening to her father's rant.

Finally, he lapsed into silence.

"You'd never believe me," Hannah said quietly, "so there's no point in telling you, Dad. But it wasn't our fault."

Mr. Dias looked worried now. "So what's going on?" he said. "Are you guys all right?"

"Yeah, we're okay," Alex said wearily. "Just tired. It's been a long time."

Mr. Dias's face grew furious again. "A long time? I don't know what you guys are talking about," he snapped. "Go to your rooms."

"I am really hungry," Alex said plaintively.

"Whatever," said Mr. Dias. "I gotta go back to the office. Make yourself sandwiches."

"Fine with me," muttered Alex.

"What was that?" said Mr. Dias suspiciously, looking at his son.

"Nothing," Alex said sullenly, turning away from his father.

Brandon's mom was not pleased. Not pleased at all.

"How could you just vanish like that?" she demanded, wagging a finger in her youngest son's face.

Brandon thought it best not to reply. This was not a discussion he wanted to have with his mother.

But Mrs. Clark wasn't giving up so easily. "You've got nothing to say for yourself? Nothing?"

Brandon's dad was standing behind his wife. He didn't say anything, but he looked mad, too.

I'm just too tired to deal with this, Brandon thought.

Suddenly, his mom stopped and rubbed her eyes. "I just don't get it, Brandon. You've been like a different child these past few months. I mean that in a good way, you know? Your dad and I have been so proud of you. It's like you matured overnight. So why mess up now?"

I want to tell them, Brandon thought. *I want them to know what's going on. Dr. Braithwaite would support me, I know he would. He'd convince them I'm a time-traveler.*

Or would he?

Brandon, with sinking heart, now imagined Dr. Braithwaite saying, "The only people who know about your time travel are Verity and me. Who else would believe it?"

There was no point in trying to tell his parents. They wouldn't understand.

"You wouldn't understand," he said dully.

"Try me," shot back his mom.

But Brandon just stared into space, as one tear after another slowly leaked from the corner of his right eye.

Chapter 14:
LOOK BACK

Dr. George Braithwaite thought back over his long life with a great deal of satisfaction. No question about it, he had started out badly: Orphaned as a young boy in England, he was evacuated to safety from the bombing of the cities during World War II, only to find himself suffering under the rule of a cruel foster mother.

But little George was rescued from this living hell. To his rescue came an unlikely band of kids: a working-class evacuee boy named Eric, a smart and rather posh young lady called Verity, and—most surprising of all—Hannah and Alex, two fellow evacuees. He also met Alex and Hannah's friend, another refugee who, like little George, was black.

Three of those children had faded from his life, but in the years that followed, the love of George's adoptive parents Arthur and Diana Healdstone, his friends Eric and Verity, and Verity's formidable grandmother, Elizabeth Devenish, had healed his ragged soul.

With their support, George Braithwaite took charge of his future. He worked hard at school and university, and as a young man in the 1950s, he emigrated to America.

For a very long time, he had lived in Snipesville, Georgia. He had served as doctor to most of the black people in town and, after desegregation, to many of the white folks too. Now, he was enjoying his retirement. He had good health, the freedom to travel, and the time to tend to his roses.

The last thing he had expected in his twilight years was to meet the very same kids who had rescued him in 1940. And they were indeed the very same: When George met Hannah, Alex, and their friend Brandon just a few months ago, they had not physically changed since World War II.

Freaky though that meeting was, George had grown fond of the kids. Once he learned that they were time-travelers, he worried constantly about them, and he was determined that so long as he was alive and able, he would care for them.

Which was why, when Brandon's mother called him that evening, Dr. George Braithwaite hurried to his car.

"I am so sorry to bother you, Doctor B.," said Mrs. Clark the moment she opened the door. "I know you're not a psychiatrist, but you know Brandon, and we just want your advice about him. Like I told you on the phone, he didn't go to school today, and he won't tell us where he went. We are so concerned."

Dr. Braithwaite gave her a reassuring smile. "Of course you are. May I speak with him?"

She nodded gratefully, and showed him the way to Brandon's room.

When he knocked, Brandon grunted. Dr. Braithwaite entered, then closed the door behind him.

"So where was it this time?" he asked quietly, moving a pile of books from the only chair onto the floor so he could sit down.

Brandon was sitting on the bed, gazing out the window. Now, he looked up at the old man, saw the loving concern written across his face, and dropping his head, he burst into tears.

When he could speak, he told the old man everything he could remember.

"I feel terrible about what happened to the Professor," Brandon hiccupped when his story was done. "But that's not the only thing that got to me."

He had described to Dr. Braithwaite so much of what had happened, and yet, still, he hadn't figured out for himself why he was so upset. He struggled with his thoughts and feelings. "It was so weird," he said, "looking into a mirror and seeing a stranger. Although it was interesting to see how white people took me seriously when I had white skin."

His face was set, and his voice was bitter. "Yes, it was *very* interesting. It felt weird being a white person, like I was a traitor or something."

Dr. Braithwaite snorted. "That's just silly. It wasn't your doing, son. You had nothing to do with it. And it didn't change who you are, did it? That's a lesson in itself."

"I know," Brandon sniffed, "But . . . I don't know how to say this . . . . It's . . . . it's like I was there at the beginning, when things went wrong in Georgia. You know? When slavery was getting started, and white people were learning to hate black people, and black people were learning to hate white people. I was a bit afraid of black people, to be honest. And I understood why they were afraid of me, because I was white, but I couldn't get them to talk to me about it."

"From what you have told me, though," Dr. Braithwaite said slowly, "it sounds to me as though you did everything you could to help everyone around you. And perhaps that's the problem."

"What do you mean?" Brandon asked dully.

Dr. Braithwaite took a deep breath. "All those adult responsibilities, that's what I mean, Brandon. You're being thrown into situations that people can scarcely imagine, without any warning or preparation, and you're expected to act like an adult. That's a lot to take on at your age. And then, being you, you do take it all terribly seriously, and you hold yourself to a higher standard than would most adults, much less kids."

"Yes, I guess I do," Brandon admitted.

Dr. Braithwaite sighed heavily. "Look, can your Dr. Harrower help you find out why this has happened to you? She's still alive in the present day, isn't she?"

"She's missing," Brandon said distantly. "Maybe when she gets back, I can ask her. If she gets back. But you know I've tried before. We've all tried. She never wants to answer our questions. And based on what I saw this time, I'm not sure she has any answers."

"Hmm," said Dr. Braithwaite. "I need to speak with her on your behalf. From what little I've learned about her, she seems a rather slippery individual. You need an adult in your corner, Brandon, and it looks as though I'm it. This woman needs to tell you as much as she knows, and to help all of you prepare for your adventures. It's time, I think, that she took greater responsibility for what happens to you."

"So you think Hannah was right," said Brandon, "that the Professor is responsible for all this? That's not what Hannah thinks anymore, you know."

Dr. Braithwaite didn't seem perturbed by this development. "Doesn't she now?" he said. "Actually, that's no longer what I think either. Not after what you have told me about her being marooned in the eighteenth century. But I am confident that Dr. Harrower could be more forthcoming. And since Verity's family keeps popping up in your adventures, perhaps she can help us, too."

"But how can Verity help?" Brandon asked incredulously. "I mean, for one thing, she's all the way across in England."

In reply, Dr. Braithwaite smiled. "Honestly, Brandon, from what you say, one would think we were still in the eighteenth century. Have you never heard of Skype?"

Hannah stood silently in the office doorway and watched the Professor as she sorted through a pile of photocopies. She was fascinated by how young the Professor seemed, at least compared with the elderly woman she had met in 1752. And it was such a relief to see her alive and well.

"Hi," she said quietly.

The Professor jumped slightly, spun around, and broke into a broad smile. "Hannah! What a lovely surprise!" She pointed to the other chair. "Have a seat, please."

Hannah smiled awkwardly and sat down. "So, you came back," she said.

"I heard you were looking for me," said the Professor, closing a window on her computer screen. "I just got home, in fact. I'm afraid I upset quite a few people because nobody could get ahold of me. I honestly didn't mean to cause a fuss, and for the record, I was absolutely fine. But what a pity I missed all the excitement about the skeleton that Sonya Barrett dug up downtown. Did you hear about that?"

"Sure," said Hannah. "My brother and Brandon found it."

"Oh, I had no idea!" exclaimed the Professor. "All I heard was that a couple of local kids were digging around in the park and found it, but I never thought that it might be the boys. Oh, my. That's interesting . . . . Hannah, why are you looking at me like that?"

Hannah gave a small smile. "No reason. We just got back ourselves. We were in 1752 . . . ."

The Professor gasped. "Without me? Oh, no . . ."

Hannah nodded and continued, "Yeah. Without you. We were in Georgia, mostly. Balesworth for a little while. So what did you find out? About the skeleton, I mean?"

"Good grief. Aren't you going to tell me about what happened to you?" asked the Professor.

"I will," Hannah said firmly. "I just really want you to tell me about the skeleton first. It's important."

The Professor cleared her throat. "Let me see what I can tell you. I just had lunch with Sonya Barrett yesterday. She says the skeleton belonged to an elderly woman, probably in her eighties. But the part she can't figure out is, ah, why the skull had modern dental work. Hannah, did you meet this woman on your travels? Have we found another time-traveler?"

"Yes, we did," Hannah said carefully. "And she was a good friend."

"In that case, I am so very sorry," the Professor said feelingly. "Do you have any idea what happened to her?"

Hannah felt her stomach drop. "Yes," she said, her voice trembling. "She was murdered. Someone shot her. We saw it happen."

The Professor, apparently unaware of Hannah's anguish, kept talking. "I am very sorry to hear that," she said. "But how fantastic that she was a time-traveler, like us. I want you to tell me everything you know about your time-traveling friend. Time travel being what it is, perhaps we can get in touch with her. She may still be alive in the present."

Hannah just stared at the floor, the corners of her mouth turned down, and she started to cry.

The Professor offered Hannah a tissue, and then suddenly her eyes widened, and she fell back in her chair. "Wait a minute . . . . Dear, are you trying to tell me that she . . . She is me?"

Hannah nodded miserably. "Yes, only old. You were, like, eighty-five next birthday."

The Professor let out a long sigh. Then, to Hannah's amazement she smiled and yelped, "Hah!"

She started rubbing her head with her fingertips, as she sometimes did while she was thinking. "So that's how it all ends . . . . Gosh . . . well, at least I live to a good old age. And I literally go out with a bang, don't I?" She laughed again.

"That's *sick*," Hannah said, laughing despite herself. It felt odd to reproach the Professor for joking about her own death, and yet it was a relief to discover that she didn't seem too bothered by the news.

The Professor patted her hand, and spoke soothingly. "Look, don't worry, Hannah. The older I get, the less death frightens me. To be honest, I'm not as weirded out by this news as I am by the fact that I didn't know I was going to end up in Georgia in 1752. I'll check my research, but I don't think there is any record of my being there, if that makes sense. Oh, dear, I'm babbling."

Hannah was confused, too. But then she remembered what the Professor of 1752 had told her. She had to give information to "her" Professor in the twenty-first century, so she would know for the future.

"There's something else," she said hesitantly. "You had a husband . . . ."

"Yes, I do know that, of course," the Professor said impatiently.

Hannah was taken aback. "How could you possibly know that?" she sputtered. "You met him there, in the eighteenth century. He was a black guy, an escaped slave called Fred."

Now the Professor looked worried. "Are you sure? Yes, of course you're sure. But I don't understand. Why would I get married again?"

You're already married? Hannah thought. This was the first she'd heard of it. The Professor had never mentioned a husband before. "You told me you were stuck there," she said. "Like, you arrived, and you didn't know how to leave. So you didn't. You were in the eighteenth century for a lot of years."

There was a long silence, and now the Professor looked somber. She almost seemed to withdraw into herself. Then she said, "Thank you for telling me, Hannah. That's very helpful. Is there anything else?"

"One thing," Hannah said falteringly. "She, I mean *you*, *you* told us before you died what happened in the end to the other people we knew in 1752, you know, later in their lives. And you told me that you learned about them from us, that's how you knew. So *she*, I mean, *you* have to help us figure out about them. So we can tell you what happens to them, and then, when you're old, you would know to tell us."

"How very confusing," said the Professor. "But yes . . . yes, of course I understand. Very well. First, I suggest you get together with Alex and Brandon, and start writing down everything you can tell me about the people you knew in 1752."

"Okaaay," Hannah said slowly. "But what kind of stuff do you want to know?"

"Let's see," said the Professor, ticking off thoughts on her fingers. "Their names, of course, how old they were, who their friends were, where they were from, any records they kept, like diaries or letters . . . ."

Hannah rolled her eyes. "I'm sorry, but that would take, like, forever. Isn't there a faster way?"

The Professor chuckled. "I wish," she said. "But what I'm asking you to do is the easy part, believe it or not. After we have exhausted what you guys know, unless any of these people have had books written about them, which I doubt, it's needle-in-a-haystack time. We have to start going through the archives."

We? thought Hannah anxiously. "You'll do that for us, right?" she asked the Professor.

"Yes, I will," said the Professor with a twinkle in her eye that Hannah didn't like the look of. "Although I think you would enjoy visiting an archive with me more than you would think."

Then the Professor gave her a kindly smile. "Hannah, thank you for coming to see me. There's something I must tell you, and I hope it will cheer you up. What happened to me, and to you, may not stay that way. There is always the possibility that the past could change. And we won't be any the wiser when it does. Do you understand?"

"Not really," sighed Hannah. "Honestly? I'm just exhausted by all this."

What she had said to the Professor hadn't been entirely true, Hannah thought as she opened her locker at Snipes Academy and started hunting for her social studies textbook. She wasn't exhausted by her adventures. When she time traveled, even when she was afraid or miserable, she at least felt alive. In Snipesville, she always felt. . . Hannah couldn't find the words. But she knew that her normal life in Snipesville didn't feel like living. Existing, but not living. Come to think of it, she had felt the same way in San Francisco.

Just then, she heard giggling behind her. She turned around to see Natalie Marshburn and Ashlee Bragg. They tried to act like they hadn't been laughing at her, but Hannah wasn't stupid. And she also wasn't in the mood for their nonsense.

"Can I help you?" she asked them with a heavy sigh.

Ashlee said, "So where's your friend today?"

Hannah stared at her, and Natalie stepped in.

"I thought you were best friends with Tara Thompson?" she said. The two girls glanced at each other, rolled their eyes, and started giggling again.

"What's it to you?" said Hannah coldly. She didn't wait for an answer, but spoke slowly and deliberately so they would know she wasn't just losing her temper. "You're both snobs and racists, but you know the worst thing? You're stupid and boring. Tara looks weird, but at least she's a real person. Ten years from now, when you're both stuck in Snipesville with your boring husbands and snot-nosed kids, guess what? Tara and me will be far away from this dump, having interesting lives."

In no hurry, Hannah locked her locker, hoisted her bag on her shoulder, and turned back to the dumbstruck girls, who were opening and closing their mouths like goldfish. "And in case you're thinking of messing with me, don't even think about it. I've done things you can only dream about, and I'm not taking any more crap from you. See you later, losers."

To Hannah's astonishment, Ashlee and Natalie, after exchanging less-than-confident eye rolls, slunk away.

Now a voice behind her made her jump.

"That was really brave. Or really stupid. Or maybe both."

Tara was giving her a lopsided smile. They both watched the other girls leave through the double doors that led to Snipes Academy's cafeteria.

"I don't care," Hannah said adamantly. "I could take both of them on, and win."

"What, you think they're gonna jump you?" Tara was incredulous. "Hannah, like I told you, you got a lot to learn about living in a little bitty town in the South. Lesson number one: They won't come after you when you expect it, or how you expect it. They'll come after you sneaky, like. See Ashlee? Her dad is Mr. Bragg, the social studies teacher. Hope you don't end up in his class anytime soon, because Ashlee is daddy's girl. And isn't Natalie Marshburn's dad your dad's boss?"

"Yes," said Hannah, puzzled. "But what does that have to do with anything?"

"It has everything to do with everything," said Tara, giving Hannah a pitying look. "Family comes first here, and you're outsiders. I don't know why Mr. Marshburn hired a guy called Dias from California, but I bet your dad wasn't his first choice. They like to keep good jobs in the family round here. Don't be surprised if your dad gets picked on because you had a little fight with Natalie."

"That's ridiculous," Hannah said. But now she was worried.

Dr. Braithwaite had been over-optimistic about Verity's confidence with computers, and it turned out that, no, she didn't know how to use Skype. When he called, she promised him that next time her daughter Lizzie or son Mark visited, she would have them help her learn to make video calls.

That was why the kids had to call her on the landline.

"Verity?" Hannah said into the phone. "I'm here with Brandon and my brother. We know who's in the portrait. Do you mind me putting you on speaker?"

"Not at all," said Verity excitedly. "My goodness, it is a very clear connection we get to America these days, isn't it? Hello, boys!"

The boys shyly mumbled their greetings, and Alex, forgetting that he wasn't on Skype, raised a hand.

Hannah brought the portrait up on the computer screen.

"Okay," she said. "The woman who looks like you and Mrs. D., she's called Mrs. Jenkins, and she owns . . . owned the Balesworth Arms with her husband.

He's not in the picture, and because she looks older and stuff, I think he must have been dead by the time this was painted."

"So he was out of the picture, so to speak?" quipped Verity.

"Yeah," said Brandon with a smile. Now he couldn't wait to tell Verity his news. "The man in the wig, that's Mr. Osborn," he said. "He's . . ."

"No first name?" interrupted Verity.

Brandon had to think about that. He had never heard anyone call Mr. Osborn by his first name, not even Mrs. Osborn. "No. I don't know his first name," he said. "But I can tell you he was the curate in Balesworth, and some time before this picture was painted, he spent time in St. Swithin's Parish, Georgia, what's Snipes County today."

Alex leaned forward. He wanted to contribute, too. "The girl isn't Hannah, like we thought. She's called Jane."

Hannah tried to stomp on his foot. "Shut *up*, Alex, I wanted to be the one who told her that!"

"One at a time, kids, please," Verity chided them. "I can't hear when you all speak at once. Now, Hannah, what is it that you want to tell me?"

Hannah studied the picture. "Jane was Mrs. Jenkins's daughter," she said, "and she was Mr. Osborn's second wife." As an aside, she said in a low voice to Brandon and Alex. "Wow, we're like twins, huh? I didn't realize at the time that we looked that much like each other."

"She didn't look so much like you then," Brandon observed. "I guess her hair got darker as she got older, and she kind of changed . . . . Man, how strange."

There was silence. Then Verity said quietly, "Now we're getting somewhere."

The kids looked at each other expectantly, but she didn't explain. "Now, I must go," she said suddenly. "It was lovely of you to ring me, but I cannot imagine what your father's phone bill will be like. Goodbye now. See you soon."

"It's okay . . . it's cheap . . . ." Hannah said, trying to stop her from hanging up. But the phone had gone dead.

"She was in a hurry to go, wasn't she?" Brandon said. "Did we offend her?"

"I don't think so," said Hannah, perplexed. "And what did she mean, 'see you soon'?"

"That's funny," said Alex. "When Dr. Braithwaite called, he said something to me that I didn't get. About us seeing Verity here."

"Duh," said Hannah, affectionately slapping her brother's arm. "She must be coming here! That is so exciting. I hope it's soon. And this reminds me, the Professor wants us to write down everything we remember about everyone in 1752. She says it's important."

Brandon's dad had just picked him up from Hannah and Alex's house when Mr. Dias returned from the office. For once, he wanted to speak with his children, and he called them downstairs.

"There's something I need to discuss with you two," he said as he sat on the sofa. "Alex, I've heard you've been saying that the Marshburns' ancestors were drunks. What is that about?"

Alex felt himself go cold. It took him a moment to remember the conversation he had had at Snipes Academy, because for him, that conversation had taken place months ago. And when he did remember, he almost told his dad that what he had said was true, because it *was* true, at least of the ancestor whom Alex had actually met in 1851. But there was no point in telling his father any such thing, and so he sat silently.

Mr. Dias took his son's silence for a confession of guilt, and giving him a glare, he snapped, "I don't want to be embarrassed like that ever again, you got me? It's tough enough in this town for a guy from California called Dias without my kids spreading lies about my boss's family. Got that?"

Alex nodded miserably. Now Mr. Dias looked at his daughter. "And Hannah, what's this about you saying rude things about Natalie Marshburn?"

"She's a bully," Hannah said flatly. "She and her friend were making fun of me, and I scared them off."

For a moment, Mr. Dias's anger wavered. He sighed heavily, and ran a hand through his hair. "Just remember that you're newcomers," he said calmly. "Maybe we can move on in a year or two, but the banking business isn't too good right now, and I need to do a good job here, okay? Help me out. Try to fit in. Try not to tick off the Marshburn kids. I mean, I would put you in public school to get away from them, but the public schools are really bad here."

"Brandon likes his school okay," Alex pointed out.

"That's great," said Mr. Dias in an insincere voice. "But what's good for Brandon and his family may not be so good for ours."

"Why?" said Alex passionately, "Because he's black? Don't black kids deserve a good education?"

Mr. Dias said in a deadly quiet tone, "Don't call me a racist, Alex. Just don't."

Hannah and Alex sat sullenly, waiting for their father to calm down. But they no longer had his attention. He had his hand under his chin, and he was looking into the middle distance. "Go to your rooms," he said in a resigned voice.

Hannah heard a gentle tapping at her bedroom door. At first, she thought her dad had come to talk with her, but it was her brother, and he was waving a brown manila envelope. When he held it out to her, she saw the Snipesville State College return address.

"Hannah," Alex said, stepping inside as she took the envelope from him. "It came in the mail. Bet I know who it's from."

After each adventure, the Professor sent pictures of themselves, for the souvenir albums she had given each of them.

This time, in Hannah's photo, she was lying on the bed in the Professor's cabin, in a malaria-induced stupor.

"Huh, how flattering. Not," she said, grimacing. "Happy times. Here's yours."

Alex looked glumly at the photo of himself as a black kid, standing in a field with some brown cattle, Tony in the background.

"Hard to see this as me," he said, shrugging, picking up the envelope and looking into it hopefully, as though a picture of the real him might suddenly appear.

"If we didn't have these pictures, I might not believe that these things happen to us," Hannah said. "But you know what? They do happen, and I want to know why."

Then she gasped. "Wait. How could she have sent us these pictures if she didn't know what happened?"

"Hey, there's a letter in here," said Alex, pulling it out from the envelope. His sister snatched the paper from him, and began to read.

Dear Hannah, it said,

I found these photos in the college museum, of all places, stuffed into an old envelope. I remembered the curator telling me just last year that he had these weird color photographs of people in eighteenth century costume, re-enactors apparently, but that they came with a note from the very first museum curator more than a hundred years ago. He had wanted me to take a look, but I was very busy then, and it completely slipped my mind until now. Hope you enjoy them.

Hannah showed the letter to Alex. "You know what? She does know where to look for stuff about our time travel. She must know something about how to control it. Alex, I want us to decide where and when we go. And I'm starting to think that it's not a skill anyone can really teach me, not even That Woman. It's more like something inside me I never knew existed before. I just have to learn to recognize it and control it."

"Oh, so that's all," said Alex with heavy sarcasm.

"Of course not," his sister said calmly. "But it's a start."

ACKNOWLEDGMENTS

I wish to thank a number of kids and adults for their particular support of this book, and I hereby induct them to the **Most Worthy and Honorable Order of the Friends of Snipesville**.

The following are dubbed **Companions of the Order of Snipesville (COS)**, in recognition of their having read and critiqued drafts, and so having made this book better than it would otherwise have been. They are entitled to use their title, abbreviated to COS, in their correspondence:

Kristi Craven	Hazel Kirby
Melinda Cannady	Sophie Lichtman
Jacob Cohen	Sara McCracken
Cristina Dover	Bryan Ogihara
Mary Flad	Ryan Owens
Dusty Snipes Gres	Cathy Skidmore-Hess
Jane Hall	Kathleen Smith
Joanna Jarrell	

The honor of **Member of the Order of Snipesville (MOS)** is hereby conferred upon the following, for their support of the creation of *Look Ahead, Look Back*:

William Thomas Ansley	Luke McGrath
Janice Bass	Matthew McGrath
Theodore Bloyd	Neil Norby
Christa Campbell	Jessica Rao
Christian Cotten-Dixon	Kaley Whittle
Nancy Cvetan	Jennie Goloboy
Adam Holsomback	LaQuita Marie Staten
Mary Keith	Janet Moores

The title of **Dame of the Order of Snipesville (DOS)** is awarded to:

Kelley Callaway, for services to book design.
Deborah Harvey, for services to cover design and marketing.
Kathleen Smith, for services to copyediting and proofreading (all errors, and I do mean this, doubtless flow from my failing to heed her sage advice.)

NOTES ON SOURCES
(for those adult readers
who care about such things)

Kids: BOREDOM ALERT. Please don't read this next bit unless you want to be very, very bored. Don't say I didn't warn you.

So much of the historical background to *Look Ahead, Look Back* depends on my knowledge of early American history, acquired over the past quarter-century. I cannot always tell you my original sources, and the lovely thing about fiction is that I don't have to! I will fess up, though, that I have far greater knowledge of eighteenth-century South Carolina than of Georgia, and I freely admit that I've transferred things that happened in rural South Carolina to backwoods Georgia, but only when I think they *could* have happened there, even if they didn't.

This sleight-of-hand in my using history does not make my primary message any less valid: We don't need founding fathers and redcoats to make the eighteenth century fascinating.

The earlier part of that period is when so many developments took place that shaped modern America, including the large-scale rise of slavery and slave societies in the South, the rise of evangelicalism, and the emergence of consumer culture (another academic interest of mine) among the planter class.

Religion and the Supernatural

My choice of an Anglican missionary as a major supporting character in *Look Ahead, Look Back* was hardly accidental: My historical scholarship has focused on eighteenth-century popular religious culture, through the lens of the Church of England in America. Mr. Osborn was loosely inspired by an Anglican minister named Brian Hunt, who was chased from his South Carolina parish in 1727 amid accusations of drunkenness and other misdeeds. I wrote about him at length in *"A Very Immoral and Offensive Man": Religious Culture, Gentility, and the Strange Case of Brian Hunt* (The South Carolina Historical Magazine, Volume 103, No. 1 , January, 2002). The fate of Brian Hunt (and, by extension, his alter ego Mr. Osborn) is not atypical: I have read accounts of English missionaries in America being required to live in leaky barns, being subjected to their parishioners' tailgating during services, and, if they complained, being accused of drunkenness and other forms of "immorality." If you're really keen to learn more, you may want to read my doctoral dissertation: *All Things to All Men: Popular Religious Culture and the Anglican Mission in Colonial America, 1701-1750* (University of California, Riverside, 1995) It's a good cure for insomnia.

In my research on missionaries in the eighteenth-century British colonies, I became fascinated by their interactions with slaves. I was perplexed to discover that most historians had assumed that slaves were indifferent or even hostile to Christianity, because the evidence, while not necessarily endorsing the opposite view, certainly didn't support that assumption. The product of my interest was the most important work of my modest body of scholarship: *"Heathens and Infidels"? African Christianization in the South Carolina Low Country, 1700-1750* (Religion and American Culture: A Journal of Interpretation,Vol. 12, No. 2 , Summer 2002). The opening anecdote is the one on which I based Mr. Osborn's encounter with slaves seeking holy communion.

The negotiation of Christianity among slaves, slaveowners, and Anglican missionaries is one that has fascinated me for a long time, and it was such fun to have the opportunity to fictionalize it. If I tried your patience with theological discussions, I do apologize. You have no idea how much I cut before this book was done.

In general, what I have tried to get across is that fascinating phenomenon we have dubbed syncretism, whereby people adapt Christianity to existing cultures and belief systems. As I have written elsewhere, it is absurd to view this as an exclusively non-Western phenomenon. The prevalence of Green Man imagery in English history is one of the most delightful bits of evidence that refutes that assumption.

Unlike the common folk of the eighteenth century, I'm a modern person, and I really don't think much in terms of the supernatural. Despite my extensive work on eighteenth century popular religious culture, I had major gaps in my understanding that became painfully apparent to me as the book developed. I realized that I needed to get acquainted with folklore, and for that, I was delighted to have the assistance of Dr. Heidi Altman, anthropology professor at Georgia Southern University (Heidi bears NO resemblance whatsoever to Dr. Sonya Barrett in the book, just in case the thought should occur to you.) She introduced me to Cherokee folklore, including the Yunwi, and to the body of literature on Southern folktales. I can especially recommend for your enjoyment *Storytellers: Folktales and Legends from the South*, edited by John A. Burrison (University of Georgia Press, 1989). Anything I got wrong is absolutely and utterly my own fault, and not Dr. Altman's.

Extensive interactions among Africans, Europeans, and Native Americans make nonsense of the idea of an entirely separate storytelling tradition for each group, something I have tried to demonstrate in action. The oral tradition on which storytelling once depended is also nicely demonstrated by Tony's having acquired the gift from Sukey, and, of course, by the kids learning from them both.

Sukey's story about the snake-man is my own retelling of a traditional Cherokee tale, as given in James Mooney's classic *Myths of the Cherokee* (1900) which is available in reprint editions, and free in Google Books. Her story of Master Smith and the h'ant is loosely based on a South Georgia folk tale that I found tacked to a bulletin board at Obediah's Okefenok (a brilliant roadside attraction/folk museum that also helped me imagine the houses of colonial rural Georgia.)

As for Tony's story of Pompey and the sinkhole, I made it up. However, it is true that there is a locally famous sinkhole in rural Bulloch County, Georgia, and it looks exactly as I describe. The legend in these parts was that the sinkhole was bottomless, until it was dredged in the 1920s after a car belonging to a fleeing murder suspect from Florida was found nearby. I am grateful to my former student Emerson Chester and his brother Thomas for this information, and for taking me to see the sinkhole, which is on their family's farm. For a wonderful description of the sinkhole, see their website: http://sinkholefarms. webs.com/aboutus.htm.

Conspicuous Consumption

I have long been intrigued by the phenomenon of those wealthy eighteenth-century planters who exchanged a once-parsimonious life, in which they reinvested their income into land and slaves, for a luxurious lifestyle characterized by conspicuous consumption. The Gordons' experience, starting with their beloved tea set, is my re-imagining of what this transition might have looked like for a couple who belonged to the emerging upper class.

Living Outdoors

The first draft of this book revealed to me a gaping and shameful hole in my knowledge of eighteenth-century American culture. First, although I once spent a stimulating and entertaining three months wandering Colonial Williamsburg, I really didn't understand what it was like to spend one's life mostly outdoors. To rectify this problem, at least in part, I bought a pass to the Georgia State Parks and learned to enjoy hiking through something other than the British countryside, while keeping a watchful eye out for snakes and other critters.

I also had an enjoyable time at Okefenokee National Wildlife Refuge. On a boat ride through the swamp, I accepted the tour guide's invitation to step from the boat onto a peat bog in my bare feet. I enjoyed the sensation for a few seconds before my left leg vanished into the muck, just as a ten-foot alligator came over to take a look at what we were up to. Two Dutch tourists helped pull me out, and a good time was had by all. I couldn't figure out how to work this little gem into the story, so here it is, for your reading pleasure. It wasn't entirely wasted experience as far as the story was concerned, because Hannah's "freeway for elves" came from my boat trip up a canal in the Okefenokee. Learning to paddle a canoe was something I did myself at George L. Smith State Park, near Twin City, Georgia, with advice from my long-suffering husband.

Crime and Punishment

Attitudes toward criminals in the early twenty-first century can sometimes mirror those of the eighteenth century, which is why I think it's good to be reminded that there is a reason to sustain a humanitarian impulse toward penal reform.

"Jane's" crime is basically lifted from the trial of one Catherine Hawes in 1744, whose case I discovered in that terrific database, the Old Bailey Online: http://www.oldbaileyonline.org/ It is impossible to overstate the importance of this resource to historians, for it has opened up to us mountains of details on the lives of ordinary people in eighteenth-century England.

As for the actual court experience at the Old Bailey, I based that on the short and sweet discussion on the same site: http://www.oldbaileyonline.org/static/Trial-procedures.jsp Apparently, the executioner did take bribes to fake brandings (see http://www.oldbaileyonline.org/static/Punishment.jsp#branding), but I have had to make an educated guess as to how on earth he faked them, since the convicted were branded in open court before an enthusiastic audience.

For my descriptions of Newgate Prison, I referred to Stephen Halliday, *Newgate: London's Prototype of Hell* (Sutton, 2006).

Thank you (I think) to Dr. Jon Bryant, professor of Georgia history at Georgia Southern University, who says that he has concluded that the story of convicts coming to colonial Georgia is a myth. The only imported felon he has ever discovered in the records, he tells me, was the state's founding father, James Edward Oglethorpe, who spent time in a London jail for killing a man in a bar brawl. Bet they won't teach that in Georgia schools. Jon did allow, however, that a boatload of indentured servants was allowed to settle in Georgia after they were detoured to Savannah following a devastating storm. I ran with this as plausible evidence that such a thing could happen, and the result is that Hannah ends up in Georgia. Phew.

Language

Recreating the spoken language of eighteenth-century people is a tall order. The language of Mr. Osborn is as close as *I* can get (without hopelessly confusing my readers) to how educated eighteenth-century Englishmen might have spoken. I make no claims for its accuracy: I am no expert in historical linguistics. I have, however, read more than 10,000 letters written by Anglican missionaries in America to the Bishop of London, and I hope that my familiarity with their written English has been helpful. I also flipped through *Moll Flanders* for inspiration. Sukey's speech is based mostly on my long acquaintance with speakers of English as a second language, my own fumbling efforts in French, and what I learned about traditional Cherokee understanding and expression of the passage of time. I probably got it wrong. The accuracy of the speech of the slaves is also my best guess, tempered with a need to keep things clear for my readers, and that is all. It is not "accurate", and as any honest and reputable historian will tell you, how on earth could we know how they spoke?

Random Stuff

I thank pharmacist Minette Ugorji for her advice on which drugs could be dispensed to a minor without too many awkward questions being asked. However, it is only fair to say that policies do vary among pharmacists.

Hannah Glasse's *The Art of Cookery* (1747) is available in a reprint edition, and also free on Google Books, for all your eighteenth-century cooking needs.

For more about colonial medicine, I recommend *Physick: the Professional Practice of Medicine in Williamsburg, Virginia, 1740-1775* by Sharon Cotner et al., (Colonial Williamsburg, 2003).

Mrs. Jenkins' characterization of Englishmen in America (that they looked and dressed like Indians) was apparently a common misapprehension in England until the Revolution. Or possibly to the present day.

If you have any questions about the historical background to *Look Ahead, Look Back*, please visit my website at AnnetteLaing.com

BRING ANNETTE TO YOU

Schools, Libraries, Museums, Arts Centers: Would you like me to give entertaining presentations to kids about the history behind one of the *Snipesville Chronicles*? For Grades K-6, I come in costume, with artifacts, prizes, music, and more, and can present anything from a one-hour performance to a five-hour workshop. For Grades 7-12, I will be glad to discuss plans with you. With nearly twenty years experience in teaching, I can guarantee that my appearance will be entertaining and interesting. After all, my work with kids was winning praise (and a feature in the Associated Press) even before I began writing *The Snipesville Chronicles*! My fees are very reasonable. Visit http://AnnetteLaing. com for information about my range of presentations, and to contact me.

Adult audiences: I give teacher workshops, and am also happy to speak to adult audiences at lunch and dinner meetings, conferences, or any venue that works for us both. Contact me at Annette@confusionpress.com to discuss your proposed event.

Book Clubs: I am always happy to be invited to speak about one or more of my books to audiences who have read them. Want me to come to your book club? Just let me know! I'll contact you when I plan to be in your area, and visit you for free if your group is reading or has read one of my books. If you want to speed things along, source me a paid booking in your area (school or library), and I will come to you, again for free, in conjunction with that visit. Contact me at Annette@confusionpress.com to register your interest, or for more information.

For more information about my books, my public appearances and performances, or simply to keep in touch:

Visit my web site at **AnnetteLaing.com**.

Sign up for my mailing list. I send out a monthly e-newsletter to keep you informed about my various activities promoting non-boring history for kids. Simply email me at Annette@confusionpress.com with 'subscribe' as your subject line.

'Like' me on Facebook. Join my great community of fans on my page at https://www.facebook.com/AnnetteLaingAuthor I sponsor fun contests and giveaways, too!

Kids and adults: Send me fan mail at Annette@confusionpress.com. I love hearing from you (yes, adult readers, that includes you!)